PENGUIN BOOKS

# THE TEMPEST BLADE

Danielle L. Jensen is the #1 *New York Times* bestselling author of *A Fate Inked in Blood* and *A Curse Carved in Bone,* as well as the *USA Today* bestselling author of the Bridge Kingdom, Dark Shores, and Malediction series. Her novels are published internationally in twenty-three languages. She lives in Calgary, Alberta, with her family and guinea pigs.

## BY DANIELLE L. JENSEN

### THE MALEDICTION TRILOGY
*Stolen Songbird*
*Hidden Huntress*
*Warrior Witch*
*The Broken Ones* (prequel)

### THE DARK SHORES SERIES
*Dark Shores*
*Dark Skies*
*Gilded Serpent*
*Scorched Earth*
*Tarnished Empire* (prequel)

### THE BRIDGE KINGDOM SERIES
*The Bridge Kingdom*
*The Traitor Queen*
*The Inadequate Heir*
*The Endless War*
*The Twisted Throne*
*The Tempest Blade*

### SAGA OF THE UNFATED
*A Fate Inked in Blood*
*A Curse Carved in Bone*

# THE
# TEMPEST
# BLADE

## DANIELLE L. JENSEN

PENGUIN BOOKS

PENGUIN BOOKS

UK | USA | Canada | Ireland | Australia
India | New Zealand | South Africa

Penguin Books is part of the Penguin Random House group of companies
whose addresses can be found at global.penguinrandomhouse.com

Penguin Random House UK
One Embassy Gardens, 8 Viaduct Gardens, London SW11 7BW

penguin.co.uk

First published in the United States of America by Del Rey,
an imprint of Penguin Random House LLC 2026
First published in Great Britain by Penguin Books 2026
001

Copyright © Danielle L. Jensen, 2025

The moral right of the author has been asserted

Penguin Random House values and supports copyright.
Copyright fuels creativity, encourages diverse voices, promotes freedom
of expression and supports a vibrant culture. Thank you for purchasing
an authorized edition of this book and for respecting intellectual property
laws by not reproducing, scanning or distributing any part of it by any
means without permission. You are supporting authors and enabling
Penguin Random House to continue to publish books for everyone.
No part of this book may be used or reproduced in any manner for the
purpose of training artificial intelligence technologies or systems. In accordance
with Article 4(3) of the DSM Directive 2019/790, Penguin Random House
expressly reserves this work from the text and data mining exception

Set in 10.45/12.9pt Times New Roman
Typeset by Six Red Marbles UK, Thetford, Norfolk
Printed and bound in Great Britain by Clays Ltd, Elcograf S.p.A.

The authorized representative in the EEA is Penguin Random House Ireland,
Morrison Chambers, 32 Nassau Street, Dublin D02 YH68

A CIP catalogue record for this book is available from the British Library

ISBN: 978-1-405-96895-9

Penguin Random House is committed to a sustainable future
for our business, our readers and our planet. This book is made from
Forest Stewardship Council® certified paper.

For my readers.
Thank you for coming on this journey with me.

# 1
# JAMES

"THREE SETS OF eyes on her at all times," James growled at his men. "This woman might well be the most dangerous individual you come across in your lifetimes. Keep her gagged. Keep her chained. And for the love of God, keep your fucking wits about you."

"Yes, sir," his lieutenant responded, but then his eyes slid to the prisoner. "How do you wish us to handle requests for privacy? She *is* a princess, and propriety demands—"

"What do you value more, propriety or keeping your throat intact? Because I assure you, if you turn your back on this woman, you will regret it." James gestured sharply to Hazel, who stepped forward, her expression frosty—as it had been since the moment the young maid had joined his company. "Hazel will ensure proper conduct, but when I say three sets of eyes on her at all times, I mean *at all times*. Am I clear?"

"Yes, sir!" The men saluted sharply, and Hazel gave a tight nod, but James's attention was all for the prisoner on her knees before him.

Azure eyes tracked him, cold as ice. James knelt before Princess Bronwyn Veliant and met her stare for stare. "To reiterate, Your Highness, you are being released not because I believe you are innocent but as a courtesy to Queen Sarhina, with whom Harendell has no quarrel."

*We'll see how long that lasts.*

Bronwyn did not so much as blink, yet James resisted the urge to reach for his sword hilt, every instinct screaming *danger*. This woman had the same training as her sister Lara, which meant she'd spent most of her lifetime under the tutelage of the Magpie and his minions. Bronwyn was a killer to her core, and her dead-eyed stare promised that the moment she got her hands on a blade, it would have his name on it. Except there were many people who felt the same way about him, so she could get in line.

"You will be delivered to Northwatch," James continued. "You will relay a message to Ithicana's king that he is to immediately turn over his sister for execution for the murder of King Edward and the attempted murder of Queen Alexandra. Should he comply, and should we discover proof Ahnna acted of her own accord, Harendell will reconsider its plans to retaliate against both Ithicana and its crown. Should Aren refuse, the full might of Harendell's military will descend upon Ithicana's shores, and you might remind Aren that we know all the ways in. That is the consequence of Ithicana's choice to betray its oldest ally." He pulled out Bronwyn's gag. "Am I understood?"

Her voice was hoarse as she asked, "And if Ahnna is *not* in Ithicana?"

"It is my understanding that Lara maintains Ithicana's spy network. A spy network unrivaled by any other nation. I suggest she put it to good use and find Ahnna before it's too late." James smiled, knowing full well it did not reach his eyes. "I'm sure Ithicana's queen will give no argument. Ahnna is hardly a friend to Lara and has caused her no end of grief. If Ithicana is innocent of the princess's crimes, then they no doubt wish to be rid of her. See it done, Your Highness— you've your own interests to protect."

The coldness in Bronwyn's gaze transformed into rage. "If you lay a finger on Taryn, I'll—"

James shoved the gag back in her mouth, cutting off the inevitable threat. "Taryn will be treated as a lady right up to the point she is recast as a prisoner of war." He stared Bronwyn down. "Deliver Ahnna to us so that we can punish her for her crimes. It's in everyone's best interest."

Rising, James exited the ship's brig, the heavy clang of steel bars filling his ears as he headed toward the stairs to the main deck. The moment he was out of sight of Hazel and the guards, he stopped and rested a hand against the wall, searching for equilibrium. Yet every time James blinked, he saw his father's corpse laid out on a table. Eyes still and glassy, the blood washed away to reveal knife wounds so great in number that they merged. His indomitable father reduced to so much meat.

*Forty-seven wounds.* The surgeon's shaken voice filled James's thoughts. *A crime of rage, of that there is no doubt.*

Nausea twisted in James's stomach, and he swallowed hard, unable to escape from the memories that plagued him.

The bloody scene of the murder had been discovered by a servant, who'd immediately called for help. James had been walking back to his own rooms, head thick with his father's alcohol and mind consumed with how he was going to make things right with Ahnna, when the alarm had sounded. He'd joined the guards, and they'd followed the small smears of blood left by the killer's boots through the Sky Palace. Not once had it occurred to him that it might be Ahnna's trail they were following, so when they rounded the corridor, lured by screams, the sight of her before a bleeding Alexandra had shocked him to the core.

*Help me*, Alexandra's voice sobbed from his memories. *Help me, Jamie.*

It had been the first time she'd ever used his childhood nickname without derision, and it echoed over and over in his thoughts. As did the memory of Alexandra reaching for him, eyes filled with agony and terror.

*A severe defensive wound to her hand,* the surgeon had told him. *The queen may never have full use of it again. The wound in her cheek will leave significant scarring, but the stab wound to the abdomen was nearly the death of her. An inch to the left and we would have lost Her Majesty as well.*

There had never been any love lost between James and Alexandra, for she had resented both his parentage and his father's favoritism, but she had set aside their conflict since his father's death. An attack on one Ashford was an attack on all, and just before James had left Verwyrd, the queen had come to him.

"I fear for our family, James." Her speech was difficult to understand due to the injury to her face, her eyes heavy with narcotics and pain. "Our enemies will see this as an opportunity. Your brother is bereft and not ready to leave. I . . ." She swayed on her feet, only James catching hold of her hands keeping her from falling. "I haven't the strength to aid him. Jamie, I know we have long been at odds, but for all my cruel words, I do know that you have ever been your brother's bulwark against those who would harm him. You are the soldier among us, the warrior, and I am trusting you to keep us safe from those who would take advantage of your father's death."

James could see that, even now, the admission cost Alexandra. She did not want to rely upon him. For her to do so spoke to the emotional toll of her brush with death, but also to her certainty that he would always do right by his siblings. "I'll find her, Your Grace. We will have justice."

Alexandra gave a tight nod, but then her green eyes welled with unexpected tears. "I went to find Ahnna, because I know better than anyone how your father's words can cut to the bone." Her eyelids squeezed shut for a heartbeat, and when they opened, tears spilled down her cheeks. "*Could* cut."

Past tense. Because his father would never utter another word again.

Alexandra drew in a shuddering breath. "I'd hoped to temper what Edward had done, but Ahnna was so angry that she would not hear me. There was no reason in her. No logic. Only rage and a knife in her bloody hand."

*A deadly combination.*

Alexandra's fingers closed on his. "Be careful, Jamie. Ahnna Kertell is more dangerous than we realized, and I believe you are the one she truly desires to hurt."

As if he didn't know that. As if he didn't wish that it had been him lying dead on that table, because his father had wanted Ahnna to be queen—to be his successor. Had wanted her to marry James so that they would one day rule together. If James had only gone to Ahnna immediately and explained, rather than wallowing in misery over his father's ill-thought methods, *none* of this would have happened.

"James? Jamie, are you all right?"

The sound of his name tore James from his thoughts. He lifted his head to find Georgie coming down the steps toward him. "Fine. Is the ship ready to sail?"

His best friend nodded. Gripping James's shoulders, he said, "You need to get some sleep. We have every huntsman and dog on her trail, and the civilians are forming militias to guard the coastline. Every ship leaving harbor is being searched top-to-bottom by loyal men and bloodhounds that have been given articles of her clothing. It's only a matter of time until we track the bitch down and make her pay."

*Hanged, and then drawn and quartered*, William's voice snarled. *I'll send her head to her brother on a spike*. Despite himself, James flinched, and he silently cursed himself for shying away from a punishment Ahnna deserved.

Georgie's face softened. "I know how you felt about her, Jamie, so I can only imagine the thoughts in your head. But this isn't your fault. We've all heard how savage the Ithicanians can be, but no one expected a lady to turn to such gruesome violence. No one predicted it."

"You did," James muttered. "At first sight, you said Ahnna was a wild thing that we could not treat as a pet—that either she'd lash out or her spirit would be broken." In the end, it had been both. "Has anyone spotted her?"

"Only from a distance." Georgie gestured to the stairs. "She's proving surprisingly adept at evading capture, but we know she's heading south."

James wasn't surprised at all. Ahnna had a fast horse and every skill she needed. "I should have gone with the trackers."

"No, you were right to think she'd head to the conservatory to seek the aid of her cousin." Georgie shielded his eyes as they stepped onto the ship's deck. "And even though that proved incorrect, we now have Taryn as a prisoner. If you hadn't moved as swiftly as you did, all three women might have evaded us."

In hindsight, it was idiocy to have thought Ahnna would go to her cousin. From the beginning, her goal had been to protect Taryn—to give her a new life—and going to her would have been the nail in the coffin of complicity. For while James suspected that Taryn and Bronwyn were both guilty of espionage and efforts on Ithicana's part to undermine Harendell, Ahnna's decision to murder his father had been impulsive and poorly planned. An act of rage, not a strategic assassination, but it was only now that he was coming to see that.

*Why can't I think straight? Why do I keep making mistakes?*

"Sleep, my friend, you need sleep, that's why," Georgie said, and James realized he'd spoken aloud.

"No matter how fast Ahnna's horse, there is no chance she'll beat us to the coast. We're ahead of her and our net is closing," Georgie continued, guiding James to the gangplank. "Everyone loved your father—all of Harendell wants vengeance." He gestured to the sky as they descended from the ship. "And now that the weather has cleared and the *Victoria* can set sail, it won't be long until Ithicana knows we are coming for their blood."

Their boots thumped against the wood of the docks, and together they headed toward the port. Everyone from the dockworkers to the merchants to the prostitutes was dressed in funeral black in mourning of his father, but—Harendell being Harendell—business carried on. Men doffed their hats as James passed, women bobbed curtsies, and from the taverns, songs exploded forth about "Good King Eddie" along with cries that Ithicana deserved to starve for its crimes.

It was all noise in James's ears, because with every blink, he saw his father's corpse. Saw Alexandra's ruined face. Ginny's tears. William's grief. All with Ahnna's angry words repeating in his head. *If any of you come near me again, I'll kill you all. I swear it.*

His anger and grief rose, fuel for the red-hot need for vengeance that had burned in his heart from the moment he'd seen Ahnna bent over Alexandra, bloody knife in hand. No matter how fast she ran, no matter how far, he would never stop hunting.

And when he found her, there would be no executioner, as James fully intended to kill Ahnna Kertell himself.

The sound of pounding hooves caught his attention. James pulled himself from his thoughts as a soldier galloped toward him and Georgie. The man threw himself off his foaming horse before it had even stopped, only James's reflexes keeping the man from falling face-first into the dirt.

"Major General," the soldier gasped out. "I've got news!"

"Have you found her?" James could barely breathe, his hands fisting and unfisting, the harm Ahnna had caused his family parading through his mind's eye.

"Yes, sir." The soldier squared his shoulders. "She was spotted in Sableton and is now on the run. The whole city is hunting her."

The world seemed to stand still for a heartbeat, then James said, "Saddle my horse. We ride for Sableton."

And if he had his way, the city's streets would run red with Ithicanian blood tonight.

# 2
# AHNNA

Ahnna stooped to pick up a small rock, bouncing it on her palm before tossing it at a dense thicket. Pheasants exploded skyward, and she swiftly nocked an arrow, aimed, and then let it fly. Green fletching soared through the air, and then one of the birds dropped.

"I told you I'd get one." She glanced sideways. "They aren't the brightest creatures you'll ever meet."

Dippy snorted and bobbed his head in agreement, then returned his attention to the thick grass. Ahnna watched him for a moment, noting that the white chalk she'd used to mark a large star on his forehead was starting to fade, though the dirt covering his coat still served as a disguise for his quality. During her journey south, she'd swiftly discovered that no matter how well she hid her own appearance, people remembered a polished thoroughbred. It pained her that he was dirty with burrs tangled in his tail and his coat marked with sweat, but it was better than trading him for a less distinguished mount.

She'd lost enough without losing her goddamned horse.

Leaving Dippy to graze, Ahnna strode to retrieve her dinner, her large overcoat flapping on the cool breeze. Her height, along with stolen clothing, a hat, and a generous amount of grime had served to disguise her as a young man as she fled Sableton, but even with her efforts to put off the bloodhounds, it was only a matter of time until they discovered she had headed to the mountains.

With her current proximity to Sableton, she couldn't afford to linger. The soldiers who'd spotted her in the city had put on hot pursuit with dogs, and it had taken all her skill to evade capture as she headed toward the mountains.

Ahnna plucked and gutted the bird, then gave a sharp whistle that had Dippy trailing after her toward the clearing where her supplies were hidden. He made soft little whickering noises, and not for the first time, Ahnna felt a sharp pang in her chest knowing that there would be a moment she'd have to leave him. Never mind that it would be impossible to transport him to Ithicana—her homeland was no place for a horse like him. He needed space to run, the freedom of wild open fields and crisp air to breathe. Not the dense jungle and tiny islands of Ithicana. To take him there would be cruelty.

But God help her, she'd cry bitter tears when it came time to leave Dippy behind. Bitter tears that she'd already wept for leaving Taryn and Bronwyn to the Harendellians, despite knowing that it had been the right course of action. To have gone to them would have rendered them complicit, as would have sending them any form of message. Both women had the skills needed to take care of themselves, yet it had still felt like a betrayal not sending them a warning.

Taking care to use dry wood to prevent smoke, Ahnna made a fire and cooked her dinner. Despite her hunger, she barely tasted the meat as she ate, her mind twisting with anxiety over how Alexandra's schemes might already be impacting Ithicana.

For all she'd been warned about Harendell's queen, Ahnna had sorely underestimated the woman. Not just in the skill with which Alexandra had framed Ahnna for Eddie's murder, every piece planned with foresight that would have put even the Magpie to shame, but also in the lengths to which the queen had been willing to go to ensure that no one would ever suspect her.

The pheasant in her mouth turned dry as Ahnna remembered how Alexandra had shoved the knife through her own palm. Sliced open her own face. Stabbed herself in the abdomen. Courtesy of Nana's teachings, Ahnna knew that the queen had selected injuries that would be horrifying without being lethal, but *no one* was going to believe that Alexandra had inflicted them on herself.

This was a noblewoman who'd never used a weapon. Who'd never suffered physical harm. While poison would have made everyone immediately suspicious, this sort of violence was so far out of Alexandra's character that Ahnna could not fault James for believing the scene his stepmother had painted for him.

A plot years in the making, and though Alexandra's strategy had clearly shifted over time, the goal had not changed: She wanted the bridge.

Casting the remains of her dinner into the fire to burn to ash, Ahnna glanced at Dippy to ensure the horse was relaxed, for his ears were the first warning she'd get of a threat. He was focused on grazing, so she turned to stare broodily at the flames and lost herself in the scope of the threat facing Ithicana.

It had been in Sableton that the full scope of Alexandra's ambitions had become clear. The moment Ahnna had seen the sign for Cartwright Foundries, she'd known that the weapons maker was the mysterious *C.F.* she'd seen in William's banking records. Alexandra had been paying the company through William using the proceeds from Maridrinian rubies. Cartwright's transport of sharpened weapons through the bridge was what had armed Silas's disguised soldiers during the invasion. A small yet oh-so-critical piece, because it had been those soldiers who had taken Midwatch. Silas had paid Queen Katarina of Amarid for the use of her navy via rubies hidden in bottles of cheap Maridrinian wine. Whether he'd separately transacted with Alexandra or whether Katarina had facilitated the payment mattered little, for it was abundantly clear that all three rulers had conspired together to take control of the bridge. When Silas had fallen to Lara's blade, Katarina and Alexandra hadn't given up their ambitions. They'd merely switched tactics, and Ahnna had been the unwitting pawn in their plans.

And she was not the only one they'd used.

Aren had played into Katarina's hand by entertaining Amarid's overtures, which, in combination with the false information Katarina then fed to Harendell's spies, caused Edward to believe that Aren conspired against him. Trade agreement with Cardiff aside, Ahnna was quite confident that Edward's belief that Aren was in league with Amarid had driven Edward to wholly turn on Ahnna and Ithicana.

All of which was but the tip of the iceberg of the machinations.

Sighing, Ahnna withdrew her mother's necklace from the neckline of her coat, tracing over the map of gemstones. In her role as commander of Southwatch, one of her most time-consuming tasks had been to go through the endless spy reports that came in from the southern nations, most especially Maridrina and Valcotta. She'd never understood how people were so easily manipulated in what seemed obvious schemes. She'd thought the individuals in the reports to be stupid, ruled by greed and emotion. Having stood in a nest of scheming spiders, Ahnna now knew otherwise.

It was hard to see clearly when in the thick of things. It was easy to be fooled when emotions were high, when instincts were wrong. It was hard to be the cleverest when those around you deceived as easily as they breathed.

"Or maybe you're as much an idiot as those you once judged," she muttered, then shoved the necklace back under her shirt. Rising, she kicked dirt over her fire before dusk fell. She'd given Dippy as long a rest as she dared, and it was time to move on. Edward had been a much-loved king, and the hunt for his killer had intensified as word of the gory details of his murder had spread.

A hunt spearheaded by James.

As always, the thought of him caused a swell of complex emotions. Anger. Grief. Betrayal.

But also fear.

James had loved his father dearly, and he believed that Ahnna had brutally slaughtered Edward as vengeance for his choice to marry William to Lestara. His choice to put Cardiff before Ithicana. His choice to deny Ahnna the queen of Harendell's crown.

*If any of you come near me again, I'll kill you all. I swear it.*

She winced at the memory of her words. At how she'd set herself up perfectly for being framed. If James caught her, he'd kill her himself. Ahnna knew that, because if she was in his position, she'd do the same. They were not like Keris in seeking out the most perfectly terrible punishment—a knife across the throat and watching the light vanish from the murderer's eyes would be sufficient.

If James caught her, there would be no explanation Ahnna could give that would convince him of her innocence. All the evidence pointed toward guilt. All she could do was continue to evade pursuit until she had escaped into Amarid, where James, at least, would dare not follow.

For while Katarina and Alexandra might be secret allies, Carlo and James were bitter enemies. It felt strange to seek protection from the Beast of Amarid, but beggars could not be choosers. And Ahnna needed to get back to Ithicana.

The sky grew darker, and Ahnna began packing up her supplies to continue her journey west. She was stroking Dippy's nose and whispering words of apology when her horse abruptly lifted his head, nostrils flaring.

Ahnna went still even as she scanned the shadows for signs of movement.

Her heart hammered in her chest, fear firing through her blood as she reached for her bow. There were bears in these rolling hills. Mountain cats as well.

But a muffled curse warned her that this predator was of the human variety.

Slinging her bow over her shoulder, Ahnna jumped to catch hold of a branch of the nearest oak, and then she silently climbed until she was hidden in the shadows.

Forcing her breathing to slow, she watched the approaching lantern.

"I'm telling you, I smelled something cooking," a young male voice said. "Pheasant, I'd bet my last copper on it."

"You ain't got any copper to bet," another male voice responded, this one older.

"Well, if I'm right and it's her, it will be gold I'm wagering in games of dice," the younger voice declared. "Gold polished to a shine by Prince James himself and offered to me with a smile for delivering Ithicana's bitch for execution. Though in truth, I might find it hard to keep from doing the killing myself to avenge Good King Eddie."

A third man gave a loud snort. "Right, Johnny. Sure you will. Can't slaughter a goat but you'll be first in line to slaughter a woman. Mark my words, you'll take one look at the Ithicanian princess and piss your trousers."

"Will not!"

The older men chuckled but then fell silent as they caught sight of Dippy.

"Might be that Johnny's nose was right after all," one of them whispered. "Weapons ready. They say she's as dangerous as a cornered mountain cat."

They weren't wrong, but leaving corpses in her wake was a surefire way to put James on her trail. Even if she could hide their bodies, the trio were victims of Alexandra's schemes, believing they were rightfully hunting the murderer of their king. Ahnna was not in the practice of slaughtering innocents to save her own skin.

They drew close enough that she could see their faces in the lantern light. A grizzled man with a thick beard and thicker-set shoulders, a man with a wild tangle of red curls, and a boy, sixteen, if that. Likely all family members.

"Good-looking horse," the boy said, approaching Dippy while the other two examined her meager belongings, none of which would give away her identity. "Though she's said to be riding a bay gelding with no markings, so this ain't him." He gestured to the star that Ahnna had colored on her horse's forehead with chalk. "But I don't recognize him either."

"Still warm," Red Curls muttered, holding his hand over the charred remains of Ahnna's fire. "Whoever it is, they're close."

"Traveler, perhaps." The grizzled man adjusted his grip on the axe he carried, his instincts correctly warning him that a threat was near. "Or another bounty hunter with the same idea as us that she'll head to Amarid."

*Don't look up*, Ahnna silently willed him as he turned in a circle. *Move along so no one gets hurt.*

The boy moved closer to Dippy, stroking her horse's neck. "You're a beauty, boy."

Anxiety built in Ahnna's chest as she willed him to leave her horse alone. Not because she feared Dippy being taken, for horse theft was a hanging offense in Harendell, but because he was the one thing down there that could be tied to her.

*Don't be friendly*, she silently instructed Dippy. *Try to bite.*

Instead, her gelding snuffled at the boy's pockets, looking for treats. The boy smiled and rubbed Dippy's forehead, and Ahnna's heart sank as the chalk smeared.

*No.*

The boy frowned. Pulling his sleeve over his hand, he used it to rub at the white star. "Da," he whispered. "His mark is just chalk. This horse is disguised."

All three fell entirely still, and from her perch in the tree, Ahnna could feel their fear. Could smell it. Her soul cringed because it was lies told about her that inspired it. Lies that she, and by association all Ithicanians, were murderous monsters who hunted in the dark.

*Go*, she willed them, despite knowing that word of this discovery would reach James. *Trust your instincts and run.*

Cold wind howled through the trees, pulling at the strands of hair that had come loose from her cap, but Ahnna didn't move. Only watched the terrified men below silently debate what they wanted to do.

"It's her," the grizzled one whispered. "I sense it in my bones."

"What do we do?" the boy asked. "She could be watching us right now."

"It's three against one," Red Curls growled. "And she's only a woman. With the reward we'll get for bringing her in, we'll live like lords for the rest of our lives."

*Go looking for me, then*, she silently instructed. *Search the woods.*

Because she'd only need a matter of seconds to tighten Dippy's girth, and then she'd be off like a shot, her escape route already planned. This was far from the first time Ahnna had been hunted.

"You think Good King Eddie went down easily?" Grizzled said. "This is no ordinary woman. We take the horse so that she's stuck on foot, and then we send word to the garrison for reinforcements. Prince

James will see us rewarded well enough for the information, and we'll be alive to spend it."

The boy untethered Dippy. If they took him, there was no chance that she'd be able to outrun the Harendellian soldiers and their hunting dogs.

It seemed that whatever luck had taken her this far had run out.

Drawing an arrow from her quiver, Ahnna dropped from her perch, landing almost silently next to the men. Leveling an arrow on the grizzled man with the axe, she said, "Do what I say, and you will exit this situation alive."

Red Curls hefted his knife, but Ahnna only shifted her stance so that her arrow was leveled at his son. "Use your heads, gentlemen. This isn't a fight you will win."

Grizzled lunged.

Ahnna took a quarter step to her left and let her arrow fly. It struck his upraised axe, knocking it out of his hand, but before he could react, Ahnna had another arrow nocked and aimed at his forehead. "Last chance."

Grizzled lifted his hands, as did Red Curls.

"Good." Ahnna didn't lower her weapon. "Remove your bootlaces. Red Curls, you tie up the old man and be sure to tie him tight. Boy, you tie up your father."

She watched in silence as they obeyed, her scrutiny ensuring that the knots were tight. When they were restrained, she nodded to the boy. "Toss me your laces and get on your knees."

He complied without argument. Once he was kneeling, Ahnna hooked her bow over her shoulder. The restraints would only slow them down, but short of killing them, which she wasn't willing to consider, it was the best she could do.

"Hands behind your back." She picked up his laces. "For what it's worth, I didn't kill Edward. Alexandra had him murdered in order to put William on the throne, then framed me."

"Liar," the boy whispered. "Everyone knows you Ithicanians are murderous savages. It was you who stabbed him forty-seven times."

*God have mercy, forty-seven?* Ahnna swallowed to clear her throat. "If that's the case, then why are you still breathing?"

Instead of answering, the boy flung himself at her.

Ahnna easily sidestepped, and he fell past her. Except rather than catching himself, his arm buckled. His head struck a rock with an ominous crack.

"Johnny!" Red Curls shouted, even as Ahnna cursed the foolishness of young men.

Ignoring the protests of the men, she crouched next to the boy and carefully rolled him over. He was breathing, but he'd split his scalp and it was bleeding heavily. He needed a physician.

Logic demanded that Ahnna tie him up, because she needed every bit of head start that she could get. Except not even in her lowest moments of the Maridrinian invasion had Ahnna stooped to sacrificing the lives of children.

"He needs a physician." She rounded on the grizzled man. "Do you know where to find one?"

"Aye," he said between his teeth.

"I'll let you go, but rather than troubling me, you're going to take him to get help. Do you agree?"

He nodded, eyes filled with fear as she tightened Dippy's girth and fixed her saddlebags in place, along with the rope she used to tether him. Approaching the old man, she shoved him to the ground so that he was prone. "Remember that I didn't kill you. And know that I didn't kill Edward either. Tell James what I said when you see him. Between the two of us, he's the backstabber, not me."

Ahnna sliced her knife through his bootlaces. In two quick strides, she vaulted onto Dippy's back, because it would be speed not words that kept her alive. Without a backward glance, she galloped into the night.

# 3
# JAMES

**M**AVEN WAS LATHERED and breathing hard when he rode into Sableton, the late-afternoon sun bright in his eyes. Only Georgie had managed to keep pace through the journey, as his soldiers' mounts were a far cry from Maven's quality.

"Report!" he demanded of the garrison captain. "Have you found her?"

The man stared at his boots rather than meeting James's stare. "No, sir, but we're hunting. A patrol spotted her trying to make her way to the harbor, but when they put on pursuit, she escaped. We're searching the city and holding all ships in port, but so far, there is no sign of her."

Georgie held out a wax-wrapped package. "An article of her clothing for the dogs."

"Thank you, sir."

"Have you found her horse?" James dismounted and handed Maven's reins to a stable boy. "Bay thoroughbred gelding, tall, no markings."

"We received her mount's description from the messenger but assumed she would have abandoned him upon reaching the city."

Though it was a reasonable assumption for most individuals on the run, James made a noise of disgust, because it was off the mark for Ahnna. "She'll not abandon her horse unless forced. She's either on a ship or on that gelding's back. If she *is* on a ship, she'll have found her horse a home before departing. Check the neighboring farms and offer a reward for information. If we find that horse, we'll find answers."

"Yes, sir." The captain saluted, then turned to set his men to the task.

"You think she managed to board a ship?" Georgie asked. "We've stopped traffic to Northwatch for Harendellian vessels, but there are merchant vessels from every nation, north and south, in Sableton's harbor. Preventing them from traveling to Northwatch would require a proper blockade."

Blockades demanded significant resources, and given the rising conflict with Amarid in the Lowlands, it wasn't a step James was ready to recommend to William. Harendell was the most powerful nation in the north, but a double-sided war was no jest. Especially because he had no certainty over the state of the alliance with Cardiff. That agreement was between his uncle and his father, and for all Will had married Lestara, his brother's sentiment toward Cardiff was unclear. If Will wanted to, he could cast aside everything James had fought to achieve and there wouldn't be a damned thing he could do about it. All he could do was pray that Lestara would sway him in the right direction.

It was not lost on James that he was counting on the support of a traitor and a murderess.

Georgie was staring at him expectantly, so James said, "A blockade would have to come by order of the king, and William's focus is by necessity on Amarid." Before James had left in pursuit of Ahnna, his brother had voiced his intent to march with Ronan and their united army to retake the Lowlands, but he'd had no recent update on William's plans. "Our mandate is not to escalate with Ithicana past the point of no return but to capture . . . the perpetrator."

*Why is saying her name so hard?*

James cleared his throat. "Ithicana isn't going anywhere," he continued, "and they are incapable of going on the offensive. Let them suffer the loss of trade with Harendell for a time and see how that changes their tune."

"Given their supposed alliance with Amarid, they may not feel the pinch as much as we might like." Georgie frowned at the gulf, which was still overcast and gusty from the last storm. "Katarina is no doubt taking advantage of openings at Northwatch to increase exports to the south."

James shook his head. "We are not certain what Katarina and Aren agreed to, but if Harendell and Amarid go to war over the Lowlands, exports will be the last thing on her mind. Katarina will need every resource she has."

James rubbed at his temples, something seeming to scratch at the back of his mind. As if he'd forgotten a detail. Or was missing a critical piece of a puzzle. Nothing he could pin down, only the sense that something wasn't quite right, and it had his hackles up.

"You need to get some sleep." Georgie clasped his shoulder. "The dogs will be out in force soon enough, and I'll ensure not a ship leaves the harbor without a full search. You head to Fernleigh House. Have a drink and get a night's sleep. If we find her while you're abed, you'll be the first to know."

James's stomach twisted at the idea of anyone but him being the one to find Ahnna. "I'm fine. You ensure the harbor searches are thorough. I'm going to take a fresh horse and join the search of the surrounding farms—I'll recognize Dippy more easily than others."

Instead of answering, Georgie furrowed his brow as he caught sight of something over James's shoulder. James turned, a band of tension tightening around his chest at the sight of a gilded coach flanked by soldiers, of horses pulling it into the market square frothing and exhausted.

"That's Alexandra's carriage," Georgie muttered. "Why is she here?"

*Whatever the reason, it won't be good.* James approached the carriage as a footman moved to put a stool beneath the door. It swung open, nearly striking the footman in the forehead.

And William stepped out.

James stopped in his tracks at the sight of his brother. "Will . . . What are you doing here? You're supposed to be on your way to the Lowlands."

Will yawned, then stretched. "Yes, about that. It seems the situation in the Lowlands was greatly exaggerated—perhaps by Father himself to manipulate sentiment in support of his desire for personal vengeance against Katarina, although who can say for sure. What I do know is that the Amaridians have *not* invaded the Lowlands. Quite the opposite, in fact. It seems they have withdrawn entirely."

That couldn't be right. Surely their father had not fabricated an invasion in order to bolster support for his plans to wage war on Katarina? To falsify it for one night would be one thing, but it was not a deception that could be maintained. His father had been a politician through and through, which meant he'd been a liar and a manipulator of the first order, but everything he did was fueled by logic.

*Are you sure about that?*

James's doubt whispered the question even as his heart reminded him that everything, *everything*, that his father had done had been motivated by a desire to avenge the murder of James's mother. Strategies a lifetime in the making all driven by emotion, not logic. "Are you certain they withdrew? It's possible they've just hidden their camp—"

"They were never there," Will interrupted. "Some have suggested that Ithicana is behind this as well. That they disguised themselves as Amaridians in order to distract us in the Lowlands while they made their move. It's not the first time they've done so, after all."

James's lips parted to argue that Ithicana hadn't been behind the attack at Northwatch, but the words didn't come. He no longer knew for certain what was truth and what was deception. All his life, he'd been wading through the endless twist of schemes that governed Harendell, but this was a knot he could not easily untangle. If he'd learned anything from his father, it was to always say less until one knew more.

Silence stretched, and Will crossed his arms. "You haven't found her yet, I take it?"

"She was spotted in Sableton trying to reach the harbor. We are hunting for her as we speak."

Will's mouth thinned, his eyes cold. "You said you'd catch her. You said we'd have vengeance for what the Ithicanian bitch did to our father and king, yet Ahnna Kertell is still free. It makes me question whether your lingering fondness for the woman has influenced your efforts."

"Will, come on now—" Georgie started.

Will held up a hand. "Reconsider your familiarity, Lord Cavendish."

Georgie's jaw tightened, but James barely noticed his friend's reaction. Shock at his brother's accusation made his words sound stilted as he said, "Rest assured, Your Grace, whatever *fondness* I might have once had for Ithicana's princess has been burned to ash. I swore that I would bring her to justice, and I will do so. Your presence here is not required—she's not worth your time."

Will met his gaze, and there was an unfamiliar coldness to his brother's stare. "Quite right. Ahnna is beneath me. I'm here for other reasons."

"What reasons?"

William scowled and faced south. To the gray seas of the gulf and Ithicana beyond. "Ithicana attacked us, James. Attacked us in a way that hasn't been seen in generations, and they must answer for it."

Unease pooled in James's stomach as his brother's hand drifted to the hilt of his sword, and he said, "We don't know that for certain. She may have—"

"You dare to defend them?" Will's voice seethed with derision. "It was Ithicana who pushed us to take her. Ithicana who sent her to get close to us. Do you truly think that Aren didn't give her orders?"

"I've no doubt he did, but this doesn't feel like a well-thought-out assassination, Will. It was impulsive and poorly planned. An act of anger, not strategy. Don't—"

"Don't think to tell me what I should and should not do!" Will snarled, rounding on him. "Ahnna murdered our father and cut up my mother, and you barely seem angry."

An accusation that couldn't be further from the truth, but he could see that Will's control over his temper was fraying at the edges.

"Bronwyn Veliant is on a ship to Northwatch as we speak. She has a message for Aren Kertell, which is that he must hand his sister over to us for execution or face the consequences. If he refuses to do so, you will have your answer on Ithicana's culpability in her crimes, and I will gladly put a sword through Aren Kertell's chest in your name."

His brother seemed to calm, tension easing in his shoulders, and he gave a small nod. "Grief causes me to say things I should not, James. You've never given me cause to doubt your loyalty before, and I know you'll not give me cause now."

"Will you return to Verwyrd?"

William shook his head. "No. We will remain here. I feel war brewing, and a king belongs on the front lines."

Clouds swirled over the gulf, and James half imagined he could see the *Victoria* sailing toward Northwatch where one man would determine whether William's words were hyperbole or prophecy.

But in his heart, James already knew the answer.

# 4

# AREN

King Aren Kertell stared at the gray seas before Northwatch Island, half imagining that he could see the continent in the distance. The storm had passed, the threat of wind and rain and wave vanquished for the time being, and yet every instinct in his body screamed that danger was at his doorstep.

"We've had five Harendellian ships miss their port times," the harbormaster said from where he stood at Aren's left. "No sign of them on the horizon."

"Perhaps they delayed over concerns with the storm."

"The Amaridians came in on the heels of it with no trouble," the man answered. "The missing vessels know these seas as well as we do, Your Grace. They know how to chase a squall, do business, and then get back to safe harbor before the next winds rise. One or two ships missing I might excuse, but *five*?"

Aren didn't disagree, and he fought the urge to reach for a weapon, his hackles up. His gaze flicked to the two Amaridian vessels moored at the piers. Their crews were busy unloading barrels of wine that his soldiers were checking to ensure their contents sloshed. *Fool me once, shame on me, but fool me twice . . .* "Any gossip?"

"None," Lara said from behind him. Aren turned to watch his wife approach, Jor and Lia at her heels. As was her custom, Lara had Delia in a sling that held their baby as close to her as the weapons sheathed at her waist.

She stopped next to him, nodding at the harbormaster, who inclined his head and went back to work.

"The Amaridian crews said little of interest," Lara murmured once the man was out of earshot. "What could be gleaned from them about Harendell is all old news and of little consequence, but they saw no reason that merchant ships would have delayed making the crossing to Northwatch. They said nothing about Ahnna."

She lifted her hand to pat Delia's bottom through the sling, swaying back and forth to keep their baby asleep. "Their silence is telling. Never have I known a ship to arrive that wasn't peddling information as much as wares, and for not one of them to have a coded message from our spies is equally concerning." Lara's blue eyes met his, her face shadowed with unease. "Something has happened on the mainland, Aren. I feel it in my bones."

Lara validating his trepidation only made the crawling sensation across his skin worse. "I should have made Ahnna come back with me. Should have dragged her home by her ankles, because I *knew* she was somehow twisting Harendell's sentiment toward Ithicana."

His wife shot him a dark scowl. "*No one* has reported anything to validate that thought. Quite the opposite: All reports speak of Edward's fondness for her."

"They also speak of his bastard's fondness for her." Aren scuffed his boot against the pier and scowled. "James acted like Ahnna was *his*. I know what that sort of possessiveness looks like, and it's not how a man acts over his *brother's* future wife. If there is something untoward between them, it would explain her refusal to return with me."

"*Untoward*?" Lara gave a soft laugh. "How very Harendellian of you. Maybe you're right and James is taken with her—it would be understandable, because Ahnna is a very beautiful woman. Or maybe his good Harendellian manners demanded he intervene given that you approached your conversation with Ahnna with all the tact of a battering ram. Did you really expect him to do nothing when he came upon you ordering her about in the dark corner of a tavern, your words having reduced her to tears?"

"I expected him to mind his own business."

Lara snorted and rolled her eyes skyward. "You disliked him from the moment you met him."

Her comment wasn't entirely inaccurate, but Aren *knew* that James's behavior wasn't just Harendellian chivalry at work. The tension between Ahnna and the bastard prince had been thick in the air, the familiarity between the two of them undeniable. Whereas when he'd watched her with William, Ahnna had appeared bored and the crown prince had barely looked at her twice, the connection between them as intense as cold oatmeal. Aren didn't want to think his sister was fool enough to cross the line with the wrong prince, but the timing of the rising animosity toward Ithicana coincided with Ahnna's arrival, and James had been at her side since the beginning. If Aren sensed impropriety, then the Harendellians would as well, and they would not view it favorably. "He's arrogant."

Lara only made a soft humming noise, patting Delia gently on the back as she swayed. "If Ahnna crossed a line, Edward would send her back and demand reparations for the slight. This is something different, Aren. I . . . I think this is something worse." Her hand moved from Delia's back to her sword, scarred fingers toying with the hilt.

His wife could handle the worst the world had to offer, but God help him, Aren wished she didn't have to. Wished he could give Lara a moment of peace and happiness untarnished by endless threats against the lives of all she held dear. In his darker moments, he felt the sickness of regret that he hadn't run away with her once Ithicana had been liberated, leaving Ahnna to rule while he and Lara carved out a simple life.

Aren said none of that, though, only murmured, "Our defenses are bolstered. Ithicana is used to defending itself." He wrapped an arm around Lara's shoulders and returned his gaze to the sea. "If nothing else, Amarid is still here to trade."

Katarina had been a paragon of courtesy of late, offering to renegotiate trade agreements and make reparations for conflict, the traffic back and forth between Northwatch and her capital of Riomar ceaseless in recent weeks. *I regret my part in what Silas did to your nation,* she'd written. *In my old age, I find myself reaching toward peace and alliance, so that I might leave a legacy of prosperity to my son when his day comes to rule.*

Aren didn't trust Katarina as far as he could throw her, but there was an air of desperation in how aggressively she was seeking Ithicana's favor that made him question whether her actions were driven not by greed but by fear.

And there was only one nation that Amarid feared.

"I wish Ahnna would write," Lara muttered. "Or Bronwyn and Taryn, though they seem to have thoroughly cut themselves off from politics."

As much as it frustrated Aren that the two had left Ahnna to her own devices, it did make him happy that Taryn was finally having a chance at the life she wanted. A life away from violence and war, where she could focus on the music she adored. Bronwyn would keep her safe—but more important, keep her happy.

A horn sounded from the lookout, indicating a ship on the horizon. Lifting a hand to shade his eyes from the bite of rain and wind, Aren made out a faint shape through the mist.

"Harendellian?" Lara squinted. "All I can tell is that it's big."

The horn blew again. Aren tensed, because the lookout was warning the rest of the island. The Amaridian sailors all turned to the sea, many of them familiar with Northwatch's signals. Especially the signal that the ship on approach was no merchantman.

Behind him, his soldiers moved to ready the island's defenses. The shipbreakers were loaded, and if that vessel came any closer, warning shots would be launched.

Jor and Lia came alongside them, and Jor handed Aren a spyglass. "Your eyes are better than mine, boy. Who's out there?"

Aren peered through the spyglass, panning the horizon until the ship came into view. A sharp hiss exited his teeth. "Harendellian ship of the line. The *Victoria*. The decks are full of soldiers."

"Just one ship?" Lara demanded, and at Aren's nod, she added, "Then this isn't an attack."

"Make sure we have eyes all around," Aren shouted, the wind carrying his orders to the soldiers behind him. "Send word down the bridge to be prepared for conflict."

The *Victoria* drifted closer, turning sidelong just outside the range of the shipbreakers and lowering the rest of their sails.

"What in the fuck are they doing?" Jor growled. "I don't like this."

Aren didn't answer, his eyes all for the empty longboat that was being lowered from the side of the ship.

It was unhooked and left to bob on the swells, Aren's rising dread bobbing in his stomach along with it.

Everyone on Northwatch, including the Amaridians, stood in stunned silence as the *Victoria* lifted its sails and headed north, swiftly disappearing into the mist.

"Get me a boat." The words croaked from his throat, barely audible over the wind, so Aren repeated, "Get me a boat!"

Lara gripped his arm. "Let someone else go."

"No." Because what if it was Ahnna in the abandoned longboat? What if it was his sister? What if his every fear had become a reality, except instead of demanding reparations for Ahnna's behavior, Edward had sent back her corpse?

"Aren, please." Lara's blue eyes were filled with the same fear that was crushing the breath from his chest, but Aren only pulled her hand from his arm and strode to where his soldiers were lowering a boat into the waves.

With the Amaridians watching in silence, Aren climbed down a rope ladder into the vessel. His soldiers took up paddles, but Aren remained standing as they approached the bobbing longboat.

"Looks empty," someone muttered. "It's sitting high in the water."

It wasn't empty.

The Harendellians hadn't sent one of their largest naval ships to deliver an empty longboat. Hadn't stayed out of range of the shipbreakers because they expected whatever was in that boat to be well received.

*Please be alive*, he silently pleaded. *Please don't be lost to me.*

No one spoke as they drew closer, and the humid air was thick with tension.

*Why didn't I make her leave?* Aren asked himself. He stood tall, trying to see into the longboat as it slid into the valley of a swell. *Why did I allow her to go at all?*

A question he knew the answer to, though admitting it made him feel sick. Allowing Ahnna to go to Harendell had been the path of least resistance. His twin had not made his life easy since they'd expelled the Maridrinians from Ithicana. Her unwillingness to forgive Lara—and her ongoing animosity toward his wife—had created a rift between them. Worse still, his people were influenced by Ahnna, and many chose to follow her lead in continuing to blame Lara for their suffering. He'd believed that after a taste of what Harendell had to offer, his twin would beg to return to Ithicana, and that when he facilitated it, Ahnna's gratitude would temper any lingering ill will she felt toward Lara.

A decision that he seemed fated to regret for the rest of his life.

The sound of something impacting wood reached his ears. Something that sounded distinctly like boot heels hitting the side of a boat.

Whoever was in there was alive.

Relief flooded Aren. Ignoring the protests of his soldiers, he put a foot onto the edge of the vessel and leapt into the longboat.

He landed on one of the benches, easily keeping his balance on the rocking boat as his eyes shot to the figure bound and gagged in the pooled water at the bottom.

Bronwyn's azure eyes stared up at him.

"Shit!" Aren dropped to his knees and pulled the gag out of her mouth. "What's going on? What's happened?"

Bronwyn spat into the pooled water next to her, coughing violently, then croaked out, "Is Ahnna here?"

Aren's stomach sank as he helped her sit. "No, she isn't. Bronwyn, tell me what's going on. Why has Edward done this to you?"

Bronwyn's blue eyes welled with tears. "It wasn't Edward." As he untied her wrists, she reached out with scraped hands to grasp him tightly. "Edward's dead. Murdered, and Alexandra barely escaped the same fate. They say . . . they say it was Ahnna who killed him. Stabbed him to death in his bed because William wed Lestara instead of her."

All the breath disappeared from Aren's chest, because Lara had been right. This was so much worse than an illicit affair. Worse than he possibly could have imagined.

Bronwyn's grip on him tightened, her teeth chattering. "James sent me with a message: Deliver Ahnna to Harendell for execution, or it will be war."

# 5

# JAMES

*A KING BELONGS ON the front lines.*

Will's words had lingered in James's mind since he'd parted ways with his brother in Sableton's harbor, Will heading to Fernleigh and James taking up the hunt. War hung in the balance, and while he did not hold his brother's belief that Ahnna had acted under orders, he did believe that Ithicana was where she'd flee.

The hounds had followed the path she'd taken out of Sableton, and today they'd found evidence a horse had been tethered on the outskirts of a large farm. The hounds had pursued, but her scent led in multiple directions. False trails set by Ahnna, and in the midst of the hunt, it started to rain. The deluge of water made short work of any evidence the dogs might find, and the trails in all directions had gone cold. Now night had fallen and they were no closer to finding her.

"It shouldn't be this hard to find one woman." Georgie scowled, exhaustion and the miserable weather wearing on his friend's temper. "Ithicana had to have agents waiting to aid her. It's the only explanation for how she disappeared into thin air."

The explanation was that Ahnna was a woman who had spent most of her existence with her life on the line, so she could survive in the worst of circumstances. "Increase the reward for any witnesses who come forward."

"There will be many false leads," the captain standing with them said. "We'll have to divide our resources."

"Better than no leads at all." James wiped rain from his eyes, knowing an update for his brother was long past due. "I'll be at Fernleigh House. Keep me apprised of any developments."

"Yes, sir."

He and Georgie mounted their horses, heading toward the royal residence. James had avoided it until now, catching a few hours of sleep in the same barracks as his soldiers when exhaustion threatened to send him off the side of his horse. But Will had requested a report, and James could no longer avoid telling his brother that Ahnna had slipped his net.

"I'm going to check for updates on the harbor, and then I'll head to Fernleigh," Georgie said. "We'll catch her, Jamie. It's only a matter of time."

James didn't answer, only reined his borrowed mount toward Fernleigh. A ship out of one of the southern ports was the obvious route back to Ithicana. But with passage on a vessel not an option, what strategy would she try next to get to the relative safety of her homeland? Civilian militias patrolled every stretch of beach and the navy was on the water stopping any vessels heading south, but this net wasn't sustainable. Logic suggested that she'd find somewhere to hide until civilian exuberance for the hunt waned, but no part of Ahnna's plan seemed based on logic.

*Forty-seven times.*

*Forty-seven.*

*Forty-seven.*

He pushed the vision of his father's corpse out of his head. Ahnna had acted rashly, her choices fueled by extreme emotion, so everything she'd done since was reactionary rather than the steps of a meticulous plan. Ahnna had to know that there would be consequences not just for her but also for Ithicana, and guilt would drive her to take every risk to reach her homeland's shores. What she hoped to gain there, James didn't know. Confession? Absolution? The chance to lift her sword in defense of the people her actions had thrown to the wolves? Perhaps some combination of all three, but regardless, James knew that hiding until the dust settled would be out of the question for her.

The guards at Fernleigh opened the gates and he trotted his horse up the main drive, the gelding's hooves splashing in the puddles. The manor looked dreary in the low light, ivy hanging heavy beneath the onslaught of the storm—although perhaps he was only projecting his own exhaustion onto the structure. As he dismounted, a stable hand emerged to take the horse, but James didn't immediately go inside. Instead, he stood outside the manor, the rain hammering down upon him as he tried to mentally compose a report that wouldn't set William racing toward war.

All his mind would give him was, *She can't run forever.*

So James took a deep breath and went inside.

To find Lestara standing in the main entrance, barefoot and wearing a velvet dressing gown. He hadn't even known she was in Sableton.

"I sensed you coming," his cousin said. "You've lost Ahnna's trail, haven't you?"

Lestara was the last person he wanted to talk to. "The heavy rains are causing the hounds some issues." His throat tried to close up, but he forced himself to add, "Your Grace."

The corner of Lestara's mouth curved. "You don't like it, do you? The idea of me as queen of Harendell."

He hated it. "My opinion is not relevant, Your Grace. But I do have a report to give to the king."

"William is asleep." She blocked his path. "He tires easily these days, for he is not yet used to the weight of so much responsibility. You can give your report to me, and I'll relay it when he wakes in the morning."

James crossed his arms and said nothing. Though he knew that his father had never intended for Lestara to be queen, it was still troubling that he'd supported her marriage to William. Since childhood, Lestara had cared for nothing but her own ambition, and she left pain in her wake from her efforts to achieve her goals.

Water dripped from his clothes to pool on the floor, the silence stretching between them, and then Lestara said, "William won't admit it, but your affections for Ahnna hurt him terribly."

James scoffed. "Please. I struggle to believe that my brother cared what Ahnna did or did not do given he was between your legs the entire time. Especially given it was Will who encouraged me to spend all that goddamned time with her. If you're going to play the game, Lestara, you'll have to do better than that."

His cousin tilted her head, silver-blond hair spilling over her shoulder. "Will only pushed you in her direction on Edward's orders. *Encourage your brother to keep her busy so that she'll not look too deeply in your direction* was what your father said. He feared that Ahnna would suspect his intentions to wed William to me and ruin everything, so we hoped to use you, and your rugged charm, to good effect. But I don't think William ever believed you'd fall victim to *Ahnna's* charm." Lestara sighed. "Though William cared nothing for her, it still broke his heart that you cuckolded him. That the one person he trusted above all others betrayed him."

"I didn't—"

"Don't lie, cousin. Hazel managed Ahnna's wardrobe, and she reported that the princess's chemise was missing. Perhaps the tornado tore it off her, but I think it was another force of nature. A woman's desire does leave a certain amount of . . . evidence."

*Drip.*

*Drip.*

*Drip.*

James listened to the water droplets fall from his clothes to pool at his feet, a fresh wave of guilt turning his mouth sour because he'd believed his brother wholly ignorant of that indiscretion.

"Even before Ahnna murdered Edward, Will hated her," Lestara said. "He blamed her for stealing you from him, and he asked me more times than I could count whether Ahnna had put a spell on you. Wept when I told him she had not, because he so desperately wanted a reason why you'd choose her over him. If you don't believe me, ask him. Ask your brother how he felt knowing that you were lying to him, that you were fucking the woman you believed he was supposed to marry. He'll tell you the same as I have, although I suspect it will hurt more coming from his lips."

"It was just once." The confession slipped out, and James instantly regretted it. Not for the admission but because it sounded as though he was looking for absolution.

"Once. Twice. A hundred times, it makes no difference." Lestara's eyes burned into him. "You chose Ahnna over William, and he believes her continued freedom is proof you still love her more than you do your own family."

James twisted away from his cousin. Though he desperately wanted to escape the guilt by fleeing out into the storm, he held his ground, William's voice rising from his memory. *You said you'd catch her. You said we'd have vengeance for what the Ithicanian bitch did to our father and king, yet Ahnna Kertell is still free. It makes me question whether your lingering fondness for the woman has influenced your efforts.*

"Catch her and kill her," Lestara said softly. "Not only to avenge your father's death, but to prove to William that you care more about him than you do your murderous lover."

James's skin prickled. "Tell me, cousin, why do you care so much for repairing my relationship with your husband? You and I might be family, but we have never been friends, and you know I think Keris Veliant should have taken off your head. What's in this for you?"

She closed the distance between them, her bare feet patting against the floor. Her amber eyes seemed to burn in the light of the lamps, and James's palms turned to ice. He'd always dismissed beliefs that many Cardiffian women were witches, but his cousin tested his certainty almost as much as her mother did.

"For the sake of my people." Lestara's stare was unblinking. "For the sake of my beliefs. The alliance with Cardiff was Edward's goal and Alexandra dared not go against him, but she has no such reticence against steering William's course. How long until she convinces him to retract the changes Edward made? I can't hold the course alone. I need you, James, as much as it pains me to admit it. And if you wish for all your life's work to endure, you need me as well."

The idea of allying with Lestara about anything turned his stomach, but James could not deny that the alliance with Cardiff hung in the balance. Especially given that there was no longer the threat of Amarid to serve as a mutual enemy. "Do you love him?"

Lestara gave a slow blink. "Every man in my life has used me to achieve his own ends. Treated me callously and cruelly. William is the only one who has shown me kindness. The only one who has cared for me. For that, I will be a loyal wife to him, but the only true love I'll ever feel is for the son in my belly."

She smoothed a hand over her stomach, and James had no doubt that if there wasn't a child inside her yet, one would be soon. It was Lestara's best way to secure her position. "Congratulations." The words came out from beneath his teeth.

She inclined her head. "Our positions are tenuous, cousin. We must prove our worth if we are to remain where we are."

Before he could answer, the sounds of hooves clattering up the drive filtered through the door, followed by a shout of, "Where is the major general?"

"Prove your loyalty to William. Hunt Ahnna down and kill her," Lestara whispered. "Everything depends on it."

"What's going on?"

They both jumped at Alexandra's voice, and James didn't miss the panic that rose on Lestara's face. She dropped into a low curtsy for Alexandra, seeming to forget herself in the other woman's presence. "Your Grace."

"Get yourself to bed, girl," Alexandra snapped.

Without another word, Lestara raced to the stairs and took them two at a time, her long hair floating behind her as she disappeared from sight.

Alexandra pressed a hand to her side with a wince, then met James's gaze. "What's going on?"

"I don't know." James exhaled a steadying breath and then opened the door. A pair of soldiers stood outside, both soaked to the bone. "Do you have an update?"

"Yes, sir," one answered. "A trio of civilians were attacked by a woman. One was grievously wounded and may not live."

James's heart skipped, then sped. "They were certain it was her?"

"Their description matches, sir. And . . . and she gave them a message to give to you."

It was hard to breathe, his chest a complex mix of emotions. "Well? Spit it out."

The soldier's gaze slid past James to Alexandra, and he grimaced. "She instructed them to tell you that it wasn't her who killed the king—she blamed another."

James went rigid. "Who?"

"The queen mother, sir."

*Alexandra.*

Though she had surely heard, Alexandra said nothing, and for his part, James felt lost for words because the accusation was insanity. He'd seen Ahnna with his own eyes with a knife in her hand, blood everywhere, and Alexandra screaming for aid. Undeniable proof she'd attacked Alexandra, and yet Ahnna expected him to believe that it had been the queen who'd arranged the murder of his father? "And what explanation did she offer for the injuries to the dowager queen? Did she blame some mystery assailant?"

Because, inexplicably, he felt a flicker of doubt.

"She offered no explanation, sir. Or at least none that was relayed to me."

Because there wasn't one. Alexandra had begged him to save her from Ahnna. Had confirmed later in no uncertain terms that it had been Ahnna who'd attacked her.

Ahnna was grasping, trying to undermine Alexandra. That was all this was. "Where did she attack the civilians?"

"Northwest of Sableton, sir."

The base of the foothills.

It was possible that Ahnna had fled to the less densely populated area to hide, but James's gut told him otherwise.

*Catch her and kill her. Not only to avenge your father's death, but to prove to William that you care more about him than you do your murderous lover.*

A hand closed on his arm, and Alexandra said, "Send George. You are needed here, Jamie."

He looked down at her, marking the swelling of her face and the way the wound in her cheek pulled up one corner of her mouth, but it was Lestara's words of caution that he heard. *Our positions are tenuous, cousin. We must prove our worth if we are to remain where we are.* Clearing his throat, he said, "I have to go. If she's headed west, it's because she aims to find salvation in Amarid. I can't let her get across the border."

"Send someone else." Her green eyes were urgent. "Your brother's emotions are high, and I fear he'll act out of grief. You need to keep him reasonable or we will soon be at war."

There was a part of him that wanted to believe she was relying on him. That Alexandra, for the first time in his life, actually wanted him here. But experience and cynicism made him suspect that she had returned to her old ways and was using this as a way to sow division between him and William. As a way to render him useless to his brother, who was now king. "That's exactly why I must go. If we catch her now, we can have justice, and reason will be restored. William charged me with this task, so I must go."

Alexandra squeezed her eyes shut, but then nodded and let go of his arm. "Return swiftly. I'll keep William in check for as long as I can."

James inclined his head and then strode through the door, both soldiers falling into step next to him. As they reached the stable yard, he shouted, "Saddle my horse!"

Maven would get no rest tonight, and neither would he.

"You wish for us to organize an escort, sir?"

"Send them after me." James strode toward the stable yard, not willing to take even a moment to change into dry clothes for the journey. Ahnna was aiming to escape into Amarid by crossing the Blackreach Peaks. The mountains were deadly but worth the risk if she could make it to Katarina's territory. For him to cross the border risked starting a war with Amarid, and also coming face-to-face with the Beast.

Which meant he needed to get to the border first.

# 6
# ZARRAH

Empress Zarrah of Valcotta opened the letter bearing Queen Sarhina of Maridrina's seal, swiftly reading the contents once, then twice, the information adding to the knots of tension in her shoulders. "Sarhina has officially taken the first steps to dissolving the Maridrinian monarchy."

Her father, Arjun Retva, took the letter as she passed it to him, his brows furrowing as he read. Shaking his head, he set the letter down. "Silas will be spinning in his grave."

Pressing fingers to her temple, Zarrah gave a slight nod. "I can't help but wonder if that's half her motivation." A wave of guilt immediately passed through her, because she knew that Sarhina was a true queen for the people. Her decision to create an elected government would ensure that the tyranny Maridrina endured beneath Silas and his predecessors would never happen again, and resenting the loss of the crown's authority because of the frustrations it caused Valcotta was selfish. "It's a remarkable achievement."

"Keris will be pleased."

"Yes." Zarrah rose and went to the window, the height of the tower allowing her to see the sea upon which her husband had sailed away. The early-morning sun turned the water orange, but the beauty was lost on her. "Perhaps Sarhina will have the opportunity to tell him herself."

Her father gave a long sigh, joining her at the window. "You were a fool to think he'd accept being locked up for something as inconsequential as his own protection. Keris Veliant has flaws beyond number, but cowardice is not one of them."

"I am aware I erred." The words came out from between her teeth. She'd been sick with regret and guilt since the argument that had driven him onto a ship north. A mistake fueled by fear, because there'd been so many attempts on his life, and her imagination too readily supplied her with visions of the moment she was told that one of the assassins had been successful. That the love of her life was lost to her forever.

So she'd let fear drive him away instead.

"It was wise of Keris to go visit his family," her father continued. "He knows his own nature, and choosing to undertake a role as ambassador was better than another quarrel. It is always wise to let tempers ease, and perhaps when he returns, he'll be more amenable to accommodations for his own safety."

"He'll never be amenable to being locked up in a palace." And she was an idiot for having even suggested it.

"Force the issue."

"I do not wish to discuss this anymore." Her voice cracked, and Zarrah cursed herself for allowing her hurt to take control. "My marriage to Keris is not your business."

Arjun crossed his arms, unmoved by her temper. "You are empress and he is prince consort. Your marriage is the business of the entire world."

It was the truth, but God help her, there were days Zarrah desperately longed for it to be otherwise. To live in obscurity with Keris, doing what they willed with no one else paying any mind.

But the stars had other plans in mind for them.

Why couldn't it be simple? Hadn't they gone through enough

for one lifetime? Even as the thoughts cycled through her head, Zarrah knew they were wishful thinking. It had been a delusion to believe their love would be enough to ease the generational animosity between Valcotta and Maridrina. All it had done was put a target on Keris's back, because many believed that if he were dead, the war would begin anew. That much was clear from the propaganda circulating through Pyrinat that kept landing on her desk.

*It never fucking ends.*

A tear ran down her cheek, and Zarrah viciously wiped it away even as she wished desperately to see Keris's ship returning to the harbor so that she could be back in his arms.

A knock sounded at the door, and her father cleared his throat and then called out, "Enter."

A soldier entered, bowing low. "Imperial Majesty, we have an urgent report."

Zarrah swallowed the part of her that was a woman, a wife, a person, and embraced that which was only the empress. "What is it?"

He stepped aside to allow one of her advisors inside, a servant also entering to set down a tray of letters before departing.

Her advisor bowed low. "Imperial Majesty. We have received word that a wasting disease is striking several cattle herds, which have necessitated culling to prevent the spread. Yet despite efforts, there are signs that it has already infected new herds. The farmers are requesting financial aid from the crown."

Zarrah's stomach dropped. With famine heavy upon Maridrina, it wasn't just her own people who depended on the meat from those animals. "When did this begin? How?"

"Recently." He heaved a large sigh. "It's believed the origin is breeding stock imported from Harendell, as theirs are a bulkier breed. They were kept separate, but an infected bull escaped his pen and entered the primary herd. The disease spreads rapidly."

"Take all measures to contain it," she ordered without hesitation. "Military support to keep it contained, and have them begin immediately culling full herds. I will compensate the farmers for their losses."

"Imperial Majesty—" her father started.

Zarrah held up a hand to forestall his protests that the crown couldn't afford the measures. "If farmers fear for their income, they will resist the cull, and the disease will continue to spread. See it done, and done swiftly."

Her advisor nodded and bowed low before departing.

Zarrah looked to her father. "I know what you aimed to say. That the coffers are drained and we can't afford it."

Arjun shook his head. "I aimed to suggest that we finally put effort into retrieving the wealth the Devil's Island current deposited in the prison. Daria told me there are buried caches in multiple places on the island."

*A small solution in a sea of problems.* "Do it."

As the door shut behind him, leaving Zarrah alone in the room, she opened one of the windows to allow in the breeze. It carried with it the scent of Pyrinat and the harbor beyond, and she inhaled, trying to find a measure of calm. She moved to her desk and refilled her teacup, feeling the weight of obligation pressing down on her.

*I need you here.*

On the heels of the thought, her eyes tracked to the stack of letters on the tray. The one on top was held closed with thick wax marked with Edward's seal. Picking it up, she slid her knife beneath the wax and unfolded the heavy paper.

*Dearest friend . . .* Zarrah broke off reading, realizing that it was yet another of Edward's letters to Keris. They kept up a regular correspondence of gossip and exchanges of trivia, which Keris found endlessly amusing. She started to set it down, but then paused, because within every letter was always some tidbit hidden within code.

Dipping her pen into a pot of ink, Zarrah began underlining the letters that matched his usual cipher, her stomach dropping as the message revealed itself.

*I will have wed William to Lestara by the time you receive this. Forgive the seeming betrayal of our friendship. As one who has risked all for love, you will one day understand everything, but know I regret the hurt my actions will cause you and your family.*

She could barely breathe, it feeling as though her lungs were being squeezed by a steel band. It took long weeks for letters to travel from Verwyrd to Pyrinat. Longer still if the storms slowed traffic to the entrances of the bridge.

Which meant Lestara and William would already be wed. Lestara, the woman responsible for the sacking of Vencia, was the future queen of Harendell.

Dragging open a desk drawer, Zarrah dug through the contents to find what she was looking for. In a few short strides, she crossed the room and flung open the door. "I need a message sent with all haste to Queen Sarhina asking to meet me in Nerastis."

The waiting guards blinked, then one asked, "Is there a letter to go along with the request?"

"None necessary," Zarrah replied, heading in pursuit of her father. "By the time our messenger reaches her, Sarhina will already know why."

# 7

# JAMES

THE RAIN HAD mercifully ceased during his ride through the night, but the wind cut deep against his soaked clothes as James dismounted outside the garrison. It was located in a small village at the base of the Blackreach foothills, a small structure sitting between an alehouse and a general store that housed only a handful of soldiers on most days. Today it was swarming with them, the picket line out front boasting two dozen horses.

"Walk her dry and then get her a stall in the barn," James instructed the soldier who took Maven's reins. "She's proven her worth when I needed her most."

"Yes, sir."

The door to the garrison swung open, and a frazzled-looking man with a cloud of fluffy blond curls sticking out in all directions stepped out. His eyes fixed on James, and he saluted sharply. "Lieutenant Arthur Holloway reporting, Major General, sir!"

"Where are they?" There was no patience left in James for protocols. "The witnesses?"

"The inn, sir. The boy's in a bad way, I'm afraid. He took a blow to the head when she attacked them."

Unbidden, a memory filled James's head of the moment Ahnna had stitched up his hand in Fernleigh's maze.

*A ruler needs an heir*, he'd said to her. *It's the way of it.*

*I know. But knowing your mother bore you because she had to is a burden I wouldn't wish upon any child. All children deserve to be wanted.*

James shook his head to clear her voice, unsure what exactly had triggered the memory, only that it caused gooseflesh to break out across his skin.

He followed Arthur's blond curls down the muddy street, past the alehouse to the inn. It was two levels, but the main floor was a common room filled with old men in conversation with their drinks, the bored barmaid drying glasses with a dirty rag. She gave James a smile and a wink when her eyes lit upon him, but he ignored her as the lieutenant led him to the stairs.

"Physician has been and gone a few times, sir," Arthur said. "He says it's in God's hands now whether the boy wakes or not. We're all saying prayers for him, but there's fear that he'll be another of the murderess's victims by week's end."

The first of many dead children if it came to war with Ithicana, and James sent a silent prayer to every higher power that William would remain reasonable. War was a powerful threat that could be used to manipulate Aren, but it was rarely kings who paid the ultimate price. William didn't really know combat, and he certainly didn't know war. James worried that with no one to temper him, William would see only the glory of bringing Ithicana low and not the true cost of such an action.

Yet another reason James needed to end this. With Ahnna dead and justice achieved, the kingdom's appetite for violence would be sated and Will would find no support for further action.

*Catch her*, Lestara's voice whispered inside his head. *Kill her.*

It was the only thing he could do to make all this right.

The lieutenant led him down the short hallway to an open door, pausing at the entrance. "His Royal Highness Prince James is here to see you," he told whoever was inside, then stepped out of James's way.

Two men stood in the small room, their caps pressed to their chests and their heads lowered. The older one said, "You honor us, Your Highness."

"All honor is deserved for those who serve Harendell." James's voice was wooden, his gaze going to the boy on the bed. He was perhaps sixteen, his face blanched pale and his head wrapped with bandages. "I am sorry for the injury that has befallen your grandson."

One of the men let out a choked sob, and the elder wrapped an arm around his shoulder. "He's a good lad. A strong lad. He'll pull through."

"Will you please tell me what happened?" James asked, his desire to get back on the hunt warring with his reluctance to press these men while their boy lay, likely dying, next to them. "Any information you can give me will aid in our pursuit of the perpetrator."

"Aye, my lord. Anything to help." The older man stepped closer, cap still clutched to his chest. "What she did to your father, our good king . . . She deserves to hang for it and it would be the greatest honor to help you see it done."

James nodded at him encouragingly despite wanting to shout at the man to get to the point. Ahnna was on horseback and moving fast, and if she crossed into Amarid, she was lost to him—as was the chance to end this before everything became chaos.

"We joined up with the militia searching the wilds for signs of her," the old man finally continued. "The three of us hunt these lands, so we know them well. Near dusk, we scented cooking meat on the wind and went in search. We came upon a camp with a doused fire. There was no one in sight, but a horse was tethered. A tall bay gelding, good racing stock from the look of him, but he had a big white star on his forehead. We thought it to be a traveler's camp, but then my boy—" His voice cracked, throat bobbing as he swallowed. "Johnny has a love of horses, and he got to stroking the gelding and discovered the star was nothing more than chalk."

*Clever, Ahnna.*

"That was when she dropped from the trees where she'd been

lurking above, deadly as a Blackreaches lion." The old man scrubbed a hand over his face, and James could smell the sweat pouring off him. The stink of remembered fear.

"I attacked her and held my own for a time, but I'm ashamed to say she disarmed me, my lord."

James doubted he held his own for more than a heartbeat.

"She was heartless as stone and forced us to bind each other. We did her bidding because she kept an arrow pointed at our Johnny, but when he tried to do as she told, the Ithicanian devil slammed his head against a rock to subdue him. He weren't no threat to the likes of her, but she treated him like a man with a sword in hand, not an unarmed boy. A cold killer if I've ever seen one, my lord."

Gooseflesh rose on James's skin, but he ignored the pricking sensation. "What was she wearing?"

"A man's clothing, my lord. Trousers and a greatcoat, and a cap to cover her hair."

"Supplies?"

"Saddlebags was all."

So not well supplied. The weather in the foothills was temperate this far south, but the Blackreaches were towering peaks, the air at the altitude near the border deadly cold. If it were anyone other than Ahnna, James would say that survival was impossible, but she knew how to live off the land. "What about weapons?"

"Bow and arrow." The mán lifted his hand to scratch his head, revealing large sweat stains on his shirt. "Who can say what else was beneath her coat?"

She'd had some weapons on her when she'd fled him, most notably a sword, and James could only imagine that she'd added to her arsenal. "And she headed west toward the Blackreaches?"

"Yes, my lord. I hope the honor of her death goes to you."

"I hope for this as well." Knowing that the men had likely been as motivated by reward as they were by desire to avenge their king, James withdrew a small pouch of coins from his pocket and handed it to the man. "In honor of your service to Harendell. I'll also see to it that the crown pays for your grandson's care."

The boy, Johnny, chose that moment to stir, and all eyes went to him.

"Don't hurt me," he whimpered. "Please don't hurt me."

His eyes opened, and he slowly focused on his father and grandfather. "Da?" Twin tears ran down his cheeks. "What happened?"

*Ahnna happened.*

James's anger, ever simmering, flared hot and bright, because she hadn't needed to hurt this child. These three were guilty of nothing more than greed for a bit of gold and cockiness that they could hold their own in a fight, which meant they hadn't deserved her violence. It made him wonder if he had ever known her, whether the kindness had been nothing but an act, because what she'd done to his father, to Alexandra, and to this boy was nothing like the woman that he'd—

James clamped down on the thought, shoving it away before his traitorous mind could voice exactly what he'd felt for Ahnna. In the silence, the specter of Lestara whispered, *You chose Ahnna over William, and he believes her continued freedom is proof you still love her more than you do your own family.*

He would prove to his family otherwise.

The boy was staring at him, and James gave him a sharp salute. "The crown thanks you for your bravery and loyalty. God speed your return to good health."

Turning on his heels, James motioned for Arthur to follow him. Once in the corridor, he said, "Your hounds are tracking her?"

"Yes, sir. Their best guess is she's headed toward the Skypass Trail."

It was a merchant road, narrow and difficult, but also the straightest shot across the border. "Choose five reliable men and strong horses, and get us all the supplies we need to go into the mountains."

He hesitated then, his focus drawn back in the direction of Sableton as he remembered Alexandra's request that he remain to temper William's impulses. Except what weight would his words have with his brother if he went back and left soldiers to chase Ahnna into the mountains? Catching her was the only way he could prove to his brother where his loyalties resided. In a matter of days, he'd return with her corpse and war would be averted. William wouldn't do anything rash in such a short period of time.

He hoped.

"We move out in an hour," James said, realizing the lieutenant was still waiting for him to finish his orders. "Get me my horse."

They left the inn, and James paused to examine the distant mountains, snowcapped year-round and cold as death. *I'm coming for you Ahnna. And there is nowhere you can run where I won't find you.*

# 8
# LARA

THE MERCHANT CAPTAIN shifted uncomfortably, unable to meet Lara's eyes as he set a letter sealed with the crest of Harendell on the table before her. "The Harendellians asked that this be delivered to Northwatch, Your Grace," he said. "Every ship flying their colors is forbidden to trade with Ithicana, but they've not yet moved to blockades. Flying Maridrinian colors as we are, we aim to run the route between Sableton and Northwatch for as long as the Harendellians allow it. Or until the Harendellians begin directing trade to Cardiff, at which time we'll make the run north into the bay."

Aren made an aggrieved noise, then snatched up the letter and cracked the wax. Lara watched his eyes skim the contents, his jaw, shadowed with several days' stubble, hardening. He handed it to her without comment, then resumed pacing the room. Lara glanced at the looping cursive, which was a request from the newly crowned King William to meet at Emesmere Island so they might hand over Ahnna and negotiate reparations. Lara set it face down on the table, then turned her eyes on her countryman. "What else can you tell me, Captain?"

The man rocked on his heels, and Bronwyn moved from where she'd been lingering next to the window. Pouring a glass of wine, she gave it to the captain and then rested her hand on his shoulder. "Speak true, friend, else you'll never see Maridrina's golden shores again."

The man's face blanched, and Lara fought the urge to roll her eyes at her sister's less-than-subtle threat.

"I only know what everyone else knows, my lady," he said after taking a gulp of the wine. "King Edward hosted a ball in the Sky Palace, but rather than announcing a date for nuptials between Prince William and Princess Ahnna, he declared that he'd formed an alliance with King Ronan of Cardiff, which included terms allowing for free trade between the nations. To cement the alliance, he had secretly wed Prince William to the witch Lestara of Cardiff." He spat on the floor. "Murderous bitch. Prince Keris ought to have taken her head for what she did. This might never have happened."

Lara didn't disagree that Keris's creativity in punishment had unleashed a problem that a beheading might have prevented, but she strongly suspected that the alliance with Cardiff had been a lifetime in the making. James's lifetime, to be specific. The marriage to Lestara was likely nothing more than the frosting on the cake of profit. "Continue. And please refrain from spitting on my floor."

"Apologies, Your Grace." The man knelt and wiped the mess up with his sleeve, his eyes jumping from her, to Bronwyn, to Aren, seemingly uncertain who was the greatest threat. "There was more to King Edward's speech. He went on about some history with Prince James's mother—apparently, she was also a Cardiffian witch, King Ronan's sister, no less, and Queen Katarina was the one who murdered her. Edward and Ronan intended to march through the Lowlands to raze Amarid as vengeance for their mutual suffering. At any rate, the Princess Ahnna took great issue with being jilted and offered threats to Edward before storming out. Late that night, he was discovered brutally stabbed to death in his bed, and when the alarm was sounded, Prince James and his men discovered Princess Ahnna in the act of trying to kill Queen Alexandra. She escaped the Sky Palace and fled into the countryside on horseback, evading all attempts at capture. She was spotted in Sableton trying to reach the harbor but fled, and she had not yet been apprehended when we set sail." The captain hesitated, then added, "Prince James heads the search himself, but the entirety of Harendell is in arms hunting the princess, all desiring vengeance for the murder of Good King Eddie."

"Ahnna didn't murder Edward," Aren growled. "This is the scheme of some power-hungry Harendellian, and my sister is nothing but a scapegoat."

The captain shifted uneasily. "As you say, Your Grace. I'm only repeating the beliefs of the common Harendellians. Tavern gossip, if you get my meaning."

Tavern gossip could be shockingly accurate, but Lara only gave the man a small smile. "We thank you for your service. Safe travels."

"Have you heard anything about Lady Taryn?" Bronwyn asked as the man began to turn away. "Any information as to where she's been taken or if she's well?"

"No, Your Highness," he answered. "Not a word."

At Lara's nod, he retreated and then exited the room.

Aren waited until the door clicked shut, then exploded, "It's not even a request, Lara! William is ordering me to meet him at Emesmere to address his demands. Like I'm a dog to be dragged, tail between my legs, to make amends for shitting on his floor."

"Colorful," Bronwyn muttered, but there was an edge to her sister's tone that matched the seething fury in her eyes. Bronwyn and Taryn had grown close in their friendship, and while her sister had been closemouthed about the nature of their relationship, Lara suspected that the two were lovers.

"The captain's story is consistent with what James told Bronwyn when he arrested Taryn." Lara rose to go to the window, looking out over Northwatch. The skies were gray and misty, but there was no sign of weather that might prevent a meeting at Emesmere. "It's consistent with everything we've been told."

Which meant this was either a very well-orchestrated deception . . .

Or the truth.

Bronwyn sighed and took a seat at the table, staring gloomily at the wood. "James believes it, Lara. That much I know. You can't feign that sort of anger and grief. While he didn't elaborate as to exactly what Ahnna was doing to Alexandra when he came upon them, it was violent. Her guilt in that crime is certain. Whether Ahnna was also the one to kill Edward, only she can say for sure, but the evidence is damning." Bronwyn hesitated, then added, "As is her motive."

"Ahnna didn't do this!" Aren slammed his fists down on the table so hard that the glassware bounced, and Lara felt a pang in her chest at the fear beneath his anger.

"I didn't believe it at first, either," Bronwyn said. "But I think we have to consider that Ahnna's anger got the better of her."

"My sister wouldn't do this! It's not who she is!"

"You're the last person who can claim to know Ahnna's mind," Bronwyn snapped at him. "You two have been at odds from the day you married Lara, and I assure you, the woman Ahnna was before the invasion doesn't exist anymore."

"Bronwyn, enough." Lara left the window and moved to rest her hands on the table. "This isn't helpful."

"Isn't it?" Her sister scoffed and then leaned back in her chair. "Because given that you two are pressing forward on the assumption that Ahnna is innocent, I think it is. Saving Ithicana was Ahnna's obsession. She went to Verwyrd on a mission to gain power and influence. Power and influence that she hoped to use to increase trade through the bridge and put enough profit in Ithicana's coffers that you could feed your people and rebuild. So that *she* could be the savior of Ithicana, not *you*." Bronwyn leveled a finger at Lara's chest. "She wanted to prove she was better than you in every possible way."

*Ahnna isn't that petty.* "Enough, Bronwyn."

"No, you listen." Her sister rose. "She was obsessed, and Edward surely saw that. Strung her along and made her feel as though she was wanted. As though she was exactly the woman Harendell needed. Made her feel as though her goals were in her grasp, and then he ripped out the carpet from beneath her and sent Ahnna sprawling in front of all of Harendell's nobility. He didn't just marry William to another princess and destroy her dream of becoming queen, but also declared his plan to direct all the gold Ithicana needed into Cardiff. And to top it all off, James, her one *friend*"—Bronwyn's voice seethed with sarcasm—"was the man behind the whole plan. Which meant he'd been lying to her the entire time. Don't tell me, Lara, that the sum of this isn't enough to break anyone, least of all a woman who has spent the past years suffering trauma after trauma."

"Stop." Lara's hands balled into fists. Her sister's words were making the air in the room so very hard to breathe.

"I will not." Bronwyn got to her feet. "Because Taryn, who has done *nothing*, is once again a prisoner, and I don't know if she will survive it. I have no doubt that Ahnna acted impulsively. I have no doubt that she regrets what she has done. But my most sincere hope is that she turns herself in and accepts all accountability, because then maybe William will have *fucking* mercy on the rest of us!"

"Get out!" Lara screamed as her own temper cracked. "Go!"

"Gladly!" Bronwyn stormed from the room, slamming the door shut behind her.

Lara drew a steadying breath, already unhappy that she'd lost control of her emotions. Aren still had his hands planted on the table but the anger had left her husband's gaze, leaving a hollowness that cut her to the core.

"What if Bronwyn's right?" Aren asked softly.

"She's not." Lara circled the table and pushed him down on a chair. Straddling him, she cupped his stubbled cheeks and forced him to meet her gaze. "Ahnna is brash and brazen. Prone to saying exactly what she thinks. But she is *never* impulsively violent. If there is anyone in the world who could have driven her to murder, it's me, but your sister has never once harmed me."

"She pushed you off the bridge."

Lara scoffed. "That was an accident and you know it. She could have killed me a hundred times over, and she never once tried. When she saw me trying to climb onto Eranahl during the attack, she could have let me fall but instead pulled me up. As someone who *is* a murderer, I say with the utmost confidence that Ahnna didn't do this. She's being framed, and my gut tells me that Alexandra is at the center of it."

"Alexandra was injured, and she said it was Ahnna who did it. There were witnesses who came upon them. *James* was one of those witnesses."

"Ahnna wouldn't have *injured* her. Ahnna would have killed her with ease. My bet is that Ahnna either walked into the middle of the attack and there was confusion, or that . . ." Her throat tightened. "Or that circumstances were staged."

Aren blinked, his bloodshot eyes sharpening. "Why?"

"To give herself an alibi."

Silence stretched between them as the weight of her words settled on them both, then Aren said, "Why would Alexandra murder Edward?"

Lara considered what she knew about the Harendellian royals. "There was no love lost between them, that is well known. Except Alexandra wouldn't have killed him over a cold marriage—she's too pragmatic. I think it's because of Cardiff. She's a true believer, so she can't have taken the news that Edward had formed an alliance with Cardiff well. His choice to marry William to Lestara behind her back must have gone over even worse. Alexandra will not want competition for influence over William, least of all a pagan Cardiffian princess. My guess is that Lestara isn't long for this world."

Aren gripped her hips, his hands warm through the thin fabric of her dress. "Getting reports will be challenging, given that the navy is patrolling their coast. The Harendellians will be searching merchant ships and reading messages, and I don't foresee receiving reports between now and when I have to meet with William."

"Agreed." The very same challenges Ahnna faced in trying to return to Ithicana.

As though reading her thoughts, Aren's fingers tightened. "If Ahnna somehow makes her way back to us, I'm not giving her up to them. I'm not letting them murder her."

"I don't think she's what they are really after." Lara stroked her fingers through his hair, feeling the silken texture as she considered Harendell's queen mother. "I think Ahnna is leverage. If Alexandra's goal is to destroy the alliance with Cardiff and ensure that trade flows south rather than north, she needs to sweeten the terms on the bridge to satisfy the merchant class. Edward dangled the prospects of free trade with Cardiff before them, which also meant better access to the nations in the far north. She has to make them whole, and that means negotiating with us using Ahnna's *crimes* as the bargaining chip.

Harendell will deem us innocent of involvement in exchange for free use of the bridge."

Aren sighed, then bent his neck to rest his forehead against her shoulder. "We can't afford that."

"We can't win a war against Harendell, so there is no choice." She stroked his back, fighting a sudden surge of anger that, after everything, they could not have a moment to just live. To be a family with no threats against them. To be happy and safe.

*That's your lot in life*, she silently chided herself. *That has always been Ithicana's lot, so quit wallowing and figure out a way to survive this. Be a fucking cockroach.*

"Harendell will be coming to this meeting looking to negotiate," she said. "Let's see what they have to say. Let's get William's measure."

"None of this would be happening if I'd made Ahnna leave." Aren's breath was shaky. "I should have tied her up and dragged her home. She only stayed because of *him*."

Lara made a soft humming sound that was neither agreement nor disagreement, because there would have been other consequences if they'd forcibly taken Ahnna back to Ithicana. Ahnna had no good choice, which she had surely known. As for what may or may not have been between Ahnna and James, Lara felt only the utmost sympathy for Ahnna, for his betrayal must have cut her to the core.

Aren straightened and met her gaze. "You can't come to this meeting. You know that, don't you?"

Her entire body stiffened. "I'm not allowing you to meet with those spiders alone."

"I won't be alone." He lifted a hand to smooth back her hair. "But if it all goes to shit, one of us needs to be alive to rule. To get Ithicana through this. To protect our daughter."

Lara's chest tightened at the mention of Delia, who slept in the next room under Nana's watchful eye. She'd not considered having to choose between protecting her husband and protecting her daughter, and every part of her hated that such a choice was now forced upon her.

Aren gestured to William's letter. "It's me he wants to speak with.

Which is not to our benefit, because I don't know how well I'm going to hold my temper through this conversation—you would do it better."

Lara wasn't so sure. What the Harendellians had done to Ahnna had lit flames of anger in her chest that she hadn't felt since her father had invaded Ithicana. The desire for vengeance had her reaching for a weapon, not words.

Her husband lowered his head to kiss her, tongue chasing over hers and igniting heat in her lower belly. She desperately desired to sate it, because fear was growing in her chest that it would be her last chance. That he would get on a ship and sail away and that she'd never see him again, and Lara wanted to hold Aren back, hold him close, using whatever means possible. Her lips parted to tell him to send an envoy, someone else, anyone else, because she could not risk losing him.

But Lara strangled the words and kissed her husband with enough ferocity to bruise.

"I love you," he murmured, hand skimming over the side of her breast. "In moments like these, I wish to take you and Delia and run as far from this nightmare as we can get. To leave it all behind and live happily. But that isn't who we are, is it?"

Lara pressed her forehead to his even as her fingers grazed the knife belted at her waist. "No," she whispered, reaching for the steel inside her heart: the warrior, the defender, the queen. "We are the ones who stand our ground and fight."

# 9
# AHNNA

Ahnna eyed the towering mountains looming ahead while using her free hand to first turn up the collar of her coat and then pull her cap farther down over her ears.

Because it was cold. Bitterly cold.

Logically, she'd been aware that the Blackreach Peaks forming much of the border between Amarid and Harendell would force her to endure temperatures she'd never before experienced. The knowledge hadn't prepared her for the icy wind that bit through her clothes and cut down to the bone. It grew worse with every passing hour that Dippy carried her higher into the mountains, and Ahnna felt the altitude keenly, her breath short and exhaustion preying upon her.

These mountains were dangerous.

Even in Ithicana, there was an awareness that the Blackreaches were usually avoided. Merchants traveled weeks north to go through the Lowlands or used ships to navigate around the peninsula. The coastline of the peninsula itself was prone to heavy flooding from the Tempest Seas and runoff from the mountains, so no one lived on the barren stretch of land but seals and gulls. Even so, Ahnna would have traveled that way to reach Amarid if not for the wall that stretched from the Blackreaches into the sea, where riptides made short work of the strongest swimmers.

The Amaridians had built the wall generations ago to dissuade Harendellian attacks. Thirty feet tall and topped with razor wire, it was watched by archers on both sides because it remained a popular route for those transporting contraband. The chances of getting caught trying to scale the wall were too high, and she didn't have time to go north to the Lowlands. The entire north was against Ithicana, and unless that ruby necklace she'd sent as a warning made it to Northwatch before all had gone to shit, it was possible Aren was entirely unaware of the threat Katarina posed.

Time was of the essence, which meant Ahnna had no choice but to risk traveling through the Blackreach Peaks. They offered not just cold and snow but also treacherous terrain with very little in the way of food for her or Dippy.

"You've gone hungry before," she muttered. "Stick to the road and you'll be fine."

A road that was little more than a narrow path, not even wide enough for two horses to travel abreast, which spoke to the lack of traffic through these famed mountains.

Yet it wasn't just the Blackreaches themselves that dissuaded trade and travel.

It was what hunted these lofty peaks.

Ahnna's skin prickled with gooseflesh, and she searched the dense conifers around her for signs of motion. The sensation of being watched only grew, so she looked back down the trail, certain that she'd see James in pursuit, murder in his eyes.

The Harendellian trio she'd encountered would have brought word by now to the local garrison, and James would be on her trail. Ahnna had no delusions that he'd be swayed by the message she'd sent with the men, but she'd had to try.

It pained her to admit it, but there was a part of her that hoped he'd see through Alexandra's schemes. That he'd believe the queen capable of stabbing herself not once but three times in order to frame Ahnna for murder. That he knew Ahnna well enough to know that no matter how angry she'd been, she'd never have murdered Edward while he slept in his bed.

That he cared enough to hear her out.

The last made her feel the most foolish of all, because James had proven, in abundance, that he cared far more for Harendell and Cardiff than he did for her.

Ahnna clenched her teeth, trying to force away anything but the most practical thoughts of survival, but in the soft silence of the mountains, there wasn't enough to distract her from the bite of betrayal that in equal parts made her burn with humiliation and want to curl up and weep.

It wasn't that she didn't understand why making peace between Cardiff and Harendell had been so important to James. It was an admirable goal, and if not for the fact it ran so goddamned counter to her own goals, Ahnna would have applauded it.

The betrayal was that, despite knowing his success meant her failure, James had still allowed ... Ahnna drew in a ragged breath, not wanting to think about what he had allowed to happen between them. His lips on hers, the taste of his tongue in her mouth, and the feel of him between her legs. How she had wept and confessed her darkest secrets in his arms, wholly convinced she could trust him with her heart.

In her darker moments, Ahnna was convinced he'd seduced her for the purpose of discovering her secrets. That he'd felt nothing for her and that it had all been an act, the sentiment—and idiocy—hers and hers alone.

Her foolish heart argued otherwise. Screamed that James hadn't known his father's plans. That he'd been as caught up and manipulated as she'd been. That he *had* cared about her as she'd cared for him.

Experience told her that the truth was somewhere in between, but Ahnna did not think there was an explanation that would cure the anger she still felt at how James had done nothing but stand in silence while Edward had stolen away Ahnna's every hope, humiliating her and Ithicana in pursuit of a better prize.

"Enough," Ahnna growled at herself. "What's done is done, and none of it can be changed. Focus on the challenges before you. Focus on what you can do to mitigate the damage. Focus on getting home."

She might as well have spit into the wind for all the good her words did. James was clever and tenacious, but more than anything else, he was angry. There was no doubt in her mind that he was with the group trailing her, their campfire smoke visible in the distance, because for him, this was personal. If he caught up to her, he'd kill her. Unless she killed him first.

But was she capable of doing so?

Ahnna had the blood of more people than she could count on her hands, but they'd all been strangers. Had all been people who'd brought violence to Ithicana. She'd never killed someone she knew, much less someone she'd cared about. *More* than cared about. As pragmatic as she could be, Ahnna worried that if it came down to it, she wouldn't be able to strike a fatal blow.

*Why didn't you kill her?* Ahnna remembered screaming at Aren when she'd discovered he'd let Lara go. *Why didn't you cut her fucking throat?*

Her brother had only blanched, eyes dark pools of misery, and when she'd demanded that he answer, Jor had told her to back off. But she hadn't let it go. No part of her had understood why Aren hadn't killed the woman who'd destroyed everything that mattered to them.

God help her, but Ahnna understood now.

"Except this is different," she muttered. "Killing Lara would have achieved nothing but revenge, whereas you might have to kill James in order to protect Ithicana."

Dippy's ears were swiveled to listen to her, and he snorted loudly and quickened his pace.

"You're right," she replied. "Better to just stay ahead of him so it doesn't—"

Motion and noise exploded from brush at her left, and Dippy shied sideways, nearly unseating her.

Ahnna reached for her bow but then spotted the birds flying up into the sky and checked the reins instead. "Easy, boy."

Dippy was as nervous as she was, but it had nothing to do with James and everything to do with what else prowled these mountains.

The white lions of the Blackreaches.

She'd heard they were a sort of mountain lion, but rather than sporting tawny fur, they were ghostly white and able to blend into the frosty landscape. They plagued the shepherds and farmers of the foothills on both sides of the mountain range, easily killing sheep and the dogs that guarded them. But what put the fear into the hearts of Harendellians and Amaridians alike was that they were man-eaters.

And very good at catching their prey.

Patting Dippy's neck to steady him, Ahnna extracted an arrow from her quiver. Ithicana had wild cats, but they weren't big enough to see humans as prey—Vitex, Aren's cat, mostly fed on snakes and rodents. But remembering how Vitex hunted had Ahnna watching the tree branches often as she scoured her surroundings, knowing full well that she was unlikely to see the attack coming.

As the sun fell low, only a thin sliver of orange between two peaks, Ahnna dismounted and lit the lantern hanging from her saddle. Exhausted as both she and her horse were, she needed to put more distance between her and James before setting up camp for the night.

The moon was rising to join the myriad stars in the sky. It was a slender crescent, barely piercing the shadows around her, leaving the lantern's glow as her only source of light. The wind was a constant, chilling howl, rattling her bones as much as it shook the trees. Each step felt like a risk, as if she were the only prey in a wilderness full of predators.

Ahnna's hand tightened on Dippy's reins as she led him onward. His hooves made sharp clacks against the loose stones, his ears flicking back and forth in a constant state of vigilance. She couldn't blame him. Every shadow seemed like a lurking beast, every sound a warning.

She glanced over her shoulder again, half expecting to see yellow eyes staring back from some hidden crevice in the rock. Her hands were growing numb, and though she wanted to shove them deep in her pockets, Ahnna was unwilling to let go of her grip on her bow.

The path narrowed again, forcing her closer to the edge, where a sheer drop fell away into nothing but blackness. She took a deep breath and focused on her footing, feeling the sting of cold air in her lungs. Dippy shuddered beside her, and Ahnna murmured softly to him, "Steady, boy," the words meant as much to calm herself as the horse.

A stone skittered down the slope above, and Ahnna froze, heart pounding. She held her breath, eyes scanning the darkness for the crouched shape of a white cat ready to pounce. The silence returned, oppressive and vast, pressing down on her shoulders like the weight of the mountain itself.

On and on they walked, and Ahnna did not stop until well after midnight when her eyes picked out the signs of a rough campsite set up in a clearing with a slope to one side that would hide the glow of a fire. Loosely picketing Dippy so that he could break free if he needed to, Ahnna gathered deadfall and set to building three fires around the perimeter of her camp. She ate the rest of her squirrel meat from a prior meal while water from a nearby stream warmed in a tiny cup next to one of the fires.

Dippy grazed the scrubby grass, and Ahnna measured out some of the grain she had in one of her saddlebags, knowing that he'd need it more when they got higher in the mountains. Already, the streams had ice along their edges, and the wind blowing in from the north smelled of snow.

Building up the fires so they'd burn for at least an hour, Ahnna wrapped up in her blanket and lay on the ground. It was rocky and uncomfortable, but with the relative sanctuary of flame and the weight of exhaustion heavy upon her, sleep came.

But so did the dreams.

Gravel and debris dug into her back, but Ahnna barely felt it as she tangled her fingers in James's hair, every part of her consumed by the sensation of his mouth between her legs. "I want you in me," she begged. "Please, James."

The sun gleamed off the hard muscles of his shoulders as he lifted his face, amber eyes dark with lust. He was so beautiful, so harshly masculine, that part of her wanted to hold him in position so her mind might freeze the vision of him forever, but her body ached with the need for more. The need for him to fill her, body and soul.

"You want this?" His voice was low, nearly a growl, and every muscle in Ahnna's body tightened, her thighs slick as she reached for him. "Yes. I want this."

He kissed her lips, and she tasted the salt of her own body on his tongue as he took hold of his cock and pressed the thick tip against her. She wrapped her legs around his waist, pulling him deep into her body.

"Ahnna," he groaned into her mouth. "You feel so good."

He pulled back and thrust again, deeper this time. She arched her back, needing to take as much of him as possible, climax rising in her body.

"Harder," she gasped, desperate to have all of him. Every part of him, most especially his heart. "Make me yours."

"You have always been mine." He slammed into her, fingers locked with hers. "You will always be mine."

Her climax began to crest, and Ahnna opened her lips to cry out his name.

Only to taste blood.

Hot sticky blood splashed, filling her mouth, and she choked, trying to scream. James stared down at her, throat sliced open from ear to ear, and through the bloody opening, his voice whispered, "I loved you."

"James," she screamed, trying to stop the blood, but a cruel laugh filled her ears. As he collapsed onto her, Ahnna saw Alexandra standing in the darkness, a knife in one hand. "Such a disappointment," the queen of Harendell chuckled. "Such a failure. But don't worry, Ahnna. At least I have the stomach for murder."

The dream shattered with a sharp, panicked whinny. Ahnna's eyes snapped open, her heart pounding as she tried to orient herself in the pitch-black night. Her fires were nothing more than glowing embers.

How long had she been asleep?

Dippy was snorting, his large shadow frozen in place, his terror palpable.

Ahnna had only a moment to snatch up her bow and nock an arrow before she heard a low, terrible growl that sent a chill straight through her. She leapt to her feet just as a white shape sprang from the shadows, all coiled muscle and glinting claws.

Ahnna threw herself sideways, barely rolling out of reach before the lion's claws raked across the spot where she'd been lying. Her hands fumbled to nock the arrow again, her fingers slick with sweat despite the cold, her breath fast and shallow as she aimed, body shaking as she drew the bowstring taut.

The lion circled her, its eyes glowing in the faint moonlight like twin mirrors, lips drawn back in a snarl that exposed long fangs. It was injured but not badly; blood streaked from a shallow gash on its shoulder where Dippy must have kicked it before she woke. Ahnna released the arrow, and it sank into the cat's flank. But rather than fleeing into the darkness, it lunged at her with a vicious snarl.

Dippy screamed and broke free of his tether. He kicked out wildly and nearly hit the lion, but the creature sprang out of the way. It circled the camp, a ghostly shadow in the red glow of the dying fires. Ahnna scrambled to her feet, her heart a frantic drumbeat in her chest as she nocked another arrow.

Only for the ghostly shape to disappear into the darkness.

Dippy snorted, nostrils flaring with the scent of the predator that had almost certainly not given up.

Ahnna held her bow at the ready, hunting the darkness for a white shape. Listening for any sound that might give her a clue as to where the predator was.

Then in her periphery, a shadow moved.

She only barely threw herself to the side, the searing graze of its claws ripping through her coat, warm blood trickling down her shoulder. The pain was sharp, but she forced herself to ignore it. The beast stalked closer, a low, throaty growl rattling the cold night air, its eyes alight with hunger.

She let the arrow fly, striking it in the shoulder. The lion staggered, its snarl turning to a rasping, pained hiss, but still it advanced. It was gaunt, the desperation for food visible in each limping step. It needed this meal and was willing to die for it.

The lion was between her and her quiver, so Ahnna dropped her bow and pulled a knife. She swiped at the lion and it recoiled, but fast as lightning, it pounced.

Ahnna flung herself sideways, claws snagging in her clothes even as her knife sliced along the lion's belly.

It screamed but though blood splattered the snow, the wound wasn't deep enough to stop the attack. The creature was hungry, and if it didn't kill her, it wouldn't have the strength to take down something else.

This was a fight to the death.

The lion circled, muscles bunching, and Ahnna braced.

But then Dippy attacked. With a scream Ahnna had never heard him make, her horse reached out and clamped his teeth down on the lion's back. He jerked the cat from side to side and then flung it across the camp.

Before the lion could rise, her horse was on it. Dippy slammed his hooves down, trampling until white fur turned red, bones were crushed, and gore soaked into the snow.

The lion let out one last wet gurgle, then went still.

Ahnna stood frozen, chest heaving. She had not known horses were capable of that sort of violence.

Dippy snorted at her, and Ahnna stumbled over to fling her arms around the gelding's neck. "Thank you," she breathed, pressing her face against his sweaty coat. "I will never let you go."

Lighting the lantern, she examined Dippy to ensure he wasn't injured, then swiftly rinsed the shallow cuts the lion's claws had left on her arm. Her coat would need mending, but she could do that while she rode. The stink of blood would draw any number of predators, so they needed to get away from this place.

Ahnna loaded up her supplies and readied to set out. But as she mounted, a speck of light in the distance caught her eye.

It was so far off as to be little more than a pinprick, but it was undeniably a campfire.

"James," she whispered, every instinct in her body telling her that it was him. Reflexively, she reached up to wipe her face, expecting her hand to come away bloody. It was clean, but from the darkness of her mind, Alexandra's voice echoed: *Such a disappointment. Such a failure. But don't worry, Ahnna. At least I have the stomach for murder.*

"We have to hurry, Dippy." Ahnna dug in her heels, knowing that for all her horse's speed, there were some things he could not outrun.

# 10
# JAMES

*J*AMES.

He jerked upright, certain that he'd find Ahnna standing before him, but there were only the sleeping shapes of his men and the glow of the campfire.

"Sir?" Arthur stepped from the shadows, a loosely nocked bow in his hands. His full head of curls pushed out from beneath his woolen cap, his face red from the cold.

"What was that?" James asked.

"Screams," Arthur answered, turning his back to the fire so that his eyes were once again on the shadows. "Sounded like a lion caught something farther up the valley."

James stiffened, and his stomach dropped.

"Not human screams," Arthur clarified, rocking on his heels. "Horse."

The world spun, James's mind filling with a vision of Ahnna's half-eaten corpse, her hazel eyes staring glassily up at him. He hunted her with the intent of killing her, but the vision made him feel sick, his mouth sour. "Wake everyone. We need to ride."

"It's not wise to ride in the dark, Major General," Arthur said. "If a lion took her horse, we'll catch her quick come daylight."

"She might be injured." The words came out without thought, and as Arthur frowned, James added, "The king will want proof she's dead. That's hard to give if she's in a lion's stomach."

All true, but not the reason his pulse thrummed with urgency. "Get everyone up."

Though the men moved swiftly, it felt like an eternity before they were mounted, and it was all James could do not to gallop Maven down the dark trail. Under any circumstances, doing so would be dangerous, but he was well aware of Ithicana's reputation for booby traps and trickery, and the idea that this might be a trick sat in the back of his mind as they pressed onward up the winding trail.

"Should've brought the dogs," Arthur called, and though he was a reliable soldier, James wished he spoke less. "She could've backtracked around us and we'd never know it. We should send someone back for them."

There was no backtracking here, at least not on horseback. The terrain was too rough, torn apart by rockslides and crisscrossed with deep ravines. On her own, she'd manage the climb, but Ahnna wouldn't abandon Dippy in the wilds, of that much James was certain. "Dogs don't survive these mountains," he called back. "If the lions don't get them, they bring bears down upon camps. No dogs."

James had hunters and their hounds with them, but he'd sent them back when they'd first encountered mountain lion scat. Though it had been tempting to keep the hounds longer, given the way they bayed and barked at Ahnna's fresh trail, James knew better. The Blackreach lions didn't just eat dogs, they ate men, and it was better to take longer than to risk his men's lives by tempting the wildlife down upon them.

Yet for all his thoughts for caution, he heeled Maven into a canter at the first glow of dawn light.

Only to draw her up short as he rounded a bend.

The small clearing had signs it was regularly used as a camp by travelers, and the remains of three charred campfires looked fresh. But it was the dead lion at the center of the site that stole his attention.

James drew his sword, hunting for signs that this was a trap even as his heart climbed into his throat with the certainty that the next body he'd spot would be hers.

But there was no sign of Ahnna or her horse.

Sliding off Maven's back, James left the mare and approached the dead lion. It was broken and bloodied, fur more red than white, but there was no mistaking the distinct shape of a horseshoe repeatedly crushed into its flesh.

Dippy had proven his worth.

Reaching down, James touched the broken arrow jutting from the cat's flank, feeling the temperature of the body, which had not yet frozen. "She's not long gone. Ride!"

# 11
# AREN

AREN HAD DEBATED sailing one of the many ships Ithicana had acquired over the years—vessels stolen from pirates, salvaged from storms, or commandeered during failed attempts to crack the Bridge Kingdom's defenses. In the end, he'd decided to arrive at the meeting with King William of Harendell in an Ithicanian vessel crewed by his bodyguard, a fleet of similar vessels in his wake.

William's letter had been specific about the rules of engagement. Twelve people, no weapons, and all vessels were to be kept well back of Emesmere Island. The island itself was uninhabited, little more than a block of rock cast into the ocean with minimal greenery clinging to its iron-gray surface. It had long been debated whether it belonged to Ithicana or Harendell, so for the sake of peace, neither nation used it for much beyond a harbor of last resort in a storm. It had been hard to resist sending someone ahead to plant an Ithicanian flag on the highest point and officially claim it as his just to be contrary.

"You'll recognize the *Victoria*," Jor muttered, resting a hand against the mast for balance. "The rest look to be ships of the line, but

I can't tell which ones from here. Seems like they're holding to their word and keeping well back."

Aren grunted in agreement, then lifted a hand to shade his eyes to better see the setup the Harendellians had elected to use for the meeting. They'd erected a large pavilion of white fabric intended to shelter those beneath it from the weather, but they'd not accounted for the stiff breeze, and it looked ready to snap its moorings and fly away like a great white bird. Beneath it sat a table set with a white tablecloth that was equally at risk of being lost to the wind, on which rested an ornate writing desk. The sight of it lent credence to Lara's belief that the Harendellians were here to negotiate.

God but he wished she were here. Lara had an eye for schemes, and all of the Magpie's training would allow her to see things in the way the Harendellians moved, hear things in their inflections, and sense things in the uncanny way only those who had survived on instincts ever could. But his wife was with Delia, Nana, and a heavy guard on one of Ithicana's more impenetrable islands. Ready to rule, to lead, to go to war if this was a trap.

Except Aren's gut told him that the Harendellians had something else in mind for this meeting.

The double-hulled canoe ran up on the narrow and rocky beach, and Aren climbed out. Waves soaked his boots as he strode up the slope toward the pavilion, but it was his lack of weapons that caused him discomfort. His bodyguard fell in alongside him, Commander Mara the only senior member of his military present, and she was here only because she knew the Harendellians better than anyone.

"They just launched a longboat," Lia murmured, her eyes on the *Victoria*. "Twelve aboard, by my count."

Aren counted the same, his eyes skipping over the shadowed figures. In the mist and gloom, it was difficult to identify anyone, but he suspected one of the smaller hooded figures was a woman. Alexandra was his guess, which called into question whether her injuries had been as serious as reported.

He reached the pavilion, the billowing silken material irritating in the relative silence.

*Snap.*

*Snap.*

*Snap.*

Aren twitched each time the fabric stretched taut. With a curse of exasperation, he pulled up the four stakes holding it in place. The white fabric launched into the air, soaring over the Harendellians as they reached the beach. They looked up at it as it flew, watching as it tangled in the rigging of the *Victoria*. Crew members climbed up to remove it, but the white fabric resisted their efforts.

Jor chuckled. Aren did not.

The Harendellians climbed out of their longboat, then formed a procession up the path to where the table sat.

"The cocky-looking one with the hooded woman on his arm is William," Jor said under his breath. "The man leading the group is Lieutenant George Cavendish, lord heir to the earldom of Elgin. Good fighter, and right-hand man to Prince James. I don't know the others in the group."

"I recognize Cavendish from when they retrieved Ahnna from Northwatch," Aren replied. "James isn't here, though. None of them are tall enough."

Which was probably just as well. Aren wasn't certain his control over his temper extended to the man who'd been seducing Ahnna while working to stab her in the back.

"Lara told me James is heading up the hunt for Ahnna," Jor replied. "His absence suggests that he, at least, doesn't believe she's here. They can't start making demands for a woman they know we don't have."

*Where are you?* Aren sent the question onto the wind, willing it to find his sister. *Please be safe.*

Because the alternative was that James wasn't here because he'd already captured Ahnna.

Aren silently watched the Harendellians approach. The majority of them were soldiers, and they scanned their surroundings for threats with a practiced eye. In truth, Aren was somewhat surprised that William had chosen to come himself. The seas always presented a risk, especially at this time of year, and the prince was not known for his bravery. Though Edward had always been one to get himself into the thick of things, so perhaps this was the son trying to live up to his father's legacy.

Or perhaps it was for another reason entirely.

Lord Cavendish dropped back next to his king, his eyes on Aren as he murmured something. Likely identifying him, though William's brow only furrowed with annoyance, and he snapped a retort that Aren couldn't make out.

"William has a hot temper and a reliance on drink," Jor said softly as they drew nearer. "He radiates pride and ego, but beneath it all, he's a boy who was never good enough for his father. Some rally in such a situation, but William is not one of them. He's a mother's boy who desperately needs the flattery of others, which is why he surrounds himself with sycophants."

For all Aren had inherited his crown in the same way as William, it struck him how unfair it was to the people of Harendell that they were stuck with such a man by virtue of birth. "So he can be provoked?"

"Undoubtedly, but if he makes a threat, he'll feel compelled to follow through on it for the sake of his pride, even if he regrets it in hindsight. Tread warily."

"Understood."

William walked with a swaggering stride, waving off the soldiers around him as he reached the opposite side of the table, the hooded woman still on his arm. She was looking down, and the fall of the fabric made it impossible to see her face.

William let go of her arm and rested his hands on the edge of the table, the cloth wrinkling under his grip. "Aren Kertell. The Master of the Bridge." His lip curled into a slight sneer. "Where is your wife?"

Aren met the other king's stare. "Occupied."

"Motherhood." William said the word like it tasted bad, and the hooded woman tensed ever so slightly, making Aren more certain it was Alexandra.

He didn't blame her for reacting—to be so dismissed by her own son must be infuriating. "Among other things."

"One hopes that motherhood has tempered her more violent tendencies and turned her into a proper lady."

"I've not found that to be the case." If anything, motherhood had only made his wife more dangerous. "I'll leave the *proper ladies* for the *proper gentlemen* of Harendell."

William's jaw tightened, but rather than rising to the bait, he gestured to the hooded woman. "Allow me to present my bride, Queen Lestara."

*Not Alexandra.*

Aren managed to keep surprise from showing on his face, but only barely given that Lara's theories were crumbling before his eyes.

Lestara pulled the hood back and lifted her face, amber eyes meeting his. She wore Cardiffian ceremonial clothes, her face painted and her blond hair braided and affixed with feathers and tiny skulls. No longer the angry, dirt-covered creature he'd seen in the mass grave in Vencia, but Harendell's queen.

Lara had been wrong about Lestara, and that did not happen often. Aren's stomach pooled with unease.

"Your Grace," Lestara said softly. "Perhaps one day we will meet under brighter circumstances."

William scoffed. "You are too gracious, my love. He should be grateful he's not taking this meeting on his knees."

Behind him, Aren's guards shifted angrily, but he only held up a calming hand, his pride not what would turn this moment to violence. "What is it that you seek from this meeting, William?"

Harendell's king raised an eyebrow. "Did you not receive Prince James's message? Even if you were incapable of reading my letter, I would think my brother's message clear enough."

"If you mean the words given to Lady Bronwyn Veliant, then the message was received."

"Then you know what we want. Hand over your murderous bitch of a sister so that she can be executed for what she did to King Edward and the Dowager Queen Alexandra, and we might consider showing mercy to your shithole of a kingdom."

Aren waited a heartbeat, then another, certain that William would segue into his real demands, but the other man only crossed his arms.

"Hand Ahnna over," William repeated, and there was no mistaking the anger in his green eyes. "Hand her over, and we might also consider the notion that you are not complicit in your sister's crimes against Harendell. Hand her over, and we might rethink our belief that you conspired with Amarid against us. Hand her over, and we will pause our plans to blockade Northwatch. Prove you are yet Harendell's ally by handing over the murderess so we may have justice."

*He believes Ahnna is guilty.*

The thought ricocheted through Aren's head right as horns sounded from the beach. All eyes shot down the slope, shouts of *deception* and *treachery* rising to lips, only to fade on the wind as the flag on the longboat snapped straight to reveal Valcotta's colors.

The vessel ran up on the beach, and a familiar dark-clad figure climbed out, strands of blond hair that had come loose from the knot at the back of his head blowing on the wind.

"This meeting is between Harendell and Ithicana." William's voice was acidic. "Valcotta was not invited, nor is their presence wanted."

"I didn't invite them," Aren replied. *But damned if they are not wanted.*

Keris strode up the slope with several Valcottans at his heels, all of whom Aren recognized as former prisoners of Devil's Island.

"Sorry I'm late." Keris clapped a hand on Aren's shoulder. "Bad weather. I don't know how you stand the endless rain, Aren. I feel like a drowned rat."

"Keris Veliant, I assume?" William's knuckles turned white from his grip on the table. "Valcotta has no part in this conversation. This is between Harendell and Ithicana."

"Which is why I'm here to moderate. Keep the peace. Unbiased third party, as they say, but one quite keen to learn the truth of this situation." Keris straightened his sodden cuffs. "My condolences for your father's death, Your Grace. Edward and I kept up correspondence, and he wrote the most entertaining of letters. He'll be missed."

"The *truth of this situation* is already known," William snarled. "Ahnna Kertell murdered my father and attacked my mother. Anyone who stands between me and justice is Harendell's enemy."

"Allegedly murdered." Keris's azure eyes moved from William, narrowing as they fixed on Lestara. "Well, well, well. I see you finally managed to suck the right royal cock to get the crown the stars promised you, Lestara. You are tenacious, I'll give you that."

William's face purpled even as Lestara retorted, "Fuck you, Keris."

"I already declined that offer." Keris's voice was mocking. "More than once."

"You call this keeping the peace?" Aren asked under his breath, but Keris's only response was to step heavily on the toe of his boot. His brother-in-law had a strategy here, and Aren bit his tongue and readied himself to see how it would play out.

"You will mind your tongue, sir," William said between his teeth. "Lestara is queen of Harendell, and we do not suffer slander against her name lightly. Make your apologies and excuse yourself from this meeting."

"I speak no slander, only the truth." Keris moved to stand at the head of the table. "Lestara conspired with Petra Anaphora and committed treason against Maridrina, which cost the lives of countless civilians, including many children. Edward agreed to take her into exile as punishment for her crimes—to serve as her jailer and keep her in appropriate misery, but it seems he chose to violate the terms of that agreement. You have wed a murderess, William. A faithless creature who will stop at nothing in her pursuit of a destiny she believes the stars have promised. It makes me question if perhaps Lestara was not willing to wait for Edward to die of ripe old age and chose to speed along the process herself."

Aren hadn't even considered Lestara as a possible culprit behind the murder, but now that Keris had laid it out before him, it made infinite sense.

"I did no such thing!" Lestara's hands balled into fists. "I was in my husband's bedroom when it happened. It was Ahnna who killed Edward. All because she was angry I was chosen over her. That Cardiff was valued over Ithicana!"

"Where is your proof?" Keris demanded. "How do you know for sure that Ahnna was the killer? How do you know for sure that she had not been framed?"

"Because she attacked my mother as well!" William slammed his hands down on the table. "You will cease with these baseless accusations, sir, for my own brother and his soldiers came upon Ahnna in the midst of attacking my mother, knife in her bloody hands! Ahnna Kertell is guilty!" He screamed the last, spittle flying from his mouth.

"Be calm, my darling." A hooded figure at the rear of the Harendellian ranks stepped forward and pulled back her hood. "We know the truth and we will have justice for what was done to your father."

This time, Aren couldn't keep shock from his face as his eyes settled on Alexandra. Even Keris fell silent as the queen mother approached the table.

Alexandra's face was swollen, a large stitched gash running the length of her cheek. She moved stiffly, indicating more injuries beneath her clothes, and as she stopped next to her son, Alexandra rested her hands on the table. Her left hand had a wound in the center of it, and it was an injury Aren had seen many times. A defensive injury taken from trying to stop an attacker with a knife.

It suddenly felt very hard to breathe, and impossible to speak, because the injuries were proof that the Harendellians had not fabricated the attack on Alexandra.

Keris filled the silence. "My condolences for your loss, Your Grace, and I hope you have a swift recovery from your injuries."

Alexandra inclined her head to Keris, but then fixed her eyes on Aren. "I see in your eyes that you struggle to believe your beloved sister has done this. It is difficult to reconcile the woman you know and love with this act of violence, so to ease your mind, I will say that Ahnna was pushed to the brink by my late husband. To further his goals with Cardiff, Edward strung Ahnna along and made her believe that he desired her to be his heir in spirit. Made her believe she would become queen of Harendell, which would ensure our alliance with Ithicana was stronger than ever. Made her believe that she would have all that she desired, and then ripped that dream away from her in the most humiliating and hurtful ways."

William's lips parted, but Alexandra rested her injured hand on his to keep him silent. "I, too, was crushed by Edward's actions, by his choice to wed my son to a woman with no faith"—she cast a sideways look at Lestara—"behind my back. Which was why I went to speak with Ahnna late that night. I hoped to make amends, to find a way forward that was true to my faith. Whether my words would have made a difference, I don't know. All I do know is that they came too late."

Alexandra drew in a ragged breath, her eyes welling slightly. "Forgive me, it is still painful to speak."

Aren didn't answer, and Keris, for once, was silent.

"I came upon Ahnna exiting her room. She was dressed in traveling garments, well armed, and carrying light baggage. It was my assumption that she aimed to flee for home, for which I did not blame her, but I still wished to speak to her, so I called her name." Alexandra swallowed hard. "Ahnna turned to me, and her eyes were swollen as though she'd been weeping for hours, so I approached."

*Oh God, Ahnna.* Aren felt sick to his stomach.

"I told her that I was sorry for what had happened, but it was as though my words set her into a rage. She drew a knife and . . ." Alexandra broke off and drew in a steadying breath. "It was so quick. I screamed for help, and I think it was only by the grace of God that James and his men came upon us."

"Not God," William growled. "Guilt. My brother was following the bloody footprints left on the carpet by the one who killed my father. They led him straight to Ahnna and my mother."

"It was God who ensured that her efforts to disguise her trail were not successful." Alexandra used her injured hand to toy with the large pendant hanging from a chain around her neck depicting the symbol of the faithful. The diamond at the center of it had to be worth a queen's ransom. "As painful as the truth may be, Your Grace, it cannot be denied unless you name me a liar. Unless you name James a liar. Unless you name every man in his company a liar, along with half the staff of the Sky Palace who watched your sister fight loyal men to secure her own escape."

That was *exactly* what Aren wanted to do. To scream in their faces that they were all liars, that his sister was innocent, that this was all a ruse to secure Harendell's most important goal: profit. But he suspected that a break in his composure was exactly what they wanted, so he clenched his teeth and said nothing.

"What is your goal here, Alexandra?" Keris finally asked.

"Reparations? Because to pit two nations in a bloody war over the actions of one individual is not the path to justice."

"Aren knows what it is we seek," Alexandra answered. "Not reparations. Not gold. Not terms. Give us Princess Ahnna Kertell so that she may be executed for her crimes, and we will be content that Ithicana was not complicit. War can be avoided."

*No!* Aren wanted to scream. *You cannot have her!* Instead, he forced himself to say, "To my knowledge, Ahnna is not in Ithicana. We do not know where she is. But I do know that you are holding my cousin Taryn Kertell against her will."

Bloodshot green eyes met his, delving deep and seeing much. Then Alexandra said, "Lady Taryn is being kept in comfort as our guest. She will be returned to you once you prove your commitment to keeping the peace with Harendell."

"Find Ahnna and turn her over," William said softly. "You have one week, Aren, and then we will take steps to blockade Northwatch. If that suffering does not serve as sufficient motivation for you to deliver her to us, know that once the calm season is upon us, Harendell will come to Ithicana and find her ourselves. And you can trust that we'll leave nothing but ash in our wake."

Without another word, the Harendellians turned and walked away.

No one spoke.

No one moved.

The only sounds were the wind and the crash of waves on the shore and the thundering beat of his heart. Then Keris said, "What do you want to do?"

Aren closed his eyes, the familiar sour taste of helplessness rising in his throat. "I don't know."

## 12

## KERIS

They sailed south, the small fleet of Ithicanian vessels moving nimbly through the maze of islands. Keris gained a new appreciation for how they evaded the vessels of other nations as they slipped through narrow gaps between sheer cliffs, surf smashing against rock with a violent force that reminded him of the route into Devil's Island.

Saam was suffering on the rough water, his friend hanging over the side while Daria absently patted him on the back.

"I didn't think you got seasick, Saam," Keris said, watching Aren in the vessel ahead of him. His brother-in-law had sat almost unmoving the entire journey, eyes downturned and expression grim.

"I don't." Saam wiped his mouth on his sleeve, his brown skin now possessed of a decidedly green hue.

"Perhaps you're pregnant."

His friend cast him a malevolent glare. "Don't tempt me to feed you to the sharks."

Keris smirked. "You sure you don't want first dibs?"

The Ithicanians who sailed the vessel gaped at him in horror, but his bodyguards, all former Devil's Island inmates, cast their eyes skyward at the jab. Saam looked him up and down, then said, "Nah. You'd be stringy," then promptly vomited over the side of the boat again.

Everyone laughed, but none of the tension in the small vessel was dispelled. A year had not yet passed since the Endless War between Maridrina and Valcotta had been declared over, and now they found themselves on the cusp of another one. It was as though the world existed in a state of balance between war and peace, and when one nation found the latter, the former rose somewhere else. Though for Ithicana, it must have seemed especially ceaseless.

"We're here, Your Highness," one of the Ithicanians said as they navigated through a narrow gap.

Daria pointed upward and Keris lifted his face, spotting the glint of steel in the heavy foliage covering the cliffs to either side of them. He suspected that for every warrior he saw, there were ten more he did not.

The gap between cliffs opened into a large cove that Keris would never have guessed was here, the water turquoise and the beach formed of white sand. It was idyllic—although as fins passed beneath him, Keris discarded any thoughts of a swim. A few of the Ithicanians swatted gently at the sharks with as much concern as Keris might expend shooing away an excited lapdog. Then the hulls ran up on the sand of the beach.

Casting a wary glance at the water, Keris stepped out. "I'll walk with Aren," he said quietly to Saam. "You follow, but give me some space."

"Her Imperial Majesty said we are not to allow you from our sight." It was Daria who answered. "I believe her exact words were: *Don't allow him to do anything reckless.*" Saam nodded in agreement.

"Zarrah will understand." Keris didn't wait for a response, only strode to where Aren stood, looking for all the world as though he'd been punched in the stomach and couldn't draw breath.

Aren didn't look up as he asked, "How did you know to come?"

"I didn't. I met Dax in the bridge and he gave me the news. I sent him onward to update Sarhina and Zarrah." Keris pulled off his coat and slung it over his shoulder, the humid heat gluing his shirt to his back. "As to why I was in your bridge, I came to see my niece. Congratulations, by the way. I've heard she inherited her mother's looks—and with any luck her intelligence as well. She'll make a good queen one day."

Aren stared at the sand and then said, "Queen of what?"

All the Ithicanians within earshot paused what they were doing, their eyes turning to their king until Jor shouted, "Get about your business! Clouds are rising in the west, and I want everything safely stowed before they roll over us."

Keris considered his next words. When he'd last been in Eranahl, tension between Aren and Ahnna had been high. Yet he knew that the siblings had once been close. Now Aren was forced to choose between war and his sister's life. Dax had made it clear that Aren believed Ahnna was innocent. That he believed the king's assassination was a strategy one of the Harendellian nobles—likely Alexandra—had in play in order to take power, Ahnna nothing but a convenient scapegoat, and Keris had wholeheartedly agreed. But now . . . Now he was much less certain.

Alexandra's injuries were catastrophic and life altering, her accusations compelling. With Prince James and many other guards bearing witness to the attack, it was hard to argue for Ahnna's innocence. "Have your thoughts on the situation changed now that you've spoken to the Harendellians?"

"I'm not giving my sister to them to execute."

That hadn't been the question Keris had asked, but it was answer enough.

"The situation is dire," he said quietly, feeling dozens of eyes upon them. "But you are king of Ithicana, and your people are looking to you for leadership. You must bury your emotions and put on a show of strength while we decide our course."

"*Our?*" Aren lifted his head, hazel eyes bloodshot and tired as they bored into Keris's.

"We're family," Keris answered. "And allies. Valcotta is with you, and Maridrina will be as well. Ithicana does not stand alone in this."

Emotion flickered through Aren's gaze, and he gave a tight nod. "I'm glad you're here. Is Zarrah—"

"She's in Pyrinat. For her to leave right now was not wise, but she sends her well wishes along with several chests full of presents. I'm not entirely sure where my baggage was delivered, but Delia is now the proud owner of quite a collection of child-sized weapons. I suggested the girl might turn out bookish, given she's my niece, but Zarrah only looked at me like I was the purest form of stupid."

The corner of Aren's mouth turned up. "Zarrah is well, though? You're both well?"

"Yes, we are very well." A partial truth, but Keris had no intention of dumping his woes on Aren in these circumstances.

His friend's eyes narrowed. "I do have spies, you know. What is it now—six attempts on your life?"

Keris crossed his arms. "People have been trying to kill me since I was a child, so that's nothing of note." Which was true, but there was no denying that not everyone had wanted an end to the Endless War, and having a Maridrinian—and a Veliant, no less—married to the empress did not sit well with them.

"You and Lara are two peas in a pod in your assessment of personal risk." Aren shook his head. "Stay as long as you like."

This had been meant to be a social visit. Short and filled with food and family and laughter, because God help him, Keris had sworn he'd never put armor back on again.

"It never ends, does it?" Aren said softly. "The fight?"

Keris looked at the sky, a cloud bank rising and appearing for all the world like a beast looming over Ithicana. "No," he replied. "It never fucking ends."

"Keris?"

They both turned as Lara emerged from the dense jungle, several guards walking at her heels with weapons in hand. His sister wore the drab clothing that the Ithicanians favored, and if not for her blond braid, she'd have blended in with the Ithicanians entirely.

Keris stepped back to give Lara space as she wrapped her arms around Aren's neck, knowing that she'd have been sick with nerves over this meeting. His sister always wanted to be in the thick of things, and while necessity demanded one of them remain in safety in case the worst happened, he suspected doing so had sat poorly with her.

He dug the toe of his boot into the sand while they exchanged muted words, lifting his head only when Lara turned to him.

"I'm so happy you're here," she said, then to his surprise, her blue eyes welled. Lara flung her arms around his neck and buried her face against his shoulder. "Everything has gone to shit."

"I know." He patted her on the back, and when Lara straightened, all signs of emotion were gone. "My plan for today was to drink Aren's expensive wine and admire your progeny, not come up with creative insults for Lestara while standing on a barren and rainy rock in the middle of the Tempest Seas. I truly regret not burying that woman alive while I had the chance."

"Lestara was there?" There was surprise in Lara's voice, and Aren responded quietly, "It didn't go as we hoped."

"Did they say anything about Taryn?" a female voice demanded.

Bronwyn marched toward them, and Keris frowned at the uncharacteristic anger in his half sister's gaze. Valcotta had spies aplenty in Harendell, so he'd known that Bronwyn was with Ahnna, as was Aren's cousin Taryn. Dax had updated him about Bronwyn's unceremonious return to Northwatch and Taryn's imprisonment, but that didn't quite account for Bronwyn's anger.

His half sister slid to a stop in the sand, arms crossed as she glared up at Aren. "Well?"

"They confirmed they have her," Aren said. "They'll—"

Keris rested a hand on his friend's forearm, silencing him. "Let's not have this conversation on the beach."

Aren seemed to finally register how many of his people were in earshot, and he gave a tight nod.

Bronwyn's hands balled into fists, and her "Fine" came out between her teeth.

Their group started up the narrow path into the jungle. Lara and Aren walked ahead, their elbows pressed together as they exchanged quiet words. Keris focused his attention on Bronwyn. "Other than the obvious, what has your knickers in such a twist?"

"Fuck you, Keris." Bronwyn kicked a stick, sending it soaring into the bushes. A red snake shot out of the same bushes. Keris tensed, but it slithered in the opposite direction.

"Taryn is my friend," his half sister muttered. "She's entirely innocent, but the Harendellians imprisoned her because of what Ahnna did."

Aren heard her, and the glare he cast over his shoulder was murderous. Bronwyn lifted her hand and flipped him her middle finger, and Keris gave her an elbow to the ribs. "Enough. Sarhina won't be best pleased if you cause trouble, and I *know* you won't cross her."

"Don't be so sure. There's not much I won't do to free Taryn."

The vehemence in her voice filled Keris with unease. "Ithicana and Harendell sit at the brink of war. If you go in blades-flashing and steal away a prisoner, you might push them over the edge. Especially if you kill anyone. I think the only thing holding William back is that they have doubts that Aren is complicit. If you liberate his cousin, those doubts are unlikely to hold. The stakes are high, so every decision needs to be thought through."

"The stakes were pretty goddamned high when you sailed to Devil's Island to rescue Zarrah, but I recall thinking that you'd let the whole world burn to free her. Lara wasn't much better when Aren was imprisoned. So you'll have to excuse me, but I find advice from both of you to be the purest form of hypocrisy."

It was a fair point.

Bronwyn caught hold of Keris's arm, dragging him to a stop while Lara and Aren pressed onward. "Aren refuses to believe that Ahnna did this," she said quietly. "If she makes it back to Ithicana, he won't give her up. It will cease to matter if Aren was involved with Edward's murder, because he'll be guilty of harboring the woman who killed the king of Harendell. How long until Taryn's head is sent to Northwatch in retaliation?"

A vision of William's face filled Keris's mind—the portrait of a man desperate to lash out. If he didn't get what he wanted, it was fair to say that Taryn's life would be forfeit.

"I know we aren't close, Keris. Not in the way you are with Lara, but I need you to be on my side in this." Bronwyn's blue eyes were liquid bright. "I know you understand how I feel better than anyone."

Keris did understand, but he also felt pulled in multiple directions by those who had his love and loyalty. "I don't have the full picture yet, Bronwyn. But I promise, I won't stand by and allow Taryn's life to be thrown away."

His half sister wanted more from him, that was obvious, but Bronwyn only gave a tight nod and led him onward.

They reached a modest-sized structure made of stone covered with moss, the roof so overgrown with plant life that one could be excused for walking past the building without noticing its presence.

He entered through the open door, and though it had been cool beneath the canopy of trees, it was almost cold inside the building. Dark, too, the only light coming from a lamp that sat on a rough wood table in the center of the main room. The back wall was lined with doors, one of which was open to reveal a narrow cot.

*Barracks.*

Keris's focus moved to Lara, who was taking a bundled infant from Aren's grandmother. Amelie was much changed from when he'd last seen her, skin ashen and shoulders stooped, and though her eyes flickered with recognition when she saw him, Amelie said nothing. Jor took her elbow and led her to the corner, and Amelie's face crumpled at whatever he told her. It was as though the spirit had been drained from everyone in the room, making the cold and dim space all the more oppressive.

"This is the most secure location in the north that we can be sure the Harendellians don't know about," Lara said. "Not luxurious, but safe."

"Safety is a luxury." He went closer to take a look at his niece, who was fussing the way babies did when they were hungry. Delia was a sweet little thing with a full head of dark hair, but it was the hazel eyes looking back at him that held Keris's attention. "She escaped the curse."

Lara's mouth crooked up in a half smile, understanding his meaning. A certain stigma came with having eyes of Veliant blue, and Keris didn't wish that legacy down upon his niece.

Delia chose that moment to let out a hungry howl, and Keris moved to join Aren at the table.

"Drink?" Aren asked him.

"Water, if you have it. I'd be less thirsty after a week in the Red Desert."

Aren picked up the pitcher and filled a chipped cup with water, handing it over before he sat on one of the chairs. He rested his elbows on the table, staring blankly at the scarred surface.

Keris sat across from him. "You've not heard anything from Ahnna? You have no idea where she might be?"

Aren gave a slow shake of his head. "I don't even know if she's alive."

"Tell me what you do know."

Keris listened in silence as his family filled him in on everything that had happened since Ahnna had left for Harendell, as well as the details that had been gleaned about Edward's murder. Halfway through the story, he took the now-fed Delia from Lara and circled the room with his sleeping niece, pausing from time to time to read the spy reports Lara fished from her stack, the full scope of the situation forming in his mind.

It was damning.

Ahnna had a motive. There were witnesses, not the least being James Ashford. But perhaps the most damning of all were Alexandra's injuries, which Keris had seen with his own eyes.

Passing the sleeping baby to Amelie, Keris rested his hands on the table. "The only person who knows what really happened is Ahnna, but I think it fair to say the truth does not matter. Harendell believes she is guilty, and I don't think there is a way to prove otherwise given that her word means nothing to them. My question is whether what Ahnna has to say matters to *you*?"

Silence filled the room, and Keris felt a sudden urge to drag everyone outside into the jungle. To find sunlight and open air, because the shadows felt as though they might consume everyone.

"Of course it matters," Aren finally answered. "I'm not allowing my sister to be executed for something she didn't do."

"What if she's guilty?" Keris didn't enjoy pressing this issue, but someone had to. "Will Ithicana go to war to protect Ahnna if you know for certain she murdered Edward and then attacked Alexandra?"

Aren blanched, his skin turning ashen in the dim light. "I . . ." He looked away. "I need to hear Ahnna's explanation. I need to hear her voice. I can't make a decision without seeing her."

"Except you don't have that option." Keris buried his guilt at pushing his friend in his time of grief. "No one knows where she is, and Harendellian patience is wearing thin. If you don't at least denounce her, they will assume that you are complicit. You must decide your course with the information you have."

"She could already be dead." It was the first time Bronwyn had spoken, and she stepped away from the wall she'd been leaning against. "Which means you're risking Taryn's life, your wife's life, your daughter's life—the lives of everyone in Ithicana—for a corpse. I looked James in the eye when he delivered his message: He's not going to stop his hunt, and if he finds her, Ahnna won't make it to execution. That kind of anger is only sated by blood."

Keris remembered a report he'd read from one of Valcotta's spies in Harendell. Much of it had detailed the commotion that Lestara had been causing in Edward's court, but tacked on to the end was an account of an incident in Sableton the night Ahnna had arrived in Harendell. James had been involved in a brawl in the tenderloin district after patrons of an alehouse had laid hands on Ahnna. The two had subsequently quarreled, and then, in full view of everyone on the street, James had slung Ahnna over one shoulder and carried her away in a manner that the spy had interpreted as *decidedly familiar, especially for a Harendellian.* Before Keris had left for Ithicana, more reports had arrived full of rumors and speculation that Ithicana's princess had seduced Harendell's most eligible bastard. If that was true, then Keris was inclined to agree with Bronwyn that James was out for blood.

For there was no more intense hatred than one born out of love gone sour.

A sharp knock sounded on the closed door of the barracks, echoing against the stone walls. At Aren's nod, Jor opened it and a sodden Ithicanian stepped inside, along with a gust of wind carrying heavy rain. "Word from Northwatch via the Amaridians."

Aren stood so abruptly that he jostled the table, toppling two cups of water. "Ahnna?"

"Yes, Your Grace." The man wiped his face, a puddle forming around his boots. "The Amaridians say that she was spotted in

Sableton but evaded capture. Every ship is being searched by soldiers and bloodhounds before departure, but the gossip in the city is that she subsequently ran afoul of civilian militia in the foothills. Prince James apparently left Sableton at a gallop and hasn't been seen since."

"Anything else?" Aren demanded, but the man only shook his head.

"Ahnna's aiming to cross the Blackreach Peaks," Keris murmured once the man had departed, drawing a map of the continent in front of him. "She's trying to get to Amarid."

"That's a dangerous trek." Jor joined them at the table, his weathered face grim. "The mountains are tall, and at this time of year, the snow will be thick and prone to avalanches. Ahnna is tough and knows how to live off the land, but this is new ground for her."

"But if she can get across the border, it's the one place James won't follow," Keris countered. "Angry isn't the same as stupid—he won't go into the Beast's territory. Those two have been at odds in the Lowlands for over a decade, and they hate each other. I can only imagine that the rivalry has grown worse since the castration."

Everyone stared at him.

"Don't you read your spy reports?" Keris demanded. "Last year, fighting came to a head in the Lowlands, and James and Carlo were in the thick of it. The word is that it turned to fisticuffs in the mud. Before they were separated by their men, James put his boot heel into Carlo's balls with such force that the physicians had to cut one of them off. I've heard that Carlo's now obsessed with killing James himself. Given his proclivities, James would have to be mad to cross that border without an army at his back."

"Ahnna needs to get to that border." Aren was staring down at the table, but then he straightened and cleared his throat. "Katarina has been making overtures of negotiating a new deal. Of making amends."

"You can't seriously be thinking of trusting her?" Katarina was sly as a fox and twice as mean.

"I trust that she's trying to profit off this conflict," Aren replied. "Northwatch's piers sit half empty, and she'll be keen to fill those spots with her merchant ships. If she can secure Ahnna and get her safely back to me, then I'll deal."

"And piss the Harendellians off even more?" Keris shook his head. "Are you sure?"

"I'll warn her to be discreet," Aren replied. "Katarina will no more want William's ire than we do, so if she can get what she wants from me with a stealthy rescue, she'll do it."

The idea of trusting Katarina to do anything made Keris's skin crawl, but the rivalry between Amarid and Harendell was as certain as the sun rising in the east. What's more, once Carlo learned that James was in the Blackreaches, there'd be no stopping him from pursuing his revenge. Keris had no grievance with James Ashford, but if the Beast killed him, it would redirect some of William's focus.

"Bronwyn, please sit," Aren said, gesturing to one of the empty chairs.

Keris watched his half sister consider refusing, then slowly cross the space to flop down on a chair, her jaw tight.

"I know you think I don't care about what has happened to Taryn, but that couldn't be further from the truth," Aren said after exchanging a weighted glance with Lara. "We need to start making plans to get her out if this goes sour. Which is why I want you to board one of the Amaridian merchant ships at Northwatch and sail to Riomar. You're a Maridrinian princess, which will get you an audience. I want you to convince Katarina to help Ahnna get safely across the border so that we can hear the truth from her lips, but I also want you to convince Katarina to aid in liberating Taryn. Tell her that if she helps us, I'll agree to renegotiate our current agreements in her favor."

Keris's half sister flicked her eyes to him, and Keris gave a slight nod to indicate he'd keep her interests at heart while she was absent. "All right," she said. "But if Katarina won't deal, I'm going after Taryn myself. Consequences be damned."

"Fine."

"There's something else to consider that I think everyone has missed." Lara's eyes were on the pages of spy reports in a pile before her. "William and Alexandra *knew* Ahnna was headed to the Blackreaches when they arrived to meet you, Aren. They know we don't have Ahnna. Which means they knew they were asking for something you couldn't give." She looked up. "I wasn't wrong. It's not Ahnna they're after. Or at least not entirely."

Keris hadn't missed that pertinent detail, but without more information, *what* Harendell was after would be pure speculation.

He sat, resting his elbows on the table and his head in his hands. This was supposed to be a short visit. A week spent in the tropics drinking with Aren, bickering with his sister, and spoiling Delia, after which he'd return to Valcotta. Return to Zarrah, because he'd regretted leaving the moment Pyrinat had faded on the horizon. "We need to better understand what is going on in William's court."

"Yes," Lara replied quietly. "We do. But it's not the sort of understanding that a spy will gain, and if we send an emissary, they'll be pushed into a corner to cool their heels."

Zarrah was going to kill him when she found out about this. "You need someone they can't afford to ignore."

"Yes." His sister's voice was tight, like she was holding back tears.

"Just what exactly are you suggesting?" Aren demanded.

Keris lifted his head from his hands, wishing that he'd had the chance to hold Zarrah one last time. To tell her that he loved her more than life, more than breath. Because there was a fear growing in his chest that he'd never get another opportunity. "It feels like a lifetime ago I walked down your bridge with the aim of escaping to Harendell." He exhaled a steadying breath. "I think it's time I finished that journey."

# 13
# AHNNA

James was gaining on her.

Ahnna had pressed hard through the day and into the following night, but in the dawn light, exhaustion was taking hold. For her and her horse.

Dippy moved at a sluggish walk, head low, barely casting a sideways glance at birds when they burst out of the brush. More than once, she'd fallen asleep on his back and woken with total certainty that James had caught her.

Discovering the trail behind her empty brought little relief, because it was only a matter of time.

Her pursuers' horses would be flagging as well, but the men themselves could take turns leading one another's mounts as they slept. They were better supplied, especially with grain for their mounts. When they did stop, they could rest easy knowing that one of their ranks was on watch against mountain cats or worse, whereas Ahnna was sick with anxiety that something would attack her while she slept or that she'd freeze to death if her fire burned too low.

Though in truth, she was so cold that part of her wondered if even a bonfire would warm her frozen flesh. Ithicana didn't get cold, and this was the first time she'd experienced snow. It was so much worse than she'd thought it would be—like trudging through sand. It melted and soaked her clothes when she walked next to Dippy but then froze whenever she was mounted, and her body ached where it wasn't entirely numb. Her toes had lost sensation, and she had to trade off which hand held the reins, the other tucked into her armpit under her coat. Her body was racked with shivers, and though the Blackreaches were covered with a carpet of green conifer forests, it felt lifeless and desolate.

She couldn't sustain this pace.

The growl of her stomach was audible over the crunch of the snow beneath Dippy's hooves, but hunger wasn't the reason twin tears rolled down her cheeks.

"James will feed you," she whispered to her horse, who'd finished the last of his grain when dawn had lit the sky. "It's me he's angry with, not you."

Dippy's ears rotated back, listening to her.

"Just wait on the trail until they catch up," she instructed. "Forage for grass under the snow and keep an ear out for mountain cats, understood?"

The only way to evade James would be to travel on foot. She had to leave the path and climb into the upper reaches of the mountains where horses couldn't go. There she could find somewhere to hide and rest, and perhaps escape.

"Do what you have to do," she mumbled to herself, taking a weary sip from her waterskin. "You need to get to Amarid. You need to find a ship. You need to get to Ithicana. You need to warn Aren that Amarid is in league with Alexandra. You need to tell him that they're trying to take the bridge."

A clear path.

A clear goal.

Yet instead of dismounting and heading into the trees, Ahnna continued down the narrow trail, unwilling to abandon the one source of comfort she had left.

From time to time, she glanced back. Though she saw no sign of James or his men, she knew they were getting closer. She'd smelled the smoke of their cook fire when the wind had shifted the prior night.

"Do it now, Ahnna," she muttered. "So that they find Dippy during daylight."

Ahnna knew it was foolish to strategize around the survival of a horse, but she couldn't help herself.

Drawing Dippy to a halt, Ahnna slid off his back. She rested her head against his steaming shoulder, snowflakes falling all around them, and then flung her arms around his neck.

"I'm sorry," she sobbed. "I'm sorry I got you into this mess, but it will be all right. James will feed you, and when you get back to Harendell, you'll be well cared for. Green pastures and a dry stall at night."

Her gelding leaned against her, and though it was likely because he was exhausted, Ahnna allowed herself to believe he felt the same grief that she did. She granted herself a moment to stand there with him, wishing that all her memories of her horse were not so entwined with memories of James.

*He lied to you*, she silently whispered. *He stabbed you in the back.*

Yet as she removed Dippy's saddle to reveal his sweat-marked fur, she was hit with the vivid memory of discovering that James had been training her horse in his spare moments. Hours of work in the rain, and all so that she might sit atop a horse she hadn't been ready for.

It was not lost on Ahnna that if James had not put in those hours of effort to train Dippy—and her—she would never have escaped Verwyrd. It made her wonder if James was cursing himself for the same reason.

Ahnna set the saddle in the snow, and then looked up the sharp slope the trail was cut into.

An idea struck.

High up the slope was a toppled tree, the roots torn from the earth and twisted horizontal. A common enough sight, but what made it interesting was that the spread of tree roots held back a pile of snow and debris from a previous avalanche.

If she could unleash the snow and debris held back by those tree roots to create a larger avalanche, it would cover the trail. James and his men would be able to climb over it, but the horses wouldn't. They'd have to either abandon their mounts or backtrack to find another route, which would put them days behind her.

It could work.

But she didn't have much time.

Ahnna swiftly resaddled Dippy and then led him at a trot down the trail until she was confident he was out of range. She tethered him to a tree, and then dug the canister of her remaining lamp oil out of her bag. With it clutched in her frozen fingers, she broke into a sprint back down the trail. The route up to the fallen tree was challenging in the deep snow, but using trees and bushes, she climbed up to the tangle of roots.

As she turned, her foot slipped and a wave of vertigo struck her as she caught her balance. The slope beneath her was terrifyingly steep, but it gave her an impressive view. Dippy was a tiny figure in the distance, her horse pawing at the snow to reach the dead grass beneath.

Ahnna looked the other direction.

"Fuck!" she hissed as riders appeared around a bend in the cliffside path. They were still a fair distance away, but there was no mistaking Maven, the black mare's head held high and proud.

Nor was there any mistaking the figure on the mare's back.

Ahnna's heart skipped, then sped. This was the first time she'd seen James since he'd chased her through Verwyrd, and her head filled with the words he'd screamed at her as she swam across the river. *You can't run from this, Ahnna. There is nowhere you can go that I won't find you!*

It felt like prophecy becoming reality, and even from here, she could feel his anger. Could see it in the way he rode, pushing Maven harder than she'd ever seen him do. If the civilians she'd encountered had relayed her message, it had done nothing to aid her cause. James wasn't chasing her through the Blackreaches to capture her.

He was here for blood.

Though it had been stupid to do so, part of her had hoped he'd have seen through Alexandra's schemes by now. The expression on his face burned that hope to ash, so Ahnna reached for her own anger.

"Fuck you, James," she snarled. "If you think I'm going to let a back-stabbing piece of shit such as yourself be the end of me, you have another thing coming!"

Ignoring the thunder of her heart, Ahnna assessed the roots of the fallen tree. Beneath a layer of snow were boulders, chunks of ice, and broken branches, all primed to continue their path of destruction down the steep slope. All she had to do was remove the barrier without getting herself killed in the process.

And she needed to do it quickly.

Sloshing lamp oil on the parts of the tree she needed to break, she cast aside the bottle and then drew her flint from her pocket.

The snow fell in heavy flakes around her, the wind bitter as it howled through the peaks. Her frozen fingers protested as she closed them around her knife hilt, but Ahnna only gritted her teeth and knocked the blade against the stone. A spark flew but fizzled in the air.

"Come on," she growled, refusing to look to see how much closer James had traveled.

She cracked steel to stone again, fear clawing at her because not a single spark flew. She'd lit a thousand fires in her life, using the dampest wood, but her frozen fingers were clumsy.

Of their own volition, her eyes turned to James. Her stomach plummeted at how close he was.

"Come on!" Her pulse roared, and she cursed herself for not bringing her saddlebags: This was going to fail, and she'd have to run with nothing but the clothes on her back. "You're an idiot! A failure! A fool!"

With each word, she struck the knife against the stone. On the last, a spark flew and landed on the oil.

Blue flame raced along the wood, but there was no time to admire the growing inferno. It would work. Or it wouldn't.

And with the way things were going, she had to plan for failure.

With reckless speed, Ahnna hurled herself down the slope. Slipping and sliding and setting off tiny avalanches as she moved at an angle toward Dippy. She risked a backward glance, certain that the fire would have been put out by the heavy snow, but the tree and its roots were a veritable bonfire.

Except that was only one piece of the plan. All of this was for nothing if there was no avalanche.

Ahnna slid onto the path and rolled, nearly falling over the cliff on the opposite side. Clawing the snow, she scrambled upright and then broke into a sprint down the trail. Her side cramped and sweat rolled in rivulets down her back, but she had to get out of the avalanche's path.

Dippy shifted restlessly as Ahnna untethered him, forcing her to vault onto his back, stirrups be damned.

Sensing her urgency, Dippy broke into a gallop. They careened down the trail at breakneck speed, Ahnna pressed low over his neck, trusting him to keep his footing as she glanced back.

To see James and Maven come galloping into view. Their eyes locked over the distance, and James leaned over his mare's neck, urging her for speed.

"Run!" she shouted at her horse even as she prayed for the thunder of falling snow to deliver her from a fight she was as afraid to win as she was to lose.

But the only sound was the pounding of galloping hooves.

## 14

# JAMES

How she'd kept ahead of them for so long, James didn't know.
Strength. Endurance. Speed.
Sheer fucking willpower.
He'd put his money on the latter.

But willpower only went so far, and as he heeled Maven around a bend into an open stretch of path, James's eyes locked with Ahnna's.

She was looking over her shoulder, Dippy galloping down the trail like he was back on the racetrack. Her slender frame was bulky with the thick coat she wore and her face was partially obscured by a woolen cap, but even across the distance, seeing her was like a punch to the gut.

Ahnna's lips parted, then she twisted back around and leaned over Dippy's neck.

"I don't think so," James snarled, and dug in his heels.

"Sir!" Arthur shouted from behind. "James! Stop!"

James ignored him, but as Maven galloped ahead of his companions, a dark cloud of smoke blew over him.

Far up the slope was a large fire, a fallen tree with its exposed roots ablaze. Perhaps an attempt at starting a forest fire, but it was a waste of effort: The trees around it were laden with snow. Even as he watched, the fire lessened its intensity, more smoke than flame.

The sound of wood snapping was deafening even over Maven's hooves, and it was followed by a far worse noise.

Horror gathered in James's stomach as debris exploded through the burning tree roots and tumbled down the mountainside.

An avalanche.

Ahnna meant to block the trail.

Instead of checking Maven's reins, he bent over the mare's neck and shouted, "Run!"

Boulders and chunks of ice smashed through trees and tore up earth, the mass of debris growing with each passing second. The noise was deafening, louder than a thousand claps of thunder rolling through the sky at once. Everything in its path would be destroyed, but James raced toward it anyway.

Because if he didn't get to the other side, Ahnna would escape.

Flecks of foam flew from Maven's mouth, his horse seeing the wave of death rolling down the slope as clearly as he did.

*Faster*, he pleaded, feeling his mare's fear, knowing she was loyal to him even if it meant death.

A large rock bounced on the path ahead of them and Maven veered to avoid it, nearly going off the cliff to their left. Smoke and embers clouded the air, and a rock clipped James in the shoulder, another striking Maven on the neck. She barely flinched, terror driving away pain as she ran for both their lives.

He'd made a mistake. He was dead, Ahnna would escape, and his father would never have justice.

The slide was upon them.

Maven leapt forward—

And the murderous tide of ice and rock washed over the trail.

# 15

# AHNNA

THE PLAN HAD worked far better than Ahnna had intended.

But God help her, the results had been so much worse.

Fear had driven Dippy at high speed for a long time after the roar of falling rocks and snow had ceased. Yet as the rush in her veins faded alongside the clouds of snow and smoke, it was replaced with a grief that threatened to consume her.

Climbing off Dippy's back, Ahnna fell to her knees and pressed her forehead to the snow. "Breathe," she whispered.

But the next breath was a sob.

James was dead.

The last thing she'd seen right before Dippy had galloped around a bend was James riding straight into the path of the enormous avalanche, and it had been all she could do not to turn around and try to save him, despite knowing that there would be no surviving that wave of death.

Her body shuddered as she sobbed into the snow, because it never goddamned ended. The suffering. The loss. It was as though life itself were a war—a ceaseless battle to survive while those you cared about fell to either side. A scream boiled up inside of her, one of rage and grief that would echo off the mountains so that even the stars in the growing darkness would be forced to acknowledge what she endured.

Instead, Ahnna swallowed it. "Alexandra drove him to this," she whispered. "Yet another death on her hands, but more will come if you do not stop her, so hold on to your rage. Let it fuel every step you take until you can put a knife in her evil heart."

Dippy snuffed the top of her head, then caught hold of her cap with his lips and tossed it on the ground with a snort as though to say, *Enough*. She looked up at him through her tears. "You're right. We have to keep going."

Clinging to her fury, Ahnna climbed to her feet and led her horse down the trail. There was every chance that the soldiers who'd been on James's heels would pursue for a time on foot, which meant that she needed to put distance between her and them.

Darkness fell, and Ahnna lit her lantern. The small amount of oil left in it wasn't enough to last through the night, so she kept it low. Which meant that she caught sight of a distant spark of light at the base of the valley.

A campfire.

She stared at it for a long time, wondering if they'd found James. Wondering if they'd bring his body back to Harendell to his awful family, or whether he'd remain buried forever in a tomb of her making.

It felt so hard to breathe.

He'd betrayed her. Hunted her. Would have killed her if he'd caught up to her, but Ahnna had not wanted this. Tears pricked in her eyes, because a deluded hope had burned in her heart that she'd escape and live to prove Alexandra's duplicity. That James would learn the truth and . . .

"And what?" she whispered. "And *what*, you lovesick idiot? Did you really think that if James learned you were innocent, something would be possible between you? Why would you even want that when he took you with lies on his tongue? What is wrong with you?"

*I love him.* The truth whispered up from the depths of her heart, and Ahnna sucked in a mouthful of air that didn't feel like it reached her lungs. "He's dead. Move on. Move forward. Focus on the lives of those who deserve your loyalty."

The snow grew deeper as she continued, up past her knees now, and exhaustion pressed down upon her as she walked through the darkness. Following the trail as it wove higher into the Blackreaches toward the relative safety of Amarid's border.

The air was frigid, her toes numb inside her boots and her teeth chattering. She covered Dippy with her only blanket, fixing it to his bridle and tucking it under the saddle so it wouldn't blow away, and then pulled her arms inside her sleeves, tucking her hands into her armpits. Yet nothing she did held back the growing chill.

She and Dippy walked through the night, mostly because she was certain that if they stopped, she'd freeze in her sleep. As dawn lit the night sky, each step was a force of will. She had to find shelter before death found them first.

The trail descended into a valley between the mountains, revealing a lake. The water was frozen, the sharp wind having blown away the snow so that the ice looked like glass. Nestled on the banks amid the trees was a shadowed structure.

Ahnna tripped in the snow and fell. Got to her feet, then tripped again.

"Come on," she whispered, her lips cracked and bleeding. "You can make it."

Catching hold of a stirrup, she dragged herself to her feet and then into the saddle. With his head low, Dippy staggered through the snow in the direction of the cabin.

No smoke rose from its chimney, and there was no disturbance in the snow around the building to suggest anyone lived there permanently. Dismounting, she drew her knife and walked toward the door. "Hello?" she called. "Is anyone here?"

There was no response, so she carefully lifted the latch holding the door closed. It was dim inside, but the watery sunlight filtering through the heavy clouds allowed her to see that it was empty. The cabin was small with only a rough table and chairs, a cot, and a fireplace; the second room was not a room but a horse stall with a separate door. A place for travelers to rest that protected them from weather and predators, and Ahnna thanked God, fate, and the stars for leading her to it tonight.

She led Dippy into the stall at the rear, then removed his tack before draping her blanket across his back. There were scraps of grass and hay from prior occupants, and she left him to forage while she returned to the living quarters.

Cold to the bone, Ahnna knelt before the hearth, which the prior occupant had left set with kindling and wood. It took what felt like an eternity to get it lit, but soon she was warming her hands over the flames, the small space heating up swiftly. She melted water in her pot and drank deeply, then melted more for her horse.

Taking up her bow, Ahnna ventured outdoors again and shot a fat squirrel, which she skinned and then cooked over the fire before eating every last morsel and licking the grease from her fingers.

She added more wood to the fire.

Melted more snow for water.

Shot another squirrel for her next meal.

Her body screamed for sleep, but without tasks to keep her hands busy, the hollowness in her chest threatened to consume her.

*James is dead.*

*You killed him.*

She pressed the heels of her hands to her eyes, fighting for control. Fighting to keep food in her stomach, because her thoughts made her feel sick.

*Murderer.*

"Stop it." Making one final patrol to ensure there were no signs of pursuit, she retrieved her blanket from the sleeping Dippy and wrapped herself up on the rough cot, boots still on. Knife clutched in one hand, she stared at the fire.

*James is dead.*

"I'm sorry." She squeezed her eyes shut, then immediately regretted it, because her mind's eye filled with a vision of him shattered and broken, amber eyes glassy and lifeless.

*You killed him.*

"Stop." Tears leaked out around her eyelids, soaking into her blanket. "It's not what I wanted."

*You could have tried to reason with him,* her guilt said, rising from her conscience. *You could have tried to explain.*

"He refused to listen."

*You could have tried,* her guilt whispered. *Instead, you just saved yourself.*

"I did it for Ithicana." Ahnna knew she was arguing with herself, but it didn't matter. "I need to be alive to warn them. I'm doing all of this for Ithicana."

*So you always say,* her guilt answered. *But perhaps it's time you admit that everything you do is for yourself.*

She rolled onto her back. "That's not true."

*Isn't it?* Her guilt's tone dripped with sarcasm. *Was it for Ithicana that you allowed James Ashford between your legs?*

"Shut up!"

But her guilt and heartache and grief refused to be silenced. All the things she could have done differently cycled through her mind, around and around, until finally sleep dragged her under.

It granted no respite, for her dreams were plagued with horrors that Ahnna could not escape, exhaustion holding her down like shackles. Nightmares where the Harendellians descended on Ithicana and put her people to the sword, her brother falling. Lara falling. Delia, the niece she'd never met yet loved more than life . . .

Ahnna jerked awake. A stifled sob tore from her lips and she rolled, burying her face in the crook of her arm as the nightmares slowly faded from her vision.

"Breathe," she whispered. "It's not real. You'll get there in time to warn them."

Vaguely she was aware that the fire had gone cold and that night had fallen, which meant she'd been asleep for hours. Though it had done her body much good, her heart felt worse for it.

Dippy abruptly snorted and shifted restlessly in his stall. Ahnna's grip tightened on her knife.

She untangled her legs from her blanket and silently settled her boots on the floorboards. She moved with total silence to open the door leading to his stall. Her horse's head was held high, ears pricked and focused. It could be anything. Mountain cat. Bear. A squirrel.

Or the most dangerous threat of all: a human.

Ahnna took a steadying breath and listened for feet crunching on snow, but there was nothing save the calls of birds in the trees outside.

Dippy's nostrils flared and he gave a loud snort, then relaxed.

Ahnna blew out a breath between her teeth and shook her head. Quietly closing the door to his stall, she moved into the main space. She'd cook the squirrel, then get more rest, because at dawn, she'd continue on into Amarid.

Except she couldn't relax.

Her heart beat violently, her breath rapid gasps and her palm slick around the hilt of her knife as she stared at the bolted door. The vision of opening her bedroom door on Southwatch filled her mind's eye. The memory of a Maridrinian soldier slashing at her, and the painful sting as his blade tip scored her face.

*Open the door, Ahnna.*

Her whole body was shaking.

*This isn't Southwatch. There's no one there.*

Yet she couldn't move.

*Open the fucking door.*

Drawing in a breath, Ahnna reached for the latch—

Right as the door exploded inward.

# 16

# JAMES

James slammed his shoulder against the door to the cabin, the force ripping the latch out of the old wood. He saw Ahnna's wide eyes only for a second before the edge of the door struck her.

She stumbled back, ankle catching in a blanket, and then she was falling.

The sound of her head hitting the table sent a jolt through him, and James stood frozen, staring down at the woman who'd torn his world apart. She lay unmoving, and the sudden certainty that she was dead almost brought him to his knees.

It was over. It was done.

Yet rather than elation, James swallowed bile as the interior of the cabin spun around him.

*This was what you came to do*, he screamed at himself. *This is what she deserves.*

Yet his heart screamed a silent plea to the stars to undo this moment, because Ahnna was dead. She was dead, and he'd been the one to kill her. A howl started to rise in his throat, but he clenched his teeth. *She deserved it. She deserved it.*

She didn't deserve this.

James grabbed hold of the doorframe to steady himself, but then Ahnna's boot moved.

A sickening mix of relief and panic surged through him.

*Kill her!* a voice that sounded distinctly like Lestara screamed in his skull. *Prove your loyalty!*

Instead he flung himself down on Ahnna, catching hold of her wrists. There was twine on the floor next to her belongings, and he used it to bind her arms tight. James told himself it was because honor wouldn't allow him to cut her throat while she was defenseless on the floor. That he'd do it after she roused. After he said his piece.

He looked up from her bound wrists to find Ahnna watching him, clearly disoriented. "James?" she murmured. "You're alive?"

"Disappointed?" The word came out as a snarl.

Twin tears dripped from her eyes, one catching on the rapidly swelling bruise on her cheek. "No. I didn't want to hurt you."

"You didn't want to hurt me?" He repeated the words as if doing so would cause them to make sense. Trying to kill him was the least of the hurt she'd caused him, and anger boiled up to chase away all other emotions. Grabbing the blanket, he tore off a strip and shoved it between her teeth.

"I don't want to hear another fucking word from you," he hissed. "You murdered my father and tore my family to shreds, and if that is not enough justice for your execution, know that your actions have caused Ithicana and Harendell to move toward war. If you have any goddamned decency in your black heart, confess and accept punishment, because it is the only way to avoid the destruction of your entire people."

Her already pale face drained entirely of color, but Ahnna slowly shook her head.

James jerked a knife from the sheath in his boot, then pinned her to the ground, his knees to either side of her. "Confess."

Her voice was garbled and muffled by the gag. "No."

The blade of his knife kissed her throat, a line of blood appearing. "Confess, and I'll make it quick."

Her hazel eyes had regained their sharp focus, and she glared at him with utter defiance. "No."

The knife in his hand quivered as he warred with himself. As his desire for vengeance for his father and absolution from the hurt he'd caused his family fought against an inner force that refused to do harm to the woman beneath him.

James dropped the knife and closed his fingers around her throat. "Why won't you confess?" he whispered, his fingers tightening enough that she struggled to breathe. "I saw you, Ahnna. Saw you holding the bloody knife with my own eyes. Saw the ruin you made of my father with the same blade. Your guilt is certain. All you need to do is confess and we can end this painlessly."

Ahnna only stared him in the eye and jerked her head from side to side.

*Kill her*, Lestara ordered from his thoughts. *Give your father justice. Prove your loyalty to your brother.*

But his hands refused to tighten. Refused to cut off her breath entirely, because it would mean watching the life disappear from those eyes.

With a scream of frustration, James flung himself away from her. He leaned against the wall of the cabin, head in his hands, raging at his inability to do what needed to be done. Lowering his hands, he stared at her. "I hate you, Ahnna Kertell. I hate you more than I believed was possible. You deserve death, and it will come for you, even if I'm too much of a coward to do it."

"James," she said around the gag. "I didn't—"

"Shut up!" he screamed. "I don't want to hear any of your poison. Don't say another fucking word."

"Please—"

He snatched up the blanket and tore off another strip. Thicker this time, and he shoved it in with the first gag, silencing her. Yet Ahnna still watched him, her gaze making his skin burn, so he threw the blanket over her face. He didn't want to hear her, didn't want to look at her, in case whatever power she had over him took control of his mind and caused him to go back on his oath to his family entirely.

Kicking open the door, James strode out into the snow to where

Maven waited, her coat crusted with blood in several places after their near escape from the avalanche. He stroked her neck, losing himself to the memory of how she'd leapt forward, just barely clearing the slide as it swept across the trail.

Small rocks and shards of ice had struck them as they galloped on, and only when the roar ceased did he rein the mare in and look back.

The path had disappeared.

The slope was a carnage of torn-up trees, rocks, and snow, with the faint haze of smoke hanging over all of it. To cross it on foot would be a challenge. No horse could make it across without breaking a leg.

On the far side of the avalanche, his men gaped at him from atop their horses.

"Major General, are you all right?" Arthur shouted. "Are you hurt?"

Blood ran down James's cheek from where a rock had struck him, and Maven had several small wounds, but James shouted back, "I'm fine!"

"Easy, girl," he'd murmured as he dismounted. Maven was snorting wildly, her sides soaked with sweat. Pulling off his greatcoat, he draped it over her neck and shoulders, walking her back and forth until her sides ceased heaving. Rubbing her forehead, he said, "I'm sorry for doing that to you."

James wished he could promise it would never happen again.

Arthur was slowly picking his way across the debris. Leaving Maven to rest, James ventured onto the mess of rock, broken trees, and snow, eventually meeting the other man in the middle.

"With the utmost respect, are you mad?" Arthur demanded. "If your mare was a fraction of a second slower, you'd both be pulp at the bottom of this mountain." He gestured downslope, where rocks and debris were still bouncing down and down.

"It would be impossible to catch her on foot, so I had no other choice." James wiped away the melting snow. The droplets that struck the ground were stained pink from a cut on his face. "To backtrack to another pass would put us days behind, and she'd reach the border long before us."

Despite the logic of the argument, Arthur stared at him as though he spoke gibberish.

Sighing, James said, "I'll take all the supplies you can spare and pursue her while you backtrack. Do you have a map?"

Arthur silently retrieved a creased map from the inner pocket of his greatcoat and handed it over. James spread it on a rock. "Resupply and get more reinforcements, then come up this trail here." He traced a route to the north of their current position. "Once I have her, I'll return via the same route and meet you."

Arthur frowned. "To do that will take you right to the border, sir."

James shrugged. "The Amaridians don't patrol deep into the Blackreaches this time of year, and besides, it's hardly the first time I've ventured onto their soil. I'll be in and out before they notice."

"Alone?"

"I can handle Ahnna Kertell." James shoved the map into his pocket. "She believes her avalanche cut us off and that we can't pursue. She'll lower her guard, and I'll catch her unaware. Bring her back for execution."

At the time, it had been a lie, because he had fully intended to cut her throat himself. Fully intended to prove to his family that they had his loyalty, no matter his past mistakes.

Except he hadn't been able to do it.

He led Maven back to the cabin, then took the rope fastened to her saddles and used it to bind Ahnna tightly. He desperately wanted to fling her over Dippy's back and lead her straight back to Harendell, but the snow was falling heavily and Maven was exhausted. James was exhausted, too, and if he didn't get some rest and food in his stomach, he might make a mistake.

He led Maven into the space at the rear, Dippy whinnying happily at the sight of his stablemate. Maven pinned her ears and snapped at the gelding, in no mood for his cheerful demeanor, although she calmed as James untacked her and brushed the sweat marks from her coat. Feeding and watering both animals, he left them to rest and returned to the living quarters.

Ahnna remained trussed on the floor, her only motion the slight rise and fall of her chest. He said nothing to her as he added wood to the fire, and then sat on the single chair while he ate and drank.

Why couldn't he do it? Why couldn't he put down the woman who'd ruthlessly butchered his father?

*What is wrong with me?*

It was exhaustion, he told himself. James couldn't remember the last time he'd really slept, and that's what was weakening his resolve. A few hours of rest would put steel back into his spine, and he'd do what needed to be done.

Triple-checking that Ahnna's bindings and gag were secure, James sat with his back against the wall and his sword across his legs. He stared at the crackling fire, but against his will, his eyes tracked to Ahnna's still form. Her wrists were bound, as were her ankles, and he'd strung a rope between them to reduce her mobility even more. Though she could probably have removed the blanket covering her face, she hadn't tried, and a sudden unease filled him that she'd hit her head harder than he'd thought. That she'd been slowly dying beneath a rough woolen blanket while he'd eaten a meal.

*Let her die!* his anger demanded. *If her skull is cracked, you can't save her anyway.*

James tightened his grip on his sword hilt and clenched his teeth, fighting the urge to get up. His heart thundered faster and faster, his eyes fixed on Ahnna's chest, which still rose and fell.

Maybe she was just asleep.

Or maybe her brain was bleeding, and the next heartbeat would be her last.

Cursing, James twisted onto his knees and yanked the blanket off her face. Ahnna glared back at him, the firelight gleaming off her eyes. Unblinking, she slowly shook her head.

"Your stubbornness will not save you."

Using her limited range of motion, Ahnna lifted one shoulder in a shrug, and with a snarl of frustration that was more at himself than her, James threw the blanket back over her head.

He returned to his place at the wall.

*Sleep*, he ordered himself. *Rest.*

And though it seemed impossible given the way his heart thrummed, his eyelids slowly drifted shut as exhaustion claimed him.

# 17

# AHNNA

AHNNA NEEDED TO escape.

Just because James was struggling to kill her himself did not mean he wouldn't drag her back to Harendell so an executioner could do the job, and while James seemed to think that her death would sate demands for war between Harendell and Ithicana, Ahnna had no such delusions. Alexandra wanted the bridge, and even if James dragged her corpse before all the nobility in the Sky Palace, the queen would only manufacture another justification for war.

Aren needed to be warned, and time was of the essence.

Which was all well and good, but Ahnna had yet to figure out how she was going to escape her bindings. James knew his business: There wasn't an ounce of slack in the rope digging into the flesh of her wrists and ankles. She could barely breathe with the two gags and the blanket over her head, and James was only a few feet away from her.

*Think.*

He had to be exhausted. While she had the benefit of many hours of sleep in the cabin, James had to have been going nonstop since the avalanche that he'd somehow escaped, on top of what would have been a severe lack of sleep over the many days he'd pursued her. If she waited until he nodded off, that would be the best opportunity she had to get free of these ropes.

Ignoring the crackle of the fireplace, she focused her ears on the sounds he made. The scuff of his boot heels as he shifted his position. His soft sigh of frustration. And then, after what felt like an eternity, his breath deepening with sleep.

Unless it was a trick.

Ahnna scowled at the blanket, not putting it past him to try to lure her into attempting to escape, but eventually she conceded that it was now or never.

Her mobility was severely constrained, her back bent with the way her wrists were bound to her ankles, but what James hadn't taken into consideration was that Ahnna was very, *very* flexible. Muscles screaming, she increased the bend in her spine and reached down and down until her fingers found her ankles.

A loud *pop* made her jump, her heart racing, but it was only sap in the firewood. She waited to see if James might stir, but his steady breathing continued.

Moving by feel, Ahnna picked at the knots holding her ankles in place, the pain in her back rivaling the pain in her battered skull as she dug her fingernails between the ropes. The first knot came loose, but James, curse his goddamned proficiency, hadn't limited himself to just one knot.

Tears of pain leaked down her face from sustaining the position, but Ahnna kept going. One of her nails pulled up as she clawed at the ropes, and she clenched her teeth around the dirty blanket forming her gag. Then the knot came loose.

Last one.

No sooner did the thought go through her mind than James shifted, making a soft noise of protest. Ahnna froze, certain that he was about to rip the blanket off her and catch her in the act, but then his breathing steadied.

Just a dream.

Her head was pounding, her whole body trembling, but Ahnna

set herself onto the last knot around her ankles as though her life depended on it. Which it did.

Finally, the binding came loose, and Ahnna carefully straightened her legs. Not waiting for the trembling in her muscles to ease, she managed to get seated, the blanket over her head falling to her lap.

Her eyes immediately moved to James.

He sat against the wall of the cabin, his head hanging down in deep sleep. The fire had grown low, but it was enough to illuminate his face, and she took in the changes in him. Shadows lay under his eyes; hollowed cheeks were partially hidden by enough growth of beard that she suspected he'd not picked up a razor since the night she'd escaped. His clothes were travel-stained, and he had a scabbed cut beneath one eye. Even in sleep, he seethed with tension, his jaw flexing and unflexing as dreams plagued him.

Alexandra had done this. Everything he was suffering was because of his bitch of a stepmother, and James didn't even know it.

*He betrayed you*, her anger whispered. *He took your heart and your body while knowing that his actions would destroy everything you fought for.*

Yet as she looked at James, and at the toll the past weeks had taken written over every inch of his body, what she mostly felt was the hollowness of sorrow. She was deeply familiar with the emotion, just as she was familiar with pushing past it, using pragmatism as her fuel. They'd both been wronged, both been used as pawns, but she couldn't risk trying to reason with him.

He'd proven he wasn't willing to hear it.

The ropes binding her wrists dug deep into her skin as she looked around the small space for something she could use to cut them. Her own weapons were sheathed and shoved far under the cot. Reaching them with her hands was impossible, and trying to get them out with her feet, never mind unsheathing them, risked noise that would wake James.

Which left only one option.

Turning to the fireplace, she used the toe of her boot to carefully nudge an ember out onto the stones forming the front of the hearth. Turning her back to it, she checked that James was still asleep and then leaned back, easing her wrists toward the ember.

The heat grew, and Ahnna grimaced as the side of her wrist grazed the ember, burning her skin. Shifting, she got the angle right and pressed the ropes against it.

This was going to hurt.

The rope began to burn, and Ahnna cringed as flames licked her flesh. Straightening, she held her wrists out as far as she could from her back to keep her clothes from catching fire even as she strained against them.

*Break*, she pleaded, the pain excruciating. *Goddamned break!*

The burning ropes snapped.

Ahnna jerked her arms in front of her, and then cast the rest of the burning rope into the fire before smothering the cuffs of her shirt, which were aflame. The smoke had an acrid smell, and James shifted slightly.

She needed to hurry.

Easing to her feet, Ahnna slipped on her greatcoat because she'd never survive the cold without it. Her burned wrists stung as the rough wool rubbed over them, blisters already rising. But that was a problem for later.

Eyes on James, Ahnna reached under the cot, her fingers closing over her sword. Once she had her weapons, she'd go for Dippy and pray to every higher power that she could get her horse out of the stall without waking James.

As if Dippy heard her thinking about him, he chose that moment to let out a loud whinny.

James jerked, his eyes snapping open to fix on her. For a heartbeat, they stared each other down.

Ahnna moved first.

Jerking her sword out of its sheath, she managed to twist in time to meet James's strike. The strength of his blow made her arm shudder, and she rolled, scrambling to her feet as she parried.

Whatever reluctance he'd had to kill her before was gone, his face a cold mask of fury as he came at her. Ahnna met him blow for blow, but there was no room to move in the tiny space.

She sidestepped as he lunged, his blade slicing through the air where her chest had been a second before. She spun away, shoving the wooden chair in his path. But James barely slowed, his gaze fixed on her with a deadly focus, his movements calculated, relentless. Ahnna's grip on her sword was slick with sweat, her breath shallow and fast.

"James, stop! Just listen to me!"

In response he came at her again, a quick, brutal swipe that she barely deflected, the force of it rattling up her arm. She countered, swinging low, aiming for his ribs, but he sidestepped her blow, catching her wrist in an iron grip and twisting.

The blisters on her burns ruptured beneath his hand, and she grimaced, her teeth bared, using the other hand to punch him in the ribs. He grunted, loosening his grip for just an instant—long enough for her to wrench free and backpedal, putting the small table between them.

"I'm not interested in your words," he growled. "I've already paid enough for allowing you inside my head."

Ahnna's eyes flicked to the door to Dippy's stall. She'd never get the latch open before he caught her. But the latch to the cabin's entrance had been torn off when James had forced his way in, just his saddlebags holding it shut. Unless she killed him, that was the only way out.

She'd get her horse back later.

Ahnna attacked, but when James parried, she allowed him to push her back, hoping to lure him into a rush. Whether it was exhaustion or anger, she didn't know, but he fell for the ruse and lunged. She sidestepped and slammed her elbow into his kidney, putting her full weight into it.

He grunted in pain and staggered a step.

She reached for the edge of the door, but James recovered quickly, catching her by the shoulder and yanking her back. Ahnna spun and sliced at him, her sword carving through his coat and into his forearm. He hissed in pain, but rather than recoiling, he grabbed her blade with his gloved hand and yanked.

Her hand was slick with sweat, blood, and fluid from her burst blisters, and he easily wrenched her weapon out of her grip, casting it behind him.

"I didn't hurt them!" she shouted. "Alexandra staged all of it!"

"He wanted to make you queen!" James screamed back, not even seeming to have heard her words. "He was going to give you what you wanted, and you killed him!"

*What?*

Ahnna didn't have time to think before James swiped his blade in a vicious arc toward her face. She ducked, feeling the air move just above her head, but then the tip of his sword caught in the doorframe.

She took advantage, bringing her knee up sharply into his thigh. James staggered back, but only a step. Just enough for her to reach down and yank the knife protruding from his boot top.

Their weapons clashed, the metallic sound ringing through the small room. She gritted her teeth, matching his blows as best she could, her arms burning with the effort. He was stronger, his attacks unrelenting, each swing faster and more ruthless than the last. The only reason she was still alive was that his sword was too big a weapon for the space.

With a desperate burst of energy, she faked a high feint, then dropped low, sweeping her leg under him. James stumbled, his balance shifting, and in that split second, she drove her shoulder into his chest, sending him crashing backward against the table. It buckled under his weight, and he fell hard, his sword clattering from his grasp.

Ahnna bolted to the open door, but James was up in a flash, lunging toward her. He grabbed the back of her coat, yanking her so hard she nearly fell. She twisted around, thrusting her knife blindly. The blade sliced through his coat, and James snarled, releasing her just long enough for her to throw the door open and dash out into the darkness.

The storm had ceased, and the moonlight reflected off the carpet of snow to turn the night brighter than Ahnna would have thought possible.

Behind her, snow crunched as James pursued her through the darkness of the trees. Ahnna didn't look back. The air was frigid, burning her nose as she ran, the taste of blood in her mouth from where she'd bitten her cheeks as sharp as the rising certainty that one of them had to die tonight.

Perhaps she'd always known that.

Ahnna's legs pumped and her breath made great billowing clouds as she raced into the cold forest. Fighting hand-to-hand with only a small knife, she knew her chances of coming out alive were not good. James was just as skilled, he was far larger and stronger, and he had the better weapon. She needed to lead him away from the cabin, then circle back for her bow.

Her eyes burned at the thought of filling his body with arrows and watching him fall—as much a victim of Alexandra's strategies as Edward—but she had no choice. He was beyond reason, exhaustion and grief and God knew what else controlling his thoughts, and she had to survive. Had to get to Aren to warn him, otherwise Alexandra and Katarina would see everyone she loved to the grave.

Her boots slid in the snow and she tripped over a hidden root, nearly falling. Fear was thick and choking in her throat, but the emotion was an old friend and it gave her wings. She headed downslope toward the lake, banking that her many hours of rest would give her the endurance to outpace him on the climb back up.

*Thunk.*

A gasp tore from her lips as her eyes latched on the shuddering arrow embedded in the tree next to her.

"I told you I'd hunt you." James's voice filtered through the trees, pursuing her as she ran on. "I told you that there was nowhere you could go that I wouldn't find you!"

She flinched and risked a backward glance, spotting James through trees that no longer felt as dense as they had a moment ago. The only thing that would save her now was speed, because with the moonlight gleaming off the snow, it was impossible to hide. Her trail would lead him right to her.

An arrow whooshed past her cheek.

Too close. Too close by far. Her breathing was ragged, a stitch forming in her side. The knee-deep snow was slowing her down, keeping her from getting ahead.

And then Ahnna stumbled out into the open.

The frozen lake stretched before her, vicious winds rushing across ice as clear as glass.

She had no idea if it was thick enough to hold her weight, but with the heavy crunch of James running through the snow toward her, there was no option but to risk it.

Ahnna's boots slid on the ice as she took a tentative step, heart hammering. If she didn't keep moving, he'd close in. And even with these winds and his injured arm, it would be too close a shot for James to miss.

The ice creaked underfoot, a low, ominous groan that vibrated through her bones. She cast a glance over her shoulder, spotting James emerging from the tree line, his silhouette dark and unforgiving against the snow. He slowed, eyeing the frozen lake, then started toward her. His every step was measured, his gaze fixed on her like a wolf tracking its wounded prey.

"It's not thick enough!" he shouted. "You're going to make this easy for me and get yourself killed!"

"Dead is dead!" She turned to walk backward. If she kept enough distance between them, she had a chance of dodging his shots. Yet with each moan of the ice beneath her, Ahnna's fear grew at the thought of frigid water closing over her head, of pounding her fists against ice, unable to find a way out. Dead might be dead, but an arrow through the heart would be quicker.

James lifted his bow and his jaw tightened as he drew the arrow and let it loose. A gust of wind caught it, sending it flying wide. With a grimace, he reached for another arrow.

There were only four left.

Ahnna forced herself to keep moving forward, each footfall sending tiny fractures spidering out across the glassy surface. She slipped, arms flailing, barely catching her balance as the ice groaned again, louder this time. Her breath came fast and shallow, fogging around her face as she edged farther out, knowing that one wrong step could send her plunging into the freezing darkness below.

James moved steadily, cautiously, his eyes never leaving her. Blood dripped from his arm, leaving a crimson trail on the ice.

*Crack.*

Ahnna tensed, watching the fractures grow. It was impossible to tell how thick the ice beneath her was, but logic told her that the farther out she went, the thinner it would be.

"There is no getting out of this, Ahnna!"

James loosed another arrow, this one tearing a lock of hair from her head as it shot by. A cry of pain tore from her lips, and she took another step back. "Will you at least listen before you kill me?"

If she could draw him out farther, his extra weight might break the ice.

"No." Another arrow flew at her, and though she flung herself sideways, it still cut a burning line across her shoulder.

"Alexandra set me up!" She had to at least try. "Your father met with me when I returned to Verwyrd. He had me brought to the throne room, and he put Alexandra's crown on my head and had me sit on the throne. He was acting strangely, and he spoke about your mother. Said that I reminded him of her, and then told me that he intended to kill her murderer. That he would see Siobhan's dreams fulfilled and that Harendell would be changed forever. A perfect storm."

James didn't answer, only let loose another arrow and Ahnna cried out as it scored a line of fire across her thigh. She took another few steps back, and the ice moaned in protest.

"He said the queen was dead." Tears were freezing on her cheeks. "I thought he meant that he intended to kill Alexandra for murdering your mother, but I also realized that to achieve your mother's dream meant peace with Cardiff. Which meant trade with Cardiff, at the cost of Ithicana. He had George lock me in my room, but Alexandra came to me, and after I told her his plans, she offered a solution. She said that the people wouldn't want this, and that I should go to the ball and challenge Edward's plans by reminding everyone that Harendell's alliance with Ithicana was old and strong and reliable. But I know now that I was just dancing to her music—she knew what your father had planned, and she wanted me there so that he'd be forced to publicly embarrass me. So that all would watch as he tore everything from me, giving me the motive for murder."

James lifted his bow, his last arrow in hand. But instead of letting it fly at her heart, he said, "She couldn't have known."

"Alexandra knows everything!" Ahnna screamed, sliding her foot back even as James took a step forward, the once glassy ice now a network of white cracks. "I packed my things that night. I was going to sneak out of the palace, take Dippy, and ride to the coast. But when I left my room, she was waiting. She told me that I had played my role to perfection. That I was every bit an Ithicanian, and not to take it personally; she just needed someone to blame."

James took another step, arrow leveled at her head, and Ahnna slid another step back, the wind tearing at her hair.

*Crack.*

"She took my knife and then told me I should run if I wished to escape with my life. And then she started stabbing herself. You know the rest. You saw the rest."

James didn't answer. Didn't lower his bow, only eased closer. Close enough that there was no chance he'd miss.

"I don't know why Alexandra went to such lengths or why she felt she needed to risk so much. I don't know if she did it to save her own skin, or if she just hated Edward that much, but Alexandra was the one who killed your father, James."

*Crack.*

This was it. This was the end. "All I have done was for the sake of my people," she sobbed, feeling failure reaching for her once more. "And though the nest of spiders you call a family all stabbed me in the back and deserve death for your faithlessness, I am *no fucking murderer*!"

His arrow remained fixed on her head, and Ahnna gave up hope as he remained silent.

"I have to protect Ithicana." The words came out as a croak. "Forgive me."

And then she dropped to her knees and slammed her knife tip into the ice.

# 18
# JAMES

*E*VERYTHING *I DO is for the benefit of William and Virginia.*

Alexandra's voice filled James's head, rising up from memory. If Alexandra knew the entirety of his father's plans, then she had known her marriage was invalid. Had known that William and Ginny were bastards as a result. Had known that James's father had intended to disinherit both and put James on the throne with Ahnna at his side.

He blinked, and saw Alexandra bloodied on her knees, eyes full of pain and fear. Could she have done that to herself? Was she capable of that sort of personal violence? It seemed like madness to consider, and yet . . .

"I have to protect Ithicana." Ahnna's voice tore him from his memory, her gaze focused on the arrow tip still pointed at her head. "Forgive me."

She slammed her knife down. The tip sank deep into a fissure that ran straight between his legs.

*Fuck.*

The ice shattered beneath him, and James plunged into the freezing darkness. The water closed over him with brutal finality, stealing his breath and slicing into his skin like shards of glass. Instinctively, he started kicking and reaching up to find the opening. But his head struck solid ice. He was trapped, the black water pressing in on all sides, numbing his limbs as he fought to stay calm.

James's lungs screamed, his fingers scrabbling against the smooth, unyielding ice above. Panic clawed at him as he tried to orient himself, his gaze darting through the icy dark for any sign of the hole he'd fallen through. Bubbles slipped from his mouth, drifting away in silvery streams. Every part of him wanted to slam his fists against the ice, but James forced himself to still as he hunted for the opening.

He ran his fingers over the ice, his vision blurring, the freezing water slowing his movements. Then in the far corner of his sight, he saw rays of moonlight filtering through a jagged hole in the ice. He kicked toward it, his body heavy, limbs numb, the darkness at the edges of his vision starting to close in.

Just as James thought his lungs would burst, his head broke the surface. He gasped, sucking in air so sharply it stung his throat, but he barely had time to recover before his hands slipped again, sending him back into the water. Panic surged, and he struggled for a hand hold even as he watched Ahnna cautiously move on her hands and knees, keeping well away from the opening.

Leaving him to die.

Shoving down his panic, James kicked his legs and tried to push himself up onto the ice. It cracked beneath him, and he plunged down, water closing over his head.

It was so cold.

His strength was faltering, his heart stuttering, but he kicked upward again, forcing himself onto the wet ice. He clawed at it, trying to get a grip, but he kept sliding backward.

Then a hand closed around his wrist.

Ahnna's face hovered above him, her expression fierce and determined. She braced herself on the ice, leaning back with all her strength, and with a final, desperate pull, she dragged him out. She hauled him along the ice until they reached shore, and then in a quick motion, she was on his back, shoving him face-first into the snow.

"I'm not a murderer." She repeated her refrain from before. "But I don't fucking trust you, James, and I never will. You live on my terms."

Her knee pressed down on his wounded forearm as she affixed her belt to his other wrist and then bound them together. Rising to her feet, she hauled on his arms. "Get up. You'll freeze to death if I don't get you warm."

James stumbled forward, his legs trembling as he waded through the knee-deep snow, each step a brutal fight against the cold that had sunk bone-deep. His clothes were soaked through, clinging to him like ice; every inch of fabric held the frigid bite of the water he'd fallen into. The belt cutting into his wrists behind his back was just one more source of pain, a reminder that he was at her mercy as he fought to keep moving.

"Come on, James." Ahnna's voice rang out sharply from a few paces ahead. She looked back at him, her expression hidden by shadows. "The cabin's close. You can make it."

Answering was impossible, his throat raw and frozen, the effort to form words too great. His legs were heavy and numb, dragging through snow that threatened to swallow him with every step. The cold had spread inward, a constant ache in his muscles, and a shudder rattled through his body, uncontrollable and violent.

The slope rose sharply before him, a slick, glistening incline that seemed steeper with every step. He could see the cabin now—a dark shape hidden beneath snow-laden pines, just at the edge of his blurring vision.

He slipped, his boot catching on a hidden root beneath the snow, and he fell hard, plunging into the icy powder. The shock of cold against his soaked skin jolted him, sending waves of agony through his freezing limbs, and he struggled to push himself up, but his arms remained uselessly bound, pinned behind him.

Ahnna came back to him, gripping his arm firmly and hauling him upright. Her face was hard, her mouth a thin line, but he didn't miss the tears rolling down her cheeks. "Not here," she muttered under her breath, pulling him onward with shocking strength. "You're going to make it inside."

They reached the cabin's door, and she kicked it wide and let go of him once they were inside. James fell to his knees.

"Lie down," she ordered.

James didn't argue, didn't so much as flinch as she pressed her knife blade to his throat and unfastened the belt binding him. She kept the blade in place as she pulled off his greatcoat, then his uniform coat and shirt. With ruthless practicality, she again knelt on his wounded arm to secure his wrists, and then tossed a blanket over his body.

He watched her go to the fireplace, carefully adding kindling and coaxing the few faintly glowing coals back to life until flames appeared. Ahnna tended the fire until it was blazing hot, then muttered, "I'm going to check on the horses. Don't die."

Easier said than done.

The fire crackled a few feet away, and he could see the flames licking the logs, bright and alive, but the heat felt impossibly distant. His whole body shook, each tremor painful in its violence, every part of him frozen to the bone.

*Hypothermia*, he thought, his mind sluggish and heavy, like each thought had to break through a wall of ice. His trousers were soaked, the chill from the lake still clinging to his skin. His arm throbbed where Ahnna had stabbed him, blood forming a small pool next to him.

*Is Ahnna telling the truth?*

James closed his eyes for a moment, but his own breathing sounded strange, faint and hollow. Part of him knew he needed to keep fighting, to warm up, to do something, but he was so tired—bone-deep, aching tired. *Just need to . . . rest for a second*, he told himself, but there was a hollow certainty settling in his chest, a sense that this rest would not be one from which he would wake.

*Did Alexandra kill my father?*

The fire crackled, pine sap snapping and popping, a few sparks leaping from the stove to singe his skin, but James hardly felt them.

*Did I fall for a ruse?*

It was hard to think, his consciousness fading.

*Stay awake*, he thought, but the ice in his mind was thickening, pulling him down, blurring the edges of everything.

Until all was darkness.

# 19

# AHNNA

"**You're an idiot**," Ahnna growled, filling a bucket with snow and putting it in with the horses to melt. "Why didn't you just let him drown?"

It would have been the intelligent choice, but logic and reason had all disappeared from her skull when James fell beneath the ice. The only thought in her head had been that she couldn't let him die.

"Too stupid to live." She kicked at the dirt, grimacing as the wound in her leg screamed. What had changed? James had heard her truth, but had said nothing to indicate that he believed a damned word she'd said. Part of her had howled in frustration that, despite knowing that Alexandra was a schemer of the first order, he refused to see her guilt. Refused to believe Ahnna's very reasonable explanation of what had happened.

But the wiser part of Ahnna understood that her truth was competing with what James had seen with his own eyes. Alexandra on her knees and wounded, begging for aid, while Ahnna knelt next to her with a bloody knife in hand. It was lunacy to suggest that Alexandra, a woman who'd never held a weapon in all her life, would inflict such awful wounds on herself, and if Ahnna hadn't watched her do it, she wouldn't have believed it either. James had what he thought was incontrovertible proof of Ahnna's guilt, and she had nothing but her own pleas of innocence to convince him otherwise.

"Which is why letting him live was a mistake." She pressed her face to Dippy's neck, inhaling his scent to calm herself.

Even if she and Dippy left now, once James was recovered, he'd pursue, and she didn't think even the threat of crossing Amarid's border would be enough to stop him. Not when he'd gotten this close to catching her.

Which meant they'd be right back to where they started: the hunter and the prey. The very thought of it made her want to scream.

Instead, she bandaged her multitude of wounds and saddled Dippy. Secured her bags, along with some of James's weapons and supplies, keeping one eye on his still form in front of the fireplace. She didn't know how long it would take him to warm up enough to pursue her, which meant she had to hurry.

Going back into the cabin, she added more wood to the fire, always keeping one eye on him.

"James," she said. "I'm going. Please don't follow me. Please go back to Harendell and do something to stop Alexandra."

He didn't move.

Uneasy, Ahnna checked that his wrists were still secure, then knelt next to him. He was ghostly pale, his breathing shallow, and when she touched his forehead, his skin felt like ice.

"Goddamn it, James," she muttered, pressing fingers to his throat and finding that his pulse wasn't half as strong as it should be. Some blood had pooled beneath his arm from where she'd sliced him open, but not enough to threaten his life, which meant that it was the plunge into the water that was to blame.

*Leave*, pragmatism screamed at her. *He betrayed you. Hunted you. Tried to kill you.*

Instead, Ahnna retrieved the medical supplies she'd taken from his saddlebags and packed in her own. Moving swiftly, she cleaned, stitched, and bandaged the wound on his arm, James not once stirring.

She had the fire roaring, and sweat ran in beads down her face. But James still felt cold to the touch.

*You could be escaping. You could be miles from here.*

Ahnna shoved away the thought and gently shook his shoulder, her voice breathy with rising panic as she said, "Wake up. Please wake up."

He didn't move, the bare skin of his torso so pale and cold that he looked like a corpse.

She needed to get him warm.

But she also needed to run.

"Curse you for a fool, Ahnna," she whispered, but then started removing her clothes.

# 20

# JAMES

WHETHER MINUTES PASSED, or hours, James couldn't have said. All he knew when he peeled his eyelids open was that he was not dead and that a fire burned bright before him.

While a different sort of heat pressed against the bare skin of his back.

James fought the urge to stiffen, for it would reveal that he was awake, and instead took account of the situation.

The woolen blanket was still over him, and as he slowly inhaled and exhaled, he felt the soft press of breasts against his back. Knees against the backs of his legs. And his hands, still bound by the belt, were pressed against the apex of a pair of thighs.

Ahnna's thighs.

Against his will, he remembered being between those thighs. The taste of her on his tongue as she wrapped those endless legs around his shoulders, her whole body taut with pleasure.

James shoved away the thought, because they were a lifetime away from that moment.

Her arm was draped around his waist, the limpness of it, along with the steadiness of her breath, suggested she'd fallen asleep while doing everything she could to keep him alive.

*I am no fucking murderer.*

He flinched at the memory, and the rest of what she'd said before he'd plunged through the ice filled his head. Ahnna must have felt the motion, because she stirred and then abruptly jerked away from him.

"I see you managed to stay alive," she muttered as she clambered to her feet and moved to put another log on the fire.

She wore only her undergarments and the same necklace she'd been wearing the night everything had gone to shit, but his eyes were all for the long legs on display, not jewels. He forced himself to stop gaping, but not before he noticed the bandage around her leg and shoulder, both wounds he'd inflicted. The one on her leg was soaked through with blood, and it struck him that if his aim had been true, she'd be dead.

"Why did you help me?" His voice sounded like it was dragged over gravel, and he coughed to clear his throat. "You could be across the border into Amarid by now." A thought occurred to him, and he added, "Intending to use me as your hostage?"

She glared at him in disgust. "Go fuck yourself, James. I should've left you to die."

"Why didn't you?"

"Because Alexandra's body count is high enough. No need to add yours to it." Ahnna tilted her head. "Not that you believe me."

James no longer knew what to believe. No longer quite trusted what he'd seen with his own eyes and heard with his own ears, so instead he said, "You're bleeding."

Ahnna bent down to meet his gaze, her hazel eyes hot with anger. "Yeah. Because you shot me. Twice. Thanks for that, by the way."

Dragging a roughly made chair next to the stove, she unraveled the bandage on her thigh to reveal the arrow wound, which was oozing blood. It needed to be stitched.

"There are supplies in my saddlebags," he told her. "Needles, gut thread, and bandages."

"I used them on you," she replied.

James realized then that his injured forearm was wrapped tight with a bandage. She must have stitched him up while he was unconscious. "Thank you."

"Take your thanks and shove it up your ass, James. I'm not interested."

God help him, he didn't know what to make of this situation.

Dipping a cloth in a pot of water, she cleaned away the blood from her leg, then grimaced and put one of her knives into the fire.

"Ahnna . . ."

She ignored him, eyes on the heating blade. When it started to glow, she donned a leather glove and extracted it. Without so much as taking a steadying breath, she pressed the glowing metal to the bleeding wound.

The sharp sizzle filled his ears, along with the distinct smell of burning flesh.

She screamed, her voice wild and furious and full of pain, and leapt to her feet. "Goddamn it!" she shrieked, and kicked the chair across the room before doubling over. "That hurts!"

James kept his mouth shut, as commenting didn't seem prudent. Instead, he watched the fire while Ahnna wrapped a length of bandage around her thigh in his periphery. She righted the chair and sat again, elbows resting on her bare knees. Her hair clung to the sweat beading on the sides of her face, the cabin now hot enough that the icy lake seemed a distant memory. Her eyes focused on him. "Why won't you believe me?"

"Because I saw you, Ahnna. I saw it all!"

"Except you didn't, did you?" Her hands fisted. "You came upon the aftermath, and you saw exactly what Alexandra wanted you to see. She inflicted those injuries on herself in order to—"

"No one could do that to themselves," he interrupted, straining as he tested the bindings on his wrist. "Alexandra has never lifted a weapon in her life. Never known violence. Never known pain. To believe she could do such a thing is irrational, but it is equally irrational to believe that she had the strength to overwhelm my father and kill him. Equally irrational to believe that the riding-boot prints left with his blood came from her tiny *fucking* feet!"

"Why are you defending her?" Ahnna shouted. "She has been

awful to you your entire life, and you've seen firsthand how she schemes!"

"I'm not defending her!" James forced himself upright, ignoring the wave of dizziness. "I'm pointing to the factual evidence of your guilt and trying to understand why, even though everything points to you having done this, I still want to believe you are innocent. I hate that you have gotten so under my skin that I'll absolve you of murdering my own father because you tell me to!"

Ahnna went still.

"I can't be around you," he snarled, the room spinning, his thoughts in a spiral. "Because from the moment you knocked me off that ship, you consumed me. Made me turn on everything that mattered just to have you, and I cannot let that happen again. I cannot put you before my family, and I will make things right by bringing them your head!"

Ahnna snatched up her knife and in a flash knocked him flat on his back. She pressed the still-hot blade to his throat. "Killing me isn't justice, James. It's just you erasing the evidence of your weakness." A trickle of blood ran down the side of his neck, but he barely noticed the pain as his body reacted to the press of her nearly naked skin. "Alexandra is allied with Katarina. This is all a scheme to take the bridge, and if you stop me from warning Aren, my people will pay the price."

James stared at her, his shock at the audacity of her claim doing nothing to temper his traitorous cock's reaction to her naked legs. "An alliance between Katarina and Alexandra? Given the history between Amarid and Harendell? I don't know whether you're lying or you've lost yourself to delusion."

Her eyes filled with anger but as her lips parted to respond, a cold draft of air struck James's naked side, and a familiar voice filled the cabin. "Well, well, James. When they told me you were hunting Ahnna Kertell, this was not the position I expected to find you in."

James's head snapped sideways, horror sucking all the heat from his core.

Because standing in the doorway was Prince Carlo.

The Beast of Amarid smiled. "Such a shame you didn't listen to the princess, my friend, because every word she said was true."

# 21
# AHNNA

Instinct took over and Ahnna flung herself off James, uncertain whether the arrival of the Amaridians was her salvation or her damnation.

Only to freeze as a sword blade rested against her throat.

"Now, now, Princess," the Amaridian man said. "Drop the knife. Mother said you are to be kept alive, which will be far easier if we are friends, no?"

Realization burned like acid through her veins, and Ahnna rolled her eyes up to look at the man who could only be Prince Carlo of Amarid. He gave her a toothy smile, but his gray eyes held no amusement. Held nothing at all beyond predatory interest. All the horror stories she'd heard about the Beast filled her head, and fear turned her heart staccato in her chest.

Carlo's gaze flicked to James. "This is a pleasant surprise, James. It is said that Harendellians are terrible lovers—staid, boring, and uptight—but it seems your Cardiffian blood gave you more than amber eyes." He huffed out an amused breath. "James Ashford likes rough sex." His gaze drifted down to James's crotch, and Ahnna blinked as she saw the hard ridge of his cock through his undergarments. "Likes it a lot, I see."

Rather than correcting the misinterpretation of the situation, James said, "Envious, Carlo?" His tone was mocking and Ahnna silently cursed him, because this was not the time for male posturing. "You're not the man you used to be."

A low growl exited the prince's lips, and he lifted his sword from Ahnna's neck.

She rolled, coming up with her knife, which she threw at the soldier just beyond the threshold. It sank into his throat and he staggered back, clawing at it. Ahnna pursued, yanking out her blade and readying to fight the next opponent.

Only to fall still.

Carlo hadn't come into Harendell's side of the mountains with a small band of men. He'd come with a goddamned army, and enough arrows were leveled at her chest to turn her into a pincushion.

The soldiers swarmed her and forced Ahnna down to the cold snow, more of them pouring inside. At Carlo's call, they dragged her back into the cabin and threw her to the floor, binding her wrists with rough rope. James was pinned to the ground by four of the men, a fresh wound bleeding on his shoulder.

"This is not how friends treat each other, Ahnna." Carlo grabbed her by the hair and pulled her head back so hard, her neck felt on the verge of breaking. "I suggest you improve your behavior, else our journey to Riomar will not be pleasurable. For you and James, at least. Mother only said you needed to be alive, not that you needed to be . . . *whole.*"

His sword blade moved down the length of her torso. Then he angled the blade beneath her left breast.

Ahnna hissed as it cut into the sensitive skin, trying to pull away, but Carlo's hand closed over the back of her neck, holding her in place.

"If you hurt her, I'll kill you!" James roared, flinging one of the men holding him across the cabin, the other three struggling to contain him.

"James, my old nemesis," Carlo murmured. "Be still, or I will maim her."

Blood ran in steady trickles down her side, and Ahnna took only shallow breaths, for any motion risked the blade slicing deeper.

James went still, his chest heaving.

"Good, good," Carlo murmured. "Ensure he is bound securely, comrades. His Highness is twice the man of any of you, and I fear what might happen should he get loose. Mother will not take it well if we do not give her what she wants."

Ignoring the sharp pain beneath her breast, Ahnna racked her brain for a way free of this situation, but came up empty. There were just too many of them, and Carlo was an experienced soldier who would not underestimate either of them.

His breath brushed her ear. "That's right, Princess. There is no way out."

Her skin crawled, every instinct in her body screaming that there was something wrong with this man. That he did not play by the same rules as she did. Did not think like she did. Would not act like she did. "What do you want?"

"He's bound, sir," one of the soldiers said, but Ahnna did not fail to notice that all three of them maintained a tight grip on James, holding him back.

"Perfect." Carlo's voice was like the sound of a snake slithering over dead leaves. He lowered his sword and set it aside. Then he let go of Ahnna's neck. Instead of easing its frantic throb, Ahnna's heart raced even faster in her chest. She braced herself.

Carlo's hands were hot as he took hold of her forearm. "You're a dangerous woman," he whispered. "More dangerous, I think, than James, and that must be tempered, Princess."

Then he jerked his hands.

*Snap.*

The breaking bone sent pain lancing through her body. Ahnna clamped her teeth down on a scream, because her instincts told her that screams were what Carlo wanted. That he enjoyed seeing others suffer.

Yet as Carlo laughed, she realized it wasn't her pain that he cared about. It was James's. These two had an old history, and a bad one, and she was now in the middle of it.

"What do you want, Carlo?" Ahnna asked between her teeth.

"I want you to tell James he was wrong to question my virility." Carlo pulled on her bound wrists, sending knifing pain up her arm, then pressed her hands to the crotch of his trousers.

Against the hardness beneath.

Ahnna gagged, swallowing the sourness that rose in her throat. "He was wrong."

"Louder."

She locked gazes with James, the fury in his amber eyes making the breath catch in her throat. "You were wrong about his virility."

"I'll be sure to remedy that." James's voice was murderously cold.

Carlo snorted and shoved her away. "Get clothes on them and take their horses. James has many faults, but taste in horseflesh is not one of them. The princess will ride with me. His Highness can walk."

Then he left the cabin.

If the Amaridian soldiers were disturbed by their prince's behavior, none showed it. Ahnna's arm was splinted, then she and James were shoved into their clothes and dragged outside.

The ropes binding James were attached to one soldier's saddle so that he'd be forced to walk behind. But Ahnna was led to where Carlo sat astride a horse.

*Her* horse.

Dippy turned his head to regard her and whickered softly, but Ahnna allowed none of her dismay to show on her face. If Carlo knew she cared about the horse, he'd only hurt Dippy to make her suffer.

The soldiers lifted her onto the saddle in front of their prince, then tied a loose rope under Dippy's chest to bind her ankles so she couldn't kick. Carlo pulled her against him, enveloping Ahnna in the thick folds of his fur coat before giving her several rapid kisses on the forehead as if she were a small child. "Such a good girl."

It was more horrifying than having her arm broken.

"Mount up," Carlo called out, and the Amaridians all slid into the saddles of their shaggy mountain horses. "Mother is waiting."

He wrapped an arm around Ahnna's waist and heeled Dippy into a fast trot, the speed making her sick because James would have to run to keep up.

"Why don't you just kill us and be done with it?" she asked. "Why keep us alive?"

Carlo chuckled. "Tempting, and it is what Alexandra wanted us to do. You know too much, Princess, and James . . . Well, Alexandra hates James almost as much as I do. But Mother thinks that we are best served keeping you alive. I'm sure you appreciate what the Harendellians are like, and Mother does not like risk. Mother likes insurance."

So the years-long alliance between Katarina and Alexandra was not without rifts. Ahnna quietly stored that fact away. "Do you always do what *Mother* tells you to, Carlo?"

"Oh, yes." He gave her a kiss on the cheek. "And soon, sweet Princess, you will understand why."

# 22
# KERIS

"ZARRAH IS GOING to kill you for this," Saam muttered from where he stood next to Keris at the rail of the ship, his eyes on Sableton's harbor. "You were supposed to deliver the gifts, admire the baby, and then return to Valcotta, but here we are, about to dive headfirst into a spider's web."

The motivations behind his visit to Ithicana were complicated, but Keris only said, "Daria will explain the situation, and Zarrah will understand the change in itinerary."

"The change in itinerary?" Saam twisted to glare at him. "Keris, you're going to infiltrate the Harendellian court as a spy for Ithicana."

"An intermediary."

"Right." Saam gave a loud snort. "I'm sure that's exactly what the Harendellians think given you insulted William, called Lestara a royal cock gobbler, and inferred that Alexandra was a liar."

"In hindsight, my choice of words was not strategic." Keris rested his elbows on the rail of the ship to catch his balance over a large wave. "Yet I find myself regretting only two of the three statements."

The ship rolled into a trough between two waves, spraying both men with surf. Keris scowled and shoved a sodden lock of hair behind his ear. This was a merchant vessel from the tiny nation of Myris, which was north of Cardiff, and the captain sailed as though he were at war with the sea. But beggars could not be choosers, and very few vessels were risking the ire of Harendell to make port at Northwatch. Soon no one would be making port, for the volume of Harendellian naval vessels they'd passed suggested that a blockade was being formed.

"I know you hate Lestara, and justly so," his friend said quietly as he wiped seawater from his face. "But she's the queen of Harendell now. That means she outranks you."

"Thank you for the clarification." Keris's tone was sharper than he'd intended, but it ground his nerves that Lestara's prophecy had come true and a crown now rested on her head. Not just any crown either. "William's a fool."

"You'll get no quarrel from me on that, but he's an entranced fool. If she tells him to take off your head, he might just do it. And let me remind you that you were supposed to be escaping assassination attempts with this sojourn to visit family, not inviting more of them down upon you."

"He's not that much of a fool." Keris was struck by yet another spray of seawater, and he spat out the mouthful before adding, "It would equate to declaring war on Valcotta and Maridrina."

"Both of which are on the far side of the Tempest Seas." Saam stepped away from the rail and shouted at the captain, "Have you ever sailed a ship before?"

The captain only waved at him with a wide grin, then spun the wheel and shouted unintelligible orders at his crew. Sails lowered, and the vessel slowed its speed into the harbor.

"The Tempest Seas will prevent Zarrah from declaring a proper war to avenge you, and given that Harendell is turning trade north to Cardiff, I'm not sure how much they'll care about the loss of Valcottan gold." Saam squeezed the cuff of his sodden uniform jacket, then sighed and gave up. "You're right that William wouldn't cut off your head, but if you succumbed to poison, it's easy enough to blame the same individuals who were trying to kill you in Valcotta. Zarrah might suspect the truth, but how could she ever prove otherwise?"

"First Dax, and now you," Keris muttered. "I'm surrounded by armchair politicians."

But Saam wasn't wrong. Going into Harendell was risky and his life was very much on the line, but Keris refused to slink back to Valcotta while Aren and Lara fought, bled, and potentially died in a war they hadn't asked for. They'd had his back when he'd needed aid rescuing Zarrah from Devil's Island. Had his back when he'd taken Maridrina to war against Petra. Keris refused to abandon them now, when he alone had the capacity to aid them. "I'll be careful."

"And you'll curb your tongue?"

"Yes, Auntie."

Saam glared at him. "Think about what it would do to Zarrah if something happened to you. It would destroy her, especially given that your last conversation was an argument."

"Low blow."

Saam didn't bother responding, and Keris allowed his friend's comment to drag him into a memory of his last conversation with Zarrah before he'd left for Ithicana. An argument fueled by an attempted assassination in the streets of Pyrinat, with only Daria's sharp eyes saving him from an arrow in the back. He hadn't told Zarrah—he didn't want to add to the strain she endured trying to erase the stain Petra had left upon Valcotta—but the Devil's Island crew were ever loyal to their empress.

"You can't be out wandering the streets in this city," Zarrah had shouted. "It's not safe in Pyrinat. Not for you."

Logically, Keris had known she was right, but he'd lashed out anyway. "I'm not staying locked in your palace, if that's what you're suggesting. I'll lose my fucking mind."

"You think I'm not losing *my* fucking mind?" Tears flooded down his wife's cheeks. "You know the risks, yet you can't find enough patience in your soul to sit still until tempers ease. Every time I'm out of your presence, I live in fear that Daria will arrive to tell me you've been shot. Or stabbed. Or had your throat slit in some back alley because you just had to venture into a seedy winehouse to play cards with people who have a generational animosity to your name."

He'd turned his back on her, irrationally angry. "You think I wouldn't change my name if I could? That I wouldn't purge every marker of the Veliant legacy from my face, if such a thing were possible? What would you have me do, Zarrah? Cut out my goddamned eyes?"

Silence had stretched between them, and in that silence, Keris had felt sick because Zarrah was the last person he wanted to argue with.

"Do you want to walk away from this?"

A knife to the gut would have hurt less. "Pardon?" In two strides, he'd closed the distance between them. "I'd rather be dead than—"

"I don't mean me, I mean *this*." She gestured around the ornate room. "From rule. Do you want us to leave Valcotta to one of my cousins and run away to someplace where no one knows our names?"

All Keris saw was his wife's luminous eyes, tears dampening her long lashes. There'd been no denying a certain appeal to the offer, but he knew that abandoning her people would destroy a part of Zarrah. That it would sink into her like rot, turning her bitter, and he'd be the one to blame. "No, I don't want that."

She rested her forehead against his chest. "Keris, if something happens to you, I wouldn't be able to—"

"What do you want me to do?" He asked the question despite knowing the answer. "What do you need me to do?"

"I . . ." Her fingers flexed where she gripped his arms. "I need you to stay where Daria and her soldiers can protect you. In the palace and under heavy guard. It's not for forever, but I need you to be safe until things settle."

*Safe*. There should be allure to that word, after all they'd been through, but Keris's mind recoiled from it. "How about a compromise? I've seen the small fortune worth of gifts you've compiled for Delia. I'll take them to Ithicana, visit my sister and Aren, admire the baby, and get all my desire for adventure out of my system under Lara's watchful eye while you have some respite from worry."

Zarrah stiffened. "Your solution is to leave? You'd rather leave than be bored for a month in the lap of luxury?"

What he wanted was for her to accept the risk that came with loving him, but instead Keris said, "Lara is my sister and Aren is . . . well, he's important. This is their first child and they deserve my time. I'll visit them, and when I return, you can lock me in a tower of safety."

A tear had rolled down her cheek, and then his wife had given a tight nod. "Fine. Make the arrangements."

"Well, would you look at that. Do you think that's for you?" Saam's voice pulled Keris from the miserable memory, and he looked to where his friend was pointing.

Dozens upon dozens of soldiers with pristine uniforms and banners waited on the wharf, along with a gilded carriage pulled by a full team of horses with white plumage attached to their harnesses.

"Likely. The only thing Harendellians like better than a ceremony is a parade. I should change into something dry."

Keris departed into his quarters and extracted dry garments from his baggage, grimacing over the selection. He'd anticipated following Aren through the Ithicanian jungles, not parades and banquets. But anything was better than looking like a drowned rat, so he swiftly changed, pulled his hair into a knot at the back of his head, and then armed himself with a variety of knives.

The ship rocked gently as it reached the dock, and when Keris came back on deck, it was to have his nose assaulted with the stench of the city. Saam and the rest of his guards all wore the uniforms of the Valcottan imperial army. Their weapons were polished to a shine, and their expressions were stern.

"Thank you for accommodating my party," he said to the captain, who grinned and said, "A good tale for my wife when I return, Your Highness. Good luck with the spiders."

He'd need it.

An ornate gangplank was pushed into place, and as Keris strode down it, a dozen hornists blasted a melody on trumpets, the noise deafening.

A man in a pristine uniform thick with medals and badges of rank waited on the dock, and Keris immediately recognized him from the meeting on Emesmere Island. George Cavendish.

"Welcome to Harendell, Your Highness." Cavendish bowed low.

"We are so pleased to host you, for long have Harendell and Valcotta been friends."

"I hope the friendship continues," Keris replied. "Thank you for agreeing to the visit. War looms, and I feel compelled to do what I can to prevent it."

Cavendish gave a tight smile. "We should all like to avoid any more violence. Has Ithicana's king decided to denounce his sister?"

Keris returned the smile. "I believe that's a conversation I'd best have with your own king."

"Of course." Though he was undoubtedly annoyed, the other man's face was a mask of composure as he gestured to the waiting carriage. "My people will arrange for your belongings to be brought to Fernleigh House. Shall we?"

They walked down the dock, Saam and his soldiers jockeying for position with the Harendellians, a multitude of glares exchanged.

"Apologies," Keris murmured. "The empress personally charged them with protecting my well-being, and her wrath is a thing to behold."

"You must sleep easy being so well cared for by your wife."

"Like a baby," Keris responded, amused by Cavendish's sorry attempt to bait him. "There's much to be said for having a dangerous woman in your bed."

"I'll have to take your word on that, Your Highness. Being a military man myself, I've always been the more dangerous one beneath the sheets."

"It does require a certain degree of nerve."

Cavendish's jaw tightened. "I've never met a woman I couldn't top."

"Then I daresay you've never truly lived." A footman opened the door to the carriage, and Keris gave Cavendish a condescending pat on the shoulder. "A bit of advice, man-to-man: The view from the bottom is better."

Not giving the idiot a chance to respond, Keris climbed into the carriage, only to freeze as his eyes latched onto a familiar face.

"Welcome to Harendell, Your Highness," Queen Alexandra Ashford said, the wound on her face twisting as she smiled. "We are so delighted to have you here with us."

Keris inclined his head. "I appreciate your gracious acceptance of my request, Your Majesty. I have seen enough war to last a lifetime, and if I can aid in averting another, I will gladly do so."

She gestured toward the seat opposite her with one gloved hand. "We all wish to avoid war."

Keris sat, but as he did, he was struck with a sense of déjà vu of sitting before his father's desk in the tower of the Vencia palace. His skin crawled, but he kept his unease off his face.

The carriage swayed as the horses made their way into the city, and Alexandra was silent, her green eyes contemplative.

"I hope your recovery is going smoothly," Keris said to break the silence.

"As well as can be hoped." Alexandra smoothed the silk of her black skirts. "The physical pain is manageable now, but . . ." She sighed and gestured to her cheek. "At my age and experience, I shouldn't care about the disfigurement, but I find it difficult to look in the mirror. The weakness of vanity."

"A weakness I share, so you'll get no judgment from me." Nor would he be so easily lured in by this pretense of fragility. North and south, Alexandra's reputation was well known. Cold. Hard. Infinitely well mannered but always aloof. Above all else, she was infamous for her ruthless intelligence.

"I appreciate the sentiment, although I suspect your vanity is rarely tested. You will have the ladies of my court swooning, of that I have no doubt."

"I'm a married man, Your Grace."

"A love story for the ages, I'm told. Edward was entranced with the lengths to which you went to rescue Zarrah." She smiled, but there was no warmth in her eyes. "My late husband believed in true love."

*Except Edward's true love hadn't been his wife.* "His letters were endlessly entertaining. While we never met, I do feel as though I knew the late king well, and he will be sorely missed."

"His loss is a hole that will never be filled." Alexandra's gaze broke from his, fixing on the gilded handle of the carriage door. "Tell me, does the empress know you are here?"

A question that logistics gave answer to, but Keris said, "Word has been sent to her. She will support my presence, if that's your concern, Your Grace. Valcotta's relationship with Ithicana is strong, and my wife counts Aren and Lara as dear friends. She has a vested interest in peace."

"As do we all." Alexandra braced her hand against the side of the carriage as they rolled over a hole in the cobbles. "Has Aren reconsidered his position?"

"Ahnna is not in Ithicana." Keris winced as they bounced over yet another hole. "But you know that, don't you, Your Grace? How could you not when Prince James himself is in pursuit of Ahnna through the Blackreaches?"

"I meant his position on Ahnna's guilt." Alexandra gestured to the city outside the carriage windows. "The people demand justice, Your Highness. Their most beloved king was brutally murdered in his bed, their queen attacked, and then yet more civilians laid low by Ahnna's violence as she escaped. We must bring her to justice, and by refusing to condemn his sister, Aren renders himself complicit. Not just himself, but all of Ithicana, for he is *king*."

"Harendell's laws require a trial in which the accused may speak for themselves before judgment is made," Keris replied. "Aren honors your own legal system by refusing to condemn Ahnna until she has had a fair trial."

He waited for Alexandra to call out his bullshit, but instead she bit her bottom lip. "You and I know there will be no trial, Keris. James is beyond reason in his resentment and grief, and he will surely kill Ahnna himself the moment he catches her. She might already be dead, for news is slow to come from the depths of the Blackreaches. Aren risks war for a corpse."

Keris's eyes narrowed. "Resentment?"

The dowager queen rubbed at her temples, then made a face. "It is a proper tangle of politics and sentiments, illicit and tawdry, as is only possible in Harendell. I don't care to reveal my family's dirty laundry, but if doing so will help Aren better understand why Ahnna was driven to such lengths, then perhaps he might come to terms with the truth."

Well aware that he was now another thread being drawn into said tangle, Keris leaned forward. "I'll convey what you tell me to his ears only."

Alexandra sighed, toying with the black lace trim on her sleeve as she did. "I'm sure Valcotta's spies informed you and the empress how . . . *taken* James was with Ahnna." She huffed out a rueful sigh. "I suppose I should not mince words. He was utterly besotted with Ahnna from the moment they met."

"We are cautious about believing rumors and speculation."

"Consider the rumors confirmed." She was quiet for a moment. "As I said before, Edward was a believer in true love, but as I'm sure you know, Edward's true love was James's mother, Siobhan. As such, he has always favored James over his other children. Favored him with his time, with love, with titles, and with accolades, demanding that everyone in Harendell treat James as a legitimately born prince. James was the apple of Edward's eye, and there was nothing he would not do for Siobhan's son. And James wanted Ahnna Kertell."

Alexandra would be using this information to manipulate him, but that didn't mean the queen's words were lies. "I see."

"For Ahnna's part, I think she shared James's sentiment, and in another life, she might have chosen him. But the sense of duty in that woman was a thing to behold, and it was very clear to me that she came to Harendell with the singular goal of delivering Ithicana from the ruins of war. To do that, she needed to be queen of Harendell, which meant marrying William. Keris, I tell you with all honesty that Ahnna put her heart into becoming a proper Harendellian lady. Adopted our dress and our customs, and put every effort into enticing William. Wasted effort given that Edward had sabotaged her chances with William, because God forbid my son get something that James wanted."

"By sabotage, you mean Lestara?"

"Yes." Alexandra spat the word. "Two birds with one stone, because not only would it leave Ahnna free for James's taking, but wedding my son to that murderous slut also cemented his alliance with Cardiff. Edward aimed to give Ahnna to his bastard like a gift, with no regard to what she wanted. He never once considered the affront of presuming that Ithicana's princess, the twin sister of King Aren, would want to be bound to a man born of an illicit affair."

Keris considered the revelation and his impression of Ahnna, then said, "Ahnna wouldn't have murdered Edward because he insulted her."

"You're right." Alexandra leaned so that their faces were close. "The laws of Harendell would never allow Edward to name a bastard as heir. James could never be king of Harendell, no matter how badly Edward wished it. But wed to Ahnna, he *could* become king of Ithicana and Master of the Bridge."

Keris's blood turned to ice. "You aren't serious?"

"I am deadly serious, Keris." Her green eyes searched his. "Edward held nothing but contempt for Aren after he forgave Lara her transgressions, but Ahnna he put upon a pedestal. Everyone knows that she is the more beloved of the two Ithicanian royals, for she has been constant and true in her devotion to the people, just as all know the conflict between the two was intense because of Ahnna's hatred of your sister. Aren cast Ahnna aside like trash, so Edward was certain that she'd respond favorably not just to wedding James, but to Harendell supporting a coup to overthrow Aren and put Ahnna on the throne, James at her side."

"Overthrow, as in *kill*."

"Obviously." Alexandra gave a slow nod. "Edward aimed to murder Aren, Lara, and baby Delia all so that his beloved son could have the woman he wanted and a crown on his head."

Keris's heart hammered, blood roaring in his ears. "Edward told Ahnna his plans?"

Alexandra sat back. "Only she and Edward know for certain, and he is dead. My husband was a clever man, Your Highness, but he erred in his judgment of Ahnna Kertell's character."

Keris leaned back in his seat, it all making horrible sense in a way that made him feel sick. Because if there was one thing he was certain of, it was that Ahnna would defend her brother to the grave. "How do you know all this, Your Grace? Because I can only assume that Edward did not include you in his plots."

Alexandra smoothed her skirts again. "There are many secrets kept in the House of Ashford, Your Highness, but not from me. At least, not for long."

It all made far too much sense, and with so much of what she'd said widely known by all, it was either the truth or the most masterfully woven lie Keris had ever encountered. "What do you aim to achieve by telling me this, Alexandra?"

She gave a slow nod to acknowledge that these revelations had a cost. "What I will tell you next is for your ears only, Keris. If you ever claim that I spoke these words, I will deny it to the grave." Her eyes locked on his. "Edward deserved his end. He deserved Ahnna's violence, and she was in the right to cut him down, because not only did he treat her like a mare to be bought and sold, but he threatened her family as well. She was in the right, and I say that as one of her victims."

"But . . ."

"But the people will not accept justification of their king's brutal murder by a foreigner. The only way to appease them is with her head, which means that Aren must sacrifice her. He must. Otherwise, it will be war. Ithicana will fall beneath Harendell's might, and thousands will perish."

"What about William?" Keris demanded. "Does he know all this? Surely he can be made to see reason. Surely you can sway him toward peace."

"He knows." Her expression hardened. "But he is under the spell of a witch. A witch who is Ronan Crehan's daughter, and I assure you, her goals are not peace with Ithicana."

The carriage swayed to a stop, and Keris glanced outside to see they had drawn up in front of a manor with ivy climbing up the gray stone walls.

"If Aren does not sacrifice Ahnna to keep the peace, it will be war on Lestara's terms," Alexandra said, then the footman opened the door. "And you, Keris, have no one but yourself to blame for that."

# 23
# AHNNA

Ahnna had thought she'd known misery. Had thought she'd known evil.

Yet the hours she spent in the saddle with Carlo made her feel like she knew nothing at all.

The Beast of Amarid had a fondness for singing—and a remarkably good voice—but there was something about listening to him sing cheerful songs while gleefully tormenting her and James that made her skin crawl. That made fear pool in her belly.

Because Prince Carlo was not sane.

He rode behind the soldier holding the ropes attached to James, his voice rising in crescendo every time James tripped or fell, forcing Dippy so close that for all her horse's efforts, he stepped on James more than once. Between songs, he'd kiss Ahnna like Harendellian courtiers kissed their lapdogs, then would squeeze the break in her arm while whispering soothing words and stroking her hair.

It took every ounce of willpower she possessed to keep from screaming.

"I like you, Princess," Carlo whispered, running his fingers down her cheek while he rode next to a stumbling James. "I think I could love a woman like you. It's a shame I can't clean you up and dress you pretty. We could have such a lovely time together. But Mother has other plans for you." He sighed and squeezed her broken arm.

Ahnna clenched her teeth, waiting for the excruciating pressure to ease, then she said, "What will your mother say if you accidentally kill James? Because if you keep this up, he *will* die."

Carlo let out a breathy laugh. "Mother's rage would be a thing to behold, my sweet beautiful Ahnna. But James will not die. Not like this. He won't allow it."

"You say that as though it were his decision." From the corner of her eye, she watched James stumble and fall, the horse dragging him several paces before he regained his feet. His face was pale with exhaustion and droplets of blood streamed from his wrists where the ropes dug into his skin, but she dared not look at him directly. "Everyone has a limit."

"True." Carlo kissed her cheek six times in rapid succession, his lips leaving damp marks on her skin. "But I know James's limits. We have been adversaries for a very long time, and there are moments when it feels like he is my soul's mate. My perfect adversary. My darling nemesis. To lose him to exhaustion? Intolerable." His voice turned vicious. "I would never allow it."

He squeezed her arm again, and despite herself, Ahnna let out a soft whimper.

"Don't disappoint me, my sweetling," he crooned. "Don't be less than I dreamed you to be. Mother only made me promise that I keep you alive, not whole. Not whole!" He sang the words, then reined Dippy sideways so that her horse knocked into James.

Ahnna bit the insides of her cheeks, digging deep into her reserves to keep from lashing out in a frenzy. To keep from doing every desperate thing she could to get free, because logic told her nothing would work.

*Bide your time*, she ordered herself. *Wait for them to lower their guard.*

But it killed her to do nothing while James was pushed to the brink, so despite herself, Ahnna turned her head—to find James watching Carlo, amber eyes filled not with defeat but with murder.

It seemed that the Beast knew what he was talking about after all.

"You should want him dead, no?" Carlo murmured. "James's list of transgressions against you is so very long, Princess. I heard that the look on your face when dearest Eddie told all his court that Lestara and Cardiff were the chosen jewels, not Ahnna and Ithicana, was the expression of one stabbed in the heart. Made all the worse because James, your only friend in all of Harendell, was instrumental in the conspiracy against you. I wish I could have been there to witness it." He stroked her cheek. "Did you weep, Ahnna? Or did you rage? Or did you do nothing but hide in your room while Alexandra framed you for Eddie's murder?"

"I'll tell you what I did if you tell me who stabbed him, because I know it wasn't Alexandra," she replied. "Edward was a strong man, and it wasn't a quick death. It took strength, and whoever did it would have been covered with blood. Alexandra was pristine when she approached me."

"Who indeed?"

"Mother didn't tell you?" It was foolish to bait him, but Ahnna couldn't help herself. "Or does Mother not know?"

Carlo gave a soft laugh. "Speaking of not knowing ... I can't help but wonder if *you* know the full depths of the schemes against Ithicana. James, do you wish to tell her what Eddie planned to do to poor Aren, or shall I?" He kissed Ahnna's cheek. "It gets much worse, Princess. Much, *much* worse."

Ahnna barely felt the kiss, because James had somehow grown paler.

"Halt," Carlo called, and the line of soldiers all reined in their horses. The Beast's breath tickled her ear as he whispered, "I wouldn't want you to miss any of this confession."

James's jaw worked from side to side, his gaze on the snow.

"Reticent, are we? Let me help you along, because there are no secrets in the House of Alexandra. You see, Ahnna, it turns out our dear prince isn't the bastard we all believed him to be. Eddie, that sly fox, secretly wed Siobhan Crehan, and as she was yet living when he stood in the cathedral with Alexandra, the king of Harendell spoke lies rather than oaths. Time passed and Eddie held his truths close to his chest, but with peace secured with Cardiff, he intended to announce James's legitimacy and to wed him to you. Isn't that right, James? Eddie never intended William to sit on the Twisted Throne—the seat was for you."

*He wanted to make you queen!* James's screamed accusation rose from Ahnna's memory, giving proof to Carlo's words.

"But there's more!" Carlo slapped his thigh with delight. "They also planned—"

"My father didn't respect Aren," James interrupted. "He thought he was a bad king who'd caused unspeakable harm to his people for the sake of a pretty face. He aimed to back a coup to overthrow Aren and make you queen of Ithicana. But I—"

"Which would have made dearest James the Master of the Bridge!" Carlo crowed. "King of Ithicana, and then one day king of Harendell as well. The true lord of the north with a pretty wife at his side. That was their plan!"

Nausea swam in Ahnna's stomach, and she swallowed hard to keep from vomiting.

"Do you know what happens during coups?" Carlo asked, and though Ahnna could not see his face, she sensed the smile on it. "Kings die. Queens die. Little baby princesses *die*."

*They planned to kill my family.* Ahnna lost control of herself and vomited into the snow, because Carlo had been right. It was so much worse.

"Ahnna, I didn't know that was his intention until that night." James stepped toward her, but the soldier holding his leash yanked him back. "I didn't want any of it. Told him I didn't support it and that you wouldn't either."

"And so vehement was he in his rage toward Eddie's plan that dear James took action and—" Carlo held up his hand in a dramatic pause.

"—sat alone drinking in his father's study while fireworks burst over Verwyrd. The true man of the hour! Huzzah!"

Ahnna's mouth was sour with vomit, her chest hollow. Edward had planned to kill her family, and James had done nothing?

"It is said that Harendellians are spiders," Carlo continued in a low voice. "That the court in Verwyrd is like wading into a web. Yet I've always found the Ashfords to be more like wolves. Did you not see how they separated you from your flock, Ahnna? How they got you alone? How they made you weak to use you to achieve their own ends? Amber eyes aside, James is very much an Ashford, because he ensured you were cut off from anyone who might aid you. Princess Bronwyn was trussed like a pig and cast on a ship for Northwatch, and your dear cousin Taryn locked in irons and sent off to prison at Verwyrd."

"Please tell me this isn't true."

*Please don't let it be true that Taryn is a prisoner again.*

"I arrested her at the conservatory." James's tone was clipped. "Taryn was to be brought back to Verwyrd to be kept as a political prisoner." His throat moved as though he were swallowing hard. "And as possible bait for you."

A shudder ran through her whole body, and Dippy snorted and sidled sideways as he sensed her distress.

"She's a lady. She won't be harmed, and she'll be kept as befits her station."

"Like Lestara was?" The words came out as a shriek, sudden and desperate panic filling her. "Why would you do that to her? They were nowhere near Verwyrd when your father was murdered. I deliberately stayed away from them when I knew your dogs were on my trail. I didn't even send them a *fucking* message, because I didn't want to give any reason for you to think they were involved!"

"I knew she wasn't involved, but . . . I'm sorry, Ahnna."

"You're sorry?" She could barely breathe. She'd naïvely thought she'd been protecting them, but instead she'd left them to the wolves who'd already been planning to exterminate her entire family. "You're *fucking* sorry? Is that all you have to say?"

"There isn't much to say, is there?" James finally met her glare. "Alexandra fooled me. I should have heard you out. I should have done things differently. But regret doesn't undo what has already been done."

"Edward planned to destroy my family to give you Ithicana like a fucking gift." Her whole body was taut with fury. "You can't blame Alexandra for that."

"I didn't ask him for any of that!"

"But neither did you try to stop it!"

Carlo shifted behind her in the saddle, his arm tight around her waist, and though Ahnna knew he was relishing this moment, she didn't care. "Fuck you, James. I should've timed that avalanche better. I should've let you stay beneath the ice. I should've let you freeze to death."

He didn't answer, only stared at the snow between them.

"You had best hope that your *dear nemesis* keeps my ropes tight," she hissed, "because if I get loose, I'm not going to run. I'm going to slit your goddamned throat, because you seem as great a threat to Ithicana as the rest of your awful family."

She thumped her heels as best she could against Dippy's sides, and Carlo didn't check the reins as her horse broke into a trot. Instead, he wrapped his cloak more securely around her and pulled her close to him. His breath was hot as he whispered, "I have more truths to share, little sheep. Let me know when you are ready to hear them."

# 24

# JAMES

James's breath came in ragged pants as he stumbled through the knee-deep snow, desperately trying to keep his feet beneath him. Because to fall meant being dragged, and he wasn't certain he'd be able to get up again.

His hands were numb while the rest of him burned with heat, and he knew the sweat soaking his clothes would turn to ice when they stopped to make camp that night.

If he made it that long.

His plunge into the lake had taken more out of him than James cared to admit, and compounded with the endless days of hunting Ahnna without rest, he was recovering slowly.

Yet that felt like a minor concern compared with the all-consuming guilt that threatened to drown him.

Ahnna was innocent. Completely and utterly innocent, and yet it had taken the truth coming from his enemy's lips to make him fully believe her.

Logically, James was aware that Alexandra's scheme had been

masterfully executed, but he still felt the purest form of stupid for having fallen for it so completely. With each step he took, it felt harder to understand why he hadn't suspected her. Why he hadn't taken a breath to hear Ahnna out. Why even when presented with the truth, he'd still clung to the lie, unable to get beyond what he'd seen with his own eyes.

Failures that he was being punished for, because he and Ahnna were now the Beast of Amarid's prisoners.

Dippy trotted ahead of him, Carlo and Ahnna wrapped in a heavy fur cloak, and James couldn't help but wonder what was happening beneath. Nothing good, was his best bet, although it was possible that the Beast's proclivities were sated for the time being.

Since they'd been in their late teens, he and Carlo had gone head-to-head against each other over the Lowlands. Endless clashes of violence as Harendell and Amarid danced the knife's edge of war over the fertile stretch of land north of the Blackreaches. The Amaridian prince's reputation had always been dark, his sadistic tendencies known, and he'd grown into them with each passing year. Carlo left many bodies in his wake, and not just on the battlefield, because Katarina was endlessly covering up the deaths of his wives. All dead by accident, Katarina said, but it was no secret that Carlo had strangled each one. His soldiers were deeply loyal, and while that was partially because Carlo was a skilled commander, it was mostly out of fear of his particular brand of punishment.

Katarina was the singular individual who controlled the Beast, and he worshiped and feared his mother in equal measure. James had always believed that if someone like Carlo feared Katarina, the Crimson Widow's cruelty must be greater than anyone knew.

Yet Katarina was also the reason he and Ahnna were alive.

Insurance against Alexandra, and apparently destined for imprisonment in the Furnace, but it was a long way to Riomar. Days on the road, and with fear of Katarina's wrath holding back the worst of Carlo's tendencies, there was a chance for escape.

*If I get loose, I'm not going to run. I'm going to slit your goddamned throat.*

James grimaced at Ahnna's words, because it was going to be

very difficult to rescue a person who aimed to kill him the moment she had a chance. Not that he could blame her.

Carlo had certainly manipulated the truth to the worst possible effect, but that didn't change the fact it was the truth. James's father had planned to overthrow Aren, and pleading to Ahnna that he hadn't known until the final hour, that his father had believed he was doing right by her, that he'd intended to offer Aren exile would seem weak and hollow. Especially given James had sat and drunk for hours rather than immediately telling Ahnna of his father's plans. James deserved Ahnna's ire for a thousand reasons, and he refused to shirk responsibility when a more proactive response on his part might have stymied all that had occurred.

He was more than culpable. He was to blame.

Yet that did not mean he intended to wallow, because that would only dig the pit they were in deeper.

And the Furnace's cells were deep enough.

# 25
# AHNNA

*WHAT'S DONE IS done*, Ahnna silently told herself. *You already knew Edward didn't have your interests at heart, and this just confirms the depths of that truth.*

Yet she couldn't help but rehash the revelations that Carlo had forced from James, anger wrapping around her chest like a vise.

*He wanted to make you queen! He was going to give you what you wanted!*

James's shouted words kept repeating in her head, but it was the latter part that made her ill—because how much of this was her own fault? How much of Edward's negativity toward Aren was because she'd made no secret of her disgust for Lara and for Aren's forgiveness of her? Had she driven that aspect of his plan? Would everything be different if she'd been vocal about her support for not just her brother's rule, but Lara's as well?

Against her will, Ahnna's imagination spiraled, showing her a future where James was king of Harendell and she was his queen.

A future where she had all that she desired, most especially the man she was in love with.

*That's not a future, it's a delusion*, her anger hissed. *You'd be as powerless in that situation as you are now. A toy taken from one son and given to another, your name used as leverage to extort Ithicana, not support it. Your goals wouldn't matter. You wouldn't matter.*

"Why so tense, sweet Princess?" Carlo asked, breaking off from his incessant singing. "Does your heart hurt, having learned how the Harendellians intended to use you? Or is it because James is not the paragon of chivalry you'd thought him to be? You should have asked for my advice, because I'd have told you the truth about him."

She shifted restlessly, hating how her body was pressed against his. "No, you wouldn't have, because that would have disrupted Mother's plans."

Carlo chuckled. "True, true. But tell me, behind the handsome face, the polished boots, and the rigid manners, didn't you sense a different sort of man? A woman such as you, who has survived on instinct, must surely have recognized the predator beneath? The wolf?"

Ahnna had, and God help her, it had been the wolf she'd wanted.

"In Amarid, we know only the wolf, especially in the Lowlands," Carlo continued. "The James we know is always in the thick of it, uniform torn and splattered with mud and blood. The ruthless major general who will not hesitate to fight dirty. Who will always kick his enemies where it hurts most." He gave a soft chuckle of appreciation. "Alas, with his interests vested in Cardiff, Ithicana was, by necessity, his enemy."

"Apparently." The word came out from between her teeth.

"I am curious about his state of mind," Carlo mused. "Did he feel torn between wanting to fuck over Ithicana and wanting to *fuck* Ithicana's princess, or were the goals one and the same?"

Ahnna's temper snapped. With a sharp jerk, she slammed her head back, skull connecting with Carlo's face.

He swore, and Ahnna braced for retribution. Instead, Carlo spat blood on the snow and then started laughing. "Oh good. I was worried you might be breaking, lovely, and that would have been disappointingly easy."

Ahnna cringed as he pulled her close and planted soft butterfly kisses up the side of her face, smearing her cheek with blood.

"I shall have to try harder," he murmured. "Thank you for being a challenge, Ahnna. I will do my best to be creative."

*Don't react. Do. Not. React.*

Carlo went back to his singing. Song after song, until the sun was little more than a glow on the horizon. Only then did he give the order to his men to make camp.

Allowing the soldiers to lower Ahnna from the saddle, Carlo jerked his chin toward James, who was on his knees and breathing hard. "Stake his leash to the ground next to a fire and get him warmed up. Food and water."

"Let the bastard die," one of the men muttered. "All of Amarid will cheer."

Carlo went still as death, and every one of the soldiers went stiff with tension. Slowly, he walked over to the man and lowered his head so that they were eye-to-eye. "Do you think it is *you* who will determine how the bastard prince of Harendell dies?"

Ahnna's hackles rose, every instinct in her body screaming *danger*.

"No, sir," the soldier whispered, gaze moving this way and that as he tried to evade Carlo's dead-eyed stare. "Apologies, sir."

"Since you are clearly a stupid person, I will explain," Carlo said softly. "I want James to walk, to crawl, and then to be *dragged* to Riomar, because I would like to watch him break before delivering him to Mother. This is not possible if your idiocy sees him frozen to death on the first night in our company, never mind the pain I will suffer if we deliver to Mother a rotting corpse. Do you understand?"

"Yes, sir." The man was trembling, and though all of these soldiers were her enemies, Ahnna felt a surge of sympathy. Because she knew a dead man walking when she saw him.

"I do not suffer fools." Carlo patted the man's cheek, then swift as lightning, drew a knife across the soldier's jugular. "So I will not suffer you."

The soldier staggered back, his hand clutching the wound. It did nothing to stanch the spray of blood that painted the white snow as he pleaded for aid from his fellows.

No one moved.

They only watched with dull eyes as he collapsed to the ground and went still.

"Strip him and leave him out for the lions to eat," Carlo ordered. "Perhaps such an offering will protect the rest of us every time we need to venture into the dark to piss."

Then he strode into the trees.

"Come on, then," one of the soldiers restraining her said. Ahnna gave no argument as she walked through the blood-soaked snow to where they were setting up camp.

The soldiers fastened her bound wrists to a stake driven deep into the ground between her knees, which allowed her enough range of motion to eat and not much else. Not that she'd be good in a fight with her right arm broken. Not against this many men, and not in the middle of the wilderness where she'd need to hunt to survive.

James was similarly restrained on the far side of the fire from her. His shoulders rose and fell with rapid pants of exhaustion, steam rising from him, but the heat of a day of running would soon turn to cold in the cruel night air. The soldiers draped blankets around both of them, as well as setting food and water at their feet. Seeming content that they weren't going to escape, the soldiers moved to finish constructing the rest of the camp.

"Are you all right?"

Scowling, Ahnna lifted her eyes from the fire to glare at James. "Oh, I'm wonderful, James. I can think of no better way to spend the day than bouncing on the lap of a one-balled sadist with a dubious claim to sanity who intends to deliver me to his mother, the queen who is working toward the destruction of my family and homeland. But enough about me. How was your day?"

James blew out a slow breath. "I know you hate me, but if we are to escape, we need to work together."

"Or maybe I escape and leave you to entertain your *dear nemesis*."

"Ahnna, you have a broken arm."

"Really? I hadn't noticed."

"Ahnna, if you'd just listen—"

She kicked at the fire, sending up sparks. "Just listen? Just give you the benefit of the doubt so that you might explain yourself? Just set aside the fact that you're a lying, scheming son of a fucking meddling prick and let you say your piece? Fuck you and your audacity, Your Highness, because you would have spared us all of this if you'd accorded me that very courtesy."

Before he could respond, Carlo approached and sat on a flat rock.

"Let us have a nice meal together," he declared as though they were all old friends. "I have a bottle of good red we can share."

He pulled the cork from a bottle of wine, the wax seal with the vintner's mark telling Ahnna it was costly enough to feed a family for a year.

Carlo took a swig straight from the neck, then held it out to Ahnna. She took it and lifted it to her mouth, her broken arm screaming protest. She forced herself to take several swallows.

"Hurts, doesn't it?" Carlo asked, taking the bottle and offering it to James, who shot him a sour glare. "But naughty girls deserve punishment." He touched his split lip.

"Broken bones grow back stronger." Ahnna ate the food she'd been given, chewing and swallowing. "I've broken many, so I know."

Carlo smiled and took another sip. "I wish we'd met before."

Ahnna shrugged. "We might have crossed paths if you'd been part of Maridrina's invasion. Were you too busy playing with James in the Lowlands or did your mother not allow you to join the fun in Silas's war?"

James gave a soft laugh. "Care to reveal your own truths, Carlo, or shall I?" When the Beast didn't answer, he added, "Ithicana has nothing to fear from Carlo, because he's scared shitless of water. Can't stomach anything deeper than his own bath without squealing like a little girl."

Ahnna held her breath, certain that Carlo would lash out, but he only grinned. "I am enjoying this game tremendously. Is it my turn now?"

James reached out, the restraints staked into the ground between his knees stretching taut as he picked up the wine bottle. "Cheers." He drank, then twisted the bottle as though to smash it, but Carlo swiftly plucked it from his hand, tutting as he did.

The Beast turned a sly eye on Ahnna. "My turn. When I left Riomar, it was with the news that William intended to meet with Aren ringing in my ears. Harendell's new king intended to give him an ultimatum: Surrender you, Ahnna, for execution or suffer a war they are sure to lose."

"Aren can't surrender what he doesn't have." Her veins turned to ice. "William knows James pursued me into the mountains, which means they know I'm not in Ithicana."

Carlo shrugged. "That's true. But tell me, do you think your brother will believe them? Will he be convinced of your guilt? It is my understanding that Alexandra intended to go to the meeting herself, and I have heard that the wounds *you* inflicted have made the lady a horror to look upon."

Throughout all of this, Ahnna had not once considered that Aren would believe the accusations. Recent conflicts aside, no one knew her better than her twin. But too easily she remembered how James had been deceived by Alexandra's injuries. Would Aren be the same?

"What will Aren think when he sees Alexandra's cut-up face? Will he suspect she did it herself?" Carlo asked. "Or will he condemn you? Will he cast you to the wolves to evade war?"

Ahnna forced her face into a mask of composure. "I want Aren to put Ithicana before me. I want him to do whatever it takes to avoid war."

"Except Alexandra wants this war. Mother's protégée walks a fine line. She must keep the Harendellians convinced you are Eddie's murderess but also ensure Aren is certain of your innocence so that he will refuse to condemn you. If she does this, war is certain."

Her hands felt like ice.

"You see, Ahnna, no matter which path Aren takes, you lose. You are the one whose name will be cursed until the end of days. Best to just lie down and die, no?"

"Carlo, shut the fuck up. Ahnna, do not listen to him," James snarled. "Alexandra wanted this war, which means she'd have it regardless of whether you were alive or dead."

"Perhaps that is so, old friend," Carlo answered. "But what will the Ithicanians believe? Will they be certain that Ahnna is innocent?

Or will they believe that, once again, their king is sacrificing them for the sake of a woman? Perhaps Eddie's plans will come to fruition and it will be a coup that hands the bridge to Harendell after all."

The food she'd just eaten threatened to come up, and Ahnna gagged.

"Ahnna, do not listen to him!" James shouted. "He's getting off on this—he's just trying to hurt you."

She knew that. And yet . . .

Carlo lifted the bottle to her lips, making her drink. Then he stroked his fingertip down her scar. "Nothing cuts deeper than the truth, does it? You will be Ithicana's damnation. And nothing you can do, whether it be escaping to fight for your people or giving up and falling on your own sword, will change that." His teeth gleamed white in the firelight as he stood. "Sweet dreams, beautiful Princess."

James was shouting not to listen to him. Cursing at Carlo and making threats, but Ahnna barely heard him.

Because the Beast was right.

*You are the damnation of your people.*

Lying down on the cold ground, Ahnna curled around the spike holding her in place. And though she knew what pleasure it would bring him, she could not fight the tears that slid down her face.

# 26

# KERIS

Keris reached up to pluck an orange from one of the trees, and then absently peeled the fruit as he stared through the glass of the orangery at the hedge maze beyond.

"A bit strange to grow trees inside," Saam said, reaching up to pick his own orange. "It's warm and wet—they'll grow outside just fine."

"The wet is likely your answer." Keris ate a piece of the fruit and eyed the raindrops pattering against the glass ceiling. "I doubt the Harendellians care to take their tea sitting in the rain. I certainly don't."

"You don't drink tea."

Keris shrugged. "I don't like to do anything in the rain." He walked through the orangery eating slices of the fruit and examining the wrought-iron benches made comfortable with thick velvet cushions and small knit blankets. At one end was a mahogany dining table with six chairs, the top well polished but also marked with dings and scratches from years of use. On one leg, three names were carved: Will, Jamie, and Ginny. Keris ran a finger over the childish script, one of many markers that this was a home that was *lived* in. The whole of

Fernleigh—at least the rooms Keris had explored—was filled with the same. Furnishings of the highest quality, but all bearing signs of heavy use, and rather than expensive artwork, portraits of the royal family adorned every wall. The shelves in the library were filled with books of fiction and poetry, stacks sitting on side tables as though awaiting the return of the family member who'd been reading them. It smelled of oranges and fresh bread, wood polish and leather, but above all else, it smelled of extreme wealth. The Harendellians were so good at being the richest people in the world that they didn't feel compelled to prove it.

"My father would have hated everything about this place," he murmured, toying with the corner of a chair where the leather upholstery had come unstitched, thinking of the Vencia palace and how everything was flawless, expensive, and utterly devoid of personality. Perhaps the Sky Palace in Verwyrd was the same, but he doubted it. Harendellians believed that if you tried to impress, it meant you weren't impressive at all, and the Ashfords epitomized what it meant to be Harendellian.

"I think it's all right." Saam was leaving small piles of orange peels littered across the orangery. Keris considered warning him that his stomach might rebel from eating so many, then decided to leave his friend to discover that information himself. "Are you going to write to Zarrah?"

Keris made a noncommittal noise. Daria would be well into her journey back to Pyrinat with an explanation of where he was and why, and though the written word was normally his forte, he'd only stared at the blank sheets on the writing desk in his room and then set his pen back down.

What was he supposed to say? He was doing the exact opposite of what she'd asked him to do, and while Zarrah would understand the logic of his choice, Keris suspected that Daria's explanation would still hit like a punch to the stomach. It made him wonder whether, for all Zarrah loved him, she wished he were a different sort of man. Someone who'd say and do all the right things. Who'd be an asset rather than the liability he undoubtedly was to her.

*You could be that man.* Keris shoved away the thought in favor of abandoning the orangery for the main house. He was waiting to speak with William, but the king and Lestara had been gone all day visiting a horse breeding farm north of Sableton. After leaving Keris in the care of her servants, Alexandra had pleaded pain and exhaustion and retired to her room, which meant he'd accomplished exactly *nothing* other than sending one of Saam's most trusted soldiers back to Ithicana with a verbal account of all that Alexandra had told Keris in the carriage.

He'd given no opinion on his interpretation of what Alexandra had said, but continuing to cling to the belief that Ahnna was innocent now bordered on delusion. Edward had threatened the lives of Aren, Lara, and Delia, and while Ahnna might not murder for pride, anger, or country, Keris suspected that she might do it for family.

With Saam trailing at his heels, Keris walked through the soft silence of Fernleigh, the rooms lit with the warm glow of lamps and hearths, but as he went to climb the main staircase, he paused. The wide landing had an enormous portrait of William standing with a horse, but in the lamplight, he noted that the paint surrounding the frame was slightly darker in hue—as though a larger piece had hung in place of this one until recently.

"Excuse me," he said to a maid crossing the front entrance carrying a tray of cakes and a steaming cup. "Is this portrait of His Grace recent? The artwork is magnificent."

The woman bobbed a curtsy. "Not new, Your Highness, but recently moved to this wall to replace one of the Good King Edward. The queen mother, God bless her heart, was brought to tears every time she looked upon his face, so she asked that it be stored away so as not to test her strength in these dire times."

Keris blinked. That sentiment was deeply at odds with the Alexandra who'd declared to him that Edward had deserved his fate for what he'd done to Ahnna. "Such a terrible loss," he murmured, then carried on up the stairs to his room.

"The Harendellians have the estate under heavy guard," Saam said as he fell in alongside Keris. "But we'll post a rotating guard of our own outside your door and below your window, and I'll also have a few doing a stroll about to keep an eye on things without stepping on Harendellian toes."

Keris only shrugged. "If the oranges were poisoned, you'll be the first to know."

His friend's stomach chose that moment to give a mighty gurgle, and Saam's lips parted in horror. "But how? They have peels."

"Inject them with a needle, I suppose. The Harendellians are masters of poisoncraft. If they want us dead, dead we shall be."

Saam's stomach gave another violent gurgle. "Oh God. My stomach hurts."

"You ate fourteen oranges. That's on you, not God."

Saam nodded, but his eyes suggested he was at greater risk of poison than indulgence as he swiftly inspected Keris's room, then said, "Don't leave." Without waiting for a response, he shut the door, his boots moving rapidly down the hall.

Going to the sideboard, Keris stared at the heavy crystal decanters filled with amber liquids, sighed, then poured himself a drink from one of them. Only for his eyes to catch on a folded piece of paper sitting on the writing desk that hadn't been there earlier.

Sipping the brandy, he examined the paper, which had a small drawing of a foxglove blossom on it.

*Cardiff.*

His hands abruptly turned cold, and he drained his glass before flipping open the page.

*We need to talk. Fabled Flask in the tenderloin. Come alone.*
*Cormac.*

It had to be Prince Cormac, who was King Ronan's brother. Which also made him Lestara's uncle.

Given that Keris had once pushed Lestara into a mass grave, shoveled dirt into her face while outing her as a traitor to the survivors of Vencia, and then exiled her into the care of the Harendellian court, meeting with her uncle seemed . . . *unwise.*

*But* Lestara was now queen of Harendell, which would not have happened if not for his choices. Cardiffians had interesting notions about fate and destiny, which meant they might see all that she'd endured as a necessary means to a royal end.

Going to the wardrobe, Keris retrieved a black shirt and his leather coat. Putting on both, he drew up the hood and checked that his knives were all where they should be, an odd sense of nostalgia passing over him.

Turning the lamps down low, he opened the window and looked out over the hedge maze, marking both the Harendellian guards and his own.

*You promised Zarrah not to take more risks.*

Keris gripped the windowsill, Cormac's note crumpled in his fist. To go at all was a risk. To go alone was foolish.

But he hadn't come to Harendell to sit around drinking the enemy's wine. There was a great deal that Alexandra wasn't telling him, and Cormac might be his only chance to discover the truth.

Stepping onto the windowsill, Keris waited for the patrolling guard to move out of earshot.

And then jumped.

# 27
# ZARRAH

Z ARRAH STRODE DOWN the ship's gangplank onto the docks, and then made her way into the city. Nerastis, always its most beautiful at night, gleamed brilliantly in the moonlight.

But after meeting with Dax on the journey north, she had no room in her heart to appreciate the city Valcotta shared with Maridrina. Her heart was too full of dread over what was to come.

Edward dead.

Ahnna accused of murdering him.

William threatening war to avenge him.

Lestara now queen of Harendell.

And Keris on the front lines of another war.

"Did Keris give any indication of what he planned to do?" she asked Dax, who strode at her elbow.

The Maridrinian man shook his head, then rubbed his temples, his exhaustion written across his face. "Only that he planned to find Lara and Aren. He ordered me to carry on to deliver the news of the murder to Sarhina, and then you, but I got stuck at Southwatch due to the storm. Everything we know is terribly outdated unless Sarhina has fresh intelligence."

Every instinct in Zarrah's body screamed that the situation had only grown worse, and she cursed the slow travel of news from north to south. Cursed Ithicana's storms for how they endlessly disrupted travel, though she knew that it was those very storms that would be preventing Harendell from retaliation.

"Lara will keep him out of trouble," Dax said. "He's probably drinking their wine and complaining about the quality of Aren's library."

Zarrah was in no mood for platitudes. "Aren and Lara are certain Ahnna is innocent?"

"Yeah." Dax was quiet for a long moment. "But Prince James isn't a witness who is easily discounted."

"Agreed." The bastard prince of Harendell was not one for schemes. Unlike the rest of his family. "Though we can't discount that he's Lestara's cousin." Another revelation that Dax had delivered. "What was Edward thinking?"

"Doesn't much matter now that he's dead, does it?"

Zarrah's mind twisted over the fragmented information, trying to put together all the pieces as they pressed into Nerastis. But her thoughts kept circling back to one point, drawn there by her rising fear.

"Lestara *hates* Keris," she said softly. "Which hardly mattered when she was being led around on a leash by Virginia Ashford and fed dog biscuits by the ladies of the court, but now she's *fucking* queen of Harendell. If she finds out he's in Ithicana, she might use her newfound power to take revenge on him."

"Trust the storms," Dax intoned, and Zarrah bit down on a retort, because every storm season had an end and every War Tides a beginning.

But she could not stop the turn of the seasons, so Zarrah fixed her sights on the Maridrinian palace where Sarhina waited.

There was no ceremony or fanfare at the gates, only covert nods as she and her small entourage passed by the Maridrinian guards. Word of this meeting would travel north eventually, but stealth might buy them time.

"Get some rest," she said to Dax. "I'll meet with Sarhina alone."

Striding down the corridor where Keris's brother had once dragged her as his prisoner, Zarrah smiled for the first time in what felt like eternity as a familiar face approached. Tucking her gloves into her belt, she lifted her hands and said, "It's good to see you, Ensel."

"You as well, Imperial Majesty." He smiled. "You've been practicing."

At her request, Ensel had provided drawings of the signs he made with his hands to speak and sent them to her in Pyrinat. Zarrah enjoyed conversations with Sarhina's husband, for he was a breath of calm in the midst of an endless storm. Maridrina's queen was a force to be reckoned with, as tempestuous as any Veliant, but she always listened to Ensel. "How is she?"

"The world has never seen anger like this."

Zarrah gave a tight nod. Sarhina's hatred for Lestara and what she'd done to Vencia was a thing to behold. Dax had told her Maridrina's queen had taken Lestara's ascension poorly, and the timing could not be worse, because Sarhina had just given up most of her power.

Sarhina's decision to begin abolishing the monarchy was commendable in many ways, but Zarrah did not think that these elected officials would be willing to risk much on behalf of Ithicana if it truly came to war with Harendell.

Zarrah silently cursed Ahnna Kertell for her rash violence, because the ripple effect of Edward's murder would be felt across the known world.

Guards opened a set of doors, and Zarrah strode into a room dominated by a large table. Pulling her hood back, she fixed her gaze on the woman who sat at the far end of the table, hands resting on its flat surface and a scowl etched across her lovely face. "I wish we were meeting under better circumstances."

Sarhina exhaled, then pushed her black braid over her shoulder and rose. "Ahnna Kertell has started a war, sure and true. The Harendellians will not let this go—Edward certainly deserved a knife to the chest for wedding that murderous sow to his heir, but he was beloved by the people."

They both circled the table and embraced, then Sarhina gestured for Zarrah to sit, pouring them both glasses of water from a carafe on the table.

"Do you have any fresh news?" Zarrah asked after drinking. "Have you heard from Lara?"

Sarhina shook her head. "The storms have been vicious. Even getting a ship across to Southwatch has been nearly impossible, so the only news I have is what came via Dax before he pressed on to give you the same information. Lara has undoubtedly sent additional messages, but they will be stuck at Southwatch until the storms ease. I hate to imagine what has been happening in the north, but imagine we must. If it comes to war, we will have to pick a side."

"I was under the impression we already had chosen a side."

Sarhina leaned back in her chair. "Yes. And no. Dax's information might be old, but on the matter of Ahnna's actions, it was clear. Prince James and his men came upon Ahnna attacking Alexandra. She had the bloody knife in her hand. Had shouted threats of murder toward the Ashford family not hours before, after Edward humiliated her in front of his entire court. It's possible that William will be placated with her execution—with luck, they've already caught her and seen it done—but Aren needs to vocally condemn her and her actions to put as much distance between Ahnna and Ithicana as he can. I say that knowing full well that he won't. Dax indicated that Aren doesn't think she's guilty."

"Would you, if it were one of your sisters?" Zarrah couldn't help but feel defensive toward Aren, for she admired his stalwart loyalty immensely.

Azure eyes locked on hers, identical in color to Keris's but for the black lashes that framed them. "Yes. Which is why I'm praying to every higher power that Bronwyn doesn't involve herself."

"Dax said she was in Ithicana."

Sarhina grimaced. "Yes, but Taryn Kertell was taken prisoner. Given she's Bron's lover, I can't imagine that my sister will sit idly."

"It's not the Veliant way." Zarrah took another sip of her water. "I have the same concerns about Keris. He'll be in the thick of things."

"He's not exactly a tempering influence, though, is he? Especially given Lestara's rise to the throne." Sarhina rubbed at her temple.

"William's a hotheaded idiot, so he'd have been easy pickings for Lestara. She's beautiful, and more than that, she's experienced with royal men. But what is Edward's excuse for such a foolish decision? Ronan has other daughters he could've chosen who aren't responsible for mass murder if a union with Cardiff was what he wanted. Why her?"

"She was convenient, and she's likely done an excellent job of convincing William that she was a victim of my aunt's manipulation."

"We can blame Keris for that. I told him to cut off her traitorous head."

Zarrah didn't bother defending her husband's creative punishment, because she was sure he was currently cursing the decision himself. "The past can't be changed, but it most certainly will influence the future. We must assume that Lestara has her claws in deep and is more than capable of manipulating William to achieve her own ends."

"Keris needs to keep his head down and out of her reach. There is no one in the world she hates more than him, and I don't think your wrath is enough to keep her from killing him, should she get the chance."

A band of tension tightened around Zarrah's chest, and she drew in a steadying breath.

"He won't hide, that much I know." Reaching into the pocket of her coat, Zarrah withdrew several folded pieces of paper. "These are the letters Lestara sent in correspondence with Petra. They were found in my aunt's quarters. Proof, in Lestara's own hand, that she knew exactly what her actions would achieve, as well as a clear statement of her ambitions to rule. If William were to see these, he might better understand the woman he married."

Sarhina spread the pages flat, and though she made no visible reaction as she read, Maridrina's queen seethed with fury. Zarrah's skin prickled, and she was reminded of an offhand comment Lara had once made that Sarhina was the most dangerous of the Veliant sisters.

Though she'd read the letters many times, Zarrah's eyes caught on Lestara's looping script. *Maridrina must be rid of Keris, Imperial Majesty. Any and all losses that the people suffer will be well worth it, for he is not fit to rule. The people will grow to understand that the short-term costs are worth the long-term gains when I am on the throne, for through my rule, I will right this nation. You and I will be the strongest of allies, for the stars themselves have foretold that to rule is my destiny.*

It was pages and pages of the same, all of it making it very clear that Lestara had cared little who died as long as Keris, whose name she slandered at length, lost the crown. Her obsession with being queen and ruling seemed to permeate the pages themselves, and just touching the paper filled Zarrah with intense unease. With luck, William would feel the same upon reading them and would set Lestara aside. Not a solution to all their woes, but not having a queen who wished vengeance upon Ithicana, Maridrina, and Valcotta alike would go a long way.

Silence stretched through the room. Sarhina quietly rose and poured two drinks, setting one in front of Zarrah, who stared at the amber liquid but didn't take a sip.

"Ahnna's choice to murder Edward may have set events in motion, but this is a multifaceted conflict." Sarhina sipped her drink, staring at a map of both continents and the bridge between them. "I'd say all nations will be drawn into it, but in truth, we're already involved. We are all connected, in alliance and in enmity, and have been for generations. I think that the revelation of Edward's connection to Cardiff's House of Crehan is but the tip of the iceberg. We must show care, else this will spiral into something that dwarfs the Endless War."

Just then, a knock sounded at the door.

"Yes?" Sarhina called out, and the door swung open.

Daria stepped inside, face shadowed with exhaustion and clothes stained from travel. At the sight of her, Zarrah's heart lurched into her throat, because her fears had shown her this moment a thousand times.

Bowing low, Daria then straightened and cleared her throat. "Imperial Majesty . . ."

Zarrah was already on her feet. "Where is my husband? Is Keris all right?"

Daria winced. "He's fine. At least, he was when I left him in Ithicana."

"But . . . ?"

"Keris sent me with a message. William has threatened war if Aren doesn't turn Ahnna over for execution. Which is complicated, because for one, Aren is not convinced of her guilt, and two, Ahnna isn't in Ithicana. The last information received before I left was that Prince James had pursued her into the Blackreaches."

Daria was looking everywhere but at Zarrah, and her skin crawled with unease. "What aren't you telling me?"

"The Harendellians are up to something, but it's hard to get information. So . . ."

"So?" Zarrah almost shouted the word, her stomach twisting into ropes. "Spit it out, Daria!"

"So Keris volunteered to be an intermediary." Daria slowly lifted her head, meeting Zarrah's gaze. "He's going to Harendell."

Where Lestara, the woman who hated him more than anyone else living, now ruled as queen.

"He said he's sorry." Daria gave a sharp shake of her head. "The Harendellians aren't going to let this go. If Ahnna isn't brought to justice, they'll come for blood, and Ithicana is in no position to defend against them. Keris is trying to stop a war."

"I know he is." And God help her, Zarrah loved him for it. "But Lestara is going to kill him before he has a chance."

# 28

# KERIS

Keris kept his hood up as he entered the tavern, the stench of cheap wine, spilled ale, sweat, vomit, and worse immediately washing over him. Yet rather than feeling disgust, Keris relaxed at the familiar scent of seedy watering holes the world over. He well knew this sort of establishment and its patrons, and the lights were low enough to hide his most defining characteristic.

Buying a glass of wine and wiping the lip marks of a prior customer off its edge with his sleeve, Keris surveyed the patrons—mostly merchants and sailors—until he caught sight of a large figure in a shadowed corner. Walking over, he set his glass down on the table. "Good evening, Your Highness."

Cormac Crehan, brother of the king of Cardiff, leaned back in his chair. "I was curious whether you would come, Veliant. One whisper says you are a soft creature who sits in libraries and drinks expensive red wine paid for with his wife's gold. The next whisper says you are a shadow in the night and not to be crossed lest the crosser discover how deeply Silas Veliant runs in your veins."

"I find the space between whispers is where the truth lies, but I'll let you be your own judge." Keris sat across from the older man, then gestured to the medallion depicting a constellation that hung around his neck. "Brave choice. I know the law prohibiting astromancy has been struck, but old habits die hard."

"We are friends now, Cardiff and Harendell."

Keris took a sip, winced, and then set the glass aside. "Then why didn't you knock on the door of Fernleigh House and speak to me there? Alexandra has good taste in wine."

Cormac shrugged. "Old habits die hard."

"Fair enough." Keris rested his boot on the opposite knee, taking the measure of the prince. He was in his fifties, his brown hair heavily laced with gray, his skin weathered. Though it was too dark to see the color of his eyes, Keris suspected they were amber as a wolf's. Cormac was a big man, both in height and in breadth, but Keris also heard the faint wheeze in the man's breath that indicated poor health. "Things are coming up rosy for Cardiff these days. An alliance with Harendell, border open to free trade, the burning of witches outlawed, and Ronan's daughter now queen of Harendell. Yet you look the opposite of pleased, my friend."

Cormac sipped his drink. "You shamed my niece."

Keris grimaced. "My only regret is not cutting off Lestara's head and staking it on what remained of Vencia's gate."

"A mistake I'm sure you'll have great cause to regret." Cormac fell silent as the barmaid approached and set a bowl of stew on the table, along with a heel of bread. He paid her, and when he and Keris were alone again, he said, "But it is my nephew, not my niece, whom I wish to speak of with you."

"James." Keris tapped his fingers on the table. "That was quite a secret to keep all these long years. Not once did I hear a whisper that Edward's mistress was actually a Cardiffian princess."

"Siobhan had been a spy in Verwyrd since she was fifteen," Cormac answered. "Her cover was deep. After her death, it was agreed to keep her identity a secret to protect my nephew."

"Why? His mother being a princess didn't make him any less the king's bastard."

The older man didn't reply, only took another sip of his drink, watching Keris as though waiting.

Understanding struck Keris like a slap to the face. "Not a bastard."

Cormac gave a slow nod of confirmation.

Edward hadn't just aimed to make James king of Ithicana—he'd aimed to make him the heir to Harendell's throne. With James's ties to Cardiff, he'd have been the most powerful man in the known world. It was a bloody ambitious plan that made entirely too much sense, and it might well have come to fruition if Edward hadn't so sorely misjudged Ahnna's loyalty to her family. "Does Alexandra know?"

"Edward took extreme measures to keep the knowledge secret to protect James."

Keris silently debated how much he wished to reveal to this man, decided the answer was nothing, so he only said, "That wasn't my question."

Cormac traced the tip of one finger around the rim of his glass, expression considering. "I think if Alexandra knew the truth, James would be dead."

"Like his mother."

The older man grimaced. "Siobhan's death was Katarina's doing, there is no question. The assassin and the poison were tied back to her agents in Riomar with little effort made to hide that she was responsible. Edward, naturally, suspected Alexandra, but no amount of investigation could implicate her beyond Amarid's propaganda machine casting blame her way."

Keris frowned. Though it made sense that Katarina desired to throw a wrench into the workings of peace between Cardiff and Harendell, there was something about the ... *obviousness* of how it was done that bothered him like an itch that refused to be scratched. "Why are you telling me all this, Cormac? What do you want from this soft creature who does nothing but read, drink, and spend his powerful wife's gold?"

Instead of answering the question, Cormac ate, dipping his bread into the stew and devouring the meal like a man starved. Only when he was finished and the barmaid had taken the dishes away did he speak. "James is the rightful heir to the Twisted Throne. We invested a great deal of effort in aiding Edward in his plans to secure James's ascension, not only because his ties with Cardiff would ensure peace, trade, and prosperity, but because he would be invested in vengeance against the Crimson Widow. Ahnna Kertell destroyed decades of labor, because without Edward to name him heir, no one will believe it."

"Because you have no proof."

"Edward's word was always the proof." Cormac drained his cup, then slammed it down with enough force that the table shuddered. "He wanted this as badly as we did, and stars as my witness, we were damnably close to seeing everything we worked for to fruition."

*Such as taking Ithicana with a coup*, Keris silently thought.

"No one will believe Cardiff's claims of James's legitimacy," Cormac continued. "It is too self-serving, too obviously in our interest, and William will only deny it. Alexandra will deny it. All of Harendell will believe them, because Edward revealed the truth to no one."

"You telling me the truth doesn't change that fact."

"No. But if *Edward* told you the truth, then all would be forced to listen, for you are the empress's consort. A prince of Maridrina. Brother to two queens."

"While I am enjoying watching my stock rise on the tide of your desperation, Cormac, there is a flaw in your plan: Edward never once mentioned any of this to me."

"Are you sure?" The prince rested his elbows on the table, and it groaned beneath his weight. "Everyone is aware that you and Edward carried on a merry correspondence and that he held you in high esteem. Letters went back and forth, your exchange of words well known and uncontestable, yes?"

Keris blew out a long breath, disliking where this was going. "Yes."

"We know he sent a message to you just before his death." Cormac reached into the interior pocket of his coat and withdrew a letter with a cracked seal, which he handed to Keris. The paper was identical to what Edward used, the broken wax sealed with the king's ring, and as he unfolded it, the writing was in Edward's hand. Keris took in the contents—all gossip from the month leading up to the murder, amusing but trivial. But Keris also saw the message within the anecdotes, the coded one Edward had often used to reveal more salacious details.

Refolding the forged letter, Keris tapped it against the table. "You want me to lie. You want me to use the weight of my name—the weight of my *wife's* name—to take the crown from William and put it on James's head."

"He is the rightful heir."

"Perhaps that is true, but this letter is a forgery, and if my deception came to light, it would destroy the relationship between Harendell and Valcotta, never mind the personal consequences that would befall me."

"If you do this and see James to the throne, we will ensure that he ends the conflict with Ithicana." Cormac went silent as the barmaid returned with another full cup for him. "An end to the blockades and a resumption of trade, all blame for Edward's murder held only by Ahnna Kertell, who will be executed."

Keris went still. "That's not in your interest. While revenge against Katarina might have been part of your goal in aiding James's rise, the majority of it is surely trade flowing north to and through Cardiff rather than through Ithicana's bridge."

"Ronan recognizes that Edward's death necessitates some concessions." Foam frosted gray stubble as Cormac drank deeply. "One lie, Your Highness, and you will spare Ithicana a war. Spare your family defeat and inevitable death. It is a good deal, especially given that your small deception will allow a great truth to come to light."

Keris resumed tapping the folded edge of the letter against the table, the wheels in his mind spinning. Because Cormac was right: It was a compelling offer. If Keris took this letter and gave it life, there was every chance that they could see James to the throne. He was well liked. A military hero. A man much more worthy of the nation's respect and loyalty than his fool of a brother. Ronan had influence over him, and if Cardiff committed to convincing James to end the conflict with Ithicana, all of this could be over at the price of—

"You believe Ahnna Kertell is guilty, then?"

Cormac frowned, clearly not expecting the question. "Don't you?"

"I . . ." Keris trailed off as the prince coughed, then reached for his throat. "Cormac? Are you well?"

The other man didn't respond, because when his mouth opened, all that came out was foam-drenched wheeze.

Poison.

"Shit!" Keris shoved the letter in his pocket, then reached for Cormac. "Help! He's been poisoned!"

But no one heard him over the din.

Cormac clawed at his throat, his face purpling as he fought to breathe, and he stumbled into the table next to them. The occupants shouted as their drinks spilled, but then they caught sight of the prince's bulging eyes. "What's wrong with him?"

Keris's lips parted to demand someone find a physician, but he knew it was too late. A heartbeat later, Prince Cormac of Cardiff dropped to the floor, amber eyes still and unseeing.

"Get the city guard," someone shouted, the patrons all crowding around to get a look at the body.

Keris took a step back. Then another.

He was innocent, and only a damned fool would poison the man sitting across from him. But no part of him thought that being involved with the situation would do any good.

Keris took another step back and turned.

To find himself face-to-face with George Cavendish.

"Your Highness. I must say, this is not where I anticipated finding you tonight." Cavendish's gaze skipped past Keris to the body, and his brow furrowed. "That's the queen's uncle."

"He's been poisoned, sir!" The barmaid bent over Cormac looked up, face pale. "Poisoned dead. And he was sitting with him!" She pointed directly at Keris.

Cavendish's face hardened, and he gestured to the soldiers who'd come in on his heels. "Shackles."

Rounding on Keris, he gave the smallest of smiles. "You're under arrest for the murder of Prince Cormac of Cardiff."

# 29

# JAMES

James was going to kill him. He was going to fucking kill that one-balled prick and he was going to make it *hurt*.

"Plotting ways to escape?" Carlo tipped the bottle, swallowing the last few mouthfuls. "That is my favorite thing about you, James. Everything has gone so utterly wrong for you, every aspect of your life has been torn apart, and yet you refuse to concede. You can be killed but never, *ever* broken." He gestured to Ahnna with the wine bottle. "Unlike this one."

Moving around the fire, Carlo knelt next to her still form, and James tensed.

The Beast leaned over Ahnna so that his cheek hovered just above hers, then closed his eyes. "I can feel the will to fight fading from her. She knows that everything she does makes Ithicana's situation worse, and I think that I'll have to take measures to keep her alive to deliver her to Mother. Do you think it's possible to die from a broken heart? Because Ahnna's heart has most surely been broken." Carlo snickered. "I did not factor you as a breaker of women's hearts, dear nemesis. What other things will I learn about you on this journey?"

James didn't answer, only watched as Carlo sighed and moved back to sit on his rock.

"If it makes you feel any better, Mother kept all these secrets from me as well," he said, then picked up a stick to poke the fire. "All these long years, Alexandra has been Mother's darling protégée—and not once did I suspect, not even when they schemed together with Silas Veliant. Do you think Silas knew about Alexandra? I suspect not. Information is power, and secrets are the greatest information of all."

"I've no interest in your mutterings." James lay down, curling around the spike that bound him to the ground. His whole body ached to the point it was hard to tell the difference between the pain of injuries and the pain of muscles pushed far past what they could endure, and the cold seeping up from the frozen earth made it all the worse.

Then warmth pressed against his back.

Revulsion pooled in James's gut, because Carlo had sat next to him. Was using him as a *fucking* backrest.

"How quickly the tides change," the Beast murmured, leaning an elbow on James's ribs. "You pursued Ahnna with the righteousness of justice and the fires of hate fueling your every step, but now you stew in the sourness of guilt wrought by the clarity of truth. How does it feel to have wrongly condemned your lady love, my friend? How does it feel to have hurt her because you allowed yourself to be a pawn in Alexandra's game?"

"The worst of what I've done, I did of my own volition," James replied. "I don't deserve the absolution of being deemed a pawn. Now fuck off, Carlo. I'm tired."

"What does it say about you that you are not brought low by such truths?" Carlo's voice was dreamy. "It is as though the darkness that resides in your heart drinks misery as if it were the finest wine."

"Spare me your bad poetry."

"My words are a song to which all others dance." Carlo sang the words in falsetto. "Dance until their minds or their bodies break."

There was no sense arguing with him. If James was to be awake, he was better off using the time to plan how he and Ahnna might escape.

Tuning out Carlo's humming, James tested the length of rope between his wrists and the stake that had been hammered into the ground, which was sadly insufficient to get around the Beast's neck.

It wouldn't just be a matter of getting free of the ropes and making a run for it. Without weapons or supplies, there was every chance they'd escape Carlo, only to freeze to death or be eaten by the Blackreach lions. They needed to secure a few necessary items in their flight, and James set his mind to determining what they would need and what they could survive without.

*You won't need much given that Ahnna will stab you in the heart the first chance she gets.*

The thought reared, sending his mental lists spinning into the ether, and James grimaced.

*Your father plotted to overthrow her brother,* his conscience whispered. *He aimed to make you king of Ithicana—which you sat back and did nothing about. And then there is Taryn—can't blame anyone but yourself for that.*

James grimaced as Carlo's humming increased in volume, hating the warm press of the other man's back against his.

He needed a bow. Arrows. A knife. Some rope.

*You destroyed her life while making her believe you were her friend. While trying to make her your lover.*

James twisted his face into the rough wool blanket, and Carlo patted him soothingly, humming a lullaby.

*Don't worry about food. Leave the horses—you'll never get them over the avalanche debris.*

Convincing Ahnna to leave Dippy might take some doing, but hopefully the chance to escape Carlo would be enough motivation.

*So your plan is to take her back to Harendell? So that William can execute her? Because no one is going to believe this story. They'll think you're trying to protect your lover.*

James grimaced, every muscle in his body as tense as a board.

Maybe it was better to steal back the horses. They could escape into Amarid, then ride north through the Lowlands and over the border to Cardiff.

*To Cardiff. Right into the arms of your family, who has already tried to murder Ahnna once. Besides, she wants to go to Ithicana.*

The food in his stomach churned, because would Ithicana be any better? Would Aren protect his sister if it meant war? *Could* Aren protect her given the force of arms that William would bring to bear once the calm season arrived? The only real option was for Ahnna to flee south, beyond Valcotta, to the southern nations that cared little for northern politics.

*Except she'll never agree to run.*

James's hands balled into fists, the ropes digging painfully into his skin as the tendons in his wrists flexed.

"Easy, easy." Carlo patted James again, and his temper snapped.

He slammed his elbow into the Beast's kidney, then twisted and caught hold of his coat. James shoved Carlo to the ground and tried to reach for his throat, but the ropes binding his wrists snapped taut.

Cursing, James caught hold of Carlo's clothes again and pulled him closer to the stake, trying to knee him in the side, but his ankles were tethered to the same stake. So instead he elbowed him in the gut, the attack frenzied. Hopeless, because soldiers were running toward them.

And Carlo was laughing.

As the Amaridians pinned James down, the Beast slowly got to his feet, a wild grin on his face though he had to be in pain. "Easy, friends, easy. It is good to see that the bastard of Harendell still holds on to his spirit. Let him sleep so that we might have more games tomorrow."

He strode away and disappeared into a tent.

Not caring if it was a waste of energy, James fought against the soldiers trying to pin him down. "How can you follow him?" he snarled. "He's fucking insane. A sadist. You should do the world a favor and put him down."

"A mad dog he might be, but he's our mad dog," one of the Amaridians answered, then slammed his fist into James's stomach. "I've lost comrades to your blade, bastard. You'll find no friends among us."

They held him down while one of the soldiers hammered the stake even deeper into the frozen ground, then they threw a blanket over James.

Aching and exhausted and furious beyond measure, James stared through the flickering fire and found Ahnna staring back at him.

Her face was expressionless, but her eyes held dull resentment that James knew was for him and him alone. He waited for her angry words, for her hatred, for her threats, but instead Ahnna turned her back on him.

Which was so much worse.

---

Merciless dawn came early, along with a cheerful Carlo who sang an aria to the rising sun while pissing on a campfire.

Not an inch of James didn't hurt, but he did his best to ignore the pain while he ate and drank what was given to him, all his focus on Ahnna.

She was pale and dead-eyed, listless as she picked at her food, and she refused to meet his gaze. Carlo had stolen the spirit out of her with his words; the sadist was a master at knowing exactly what would hurt the most.

Nothing mattered to Ahnna more than her people's welfare. Knowing her efforts to aid them had been used to damn them was bad enough, but being powerless to do anything about it was torture.

"Are we ready to start our day?" Carlo asked as he approached. He held out a gloved hand to Ahnna. "I do so love a ride in the snow. Especially with a beautiful woman."

Ahnna didn't look at him, only stared blankly at the ground. Making a noise of exasperation, Carlo reached down and closed his fingers around her broken arm. A sob of pain tore from Ahnna as he hauled her to her feet, the sound of it nearly throwing James's tenuous control over the edge.

"Enjoy your exertions today, James," Carlo called over his shoulder as he pulled Ahnna toward the waiting Dippy. Then he skipped and kicked up a cloud of snow. "It's getting so deep! How fun!"

"He doesn't understand the meaning of that word," one of the soldiers restraining James muttered when Carlo was out of earshot. "He's going to accidentally kill you and then she's going to have the rest of us flayed for allowing it to happen."

James didn't recognize him from the night prior, so he asked,

"Why do you put up with him? Tear out his throat and say it was the lions."

The grizzled Amaridian soldier huffed out a breath. "Katarina would only flay us for not keeping him safe. Of all her jewels, Carlo shines the brightest in her eyes." His eyes flicked up to meet James's. "I'd think you'd be familiar with such a dynamic given the way Alexandra dotes on your simpering whelp of a little brother. All of us hate your bastard self, but none of us would deny you're the better man. Must be the Cardiffian in you."

The soldiers all smirked but James said nothing. William was being used as a puppet by Alexandra, and while she no doubt did it for *his sake,* James feared what would be done in his brother's name. William had his weaknesses, but he didn't deserve to be manipulated. As for Cardiff, James had no doubt that his family there was also at risk. How long until Alexandra put an end to the hard-won peace he'd fought to achieve? How long until the burnings resumed, the border closed, and the hatred rose hot as ever?

How much worse would it be with Alexandra in control?

And what could James do about it if he escaped?

All his authority, all the respect accorded to him, had been because his father and siblings had demanded it. Now his father was dead. Alexandra hated him. And if what Lestara said was true, then William's sentiments toward him were also badly tarnished. James knew he deserved his brother's ire, but the very real consequence was that even if he returned to Harendell to shout the truth of Alexandra's treachery, William might not listen.

And it likely wouldn't be long until James met a knife in a dark alley and said nothing at all.

The soldiers were examining his wrists, which were bruised and scabbed from the ropes around them. After a muttered exchange about how the wounds would foul if they got worse, they set to shoving fabric beneath the bindings and then dragged him over to a horse, fastening his leash to the animal's saddle.

"Good luck, bastard," the grizzled Amaridian muttered, then climbed on the horse and urged it into a trot.

After that, James could spare no thought for anything beyond staying on his feet.

The snow fell heavily, thick fluffy flakes that piled higher and higher on the trail. Wind whipped through the pines, turning his face and hands to ice even as the rest of him dripped sweat. Sweat that turned to ice whenever they slowed the horses to give them a rest, his whole body swiftly racked with shivers as the cold bit down to his bones.

*Just keep running*, James ordered himself. *Just stay on your feet until dusk.*

It would only be another few days of travel until they were low enough in altitude that the snow turned to rain, but every minute felt like eternity as his feet betrayed him. As he tripped and fell, dragged onward by the horse while the piles of snow threatened to smother him.

The tension on his wrists eased and James pushed himself up to find that the grizzled soldier had stopped his horse.

"Deadfall on the trail, sir," he called back. "We'll have to clear it."

Carlo didn't answer, only continued singing, his voice drifting through the falling snow like a murderous lullaby.

A soldier draped a blanket around James's shoulders and then shoved a waterskin into his hands. He drank greedily between panted breaths.

"I need to relieve myself."

James stopped drinking at Ahnna's voice, the first time he'd heard it in what felt like an eternity.

Carlo made a noise of disgust, then shouted, "One of you take her into the bushes. I want none of this."

Two soldiers pulled Ahnna off Carlo's lap and escorted her into the brush. James heard one of them say, "Just tie her to a tree while she does her business," then a muttered argument.

It was hard to see them through the brush, but James knew their backs were to Ahnna. He tensed, certain she had a plan. Certain he'd see her figure racing away into the trees. But a few moments later, the soldiers returned with Ahnna between them. Her shoulders were slumped, every part of her exuding defeat, and his heart twisted.

Carlo stared at her with disgust, and as the soldiers moved to lift her into the saddle, the Beast drew back his foot and kicked Ahnna in the face.

She screamed and fell to the ground, sobbing in pain.

Despite knowing his reaction was what the man wanted, James hurled himself at them. The ropes binding him went taut, jerking him off his feet, and he screamed threats and profanities, unable to control the rage in his heart.

"You are a joy, James," Carlo crooned. "You'll die before you break. Unlike *her*."

He spat on Ahnna's back, then heeled Dippy forward. "Someone else take the woman. I've lost interest."

Ahnna lay crying in the snow, and she remained limp as the men hauled her up and loaded her onto one of the horses. James tried to catch her eye, certain that this was nothing but a ploy to put distance between her and the Beast. Except when their gazes locked, hers held no hate, only despair. She rested her cheek against the mountain horse's neck, body shaking with sobs.

"Disappointing, isn't it?"

James slowly turned to find that the prince had taken hold of his leash and was fastening it to Dippy's saddle. "You thought she was better than this, yes? Stronger? Yet the truth of her circumstances has entirely destroyed her will to live." Carlo's expression held no cheer as he said, "You deserve better than her, my old friend. I have shown you the truth."

"What truth is that?"

"That there is a reason the Ithicanians gave their princess to Harendell." Carlo urged Dippy onward. "Ahnna Kertell is worth nothing."

*She's worth everything to me*. It was the last thought James had on the matter, because a heartbeat later, the rope was dragging him down the trail.

# 30
# KERIS

"HE MURDERED MY UNCLE!" Lestara wailed, tears rolling down her cheeks. "He needs to be punished!"

"I did no such thing," Keris retorted. "Why would I poison a Cardiffian prince? And even if I had a reason to, do you really think me so stupid as to do it while sitting directly across from him?"

"He's lying!" Lestara shrieked. "He's trying to harm Cardiff because of his loyalty to Ithicana!"

"Darling, please. It's not necessary to be so loud." William pressed his fingers to his temples, the king of Harendell clearly in the early stages of what would be an impressive hangover in a few hours. The stench of far too much wine clung to his breath, and Keris had not failed to notice the sway to William's step.

"What precisely would murdering Cormac Crehan achieve for Ithicana?" Keris asked, trying to extract his arm from Cavendish's grip, but the Harendellian lord's fingers only tightened.

"He was trying to make it look like Harendell's doing. That's why he used poison and not a knife in the alley." Lestara wiped away her tears with the sleeve of her velvet robe. "He's trying to destroy the peace between Cardiff and Harendell. Don't let the fact he misjudged how swiftly the poison would work put you off, William. Keris meant to escape the scene and get back into his room so that no one would suspect him."

It was an entirely plausible explanation. Keris silently cursed, because while he doubted Lestara believed he'd murdered her uncle, she was clever enough to try to use Cormac's murder to achieve her own goals. Which begged the question of *who* had arranged for the Cardiffian prince's death?

Keris's bet was the very silent Alexandra, who was listening to Lestara's wails with an expression of irritation.

"You need to execute him!" Lestara demanded. "He broke Harendellian laws—your laws! He's a murderer!"

William frowned. "Darling—"

"Why is he even here?" Lestara's hands balled into fists. "I've told you all the awful and unjust things he did to me in Maridrina. How he blamed me for Petra's actions despite it being his choices that provoked her. Right in front of you, he insulted me to my face. Yet here he is, treated as a favored houseguest. He's murdered my uncle and put our alliance with Cardiff in jeopardy, and everyone seems more concerned that their sleep has been disrupted."

William's frown deepened, and Keris was struck with the sense that the king was actually considering Lestara's demands.

Alexandra, who had said nothing until this moment, gave a loud huff of exasperation. "Lestara, calm yourself. This is not good for the baby." She flicked her fingers at Cavendish. "Georgie, this behavior is beyond the pale. His Highness is a prince of Maridrina and consort of the empress of Valcotta. What possessed you to treat him like some common criminal? Get those shackles off and unhand him."

"With respect, Your Grace—"

Alexandra cut Cavendish off. "Precisely. Show some respect. This is Harendell, not Maridrina, so we will conduct ourselves with civility."

Keris bit his tongue to silence the rising retort, but the moment

Cavendish removed the shackles on his wrists, he stepped away from the man.

"Now let us get to the bottom of this." Alexandra smoothed her dressing gown. "Georgie, do we have an idea of what poison was used on poor Cormac? While I'm thinking of it, Lestara, I think tomorrow we should sit together to write a message to your father. This will be quite a blow, I'm sure."

Lestara gave a miserable nod.

"My best guess from the descriptions given by the patrons is hemswart." Cavendish crossed his arms and glared sullenly at Keris.

"Then this was surely Amarid's doing." Alexandra pushed her light brown braid over her shoulder. "Really, you ought to think these things through, Georgie. Katarina fears our alliance with Cardiff and seeks to turn Ronan against us. Keris was merely in the wrong place at the wrong time."

Her green eyes fixed on Keris. "Precisely what were you doing in the tenderloin in the middle of the night?"

"I was invited," Keris answered, for there was no sense lying when Cavendish had searched his pockets and found Cormac's note. "He requested I come alone, so I took the necessary measures to do so."

"I found these on him when I searched him." Cavendish held out the note, but also the forged letter from Edward. The latter was the far more damning document, and it was a struggle not to hold his breath as Alexandra looked it over.

Her face fell as she read. "Edward wrote of such trivialities. Such inconsequential pieces of gossip."

Keris had wanted no part of this scheme. Had fully intended to reject Cormac's request. But the moment Cavendish had extracted the crumpled letter from Keris's pocket, he'd had no choice but to give it life. "I received Edward's letter when I arrived at Southwatch. It was the last time I was wearing this coat, so I forgot I had it."

*Set it aside*, he silently willed her. *Take it for nothing more than idle gossip, and set it aside.*

Instead, Alexandra traced a finger over the words, her eyes glittering with unshed tears. "It is like having Edward in the room with us."

Keris fought the urge to tear the letter from her hands and cast it into the fire. "I'm afraid I didn't get the chance to read it, as I received it in conjunction with the tragic news of His Grace's passing."

Alexandra gave a soft choking sob.

"Mother, this is too much for you." William patted Alexandra on the back, giving the letter she held only a quick glance. "You should be abed."

*Set it down*, Keris willed them. *It's meaningless.*

Yet though the queen mother's face showed nothing but grief, his skin crawled with the sense of imminent danger.

*She sees the code.*

Alexandra lowered her hand. "Do you mind if I keep this, Keris? It would be a comfort in my dark hours."

*Fuck!*

Keris gave a slight smile. "Of course."

"Why did Cormac want to speak to you in secret?" William asked. "I do say, it has a bad smell—you sneaking out the window of my house in the middle of the night to meet him."

"A bad smell that matches his true colors," Lestara angrily muttered. "It smacks of villainy."

He'd anticipated the question from the moment of his arrest, and given the circumstances, Keris was wary of lying. "He wished to speak of Your Grace's brother, Prince James."

Though his eyes were on William, Keris did not fail to notice how Alexandra's fingers tightened ever so slightly on the letter she still held.

William's eyes narrowed. "What about him?"

"He wished to know if James was with Ahnna in Ithicana." Lying was a risk, but if Alexandra knew the truth about James's legitimacy and suspected Keris knew the same, his life was very much on the line.

The king of Harendell's expression hardened. "Why would he ask that? My brother is hunting Ahnna Kertell in the Blackreaches."

Keris shrugged. "I'm afraid that the poison took hold before we could get further in the conversation, Your Grace. All that came before was his criticism of my treatment of your lovely queen."

Lestara scowled at him but said nothing.

"It's known that Prince James was quite ... *taken* with the charms of the princess," Keris said, straightening his coat, which was askew after Cavendish's manhandling. "Perhaps the Cardiffians are concerned that James has deserted for reasons of the heart. He'd not be the first."

Alexandra's eyes narrowed slightly, but she said nothing, and Keris could not tell if she believed his deception.

"James is in the Blackreaches *hunting* Ahnna Kertell." The words came out from between William's teeth. "I do not care for the insinuation that my brother is anything less than loyal, or that he'd be taken in by the charms of the woman who murdered our father. James is a true man of Harendell, and an Ashford to the core. If Cormac suspected James was in Ithicana, it would be because he feared my brother had been taken prisoner by those snake charmers. If Cormac had had the balls to level these accusations within my hearing rather than whispering them to you in dark taverns like a coward, I'd have set him straight."

There was true anger in William's eyes. It made Keris abruptly certain that William, at least, had no idea that his elder brother was the rightful king or that it was his own parentage being called into question. "As you say, Your Grace, Prince James is in the Blackreaches, so Cormac's concerns about his loyalty were unfounded."

"Not only unfounded, but offensive. Cormac deserved his lot," William snapped, but when Lestara made a noise of protest, he waved a hand. "I speak from emotion and lack of rest."

Keris gave a sympathetic nod even as he stored away the other man's reaction for later consideration.

"Our family is unified in all things, Your Highness," Alexandra said. "Which I realize is unfamiliar to many people, yourself included. But know that to attack one Ashford is to attack all. That said, the hour is too late for the discussion of such weighty subjects. It is clear in my eyes that Cormac's death was Katarina's doing—she does not benefit from an alliance with Cardiff. Your presence at the moment of his demise is merely poor luck, but it makes me fear for our safety in Sableton. I think it best we return to our home in Verwyrd, where we can protect ourselves. There is no place more secure than the Sky Palace. I assume you have no objections to traveling with us, Your Highness?"

To be in the Sky Palace was akin to being in a prison, for there was no way out of that castle in the sky other than a very long drop. To go there with them was akin to wrapping himself up in the spider's web, and his chances of returning to Zarrah grew slimmer.

A knock sounded at the door to the house, and Keris was spared having to provide an immediate answer as Cavendish opened it. A soldier stood beyond the threshold, and he bent his head with the lord, explaining something in terse terms before departing.

"An unfamiliar girl was in the kitchens when Prince Cormac's meal was served," Cavendish said. "My men tracked her down, but when she realized there was no escape, she poisoned herself."

"Amarid." Alexandra snarled the word, then gave a sharp shake of her head. To Keris, she said, "Excuse us," and then drew Lestara and William across the room, Cavendish joining them.

Keris leaned against the wall, hearing some of what they said and seeing much more as he watched Alexandra's lips move. Over and over again, she said "Amarid" and "Katarina," and though his ability to read lips was middling, it was clear she desired Lestara to ensure that Ronan understood Cormac's murder was intended to undercut the alliance.

"Amarid fears the rise to power your father set in motion . . . will undercut . . . overtures to Ithicana."

Keris kept his face a mask of mild curiosity, because it was not lost on him that Bronwyn would soon be in Riomar speaking with Katarina on this very topic. No part of him trusted the Amaridian queen, because he remembered all too well her alliance with his father, but neither could he deny that a strong alliance between Cardiff and Harendell would inevitably cause trouble for Amarid, especially in the Lowlands.

What Alexandra had told him about Ahnna's motivations for killing Edward made it hard to argue that Ahnna hadn't done the deed, but those same motivations would ensure that Aren never turned on his sister. Ahnna had killed to protect him, Lara, and Delia.

*Will Ithicana go to war to protect Ahnna if you know for certain she murdered Edward and then attacked Alexandra?*

It was the question he'd asked Aren, but Keris knew the answer now without a shadow of a doubt. Aren would protect Ahnna, no matter the cost.

Which meant they needed to pursue another strategy to survive this.

Desperation made for strange bedfellows. If Ithicana allied with Amarid, with the support of Maridrina and Valcotta, it was just possible that Harendell would step back from war rather than risk heavy losses. Bronwyn was already on the front lines of creating an alliance, which left Keris to fight for the latter.

Alexandra approached him, one hand keeping her dressing gown tightly closed as she walked. "It has been made clear to us tonight that Sableton is not safe and that we must retreat to Verwyrd. I understand that your time in Harendell has not been without incident and that you'd be justified in departing to rejoin your wife, but we would so like for you to accompany us, Your Highness."

Zarrah's face filled his mind's eye. He belonged with her. Needed to be with her. But he could not leave his family to fight this battle alone. Inclining his head to Alexandra, Keris said, "I've always wanted to see the Sky Palace."

# 31

# JAMES

"I'M EXCITED TO see what you'll try tonight, my old friend." Carlo sat next to James, sipping from a bottle of wine and eyeing him as if James were a particularly delightful display of entertainment. "Though do try not to get yourself killed. Mother would be furious at me."

Several excruciating days had passed of James being dragged down the mountains by Dippy, and despite his every effort, James had not been able to win himself free. He'd killed six guards in separate attempts, and several others were nursing near-fatal injuries from him hurling rocks and beating them with sticks he picked up on the trail, all in an attempt to whittle down their numbers. He'd spooked and tripped up their horses, lit tents on fire, and set off a small avalanche, but while the soldiers all glared at him with wary hatred, Carlo relished his efforts with ever-rising fervor. Not even James enticing Dippy to kick the prince seemed to diminish the Beast's enthusiasm for James's desperate attempts at freedom.

James had pushed himself to the brink, his body battered and exhausted, but for all his efforts they had nearly reached the western foothills of the Blackreaches. Once they did, all chances of escape would be lost.

He couldn't help but wonder if Ahnna even cared.

Carlo had lost interest in her entirely since he'd broken her spirit, but that was little mercy, because even without his cruel attentions, she was withering away. While they traveled, she sat slumped and listless on her mountain pony, and when they camped each night, she made no protest as the soldiers ordered her about like a kitchen drudge. Only wordlessly obeyed, scarcely recognizable as the woman he'd fallen in love with. At night, James heard her softly crying, ceasing only when one of the soldiers would kick her and shout at her to be quiet.

James hunched over the stake binding him to the ground and watched Ahnna across the camp. A bored soldier held her restraints, but there seemed no need for them as she lifelessly stirred the large pot of stew that would be dinner. Her eyes were on the trees, but her expression was blank in a way that suggested she saw her own demons rather than the forest around her. It made James sick to see Ahnna this way, especially knowing that it was his actions that Carlo had used to break her.

James might as well have broken Ahnna himself.

"Don't look at her!"

Carlo's snarl pulled his attention back to the prince, whose gray gaze was filled with rage.

"She is nothing," the Beast hissed. "A broken thing unworthy of your attention. If I could kill her, I would, because that woman does not deserve the air she breathes. Rotting to death in the Furnace is a worthy fate for her."

James had always known that Carlo was not right in the head. But spending days in the man's company had given James a whole new understanding of the depths of Carlo's depravity. He was not unique in his proclivities, but men like him typically were tempered by consequence or were put down by the law. For the Beast of Amarid, there was no temperance. No consequence. No law.

Which meant Carlo was uniquely able to be wholly himself.

A monster.

"Her noise irritates me," Carlo muttered. "I ought to cut out her tongue to keep her silent."

He started to rise, and James hurled himself at the prince. In a flash, he had the rope stretched between the stake and his wrists around Carlo's neck, cutting off his air. He pulled it tight even as he forced Carlo to the ground, knee pressing against his back as the other man struggled to get up.

The soldiers flung themselves at James, trying to get him off their prince, but the very ropes they'd used to bind him held him tight to Carlo. Fists and feet flew, but James barely felt the pain.

*Hold on*, he ordered himself. *Hold on until he's dead. That's all you have to do.*

He strained, pulling the rope tighter—

Only to have it go slack.

The old Amaridian soldier had cut his restraints, and the man now turned on him, the long knife Amaridians favored held at the ready. "I've had enough of you, bastard. Time to die."

James tried to get free of the others holding him, but there were too many.

"No!" Carlo rasped the word and then lunged at the older man, wrenching the knife from his grip.

He stabbed the man. Once. Twice. Three times, and then James lost count as blood sprayed, the old Amaridian screaming as his torso was filled with holes.

The soldiers holding James's arms let go. He fell on his ass, watching as Carlo slaughtered the soldier who had saved his life, blade sinking into flesh again and again, despite the man having ceased to draw breath.

"He's mine!" the Beast screamed. "You cannot have him!"

It seemed to go on forever, and James was struck with the thought that *this* was how his father had died. Only once the man was so much meat did Carlo lift his blood-splattered face to meet James's gaze. "I won't let any of them hurt you."

The perverse protectiveness on Carlo's face turned James's stomach, but he bit his tongue.

With one gore-stained hand, the Beast gestured to the fire. "Let us sit and eat."

The visibly shaken soldiers found new ropes to tie James to the stake and carefully draped blankets around his shoulders before filling up his cup with water. He could smell their fear, and it made James wonder if this was the worst they'd ever seen their prince. If, for reasons that no sane individual could understand, James's presence brought out the worst of the monster within Carlo.

A bowl of stew was placed in front of him, and James forced himself to take a sip.

And nearly spat out the contents.

It tasted like a handful of pepper had been added to his dish by a disgruntled soldier, rendering it entirely inedible. James said nothing, because Carlo would only see it as an opportunity to blame Ahnna, and he was in enough of a mood that he might get over his boredom and hurt her. Waiting until the prince's focus was on his own meal, James tipped the contents out and then used his foot to bury the stew with snow before feigning finishing the meal.

"It's hard to swallow," Carlo said dreamily between mouthfuls, blood drying on his face and the marks from where the rope had been around his neck livid. "Even after all you've endured, you're still strong."

James didn't answer, only angled his body so that he could lie down next to the stake. It hurt to breathe. Hurt to move, and he prayed that sleep would soon take him despite knowing it would only deliver him to another day of horror.

Beyond, Ahnna moved among the men to collect their bowls, then set to washing them, her hair hanging in clumps around her face as she silently did their bidding. James couldn't watch it, so he forced his eyes shut.

Exhaustion claimed him. Dragged him down and down, so that when the screaming began, James thought it was part of his dreams. Except the screaming didn't cease when he woke, and he sat up to find the camp had turned to chaos.

Some soldiers were running in circles and screaming, while others sat on the ground weeping. The air was a cacophony of voices, men talking to themselves, talking to trees, talking to the sky, and at least two of the tents were on fire.

A nightmare. It had to be.

Then Ahnna appeared before him. All traces of apathy and defeat were gone from her face, replaced with fierce determination. Her wrists were bound, but she had a knife gripped in one hand. "Cut me loose," she hissed, shoving the blade into his grip. "We don't have much time."

*We.*

Only a lifetime of training on the battlefield kept James from gaping at her in shock, because gone was the broken woman who'd refused to even meet his gaze and back in her place was the indomitable Ahnna Kertell who'd saved his life so many times before.

And was now saving it again, despite all that he had done.

Gripping the knife hilt, James sawed at the ropes binding her wrists, trying not to jostle her broken arm. In the snow by his feet, he saw the remains of his over-peppered meal and understood immediately what she'd done. "Poison?"

"No such luck, but there's a hallucinogenic lichen that grows on the trees." She took back the knife with her left hand and then cut the ropes binding his wrists. "These idiots can't stomach watching a woman answer the call of nature, so I've been able to gather it without anyone noticing. Sorry if that offends your sensibilities, Your Highness." There was a bite to her tone that suggested that for all she was saving him, James was far from forgiven.

He wouldn't have it any other way.

"Your tongue is as shocking as always, Princess." James swiftly unbound his ankles. "Where is Carlo?"

"I don't know. Did he eat?"

"Yes." James scanned the chaos that was the camp, but he saw no sign of the prince in the darkness. "I'm going to kill him."

"If we cross paths with him, I'll fight you for the privilege." Ahnna picked up a sword that one of the hallucinating soldiers had dropped. "But we can't linger. I don't know how long this will last, so we need to get the horses and put distance between us and them."

She hefted the long blade in her left hand, and he asked, "Can you fight off-handed?"

She gripped the weapon, hazel eyes murderously bright as she lifted it so the tip rested against his throat. "In my sleep. So watch your back, James. The only reason I'm not killing you now is that tonight, you're the enemy of my enemy."

It was no idle threat, and despite the sting of the sword tip against his throat, James felt the overwhelming urge to kiss her, because seeing Ahnna like this ignited every part of him. "Understood."

They set off through the camp toward the horses. Some soldiers barely seemed to see them, but others had not wholly lost their wits and attacked. He and Ahnna cut them down, fighting back-to-back as they worked toward the lines of horses.

"Get Dippy and Maven!" she shouted, not seeming to be hindered at all by the broken arm hanging at her side. "I'll hold them off!"

It felt wrong leaving her to fight, but untying the horses required two hands, so James flung himself first at Maven and then at Dippy. Both animals were agitated and skittish, but he got their bits in their mouths, not bothering with saddles. Catching hold of Ahnna's hips right after she stabbed a soldier in the chest, he lifted her onto Dippy's back. "I'll lead him. You hold on!"

He cut the lines of the other horses and then vaulted onto Maven's back, heading down the trail at a gallop with Dippy's reins in his hand. The other panicked horses followed, and it was a chaos of animals fighting for space on the trail until their faster mounts pulled ahead.

Only for a familiar figure to step into their path.

"A marvelous turn of events!" he shrieked. "A fight to the glorious end!"

Carlo tipped his face into the moonlight, and James sucked in a breath as horror pooled in his stomach. The Beast had pulled out one of his own eyes, and it now dangled bloody and mangled against his cheek.

Carlo held his arms up to the sky and laughed wildly, not even seeming to see the horses galloping toward him.

James lifted his sword and dug in his heels, the primal desire to kill surging through his veins. He was going to take off this monster's head and rid the world of his villainy for good.

Carlo lowered his face, his remaining eye glittering as he leveled a finger at James. "Let the chase commence!"

Then he sprinted into the trees and into the darkness.

James gathered his reins, readying to veer Maven off the path in pursuit, but Ahnna shouted, "James, no! You'll never find him in the dark! We need to run!"

There was logic to her words, but the thought of letting Carlo go went against every instinct in his body.

As if sensing his thoughts, Ahnna shouted, "I will not wait for you," and then she leaned over Dippy's neck and urged the racehorse for more speed.

As fierce as his desire to kill Carlo was, James wanted Ahnna more. So with a curse, he galloped after her.

Moonlight illuminated the thin layer of snow on the trail, but it was still reckless to ride this fast on the bad terrain. Ahnna didn't seem to care. She balanced easily on Dippy's bare back, sword and reins held in her left hand and her right arm held to her stomach. Her long hair blew out behind her in the icy wind, and her skin seemed to glow in the moonlight. The most beautiful woman he'd ever seen. He urged Maven alongside her. "You might have hinted that you planned this and spared me all those beatings."

"I needed you to keep them distracted, especially Carlo. Besides, why would I have wanted to spare you from suffering? It was a pleasure to watch."

James knew that he had no right to pursue her forgiveness. That he should aid her escape and then let her go her own way. But her wild and relentless tenacity in the face of all adversity was alluring in ways he could not explain, even to himself. Ahnna was untamable. Unclaimable.

Yet even with death readying to hunt at their heels, he wanted to make Ahnna his again.

"We don't have the supplies we need to backtrack down another trail into Harendell," he said, shoving away the thought. "Our only chance is to head into Amarid and up through the Lowlands. We can go to Cardiff and seek the aid of my uncle."

"There is no *we*." Ahnna's eyes remained fixed on the trail. "Go where you will. I'm heading to the coast and then back to Ithicana."

"Carlo will know that's your goal," James protested. "You won't be able to fool him twice, Ahnna. If Carlo catches you, Katarina will put you in a hole so dark you'll never see the light of day. Better to go north and get help from Cardiff."

"Even if I was willing to consider going anywhere with *you*, there's not enough time for anything but the most direct route." She gave a sharp shake of her head. "Carlo wasn't wrong. Edward's murder and everything that has happened since might not have been my fault, but there is no denying that Alexandra used me, and is continuing to use me, to achieve her ends. There is no risk I won't take to try to save my people, and if I have to die, so be it."

For that to happen, he'd have to be dead first, but James said nothing.

Her eyes shot to his. "You put the lives of my people on the line. You and Edward aimed to use me to steal my brother's crown and put it on *your* head. You manipulated and used me to try to make yourself a king!"

James reached down and caught hold of Dippy's reins, pulling both horses to a stop.

"We don't have time for this!" Ahnna objected.

"I'm making time," James snapped. "What Carlo told you about my father's plans for a coup in Ithicana was true, but I had no part in their creation. I didn't even know his intent until after you slammed your door in my face and I went to call him out for how he'd treated you. When he revealed his intentions for Ithicana, I told him he'd misjudged your feelings toward Aren. Told him you'd oppose it on every level, and that no one, least of all me, would be able to convince you to turn on your family. And I never intended to try, Ahnna. I never asked to be king. Never wanted to be king. That was my father's dream, and as much as I grieve his death, there is a part of me that rages at him because there was no one he used more as a pawn than me."

"Don't pretend you're innocent." She thumped her heels against Dippy's sides to try to get her horse to pull free. "Bronwyn and Taryn were innocent, and you went after them. My cousin is a prisoner of war because of *you*, James. You can't blame Daddy for that one."

"Don't take this out on your horse," James snapped. "Bronwyn is safe in Ithicana, and Taryn—"

"Is being forced to relive the trauma that nearly killed her!" Ahnna lifted her sword. "I brought Taryn to Harendell to give her a chance. To help her find a haven to heal, and I can only imagine how you've destroyed that. And separating her from Bronwyn? Why? Why would you do that to her?"

"Because I knew it would hurt you!" Maven squealed and pinned her ears, but James barely noticed the mare's reaction. "Obviously I regret my actions knowing what I know now, but I can't undo the past."

"Would you have regretted it if I'd been guilty?" she demanded. "Would you care that you'd destroyed Taryn's life even though she was innocent?"

"The Beast of Amarid is on our heels and you want to quarrel about hypotheticals?" James gestured behind them, fully aware of his hypocrisy given that he was the one who held the horses still.

"Answer the goddamned question, James," Ahnna snarled. "Answer it, or we part ways *now*."

"Fine. If you were guilty, I would have been glad to hurt Taryn in order to make you suffer," he shouted. "And the suffering wouldn't have stopped at her. Is that what you want to hear?"

"Better I know the truth. Better I know who you really are!" she shouted back. "You might pretend to be the civilized prince but it's all an act, just like Carlo said!"

"Yes, it is." James glared at her. "But don't pretend you were ever fooled by it. You fucking wanted it, Ahnna, and if I am to stand here and spill every dark truth lurking in my heart, perhaps you might be honest about what lurks in your own."

"Fine." She lifted her chin, eyes gleaming in the moonlight. "You want the truth, James? I'll give it to you. I wasn't fooled. How could I have been fooled when the real version of you was the one I met in the tunnels beneath Northwatch? I knew what lurked beneath the manners and civility, and I wanted it. Wanted *you*. I was in Verwyrd to marry your brother, but it was your face in my mind every night that I slipped my hand between my legs to make myself come. It was your mouth I dreamed of kissing me, your hands I wanted to touch me, your cock I desired inside me. I wanted you like I wanted breath, and though it was folly, my heart wanted you as much as my body. Is that the truth you want?"

James's lips parted, but no words rose to his tongue because he'd not expected her to rise to his challenge. Which made him the purest form of stupid, because Ahnna always shattered expectations.

"You want more truths?" she spat. "Even after you blamed me for a crime I didn't commit and then hunted me across Harendell, I still wanted you. I couldn't get you out of my mind, because you have a hold on me that makes every part of me ache in every possible way. I hate myself for it. Hate that there is a part of me that wants you to pull me off my horse and fuck me in the snow despite evil stalking our steps."

His cock stiffened, not caring about the threat on the trail behind them because his head was filled with a vision of Ahnna beneath him, those endless legs wrapped around his waist.

Whether it was because his body was betraying him or because Ahnna was just that quick, James was too slow to react as she abruptly lifted her boot heel and slammed it into his hands. James cursed, dropping his sword and Dippy's reins. She was instantly moving, circling around Maven.

"But here's another truth, James. You use your name, your size, and your force of will to intimidate people into doing what you want. It's your way, in all things, and to hell with anyone who has a problem with it. Except I'm Princess Ahnna Kertell. My family has ruled the wildest and most dangerous kingdom in the world for generations, and I have lived and breathed violence since I could hold a blade. No one intimidates me, and you would do well to remind yourself that you live because I willed it so. You stand here now because I chose to free you. And you will ride with me only on my terms, is that clear?"

His knuckles stung from where her boot heel had connected with them, but James barely felt the pain as he slid off Maven's side to retrieve his sword. Every part of him was twisted up with anger and desire for this woman who infuriated him like no other. Watching Ahnna circle him, James bowed low. "Your will, my sword, Your Highness."

"Fuck you, James," she snarled.

"That wasn't the sword I was referring to, but I'm happy to oblige, Princess." He gave her a dark smile, feeling the thrill of the chase settling upon him as her lips parted, her throat moving as she swallowed. "Though perhaps we might put some distance between us and the Beast first."

"We're riding to the coast." Her words were an order, but he did not mistake the slight breathiness to them. "Aren needs to be warned that Amarid is no ally, but rather the anvil Alexandra's hammer will smash Ithicana against."

That route was a mistake. James knew it was a mistake.

But some mistakes were worth making. "Then let's ride."

## 32

# AHNNA

THEY RODE THROUGH the night, the path a steep decline from the lofty elevations of the Blackreaches, and as dawn lit the mountains behind them, Ahnna got her first view of Amarid.

Gone was the snow and endless forest of conifers, and before her stretched rolling hills covered with dry grass and rocky outcroppings. Streams fed by the mountains ran narrow and fast, converging into rivers that cut across the landscape. While Harendell was always foggy and damp, Ahnna knew that some trick of the winds made Amarid a much more arid place, and that they relied heavily upon clever systems of irrigation to feed their croplands, including the coastal vineyards that were famous the world over.

The air had grown warmer with every passing hour they'd traversed the steep descent, and she'd already removed her greatcoat and tied the arms around her waist, the sun's warmth familiar and welcome. "Finally some grass for you to graze on," she murmured to Dippy, but as he and Maven finished drinking from the stream, she was quick to urge both horses on.

Because every instinct in her body told her that the Beast hunted at their heels.

James shifted and grumbled something in his sleep, and Ahnna cast a sideways glance to him. Hours ago, she'd insisted that he get rest while she led his horse, and he'd obeyed without protest. She'd thought that it was to make a point on the heels of their argument, but in the dawn light, she was rapidly revising that belief.

While she had her share of injuries, Ahnna had been on horseback the entire journey with the Amaridians, stuffing her face with their food, and getting as much rest as she could in preparation for her escape plans. All while James had been dragged on foot through the snow, picking fights at every chance, and using every bit of his strength to try to escape their predicament with force. There was no mistaking the toll it had taken on him. Both his eyes were blackened, the bruises stark against skin that was paler than she'd ever seen it. His knuckles were torn to shreds, and beneath the cuffs of his ruined coat, his wrists were even worse. His beard had grown thick after so many days without a razor, but it did nothing to hide the hollows in his cheeks, the strain of what he'd endured having stripped away spare flesh and left behind only lean muscle.

For all her bluster and harsh words, it had taken all her will to do nothing as Carlo had pushed James to his limit, and she'd marveled at James's capacity to endure. Her people were as hardy as they came, used to being pushed to the limits, but Ahnna had never met anyone who could have gone through that ordeal and still been standing. Not just standing, but burning with almost feral virility as he'd stared up at her, ready and willing to claim every part of her.

Ahnna's jaw tightened, but so did parts low in her core, for though James's hold over her was stupid, foolish, and irrational, it was also undeniable. He was every bit the man she'd always known him to be, good and bad, and God help her, she wanted him.

Except even if they managed to evade Carlo and escape Amarid, there was no future between her and James. How could there be with all that they'd said and done to each other? How could there be when they stood on opposite sides of the coming war?

*Maybe he'll choose to fight for Ithicana*, her heart whispered. *He wants to bring Alexandra down, too.*

"When has he ever fought for Ithicana?" she growled at herself. There was no doubt in her mind that James would do everything in his power to bring Alexandra down, but even if he succeeded, it wouldn't change that his loyalty was to Cardiff. Which meant Ahnna would be in Ithicana doing what she'd spent her life doing: fighting so her people could survive.

The divide between her and James was not one that could be bridged.

James stirred, then groaned as he shifted upright. "You shouldn't have let me sleep that long."

"You needed it."

James cast a backward glance over his shoulder as he pulled off his coat, his hair damp with sweat from the growing heat of the sun. "I'd love to say that there is a chance Carlo ripped out his own heart in the throes of his delusions, but he's not that easy to defeat. The Beast is alive, and he'll drive his men hard. Unlike us, Carlo won't care if he runs his horses to death. He has the means to switch out mounts once he reaches the farms in the foothills. Villages will have boats and he'll send men ahead to secure the coast, so not only do we need to be swift, we must be cunning."

"What do you suggest?"

"False trail." James shifted, wincing, and Ahnna couldn't help but wonder what injuries lurked beneath his clothes. "We move at speed to one of the villages and trade the horses for a small boat. But rather than heading downstream directly, we hide in deep cover until they pass us by. Then we head to the coast on foot until we can secure new mounts. Carlo and his men will be looking ahead on the rivers, not behind on the roads, which means we can make strategic choices rather than desperate ones."

Ahnna ground her teeth, grief gathering in her stomach as she stroked her horse's neck. Dippy's fur had grown thicker, and she liked how fuzzy he looked.

"I know you don't want to give Dippy up," James said softly. "I don't want to give Maven up either. But I also don't want to run them to death to escape, and going any slower will see us caught. They're valuable mounts—whoever we trade with will likely sell them to some

Amaridian lord and they'll grow fat as saddle horses in some coastal vineyard. A good life."

It was a smart plan, Ahnna knew that. Yet her heart didn't care much for smart plans, and agreeing to this hurt. "I know. He's probably better off away from me, anyway."

Not waiting for James's response, Ahnna nudged her horse into a canter, Maven following at his heels.

There was peace in having her focus be on staying astride. With a broken arm, she couldn't hold on to Dippy's mane for balance, and each jarring impact on the rough terrain sent stabs of pain through the break. The Amaridians had put care into setting the bone, but the ferocity of the pain caused her to suspect that she'd done more damage in the fight to flee the camp. She could fight left-handed, but Carlo's soldiers were angry and experienced, and they'd want revenge for what she'd done to them. Speed was of the essence.

The trail widened into a proper road as they moved through the foothills, and the river running alongside it grew as well, fed by dozens of tributaries filled with melted snow.

"I see chimney smoke ahead!" James called, the first thing he'd said to her in hours. "You do the talking. They'll be put off by my accent."

"You could fake being something you're not. Since you're so good at that."

He cast his eyes skyward. "Keep this up, Princess, and you'll make Carlo's job easier."

"Kiss my ass."

"Bend over."

Ahnna's face burned hot, but she bit down on her retort. "Give me your reins and pretend to be hurt."

"Not hard. I had my ass kicked for days because you couldn't be bothered to share your plan."

"If you are looking for sympathy, you'll be waiting a long time."

James only smiled and handed over Maven's reins, then dutifully slumped over the mare's neck.

Ahnna headed toward the grouping of perhaps ten structures. Children paused in their playing to watch them pass, and Ahnna smiled to ease their fears as she headed to the small wharf alongside the river.

Two older men sat on rough benches sewing fishing lures, neither pausing in their task as she slid off Dippy's side and approached.

"Good afternoon." She leaned into her Ithicanian accent, which most would mistake for Maridrinian. "I'm hoping you might be able to aid us. We were accosted by bandits in the mountains. Our companions were killed, our supplies stolen, and my"—she looked at James—"*servant* was badly injured. We need to make it back to the coast for aid, but he will not make it on horseback. Do you have a boat and supplies we can trade our—" Her throat tightened and she swallowed hard, her anger at James having caused her to briefly forget what she'd be giving up in this moment. "—our horses for?"

One of the men set aside a finished lure, and then picked up another set of threads and feathers, starting a new one. All while slowly looking Ahnna up and down. "What's a Maridrinian and a"—he squinted at James—"godless Cardiffian doing in the Blackreaches?"

"We heard that the Harendellians had formed an alliance with Cardiff," Ahnna answered. "We hoped to find opportunities to trade north."

The old man pursed his lips, fingers moving rapidly as he made the lure entirely by feel. "That don't sound right, girl. The Harendellians like those amber-eyed witches even less than they like us. Sounds like false news. It's no wonder they beat you bloody and sent you back. You a witch too?"

Of course they wouldn't know. Not up here in the middle of nowhere. "I'm not a witch. Are you able to trade?" James groaned from where he was slumped over Maven's neck. "I need to get him to a physician."

Part of her, a big part of her, hoped that the man would say no. That he wouldn't want to give up a vessel because his business was fish, not horses. If he refused to trade, she could tell James to piss off to the Lowlands while she made her own way. But the old man looked Dippy up and down, then Maven, and turned to his silent companion. "You ever fix that old rowboat?"

"Which one?"

"The one with the leak."

This didn't sound promising.

"Ain't got a boat with a leak."

The first old man made a sour face. "Ya do. I know you do, because you were complaining about it. But then you stopped complaining."

"Because I fixed it."

The first old man threw up his hands in exasperation. "You've shit for brains, Lloyd. Go git your woman to put together a basket and then find the boat that don't have the leak to trade for these horses."

"What do I need riding horses for, Issac?" Lloyd asked, setting aside a finished lure. "My business is fish."

Issac cast his eyes skyward, then shouted, "Margo!"

An old woman appeared, wiping her hands on her apron. "What do you want that you couldn't get up to do yourself?"

Ahnna could feel James's seething frustration from where he remained slumped on Maven's neck, and only the practicality instilled by Nana kept her from mounting and abandoning this strategy.

"These folks"—Issac gestured at her and James—"Maridrinian and Cardiffian, they are. Fools had the false belief the Harendellians would truck with them and found out the hard way. They want to trade them horses for Lloyd's boat that don't have the leak anymore, as well as some supplies, since they lost theirs. But Lloyd says he don't need horses."

Margo looked the horses up and down and then gave Lloyd a disparaging glare. "Yeah, all right. What all do you be needing, girl?"

"Food. A pot or a kettle," Ahnna replied, tears burning in her eyes, because Dippy and Maven deserved better than this. "Bandages."

Margo nodded, then squinted at James. "You'd be better off heading up north through the Lowlands and into Cardiff, girl. Harendell is full of spiders."

Ahnna knew that better than anyone, but she only nodded. Leaving Lloyd and Issac to retrieve the boat that hopefully had been repaired, Ahnna led Dippy over to James. "I'll look at the boat before I agree to it. Make sure it doesn't leak."

Then she turned her back on him and stroked her horse's nose. "I'm sorry, Dippy," she murmured. "I wish there was another way. But at least here, you will have a break from running. There's grass to eat. Wouldn't be that way with me."

He snuffled at her pockets, and a tear escaped down her cheek.

She felt the warmth of James's breath on the back of her neck, he having dismounted without her noticing. "You're a shitty actor," she muttered. "You're supposed to be near death."

"The woman recognizes their worth. They'll get them sold to someone with a need for saddle horses." He reached past her to stroke Dippy's neck. "Once we're on the far side of this, I can try to buy them back."

Ahnna didn't answer, because allowing that sort of hope into her heart seemed like the greatest sort of foolishness when *the other side of this* was looking worse with each passing day. "No need for horses in Ithicana."

*No need for you either*, her self-doubt whispered from deep in her mind. *All you do is make things worse*. The thought made her feel shittier, so she growled, "You want to do something for me, James? Get Taryn freed before she jumps off the Sky Palace walls."

James drew in a breath, but before he could respond, Margo reappeared with a basket.

"Put in as much as would fit," she said, handing Ahnna the basket. "Boat's fine—fixed the leak myself, so no fears there. But you're still getting the raw end of the bargain, girl."

"Take care of the horses and we'll call it good."

"I'll take better care of them than you, I reckon." Margo took the reins of both horses, then cast a cool look at James. "Pretty girl like her deserves better than whatever you put her through. Man up and row, and while you are rowing, do some thinking about whatever it is you've done."

"Thanks for the advice." James muttered the words, hiding his accent. He moved stiffly over to where the two old men stood next to an old rowboat, and Ahnna followed. The boat had seen better days, but there was a fresh patch on the hull. When they lowered it into the water, it floated well enough. And it wasn't as though they needed it for long.

"Thank you," Ahnna said to them once they were both inside, the basket at their feet. "He's Dippy and she is Maven. Treat them well."

Margo nodded, then Issac gave the boat a shove and the current caught hold of them, drawing them out into the river.

Feeling a sudden rush of unease, Ahnna called to the woman, "Hide them. If anyone comes looking for us, tell them we stole this boat and which way we went."

The woman's expression didn't change, which told Ahnna that Margo had seen right through their story, but she gave a small nod. "Get rowing."

The current drew them farther down the river, the boat picking up speed like it felt the urgency. There was a bend ahead, and after they were around it, the village would be out of sight.

*Don't look*, Ahnna ordered herself. *Do not look.*

But her heart took over and forced Ahnna to turn her head. A hot flood of tears poured down her cheeks as she watched Margo lead the horses away. Tears that almost immediately dried, because high in the foothills, a cloud of dust rose into the air. The sort of cloud that could only be made by many horses moving at speed on a road.

"James . . ."

"I see it." His tone was grim and he reached for the oars, fitting them into the locks. "The Beast is on the hunt."

# 33

# KERIS

KERIS TIPPED HIS head to the gray sky, which was producing an annoying sort of almost rain that made him long for home. But riding in the damp was infinitely preferable to riding in the tight confines of a carriage with Lestara.

The journey to Verwyrd was proving to be painfully slow, partially due to the thick mud on the roads, but mostly because the Harendellian royals seemed intent on visiting every nobleman's estate they passed along the way. Breakfast, morning tea, lunch, afternoon tea, and dinner were all at different households, the dinner hosts all accommodating the procession overnight, which meant after-dinner drinks that went into the late hours, necessitating equally late starts to the day. Which might all have been tolerable if it had been productive, except instead of having the opportunity to dig information out of Alexandra or bend William's ear, Keris had been forced into endless conversation with their various hosts, who all seemed bent on ingratiating themselves with the empress's consort.

"How do they eat so much?" Saam muttered from where he rode

at Keris's left. "Six meals a day is madness. Who has the time for that?"

"They don't eat much—it's all for show." Keris shifted in the saddle, his eyes on the carriage splashing through puddles ahead of them.

"That's worse." Saam scowled, his friend having strong opinions about wasting food, given that he knew starvation and knew it well. "They're readying to blockade Northwatch and starve Ithicana, all while they let their cream puffs and puddings go to rot for the sake of impressing one another."

"I suspect the servants eat them," Keris replied absently, his mind on those very blockades. Aren had been wholly silent, which William had taken for a resounding *no* to his request that Ithicana turn on Ahnna. Which was no great surprise to him. Keris's messenger would have reached Ithicana already, and while the information he'd sent made Ahnna look damnably guilty, it also made her actions feel justified. That same messenger carried all the information that Keris had learned from Cormac before the man had died, as well as the belief that Katarina was behind the murder. He wasn't ready to advise that Aren push for a military alliance with Amarid just yet, but depending on what information Bronwyn sent back, his brother-in-law was likely already considering that step.

"My God, Veliant. What a suggestion. I assure you, my good man, the servants do not eat the nobles."

Keris stiffened, then turned to find Cavendish had ridden up behind them. The man looked entirely too pleased with his jab, grinning as he added, "The cream puffs go to the pigs to fatten them up."

"Which type of pig?" Saam asked with feral interest, and Keris hid a smile as Cavendish paled, it seeming to occur to him that mocking the Devil's Island survivors might not be the best of ideas.

Cavendish gave a nervous laugh. "You've a sense of wit, my good man. Impressive given your years of incarceration." His eyes flicked to Keris. "It's commendable that you took them on."

Saam's smile grew to reveal his straight white teeth, but Keris said, "There's a certain bond that grows out of shared adversity." He gestured to his guards, every one of them once an inmate at Devil's

Island. "It's stronger than blood, and it is my honor and privilege to call each of my guards a friend."

Cavendish gave a forced smile. "No one will ever deny that Veliants have balls."

Keris yawned, then said, "Most especially my sisters. Speaking of which, Bronwyn has asked me to ensure the well-being of Taryn Kertell. I trust you will arrange for me to see her upon our arrival to Verwyrd."

"The lady is considered a prisoner of war, so there are restrictions on—"

"You can deal with me or you can deal with Bronwyn," Keris interrupted. "Choose wisely."

Cavendish inclined his head. "Of course, Your Highness."

The man checked the reins of his horse so that it fell back, but Keris's focus had already moved to the carriage. William was hanging out the open door and gesturing with irritation at one of his soldiers. The carriage stopped and William stepped down, mounting the soldier's horse and leaving the man to clamber aboard to sit with the driver.

This would be the first and potentially only chance Keris might have to speak to Harendell's new king on his own, but he curbed the urge to ride up to the other man. The Harendellians already had the advantage, and Keris had no interest in fueling William's confidence.

His patience paid off, because it wasn't long before William drew in his mount, watching Keris approach over his shoulder.

"Give me some space," Keris muttered to Saam, who responded, "Don't do anything stupid."

Falling in alongside the king, Keris inclined his head. "Your Grace."

"I hope you'll be better company, Veliant. I'd rather fall on my own sword than spend another minute in that carriage." William stretched back, face tilted to the sky. "I can see why you fled north. Better to negotiate the losing side of a war than to listen to a wife's endless nagging, am I right? Worse for you, though. At least I outrank Lestara." He laughed, slapping a gloved hand against his thigh. "Now I understand why my father drank so much. Nothing I do suits them, and they let me know."

Keris huffed out an amused breath, more interested in establishing camaraderie than in correcting William's interpretation of his presence.

"I was perfect in her eyes right up to the moment I put a ring on her finger," William grumbled. "Never said a damned thing against me, though that might be because it's hard to speak with a cock in your mouth."

*Or a leash around your neck.* Keris shoved away the thought, having no interest in developing any form of sympathy for Lestara. She'd dug her own grave.

"I'd have thought your father would have taught her to hold her tongue and that her opinions don't matter," William continued. "Mother will train her, of course, but I thought I was getting a well-broke filly. Joke's on me, and I can only imagine my father is cackling from the grave."

Silas Veliant had made that abundantly clear to all his wives, with perhaps the exception of Keris's aunt Coralyn, but Keris was not about to advocate for his father's methods. "It's likely the title. My father's wives had only the titles they came with. *Queen* has a certain ring to it, and Lestara has sought that ring for a long time."

William snorted. "Careful, Veliant. I can say what I want about my queen. *You* can't."

"Understood."

"Speaking of your father and his harem, I confess that I thought you mad to give that up for one woman, and a woman you have to bow to, no less." William reached into his coat pocket and withdrew a flask, sipping from it. "It seems a perfect situation, because if one annoys you, you can bed another. If they all annoy you, you can marry someone new."

Keris took the flask as William passed it over, feigning drinking as he considered what response would best entice the king to reveal useful information. "I wanted nothing to do with anything I associated with my father. I hated him, and I wanted to erase every aspect of him from my existence. He spent my entire life trying to make me into a certain sort of man, and I was never good enough in his eyes compared with my brothers. Dismantling everything that mattered to him brought a certain pleasure."

William was silent, and from the corner of his eye, Keris saw that the king's expression had gone slack, his gaze distant as though he was lost in memory. "I understand that feeling better than you know. I fucking hated my father. He put James on a goddamned pedestal, and nothing I ever did was good enough."

"As though soldiering were the sum of a man's worth."

William turned to look at him, his expression intent. "Right? Anyone can swing a sword, but it takes a certain caliber of man to succeed at politics. Ruling Harendell is something that happens in the courts and it takes the sharpest sort of mind, but my father acted as though James was a paragon for tussling in the mud in the Lowlands. Which isn't even a real war—just back-and-forth skirmishes with Carlo, like two children fighting over a toy. James is terrible at court—it's almost laughable how stilted he is."

"I was under the impression you two were close."

William sighed and toyed with the reins. "In a manner of speaking. We're nothing alike, but James is loyal. He's defended me since we were children, and other than my mother, he's the only one who stood up for me against our father."

"My brother Otis was the same way."

"He's the one you killed."

Keris flinched at the memory, covering it up by taking an actual drink from William's flask.

"Why did you kill him? The spies never got a clear answer—the inner sanctum was always a difficult nut to crack."

These were all memories that he wanted to keep buried, but for the sake of knowing his opponent, Keris dug them up. "Zarrah was my father's prisoner. Otis learned that we were together, and he attacked her."

"So you killed him to protect your woman?"

Memory of that night filled Keris's mind, but he found it increasingly difficult to remember exactly what he'd been thinking in that moment. *It was an accident*, he reminded himself, even as his conscience asked, *Was it*? "Something like that," he finally said. "But I don't relish it."

William gave a sympathetic nod. "James was only able to intervene in my father's abuse of me because he valued James so much. So even though he was defending me, the reason he was able to do so made me want to shove him off the Sky Palace more than once. If James . . ." Harendell's king trailed off as Cavendish moved within earshot, rolling his shoulders as though to cast off an uncomfortable thought. "This pace grinds on my nerves, Veliant. You ride well enough—fancy a gallop?"

"A race?"

William's eyes lit up. "Ah, yes! Let's make a match of it!"

"With respect, Your Grace, I must advise against it." Cavendish had pressed closer, looking ready to grab William's reins. "These are dark days and your life is not safe, even this close to Verwyrd."

"Fuck off, Georgie." William pulled a foot from his stirrup and kicked at the other man's horse, the animal moving out of range. "I'm bored, and Keris has a reputation for liking fast things. Let's make this a proper matchup between Harendell and Maridrina. Ashford against Veliant, with pride as the stakes. There are two white pillars outside the western bridge town. First man across wins, that suit?"

"Rules?"

William made a rude noise. "No rules in off-track racing."

"Your Highness," Saam said, moving to cut off Keris. "This is not wise. The roads are muddy and—"

"Go!" William shouted, and Keris dug in his heels.

The wind howled through the trees as Keris leaned low over his mare's neck, his pulse thrumming in time with her pounding hooves. The forest trail ahead twisted and dipped unpredictably, the scent of mud thick on the air as his horse splashed through the puddles. Keris's hands were steady on the reins, his focus razor-sharp. Behind him, the relentless drumming of hooves told him that William was hot on his heels.

*Let him win. The smart choice is to let him win.*

But when had he ever done the smart thing?

Keris yanked hard on the reins and cut left, veering off the beaten path. His mare lurched through the undergrowth, branches snapping against his boots, the rough slap of leaves stinging his arms. He barely had time to see the low-hanging branch ahead before instinct took over—he ducked, flattening against his mare's neck as the gnarled limb scraped just above his back.

A sharp burst of laughter—half exhilaration, half defiance—escaped his lips, because it felt like eternity since he'd ridden like this.

The ground dipped suddenly beneath them. Keris clenched his thighs, steadying himself as his mare stumbled for half a heartbeat before finding her stride again. Only for a fallen tree to appear ahead, its bark slick with moss. There was no easy way around.

Keris gritted his teeth and urged his horse forward. "Come on, girl."

The mare gathered herself and leapt.

For a moment, the world dropped away—air rushing past, the weightlessness of the jump pressing against his ribs. Then impact—his mare's hooves struck the ground, sliding through loose dirt. A heartbeat of panic gripped him as she fought for balance, her muscles bunching, her head jerking up. Keris leaned back, coaxing her to steady. She caught herself and surged forward, but he could hear William's gelding galloping down the path, flashes of the king's dark coat visible through the trees.

The forest thinned as Keris crested a slope, a valley stretching out before him. A wide green river split into two around an island city, and in the middle of it rose a structure that defied reason. A tower that stretched to the clouds, a gleaming white palace perched atop it. It gleamed like a beacon. A prize.

The finish line.

A shadow flickered at the edge of his vision.

William.

The king had stayed on the trail and was moving at reckless speed in the slick mud. Keris's eyes tracked down a slope to the town that sat on the banks of the river, two white posts on its outskirts exactly as William had described.

Keris cursed and pushed his mare harder. They tore down the slope, loose earth kicking up behind them. A jagged rock outcrop loomed ahead. He wrenched the reins, barely managing to angle his mare away in time. But then her hooves were on the road and they were tearing down it just ahead of William.

The king was shouting, urging his taller horse for more speed as they hit the straightaway. Keris remained silent, flat against his mare's neck, her hooves barely seeming to touch the ground as she flew toward Verwyrd.

William was right behind him—so close he could hear the other man's labored breaths.

Then—by inches, by a breath, by the space of a heartbeat—Keris shot ahead, his mare galloping between the two posts a full length ahead of Harendell's king.

Victory.

Keris's chest heaved as he slowed his horse, his legs splattered with mud. Behind him, William pulled up hard, his jaw tight, his eyes flashing. Not a man who did well with losing, and Keris silently cursed himself for letting his own pride get the better of him.

Then a grin formed on William's face. "I'd been so anticipating your arrival in Harendell when you'd planned to come to our university, only to have dreams of our friendship ripped to shreds by your father's designs on Ithicana. How fitting that it should be Ithicana that brings us together now."

That felt like a lifetime ago, that version of himself almost another person. Would he have been friends with William if he'd arrived in Harendell as planned? Nights of drinking and carousing, days at the races, every minute of their lives dedicated to indulgence and pissing off the men who'd sired them? Keris allowed that alternative version of reality to spool through his mind, and felt nothing but disgust.

None of which he allowed onto his face as he gave the king of Harendell a smirk. "I'm keen to see your palace, Your Grace. Shall we carry on?"

Cavendish chose that moment to careen toward them, his winded horse sliding to a stop next to them, Saam on his heels.

"I always thought you and James let me win," William said to him. "But it strikes me now that you're just slow, Georgie."

The lord grimaced, then patted his mount on the neck. "She's no racer."

"Makes me think that Veliant deserves a better prize than just bragging rights for beating me," William said. "What say you, Keris? Name your prize."

"For my sister's sake, I'd ask to see Lady Taryn Kertell," Keris said, knowing full well that Cavendish had intended to stymie that request. "They are close, and Bronwyn fears for Taryn's . . . *state of mind.*"

"I'm afraid you'll have to ask for something else," William said, and out of the corner of his eye, Keris saw Cavendish wince. "It's not possible for you to see Taryn."

Unease caused gooseflesh to rise on Keris's skin. "Why is that?"

William shrugged. "Because she never made it to Verwyrd."

# 34

# JAMES

WITH JAMES'S EFFORTS on the oars and the swiftness of the current, they made good time down the river while they searched for a wooded area dense enough to take cover.

Ahnna used the time to wash using the soap that had been included in their basket of supplies, leaning over the side of the boat to rinse her hair in the river. It was a process made difficult by a broken arm, but she did not complain. She said very little at all, in truth, and James could tell that she was deep in thought. He desperately wanted to know what was going on in her head, but he stayed silent until she was finished cleaning up and had eaten before asking, "Can you manage to keep us to the center with one arm?"

"Why?" she asked. "Do you need a nap?"

"A wash." He handed over control of one of the oars and then pulled the other into the boat. He could feel her eyes on him as he removed his filthy and bloodstained shirt, the skin of his torso just as grimy. The Amaridians had kept his bandages clean for fear of him succumbing to wound rot, but he removed them and cast them into the water. Carlo would inevitably secure hunting dogs, and the bandages would give more proof that they intended to ride the river to the sea.

James rinsed the worst of the grime off his shirt and then set the garment out to dry. He rested his sword against the bench and removed his battered boots, and then stood up and jumped into the river.

Frigid water closed over his head, the shock of the temperature like a slap to the face, but James stayed under. The icy water pulled through his hair and rinsed his injuries from the filth of their ordeal. His chest ached for air, but he stayed under until he could take it no more. Then, gasping in a breath, he looked up into Ahnna's wide eyes.

She was standing, appearing ready to leap into the water.

"Were you going to jump in and rescue me?"

A sharp noise of disgust pulled from her lips, and Ahnna sat down on the oar bench. "You speak as though I haven't had to save your ass time and again."

"Could you pass me the soap?"

She rolled her eyes but retrieved the soap. "Catch."

He lifted a hand, but she tossed it over his head, forcing him to swim hard to retrieve it before it sank. Kicking to keep pace with the boat, he scrubbed his hair and beard, then set to work on the rest of his body, a cloud of gray froth floating away from him. Deeming his trousers as clean as they would get, he tossed them in the boat and scrubbed the rest of his body.

Ahnna was staring at him, her expression unreadable.

"You're supposed to be scouting for threats," he said as he tossed the soap into the boat. "Not watching me bathe."

"Trust me, I know a threat when I see one."

"Are you just jealous that I'm properly clean and you're not?"

Ahnna snorted. "Please. If you think you can bait me into removing my clothes, you are mistaken."

"Your loss, Princess. We might not have another opportunity until we reach the sea."

"You'll just have to suffer my stink," she muttered, but James didn't miss the longing look she gave to the water.

Catching hold of the side of the boat, James heaved himself in, muscles straining. Ahnna looked away, but then her eyes tracked back to him. He pretended not to notice, but James could not deny the rush of heated satisfaction that while she might be angry at him, that anger was not the extent of what she felt. He turned his face to her, and though her cheeks flushed, Ahnna looked him slowly up and down before saying, "You're more colors than a rainbow."

He scowled and yanked his trousers up over his ass, self-scrutiny forcing him to admit she was right. His torso was mottled with bruises from fists and boots, all purples, greens, and yellows. The stitches in his arm needed to be removed, the wound healing well enough, but his wrists were a mess of raw flesh and scabs from where he'd been bound. "Nothing that won't heal."

"A part of your body could be rotting off and you'd say the same." Ahnna dug bandages and a small tin of salve out of the basket and then knelt before him. "Sit down."

James sat. His pulse thrummed as Ahnna leaned closer to examine his injuries, the clean scent of her hair filling his nose. She had the hands of a warrior, skin marked with old scars and new scrapes, but her touch was gentle as she pulled out the stitches, smeared salve over the wounds, then deftly wrapped bandages around his wrists despite only having use of her left arm. The sensation of her hands on James made him ache to touch her, to kiss her, to fuck her, but instead he said, "Let me check that break."

"It's fine," she muttered, putting away the supplies.

"If it's not healing well, you risk your ability to fight with that arm." He prayed the Amaridians had set it well, because the thought of having to rebreak it turned his stomach. "Let me look."

"If you insist."

James wanted to insist, but he only said, "I live and breathe on your terms, Princess." Ahnna rolled her eyes but allowed him to take hold of her. James unraveled the splint and bandages to reveal her forearm. She had a slender bone structure, but the muscles were hard and defined, even with the slight swelling. He carefully ran his fingers over the break, hearing her breath quicken, though his touch was too light to hurt. "It's set straight, but it will be a few weeks before you can do much with it. Can you move your fingers?"

She flipped up her middle finger.

"I'm so pleased to see you haven't lost mobility." He took one of the clean bandages from the basket and wrapped it snugly around her arm, then set the splints and bound them with more fabric. When he finished, James looked up to find Ahnna watching him, her bottom lip clenched between her teeth. "Is the pain bad?"

"I've had worse."

He fastened a sling from another length of bandage, then settled her arm into it. Ahnna didn't move away, only watched him with steady eyes, though he noted one was still badly bruised from when Carlo had kicked her in the face. James gently ran a thumb over her blackened cheekbone, checking that it wasn't broken. "I'm going to kill Carlo for hurting you." Not just kill him, but make him suffer in the worst sort of ways.

"He was harder on you than he was on me."

James shook his head. "No, he wasn't."

The sunlight reflected off her hazel eyes, illuminating the greens, browns, and golds, dark lashes so long they brushed her cheeks when she blinked. So impossibly beautiful, so defiantly fierce, and though she hid her fear over what was to come, James could feel it in his own heart. "The Tempest Seas are at their worst this time of year," he said softly. "No matter what schemes Alexandra and Katarina have concocted, there isn't much they can do besides stop trade until the calm season comes. William won't send Harendell's navy into a typhoon, and Katarina knows all too well what happens to a fleet in Ithicana's storms. There is time for you to get home and warn them."

Ahnna's throat moved as she swallowed, and James swore she leaned closer to him, her breath warm and sweet as she asked, "Where will you go once we reach the coast and I steal a boat?"

No part of him wanted to let her go when they reached the coast, and the thought of her sailing into the storms by herself on a tiny vessel with a broken arm made James feel unwell, but he wasn't ready to open up that argument. "Cardiff. I'll tell my uncle everything, and then go to speak with William in secret. My brother has his faults—no one knows that better than me—but when Will learns what Alexandra has done, he'll want no part of this. She murdered our father and then tried to use his death to start a war. I'd not go so far as to say he'd turn on her, but he will stop her plots in their tracks."

Ahnna tilted her head. "You think William will believe you?"

There'd been a time not that long ago when there would have been no doubt that his brother would side with him. They, along with Ginny, had been thick as thieves as children, always ready to defend each other to the end. But Lestara's voice filled his head, whispering, *He asked me more times than I could count whether Ahnna had put a spell on you. Wept when I told him she had not, because he so desperately wanted a reason why you'd choose her over him.* James shoved away the voice. "He'll listen. So will Virginia, and my sister loved our father a great deal. She won't let her mother get away with murdering him."

Ahnna gave a tight nod. "If Alexandra learns you are alive, she'll try to kill you. She won't risk you destroying her plans, and you no longer have the protection of your father. Harendell is no safer for you than it is for me."

"I'm aware, but given I'm the only one who might be able to sway William away from his course, it seems worth the risk."

She didn't reply for a long moment, but then she said, "Does William know you are the rightful heir to the Twisted Throne?"

It was a fact that he kept forgetting. Or perhaps his mind just wanted nothing to do with it, so it kept pushing his legitimacy to the deepest corners, where it could be ignored. "Until the night of the ball, I didn't even know myself that my father had married my mother."

"But Alexandra knows the truth. Do you think she told William in order to turn him against you?"

James considered the question, as well as his brother's character. "He'd take the knowledge poorly. It would rattle his confidence. And there is no need for it given that Katarina and Carlo were supposed to get rid of me. If Alexandra learns I am still alive . . ." He shrugged. "Who can say for certain what she'd say or do?"

"Would it turn William against you, if he knew?"

James rested his elbows on his knees, not wanting to dig too deeply because it would rip up old wounds, both his and William's. "You saw the way my father treated him, Ahnna. I never asked for his favoritism and did my best to discourage it, but my father was the way he was. I had the skills he valued and I was the son of the woman he loved, and it always felt like he hated William for being the legitimate one. But for all his mockery and cruelty, Will was heir, and my brother clung to that fact like driftwood in the open sea. It made him *more* than me, which made all the rest tolerable. To have that taken away . . ." He sighed. "I don't know how he'll respond, but I do know he won't take it in his stride."

Silence stretched between them, the only sound the rush of the river, but then Ahnna said, "Do you want to be king of Harendell?"

"No!" The word tore out of him, and James gave his head a sharp shake. "No, and I never have. That was my father's dream, not mine, and I want no part of it. No part of ruling *any* nation, just so we are being clear." He met her gaze. "When my father explained his vision of my future, it felt as though he didn't even know me—or, perhaps more accurately, didn't care what I wanted. It was all about putting my mother's son on the throne. I think it has always been about her, because he could not let her go, no matter what it cost him."

Ahnna sighed. "My parents were like that. The sort of love they write songs about, but in its own way, it was as harmful as hate because they didn't care who they hurt if it was done for the other's sake."

"All I wanted was peace with Cardiff," he said quietly. "And you. I wanted you. I still want you, Ahnna."

Her gaze broke from his, her eyes fixed on his knees. "That's not possible."

"Why?" James knew he shouldn't push this. For one, the Amaridians were on their heels and neither of them was paying an ounce of attention to their surroundings. Two, he had no right to her after everything he'd done. But he could not let her go. Could not give her up. "Because of circumstances? Or because you don't want to be mine?"

Her breath caught, and he took hold of the sides of her face, her wet hair tangling in his fingers.

"You shouldn't touch me," she whispered. "I'm not yours to touch."

"Then tell me to stop. Tell me that you'll never be mine again."

Ahnna made a soft noise of protest but didn't answer. Didn't pull out of his grip. James's heart hammered in his chest, his pulse a loud roar, because there was only one power in this world that would keep him from making Ahnna his again, and that was Ahnna herself.

Reaching down, he retrieved a sword and pressed the pommel into her left hand. Then he angled the tip so that it dug into the muscle above his heart.

"James . . ."

He waited a breath for her to tell him to fuck off. For her to shove the sharpened blade deep for his audacity, but when Ahnna did neither, James lowered his head to kiss her. A soft brush of his lips against hers, but the feel of her turned his hardening cock rigid. "You are so beautiful. The most exquisite woman to walk this world."

She shook her head slightly in protest, not of the kiss but of his words, and it drove James to madness that she'd deny such an obvious truth. Kissing her again, he trailed his tongue up the scar bisecting her face, the taste of her skin making his cock ache. She shuddered in his grip, his name a whisper on her lips.

He kissed her again, sliding his tongue into her mouth and tightening his grip on her hair. Her tongue stroked over his, and James fought the urge to knock the sword aside and pull her into his lap. The urge to strip her naked and bury himself inside her over and over until his name was not a whisper but a scream of pleasure. Instead, he kissed her jaw, catching the lobe of her ear between his teeth and relishing her moan. "I love you." The words escaped his lips, the truest thing he'd ever said, though he'd denied it for so long.

A sharp sting exploded across his chest, and Ahnna pulled away from him, dropping the sword with a clatter. "Stop. What I want, what you want . . . it doesn't fucking matter, James. I'm going back to Ithicana and you know it will be war, one way or another. A war we stand on opposite sides of, because I don't believe for a heartbeat that you'll fight for Ithicana. You never have."

Blood ran in rivulets down his torso, but James barely felt the sting of the shallow wound. "Ahnna—"

"No!" she shouted at him. "I'm not allowing myself to fall into your arms knowing that there will come a moment when we part ways and fight each other. I'm not going to allow you to break my heart twice. We are allies in this escape. Allies in stopping Alexandra and Katarina. But that is where it ends. Do you understand?"

He desperately wanted to argue. To offer a path forward other than the conflict she foresaw, but it would only be spinning lies to satisfy his own desperate desire to have her back. She was right not to invite hurt upon herself, but watching her wipe at her eyes from across the boat, it felt like the sword had sunk deep into his heart. "I understand."

Picking up the oars, he started rowing. "We need to find a place with cover deep enough to hide us. Carlo will have made it to the village."

"Agreed."

They sped onward in silence down the river, Ahnna hunting for likely hiding places while James searched for signs of pursuit.

"Up ahead," she finally said, and James looked over his shoulder at the copse of trees that had replaced the fields to either side. More than a copse, for the trees stretched on for as far as his eyes could see.

Ahnna stood up. "I think it will do, especially with the sun about to set. It will be fully dark by the time they get this far on horseback."

He rowed to the bank and Ahnna jumped out, wading through hip-deep water with the mooring rope in her hand. She tied it off and then disappeared into the shadows while he stowed the oars and climbed out.

"There are lots of good spots to hide." Ahnna reappeared and came down the bank, splashing softly to the boat. Before he could pick up the basket of supplies, she snatched them and carried them up the bank. Returning, she said, "Let's get the boat hidden."

"I'll do it," he said. "You take the oars."

"You'll need my help. If we leave drag marks on the banks, we might as well light a signal fire for Carlo. Same with damaging the branches. I suspect I've had a great deal more experience hiding boats than you have."

He didn't doubt that. "I don't need to drag it. I can lift it on my own. You can guide me."

"Are you trying to change my mind with manly acts?"

He could tell she was trying to break the tension with levity, but he'd heard the strain in her voice. Still, he kept up his end and said, "Are you trying to prove a point by rebreaking your arm?"

She huffed out a breath. "I suppose that's valid."

James moved the oars into the trees while Ahnna sat on a rock. She watched him in silence, yet the ease with which she'd conceded caused James to suspect this might not go as well as he liked.

Icy water filled his boots as he went to the back of the rowboat and struggled to overturn it. The old wood was waterlogged, the cursed thing heavier than he'd anticipated. The current caught the edge and James abruptly found himself sitting on his ass in the freezing river.

"I'd clap but my arm is broken," Ahnna said. "So you'll just have to imagine the sound of me celebrating this display."

"Noted." Standing, James heaved the back of the boat up, but the front dipped beneath the water and the current shoved him back. Cursing silently so as not to give her the satisfaction of commenting on his profanity, James shuffled beneath the boat. Every muscle in his body groaned under the weight of the waterlogged wood as he tried and failed to get the piece of shit up and out of the water.

And then the fore of the boat was lifting.

He raised his head to find Ahnna heaving it up with her good arm, and then resting it on her shoulder. "Chivalry and efficiency rarely walk hand in hand, James. Carlo isn't far behind us. Let's go."

They climbed the bank together and eased carefully through the dense trees until Ahnna found a thicket that satisfied her. While he went back to retrieve the oars, she set to hiding the boat with dirt, branches, and debris with shocking efficiency. The oars joined it, and even in broad daylight, James suspected no one would see the old rowboat unless they tripped over it.

As the darkness of night fell, Ahnna set to curling up in a pile of leaves. Once she was settled, she muttered, "You take the first watch."

James sighed and settled his back against a tree, trying not to think about what had happened on the boat. Trying to forget the taste of her skin and the feel of her tongue against his, but despite his heart feeling cut through, his desire surged at the memory.

*Quit thinking about Ahnna's legs and focus on the fact you're being hunted by a bad man*, he silently chastised himself, and the thought of Carlo did well to drag him from lust to misery. Though the weather was infinitely milder here than in the mountains, he was soaked and freezing, which contributed to his sourness. Hooking a foot around the food basket, he drew it closer and investigated the contents, eating a bit of the bread and cheese. Wind rustled the branches above him, the river gurgled, and all the small animals of the night called out to one another, which meant it was impossible to hear the cadence of Ahnna's breathing.

Yet he knew she was still awake. Could feel the tension seething from her beneath the branches and leaves, so he said, "When I'm back in Harendell, I'll make Taryn's freedom my priority. Her imprisonment is my fault, but I know you feel partially to blame."

Ahnna was silent for so long that James half wondered if he'd been mistaken in thinking she was still awake, but then she said, "Why do you say that?"

James opened the bottle of spirits that the old woman had included in the basket and took a large mouthful of something that burned all the way down. "Because you blame yourself for everything. You can't help but think if you'd done something different, Taryn would be free." He took another mouthful. "But the fact of the matter is that if you'd gone to them, I'd have caught you and Taryn as well. If I'd caught you then, you'd have already been tried and executed, and Alexandra still would have found ways to blame Ithicana in order to gain support for this war." Another sip. "Sometimes you need to accept that your enemy bested you in a battle, because dwelling on the heartbreak of loss when there are more battles to come only ensures you'll lose the war."

"I know who the enemy is," she muttered. "You were the one who struggled to grasp the truth." Then she made a noise of exasperation. "I'm sorry. It feels as though the truth is this ever-changing beast, and the moment I think I understand who is behind each scheme, each lie, each strike against those I love, the facts change. It's easier to be angry at everything and everyone, myself included."

God help him, but James understood that. Yet he also had seen what succumbing to rage turned him into, and how those who did not deserve his anger fell victim to it anyway. "Get some rest, Ahnna. This might be the last chance."

Ignoring his own exhaustion, James rested his back against a tree and watched the shadows, ears peeled for any sound of Carlo and his soldiers.

Clouds grew in the sky, blocking out the moon and stars, the wind rising.

It whipped through the trees, making them moan and shift, branches scratching against one another. Whether she was too exhausted to notice or too Ithicanian to care about wind, James didn't know, but Ahnna didn't stir as the hours passed. James was readying to wake her to switch shifts on watch duty when he saw flickers of light in the distance.

And heard the bark of a dog.

He gently touched her shoulder. "Ahnna." She jerked awake and lifted her blade.

"Shhh," James whispered. "They're here and they have a dog. We need to hide."

Ahnna reacted without hesitation. She snatched up the basket of supplies and began hurling the remaining food items toward the river before catching hold of his hand. "Step only on the tree roots so you don't leave tracks in the dirt. With luck, the dog isn't well trained and will be lured away by food—otherwise we will have to fight."

Ahnna led him through the trees, nimbly stepping from twisted root to twisted root, her balance superb. Only her grip on his hand allowed him to do the same.

"Down here," she whispered, and pulled him through a tangle of bushes into a hollow he'd never have known was there. It was small, which necessitated her sitting on him as she gently rearranged the brush to better hide them. Their proximity was necessitated by the direness of the situation, but it was impossible not to feel the tension between them. Impossible not to notice exactly where her body pressed against his.

Ahnna rubbed her hand into the dirt and smeared it over her face before twisting to do the same to James. "When they get close, squint or shade your eyes," she murmured. "It's always the eyes that give people away."

He'd known the Ithicanians were masters at camouflage, especially when it came to ambush attacks, yet it was another thing seeing it in action.

And not a moment too soon.

Flickering lanterns came closer. Far more than there should have been, given Carlo's much-reduced force.

James understood why as he caught sight of the weapons they carried. Scythes and sickles and pitchforks, because they weren't soldiers.

They were civilians.

"Search carefully, my friends!" Carlo's voice cut through the darkness. "For Harendell's bastard is not a man to be trifled with. He will cut you down as sure and true as he did your countrymen. For the sake of stealing a boat, he burned an entire village and slaughtered everyone who lived there. He will do the same to you if given the chance. Be wary!"

Ahnna tensed against him, and James felt sickness pooling in his stomach. He'd been certain that Carlo would act with discretion for the sake of his mother's schemes, but he'd been wrong. Carlo had slaughtered his own people to rally the Amaridian population to join the hunt. James's hand tightened on his sword but Ahnna's fingers wrapped around his, silently urging caution.

"He has the Ithicanian princess as his prisoner," Carlo intoned as though he'd repeated this same refrain countless times already, and James caught sight of him walking with heavy strides through the shadows. He was leading a tall horse, and James silently cursed, because it was either Maven or Dippy. "Ithicana is our ally and Ahnna Kertell our hero for putting an end to the villain Edward's treachery. At all costs, she must be rescued from Edward's Cardiffian bastard. We cannot allow him to bring her back to Harendell, for her life will be forfeit."

Ahnna's fingers tightened on his, her shock at Carlo's words as palpable as his own.

"The bastard prince has killed our brothers and sisters in numbers beyond counting in the Lowlands," Carlo continued. "He is merciless. He is cruel. And the princess of the Tempest Seas is injured and unable to defend herself from him or his foul advances."

An angry mutter seethed through the line of civilians, several of them calling out threats of what they'd do to James if they caught him.

"She fled to Amarid for our aid," Carlo shouted, drawing closer. "She fled to us because no one knows better than we do the evil of King Edward. She has done Amarid the greatest of services, and we cannot leave her to stand alone. Search, my friends, my comrades! Hunt the bastard down! A thousand golden coins to the man or woman who delivers the princess alive! Two thousand golden coins to the man or woman who delivers James Ashford, so that he can be executed by Her Most Royal Majesty as an enemy of Amarid!"

"Death to the bastard!" the civilians shouted, and Carlo's smile was illuminated by lantern light.

Yet as he turned his head, that same light did not pierce the shadows of his empty eye socket, the skin around it swollen. James clenched his teeth, knowing that the blow to the Beast's vanity would only drive the man harder, and fear tightened his chest as Carlo stopped walking.

The two soldiers with Carlo paused next to him as the civilians pressed onward, holding their lanterns up to search the shadows. The dog, a bounding retriever, raced onward and began snuffling near where James and Ahnna had been resting, right next to the hidden boat. James flexed his fingers on his blade as the dog lifted his head, nose moving as he sniffed the air.

With a bark, he raced in the direction of the river, no doubt making swift work of eating the food Ahnna had discarded to lure him off.

*Keep going*, he willed the dog as the civilians moved downstream, none of them seeing the rowboat hidden with Ahnna's skilled handiwork.

Yet Carlo remained where he was, idly tracing his empty eye socket with his index finger. "I want him alive," he said to his men. "If anyone accidentally kills James, I will make them suffer. He's mine. Is that understood?"

"Yes, sir," one of the soldiers answered. "Each team is repeating the message to the civilians. We have vessels on the water pressing downstream, men changing out horses to get the message westward as swiftly as possible, and bands of civilians hunting the banks and open ground. We'll get bloodhounds on the trail soon enough."

Carlo didn't answer, only turned to stroke the horse's nose.

It was Dippy.

Ahnna's body went rigid, and James fought the urge to wrap an arm around her waist to restrain her.

"Carry on," Carlo ordered. "Keep the people in check. Angry but not irrationally so, understood?"

"Yes, sir."

They hurried after the chain of civilians and the barking dog, but Carlo did not follow. The Beast cocked his head as though he was listening, and it was all James could do not to hold his breath.

Slowly, Carlo pivoted, now nothing more than a shadow in the night. Hunting the darkness like some form of demon. His focus passed over the hollow where they hid, and Ahnna pressed her back against James.

"Where are you, James?" Carlo crooned. "Won't you come out and play?"

A tremor ran through James, and he wasn't sure if it was terror or rage. Wasn't sure whether he wanted to melt into the mud or explode from the brush and attack.

Ahnna's nails dug into his hand, her spine glued to his chest, and her hair soft against his cheek.

"We have a connection, you and I," Carlo whispered, reaching a hand out in the darkness with uncanny accuracy. "I can feel you. It won't be long now."

He took a step closer.

*Kill him!* instinct screamed in James's chest. *Put him down!*

Except even if he killed Carlo before he made a sound, it wouldn't be long before the Beast's absence would be noted. They were vastly outnumbered. He and Ahnna would be on the run with no supplies, no head start, and there would be no escape.

Carlo dropped Dippy's reins and took another step. The wind blew, and it carried with it the man's scent. Sweat and blood and smoke, and Ahnna trembled in James's arms. Not from fear, no. He could feel her fury, and James interlaced his fingers with hers. Both of them warring with the desire to put this monster down.

"You have made this a true joy." Carlo gave a contented sigh. "A hunt for the ages. But all hunts must end, my old nemesis."

He abruptly twisted on his heels and mounted Dippy. With a few soft clicks, he drove the gelding into a trot and disappeared into the forest.

Everything fell silent, even the insects seeming to be holding their breath, the smell of blood and sweat fading.

But the smell of smoke lingered, as though Carlo left a trail of evil everywhere he walked.

Ahnna released a shuddering breath. "He killed them, didn't he? Those Amaridians who helped us."

"Likely." James swallowed to clear his throat but didn't let go of her. "I don't know if this plan will work. I had thought he'd keep our presence secret so word we were alive wouldn't reach Alexandra, but his choice to engage the civilians in the hunt changes everything. News of our presence will travel faster than we can, and with the sort of reward he's offering, everyone will be hunting for us."

He could feel her thinking, the wheels in her mind searching for a sure path to escape. James racked his own brain, but as he discarded option after option, the stench of smoke seemed to thicken.

"Do you smell that?" Ahnna pulled out of his grip and eased out of their hiding place. James followed, searching the shadows as he got to his feet.

To the east an orange glow bloomed.

At first, he thought it was the dawn. But the glow was too bright. Too fierce. Too *early*.

As the wind blew over them, it carried with it a thick cloud of smoke and James realized what he was seeing.

"God have mercy," Ahnna breathed, face no longer lost to shadows but illuminated by a wall of light racing toward them. "He's set the forest on fire."

James caught hold of her hand, anger fleeing in the face of the firestorm. "Run!"

# 35

# AHNNA

THE INFERNO RACED forward in a wall of flames. The only direction to run was either toward Carlo or toward the river.

An easy choice, which Ahnna suspected meant it was no choice at all.

She slid to a stop at the riverbank, and James cursed as he nearly ran her over. "Swim," he gasped. "We need—"

He broke off, and silence stretched between them. No words were necessary as they took in the inferno on the opposite side of the bank. Carlo had set a merciless trap and he'd set it well, the wind rushing down from the mountains driving the flames west. Flushing them toward the edge of the tree line, where there would be nowhere to hide. No way to outrun mounted soldiers. That he'd leave miles of scorched ruin in his wake clearly troubled the Beast not in the least.

"We have to get into the water," James urged. "The fire is coming fast."

Ahnna clenched her teeth and gave her head a sharp shake. "It's a trap, James. He has to know that if we are in here, we'll take to the river."

The wall of flame racing in their direction illuminated James's dirt-smeared face as he caught hold of her shoulders. "If he catches us, we still have a chance. If the fire catches us, we are *done*."

Ahnna coughed as the wind blew over them. "What if we wade out as deep as we can and wait for the flames to burn past?"

"The smoke will be too thick." He struggled to get the words out between coughs. "In another few minutes, we won't be able to breathe."

Fire like this wasn't something Ahnna knew. Ithicana was saturated with rain daily, and even fires started by lightning or humanity never took hold. "We can try. If I'm wrong, we swim."

James opened his mouth to argue, but then caught hold of her left hand and pulled her out into the river. It was fed by melted snow, and the cold cut down to the bone. But with the wall of heat blowing over her, Ahnna didn't hesitate to wade deeper.

The current was fast, and it was hard to keep upright on the slippery rocks of the riverbed. It rose up her thighs, and Ahnna leaned against it to keep from being knocked down. Yet as the water reached her waist, her boots went out from her.

James's hand tightened on hers and he hauled her upright, wrapping an arm around her waist and keeping her back against his chest as he edged deeper. He was warm and solid, his height and weight keeping them upright where hers had failed.

Around them, the smoke hung like a shroud, thick and suffocating, pressing into her lungs and coating her throat with ash. Her breaths were shallow and desperate, the air so heavy with soot it felt like trying to breathe through cloth.

James coughed violently, his body shaking from the effort of keeping them upright in the current. From the effort of *breathing*.

The smoke was everywhere, clinging to them like a second skin, wrapping around her throat like a noose. "I was wrong." Her voice was raw and barely audible over the trees exploding from the heat. "We have to go downstream."

"Carlo will be waiting." James's grip around her waist tightened, and he reached down to pull her sodden shirt up over her mouth and nose. "He's angry, Ahnna. He'll hurt you again."

As if she didn't know that. As if she couldn't picture Carlo standing just outside the range of the flames, illuminated red like the demon that he was. Waiting, waiting to punish her for her infractions against him.

*For the loss of his eye.*

"Unless you've got another plan, we have no choice."

James didn't answer, only gave a grunt of effort as he started wading upriver, his movements sluggish but deliberate as he finally said, "We just need to get past the worst of it. The wind is blowing the smoke the other way."

The smoke pressed in closer, its tendrils swirling like living things, clinging to her skin and filling her nose with the acrid stench of burning wood. Ahnna's vision blurred, the riverbank lost in crimson and flame, and her face felt like it was on fire.

*I can't breathe. James can't breathe.*

*We are burning burning burning.*

"James, this isn't working!"

No answer, but she could feel his determination to go any direction other than Carlo's. Even if that direction was death.

"James!"

With a desperate burst of effort, Ahnna slammed her feet into James's shins and knocked his feet out from beneath him.

The current caught hold and ripped them downstream, the water mercifully cold against Ahnna's flesh as she fought for air.

The smoke eased as they outpaced the blaze, and James caught hold of her shirt and pulled her against him in the water. "I'll try to distract them. You run."

"No!" She shoved at him with her left arm, treading water to keep afloat. "If anyone is going to beat you bloody for being an unrepentant stubborn prick, it's me!"

"Ahnna, this is not the time! We're reaching the end of the forest!"

Where Carlo and his men would be waiting, on land and on the river.

Ahnna twisted in James's grip and looked into the darkness downstream. The light from the fire was behind them now, which meant they still had the cover of night. "Quit shouting," she snapped. "In this darkness, they won't see us coming."

The water ahead held only deathly silence, but as they rounded a bend, torches glowed.

Perhaps a hundred paces beyond where the trees ended waited masses of armed men. Soldiers and civilians with a chain of boats tethered across the river. A wall nearly as terrifying as the one of fire racing up behind them.

"The river is deep," she whispered. "Just before we come in range of their light, swim to the bottom. We'll go right under them. Hold your breath as long as you can on the far side. With luck, they'll think either the fire got us or that we were never in the woods to begin with."

"All right." James pulled her closer, his breath warm on her face. "You still have your sword?"

"Yes." She briefly touched the hilt, the weapon pinned tight to her side by her belt. "If they catch us, we fight. I don't think we can escape a second time."

They turned in the water, eyes on the approaching wall of torches and boats.

"Deep breath," she whispered, then sucked in a mouthful of air and sank, pulling James down with her.

They moved into the depths of the river, but as her fingers brushed the slick rocks of the bed, Ahnna looked up through the blackness. The glow of the torches grew closer and closer, and triumph mixed with her fear because the lights didn't move, the Amaridians having no idea their prey was near. No one would even notice as she and James swept right beneath them and downstream to safety.

Her chest tightened, lungs abused by smoke wanting no part of this gambit, but Ahnna ignored the pain.

The glow grew brighter.

Closer.

Her triumph swelled, and then was abruptly vanquished as the current slammed her into something coarse and ropy.

A net. They'd strung a fucking net.

Ahnna wrenched her hand free of James's grip and clawed at the tangle of fishing net. She tried to swim backward, but her legs had gone through and she was caught. The relentless current shoved her forward, her fingers snagging on another loop of rope, and she tried to climb. But it was weighed down. Holding her under.

And she needed to breathe.

Bubbles exploded from her face as she fought the net, desperation making her pull her injured arm from its sling and try to climb. Pain ricocheted through her as the break snapped again, but it meant nothing compared with the need to breathe.

*James.* Where was James?

The net jerked with his motions but she couldn't see him. Couldn't reach him.

Couldn't breathe!

Blackness was rolling in, deep as the oceans, and Ahnna wordlessly screamed her rage that this was it. That this was how it would end. That she'd fail to get home because the Beast had caught her as easily as a morning meal.

And then the net jerked her upward.

Ahnna sucked in a breath and stared into Carlo's one remaining eye.

"There you are, my darling," the Beast crooned as he drew back his fist.

After that, there was nothing but darkness.

# 36

# LARA

Lara sat unmoving in her chair as she listened to the valcottan man relay the message Keris had sent. She kept her expression blank, but her hands were leaving sweat marks on the silk of her skirt as she took in his words.

"His Highness didn't wish to risk writing anything down, even in code," the messenger, whose name was Adrius, said. "I've done my best to remember everything exactly as he said, but His Highness is . . ."

"Verbose?" Lara offered.

Adrius shrugged. "He's not succinct."

"If you remember anything else, please bring it to me directly." She rose to her feet. "Please make our house your own while you rest. I know the journey was difficult." The seas had been vicious, a testament to the ship captain's skill and bravery that he was able to get through the storms to Midwatch.

"Thank you, Your Grace." Adrius inclined his head. "I'd like to return to His Highness as soon as I'm able. He doesn't have half as many guards as I might like, and he . . ."

"Is reckless?"

Adrius lifted one shoulder and replied, "Has a high tolerance for risk when it comes to things that matter to him."

Lara's chest tightened, because the risks her brother was taking were very much on her behalf, and she hated it. Hated hiding behind the defense of Ithicana's typhoons while those she loved danced with the enemy, but there was no helping it. "It may be some time before we are able to secure passage. The storms prevent sea travel, and the blockades . . ." Instead of finishing the thought, she pivoted. "Did the Harendellian blockade give your vessel any trouble?"

"No, Your Grace, though they surely saw us." Adrius's brow furrowed, brown eyes thoughtful. "If anything, they seemed to *want* me to deliver the messages. Perhaps they are losing their taste for conflict and hope that an agreement can be reached."

Every part of Lara wanted to look to Aren where he stood by the window, but she kept her focus on Adrius. "With luck, they'll be equally amenable to your return. Thank you, Adrius."

He bowed low, his loose dark curls spilling over his forehead. "Your Grace."

He left the room, and as Lara met Lia's gaze, the other woman gave the slightest nod and followed him out, shutting the door behind her.

For a long moment, Lara stared at the notes she'd taken while Adrius had relayed all that Keris had learned from both Alexandra and Cormac, eyes catching on certain lines. *Edward planned to wed Ahnna to James. He aimed to start a coup. Planned for James to be king of Ithicana.*

"Ahnna did it to protect us. To protect *me*." His voice was barely a whisper. "I thought it was her fault that the Harendellians were turning on us, but it was Edward. Edward scheming not only to give my sister to his fucking bastard like a broodmare, but to steal my entire kingdom."

A tremble ran through his body, a barely suppressed urge to lash out, and Lara tightened her arm around him even as she pressed her face to his shoulder. Her own rage seethed barely checked, memory of Harendell's lavish gifts and Edward's long letter welcoming Delia to the world now feeling like a knife to the back because the whole time, he'd been aiming to kill her baby girl.

"And it's that same fucking bastard who is hunting Ahnna." Aren's words were a snarl.

*Not a bastard*, Lara thought, Cormac had given Keris that piece of information before he'd succumbed to Amaridian poison, but then Aren drew her attention back to him.

"I'm going to kill James Ashford. I'm going to gut that prick, stake him out for the carrion, and send his head to the Ashfords. Give them a real reason to go to war."

Such an action would only make a bad situation worse, especially given that Keris was in the thick of it, but Lara bit her tongue and let him rage. Let him seethe while she buried her own anger deep to simmer. "We need to consider why Alexandra gave Keris this information. She wasn't using him as a confessional, which means she *wants* us to know these details. You heard Adrius—the Harendellians did nothing but watch as his ship sailed right through the blockades."

"Because Alexandra wanted me to know the reason why Ahnna did it. She thought it would be the proof I needed to turn on my sister."

"No." Gripping her husband, Lara twisted him to face her. "It's the exact opposite. She gave you the justification you'd need to stay loyal to Ahnna."

His hazel eyes were bloodshot as they searched hers, the toll of recent weeks written across his face, and it hurt her heart. "Why would Alexandra want that?" He squeezed his eyes shut. "I can't think clearly, Lara. Every instinct is screaming at me to attack those who are trying to hurt my family, and I can't think through Alexandra's schemes."

But she could. This is what Serin had raised her to do, and as much as she hated to do so, Lara thanked the Magpie for his efforts now. "What does a ruler do when they want to incite their populace against another nation? What did my father do? What did Petra do? What did Edward do?"

Aren scrubbed a hand through his hair. "Demonize the other nation. Make them the source of every woe. Turn your target into the villain."

"Yes." Her fingers tightened on his shoulders. "Edward sowed the seeds against us to prepare his people for the moment he incited the coup so that they'd support his actions. But with Edward's murder, Alexandra has so much more to work with. The people loved Edward, and rightly or wrongly, Ahnna killed him. If she is caught and executed, they will have their justice, but if we protect her? If we stand by her? Then we are complicit, and their rage will turn on us."

All the color drained from Aren's face as understanding took hold. "Alexandra aims to see Edward's plans through. She aims to take the bridge."

Lara gave a slow nod, using the anger in her heart to stifle the fear that had been rising in her chest since Adrius had conveyed Keris's message. "She would have been infuriated to know that Edward planned to give Ithicana to James, so it makes every bit of sense that she'd aim to take it for William. That's why she's putting up with Lestara—as much as she might loathe Cardiff, she needs that alliance for a campaign this ambitious, else she leaves the Lowlands open for the Amaridians to take. Katarina must have known some or all of Edward's ambitions, and that's why she was working so hard to get rid of James. If Harendell is allied with Cardiff and holds the bridge, it's only a matter of time until they come for Amarid."

"But why tell us?" Aren demanded. "Why did Alexandra give us insight into her plans via Keris?"

"Maybe she thinks we won't see to the heart of it." Lara looked at the ceiling as she thought, but then shook her head. "Or maybe she wants us to know. Maybe she thinks to intimidate us into conceding, to abdicate rule to Harendell, and that we'll choose to go live in Maridrina and Valcotta rather than fight a war we can't win."

"If Alexandra thinks that, she's a fool!"

Except that the dowager queen was no one's fool. Harendell was the greatest power of the north, wealthy beyond measure with a well-trained army and large navy. They had everything they needed to supply themselves through a long and drawn-out war, not the least being tight ties with Cardiff through Lestara and James.

Her thoughts snagged on the prince's name, because for all James had been the beneficiary of his father's schemes, he was surely

Alexandra's target now. It struck Lara that if Alexandra could pin James's death on Ahnna, that Harendellian rage would go far beyond the tipping point. *We need to keep him alive.*

Before Lara could dig deeper into the thought, a knock sounded at the door. "Yes?"

Lia stepped inside. "The Maridrinian delegation is here."

"They're early," Aren snapped, going to the sideboard to pour a drink. "Put them off. I don't want to deal with them right now."

Lara wasn't keen to engage with members of Sarhina's new parliament either, but if Alexandra was coming for the bridge, Ithicana needed to know its allies were at its back. "Send them in."

Ignoring Aren's sharp look, she smoothed her skirts, cringing slightly at the frayed hem she hadn't noticed earlier. All her gowns were beginning to show wear, but there was neither the time nor the means to replace them.

Moments later, Lia appeared with two men and a woman, their hair wet from the rain but their garments dry, which suggested that they'd been at Midwatch long enough to change their clothes. She and Aren had known they were coming through the bridge, but their arrival hadn't been expected until later in the day.

The woman curtsied and the men bowed, and Lara inclined her head. "Welcome. We are so pleased to host you at Midwatch."

"Thank you, Your Grace," one of the men said. "It is an honor. I am Hector Adrias."

He introduced the others, and their eyes turned to Aren, who gave a slight nod. "Welcome to Midwatch."

"Please sit." Lara gestured to the chairs surrounding the large table. "We are not much for formality in Ithicana."

"Maridrina moves away from it as well," Hector replied. "Queen Sarhina believes much of the ceremony favored by royalty is a method of oppression, as it implies a monarch is an entity above all others, closer to God than human. She seeks to dissuade such beliefs in favor of equality."

"My sister is a force to be reckoned with."

Lara sat, Aren taking the place next to her, and one of their servants circled the table with drinks.

Hector gave a slight cough, then said, "As much as we desire pleasantries, Your Graces, the situation in Maridrina has grown quite dire with the loss of trade with Harendell. Famine had long been an issue even during King Silas's reign, but the destruction that Empress Petra brought down upon Vencia has made the situation worse. We were heavily reliant on Harendell's exports of cattle, pork, and grain, all of which have been lost to us due to the conflict with Ithicana. To make matters worse, Valcotta's herds have suffered a wasting disease that required culling, and they are no longer selling north."

Sickness pooled in Lara's stomach, because it seemed all crises were coming to a head at once. "I understand. Ithicana also suffers the effects of Harendell's blockades, but there is little to be done about them."

"I recognize this is a sensitive issue, but is that entirely the case?" Hector rested an elbow on the table. "Because it is our understanding that all the Harendellians want from you is the condemnation of Princess Ahnna for the crime of murdering King Edward, as well as her unprovoked attack on Queen Alexandra."

Aren stiffened, and Lara took his hand under the table, willing him to keep his temper in check. "It is a complex situation."

"We have been informed that there are witnesses," Hector pressed. "That there can be no doubt in any mind that the princess was the perpetrator, and that there is no argument for self-defense, for the only injury done to the princess was to her pride."

Aren's hand tightened, and Lara felt her own anger rise. Biting down on it, she said, "We have come to understand that there was, indeed, provocation."

Hector tilted his head, and Lara found herself wondering who he was before he was voted into Sarhina's parliament. Not a nobleman, for his hands were thick with calluses, and she knew that the majority of those voted in were of the common civilian population.

"In what sense?" he asked. "Because we were told that King Edward was stabbed to death in his own bedchamber. In his own bed, in fact."

Lara considered how much she wished to tell this man, who was a stranger, and instead asked, "What is it you are hoping to achieve here, sir?"

He met her gaze for a long moment, then looked away, his discomfort palpable. "Princess Ahnna broke Harendell's laws, and it is within their right to demand she be punished accordingly." His throat moved as he swallowed hard, but then he met her stare again. "What is the punishment for murder in Ithicana, Your Grace? Is it not execution?"

It was, and Lara hated where this was going.

Her countryman cleared his throat, glancing at his peers once before pressing onward. "We are sympathetic to the pain of condemning a family member, but trade *must* flow. Maridrinian families are starving, and if what we learned during our travels through your bridge is true, Ithicanian families are living one meal to the next with that unlikely to improve until storm season ends. How many must suffer, how many must *die,* for the sake of familial loyalty, Your Graces?"

Aren jerked his hand from Lara's grip, on his feet in a flash of movement. He slammed his fists down on the table with such force that all the glasses jumped. "Edward was scheming to kill my family and take my throne in an act of war. My sister's actions were in defense of herself, her family, and of Ithicana, so she is guilty of *nothing.*"

He wasn't wrong and Lara had no intention of undermining him, but neither did she want this to spiral out of control. They needed Maridrina, and Sarhina had sorely undermined her control over her queendom. If her parliament voted against aiding Ithicana, there would be nothing Sarhina could do unless she dissolved all that she had built.

Lara's gut told her that her sister, no matter the circumstances, would refuse to do that.

There was fear in the eyes of the Maridrinians as they regarded Aren, who was bigger than most men, visibly armed, and possessed of a dangerous reputation, but to their credit, they didn't stand down.

Hector stood to face Aren, holding tight to his composure. "Our nations were not built around what they can create, grow, farm, or hunt for themselves, Your Grace. For living memory, we have been united by trade through Ithicana's bridge, and this conflict has stopped that trade in its tracks. Some nations will fare better than others—Harendell being one of them—but Maridrina will falter swiftly without access to the livestock raised in the north. We have been given the power to govern by the people of Maridrina, and we will act in defense of them. But that does not mean we are without compassion, for we desire Ithicana to thrive as well. Even if you are able to repel Harendell's inevitable invasion during the calm season, I must ask, what is Ithicana without the bridge? What life is there in this nation besieged by storms if the bridge does not provide?"

Aren didn't answer, and Lara struggled to keep grief from rising to her face because she knew these questions were what kept him awake night after night.

"For the sake of all who depend on the bridge, we beg of you to reconsider your stance and make peace with King William, Your Grace."

"You want me to condemn my sister?" Aren's voice sounded as though it had been dragged across gravel. "You want me to let them take her to be hanged, drawn, quartered, and then leave her corpse for the crows to pick at?"

The other two Maridrinians rose, adding strength and support to their countryman as he said, "One life, for the sake of tens of thousands, Your Grace. Your noble sacrifice will stop a war in its tracks."

*Except that it wouldn't.*

Aren huffed out a breath. "You think so, do you? You think that if we concede and give Ahnna to William to execute that all will go back to normal, and endless fucking cows will run through the bridge to fill Maridrinian bellies, just as they always have? Because I don't."

He slammed his fists down again on the table, and the Maridrinians twitched in alarm.

"If I give them my sister, who is innocent, they will not see a king making a *noble sacrifice* but rather weakness. And weakness is something Harendell will always seek to exploit, so rather than gathering up cows to send to Maridrina, they will ask for us to sacrifice more. And more. Until William is the Master of the Bridge and Ithicana is no more."

Silence stretched for a long time, and Lara all but held her breath as she waited for Hector to respond. Sweat beaded on his temple, but Lara could see that he was thinking through what Aren had said. Finally, Hector cleared his throat. "If that is what you perceive to be

Harendell's goal, and if you see them taking the bridge as an inevitability, then perhaps that is the concession you must make, Your Grace."

*God have mercy*, Lara silently whispered. *Give us the strength to endure this moment.*

"You're suggesting I abdicate to William?" Aren's knuckles whitened, and Lara found herself staring at his fists, wondering how much harder Hector could push before Aren used them. "You're suggesting that I *give* them the bridge?"

"From your own lips, this will be a war you cannot win," Hector replied. "I lived under Silas Veliant, a man who'd sacrifice any number of his people's lives for pride. The high road is one worth considering, especially given the empress of Valcotta will surely grant Your Grace and his family asylum. It might also be a way to save Princess Ahnna's life, as the empress can protect her."

Every part of Lara wanted to intervene, but she did not move from her place at Aren's side as he shouted, "Get the fuck out of my house!"

Hector crossed his arms. "Pride it is, then? This is why Sarhina has the right of it: No one man should have this sort of power over a nation."

"Get out!" Aren screamed, and the door flung open, Jor and others pouring into the room. "You are not welcome here!"

"As you like." Hector looked to his peers, who all stood with their chins raised in defiance. "But know this, Your Grace. If it comes to war and there is a vote as to whether to send Maridrinians to fight, I will vote *Nay*! because I will not send my countrymen to die for the sake of the pride of yet another king!"

Aren lunged, and Lara surged to her feet, catching hold of his arm to keep him from hitting the man in the face. "Get them out of here," she snapped at Jor. "Now!"

Holding tight to Aren's arm, she muttered, "They're leaving. They're going," but she wasn't even sure he heard her. Aren was shaking, and Lara didn't know if it was rage or something worse.

Jor and Lia urged the Maridrinians from the room, the door slamming behind them.

"They're gone," she said. "They've left the room."

"Good!" Aren roared. "Who the fuck does he even think he is? Some farmer from a field thinking he can play at politics?"

Like a cord stretched too tight, Lara felt her control snap. "At least he kept his temper! My God, Aren, what are you thinking? We *need* Maridrina, and you just shouted those who rule out of our house."

"He told me to abdicate, Lara. What would you have me do, pour him a drink?"

"Play the fucking game!" she shouted. "That's what I want you to do, Aren. Because that's what kings do."

They stared each other down, and Lara hated every second of it because she wanted to be united with him in all things. But the stakes were too high for her to concede just because quarreling with him hurt her soul.

"I need some air." Aren twisted away from her and stormed toward the door. "You can go play the game, Lara. You've always been better at it."

She flinched as the door slammed a second time. Above the house, thunder boomed and rain hammered the windows. The room grew darker as the servants hurried to close the exterior shutters to protect the glass, and it felt like a shadow was falling over all that Lara held dear.

For a long moment, she debated what to do, but it was a short debate. Aren was her heart, and she would always put him before reason. Lara flung open the door, only to stop in her tracks as she discovered Nana standing outside, hand outstretched as though she'd been about to open it.

Except gone was Aren's irritating, harridan of a grandmother, and in her place stood Amelie, former spy and harem wife, dressed in swaths of green and gold silk. "Delia is with her nurse," she said. "Jor is with them. I'll smooth the Maridrinians' ruffled feathers—you go."

But before Lara could move, Amelie's hand closed on her arm. "You fought hard for Ithicana once before, girl. Fight for us again."

Lara nodded once, then broke into a sprint through the halls of her house and stepped out into the storm.

Wind lashed across her face, the rain it carried hitting her with such force it was like being pelted by rocks, but Lara ignored the pain in favor of scanning the ground for clues to where Aren had gone. The ground was covered with puddles, torrents of water running downhill toward the sea, but she caught sight of a fading boot print in the mud and instantly knew what direction he'd gone.

Hiking up her skirts, Lara broke into a run. Mud flooded into her sandals and squished between her toes, rain gluing the blue silk of her dress to her skin as she headed in the direction of Midwatch's tower.

Covered with fallen branches and debris, the trail was more river than pathway. The trees themselves were shredded, leaves everywhere, and it felt as though she were running through a battlefield, fear as much as exertion causing her heart to thunder. A branch tore loose from above and fell right in front of her. Too close to stop, so she jumped, her dress catching and tearing. She nearly lost her footing, her ankle twisting, but panic Lara couldn't quite justify refused to allow her to slow her pace.

Or perhaps it was justifiable, given everything they'd fought and bled for was slipping through her fingers.

The wind grew worse the higher she climbed, and Lara winced as debris whipped into her, leaving scratches across her arm. But through the rain and dark shadows, the thick stone tower reared ahead of her.

"Aren!"

No response came, but it might be because he couldn't hear her over the storm. She stumbled into the tower, sodden sandals slapping against the stone steps as she circled around and around, exploding out onto the top.

To find her husband sitting on the rough stone, staring at crude drawings some Maridrinian soldier had carved into the wall.

"I told Lia to have this fixed," he said, staring at the drawings. "Twice."

There were countless such reminders of the endless months Maridrina had held Ithicana in its grasp, and erasing them had not been a priority. Scraping mud off her sandal, Lara walked to the wall and smeared it across the drawings, hiding them from view. A stupid and impermanent gesture, but the tension in Aren's shoulders released and his eyes moved to her.

"You're bleeding." He was on his feet in a flash, reaching for her.

"It's nothing, just a few scratches." Her pulse was roaring in her chest, and Lara shoved away the fears trying to drown her, because she'd found him. He wasn't lost to her.

*Not yet.*

He bent to examine her arm, rain turning her blood watery and pink. "You shouldn't be out in this storm. It's getting vicious."

"You shouldn't have left me."

Aren lifted his face to meet her gaze, rivulets of rain running down his cheeks and his hair whipping in the wind. "I'm sorry. I felt like I couldn't breathe in there."

"Don't be sorry." Standing on her tiptoes, she wrapped her arms around his neck, her hair swirling and sticking to her face. "We are all at our limits."

Aren slid a hand down over her backside, then lifted her into his arms. Holding her close, he carried her over to sit next to the wall of the tower so that the worst of the wind was blocked. Together they sat and listened to Ithicana's tempests scream and rage, the blackened sky crisscrossed with endless lightning.

"Is he right?" Aren finally asked. "Is refusing to concede to Harendell benefiting only my own pride? Am I just another variation of Silas or Petra, flush with my own importance?"

"No." Lara twisted in his arms so that her knees were to either side of him. She cupped his cheeks, feeling the roughness of stubble against her palms. "You are nothing like either of them, and none of what you have chosen to do in this situation is a matter of pride, because all of it is about preservation. Preservation of Ithicana, its people, and our way of life."

"Is it, though?" His eyes searched hers. "Is fighting a war we are likely to lose the right choice for our people? Or is it better if I give it all up to Harendell? Let them rule, let them protect the bridge, let them protect the people?"

Lara drew in a steadying breath. "Except they only care for two of those things. All Alexandra wants is the bridge and the income that will come with controlling it. All she cares about is commerce and satisfying the ruling class who stand to benefit from it. She won't use that revenue to support Ithicanians. At best, she'll hire them at a pittance to work for the crown, but it will be endless toil with people cast away when they can no longer serve. We live life differently here, and it will be our people who are forced to change and adapt, not Harendell. Not Alexandra. If she takes control, our people will lose everything they've worked to build and become little better than slaves to a foreign monarchy, because where can they go? To flee to Maridrina or Valcotta means starting over with no wealth and all the wrong skills, and if you think that won't cost countless lives, you are deluded, my love."

Aren closed his eyes, nodding slightly.

"It's never been about the bridge. It's just a structure, a tool." She stroked his cheek. "It's always been about the people, and that is who we must fight for. Who we must die for, if need be." Her breath caught. "Delia's legacy isn't a crown. It's the people around her who have cared for her and the children she'll grow up with to fight alongside. To run to Valcotta would mean stealing that from her."

"But it will be safe."

Lara shook her head, for though there was an allure to that dream, she knew better. "Ask Keris how safe it is. There is danger everywhere, Aren. We can spend our lives running toward a sanctuary that doesn't exist or we can stand our ground and fight for our home."

"But how can we win?" He leaned his head back against the rough stone. "Sarhina has given up all her power to help us, and we've heard nothing from Zarrah. It feels like we stand alone in a way we never have before."

Lara smoothed his hair off his face, wishing there was a solution she could offer him but knowing that platitudes and false hopes would only make them both feel worse.

The voice of a man she hadn't thought of in a very long time rose in her thoughts. *Ice and fire might ravage the world, but still the cockroach survives*, Erik said, her old weapons master visible in her mind's eye. *Just like you.*

And just like Ithicana.

"We will win this," Lara said, a sudden rush of determination filling her, fueling her. "I swear it."

"When you say it, I believe it." Aren tangled his fingers in her sodden hair with one hand, then traced a finger down the line of her cleavage to the plunging neckline of her gown. "This is what you were wearing when I first saw you. What you were wearing when I married you."

Her breath quickened beneath his touch, and Lara rocked against him, feeling his cock hardening where it pressed against her. "I didn't think you remembered. I've worn it many times before, and you've never said anything."

"It might be because you're as wet as you were that day." His finger moved from the tiny blue beads embroidered on the neckline, tracing over the wet silk to circle her nipple, and a soft whimper pulled from her lips, an ache forming between her thighs. "Wetter, I think," Lara murmured.

Aren made a noise low in his throat, and then bent his head to kiss her. "If I live to be an old man, I'll still be able to close my eyes and see you walking toward me, this goddamned dress clinging to every curve like a second skin. The most beautiful woman alive, and I wanted you like I wanted breath."

"Whereas all I got to see was that awful helmet. Where did that thing go? Perhaps you can wear it for me later."

Aren laughed into her throat, then bit at her collarbone. "Dissolving into rust somewhere, so you'll have to let that fantasy go."

She smirked. "Find another way to satisfy me, and I'll banish it from my thoughts."

"Gladly," he murmured, pulling the narrow straps of her dress over her shoulders to reveal her breasts. Rain pelted against them but all she felt was the heat of his mouth as he closed his lips over her nipple, a fierce need to be filled by him consuming her soul.

Rocking against him, she unfastened his belt, weapons clattering to the stone beneath them as she caught hold of his soaked tunic and pulled it over his head. Beneath was all hard muscle and suntanned skin, and Lara traced her fingers over his shoulders and back, every inch of him familiar and yet as thrilling as the first time.

Dragging Aren's face up from her breasts, she kissed him, his tongue delving into her mouth and claiming her. "I want you in me," she growled, dragging her lacquered nails down his back, then reached between them, sliding her hand into his trousers. She closed it around his thick cock, stroking him hard, the feel of him against her palm almost pushing her over the edge. "I want to fuck you now."

He groaned her name and pushed her onto her back, but Lara caught hold of his leg with her ankle and flipped him onto his. Straddling her husband, she let the tempest tear her hair this way and that as she looked down at him, then slowly drew his trousers over his hips. She took hold of her ruined dress and lifted it over her own head, so that all that she wore were two thigh sheaths and a long knife strapped to the small of her back.

"You are the storm," he breathed, his fingers tracing up her thighs, his thumb finding her clit and circling it until she moaned. "Beautiful and terrifying and mine."

"Yours." She tilted her face back, rain sluicing down her cheeks and her breasts as she mounted him, her body taking in the hard length of his cock. "Till my last breath."

Lightning cracked overhead and thunder boomed as she rode her husband, the wind lashing them with violent ferocity that Lara barely felt, because all that mattered was the taste of him. The feel of him. The hold he had on her heart and her soul.

As Lara crested, she pulled him over with her, screaming Aren's name at the sky, every part of her raging in defiance at those who sought to take from them.

She'd fought for Ithicana before and won, and little cockroach that she was, she'd do it again.

# 37

# JAMES

James's head bumped against the side of the wagon. Every inhalation smelled of dust, and his ears rang with the teeming noise of a city. Merchants shouted their wares, aggressive and loud as they bargained with patrons. Animals bleated and brayed, some pulling carts while others were intended for slaughter. Bells rang out from the fourteen cathedrals, tolling the hour, tolling various ceremonies, tolling as one of the largest cities on the continent toiled.

Riomar.

It was the capital of Amarid, and while James had never stepped foot in Riomar, he knew its reputation well. It epitomized the extremes of human existence. Wealth built on wineries that shipped their bottles throughout the known world, the families who owned them equal parts nobles and criminals, each of them running an extended network of deeply illegal activities that earned them as much as or more than the wine. They lived like kings in their walled palatial estates as they conducted what amounted to warfare against one another. Battles fought by street thugs and urchins in the dark of night. By poisons slipped into cups and or dusted across pillows. By riots and marches, the middle class pitted against one another to achieve their master's ends.

Yet there was also poverty and misery of an unrivaled magnitude. Tens of thousands who lived on the streets, great slums that multiplied only blocks away from white stone buildings capped with enamel-tiled roofs. Children starved on the streets while carriages passed them by carrying children playing with golden rattles. Every morning, hundreds of city workers swept through the slums with wagons to retrieve the dead, and James had heard that great pits outside the city limits never stopped burning the corpses spat out by Riomar.

Above it all, in her palace of gold, ruled Queen Katarina.

Ahnna shifted where she lay tied on the other side of the wagon, both of them trussed like hogs and gagged so they could not speak. As they'd been since they were dragged out of the river, both of them half drowned. Carlo had shrieked above the cacophony that he hadn't realized fishing was so enjoyable. He cast handfuls of coins into the air so that they showered down around the civilians who had aided his hunt. As the civilians had fought over the gold, Carlo's soldiers had fallen upon them. Killed them with sword and knife and arrow, merciless in their need to keep his and Ahnna's fate a secret.

The wagon rocked and bounced over ruts, the man driving shouting oaths at anyone who got in his way. Which meant the soldiers were not making a fuss. Katarina did not want anyone to know who her new prisoners were, most especially not Alexandra.

A bead of sweat rolled into James's eye and he blinked at the sting, desperately thirsty. It was hot and dry, made worse by the canvas over the wagon, and it felt like he'd sweated out every drop of moisture. Though he anticipated that it would get much worse once they were delivered to Amarid's infamous prison.

The Furnace.

Its reputation rivaled that of Devil's Island. Not the main prison, which contained petty criminals who would be released upon serving their time. It was the infamous cells at its center that put fear into hearts. Cells where those who would never again know freedom were incarcerated. It was said there were thirty of them. Small cells made of solid stone set into the earth within which prisoners were sealed with only a small hole left open for food, water, and waste. There was no way out of them, no locks to pick, no bars to break, no guards to bribe. Because there was no way out unless the masons were called to break a cell open.

And that only happened when the prisoner was dead.

James was not one to dwell on fears, but the idea of being effectively buried alive for the balance of his existence filled him with irrational terror. A terror made worse with the knowledge that the woman he loved would be confined in the cell next to him, which he knew would be a fate worse than death for Ahnna Kertell.

Yet as her hazel eyes gave a slow blink, he knew it wasn't herself that she thought of. It was Ithicana. Her people.

If Carlo and his soldiers had heard any updates on the escalations of tensions between Harendell and Ithicana, they'd said nothing. Yet James could only assume that in the time that had passed, William, on Alexandra's urging, had escalated to blockades. Possibly all-out attacks, though at this time of year it was possible that the storms were keeping the Bridge Kingdom safe. Likewise, James had learned nothing about Cardiff, but that concerned him far less. His mother's homeland was in a much stronger position, and right now, James did not think that Cardiff was Alexandra's primary focus.

She wanted the bridge, as did Katarina, and they would stop at nothing to get it. Even if it meant working together.

The wagon bounced and jostled, the quality of the noise telling James they were crossing over a bridge. Wind rustled the canvas, smelling of surf and sand, and faintly, he heard the cry of seagulls circling above.

Ahnna's eyes sharpened into focus, and she struggled to prop herself upright on the moldy straw. Her head turned into the wind, her eyes closing as she inhaled the scent of the sea. For her, he thought, it must smell like home. No sooner did the thought pass through his mind than a tear leaked out of the corner of her eye, rolling down her cheek to soak into her gag.

*Don't give up*, James silently chanted. Not at Ahnna, because he knew she never would. But at himself.

*There has to be a way out. A way through this.*

The cart stopped. A portcullis rattled, and muttered conversation filled the air. Dozens of footfalls against stone, and then the canvas was jerked back and Carlo looked down at them.

"Hello, my friends," he said, his tone loud and not unlike the ringmaster in a traveling circus. An effect ruined in no small amount by his gaping eye socket. "It has been an exciting journey, so I am pleased to share that we have made it all the way to the end. Welcome to Amarid's Furnace!" Carlo held his hands wide.

James blinked, taking in thick limestone walls and ceiling, which was all he could see of the prison from this angle.

"Get them out," Carlo barked. "Get them washed. Mother's nose is easily offended."

The Beast stepped off the back of the wagon, and men and women approached. Not uniformed prison workers, but black-clad individuals, their plain and unremarkable faces turning James's palms cold. Because unlike prison guards, Katarina's dark guild made no mistakes.

Two men reached for his ankles and yanked, dragging James out. They hauled him upright while two of the women reached for Ahnna.

The best-trained members of Katarina's military, they were infamous for their ability to blend in and call no notice to themselves, their faces carefully selected to be so ordinary that no one remembered them. They served as spies and as assassins, but also as Katarina's bodyguards and her jacks-of-all-trades for anything she didn't trust anyone else to achieve. Which James supposed was why they were here.

Yet Carlo only wagged a finger at the women who had Ahnna suspended between them. "Clean as a whistle," he sang. "And perhaps some cosmetics to cover up the most exciting moments of our adventures. Mother does hate ugly things." Reaching over, he dragged a finger along the scar on Ahnna's face.

"Yes, Your Highness," one of the black-clad women said. "She will be pristine."

"Wonderful!" Carlo snapped his fingers at the men restraining James with an iron grip. "Bath time!"

Ahnna lifted her head. "Where is my horse?"

"On his way back to Harendell with James's mount." Carlo grinned. "Those who sought your deaths will understand the message."

With his bare feet bound, James had to shuffle across the empty yard while Carlo sang children's bathing songs about ducks before moving on to one about sea creatures and sponges. James forced the noise out of his head, taking in the prison's defenses. The walls were thick, and the portcullis was solid steel. Beyond it a bridge stretched over what he expected was a moat, with another heavy set of gates on the far side. Their progress took him out of sight of the entrance. The dark guild soldiers led him into a chamber with a floor of polished stone that was slightly sloped toward a drain in the center. They proceeded to fasten him at ankles and wrists with steel manacles set into thick posts, and then began cutting his filthy clothes off him.

Carlo sat on a stool, now singing a song about muddy animals being instructed on washing by their exasperated parents. As James met his gaze, the Beast broke off and grinned. "I used to sing to my babies when they were little and did not want to wash. They never said no when I sang, so we shall see if it works for you."

Carlo had three daughters. All by different wives.

Every one of those wives had met a violent end.

James said nothing, only ground his teeth and stared at the drain as the men tossed buckets of water on him. All dignity was lost as they set to scrubbing him with soap that smelled like bergamot, of all things. The men were thorough, their eyes bland in the way of someone performing a mundane task of little interest, and they inspected him down to his fingernails, which were cleaned and clipped and buffed.

All while Carlo kept *fucking* singing.

They dressed him in the cropped coat and tight trousers favored by Amaridian lords, the short red boots they shoved on his feet possessed of long pointed toes that looked entirely ridiculous. When they took pomade to his hair, James's tolerance reached its limit, but his violent protest was brought to a swift end by the arrival of two more men who helped hold him steady while one slicked his hair back from his face, another painting him with cosmetics.

The only mercy was that Carlo had finally shut up. The Beast's expression slowly darkened through the process, the muscles in his jaw clenching and unclenching as he surveyed the results. "You do not look like you," he said sourly when they'd finished. "This is not the face of my nemesis."

"You don't look much like yourself either," James growled, jerking his face away from the man trying to rouge his cheeks.

Carlo barked out a laugh and touched his empty eye socket. "Perhaps I ought to remove the other one, for with only my ears to guide me, you are still James." Reaching over, he caught hold of the guild member's wrist and twisted. "Enough."

"Yes, Your Highness." The man lowered his arm, no pain registering on his bland face though Carlo's grip had to hurt.

"Mother awaits." Carlo snapped his fingers. "Put a hood on him so that no one sees his face. Then bring him."

A hood descended over James's head, and he was hauled onward. The fabric was dense enough that he could see nothing, but his ears picked up the sound of a harp with a young woman singing in accompaniment. They climbed stairs, and the air smelled not like any prison he'd been in, but rather like he'd stepped into a garden. He could practically taste gardenia and lily with each breath, and when they reached the top of the stairs, his boots sank into thick carpet.

The sound of the singing grew louder, the girl possessed of a lovely voice. Next to him, Carlo gave a soft curse and then demanded, "Give me that scarf."

They moved onward, and James heard a door shut behind him.

"Your Highness," two voices, male and female, said in tandem. "Welcome to the Furnace."

"Wardens. Is—" Before Carlo could finish what he was saying, the singing broke off and the girl cried out, "Papa! What has happened to your face?"

One of the soldiers pulled off James's hood in time for him to see a girl of perhaps twelve years of age bolt across the room, white skirts trailing behind her, her expression drawn with fear and concern. She flung herself at Carlo, who had wrapped a dark scarf around his missing eye. James took the opportunity to look for Ahnna, but there was no sign of her in the room.

"My sweet Nina, it is nothing." Carlo swept his daughter up into his arms and turned in a circle, her skirts swirling around them. "All is well now that I am returned to you."

"It is not nothing, Papa." The girl pulled up the scarf and made a noise of distress. "Your eye!"

"I will get a patch and we will play at being pirates."

The girl's face twisted in annoyance. "I am too old for pirates and this is no jest, Papa. Who did this to you? Grandmama will have their heads. Was it him?"

The girl turned her head to glare at James, the fury in her brown eyes blistering. It struck James that this daughter, at least, held affection for her madman of a father.

"Alas, no," Carlo said, putting the scarf back into place. "But since you are too grown for games with your father, perhaps you might find a worthy gemstone to put in my eye's place. You do admire all that glitters, sweet Nina, and I do not wish you to look at me in horror."

"I would never!" Her lips parted for further protest, but Carlo shooed her back toward the instrument. "We shall go to the market later, dearest. Grandmama is waiting."

James's focus moved from the girl to the wardens. A man and a woman, dressed in identical short coats and tight trousers, both with hair dyed bright red, and both with their faces painted stark white with a black beauty spot adorning the same site on their cheeks. Sharp eyes regarded James with interest, and the man said, "He will make a fine addition to the Furnace, Your Highness. That sort of strength will endure for many years."

Carlo huffed out a disgusted breath and shouldered past the man, and James's escort pushed him onward. They moved through the sumptuously appointed room toward a silk screen, which rustled with the ocean breeze. On the far side of it was a wide stone balcony on which stood a tiny woman with her back to them. It was hard to see the details, silhouetted as she was by the sun, but *presence* seethed from her.

Queen Katarina of Amarid. The Crimson Widow.

"Mother," Carlo said, his tone a strange twist of adoration and terror. "I have accomplished the task you set for me."

"And do you think you deserve a pat on the head for your efforts, my son?" Katarina's voice dripped with condescension. She did not turn, keeping her attention fixed on whatever the balcony overlooked. "My guild whispers in my ear of how sorely you botched this task. Dozens of soldiers dead, acres of forest burned, civilian corpses that will require effort to explain away, and your face maimed in a way that will never heal. I stand in the most precarious moment of a plan decades in the making, yet rather than exercising a deft touch you smash at my schemes like a child with a hammer."

Carlo hung his head. "I am sorry, Mother. They proved more difficult—"

"Do not *lie* to me, my son." Tiny pale hands rested on the balcony. "James Ashford has always been your favored playmate, yet despite the fact he has gotten the better of you before, you made a game of his capture rather than treating it like the duty it was."

*Playmate?*

James knew the Amaridians hated him because of his time in the Lowlands. Because he'd been responsible for driving them well past the border and because of the body count he'd left in his wake. Yet Katarina spoke of him and Carlo like two boys in a schoolyard.

"I am sorry, Mother," Carlo whispered, his eye fixed on Katarina's hand, her index finger tapping up and down on the stone. "I could not help myself."

"You understand that you must be punished?"

"Yes." Carlo snuffled, and James could not keep the astonishment from his face, because the Beast was weeping. "I shall deliver myself to the drowning chamber."

*The what?*

"No." Katarina's index finger stilled, but she didn't turn. "Not that."

Silence stretched, and next to him, Carlo seemed to wither beneath it. Seemed to shrink in on himself, so sick with terror was he at the woman before him who was barely half his size.

"Your prize for doing a good job was to be that I'd give you the bastard prince when he had reached the end of his usefulness," Katarina finally said, speaking about James like he was a goddamned toy. "You did not earn your prize, so his fate is the Furnace."

Carlo let out a ragged sob, and it was then that Katarina finally turned.

Older than Alexandra, she was gaunt as a skeleton, her bones protruding and her cheeks hollowed. Her skin was covered with thick white paint that settled into the creases and wrinkles, and her black eyes were sunken deep into her skull. She wore a brilliant crimson wig, the looping curls hanging to her waist, and her black gown was made of layers upon layers of delicate lace.

She trailed her tiny fingers down the necklace James recognized as Ahnna's, taking in her son. Her face abruptly filled with sorrow. It was like watching an animated skeleton in a wig, not a woman, but more shocking was her abrupt change in demeanor. "Oh, my dearest boy. I was told about your poor face, but it's worse than I dreamed."

Katarina stepped up to Carlo and cupped her hand against his cheek, the Beast leaning into her palm. "I will make the Ithicanian bitch suffer in ways she cannot dream of for doing this to you. She does not yet know the meaning of pain."

"You mean it gets worse than wearing this dress?"

Ahnna's voice came from behind the screen, but then she appeared, as tightly bound as James and restrained by two female members of the dark guild. Her hair had been teased up into a tower that rose at least a foot from the top of her head, and she wore a yellow gown of tiered lace that ballooned out around her like a parasol. Her face was painted white, false eyelashes brushing her cheeks as she blinked, and her lips were the color of blood.

She looked awful.

"Carlo, take Nina and go," Katarina said. "You have another engagement to attend to, and you do not wish to be late."

The Beast left with no argument, although the glare he gave Ahnna was murderous.

Ahnna ignored him and took James in, one eyebrow rising. "You look like a jester."

"You look like the doll in the shop that no child wants lest she be given nightmares."

The corner of Ahnna's mouth turned up, but then her attention turned back to Katarina. "Let me see if I have this straight, Katarina.

You and Alexandra are conspiring together to take control of the bridge, but you don't trust your dear friend across the mountains to hold true to the arrangement. So your intention is to keep James and me alive as insurance against her double-crossing you, because we know that it was Alexandra who killed Edward. Which isn't the sort of thing the Harendellians are likely to be very forgiving about, should they discover the truth."

"That's why I captured James," Katarina answered. "As I'm sure you've come to understand, no one believes your truths, Ahnna Kertell." The queen of Amarid smiled, revealing teeth that were concealed by gold and jewels. "You, I will keep alive to control James. To give him something to live for, lest he find a way to end things. His death would vex me."

"Why? Don't you trust Alexandra?"

Katarina chuckled. "No one knows her as well as I do. It seems like only yesterday when she offered an alliance in exchange for getting rid of Edward's whore." Her black eyes rolled to James as he stiffened. "Alexandra was young and idealistic once. She believed in love, but Edward soon crushed those dreams to ruin. She blamed your mother and believed that if Siobhan were gone, Edward would come to love her. I warned her otherwise, but . . ." Katarina waved a hand from side to side. "You know how that went better than anyone, don't you, *Jamie*?"

He bit the insides of his cheeks, refusing to give her the satisfaction of a response.

"Siobhan's death put a damper on dreams for peace with Cardiff, which of course was to Amarid's advantage, but it also gave me leverage over Harendell's young queen. For if Edward learned of the murder that bound our friendship, his wrath would have been a thing to behold. Your father could be so profoundly cruel when he was angered." Gold and jewels gleamed as she grinned at him. "But Alexandra is no longer a young debutante with dreams of love in her heart, and with Edward long in the grave now, she grows bold. You will be the insurance that keeps my dear protégée in check, and Amarid will rise to heights it has never seen when Ithicana falls."

"Ithicana will not fall." Ahnna's voice was frosty, and if James didn't know her as well as he did, she would have seemed the epitome of confidence. "You've tried before. Tried and *failed,* Katarina. How many ships did you lose in the battle for Eranahl?"

"Many." Katarina's tone was unmoved, and James was again struck with how it was like speaking to a corpse. "But it was because Silas was driven to action when patience would have served him better. Driven, it is rumored, by his own son's strategy to save Zarrah Anaphora. Alexandra and I will make no such mistakes. When Ithicana falls to us, it will not rise again. The bridge will run through a dead nation inhabited only by snakes."

It was final confirmation of Alexandra's alliance with Silas and Katarina in Maridrina's invasion of Ithicana. James's father had been enraged by the invasion, smashing cocktail glasses and shouting that Silas hadn't just broken his treaty with Ithicana, but broken his treaty with Harendell as well, his vitriol toward Lara Veliant ferocious in its intensity. Through it all, Alexandra had stood in near silence, offering only the occasional, *Veliants are always the worst sort, darling. Only to be tolerated, never trusted. You warned Delia time and again, but she would not listen, and it seems the apple didn't fall far from the tree with her son, both idealists.* Not once had James ever suspected that she was involved, and it made him realize how badly he'd underestimated Alexandra's ambitions. How badly *everyone* had underestimated her.

Ahnna huffed out an amused breath. "And just how do you plan to achieve that goal when every other nation has failed?"

Katarina rested her hands against the balcony and leaned back, dark eyes calculating and cruel. "It would be a kindness not to tell you my plans, because I think the knowledge will destroy your mind once you are in a Furnace cell. Yet I am told that it was your actions, Ahnna, that caused my son to lose his eye, so I will show you no mercy."

Ahnna smiled. "Carlo did that to himself, Your Grace. Perhaps if he'd not been such a glutton and eaten twice his share of my mushroom stew, he'd see twice as well as he currently does."

Katarina's right index finger tapped twice on the stone, eyes glittering like onyx. "All right, Ahnna. I will play the game of hard truths with you. While you and James were galivanting around the

Blackreaches, William gave Aren an ultimatum: Deliver you to Harendell for execution or face a blockade. Obviously Aren could not hand over that which he did not have, but he has also stood his ground and refused to name you as Edward's murderer. Every bit as loyal as we had heard, which made him so very predictable.

"True to his word, William has put the full might of Harendell's navy to blockading not just Northwatch, but all sea traffic into the gulf. An easy enough task given that the Tempest Seas have been fierce in their storms, so Ithicana is entirely cut off from the north. Those same storms strip the trees and flood the land, but worse, they keep your people from turning to the seas for sustenance. Silas stripped all the stockpiles and stores, and Aren has had neither the time nor the funds to replenish them, so I expect your people will soon be subsisting on snakes and rats."

"The bridge has two ends." Ahnna lifted her chin. "You're underestimating my people's resilience, and we've endured similar circumstances before."

"There is Southwatch," Katarina agreed. "But Maridrina is broken and suffers its own famine, Vencia still in ruins. Sarhina might have used the power of her crown and name to force her people to supply Ithicana, but instead she has diminished her influence by establishing an elected government. Zarrah may aim to aid, but Valcotta is still reeling from its own war, wasting disease has infected their herds, and her people have no interest in a quarrel with Harendell. Cardiff is flush with Harendellian trade, and Ronan's daughter sits on Harendell's throne, so they will not intervene, and the nations of the deep north know better than to involve themselves. Which means that Ithicana, for all intents and purposes, stands alone."

The wind blew in from the sea, lifting Katarina's crimson hair around her like a fiery halo before settling, all while the gulls cried above. Ahnna swayed slightly; James tried to move to her, but his guards yanked him back.

"Alone. Hungry. Broke. Desperate." Amarid's queen punctuated each word with a tap of her index finger on the balcony. "Beggars can't be choosers, Ahnna, so if Amarid comes with a compelling offer of aid, are you so sure that your brother won't take it?"

"Aren knows you are a liar who cares only for achieving your own ends," Ahnna hissed. "He'll never trust you. Never let you in."

"Because you warned him?" Katarina slipped a hand into her pocket and withdrew a glittering ruby necklace. Closing the distance, she fastened the choker around Ahnna's neck, and to James, it looked for all the world like her throat had been slit with the way the gems glittered in the sunlight.

"Alexandra and I were both delighted at the cleverness of your warning," Katarina said, stepping back. "What a bright girl you are to put together the pieces that even great minds like Edward never considered. Shame it didn't work out, because I'm sure Lara, at least, would have taken the message to heart. She's another clever one, though she lacks your honor."

James could see Ahnna's pulse throbbing rapidly above the choker, betraying her distress even as her face remained unmoved.

"Lara won't trust you," Ahnna retorted. "She'll see right through your offers."

"But will she trust her brother?" Katarina gave a soft chuckle. "Bronwyn told me that Keris planned to go to Harendell, and I can only imagine that his ears are being filled with slander against my name, against Amarid's name, all of Harendell's woes cast at our feet. He is clever, but my protégée is unmatched at her ability to manipulate the truth. How long, do you think, until Keris suggests that an alliance with Harendell's oldest enemy might be the path to salvation?"

Ahnna blanched.

"Lara is distrustful, that is true. But her dear half sister Bronwyn has been my honored guest, and I have been a paragon of sympathy over James's cruel treatment of her and his imprisonment of her lover, the lady Taryn. Over glasses of wine, I confessed to her all my attempts to put James in the grave, but also my aim to prevent an alliance in Cardiff. I filled her ears with my fears for Amarid's sovereignty now that such an alliance has come to pass, for how long until Harendell and Cardiff's united force takes not just the Lowlands but also Riomar itself?" A tear cut down Katarina's waxy makeup, and she flicked it away with one painted nail. "Fear does unite even the most unlikely of individuals, no?"

James felt as ill as Ahnna looked, because Katarina was displaying what made her and Alexandra infinitely more dangerous than Silas had ever been.

"But there are those in Aren's council who may not be swayed by the advice of two Veliants," Katarina continued, her smile again revealing the strange fabrication that encased her teeth. "Thankfully, James provided us with the trump card. Come!" She gestured to both of them. "Come stand with me!"

The guards shoved at both him and Ahnna, and James reluctantly shuffled to stand at Katarina's right while Ahnna moved to her left. The queen linked her arm through his, and if James's wrists hadn't been chained to his ankles, he'd have bodily flung the old woman over the edge and to her death.

Instead, he was forced to stand motionless, his eyes moving across the wide moat encircling the prison to a broad expanse of gardens. Men and women promenaded together along the cobbled paths, servants holding sunshades over the ladies' heads. A band of marching musicians in matching outfits struck up, drums and cymbals banging, and the nobility laughing and clapping in delight.

Then Carlo appeared, walking next to two women who were arm in arm.

One of the women was Bronwyn Veliant.

James squinted and leaned, but the Beast blocked his sight of the other woman as they walked down the edge of the garden. Carlo wore a patch over his ruined eye and he was laughing and gesturing at the band, adeptly performing the role of courteous prince.

"Alexandra and I had mused over how best to deliver my overtures of alliance," Katarina murmured. "Who in our arsenal would Aren trust? Who would his council trust? No one quite fit; but then you, James, delivered to us the perfect messenger."

His hands turned to ice, because James knew.

The Beast stepped sideways and gestured to the distant prison as though explaining its purpose. Revealing the other woman's face.

"Your cousin, Princess," Katarina said. "Taryn Kertell."

# 38

# AHNNA

"**T**ARYN!" AHNNA SCREAMED her cousin's name. "Taryn! Bronwyn!"

But over the wind and the gulls and the cursed *marching band*, her shouts were drowned out. Ahnna lifted her hand as high as her restraints would allow to wave, and a rush of adrenaline filled her as her cousin's eyes latched upon her. Yet Taryn only frowned in confusion, and when Carlo affably waved back, so too did Taryn and Bronwyn.

Because all they saw was a peculiar noblewoman with wild hair and cosmetics, not Ahnna. Not James.

Katarina lifted a hand and waved. A horrifying moment ensued with them all staring at one another, and then Carlo gestured down the path. Taryn and Bronwyn carried on with him, all three laughing and smiling.

"It was most fortuitous that members of my dark guild were nearby when James so viciously arrested Lady Taryn," Katarina said. "They were able to slay the guards watching over her and flee, using Amarid's channels to *escape* Harendell. When Bronwyn arrived so desperate to save her love, I was able to ease her heart with the knowledge that Taryn was already safe and on her way to Riomar. Taryn was distrustful of me at first, which was no surprise given the history between our nations, but gratitude goes a very long way. Once there is a break in the storms, I have promised to dispatch both women back to Ithicana on my swiftest ship, one capable of evading the Harendellians, and I will ask for nothing in return other than that Aren agree to a meeting."

Tears poured down Ahnna's face, floating over the waxy makeup and splattering against the balcony stone. Taryn was no fool. She knew the nature of Amarid and its queen. Had fought Amaridian raiders countless times, and there wasn't a chance she'd forgotten that Katarina had aided Silas.

None of which Ahnna spoke aloud, and yet Katarina said, "Taryn might not have been amenable if James had not acted as he did. Barging into her sanctum in the conservatory, destroying the dream she'd finally achieved, and tearing her away from the Veliant princess she loves so dearly. The mind is a funny thing, Ahnna, because somehow, all the resentment and hate Taryn once held for Amarid and Maridrina is now fixated upon Harendell—James, most especially. When I deliver her to Aren, everything Taryn says, everything Taryn does, will center upon her need to destroy that which she hates most. If you think that she will not stoop to allying with an old enemy to do it, you are mistaken."

Ice pooled in Ahnna's stomach that her cousin was being so cruelly manipulated. But she could not deny that the manipulation was masterful in its understanding of Taryn's psyche, and Bronwyn did not have enough experience with Katarina to see through her schemes.

Then, out of the corner of her eye, Ahnna saw James move.

With Katarina's forearm trapped where it was linked through his, James tried to throw himself over the balcony so as to drag the old queen with him. Katarina screeched, her nails digging deep into Ahnna's arm, holding on just long enough for the dark guild soldiers to yank James back.

Katarina staggered into Ahnna, off balance. Ahnna dropped low and hooked her shoulder under the old woman's bony ass, lifting.

The queen screamed, but before Ahnna could fling her into the moat below, the wardens were on her. The man caught hold of Katarina even as the woman jabbed Ahnna with a sharp needle.

Almost instantly, the world began to spin. Around and around, and Ahnna fell to her knees. Slumped on her side, the sky above swirling blue and white, her ears filled with the incessant noise of the marching band. Not unconscious, but unable to move.

"Ahnna!" James was shouting her name, the guards cursing as they struggled to contain him. Then he fell silent, no doubt to the same narcotic.

Above her, Katarina's awful face appeared, lip bleeding where it had been cut on the jewels adorning her teeth.

"Poison has always been my favorite weapon." The queen's black eyes glittered with malice. "Aren fears armies and swords. He fears starvation and disease. But when he falls, choking on his own blood and surrounded by the corpses of his people, the fear he feels as his heart beats its last will be of *me*."

# 39
# JAMES

PARALYZED BY THE narcotic, James had been powerless to fight back as they'd dragged him to the showers, stripping away the finery and paints to dress him in a rough tunic and trousers. From there he was hauled through the prison and out into a massive courtyard. It was entirely paved, with smoking chimneys at all four corners, the walls high and smooth and heavily manned. But it was to the small slitted openings in the paving that James's focus went.

There were dozens of them, and from them shrieks and gibberish poured forth. These were the Furnace cells, filled with men and women who were incarcerated for life. The screams were from prisoners who'd lost their minds to the horror of their circumstances, and he and Ahnna were about to join their ranks.

There were two larger openings in the ground, and James was lowered into one. Left to lie on his back, staring up as masons worked to fill in the opening so that only a small slit remained.

He could not move.

Could not scream.

Could do nothing but lie motionless and stare at the small opening that showed the sky. A sliver of freedom to long for but never achieve, because the only freedom to be won in this place was in death.

The stone beneath him was hot, warmed by the heating system beneath these cells that gave the prison its name. The air grew close and stifling, stinking of the filth of those who had lived and died in this space. Panic filled his chest because it felt like he was being cooked alive.

*Ahnna.* James tried to scream her name but all that came out was a breath of air. They were burying her in the chamber next to him, bricking her in. For a woman like her, there would be no greater torture. She was a storm over the Tempest Seas, a wind that needed to race free over open spaces, not be locked in a hole in the ground.

"Ahnna." Her name was no more than a whisper, but with it, James felt the narcotic beginning to lose its hold. His hands twitched and then his feet. With concerted effort, he turned his head, taking in the stone walls of the chamber. A single wooden cup. A tiny wooden pitcher. A bucket, made in the same rectangular shape as the small slit above.

James rolled his head in the other direction. There was enough light that he could make out a small opening in the side of his cell. "Ahnna!"

His voice was loud now, and in the silence that followed, he faintly heard, "James?"

No part of his body wanted to obey, but James painstakingly forced himself to edge sideways until his face was in front of the opening. Through it, he could see Ahnna lying on her back in the small beam of light from above. So painfully still, the only sign of life the faint rise and fall of her breasts. "Ahnna! Ahnna, I can see you. When you can move, look to your right. There's a small hole."

Ahnna's chest shuddered as she drew in a heavy breath. "James?"

"I'm here." He didn't add that he was on the far side of a wall. Or that they'd been encased in a cell in the ground with no way out. "You'll be able to move soon enough."

Now that the narcotic had lost its hold, James's strength was flooding back to him. "Keep trying to move."

He stood, noting that the floor was curved. As were the walls themselves. James pressed a hand against the stones, grimacing at the scratches in them. Nail marks and dried smears of blood turned black from age. Stretching up high on his bare toes, he reached for the fresh masonry at the very top, but even when he jumped, it was too high.

Sweat ran down his back from the oppressive heat. James retrieved the water pitcher, filling the small cup. He drank without concern. Katarina wanted him alive, and filthy water in these conditions would make short work of that.

He took another mouthful of the water, glaring at the opening above, which might present an opportunity.

*For what?* his doubt whispered. *They've built the cell around you.*

His scowl deepened, but then he picked up the sound of rapid breathing. Too rapid. "Ahnna?"

She didn't answer. James dropped to his knees, looking into the hole. Ahnna was sitting, broken arm resting on her lap. "Ahnna, just breathe."

"They walled us in here. We're trapped."

She wasn't wrong.

His lips parted to tell her not to panic, but James thought better of it. "Katarina needs us alive. If we are alive, there is hope."

"Why is it so hot?" She gasped out the words, struggling to breathe. Then she pressed her hand to the ground. "James, why is the ground so hot? Are they . . ." Her throat moved as she swallowed. "The Furnace. That's the reason for the name, isn't it?"

"They heat the ground beneath us." There was no point in lying. "There's water in the pitcher next to you."

She snatched it up, taking several big gulps before stopping to stare at it. "When do we get more?"

Likely not soon, and seeming to recognize that, Ahnna set the pitcher aside. "She's going to murder my family. My people. And I can't do anything about it."

"Nothing will happen quickly." He hunted for something to say that would keep her calm. "Katarina said the storms have been bad. No one can do anything to Ithicana if the typhoons are battering the Tempest Seas. We have time."

"Time to do what?" Her voice was breathy, like she wasn't getting enough air into her lungs. "There is no way out!"

"Come here." She didn't move, so he repeated, "Ahnna, please."

Slowly, she moved closer to the wall and lowered her face to look through. It was nothing but shadows, but James swore his nose picked up the scent of the sea.

"It's hard to see," she whispered. "Part of me wonders if it isn't even you. If I've already lost my mind."

James retreated to the center of the cell, the beam of light illuminating his face. Almost instantly, her breathing steadied, and he returned to the wall. "Never lose sight of the fact that they need us alive. Need us sane enough to be useful. I'm sure that's why they left this opening between us."

Ahnna moved, and then her hand was reaching into the opening. James slipped his own arm in, closing his hand around hers. Feeling the familiar texture of her skin, callused from toil and war. And she whispered, soft as a breath, "That was her first mistake."

# 40

# KERIS

"I NEED TO get another message to Aren and Lara." Keris paced the floor of his suite in the Sky Palace, barely noticing the expansive view out the floor-to-ceiling windows. Extreme heights had lost a great deal of their appeal to him. "If for no other reason than to get the news about Taryn to Bronwyn so that my sister doesn't do anything stupid."

Saam sprawled across a sofa, disappearing into a pile of decorative pillows. "If the Amaridians actually have Taryn, then Bronwyn might already know." He dug himself out, then rolled on his elbow to regard Keris like a courtesan in a brothel. "I'm not sending another member of your guard to deliver messages. You have to wait for Adrius to return from delivering your first message."

"One more guard isn't going to make a difference to my safety." And Keris had no intention of committing any of this to writing given that everything he sent would be read by Alexandra's spies.

Saam made a face. "It's not about *your* safety, jackass. It's that I want proof the Harendellians didn't slit Adrius's throat the moment he was out of our sight."

It was a valid concern. Alexandra was well aware whose side Keris was on, and all the smiles and easy words about him serving as an intermediary could be lip service. The Tempest Seas were notoriously dangerous, so it would be easy for them to offer up thoughts and prayers for endless missing envoys.

"Daria should be well on her way to Pyrinat by now, if not there already." Saam gave him a long look. "What are you going to do if she brings back a message from Zarrah asking you to leave the Sky Palace and come home?"

"Zarrah won't do that." At least, not if his wife thought his presence was accomplishing something. Unfortunately, Keris was feeling decidedly ineffectual. Since arriving in Verwyrd and learning that Katarina's spies had stolen Taryn from the Harendellians by force, all he'd done was serve as William's favored drinking companion. The king of Harendell seemed to have half forgotten he was on the verge of war, dragging Keris to endless horse races and then out to wine-houses and brothels to drink until the wee hours, after which the king would sleep late, only to begin anew. The idiot courtiers William surrounded himself with knew nothing and seemed not to care a wit about what might be happening in the south. All that mattered was entertainment, women, and spending endless, *endless* amounts of coin.

It was not lost on Keris that with her son focused on carousing, Alexandra was able to exercise almost total control over the nation. "I need to get an audience with Alexandra."

"You have a horse race to go to with Will and his chums."

Spending any more time with William would accomplish nothing. "Get a message to his servants telling him that I'm nursing a hangover and still abed, but will join them later. When they go, I'll find his mother."

Saam shrugged, then extracted himself from the cushions. "All right. Stay put."

---

KERIS SPENT THE next hour pacing his room, eventually ending up at the windows. They were broken into frames, one of the smaller set able to open on hinges to let in a breeze. Keris twisted the mechanism to open it, and then rested his hand against the frame to look out.

Verwyrd appeared tiny below, the figures moving in the streets little more than ants, and a wave of vertigo passed over him. All his life, Keris had been comfortable with heights, even after Otis's fall. But ever since he'd nearly lost Zarrah to the fall that had taken Petra's life, he'd no stomach for them. Only under duress would he climb out this window, and even then, part of him wondered if he could do it or whether he'd freeze, panic sending him plunging to his death.

"Get over it," he muttered, aware that this window might be his only method of accessing the rest of the palace undetected.

"Don't fall out."

Keris twitched, so lost in his own thoughts about heights and what happened to those who fell from them that he hadn't heard Saam come back in.

"William and his friends have departed the Sky Palace," his friend said. "Judging from the guards outside, Alexandra is in the king's study."

Protocol demanded he request an audience, but Keris only said, "Let's go."

With Saam and another of his guards on his heels, Keris wove through the Sky Palace corridors. Servants bowed and curtsied as he passed, and he nodded politely at them without slowing his pace. He reached the study, which was flanked by two soldiers in livery. "I was hoping to take a moment of Her Grace's time."

"Do you have an appointment, Your Highness?" one of them asked.

"It's a matter most urgent."

The guard gave him a smile that didn't reach his eyes. "Unfortunately—"

He broke off as the door opened behind him, Alexandra appearing at the entrance.

"Oh, Keris." She gave him a smile. "I thought I heard your voice. Please excuse the added security. Since the incident, Lord Cavendish has insisted on added precautions. Do come in."

Keris followed her into the room, which was yet another example of Harendellian style. Comfort mixed with a thousand subtle signals that together screamed of wealth and power.

"Do sit." She gestured to one of the overstuffed leather chairs. "Hazel, refresh the tea."

"Yes, ma'am." A young servant girl picked up the tea service and left the room, leaving Keris alone with the dowager queen.

Alexandra still moved stiffly, but the wound to her face seemed to be healing as well as one could hope, her smile twisted by what would be a formidable scar. She touched it absently as she settled herself across from him. "I had thought you off to the races with William."

"I'm afraid I haven't His Grace's stamina for revels."

Alexandra's lips pursed. "We all grieve in our own ways, and for William, it is with distraction."

"Understandable." Except that William didn't appear to be grieving in the slightest for the father he had hated. "I hope Your Grace is recovering well from your ordeal."

"Slower than I might like." She fell silent as Hazel entered with a fresh tea service, two other servants with towers of tiny cakes following on her heels. They set the lot of it on the table, then poured tea for both him and Alexandra. Keris balanced his saucer with practiced ease on one knee, sipping at the hot liquid.

Alexandra took her own delicate sip. "I heard you say to the guards that it was urgent?"

"My man has not returned from Ithicana," Keris said. "I'd hoped you might have word about the well-being of Taryn Kertell."

Alexandra set down her cup with slightly too much force, and it made a loud clink. She winced. "Apologies. I just signed the documents allocating pension amounts to the widows of the men Katarina's spies killed to secure Lady Taryn. It is a painful business. But to answer your question, no. Our spies have not seen any sign of her in Riomar." She waved her injured hand. "Perhaps when your messenger returns, it will be with word that the Amaridians have delivered Lady Taryn to Ithicana."

There was an edge of accusation to her voice, and Keris glanced at his tea, reminded at how easily he could be dispatched with a drop of tasteless poison. "Aren didn't order that attack, if that is what you are suggesting. Nor has he agreed to an alliance with Katarina, despite the rumors."

"And yet Princess Bronwyn was seen in Riomar being hosted with all respect by Katarina herself." Her tone was frosty. "We are aware of the relationship between Bronwyn and Taryn, and you'll excuse me for finding this all very convenient."

It was a damning coincidence, was what it was. Not in a thousand years would Keris have advised Bronwyn going to Riomar if he'd known Katarina's spies had already moved to liberate Taryn, because it screamed collusion. "Bronwyn had not yet reached Northwatch when Katarina's spies attacked your soldiers. She has nothing to do with Katarina's actions, although I will not lie and claim she won't be relieved if Amarid delivers Taryn to her safely."

Alexandra's expression hardened. "You take advantage of our hospitality in the name of mediation. Yet I find myself unconvinced that you act in good faith. Harendell has been injured, first by Ahnna's outburst, then by her attack on our civilians, and then again in the liberation of Taryn by the Amaridians. Edward, murdered. Me, maimed. Civilians, injured. Harendellian soldiers, slaughtered. Harendell has done *nothing* but demand King Aren condemn his sister's actions, but instead he chooses to seek alliance with our greatest foe."

The door opened without a knock, and Keris turned to see William appear, his arm slung around Adrius's shoulder.

"Look who I found coming up the spiral," the king said, the lightness of his voice not reaching his eyes. "His report seemed worth missing the races. How is that hangover of yours, Veliant?"

Keris didn't answer, and William gave Adrius a push forward. Adrius bowed low, his uniform travel-stained and his face marred with exhaustion.

"Well?" Alexandra had abandoned Harendellian civility, her anger palpable as William circled the table to flop on the sofa next to her. "What does Aren have to say for himself? Has his murderous sister returned?"

Adrius's eyes shifted to Keris, and he gave a slight nod, trusting that the man would know what information should best be held back.

"There is no word from Princess Ahnna, Your Grace," Adrius

answered. "It is assumed she remains in the Blackreaches. His Grace, King Aren, will not condemn Lady Ahnna without first hearing her account of circumstances. It is hoped that, should Prince James arrest her, she will be given a fair trial and the opportunity to speak."

"I didn't agree with my father on much," William muttered. "But he was right about Aren being an inept ruler who is wholly self-interested. How Ithicana doesn't grow weary of him putting his favored women before all others is beyond me. One of them should put a knife in his gut and liberate the nation of his idiocy."

The hypocrisy of William accusing anyone of self-interest was a thing to behold, but Keris bit his tongue as Alexandra abruptly rose. She strode to the sideboard and poured a large glass of wine, taking a mouthful as she stared out the window.

"Aren's request is fair and holds to the rule of law of both your nations," Keris finally said. "Guilty or not, Ahnna deserves a trial and the chance to speak her piece." He hesitated, then added, "Have you heard word from Prince James?"

"No," William responded even as Alexandra said, "Yes."

William stiffened, looking to his mother in surprise. "You've heard from Jamie?"

"From his men. I didn't wish to alarm you until I'd heard more, but . . ." Alexandra exhaled a long breath. "James was separated from his men by an avalanche that Ahnna set off. A malicious trap that was nearly the end of him. He's not been heard from since."

*Fuck.* "How do they know it was Ahnna who set off the avalanche? They happen naturally all the time."

"Because she was seen fleeing the scene." Alexandra didn't turn from the window. "There is no doubt that it was her."

Which, assuming this was the truth, meant that Ahnna was alive. Unless James had caught her.

Though it was possible she'd caught him.

William rested his head in his hands, and for all the conflict of sentiment the king of Harendell had for his half brother, his distress seemed legitimate. "If she hurts him, I'll . . . I'll . . ."

"How much more injury must we suffer, Your Highness?" Alexandra asked softly. "How many more attacks on my family and people must I endure until the proof of Ahnna's guilt is sufficient for Aren to give us justice and condemn his sister? This is not the behavior of an ally."

Given that Ahnna had acted to protect her family and then in self-defense, there was no chance of Aren turning on her.

"Ahnna's actions are her own and not reflective of Ithicana," Keris said, ignoring the thrum of anxiety rising in his veins, because everything was going wrong. "Aren desires peace. Desires trade. Desires the bridge to serve to the benefit of all nations. It is imperative we keep level heads, lest those we rule suffer the consequences."

"Your homeland already suffers the consequences." Alexandra strode to the table and retrieved a folded piece of paper from a stack, tossing it before him. "It is a plea from Maridrina's new parliament that we resume trade, because their famine has grown worse."

Keris skimmed the document, his stomach souring at the desperate plea for grain and livestock. At the account of fatalities and rise of disease. Maridrina was always dancing with hunger, but all that had happened beneath his father's rule, and his own, had put the nation in a state that it struggled to extract itself from. "Valcotta will—"

"Valcotta *cannot* aid." Keris's heart skipped as Alexandra withdrew another report, tossing it before him.

"Wasting disease in the cattle herds," she said. "Harendell knows that illness and we know it well. The empress will have to order mass culls to prevent the spread, and the dead animals will need to be burned, for infected meat is fatal. Valcotta will scarce be able to feed itself, much less Maridrina and Ithicana. Hunger will reign in the south, and it will be because Aren refuses to condemn a murderer. Every life lost is on *his* hands, so I ask you to urge him to reconsider his position."

"If you care so much for civilians, then reopen trade and negotiate with civility," Keris snapped. "Ithicana has acted in good faith and all Aren asks is for a chance to hear Ahnna's testimony, but you won't even commit to that. What is it that you are so worried she'll say?"

"Obviously she'll lie to try to save her own neck!" William leapt to his feet. "Why are you defending her, Veliant?"

"I'm not." Keris met the king's gaze. "But it troubles me that you will punish Aren, punish Ithicana, punish the whole fucking south for the actions of one woman. Whatever she did or did not do, Ithicana has only ever acted in good faith. Yet you treat them like the enemy!"

The door opened again and Keris nearly turned to curse at whoever had interrupted, but he bit his tongue when Cavendish stepped inside.

"We've received a report from Riomar." His expression was grim. "Taryn Kertell has arrived and is being treated as an honored guest alongside Bronwyn Veliant. Katarina has committed to returning both women to Ithicana. The Amaridians sing Ahnna's name in the streets for killing King Edward." He drew in a deep breath. "But worse are the rumors gleaned by our spy in deep cover in Katarina's palace. King Aren has promised Amarid choice trade on the bridge if Katarina delivers Ahnna safely, and the Beast was set to the task." Cavendish's throat moved as he swallowed. "Carlo knows James is in the Blackreaches, and he aims to kill him."

Every eye in the room slowly tracked to Keris.

"Ithicana has only ever acted in good faith," William said softly. "And yet Aren conspires with our oldest and most dangerous enemy to steal justice from our grasp. Worse still, he has set the Beast to hunt my brother down."

What could Keris say? It was a twisting of the truth, but no one here would believe Aren's true intentions. "Aren does not seek James's death. If Katarina, or Carlo, takes advantage of circumstances, then that is between Harendell and Amarid. One can hope that James had the wisdom not to cross the border."

All three of them were staring at him unblinking, and Keris was struck with the sudden certainty that he was a fly trapped in a spider-web.

"Until this moment, I had been so certain that Aren had no involvement," Alexandra finally said. "I thought him a brother moved by grief, touched by his sister's desire to protect him and his family. That certainty fades the more we learn of the conspiracies to undermine my family and Harendell itself."

"He wasn't involved." The words came out from between Keris's teeth.

"We know of Ithicana's dire straits," Alexandra replied, then took another sip of wine. "We know they had aspirations for Harendell's wealth, but it strikes me that they were looking to secure Amarid's wealth as well. They were playing both sides, and when Edward did not give Aren what he wanted, he climbed into bed with Amarid entirely. The alliance is dead, and it is Ithicana who tore it to shreds."

Keris's lips parted, but William cut him off before he could speak. "Family or not, how can you defend him, Veliant? Maridrina is starving, and it is because of the Kertell family's focus on satisfying their own impulses and self-interest. For generations, it has been said that trade hung on the Kertell family's whim, but I think it's time that ended. They have proven themselves unfit in every possible way."

His hands felt like ice, because Keris could see where this was going. Could see how anger and the desire for vengeance had spiraled into ambition. How the oh-so-Harendellian eye for profit saw an opportunity. "What, precisely, are you suggesting?"

"We've suggested nothing," Alexandra's voice was cold as ice. "But Sarhina's parliament has suggested abdication as the solution. It seems no one wants Aren Kertell to rule anymore. All his reign has brought is disaster and death."

It had been the ambitions and greed of other nations that had brought disaster and ruin, but they already knew that. This wasn't about Aren, not anymore. It was about the *fucking bridge*. "Abdicate to *whom*? Because I presume that you don't aim for an infant princess to rule a nation. Nor do I believe that you have another Ithicanian family in mind to wear the crown."

"It never made any sense for a structure dedicated to trade to be managed by a half-feral warrior nation," Alexandra said. "It requires the guiding hand of those with heads for business. Those who are governed by civility and who possess strong relationships with other nations. Those with the might to dissuade the sort of violence that plagues the bridge year after year."

"Harendell." Keris all but spat the word.

Alexandra lifted her glass and took a sip of her wine. "It is the logical choice."

William shifted restlessly, betraying what Keris had already known: The king of Harendell was nothing more than a puppet played by his mother.

Keris met Alexandra's green-eyed gaze, and though he'd always known she was a threat, he understood now that he'd sorely underestimated her. She had the ambition of his father. The cleverness of the Magpie. The skill at emotional manipulation of Petra. But what made Alexandra Ashford dangerous was her capacity for calculated logic and patience. "My father caught Ithicana off guard and infiltrated it from the inside, yet I can attest to the incredible toll in life and coffer that the invasion took upon my homeland. Would you bring the plight that plagues Maridrina down upon Harendell?"

"Don't be ridiculous by suggesting that we'd pursue Silas Veliant's strategies." Her smile was chilly. "If Aren is wise, he'll abdicate to William without protest. If he is not, we will enforce a full blockade on the north and launch a campaign educating the Ithicanians that everything they suffer is a result of Aren's desperate desire to cling to power. His selfishness in putting his women above his people. His ambition in courting the Crimson Widow. I think it won't be long until the Ithicanians bring us his head. Trade will flow, and under William's rule, all will be brought right in the world. The people will rejoice."

And Alexandra could do it. Harendell was a titan with near-infinite resources, and courtesy of James and Lestara, it had Cardiff at its back.

"We do not wish death upon Aren and his family, despite the injuries that they have caused us." Alexandra set down her glass, then rested her hand on William's arm. "You would be doing all nations, not just Ithicana, the greatest of services if you left us and traveled to meet with Aren. If you convinced him to make the wise and selfless choice to turn over power so that we are not driven to secondary measures."

To leave would be the easiest. To board a ship and rejoin Aren and Lara, bringing with him what he'd learned. Except what good would that do them? Words would not save them. Advice would not save them. His sword arm certainly would not save them.

Then there was Zarrah and the challenges his wife would be facing in Valcotta. His place was at her side, and that was where his heart was and where he wanted to be. Except he knew what wearing the crown meant to Zarrah. Knew that doing what was best for her people held a huge portion of her heart, and that meant he needed to do what was right for her crown. And the bridge falling under Harendell's control would benefit no one but Harendell.

He had to take every risk, make every sacrifice, to keep that from happening. That meant holding his ground, because within Verwyrd, he could snip away at the spider's web from the inside.

And Keris knew exactly how he would start.

# 41

# AHNNA

THE FIRST FEW days of imprisonment had been shockingly easy to endure, for she and James had spent every waking moment testing the limits of their cells and learning the routines of the prison. Ideas whispered back and forth in the small opening between them, both of them well aware that there was likely someone tasked with listening to their every word. They were kept fed and watered, so while the hope they might find their way free endured, Ahnna had not felt the impact of being confined.

Yet as each of their ideas failed, and days turned to weeks, the walls seemed to press closer. The air seemed to grow hotter. This prison was old, and it became abundantly clear that given the countless prisoners who'd lived and died in these cells, there was no method of escape the Amaridians had not seen attempted.

Which meant they had stymied them all.

"Water!" a voice called from above, and knowing from experience that if she wasn't ready the wardens wouldn't wait, Ahnna rushed to lift her pitcher up beneath the small opening. A moment later, water flooded down, filling her pitcher even as it drenched her hair and clothes. She'd learned to get as much of it on her as possible, for it was the only respite from the heat.

And it was always so painfully short-lived.

"Waste!" A thin cord dropped from above, and Ahnna swiftly tied the waste bucket with a tight knot, watching as it was lifted up and through the opening. A clean one dropped through a moment later, and she caught it and set it next to the thin piece of rope she'd yanked out of the warden's hands on the first day. Rope, she'd swiftly discovered, that was made of some sort of weed or vine. It was far too weak to bear more weight than a full bucket, and within a day of her stealing it, it had dried up in the heat and was crumbling apart.

"Rations!"

She lifted her hands and caught the bread, sliced apple, and piece of ham that fell from above. There would be no more communication from above until the following day, so she sat next to the opening to James's cell. The walls were curved, and when she sat, the opening was at about shoulder height. It was six inches across and the wall itself was about a foot thick at that point, which meant they could both reach into each other's cell, and it was possible to see each other when the light was right.

She heard James's soft sigh as he sat on his side of the wall, and the faint crunch of him biting the apple. Normal human sounds that she'd once taken for granted but never would again.

"This is how Zarrah must have felt." She chewed slowly on her bread. "I never really appreciated what she went through on Devil's Island until now. What it was like to know that those you care about are in danger but being helpless to aid them."

"She escaped."

"She was *rescued*," Ahnna corrected. "As was Aren when he was trapped in Silas's inner sanctum. But no one even knows we are imprisoned, James. No one other than Katarina's family of ingrates, the wardens, and her dark guild even knows we are in Amarid. Carlo killed everyone else who might have carried the news. Even Alexandra will have been told we're dead. Which means no one even knows we need to be rescued."

"We don't need to be rescued."

Ahnna sensed James's stubborn scowl, and despite herself, she smiled. "I believe you are exhibiting what is known as denial."

"You mispronounced perseverance."

She rested her head against the stone, watching the small rectangle of light in the ceiling fade into blackness as night fell. "Not knowing is the worst part," she finally said. "Maybe the storms have held true and Taryn has not even returned to Ithicana yet. Or maybe Aren is already on his way to meet with Katarina to hear the offer that will be Ithicana's damnation." Her chest tightened. "Do you think she'll come to brag about her success, or do you think I'll spend days, weeks, months, *years* wondering about a family that is dead and buried?"

"You can't think like that. It will drive you mad."

"To think about anything else feels like I'm betraying them. It feels right that I should suffer, because everyone I love is suffering." She traced a finger along the mortar joining the stones that formed her cell. "Which is not to say that I'm giving up. Only that it feels right that I be miserable while I try and fail and try and fail."

"Entirely reasonable."

"Thank you for the validation, Jamie."

His huff of annoyance filled her cell. "If you call me that again, I am going to fill in this hole myself."

She moved her hand down to the opening, picking at a rough patch of stone with her fingernail. "Why? Everyone else who is close to you calls you Jamie."

"Only those who met me before the age of six. And just because I tolerate the nickname does not mean I like it."

"You shouldn't have told me that . . . *Jamie.*"

"The idea that being trapped with *you* would be motivation to stay alive was a significant error in Katarina's judgment, *Princess.*"

His tone brought to her mind the moment in the boat when he'd kissed her, the remembered sensation of his tongue tracing the scar on her face sending a pulse of remembered pleasure between her legs. It was hard to remember what she'd been thinking, pushing him away. Hard to recall the anger over what had been done and her fear of what was to come, though she knew that had been what had driven her. All she felt now was regret that she'd not allowed herself to give in to desire, because it felt as though she'd never get that chance again.

"Have I mentioned that I like it when you call me Princess?" And then, because she knew it would get a rise out of him, she added, "Although not as much as when you tell me I'm a *good girl*. There's no one else alive with that sort of audacity."

James laughed softly. "You haven't earned that one lately."

"I'll have to remedy that failing."

They fell into silence, listening to the shrieks and moans of those trapped in the other cells of the Furnace as the wardens fed and watered them. She laid her cheek against the hole, knowing that she should rest. That no solutions would come if she was exhausted. But the screams of the imprisoned grew louder, fueled by food in their bellies, as was the case every day. Cries for help. Desperate pleas for loved ones. Demands to be put down. Ahnna's heart beat faster, and with the oppressive heat, it felt for all the world as though she had fallen into a hellscape from which there would be no deliverance.

Lifting her unbroken arm, she reached into the opening between her cell and James's, and a gasp pulled from her lips as her fingertips connected with his.

"Are you all right?" His voice was low.

She shook her head, then whispered, "No."

The heat of the floor seemed to grow hotter, and Ahnna imagined that whoever tended the great furnace below had added fuel to the flames. Making the cells hot enough to madden but not hot enough to kill.

"They feed the furnace six times a day." James's breathing was as strained as hers, both of them trapped in a box of steam. "It's a regular pattern. The worst of the heat lasts for about the count of two thousand, but it's worse after water rations due to the steam."

Only half an hour. Yet having endured it so many times, Ahnna knew it would feel like eternity. "What is the count at?"

"I confess, you caused me to lose track."

Ahnna dragged in breath after breath, feeling as though she were suffocating. "James?"

"Yes?"

"I changed my mind."

"About what?"

"I want you to touch me."

James gave a soft laugh, then coughed. "Is your goal to drive me to tear down the wall between us with my bare hands, Princess? Or are you only aiming to add to my torment?"

Her mouth curved with a small smile, each breath a challenge as the water that had been poured into her cell evaporated off the hot stone. "Both?"

"Wicked woman." But then his hand closed around hers. "I've got you."

Ahnna tightened her grip on him, feeling as though his touch was the only thing holding her sanity in place as the prison raged with the howls of its inmates and the furnace beneath slowly cooked her alive. "Don't let go."

"Never."

He held tight to her hand through the worst of the heat, but it gradually eased, the steam dissipating through the small hole above them. It became easier to breathe, but Ahnna kept her cheek pressed to the wall, her hand locked in James's.

"I'm afraid I'm going to lose my mind," she whispered. "I'm afraid I'll go mad, and that everything that matters to me will burn and I'll never know it."

"I won't let you lose your mind. We'll find a way out of here—it's just a matter of figuring out how."

Panic started to rise, as choking as the steam, but then James's fingers moved from her hand. Slowly, he traced up the veins of her wrist to her elbow, and then back down, and the sensation made her pulse hum in an entirely different way. Up and down her wrist, and then he said, "Would you like to know what I'd do to you, should I find myself on the far side of this wall, Princess?"

"Yes." The word came out as almost a moan, and she struggled to comprehend how the feel of his fingers on her wrist was somehow the most erotic sensation she'd ever experienced in her life.

"Are you sure you can handle it?" His voice was low, and it stroked places that his fingers couldn't reach.

"I am certain." There was no other answer, because if he stopped touching her, stopped speaking to her, her mind would surely crack.

"I hadn't finished kissing you when you decided to stab me with my own sword," he murmured, tracing a finger over her palm and making her fingers curl. "And I'm a man who finishes what he starts, so I'd surely start there. Tasting those sweet lips while my tongue explores that mouth of yours, all while I think about how it will feel when those lips are around my cock."

Ahnna's breath caught, heat rising to her cheeks because no one had ever spoken to her like this. No one had dared. "Your Highness, this hardly seems appropriate language for a prince."

"Nor for a princess. Shall I stop?"

"No." She squirmed, rubbing her thighs together, an ache forming between them. "No, my curiosity is piqued."

"I wouldn't dare leave you unsatisfied, even if it is only your curiosity." His fingers locked with hers, and he pulled, forcing her shoulder deep in the hole, her cheek pressed hard against the stone. His lips brushed her knuckles, and Ahnna whimpered, wishing desperately that her other arm wasn't broken so that she might put fingers between her legs.

"I'd move to your throat," he murmured. "And leave my mark on your skin, because you are mine, Ahnna, even with walls and circumstances and bad history between us. I'd rid you of those clothes and lay you down on the ground while sucking on your perfect breasts, tasting those nipples that I recall are the color of roses. I'd make them pinker still because I know you like the feel of teeth on your skin."

Ignoring the pain in her arm, Ahnna moved her right hand between her legs and found her clit.

"You're touching yourself, aren't you?" He tugged harder on her arm, stone digging into her shoulder, grip on her wrist implacable. "Enough of that, Princess. You'll come when I'm ready for you to come."

Ahnna's pulse roared in her veins, desire running so hard and hot that she felt almost feral with the need for climax. But she obeyed him.

"This entire time, of course, those long legs of yours will be wrapped around me." He kissed her knuckles again, then sucked on one of her fingers. "I confess to having a small obsession with your legs, Princess, and I've stroked my cock to completion more times than I care to admit with thoughts of them filling my head."

Ahnna's back arched, her nails digging into the skin of her thigh to keep from touching herself. Her climax was rising on his words, on his voice, and on the feel of his mouth on her fingers.

"I think next, I'd spread those legs wide to look at that pretty pink pussy of yours. Admire how wet you are and how much wetter I intend to make you, and then I'd—"

"Oh, nemesis! What are you whispering about down there?"

Ahnna sucked in a shocked breath at the sound of Carlo's voice. "Oh, James!"

The snarl that tore from James's lips sounded barely human as he shouted back, "Fuck off, Carlo."

The Beast gave a low laugh. "I think not, James. I have some crushing news that I'm desperate to share with you."

Ahnna almost whimpered as James let go of her arm, the ache of being left on the brink of climax almost painful, but then Carlo said, "It is the beginning of the end for Ithicana."

# 42

# JAMES

JAMES'S FURY AT having been interrupted with Ahnna vanished like flames doused with water, replaced by dread.

Rising to his feet, he went to stand beneath the opening above and looked up. Carlo was nothing but an outline, backlit as he was, but he could smell the Beast's cologne from here.

"There you are," Carlo murmured. "In no way diminished, I see. Not even the Furnace is enough to break you." Then his head tilted and he made a retching sound. "But God help me, you stink."

"So sorry to offend," James retorted, but his tone belied the panic churning in his stomach. "I'm afraid my cell wasn't equipped with a bathtub. Or soap. It does, however, sit over a fiery pit of some version of hell."

Carlo gave a soft snort. "Nothing so fantastical, I'm afraid. Just a large room with a big stove and a man who must be replaced every year because his lungs turn black from the labor." He lay on his stomach, looking down at James. "This is beneath you, James. I told Mother that, but she says there is no other place we can be certain that you will be contained, which I cannot argue with. Still, it grieves me that you will meet your end rotting in your own filth. You deserve a glorious demise."

"And yet here I am," James said even as he silently screamed, *Get to the point!*

"Here we are."

A cloud must have passed overhead, because the light of the sun fell away and James could make out Carlo's face. His missing eye had been replaced with a polished red gemstone that glittered as he moved.

"Are you going to get on with it?" James finally asked. "Or do you just wish to discuss my accommodations?"

"Ah, yes. Thank you for reminding me." Carlo cleared his throat. "It has been such an uneventful span of time. Ithicana's typhoons have prevented any sea travel south, so Mother's plans to send Lady Taryn home to serve as our poisoned apple were much delayed. I have just returned from the deep south, where we were waiting for a break in the storms. I am pleased to inform you that Lady Taryn and Lady Bronwyn should be arriving in Ithicana shortly to begin making their appeals to Aren for an alliance with Amarid. Which will be timely, because Prince Keris's messenger should be arriving at nearly the same time to deliver Alexandra's threats. The titan of the north breathing hot fumes down Aren's neck right as Mother's poisoned apple promises deliverance. It is a beautiful thing."

James's chest hollowed.

"Mother has them convinced she's terrified of the alliance between Cardiff and Amarid. Truly, she has such a gift for the theater. Though between you and me, I do think she fears the Crehan clan, Ronan most of all. Alexandra does as well, which is why she put an end to your uncle Cormac. Poisoned him right across the table from Keris himself!"

*Cormac is dead?*

"We'd always intended to kill him, of course. He knew the truth about William's pedigree, and Mother has taught her protégée not to leave loose ends. But this was two birds with one stone, for now Keris believes that Amarid has grown so desperate to stymie the northern alliance that we have reduced ourselves to sloppy attempts to frame

Harendell for assassinations. Alexandra has ensured that no one stands in the way of Keris's messages back to Ithicana." Carlo snickered. "I do not normally care for these sorts of manipulations, for they are a woman's weapon, but it is delightful to watch nations north and south dance about on Mother's web."

"Mother's? Or Alexandra's?" James asked between his teeth. "She's the bigger spider."

Carlo made a soft humming sound. "That is why we keep you, James. The biggest threat of all to William's reign is you. And you are ours."

"Unless I rot to death."

Carlo was silent for several long moments, the only sound the endless wailing of the Furnace inmates, then he said, "Cormac is just the first to die, James. Ronan will meet an accident soon enough, and then we will pick away at the House of Crehan until Lestara is the heir apparent. Or, more accurately, the child in her belly. The baby will be king of Harendell. King of Ithicana. King of Cardiff. Yet Alexandra will rule him, and Mother rules Alexandra. It is stunning, isn't it? A proper masterpiece of plotting, because the largest roles of manipulation go to those Aren trusts the most."

Logically, James had known that it would come to this, but hearing the plans to murder his family from the heartless lips of the Beast made them so much more real. So much more *certain*. And trapped as he was, there was nothing James could do about it.

"Enjoy the balance of your day, dear nemesis." Carlo got to his feet. "Not even the misery on your face is enough to keep me in this stink."

The Beast disappeared from sight.

As he departed, so did the cloud cover, and sunlight streamed through the small opening, stinging James's eyes. He endured it for a heartbeat, and then returned to the opening between his cell and Ahnna's, leaning his back against the wall.

"I'm sorry, James." Ahnna's voice filled his ears, and he reached up to take her hand through the opening. It felt like she was the only thing keeping him alive.

"I hate this," he replied, running his thumb over her knuckles. "I hate not being able to do anything."

"I feel the same way." She was quiet, the only sound her breathing, then she said, "But I think Alexandra made a mistake."

James turned his head, looking at the shadow of her face. "How so?"

"I don't think killing Cormac was part of her plan. I think she was rushed into it by whatever drove Cormac to meet with Keris. I think she was worried what Cormac might tell Keris and chose to silence him."

He shook his head. "It sounded to me as if Keris is very much part of their plan. They are using him to soften Aren up for an alliance with Amarid so they can strike Ithicana from the rear."

"I know, but they couldn't have predicted that Keris would go to Harendell. I think they've pivoted to use him, but in doing so, they've overextended their hand." Her fingers flexed in his. "I think Alexandra reacted impulsively, murdering Cormac to silence the spread of William's secrets and then blaming Amarid to further that scheme, but it lacks her usual foresight. Because Ronan will not take this death lightly, will he? He already wants revenge against Katarina for Siobhan's murder, and that desire will be compounded by Cormac's murder."

"He'll push William to move with him to attack Amarid." The wheels in James's mind began to spin, following her course of thought. "And if William refuses, or if Alexandra digs in her heels to protect her ally, Ronan might withdraw his support from the alliance."

"Exactly. Alexandra has woven so many threads, and I think she's finally tangled herself in this one. William is the one thing that causes her to act impulsively, because she'll do everything and anything to protect him and his reign." Ahnna's grip tightened. "She's made a mistake, James. And if she makes one, she'll make more."

There was a fierceness to her voice, and James relished her strength. Hope was dim for them in this place, but she had not given up and neither had he.

"Carlo does not like that you are imprisoned," she whispered, her grip tightened. "Katarina is punishing him as much as you by keeping us in here, and that might be something we can exploit."

"How?"

"I don't know yet, but my gut tells me that Carlo might be our one ally in escaping this place."

James's lips parted to remind her that if Carlo released them from the Furnace, it would only be because he had a more vicious end planned for them, but then the warden's voice called down from above, "Prisoner, approach!"

# 43
# AHNNA

"WHAT NOW?" JAMES muttered, letting go of her hand.

Ahnna bent her head to watch him walk back into the beam of light, looking up at the male warden above. "What do you want?"

"His Highness finds your smell offensive and has ordered you bathed." The warden's voice was tight with irritation. "Strip."

"I'll pass," James growled. "I'm not interested in you turning my cell back into a steam box."

"The furnace fires are banked and will be kept so for the balance of the day," the warden snapped, and it struck Ahnna that the man resented this. The Furnace cells weren't just a prison. They were also torture chambers, and Katarina's need to keep them alive and sane undermined that purpose. "Strip."

"Or what?" James asked. "You going to come down here and punish me for disobeying?"

The warden gave a soft chuckle. "Perhaps we starve your woman."

An unsubtle way of reminding them that Ahnna was being kept alive to manipulate James.

"No, you won't." James's tone was bored. "Katarina wants her alive. Katarina wants her sane."

Silence stretched, but James only stood with his arms crossed in the beam of light from above. Finally, the warden said, "We'll give your woman wash water. And soap."

Ahnna's toes curled at the mention of soap, the thought of washing away the sweat and filth coating her skin more alluring than anything else they might have offered, but James didn't respond.

"And the furnace stays banked until tomorrow," he finally said. "That's the deal, and if you go back on your word, Warden, this will be the last concession you ever get from me."

The warden was silent, but Ahnna could feel his rage seething through the stone above her. His unbridled fury at having his shrine to sadism bent to a different purpose. But she also suspected that his fear of Carlo, and of Katarina, was more powerful than his rage. "It will be so. Strip."

Ahnna knew that it would be appropriate to look away, but she remained where she was as James pulled off his prisoner garments and stood naked beneath that golden beam of light. It illuminated his skin, and Ahnna couldn't help but admire the hard lines of his body, shoulders broad and waist narrow, the muscles of his ass worthy of a sculpture.

He caught a small block of soap that the warden dropped, then turned his face up as water was poured down. It cascaded down his body, and he set to scrubbing himself with the soap, hands moving over his body with vigorous efficiency, and a memory of his words filled her mind. *I confess to having a small obsession with your legs, Princess, and I've stroked my cock to completion more times than I care to admit with thoughts of them filling my head.*

The ache of need returned with a vengeance, her breath quickening as she watched his hand move over his cock, more water sluicing down from above to pool at his ankles. She'd seen him nude before, but Ahnna found it impossible to take her eyes from him, her imagination filling with images of her hands on him, her mouth around him, and a soft noise escaped her lips.

James must have heard, because his head turned in her direction, and she knew that he knew she was watching. His cock stiffened beneath his grip, and Ahnna's lips parted, lust for him making her feel almost feral with need.

He lifted his face. "All right, Warden. Time for you to fulfill your part of the bargain."

"Prisoner, approach!"

Ahnna twitched at the female warden's shout from above. Biting at her bottom lip, Ahnna moved beneath the opening, the sunlight stinging her eyes.

"Strip."

It wasn't easy getting her clothes off with a broken arm, but Ahnna managed, standing naked but for the splints bound to her forearm. The warden dropped a piece of soap, and Ahnna held it to her nose, inhaling the scent of lavender.

Then water poured down. It was icy cold, and she gasped with shock as her nipples peaked, but the shock faded with the sweet pleasure of sweat being washed from her skin. She rubbed the soap over her body, building a lather on her breasts, then ran a soapy hand down one leg. Then the other.

Water poured from above, but over the splash against the floor of her cell, she heard James's intake of breath. Heard the sound of his hand working himself as he watched her, and Ahnna pivoted so that he could see her ass as she ran the soap over it. More water, and she moved to her hair, cleaning the long lengths so that it hung in loose curls to her waist.

Her body ached with the need to be touched, and as more water sluiced down, she slipped her fingers between her legs, aroused beyond reason knowing that James was watching her. She heard his intake of breath as he climaxed, and it was nearly her undoing, but then the warden snarled from above, "Get your clothes on, prisoner."

Ahnna ignored her. Discarding the remains of the soap outside the pool of water, she walked slowly toward the hole between their cells, then leaned against the wall. "Touch me."

"You never cease to surprise me, Princess."

She closed her eyes, a soft gasp tearing from her lips as he reached through, his index finger parting her sex.

"You must have enjoyed your bath," he murmured, his finger slipping inside her. "You're very wet."

"I enjoyed watching yours more." Her nails scratched against the wall, her body shuddering as his finger curved, stroking inside.

James made a soft noise of amusement. "Liar. I was watching you. I should have negotiated for a bath every day."

She'd known that he had been, but the confirmation sent a thrill through Ahnna's veins. "Consider it an incentive to find a way out of here."

By way of answer, he slid another finger into her, his thumb finding her clit, the sensation making her knees weak. She'd already been aroused close to the point of climax, and his touch was on the verge of sending her over the edge. "Don't stop."

"I am yours to command, Princess."

Her body was rigid with tension, the aching build between her legs so intense she could barely breathe, but Ahnna clung to the edge and refused to go over. Because she didn't want this moment to end, didn't want his hands to leave her body, but her control trembled as he teased and stroked her sensitive flesh.

"Come for me, Ahnna," he growled, his words punctuated by his fingers plunging in and out of her. "Give in to me."

Her control shattered, and her climax exploded through her body with such force that she sobbed his name. No part of her cared who heard, because she was consumed by pleasure that would have brought her to her knees if not for his fingers inside her. Stroking and teasing out every last tremble until she was spent.

Ahnna nearly wept as he withdrew his hand, and she slid down the wall until her cheek rested against the edge of the opening. Through it, she could see the shadow of his face. Hear the rapidness of his breath, and she knew that there was no other man in the world for her but James. She was his, circumstances and wars and fucking prison cells be damned.

Reaching through the opening, she took hold of his hand and gripped it hard, whispering, "I'm bringing this wall between us down, one way or another."

---

AHNNA FELL ASLEEP with her fingers locked with James's, drifting in and out of fitful slumber, her unconscious mind stewing over the knowledge that Taryn was on her way back to Ithicana and that time was very much of the essence. When she woke, her eyes felt full of sand as dawn light poured in through the opening above. Her mouth was equally dry, the awful heat having returned to the cell floor. It cooked the moisture out of her body and left her with a blinding headache.

Pulling her hand from James's grip, Ahnna crawled over to her water pitcher and filled her cup. She drank long and deep, but as she lowered her arm into the sunlight, Ahnna went still. Her skin was smeared with white dust, noticeable now because the rest of her was relatively clean. Powdered mortar left behind when they'd cut the hole between her cell and James's. *Gypsum.*

She squinted at the walls of the cell. The builders had used lime mortar to build the Furnace, but lime mortar took a long time to set. The modification to her cell and James's had been done quickly, so they'd used gypsum. Wheels began to turn in her mind, and Ahnna scratched at the thick white crust that had caked in the lines between the stones of the floor from years of piss building up. *Saltpeter.*

Neither was ideal or a pure source, but Ahnna was Ithicanian, which meant she knew explosives.

And she knew them well.

She surveyed the meager supplies in her cell, and then picked up the soap and the dried vine ropes scattered about.

It was a start, but it wasn't enough to accomplish the plan growing in her head. Crawling over to the hole, she hissed, "James!"

"Is something wrong?"

"No, I have an idea." Pressing her face to the opening, she softly whispered her plan, finishing with, "What do you think?"

"The wardens will be tough to trick. Keeping people imprisoned is their expertise."

"True, but none of their other prisoners are Carlo's precious nemesis."

He made a sound of aggrieved agreement. "Fair."

A thrill of energy coursed through Ahnna, and she said, "Tell them you want to speak to Carlo."

# 44
# AREN

THE STORMS HAD been relentless, which had driven off the Harendellian blockade and kept Ithicana safe from attack, but also kept everyone hidden inside, travel only possible through the bridge. While his people were used to the long periods of confinement, no one had handled the idleness well this time, and the endless discussions of how to bolster Ithicana's defenses had frequently devolved into arguments and shouting matches.

He and Lara had traveled through the bridge to the northern islands to begin the process of evacuating anyone vulnerable farther south, as well as to consider what changes could be made that would counter the information Harendell had of their defenses. New shipbreakers were constructed, new traps set, but now that there was a gap in the storms, all hands and vessels were on the water with nets and lines, barrels of salt ready to preserve the catch for lean times to come.

Ships from neutral nations were taking advantage of the gap to make the treacherous run between continents, and Adrius had secured passage on one such vessel, his aim to return to Keris. Lara had filled the man's ears with what information they could risk sending, it not lost on anyone, including Keris's bodyguard, that there was a chance the Harendellians might risk Zarrah's wrath by putting Adrius to the question.

Aren had also opened Southwatch's market to general trade, not just transport through the bridge, and eliminated all taxes and fees. It undercut trade at Vencia's market, but Aren didn't care. He hadn't been south himself, but he was told the water around Southwatch was thick with ships from the north, mostly Amaridian, only Harendellian and Cardiffian vessels traveling on to Vencia. The south was buying up goods with greed, as was Ithicana, every bit of gold and silver Aren could get his hands on going to buy the supplies Ithicana needed.

To prepare for war.

It didn't feel like enough. Not even close. Which was why Aren had spent the day in the water rigging traps for any ship that might venture too close. Now dusk was falling, but as he retrieved his shirt from where he'd left it on some rocks, a shout of warning caught his attention. "Ship on approach!"

"It's Amaridian." Lia walked toward Aren, handing him a spyglass. "They're flying a white flag. What do you want to do?"

For most of his life, Amarid had been a thorn in Aren's ass. A thorn that had dug painfully deep when Katarina had allowed Silas to use her navy at the price of a small fortune in rubies. Ithicanians beyond count had fallen on Amaridian blades, but it was not lost on him that they were also Harendell's enemy. Katarina had been aggressively pushing for a renegotiation of trade terms since the moment Ahnna had left, as well as a desire to *mend fences,* but he'd received no information from Bronwyn since she set sail to Riomar. That could be because of the storms, but it might also be because Amarid wasn't willing to risk Harendell's wrath by aiding Ithicana in any capacity. It was possible that this vessel carried the answers he sought. "Send out a boat to see what they want."

Lia trotted down to the hidden cove to give the order, and Aren said to another of his men, "Bring word to Lara that Katarina wants something."

Because his skin was crawling with the certainty that this ship wasn't here to sell him expensive wine.

The Amaridians anchored just outside the shipbreakers' range, and Aren watched how they nervously surveyed the seas. How they looked ready to raise anchor and flee at the sight of Harendellian sails, which were a common enough sight this far north. William had made it clear that there was no tolerance for his lines being crossed to trade with Ithicana, and any ship, from any nation, would suffer the consequences. For the Amaridians, that would mean being sunk.

A small boat navigated out of the cove, several of his soldiers aboard. Raising its sail, it skipped across the whitecaps until it neared the Amaridians, then slowed. The soldiers aboard switched to paddles to maneuver close.

Amaridians leaned over the rail of their ship and conversation was exchanged, but even with the spyglass, they were too far for Aren to read expressions. Then a lean woman walked to the rail, and his heart skipped with recognition. "Bronwyn's with them."

More figures massed around the Maridrinian princess, but then the ship rotated and he lost his view of those climbing down to the longboat. He lifted his hand to shade his eyes, seeing the flash of a long brown ponytail before Bronwyn blocked his view of whoever it was.

Aren's heart lurched, and he took a step toward the water.

"What's going on?"

At Lara's voice, he turned. She was approaching with Delia in her sling, sword bouncing against her hip. Jor was at her heels, as was Delia's nurse, Becca.

"Bronwyn's with them," he replied. "Another woman as well."

"Ahnna?" The hope in his wife's voice hurt his heart, and he handed her the spyglass.

"I can't see her face," she muttered. "But Lia is hugging her. Whoever it is, she's one of ours."

Aren had known that from the way the unidentified woman had balanced on the boat, and yet his skin was crawling with unease. Unease Lara must also be feeling, because she motioned for Becca to take Delia. The jostling woke her and Delia made a squawk of protest, but swiftly settled under the nurse's experienced hand as the woman headed in the direction of the barracks, Jor following with a hand on his weapon. More guards shifted out of the cover of the trees to follow Ithicana's heir, but as they did, a scout approached.

"Your Grace," he said, out of breath. "One of our vessels is on approach. Prince Keris's man Adrius is with them."

Back so soon. Adrius would, no doubt, have valuable information, but Aren felt nothing but trepidation. "Bring him up the cliffs so the Amaridians don't see him."

The scout nodded and departed at a run.

"Let's go down to the water." Lara pushed her braid over her shoulder and then drew her sword. "The Amaridians wouldn't risk running afoul of the Harendellian fleet for the sake of returning Bronwyn to us." She gestured with the tip of her blade. "They aren't making ready to sail—they're waiting."

"Keep a close watch for Harendellian vessels," Aren said to one of his soldiers, and though it felt like a strange request to make given Amarid had always been the enemy and Harendell the ally, he added, "Warn the Amaridians if you see sails on the horizon."

"Yes, Your Grace."

Aren shadowed Lara as they wove down the narrow trail to the water. She moved at a swift trot, but the knuckles on her right hand were white from how tightly she gripped her weapon. Equal parts eager and terrified as he pleaded to every higher power that it was Ahnna whom Bronwyn had brought home with her.

His pleas floated away on the breeze as his eyes latched onto the woman climbing out of the boat, the soldiers around her laughing and cheering. "Taryn?"

Lara had drawn up short as well, her eyes wide with shock.

Aren shoved down the unwelcome sense of disappointment as his cousin strode up the beach toward him, her arm linked with Bronwyn's. They stopped, and Taryn inclined her head. "Your Grace."

"None of that." Aren wrapped an arm around her, pulling her close. "How are you here? Bronwyn told us you had been arrested by Prince James for espionage and were being taken to Verwyrd."

"I was." Taryn pushed back from him. Her eyes slid to Lara, but then locked with his again. "Amaridian spies witnessed my capture.

On the way to Verwyrd, they attacked my guards and rescued me, then brought me through their channels to Riomar. Where Bronwyn was waiting." She turned a smile on the Maridrinian princess, who pulled Taryn close. "We'd have been back sooner, but the storms made passage impossible."

Everyone fell silent, because in that moment, several soldiers approached with Adrius in tow. The Valcottan man looked exhausted beyond measure, but he bowed low. "Your Graces." His gaze went from the Amaridian vessel to Taryn and Bronwyn. "Lady Taryn, I assume? Your liberation was my one piece of happy news, but it is good that you were able to deliver it yourself."

"You've seen Keris?" Lara asked.

Adrius nodded. "Yes, and circumstances are dire. Though the information he sent back with me is best kept to as few ears as possible."

Aren nodded at Lia, and she softly murmured orders to nearby soldiers to move out of earshot.

"The Harendellians took many casualties when the Amaridians liberated you," Adrius said to Taryn. "If they weren't so occupied with Ithicana, I think they'd be making plans to retaliate."

"Did Katarina indicate why they freed you, Taryn?" Lara asked. "It all happened so quickly that the order couldn't have come from Katarina in response to Edward's death. Why would she risk his anger?"

"Don't think I'm worth it?" Taryn snapped, but then she winced. "I'm sorry. It's a fair question." She was quiet for a moment, then said, "Katarina fears Harendell's alliance with Cardiff. Fears that after Harendell has its way with Ithicana, they—with Cardiff at their backs—will come for Amarid. Her spies . . . they know her goals, and I think they saw rescuing me as an olive branch Katarina might offer to Ithicana. Not as good as Ahnna, but . . ."

"The difference is that you didn't do anything wrong," Bronwyn growled.

Aren gave her a flat stare before asking, "Is there any word about Ahnna? Any sign of her?"

Adrius cleared his throat. "She was last seen weeks ago deploying an avalanche trap that nearly killed Prince James. The trail was wiped out, but he chose to pursue her alone. He's not been heard from since."

Anything could have happened in the intervening time period, but Aren's heart still leapt at the confirmation she'd been seen.

"Katarina sent word to Carlo as soon as I arrived in Riomar," Bronwyn said. "But he and his men found no sign of Ahnna, or James, in their search."

"The Harendellians know about your request for aid," Adrius said. "Spies in Katarina's household. They see it as an attack on the Ashford family, and their anger is a thing to behold."

Aren listened in silence, his chest hollowing as Adrius relayed all that Keris had learned, finishing with, "Alexandra aims to take the bridge, one way or another. Keris suggests you bolster defenses and call in all favors, all alliances, because the Harendellians show no signs of standing down."

All that Adrius had said rattled in Aren's skull, and his gaze slowly moved to the Amaridian ship bobbing on the waves. "Taryn, what does Katarina want? Because the Crimson Widow didn't send you back to us out of the goodness of her heart."

"A meeting," Taryn answered. "Between you and her, face-to-face, to discuss an alliance against a mutual antagonist."

Aren drew in a deep breath, seeing Lara's gaze narrow in his periphery. It was one thing to renegotiate trade terms, quite another to ally himself with a lifelong enemy.

"Harendell is as dangerous to Amarid as it is to Ithicana," Bronwyn said. "Katarina told me herself that she believed Harendell would move to take control of the bridge, and that threat has now been conveyed by Alexandra herself through Adrius. If Ithicana falls to Harendell, Amarid will be locked in on all sides, reliant on ships risking the Tempest Seas to reach the southern markets, and that would be catastrophic for them. Katarina fears Amarid will weaken in its isolation, and that Harendell will first claim the Lowlands and then use it as a staging ground to invade Amarid." She gave a slow shake of her head, azure eyes distant. "Katarina's not a good person, Aren, and Carlo is no better. But they fear what is to come as Harendell's power grows, make no mistake."

Taryn nodded in agreement. "I know better than anyone what Amarid has done to us in the past, but no one knows the Harendellians like they do. That rivalry is as old as the nations themselves, and with Ronan of Cardiff set on vengeance for his sister's murder, it's only a matter of time. They are desperate."

So was he.

Katarina would never be his friend. Yet as Aren stared at the bobbing mast, he also knew that when one stood alone, one could not afford to be particular. "Do you have a time and a place for this meeting?"

"Yeah," Taryn said. "I do."

# 45

# KERIS

"I BOUGHT YOU SOMETHING."

"You shouldn't have," Keris responded, not lifting his head from the book he was reading detailing the history of the conflict between Cardiff and Harendell. "Our friendship doesn't rely upon material goods."

Saam snorted. "Maybe not, but my longevity does depend on keeping you alive."

"Zarrah won't punish you if I meet my end on your watch." Keris flipped the page, then cursed and snapped the book shut, nothing inside telling him anything he didn't know.

As it was, he was having difficulty focusing, his mind going back to his parting words with Adrius before the man set off to Ithicana again. Or, more accurately, to Adrius's words. He'd confirmed the disease in Valcotta's herds, but also that Zarrah was not responding to Aren's letters requesting aid. It made Keris sick with unease, because as angry as she might be with him, Zarrah would *never* take that out on Aren, whom she considered a dear friend. There was something keeping her from responding, but with news from the south patchy due to a particularly bad storm season and the absence of traffic on the bridge, he'd been unable to learn more.

*Please be safe*, he silently pleaded, turning his head to the window and staring south, feeling torn between the welfare of the love of his life and the family he held dear. Then a yip caught his attention. "What in fuck is that thing?"

"A poison-sniffing dog." Saam grinned and set the white creature on the floor. "Sit!"

It sat.

"That's not a dog," Keris said, eyeing it. "That's not even a cat. That's a fluffy rat."

"She is a dog and her name is Fiona. She's from the most pre-eminent breeder and trainer in Harendell, and there is typically a seven-year waiting list for one of their dogs. Fortunately, Zarrah's name goes a long way." Saam patted the animal on its head, then deposited a folder of paperwork on the desk. "Her documents, as well as the jeweler's certificate for the diamond collar she came with."

The fluffy white animal did indeed have a glittering collar around her neck. "That she ... came with? Saam, precisely how much did you pay for this *dog*?"

"One cannot put a price on safety," his friend replied, which Keris suspected was how this dog breeder had sold him on this thing. "She is trained to identify three hundred and forty-two types of poisons, and the demonstration they gave me was very compelling. Don't worry about the cost. One of the banks in Verwyrd gave me the coin."

"That's not free gold!" Keris scrubbed a hand over his face. "They withdrew it from my accounts."

Saam shrugged. "Fiona is worth it, trust me."

Keris highly doubted that, but he also had bigger concerns. Namely that he needed to make progress in his goal to undermine the alliance between Cardiff and Harendell. Having Ronan withdraw his support would undercut Harendell's ability to go on the offensive, especially if he stirred up conflict in the north. The peace between the two nations was tenuous and new, and with James absent, probably dead, the only thing binding the two nations was Lestara. Especially given that whatever profits in trade Cardiff hoped to gain in the alliance would be much reduced if Harendell held the bridge. It was an alliance destined to fail eventually, Keris only needed to hurry the process along.

Which meant turning the nation against its new queen.

Keris exchanged stares with the tiny dog, but then the door to his suites flew open and William appeared. "Veliant, my good man! Care to go on an excursion?" Then he caught sight of Fiona and grinned. "Have you got yourself a Fitzgibbons? My God, mate, you have either choice dirt on them or bottomless coffers."

Keris gave Saam a sour glare, but his friend only shrugged as William dropped to his knees next to the wriggling cotton ball, petting her with enthusiasm.

"Mother has a Fitzgibbons, of course, and Virginia had one for years. Ginny wept like a babe when he died. I should really get her another to make up for . . ." William trailed off, then shook his head and stood. "At any rate, no sour feelings about Ithicana and the bridge, right? It's just politics, and Mother has a way of getting me riled up. No need for it to come between friends."

William was looking everywhere but at him, and Keris nearly sighed at the sad predictability of the other man. At his need for validation. At his need to be liked despite constantly engaging in behaviors that made him profoundly unlikable. "Where is Princess Virginia?"

"At Whitewood Hall, our hunting lodge in the north. Ginny and Lessy don't quite see eye to eye, and grief has a way of making my sister harsh with her tongue. I thought it best Ginny take some time away from the stir of the court to recover. Her ladies are with her."

Keris's eyes turned to the diamond collar around Fiona's neck. Virginia Ashford had been the ringleader of the Harendellian noblewomen who'd taken Lestara's punishment as their personal mission, and it was no shock that Lestara had them all removed from court. Though it was a bit strange that Alexandra had allowed her daughter to be sent away on account of Lestara's pride. It supported his certainty that Lestara's life and reign would not continue after she produced an heir.

"Ginny's behavior was abhorrent," William continued, his eyes also having moved to the dog. "Lestara has been a paragon of forgiveness, but she still finds seeing those women very upsetting. I've already made it up to Ginny by agreeing to wed her to Georgie, and once she's on the Cavendish estates with a baby or two, she won't mind not being allowed at court. Even if she does, it's your fault, Veliant, not mine. You had everyone convinced that Lestara was to blame for what happened in Vencia, but the reality is that she was Petra's victim. Virginia wouldn't have acted as she did if you had been truthful. You just wanted to be rid of the harem so you could chase after Zarrah."

Keris's eyes filled with the memory of Lestara glaring up at him from a mass grave, hair covered with the dirt he'd shoveled upon her, and it was hard to keep the sarcasm from his voice as he said, "No sour feelings though, right?"

William huffed out a breath, then slowly lifted his face to meet Keris's gaze. "Bygones. Let's head out of the city and find some fun."

Keris retrieved his coat from where it was tossed across the back of a chair and followed William into the corridor, mechanically responding to the other man's mindless chatter while he considered how he might leverage Virginia Ashford. William's friends met them in the courtyard, Cavendish among them. As they started down the spiral on foot, William drinking and laughing with his courtiers, Keris fell in alongside Cavendish. "I heard you're to wed Virginia Ashford."

"Yes."

"Then her exile from court must be a bitter medicine to swallow."

Cavendish scoffed and shook his head. "Exile? Hardly. It's temporary and understandable."

"That's not what William said," Keris took a flask from one of the courtiers, watching the man run to the railing and howl like a wolf, already drunk. "He said that Lestara can't bear the sight of her."

"William says a lot of things. Those of us who know him well know when to take him seriously or not." Cavendish shook his head as Keris offered him the flask. "Virginia will be back at court before the year is out."

"I'll pray that is the case." Keris broke into a trot and caught up to

William, pushing the flask into the king's hand. "It's a beautiful day in Harendell, Your Grace. Let's live it up."

---

IT WAS NO different from the strategy he'd employed against his father. A pocket full of silver, a deck of cards, and endless alehouses full of men more than willing to talk if he kept their cups full.

Shuffling the deck, Keris dealt the cards to the men before him, one eye on the bar where William was surrounded by his friends.

"You enjoying your time in the Sky Palace, Your Highness?" one of the men asked after looking at his cards. "Are they keeping you properly entertained?"

"It's a bit quiet, to be honest." Keris increased his bet. "I've heard it's livelier when Princess Virginia and her ladies are at court, but they are at Whitewood Hall."

"She'll be back soon enough, I reckon. Miss Ginny likes to be at the center of things."

It was the way all the civilians spoke about Virginia. *Miss Ginny*. As though she were everyone's favored little sister, and Keris had not heard a word against her. "Apparently she's at Whitewood Hall grieving."

"My cousin is friends with the sister of Lady Elizabeth's chambermaid," one of the men muttered. "She said Lady Elizabeth was informed that she was not welcome at court."

Keris made a noise to indicate mild curiosity.

"Is it the same for Miss Ginny?" the first man asked, his brow furrowed.

"Surely not," Keris said. "She's the king's beloved sister."

All the gamblers at the table went still, then their eyes shifted to where William was laughing at the bar, his friends encouraging him to chug the contents of a glass.

"The Ashford siblings were always tight as ticks," one of the men grumbled. "Now James is missing and Miss Ginny is all but banished. It's not right."

Keris took a sip of his wine and frowned at his cards.

"The Cardiffian witch cast a spell on him, mark my words," another said. "Must have cast a spell on Good King Eddie too. There ain't no other explanation for it." His eyes slid to Keris. "Did she try any of her witchery on you, Your Highness?"

Keris shrugged, seeing Cavendish's scrutiny out of the corner of his eye. He spoke loudly enough that the man would hear. "I've eyes only for my wife."

They all nodded approvingly, but then the first man said, "We all heard the horror of the sacking of Vencia, Your Highness. Nasty work, that was."

Visions of his home in rubble flashed through Keris's mind, and he didn't fight the remembered panic as he dug through the ruins of the inner sanctum, certain that he'd find his half sister Sara's body. The bodies of all his family. Sarhina had kept them all safe and evacuated the city, but so many refused to go. And lost their lives for it. "The sad truth is that when asked to abandon everything to evacuate, many chose to stay. To fight to protect their homes and livelihoods, and they lost their lives to Petra's vendetta. If I am fortunate enough to live to be an old man, I will still remember the smell and the sound of carrion birds. Still see the splashes of blood and the bodies of the very old and very young lined up in graves. Sarhina was and is a leader without equal, but she made the mistake of believing the greatest threat lay outside Vencia's walls when the real danger stood at her back." He folded his hand and stood. "I'm out, lads, but I'll buy another round before I go."

It was the third time he'd had a variation of this conversation. He always allowed the civilians to bring up the topic and never overtly said a word against Lestara. There was no need to, because all knew what she had done. Joining William at the bar, he dutifully drank the cup of shitty whiskey pushed in front of him. "If I win any more off your people, they'll riot. Time to move on."

William hiccuped, then grinned. "All right."

Arm slung around a courtier by the name of Archie Bennett, William staggered out the door. Keris followed, but the moment he was outside, Cavendish slammed a palm into his chest, drawing him up short. "That conversation looked serious for a game of cards with low stakes."

"It wasn't low stakes for them." Keris took a step back, then moved to go around, but Cavendish blocked his path again.

"What were you discussing?"

"If you must know, they asked why Virginia had not returned to court. I lied and told them I didn't know, but apparently a lady by the name of Elizabeth has complained to her servants that she's banished from court."

Cavendish's face soured at mention of Elizabeth. "Stay out of it, Veliant. You know damned well why they aren't in Verwyrd. Once tempers cool, Ginny and her ladies will return."

"I'm sure it's only a matter of months until Lestara forgets being led around by a collar and made to piss in the corner while Virginia and her ladies laughed."

Keris pushed past Cavendish and trotted to catch up to a singing William, noting that the soldiers forming the king's bodyguard all had expressions of disgust on their faces. His behavior was not kingly in any circumstances, but with Harendell teetering toward war, his blatant carousing would be rubbing many the wrong way. Which of course meant that Keris intended to encourage it.

He slung an arm around William's shoulder, then said, "Join me for a game, Majesty? I grow weary of playing for coppers."

"I've already lost enough coin to you at the races," William replied, veering sideways and into an alehouse.

It fell entirely silent as they entered, all eyes turning to them, and Keris had to fight back a cold smile as he recognized men from earlier establishments.

"Well, this is a dour crowd," William muttered. "Perhaps we try another?"

He turned, then someone shouted, "The witch let you out to play, Your Grace?"

William stiffened, then whirled, staggering into Keris before righting himself. "Who said that?"

No one answered.

"Who the fuck said that?"

Silence.

"Let's leave, Your Grace," Cavendish muttered. "It's just drunks speaking out of turn."

William looked ready to argue, but then allowed the other man to pull him back. But as he turned, someone shouted, "Queen of Carrion!" and another followed up with, "Butcher of Babies!"

"Silence!" William shrieked. "Bring forward those who dare to speak such slander!"

No one so much as twitched.

"I will have your tongues!" William shook with rage. "Who dares to speak against my queen?"

"Where is Miss Ginny?" It was one of the barmaids who spoke, a broad woman who looked as though she took no nonsense from patrons. "Where is the princess? Your sister, Your Grace? Why is she not at court?"

William stared at her, his alcohol-addled mind not putting together the connection. "Grieving, you fool!"

"Ain't got anything to do with her treating the *Good Queen* as she deserves, do it?"

Next to him, William purpled with anger. "Guards!" he shouted. "Arrest her!"

"She ain't saying anything we aren't all thinking!" The man who spoke abruptly stood, banging into his table as he did. His cheeks were ruddy with drink. "The witch betrayed Maridrina to Empress Petra to get rid of this useless tit"—he jerked his chin at Keris—"and the whole damned city burned. We all know the truth of it."

"That's lies!" Spittle flew from William's lips. "Petra was the villain. She manipulated Lestara. Tricked her!"

"Harendell don't want a queen who can be manipulated or tricked any more than we want a murderess!" the man roared. "Cast the witch back to Cardiff! Bring home Miss Ginny!"

"Cast back the witch! Bring home Miss Ginny!" The crowd filling the common room erupted into a chant.

William released a howl of rage. "Arrest them! Arrest every last one of them and throw them in the stocks for slander!"

"You're under her spell, William," the barmaid screamed. "Cast out the Carrion Queen!"

This was going better than he might have hoped, but as Keris fought back an expression of delight that the populace had risen so quickly, William withdrew his sword. In a flash, the tip was digging between Keris's ribs, right above his heart.

"Tell them!" William screamed the words, but tears were flooding down his cheeks. "Tell them the truth, Veliant! Tell them what happened in Vencia was your fault, not Lestara's! Tell them, or I'll skewer your heart, empress be damned!"

The blade cut through his clothes. Keris tried to step back, but his shoulders struck the door.

"Your Grace, stop!" Cavendish reached for William, but the king swung wildly with his free hand, clipping Cavendish's jaw even as soldiers poured in. All around was chaos as the civilians fought to flee, even as William screamed, "Arrest them! Arrest them!" his blade digging ever deeper.

Blood ran down Keris's chest, and his options spiraled through his head. If he drew a weapon on the king, he'd be arrested, but if he stood his ground, William would kill him. There was a third option, and that was to absolve Lestara, but then the one method he had of destroying the alliance with Cardiff would be spent and wasted.

"Tell them!" William wiped at his tears, face crimson with distress. "Tell them she's not guilty!"

Despite the situation, Keris felt a flood of empathy for this child of a man. It was not witchery that Lestara had used to control him, but a simple manipulation of his weakness. Of his desperation for validation. He refused to see the truth of what Lestara was, because doing so would erase all that she had done to bolster William's opinion of himself.

"Queen of Carrion! Widowmaker! Butcher of Babies!" The shouts echoed through the alehouse as soldiers slammed patrons to the ground, manacles clinking as men and women were arrested. "Cast her back! Cast her back!"

"Tell them!" William screamed. "Make them believe she's innocent!"

He wouldn't. He couldn't. Not with dozens of eyes on him, even those pinned to the ground watching to see what he would do. Keris clenched his teeth—

Only for Cavendish to tackle William to the ground. "Think clearly, man! If you kill him, you martyr him. Martyrs only tell truths!"

Cavendish hauled William to his feet, then pulled him out of the alehouse. More soldiers fell in around their king, and they started back to the spiral, leaving Keris standing bleeding in the doorway while soldiers arrested every patron to the man.

Saam and the others leaned against a stone wall, their arms crossed. "You're fucking insane," his friend snapped. "You should just fall on your own sword and be done with it."

Blood dripped down his chest, soaking his shirt. Keris leaned against the same wall, watching as soldiers dragged out civilian after civilian, loading them into a waiting prison cart.

"You've been bad, haven't you, Your Highness?"

He turned his head to find a pretty woman approaching.

"I like that in a man."

Keris rolled his eyes, pressing his hand to the wound. "Not interested, love. Move along."

"Not peddling that sort of ware," she replied. "The name is Elsie, and my grandfather once wrestled a bear. You can see it in the sky when the moon wanes."

*Cardiffian.*

"You're playing with fire, Your Highness," Elsie said, leaning against the wall next to him. "Your desire to dethrone the woman who betrayed you and Maridrina won't just cost her—it will cost all of Cardiff. You fuel accusations of witchery, but she won't be the only witch to burn, you understand? Yours is not the path to longevity."

"I've never sensed that old age was in the cards. Or the stars." He watched the soldiers fighting with a big drunk, it taking three of them to get the man in a cart. "Are you here to threaten me into leaving Lestara alone?"

"No. I'm here to discover if you've heard anything of James's fate."

There was something in her tone that suggested she cared more about the prince than a simple spy should. "Hope that he lives is fading. He was separated from his men and pursued Ahnna on his own, and there is the added complication of the Beast being dispatched in pursuit. But I'm sure you know all that."

"Yet another death to add to the tally." Elsie closed her eyes, pressing a hand to her chest as though it hurt. "Ronan will grieve."

Keris gave her a moment, then asked, "You have Ronan's ear?"

"He hears all. You have something to whisper?"

"Something to shout. Alexandra aims to take the bridge, and once she has it, she'll have no need for Lestara or Cardiff. What she will have is wealth beyond measure, which means the strength to spread her son's empire."

"To the Lowlands. To Riomar itself, and Cardiff will have its vengeance on the Crimson Widow," Elsie said. "Siobhan, Cormac, and James will be able to rest easy once their murderer is put to the sword."

Her words echoed Petra's, and Keris could not help but think of all the ruin the dead empress had left in a similar pursuit.

"And what then?" He met Elsie's golden-brown eyes. "Is vengeance worth creating an empire so vast and powerful that no one can stand against it? Or does Ronan's quest for blood just blind him to the truth that power so vast cares nothing for friends or allies, only conquest? I understand the desire to hate Katarina for what she has done, but her efforts to curb Harendell's rise serve all of us. Amarid is not the threat."

Fury flashed in the woman's eyes, her lips pulling back as she spat, "You think me a fool, Veliant? All that you do here is to serve your own interests in Ithicana. You care nothing for Cardiff. Care nothing for the harm that has been done to us by the Crimson Widow."

Keris pushed away from the wall, feeling dizzy though he wasn't certain if it was from loss of blood or too much wine. Nodding at Saam, he started down the street, but looked over his shoulder. "Scream of the threat of Harendell in Ronan's ear, Elsie. Scream and scream until he hears, because the flames are licking at Cardiff's heels, and the fire has been set by Alexandra Ashford."

# 46
# AREN

KATARINA HAD SELECTED an island located just inside Amaridian waters and well west of where the Harendellians patrolled. As though showing favor for the meeting, the Tempest Seas were entirely quiet, the wind gentle and not a cloud in the sky. Not that a storm couldn't appear in a near blink of an eye, but Aren could not have asked for better days to travel the high seas.

Especially given Lara was with him.

"Are you feeling all right?" Aren rested his hands on the railing, arms on either side of her. Every breath he took brought with it the sweet smell of her hair, and he rested his cheek against it as he watched the waves.

"No." Lara leaned back against his chest. "I wish the seas were wild. Then I'd at least know that the storms are protecting Ithicana while my back is turned. Harendell will take advantage."

"She's safe. Becca and Nana are with her, and Jor as well." Lara didn't like to be separated from their daughter. It had been a challenging birth, but despite being bloodied and exhausted, Lara had wanted to care for Delia herself from the very first time she'd held her. A stark difference from his own mother, who'd left his and Ahnna's care to others. Aren had always believed that she'd done so because it was impossible to rule and parent a small child at the same time—had defended his mother against Ahnna's hurled accusations of neglect—but watching Lara balance both made him realize that his sister had been right. His mother had simply not wanted to be present, and his father had never been far from her side.

"I'm aware." Lara's tone was clipped, but then she sighed and rested her hands on top of his. "I'm sorry. I know Taryn and Bronwyn think we can trust in Katarina's desire to outmaneuver Harendell, if not in the woman herself, but it's hard to set aside that she was partners with my father. With him, she had free usage of the bridge, and I can't help but think that's her goal. Or at least, close to it."

"I'm sure it is." He caught sight of the island in the distance, a large Amaridian naval vessel anchored next to it. "But it won't hurt us to hear what she says. If nothing else, it will satisfy my curiosity—I've never been face-to-face with her before."

Lara made a soft humming noise that was neither agreement nor disagreement, and not for the first time since Taryn had returned, he felt the weight of the unspoken question between them: How far were they willing to go to protect Ithicana?

How low were they willing to stoop?

And would his people accept allying with a ruler who'd actively tried to destroy them before?

They drew closer to the island. It was small, the center of it thick with jungle but the beach wide and white, gentle waves rolling onto shore. On the center of the beach a large blanket was spread, and sitting on it was an old woman with a young girl having a picnic beneath sunshades held by servant women. Soldiers watched over them from afar, all armed to the teeth, but they seemed relaxed and their numbers were as promised.

Sails were lowered, then the anchor rattled its way down.

Unlike the Amaridians, Aren's soldiers seethed with tension as longboats were lowered, and sweat dripped down Aren's spine as he debated just what Queen Katarina would ask for in this idyllic scene she'd painted.

He helped Lara into a longboat, the light breeze catching at the blue silk of her dress and sending it swirling up, revealing golden sandals adorned with pearls. Her hair was long and loose, the only jewelry a pair of sapphire earrings that Zarrah had sent along with all of Delia's gifts. Beautiful as she was, his wife needed no more adornment to look like a queen.

Waves and oars brought them swiftly to shore. He stepped out into the shallow water and then reached into the boat to scoop Lara up. "Wouldn't want to ruin your fancy footwear," he murmured, setting her down on the dry sand.

"Liar," she replied. "You were counting how many knives I have under my dress."

"Three."

Lara sniffed. "Five. But two of them would have necessitated you getting somewhat more handsy than is appropriate on a beach with the queen of Amarid watching."

"I'll find them later."

Lara shot him a smile, but he saw the nerves in her azure gaze as she took his arm. Together, they strode toward Katarina, their guards matching the distance the Amaridian soldiers had given their queen.

As they drew closer to the picnic, Aren took in the queen who had caused him so much trouble over the years. He knew her to be near sixty years of age, but with her gaunt face and heavy wrinkles, she seemed closer to seventy. Her hair, wrapped in a tight knot behind her head, had likely once been red, but it was now so mixed with white that it looked almost pink. She was extremely short of stature and painfully thin, her subdued blue dress covering her from neck to practical leather shoes. She wore large diamond earrings that made her earlobes sag, and her smile revealed teeth gone to rot, several of them missing. Age took a different toll on everyone, but on Katarina of Amarid, the toll had been steep.

Yet the dark eyes that fixed upon him were sharp as tacks, so he would not make the mistake of believing her mind equally diminished.

"Welcome," she said, voice soft. "It is a pleasure to finally meet you, Aren."

"Katarina."

Amarid's queen looked Lara up and down. "Every bit the beauty I was told. Please, sit and join us. We were enjoying the sea breeze."

Aren held Lara's hand as she lowered herself to the blanket and tucked her feet beneath her, adjusting her skirts as she did to keep the knife strapped to her calf from showing. He sat cross-legged next to her, the position feeling awkward for the magnitude of this meeting.

"This is my granddaughter, Nina." Katarina gestured to the pretty young girl next to her wearing a white dress. She had dark red hair and dark eyes that were as sharp as her grandmother's. This was the Beast of Amarid's eldest daughter.

"Your Graces." The girl inclined her head. "It is an honor to meet you both."

Aren nodded at her, and Lara smiled warmly at the girl.

"Thank you for agreeing to meet." Katarina gestured to the servants, who set out plates of cakes and poured small glasses of wine, which were set on trays before them.

"I know that your first concern is for your sister, Princess Ahnna, and I wish I had better news." Katarina withdrew a small pouch from the pocket of her skirt and handed it to Aren.

With shaking hands, he upended the contents into his palm, staring at the familiar necklace of gold, black diamond, and emerald. Once his mother's. Then Lara's.

A gasp tore from Lara's lips. "Oh God. I packed it for her in Bronwyn's things. Ahnna had it with her."

He couldn't breathe.

"It was found among bones," Katarina said. "The white lions had . . . *disturbed* the remains, but this was found nearby." Reaching down, she unwrapped an Ithicanian blade, and Aren nearly vomited at the sight of it. "I'm so sorry for your loss."

Ahnna was dead. His sister was dead.

"We have the remains on our ship," Katarina continued. "I have experts in my employ, and they indicated that there were signs of multiple stab wounds on the ribs and a blow to the skull. It was not the lions that killed her—a statement supported by the fact that my men found male remains in near proximity. He also shows signs of having succumbed to trauma inflicted by a blade."

She reached back into her pocket and retrieved pieces of fabric. Badges of Harendellian military rank that were affixed to a uniform, and Aren recognized it as belonging to a major general.

"Who can say precisely what occurred," Katarina said, handing them over. "But it seems James caught up to Ahnna and they fought, both of them eventually falling to their injuries. A loss for Ithicana, but also a heavy blow to Harendell. All of Amarid sings Ahnna's name, for she has accomplished what we could not."

Her words were little more than noise in Aren's ears.

"Self-defense is not murder." Lara's voice was strangled, and he slowly turned to look at his wife, finding her white as a sheet.

"Fair. Although the Harendellians have already judged her guilty, and in your refusal to do the same, you have invited William's wrath. They are prideful, the Harendellians, and the Ashfords most of all. They will not let this go. We will do our best to keep these deaths secret, but when James fails to return, William will blame either Ahnna or Amarid, depending on which serves Alexandra's purpose." Her lip curled with disdain. "The irony, of course, being that Ahnna rid her of Edward's bastard."

*Not a bastard.* The thought pushed through Aren's grief, but his tongue still felt too thick to speak, a band of tension wrapping tight around his chest.

"I am so sorry for your loss," Katarina said, then took a mouthful of cake, watching him as she chewed. "I can only imagine the pain in your heart, and you have my sympathy for the need to look past your own suffering to the practicality of facing the rising threat of Harendell."

Except losing Ahnna was like losing a part of himself. His twin had been a constant since his first breath. Sister. Commander. Confidante. And she had died trying to protect all they both held dear. Yet he knew that if Ahnna was watching from the Great Beyond, she'd be shouting at him to keep fighting, and she'd never forgive him if he allowed Ithicana's enemies to get the better of him in his grief.

Aren took a small sip of wine, burying the pain as deep as he could. "Let's not pretend your motivations are that altruistic, Katarina. What do you want?"

The queen took another mouthful of cake, again watching him as she chewed. It reminded Aren of being watched by a rat. Swallowing, she dabbed her lips with a napkin and looked at Nina, who had sat quietly this entire time. "Would you play for us, my sweet?"

The girl picked up a lute and began to play a soft melody while staring off at the sea.

"Ithicana has always favored Harendell at Northwatch," Katarina finally said. "Your alliance with them was strong, and you gave them priority in every possible way. It was the reason that I agreed to ally with Silas—he was willing to give me the terms I wanted once he controlled the bridge."

Aren said nothing, only took another sip of wine. Expensive beyond measure, yet it tasted sour on his tongue.

"All nations covet the bridge, but a ruler's greed is not sufficient motivation for an army of living, breathing men to fling themselves against Ithicana's defenses. Ahnna, however unwittingly, has given the Harendellians sufficient motivation," she continued. "If they go to war, it will be for keeps, and at the end of it, William will be Master of the Bridge. This bodes poorly for Amarid, for of a surety, Harendell will either deny my merchants access to the bridge or extort them with horrific tolls. Worse still, once they have defeated you, they will turn their eyes on the Lowlands. Since their marriage-alliance with Cardiff is soon to be cemented with an heir, Amarid will stand no chance against them. From my perspective, it behooves me to support Ithicana in its fight, because if Harendell is occupied with you, they will not come for the Lowlands."

"Support how?" Lara's voice was toneless, and it was only because he knew her so well that Aren heard the distress within it. "It will be many years before you can rebuild your navy after the losses you took in your alliance with my father."

"Oh, I will not risk an all-out war with Harendell," Katarina replied. "However, I will covertly support Ithicana by supplying weapons and steel. Everything your warriors need to keep up your resistance."

"You'd have us do all the fighting while you sit back and sip your wine?" Lara demanded.

"It may be water that I'm forced to sip, because funding your side of the war will take a terrible toll on my coffers. But yes, Lara. It will be Ithicanians on the front lines." Katarina took another mouthful of cake. "You should try a piece, Aren. My pastry chef is the best in the north, if I do say so myself."

Ithicana had run through its supply of grain, so his people didn't have bread, never mind cake, and despite not having much of a sweet tooth, Aren took a slice. The frosting tasted of oranges and ginger.

"May I have a piece of cake, Grandmother?" Nina asked, pausing in her playing.

"As many as you like, dearest. We have plenty."

The girl set into the tray of cakes with gusto while Katarina watched her with affection. "This one will make a fine queen one day. I must fight for a future where that is possible, for if the Harendellians have their way, they will rule the entirety of the north. They were quiet in Edward's reign, but anyone who knows their history will remember that their might grew from conquest. It's in their blood to *take,* and William's youth makes him brash and ambitious. In combination with Alexandra's intelligence, he will be deadly."

Harendell's history was something Aren had known from his childhood lessons but forgotten. No . . . not forgotten but rather dismissed as a relic from the past that held no threat for the present, because Edward had never shown the same inclinations as his forefathers. Or at least, Aren hadn't thought so.

Lara shook her head as Nina offered her a piece of cake. "Do not think I'm fooled by this charming picnic or your pretense at being a doting grandmother building a future for her granddaughter. You don't make sacrifices. You execute strategies."

"Lara," Aren snapped, holding to the roles they'd agreed upon before stepping onto the beach. Before they'd learned that Ahnna was gone. "We have enough enemies without adding Amarid to the mix."

His wife's voice was like ice as she said, "They already are our enemies."

Forcing a grimace onto his face, he met Katarina's ratlike gaze. "You are forever tarnished in my wife's eyes by your association with Silas, I'm afraid."

"*She* is sitting right here," Lara snapped. "And *she* has no interest in alliances with liars. Zarrah can supply everything she offers. This conversation is over."

"You cannot afford to turn me down."

"Yes. We can."

Lara rose. Aren made a noise of protest but broke off as she cast him a blistering glare, and he got to his feet as well. She caught hold of his hand and started to haul him away, but then Amarid's queen spoke. "Fine. I'll sweeten the pot."

Aren dug in his heels.

"Yes, Valcotta can supply weapons." Katarina picked up yet another piece of cursed cake, the frosting sticking to her awful teeth as she took a bite. Chewed. Swallowed. "But what about food?"

Aren dropped Lara's hand, and Katarina's mouth quirked in a smile. "Your wife doesn't know famine as you do, does she, Aren? But you remember the first war with Maridrina, don't you? You remember what it's like to be confined to your islands while typhoons rage across the Tempest Seas. Fishing, impossible. Foraging, impossible. Forced to eat vermin because the bridge sits empty. You remember how disease walks hand in hand with that sort of confinement and hunger, taking first the very old . . . and then the very *young*. Maridrina endures a famine itself, and Valcotta's herds are infected by wasting disease. Though I'm sure you are aware of that."

"What are you offering?"

"A trade. I will sell you a shipload of our best vintages at fair market value, which you can resell at Southwatch to recoup your costs. In exchange for your services, I'll give you a shipload of grain of the best quality."

"I could buy three shiploads of grain with the tolls on that much wine."

"Except there is no grain for you to buy," she countered. "It is simple economics, Aren. That which is in short supply is very valuable indeed. One cannot eat gold or steel."

335

"We aren't agreeing to extortion!" Lara grabbed his hand and pulled as though she could physically force him away from the conversation. "We're through here."

He allowed her to tug him a few paces down the beach.

"Two shiploads of grain for each ship filled with wine," Katarina snapped.

"No!" His wife, ever the consummate actress, was crying. "I will not negotiate with this woman, Aren. She was my father's ally!"

"Three." Katarina rose to her feet. "And to prove my commitment to the agreement, given we shall have nothing in writing, my granddaughter will return with you as your ward for the duration."

The girl's face paled. "What do you mean, Grandmother? I don't want to go with them!"

"You will do your duty, Nina." Katarina rested a gnarled hand on the girl's shoulder. "One day, you will be queen of Amarid, and having a strong relationship with Ithicana will be to your benefit."

"Agreed," Aren said, and reaching into his pocket, he withdrew a map and circled three locations. He handed it to Katarina. "Tell your captains to come in the next storm break."

The queen took the map, but her eyes were on Lara. "Clever like your father."

Lara stiffened. "I'm nothing like my father."

"You keep telling yourself that, girl. Silas was also very good at getting what he wanted with duplicity. He learned the hard way about what happens when one leaves a trail of those one has duped in one's wake. I would not want you to have the same fate as he did." She snapped her fingers, and a pair of servants came forward with a traveler's chest. "Do take care of my granddaughter."

The weeping child walked toward them, and Lara gently took hold of her arm and led her toward the longboat. Leaving Aren alone with Katarina.

Katarina settled back down on the blanket and reached for a piece of cake. "I think I shall enjoy the weather while it lasts. In recent years, I have learned to savor the small moments of pleasure."

A wave of loss rushed over him, because there wasn't anything

Aren wouldn't have given to have Ahnna here to wield a weapon at his back.

Katarina took a mouthful of cake, chewed and swallowed, then looked up at him. "Fight hard, Your Grace. Fight until the Harendellians decide the economics are not in their favor. Fight and win, for all our sakes."

## 47

# KERIS

"We need to leave, Keris." Saam held a needle over a candle flame, a mountain of medical supplies on the table next to him. "The king of Harendell *stabbed* you."

"He didn't stab me."

Saam waved a hand over the bleeding wound. "Then what do you call this?"

"A prick. Just give me a few stitches and I'll be fine."

"He didn't do it with a pin, you lunatic." Saam threw up his hands, eyes going to the three other members of guard for support but receiving only shrugs in response. "Get out, the lot of you. And one of you take Fiona out to the courtyard for a stroll."

Keris watched the dog prance out with one of the guards, noting that her leash glittered with what looked suspiciously like diamonds to match her collar. "I can't believe you bought that thing."

"The only unbelievable thing is that we are still here." Saam threaded the needle and set to work. "You pissed off Alexandra. Drove William to *prick* you. Inspired all of Verwyrd to call Lestara the

Carrion Queen, which saw thirty people arrested and put in the stocks. To top it all off, King Ronan of Cardiff now sees you as a threat. We should be racing for a ship to get out of Harendell, but instead you're lying here drinking the Ashfords' liquor."

"I made progress today, Saam." Keris stared at the ceiling. "Alexandra needs Ithicana to be the great villain in the eyes of the people, which means keeping their emotions firmly fixed on Ahnna's actions. Today I turned that focus to Lestara. If I can fuel the fire of their outrage inward toward their queen, Alexandra's campaign will lose momentum. To regain it, she'll need to convince William to set aside Lestara, which, with luck, will create conflict with Cardiff. Every time I step out of the Sky Palace, the civilians are reminded of what their queen did, whereas if I flee, I risk Alexandra redirecting them back to Ithicana. It's a game of public manipulation and propaganda, and no one does it better than Harendell."

"It's going to get you killed."

A sudden commotion sounded from outside. A shrill female voice and words of protest, but then the door opened and Lestara stormed inside. Her face was streaked with tears. "Why, Keris? Why must you be so endlessly cruel to me?"

He waved Saam aside and sat up. "You know the answer to that question, Lestara. Besides, I haven't done anything to you."

"They're calling me the Carrion Queen! The Butcher of Babies!" Her hands balled into fists. "You're making them hate me!"

Keris reached for his bloodstained shirt, pulling it over his bare chest while he debated how best to get rid of her. "I'm not *making* them do or say anything. North and south, everyone knows what happened in Vencia. Everyone knows that you made it possible. If you didn't want to be known for the deaths of innocent civilians, you should have put your mind to protecting them, not throwing them to the wolves for the sake of getting rid of me. Your life is what you made of it, good and bad. Own it."

"You think that I haven't owned it?" Lestara scrubbed tears from her face, then cupped a hand over her swollen belly. "You think I don't regret my part in what happened in Vencia? You think that I don't hate myself for allowing Petra to take advantage of my hurt and grief?"

Keris crossed his arms, ignoring the slice of pain as his stitches pulled. "No, I don't. The only thing you regret is getting caught."

Silence stretched between them, then she said, "Do you have any forgiveness in you?"

"No. I'm sure many consider that a profound character flaw, but it's one I'm willing to accept."

Logically, he was aware that provoking her was a bad idea, but Keris didn't care.

Her chin quivered but then stilled as she clenched her jaw. "Virginia and her ladies tortured me, day in and day out, as you knew they would. At first, I could not see beyond my hate for you, but I came to understand it was my penance. Came to understand that I needed to do good in the world in order to atone for the consequences of my mistakes. I have taken up my cousin's mantle in his absence and am doing all that I can to ensure peace continues with Cardiff. I do everything I can to temper William's anger toward Ithicana. I spend my days on charity, donate all of my allowance to good causes, and use my power to protect those who have none. I am trying, Keris."

He clapped slowly, mockingly. "Well done, Your Grace. Tell me, does it require giving up one new gown or two to atone for the death of a child? What is the accounting on such matters?"

Pink flushed into her cheeks, the muscles of her jaw so clenched she had to be risking broken teeth. Then she said, "You judge me harshly, Keris, but do you ever look in the mirror and judge yourself for the harm you caused?"

"Every fucking day." Keris shook his head. "I am no paragon, Lestara. I know I am not fit to rule, because I always act in the interest of those I love, no matter the cost to others. It's one of the reasons I gave up the crown to Sarhina. It is the reason I've refused all power in Valcotta. Whereas you just keep clawing your way higher. Keep finding ways to gain more power, and that is the reason the common folk resist you. They know you'll bury them all to get what you want."

"You're wrong." Lestara squared her shoulders and pushed her blond hair back. "I will bring forth the longest era of peace in living memory. That will be my legacy, stars as my witness."

"I pray that I'm wrong." He stared into her amber eyes, struck with the sudden certainty that Lestara believed what she was saying. "I pray that you have the capacity to change. I pray that you will do good things."

Her mouth curved in a slight smile. "I appreciate—"

"But I've never once had a prayer answered, and so I'll plan for you to be exactly the woman I know you to be."

Lestara's smile melted away, and her eyes burned with rising hatred. "Then I'll leave you with a warning, Keris. William knows that I was cruelly used by Petra. He knows I didn't plan for what happened in Vencia. He believes in my ability to do good, and he will put down anyone who stops me from doing so." Her eyes moved to the bloodstains on his shirt. "Including you. I suggest you run home to your wife while you still can, but I've heard neither she nor her people miss your presence. I wonder what they must think knowing that you're partially to blame for the loss of trade through the bridge. Yet another nation you can claim to have starved."

With a swirl of skirts and gleaming jewels, the queen of Harendell strode from the room.

Saam came back in, Fiona's leash in one hand. His expression was drawn, eyes grim. "There's news from the spies in Riomar."

"Well?"

"James Ashford's body was found in the Blackreaches," his friend said, shutting the door behind him. "They say Ahnna Kertell killed him."

## 48

# AHNNA

It had been no easy thing getting all the supplies they needed ready, but with James bitterly complaining to Carlo about foul smells, he'd secured vinegar to clean his cell, which Ahnna had used to separate the fats from their soap into oil that would burn. "The rope vine will serve as a wick," she softly explained. "And we'll have what amounts to an oil lamp, though it won't last as long as we might like."

Neither of them bothered mentioning that time was the one thing they were running out of. While pouring vinegar down on James, Carlo had gleefully told them that Aren had agreed to meet with Mother to discuss an alliance.

"I don't know what he's thinking," Ahnna muttered, carefully setting her cup full of oil where it was out of sight from above, wrapping her shirt around it so there was no risk it would spill. "Katarina has attacked us so many times over the years. How can Aren possibly believe that she's negotiating in good faith?"

"I doubt he does." James sighed, the sound barely audible through the opening. "He's banking on the old enmity between Harendell and

Amarid forcing Katarina to play fair. This entire strategy hangs upon Harendell being the mutual enemy, and it sounds as though Alexandra is doing everything she can to convince Aren that Harendell is coming for blood."

"It seems so obvious that it's a trick."

He gave a soft snort. "Harendellians and Amaridians hate each other the same way Maridrinians and Valcottans do. Or used to, at any rate. The idea that the queens are allied won't even cross anyone's minds."

The sun began to fade overhead, and Ahnna looked up, watching as dusk settled over Riomar. "You ready?" she asked as she heard the wardens doing their rounds.

"As I'll ever be."

"Prisoner, approach!"

At the sound of the female warden, Ahnna scurried beneath the opening. "Help! We need help!"

The warden ignored her, and water rained down, soaking her.

Wiping it from her eyes, Ahnna shouted, "It's James! He's sick!"

The warden's voice was amused as she said, "You aren't the first to try this, prisoner. I'm sure you won't be the last to fail."

"It's no trick!" Ahnna sobbed. "Someone came by last night and threw extra food into our cells. I told him not to eat it, but he was so hungry."

"Waste!"

The thin lines of vine dropped down, but Ahnna didn't fasten her bucket. "Please! He needs help."

James groaned audibly from his cell, and knowing the warden could see her from above, Ahnna cast a panicked look in his direction. "I think he's been poisoned."

"Very convincing." The warden dropped food on Ahnna's head. "You missed your calling on the stage."

"Please!" Ahnna shrieked. "You know she wants him alive!"

"And I know this is just a trick."

The warden moved away, and Ahnna bit down on a curse and instead shouted, "What will Carlo do to you if you allow his *glorious fucking nemesis* to die in a hole while you do nothing?"

The retreating shadow stopped moving for a moment.

"If this decision is above your rank, send for Carlo," Ahnna called up. "But if you do nothing, I would not put it past him to wall you into one of your own cells, you stupid bitch!"

The shadow moved on, and Ahnna let a string of curses loose before retrieving her food. James kept up the act, groaning and retching, but hours passed with no sound from above.

Four times, she heard the deafening racket of the cathedrals all ringing their bells on the hour, and doubt that this plan would work began to twist her stomach. Except then the faint sound of singing filled her ears.

A shadow appeared above. "I hear you are singing my name, Your Highness. You must be desperate indeed, for I am no friend of yours."

"James is sick," she pleaded. "I think it's poison. He needs help."

"This is a well-worn scheme in the Furnace," the Beast replied. "Try again."

"It's no scheme, Carlo." She stared up, knowing that he wouldn't be able to see her in the darkness. "What will Mother say if you let him die?"

"James is strong. He will endure. And Mother was clear that neither of you is to be let out."

"Are *you* content with that?" she demanded. "Will you be satisfied if James dies in a hole in his own filth? Is that the end you envisioned for him?"

Silence.

Ahnna held her breath, watching Carlo's shadow. Then he disappeared, his boots making soft thumps as he tracked over to the opening above James's cell. "Nemesis," he crooned. "I hear you are not well."

"Fuck off, Carlo," James groaned, and Ahnna winced at the filthy scene that he'd had to paint to make this realistic.

"Carlo!" she shouted. "Charcoal! If nothing else, get him charcoal. If he has been poisoned, it can help."

The prince was no fool. She knew he was considering what scheme they might concoct with anything he gave them, but she also knew that he had dreamed of one last epic fight between him and

James. His mother had denied him that, but she might yet change her mind. Except if James died, so too did the Beast's fantasy.

*Come on*, she silently willed him, refusing to allow herself to dwell on what he'd said about Katarina meeting with Aren. *Fall for it.*

"Get the charcoal," she heard him finally snap. "And I want patrols at night. All of Amarid wants James Ashford dead, so if someone has learned his identity, poison is not a stretch. Have every one of them searched while you are at it."

"Yes, Your Highness."

Ahnna paced back and forth through the tiny space, but then she heard the small thud of a package being dropped and Carlo said, "Eat a spoonful of that, nemesis. You cannot aim to rescue your lady love if you are shitting yourself to death."

James didn't respond, only groaned.

"Eat it!" Carlo shouted.

"James, you must eat it," Ahnna sobbed. "It's the only thing that might stop the poison."

"Can't. Find. It." James muttered. "Can't. See."

Carlo made a noise of exasperation, and there was an argument above between him and the wardens, but then a torch dropped into James's cell. She watched as James crawled and retrieved the packet of charcoal and ate some of it before slumping to the ground next to the flames.

The Beast's voice filtered into Ahnna's cell from above. "Call the warden if he grows worse."

Her lips parted, but he swiftly said, "I've no interest in your thanks, woman."

"And I have no interest in giving them," she snapped back. "Don't stray too far, Beast. When I get out of this place, I'm going to slit your throat."

Carlo snickered, then disappeared, and as he did, James moved. He took the cup Ahnna passed through the opening, lighting the vine wick and then handing it back to her. Ahnna watched it burn down to the oil, holding her breath as it guttered, then steadied. A tiny flame that she prayed to every higher power would last until they were ready.

They could not act that night. Not with the wardens pacing

anxiously above, everyone terrified that James might succumb to poison and that the Beast would kill them all as punishment. James moaned and groaned to keep up the pretense, and while he did, Ahnna took the rest of the charcoal and got to work, knowing full well that with her impure sources of ingredients, all this could be for naught.

Dawn came, and Ahnna made certain that everything was out of sight of the wardens as they began their morning rounds.

"Prisoner, approach!"

She stepped beneath the opening, looking up at the woman's painted face, the warden looking like a terrifying doll from a toy shop of horrors.

"Is he alive?"

Ahnna gave a tight nod. "Yes. He's better. Thank you."

The warden's response was to dump Ahnna's water rations on her face. They moved on to James, who spoke words assuring that he was going to live.

The wardens circled the furnace grounds, endless snarls of *Prisoner, approach*! filling the air until they were finished.

"You ready?" James whispered. "It won't be long now."

"Yes." She picked up her oil candle, her throat constricting because it had burned down to almost nothing, the flame a tiny glow. They had only minutes until it went out.

If that.

*Come on!*

The flame guttered and flickered, and Ahnna's eyes stung with panic and tears.

*Bong!*

The first of the cathedral bells tolled, the others swiftly following suit. It was the sixth hour, which meant six bells.

*Bong!*

She had to hurry.

"Stay back," she whispered to James. "This may not work. Or it might be bigger than I expected."

*Bong!*

Holding the flame to the dried piece of vine that served as a fuse,

Ahnna stepped back the moment it caught. Going to the far side of the cell, she crouched down, closed her eyes, and plugged her ears.

*Bong!*

*Please work.*

*Bong!*

It wasn't going to work. The ingredients weren't pure enough. She hadn't gotten the mixture right.

*Boom!*

Her whole body twitched as the small explosion went off at the same time as the bells tolled, and she twisted in time to watch a small puff of smoke rise. Stones clacked and clattered, then all fell silent, and Ahnna clenched her teeth, waiting for the guards to take notice even as her elation grew.

Because above the small pile of rubble was a much larger opening.

She waited and waited, but when no boots sounded overhead, she determined that the guards had not noticed the small bang over the noise of the bells. Or if they had, they'd thought it something that had come from the city itself. Ahnna dropped to her knees and looked through. To find James looking back at her.

"Think you'll fit?"

She eyed the small opening. "For the first time in my life, I'm glad I wasn't graced with memorable breasts."

"I beg to differ," he replied. "That sort of perfection isn't easily forgotten."

Her cheeks warmed, the thrum of fear mixing with the thrum of something else entirely.

"Tonight, we escape." James reached through the opening to grip her hands. "For now, we need to cover the evidence."

They swiftly moved to push the rubble into the gap, and Ahnna had tucked in the last piece of rock when the warden called out, "Water!"

The woman went to James first, and when she came to pour water down on Ahnna, she said, "I see he's not dead."

"Which means Carlo will let you live another day."

Instead of water, the warden spat down on her but Ahnna only lifted her middle finger and smiled.

Yet her smile retreated as Katarina appeared above her. "I was gone for a matter of but days and yet so much excitement occurred. I *knew* that imprisoning you two together would prolong your usefulness, and it pleases me to have been proven right."

Ahnna's hands turned to ice, and it suddenly became so very hard to breathe.

"Your brother and his Maridrinian wife are a perfect match," the queen of Amarid continued. "It was truly a thing to behold watching them work together to extract more from me than I wanted to give. Three ships full of grain for every ship filled with wine, which means my profit will be slim indeed."

She smiled down at Ahnna, teeth encased with gold and jewels. "The seas are high but not so high as to trouble my captains, which means the ships will sail tonight. One with wine. And three with grain laced with a very special poison. It takes time to take effect once ingested, and then it slowly eats through the stomach."

"You're a fucking monster," Ahnna hissed, but her voice shook with rising terror. "There is no hell deep enough for the likes of you."

"History remembers the victors, Ahnna Kertell," Katarina replied. "Which means that it won't be long until Ithicana, and its people, are entirely forgotten."

# 49
# JAMES

James didn't offend Ahnna with platitudes. The situation was dire, the time short, and the chances of success slim—to say otherwise would be an affront to both her intelligence and her fortitude.

Because despite being quite visibly sick with fear, Ahnna had not given up.

The moment the sun set, they scrambled to clear the rubble from the small opening she'd blasted.

"You need to be careful of your arm," he warned. "This is going to be tight."

"Fuck my arm and get pulling," she snapped. "We need to get out tonight."

The chances of that were slim to none, but James only reached through to take hold of her ankles. He pulled slowly, mindful of the rough rock beneath her, but stopped as her hips stuck. "I don't want to hurt you."

"You think hearing that my family and all my people are dead won't hurt? If you can get my ass through, the rest will be easy."

He tugged on her legs, carefully shifting her from side to side, but her hips were still stuck.

"James," Ahnna hissed, "with the utmost respect, grow a pair of balls and *pull*."

Gritting his teeth and grimacing, he tightened his grip and leaned back, using his far greater weight as leverage.

For a heartbeat, he thought it wouldn't work. That nothing short of breaking her pelvis—a line he would *not* cross—would get her through. But then Ahnna's hips started to edge through the small opening. She was entirely silent, except he felt the muscles of her legs go rigid, betraying the pain she was suffering.

He pulled harder, knowing that his hands would leave bruises on her skin. Except there was no turning back now. No pushing her back through.

*Come on!* His toes dug into the grooves in the stone floor of his cell, and then he abruptly fell backward onto his ass as her hips slid through.

"Almost there." It sounded like she was forcing the words between her teeth.

Scrambling to his feet, he eased her the rest of the way through the gap. James lifted her upright, wishing he could see her face in the blackness. Ahnna slipped her unbroken arm around his neck, and he pulled her tight against him, feeling the rapid thunder of her heart. With one hand, he tentatively reached down to touch her left hip and felt the warm dampness of blood. "How bad?"

"Nothing a swim in the sea won't cure. We need to get to work."

Yet for all her words, she didn't let go of his neck, her nails digging into his shoulder as she slowly steadied her breath. An irrational part of him wanted this moment to last forever, because she was back in his arms. Yet all too soon, Ahnna pushed away.

He heard her digging in the rubble for a sharp piece of rock, and then she whispered, "Lift me up."

Mindful of her many injuries, James knelt on one knee and helped her climb onto his shoulders. Holding tight to her thighs, he carefully rose, noting that she was much lighter than the prior times he'd done this, this ordeal having taken its toll on her. "Can you reach?"

"No." She pushed his hand off her thigh and lifted it so that she was kneeling on his shoulders. "I can reach it now."

With the other inmates taking up their nighttime howling for mercy, freedom, and deliverance providing them cover, Ahnna set to chipping away at the mortar with her rock. There were two arches in the cell's ceiling, and it was the gap between the arches where stones were removed to put a prisoner in the cell.

And to take the corpses out.

The mortar there was fresh and weak, and both he and Ahnna had noted that the wardens were careful never to put their weight on the area around the small opening. The goal was to weaken it enough that Ahnna would be able to pull part of the roof down.

As to what would come after . . . there was no way to plan for it precisely, but James suspected it would come down to speed and violence.

Dust rained down on his head as she worked away and his shoulders began to ache. Ahnna's body trembled from the effort of maintaining her balance while she worked, but she never paused in her labor other than for the quick sips of water he forced her to take.

"I'm going to try to pull it down." She handed him her rock, and James felt her body elongate as she reached up with her left hand and slipped it through the opening. "Move."

His heart hammering, James bent his knees and moved out from beneath her. He could very faintly see her shadow, hanging with only one arm from the tiny opening above.

"Grab onto me," she whispered. "My weight isn't enough."

"I'll pull you down."

Ahnna snorted softly. "I'm stronger than you think."

Shaking his head, James jumped and caught hold of her waist. Her whole body shook from the effort it took to hold both their weights with one arm; she could only last another few seconds. Then she hissed, "It's giving. I can feel it giv—"

"Oh, nemesis!" Carlo's singsong voice filled James's ears. Ahnna gave a soft gasp and let go. His feet hit the ground, and he barely kept his balance as he caught her weight. Pushing Ahnna to the side of the cell, James looked up into the opening right as Carlo's shadow looked down.

"Oh good, you are still alive."

"What do you want?" They didn't have time for this. Didn't have time to sit and listen to Carlo sing all night while ships full of poisoned grain began their trek to Ithicana.

"Your glorious company." Carlo paced in slow circles around the opening, and James felt tiny bits of crumbled mortar and dust fall against his cheeks. "I detest Riomar. It is full of painted fools. Weak men and women who weep at the smallest sliver, and are therefore no sport. Not like you."

"So you're here for conversation?"

Carlo made a noncommittal noise. "Mother's scheme with the Ithicanians went as planned."

"So I heard."

"Poison is a woman's weapon."

"Dead is dead."

Carlo sighed. "Is it, though? The taking of a life should have meaning, James. It should fill your veins with the same rush as a mouth around your cock, and how is such a thing possible if one is not even there to witness it? There is no resonance, no pleasure. Empty kills to achieve political ends." The Beast spat, his disgust palpable.

"It's no loss to you, Carlo," James replied. "The high seas sit between Amarid and Ithicana, so none of those lives were ever at risk from you. At least your mother can get the job done."

The Beast gave a soft laugh. "You are the only one who does not fear me."

"Why should I fear you? I have your mother to keep me safe, because she is the *only* person you fear."

Carlo was silent, but over the cries of the other prisoners, James could hear the scuff of his boots against stone as he circled the opening above.

Then the Beast said something entirely unexpected. "She gave the Ithicanians my Nina. A royal hostage as a sign of good faith."

Carlo's eldest daughter. James hesitated, then asked, "Does Nina know about the poison?"

"No."

"Then your mother has signed your daughter's death warrant.

Even if she is lucky enough not to eat poisoned bread, once the Ithicanians realize what has been done, they are sure to execute her in retaliation."

Ahnna shifted slightly in the shadows, but James reached out a hand, steadying her even as a plan formed in his head.

"Do you know how Ithicanians execute people, Carlo?" He watched the Beast's shadow pass over the opening as he circled. "They dangle them waist-deep in the waves and then chum the waters."

"She's only a child. She had no role in this."

James chuckled but there was no amusement to it. "One could say the same of every Ithicanian child who will soon eat poisoned bread. Do you think the survivors will see Nina as innocent when faced with burying their children? Or do you think it will be an eye for an eye?"

Carlo cursed, and there was no mistaking the fury in his tone. Which meant it was possible that Katarina had taken a step too far for her madman of a son, and James fully intended to exploit her mistake.

"Are you going to stand around and wait for your daughter to die, you fucking coward?" James demanded. "Sit here in Riomar with these painted fools while your mother sacrifices your Nina for the sake of unsatisfactory kills? You could still stop this. You could save her."

Carlo barked out a laugh. "Sloppy, nemesis. I am angry, not stupid."

"You are no nemesis of mine, Carlo. You're afraid of a little old woman—it's pathetic."

The Beast stepped close to the opening. "Everyone fears her, and rightly so!"

Dust rained down on James's face. "You disparage my brother, but you are no different than William. A patsy. A pawn. And just like William, you don't even seem to know it!"

The faint light of the opening was blocked out as Carlo fell to his knees, and James heard the man's nails scratch against stone as he gripped the opening.

"All you asked for was one thing," James said, circling beneath and knowing the monster above was trying to pick him out of the shadows. "To kill me in a glorious fight to the death. And she won't even give you that. She'll take your daughter's life but not even give you mine in exchange, because the truth is, Carlo, your mother is the biggest coward of all."

"Lies! She fears nothing."

"She fears Alexandra. She fears Harendell. It is fear that controls you, Carlo, and how am I supposed to call you nemesis knowing that?"

Carlo snarled and shoved his arm into the hole, the shadow of his hand slashing through the air with a knife despite James being far out of reach.

And already moving.

Catching hold of Ahnna's waist, he flung her up high—

Where she caught hold of the Beast's arm. He snarled in protest even as James jumped, climbing Ahnna's lean form to latch his own hand around Carlo's arm.

The ground around the opening trembled and Carlo shrieked for help, but his voice was lost to the cries of all the prisoners. Seeming to understand this, Carlo whispered, "Well played."

Then all three of them were falling into blackness.

# 50
# AHNNA

She let go of Carlo's arm as the ceiling of the cell collapsed, throwing herself sideways the moment her feet hit the ground. Her shoulder struck the wall hard but she ignored the pain in favor of lifting her arm, rubble striking her even as it rained down upon the two grappling shadows before her.

It was impossible to tell who was who in the darkness, but she picked up a piece of rock and held it at the ready. "James!"

He didn't answer, but one of the shadows had the other on the floor and was slamming him repeatedly against the stone. Certain Carlo had the upper hand, she raised her rock high to dash it down on his head, only for the pair to roll. Back and forth they fought, the heavy thud of fists and feet against flesh seeming deafening in the tight space, but she could not see enough to successfully intervene.

The pair ceased rolling, and her ears filled with the strangled noises of someone being choked out. "James, I can't tell if you need me to save your ass or not."

"Not today, Princess." The words came out as a growl, punctuated by Carlo's heels drumming against the floor, the Beast desperate to breathe. "I've waited a long fucking time to end you, Carlo, and my only regret is that it's going to be quick."

"Don't kill him!" The words exploded from her lips. "We need him alive!"

"What?"

"We can use him as a hostage to get out." She dropped to her knees next to them, and catching hold of the fabric of her shirt with her teeth, she ripped the filthy material. "Choke him out and then we'll tie his wrists."

"I'm not letting him draw another breath after what he did to you!"

"If you want to impress me, try listening to my good sense!" she snapped. "We have dozens of guards to get past, and the moment they call an alarm, more will descend. We can use him to get through—they won't risk us killing him."

"No!"

Carlo's heels had ceased drumming, which meant he was unconscious or near enough to it.

"Quit letting emotions make decisions for you." She pulled on James's wrist, trying to ease the deadly press of his arm on Carlo's throat. "You're very thickheaded when you're mad."

James let out a string of curses, but then eased his grip on Carlo's neck. In one quick move, he rolled the Beast onto his stomach and wrenched his arms behind his back.

"You'll have to tie him. I can't do it tight enough with one hand."

She fumbled around in the dark and the rubble, finding the knife that Carlo dropped. While James bound Carlo's wrists, she pressed the blade to the Beast's throat. She could hear him breathing. Knew that he'd rouse in seconds. "Gag him."

Fabric tore, but before James could shove it in Carlo's mouth, the prince began to chuckle. "You never disappoint, James. This is a wonderful turn of events."

"You're insane."

"Possibly." Carlo's voice was dreamy, and if she hadn't known better, Ahnna would have thought he'd taken a blow to his head. "But I—"

His words cut off as James shoved the gag into his mouth. More fabric ripped, and leaving James to ensure the Beast was secure, Ahnna looked up.

The hole was not overly large, but it was big enough to allow a blissfully cool wind to blow in, and she tasted her first mouthful of fresh air in what felt like an eternity.

"Unless you have a good idea of how to get him out, I'm going to kill him now."

A thud filled the cell as James's foot connected hard with Carlo's trussed form, but the Beast only laughed around his gag. Yet she knew that for all he delighted in what he saw as a game, Carlo would be looking for ways to win it. The most dangerous hostage imaginable.

"We'll make a rope out of his clothes and lift him up. What does he have for weapons?"

"Just the knife."

They set to tearing up Carlo's clothes, forming a rope of fabric that they fastened to his arms. Holding on to the end of it, Ahnna allowed James to lift her again onto his shoulders. Balancing carefully, she rose to her feet and took hold of the lip of the opening. James gripped her ankles, and with shocking strength, lifted her higher. High enough that she rose out of the hole and rolled onto the ground.

She was immediately assaulted with the shrieks and cries of the other prisoners, the noise seeming to be coming from every direction in the darkness. Ignoring them, Ahnna took in the lights from the main prison that surrounded this hellhole of a courtyard. The roof glowed with torchlight, guards patrolling around and around. Yet in their desire to make these cells as horrifying as possible, they'd eliminated their ability to see the center of the courtyard in the darkness. Or perhaps they were just that confident that no one could escape.

Going back to the edge of the hole, she whispered. "Give me a minute to brace and then climb up."

She planted her feet in the slit in the ceiling of her cell, wrapped the rope around her good arm, and anchored herself.

Her body shuddered as James began to climb, it taking every ounce of strength and willpower to hold up his weight. He rolled over the edge, took the chain of fabric, and heaved. Hand over hand, he dragged the struggling Carlo up and over the edge.

The Beast thrashed wildly and tried to shout through his gag, and Ahnna gave him a sharp kick in his remaining testicle. Not because it would do any good but because it was goddamned satisfying.

"Now what?" James muttered, his shadow rotating as he took in the fortified prison around them. "The moment we approach the walls, we'll lose the cover of darkness and the guards will see us."

"If they kill us, Katarina loses her insurance against Alexandra, and they definitely won't risk her son," she whispered back. "We are at the advantage, but only if we are quick."

She took in the smooth walls of the prison surrounding the square of furnace cells. Even without a broken arm, there was no way to climb them, which meant the only way out was the singular gate into the square. The soldiers might open the gate at the threat of Carlo's life, might even let them out of the prison, but as the alarm was sounded, more soldiers would come. With them would be those skilled enough with narcotic darts to take both her and James down.

"We need to get up the walls onto the roof," James muttered. "Escape into the moat."

The moat had stakes, so to jump would be madness. She'd also noticed crocodiles in it.

"No," she whispered, then clamped her hands on Carlo's ears so he couldn't hear her. "We go down."

Carlo jerked from side to side, trying to escape her grip as James asked, "What?"

"Into the furnace." She jerked her chin toward the corner of the yard where torches on the wall faintly illuminated a grilled vent from which wisps of smoke drifted. "There are chimneys in each corner of the yard. If we can get into one and drop down, there will be open space below the cells where the furnace is. There needs to be a way in and out for those who work to fuel it."

"We'll be cooked alive."

"It will be miserably hot, but it's the smoke that will kill you, so you'll have to hold your breath." She frowned. "But we need a distraction so we can get into the chimney without them noticing." Her eyes flicked to Carlo, who had gone still beneath James's grip. His hair was sweaty beneath her hands, and though she was filthier than she'd ever been in her life, touching him made her stomach twist with disgust.

Moving so that her lips were close to James's ear, she whispered her plan.

"You want to leave him alive?" The words sounded like they were coming from between his teeth.

"No, but do you have a better idea?"

"None of this is a good idea." But James dragged Carlo upright. "Ready?"

*No.* "Yes."

Pulling off Carlo's coat, James covered the man's head and then dragged him in the direction of the wall where torches were mounted on sconces. The second that they moved out of the shadows, shouts sounded from above.

"That's right," James roared. "I have your prince. If you want him to stay alive, you'll open that gate."

He tore the torch from the sconce and shoved Carlo toward the gate while Ahnna moved slowly in the shadows, evading the pool of light as she edged closer to the grate covering the furnace in the corner.

The prison was an uproar of noise, alarms ringing and boots pounding, and the gate at the end opened.

*Hurry*, Ahnna silently urged him. *We're running short on time.*

As if hearing her, James said something to Carlo that she couldn't make out, and then held the torch to the back of the Beast's shirt.

Flames licked up Carlo's back and he screamed, and when James shoved him, the Beast broke into a blind sprint forward, trying to outrun the pain.

James dropped his torch into one of the cells and was immediately lost to darkness, but Ahnna was already moving.

With all eyes on Carlo, whose shirt was entirely aflame as he ran toward salvation, she sprinted to the corner and caught hold of the grate. It was hot but not unbearably so, and she heaved with her unbroken arm, trying to drag it aside.

It wouldn't budge.

"Shit," she hissed, her heart racing chaotically in her chest, the stink of woodsmoke filling her nose with every inhalation.

Then James was there.

He caught hold of the grate and heaved, the heavy metal dragging sideways. "You sure about this?"

"We'll never get another chance at freedom," Ahnna answered, and sucking in a deep breath of air, she jumped.

Her shoulders and hips banged against the brickwork as she dropped into darkness, her eyes stinging with smoke, the heat intense.

Her heels hit rock with enough force that her knees gave out, and Ahnna fell sideways, rolling to her feet.

All around was thick woodsmoke, the space beneath the cells illuminated by an enormous glowing furnace. Flames flickered in its core, pumping out the endless heat that kept the cells so ungodly hot, but someone had to fuel those flames, which meant there was a way out.

James landed with a thump next to her. She caught hold of his hand and dragged him along the perimeter of the space.

Her eyes burned, tears running down her cheeks, but what scared her more was the need for air. It wouldn't take many breaths of this smoke to knock them unconscious, and by the time the soldiers found them, they'd be dead.

Though it hurt to do so, she used her broken arm to feel along the walls, searching for a door. A hatch. Any form of escape from this hell she'd delivered them to.

James broke first, drawing in a breath that immediately set him into a fit of coughing, and if she'd had the air to do so, Ahnna would have screamed.

Another few seconds and they'd be done, be dead, and they'd only be the first to fall.

Clenching his hand, Ahnna kept moving, and then through the smoke and her own tears, she caught sight of another flickering flame. A lantern, and next to it was a narrow door.

She slammed into it and it mercifully burst open, and once James was through, she sealed it shut behind them. He fell to his knees coughing as she sucked in a mercifully pure breath of air, taking in the narrow hall, which was lined with endless bundles of sticks.

A skinny man with soot-stained skin stood in the center of the hallway, gaping at them.

"I won't call the alarm," he pleaded. "Just please don't hurt me."

"On your knees," she ordered, and when he fell to the ground, Ahnna snatched up some discarded twine. James was still coughing, but he deftly bound the man and they pressed onward down the dark tunnel.

It stank with the smell of smoke, a faint haze swirling overhead in the light of the lantern she'd taken from the man. On and on they walked, and at one point, water dripped from above.

"We're beneath the moat," James said softly. "They've designed this so that the workers can access the furnace but not the prison."

"You think that the entrance to this tunnel isn't guarded?" she asked.

"Not a chance." He pushed the knife into her hand. "Make it count."

The light from the lantern revealed a heavy door ahead, and Ahnna's heart lurched as she saw there was no way of opening it from the inside. "What do we do?"

James gave a soft cough, still suffering from the smoke he'd inhaled, and reached for the door. But Ahnna caught hold of his wrist.

Lifting the lantern, she looked at him. Truly looked at him for the first time in so long, because she'd lost track of the days they'd spent in those tombs. He was filthy, his beard thick, and his cheeks gaunt, but he was still the most beautiful man she'd seen in all her life. "Show no mercy," she whispered.

He huffed out a breath. "You know that I never do."

Then he rapped his fingers against the door.

"You're not done," a voice called through the door, but it started to swing open. "I told ya—"

James's hand closed around the soldier's wrist, and he yanked him into the corridor. Ahnna saw him slam the man's skull against the wall with a brutal crack, and then she was out in the open.

There was no chance to take a mouthful of air and relish her first breath of relative freedom, because four Amaridian soldiers were gaping at her.

Ahnna didn't hesitate.

Lunging, she slashed Carlo's knife across one man's throat, then twisted and slammed the blade into another's chest. The third reached for her, but then James was on him. He caught hold of the soldier's skull, and just as the Amaridian began to shriek for help, he twisted, breaking the man's neck.

James dropped the body and picked up the man's sword, his eyes going to the prison. It was blazing with torches, the alarm bells now silenced but not the shouts and running boots. "They're coming. Run!"

They sprinted through the city, weaving through the dark alleys and racing across streets. Ahnna stole a cloak from a wash line to cover her filthy clothes, and then another for James.

"They know our goal is a boat," James hissed, then gestured toward the harbor. "Look at the torches heading that way. We'll never get through that many soldiers."

All of Riomar was coming awake and civilians poured onto the streets, gasps of horror rising to their lips as they learned that prisoners had escaped from the Furnace. Shouts from captains filled the air as they dispatched soldiers on horseback to secure any vessel that floated within a day's ride. Ahnna cursed, because they were as trapped as they had ever been.

"We go out of the city and head east and north," James whispered, pulling the hood of the stolen cloak forward to hide her face. "They can't guard the entire coastline. We just need to keep going until we get ahead of them."

"We don't have time." Her hand balled into a fist. "Ships full of poison are already on their way to Ithicana, James. Within a day or two, they'll be unloading the grain and dispersing it, and it will be too late."

"We can't stop them if we get caught!"

"I know." She crouched low, trying to curb her rising panic so that she could *think*. Then she lifted her head. "We swim."

"What?"

Smearing her finger in some mud, she drew a basic map. "There's an island within spitting distance of Riomar. It's full of villas owned by Amarid's wealthy, and they will have vessels that they use to go back and forth from the mainland. If we can swim across, we can steal one of those ships and be gone south before they know it's missing."

"Never mind the waves, the current, the sharks, and your broken arm, Ahnna."

"We find something that floats to hold on to. It's not that far." And because she knew it would piss him off, she added, "I'll go by myself if you don't think you can manage."

His shadowed eyes fixed her with a glare. "Or how about I tie you up, flip you over my shoulder, and carry you away from this plan that is sure to get you killed?"

"You'll have to catch me first!" Ahnna broke into a run, heading through the crowded streets toward the water. Many people were running, keen to get a look at the Furnace prisoners when the city guard finally hunted them down, so no one paid her any mind. Not once did she look back, because Ahnna knew that James was hot on her heels. Knew that the only reason he wasn't shouting at her was because his Harendellian accent would draw immediate interest.

Riomar's harbor was huge, but Ahnna headed south of it even as she bent her mind to remembering what she knew about Riomar. Vaguely she recalled that the city was protected by a high seawall where no vessels would be moored, which meant it wouldn't be a priority for those hunting them.

Carlo included.

Her skin prickled, and Ahnna pulled her hood farther forward even as she hunted the crowd for any sign of the prince. He was injured but not so badly that he wouldn't be dead set on being the one to find them. It struck her that the Beast might rather die than allow anyone else the pleasure of killing James.

James drew alongside her, hood casting his face in shadows. "You're going to be the death of me, woman."

"You like the thrill of it. Don't pretend otherwise."

"Ahh, yes. The thrill of being swept out to sea. The thrill of being eaten alive by sharks."

"But when you survive, you'll never feel more alive. This way."

They headed down an alleyway, and Ahnna couldn't help looking over her shoulder. Her skin was crawling with the certainty that they were being watched, but the alley was empty. The streets grew less and less crowded the farther they moved from the harbor, and when they broke out onto the pathway atop the seawall, they were entirely alone.

Going to the edge, Ahnna looked down. The tide was out, revealing a small stretch of rocky beach onto which the waves rolled. Dawn was beginning to glow, and very faintly, she could make out the shadow of the island in the distance. With two arms, she could likely have swum the distance in half an hour, but this would be slower going.

Sitting on the edge, Ahnna slid down the steep incline of the seawall, wincing as her bare feet struck rough rock. James landed next to her.

"Find some driftwood or debris," she said, hunting the rocks for something that would serve to keep them afloat as they kicked across. "We want to be in the water before the sun rises."

"The thrill intensifies," James muttered, but he started searching in the other direction.

Then the sound of a man singing a nursery song broke the silence, and Ahnna's hands turned to ice. Whirling around, she watched as Carlo jumped down from the seawall. He sang the final notes of his song, and then drew his sword. "I sent my men off on a fool's errand so that we might have a final moment alone, my dear nemesis. Let's finish this before they return."

James drew his sword. "Ahnna, get in the water and start swimming."

"No." She pulled her knife. "We kill him together."

He moved between her and Carlo. "There's not enough time. His men will be along soon enough, and if they see you in the water, they will catch you."

The logic of his words caused sickness to pool in her stomach, because Ahnna knew what he'd say next.

"My life is not worth the lives of everyone in Ithicana. Go. Warn your brother. Save your homeland."

"James . . ." It hurt to breathe. "I can't . . ."

"Oh, I love this," Carlo breathed. "I could not have envisioned a better moment."

James ignored him and turned, his hand coming up to grip the side of her face. "I love you, Ahnna Kertell."

Her lips parted to tell him that she loved him. To tell him that despite having every reason to hate him, if she could have chosen her own future, it would have been with him. But James's lips descended on hers, silencing her as he kissed her with enough ferocity to bruise. Like he knew what she would say and could not bear to hear it, because that dream would never be.

"Go." He pushed her to the water. "Save them."

"I will." Tears were pouring down her cheeks. "But only if you promise to slit his fucking throat."

Knowing that if she didn't leave now, she wouldn't leave at all, Ahnna turned and sprinted into the waves.

# 51

# JAMES

"I ALMOST HOPE that she escapes and survives," Carlo murmured, his focus over James's shoulder where Ahnna was surely carving through the waves. "To have to live the rest of her days knowing that she sacrificed the love of her life . . ." The Beast sighed happily. "It pleases me so greatly to have discovered this aspect of your character, James. To know that you are capable of passion in the bedroom *and* such viciousness on the battlefield makes me love you more."

"You do understand that your affection is unrequited?"

Carlo ran a finger along his blade. "Is it? You're here, aren't you? You two could have raced out into the waves together full well knowing that I would not follow, and yet you remained. Because the chance to kill me is worth dying for, and what is that if not a sort of love?"

James considered pointing out that killing Carlo so that Ahnna had the chance to escape was why he'd stayed, but the truth was, Carlo was not wrong. Killing him was worth dying for.

The tide slithered up the shore, whispering against the sand before retreating as though it feared the Beast as much as he did the midnight water. Moonlight gleamed off steel as James circled Carlo, boots digging into the damp ground. They'd fought so many times before, but this fight felt different.

Carlo grinned, teeth flashing white in the dark. His shirt was ripped and blackened, hanging off his shoulders and exposing the raw, charred flesh of his back. If he felt it, he didn't show it. In fact, he looked almost . . . amused.

"You're smiling," James said, flicking his sword in a lazy arc. "Should I be concerned?"

Carlo tilted his head, eyes glinting. "Are you?"

James lunged—a quick, testing thrust toward Carlo's ribs. Carlo twisted to avoid it, and the movement must have hurt, because a strangled noise slipped from his throat. But instead of pulling away, the Beast laughed.

James hesitated for half a breath too long.

Carlo struck like lightning. Their swords clashed, sparks flying as metal screamed. James barely yanked his head back in time to avoid a brutal slice aimed at his throat. He kicked sand at Carlo's face, forcing him to fall back, but it didn't wipe the wild grin off his face.

"Why do you enjoy this so much?" James asked, leveling his sword.

Carlo twirled his own blade, rolling his shoulders as if stretching, though James knew every motion had to be agony. "Why shouldn't I? Life is fleeting—it's best to relish every moment."

James snorted. "You look like a side of pig that was left too long on the grill."

Carlo hummed as if considering this. Then, suddenly, he launched himself forward. His strikes came fast and erratic—wild, almost reckless, but each blow was deadly precise. James barely kept up, blocking and dodging as he backpedaled through the sand.

The Beast laughed again, eyes bright with an inhuman brilliance. "You're holding back, James. Don't insult me."

James exhaled sharply. "I'm not holding back."

"Yes, you are." Carlo parried another strike, then leaned in close, voice dropping to a whisper. "I wonder . . . Do you not wish to kill me?"

James shoved him away, their swords clashing in a shower of sparks. "I just don't want to end it too swiftly."

Carlo's head tilted again. "Why? Would you rather spend the time with me than chase after your lady love?"

He lunged, forcing James back step by step, their boots kicking up sand. The burn was slowing Carlo, but not enough. He was fighting like a man who didn't care if he won, lost, or died. That made him dangerous.

James needed to end this.

They dueled back and forth, but the moment Carlo stepped wrong, James struck. A swift twist of the blade, a calculated sweep of the leg. Carlo's footing gave out, and he hit the sand hard.

James's sword punched through flesh. The Beast fell back, and James went with him, and his weight forced the blade deep into the rocky beach, pinioning Carlo to the ground. Instead of screaming, Carlo wrapped an arm around him and laughed. "It was well fought, nemesis."

James jerked out of his grip but left the sword in place, and as he staggered upright, a wave rolled up and immersed Carlo to his ears. His face drained of color, and Carlo tried to get an arm beneath himself to push up. To use his body to drag the sword out of the ground so that he could escape the next wave.

James took hold of the hilt and rested his weight on the sword. "The tide is coming in, Carlo."

A wave washed in, this time going over his face. As it retreated, it took with it a crimson cloud. Carlo spluttered and cried out in fear.

James lifted his head, searching the waters for Ahnna. They were cast in pinks and oranges from the dawn light, but he saw no motion. *Please be all right*, he silently prayed. *Please make it home.*

Carlo's terrified splutters as another wave rolled in drew his attention back to the man at his feet. "You're right," James said to him. "The method of death does matter. Watching you slowly drown is exactly how I would have dreamed of your death, if I dreamed of such things."

Another wave rolled over Carlo, deeper this time, but as the froth cleared, it took with it the fear in the Beast's eye. Except no . . . that wasn't quite right. The fear was still there, but it was mixed with pleasure.

Between coughs, Carlo whispered, "You're right. It's perfect."

Another wave rolled in, this one coming up to James's thighs. It took a long time to retreat, and Carlo desperately gasped for breath when it did, only to be hit by another, the froth tinged pink with blood as it pulled back into the sea. It wouldn't be much longer now.

James glanced out to sea. *Please have found a boat. Please be safe.*

"Stay until the end," Carlo managed to croak out. "I want you to see it."

In the distance, James heard shouts of alarm. He and Carlo had been spotted by soldiers, and they were racing this way. Too late to save their prince, but if they thought they'd take James alive, they were going to be disappointed.

Another wave rolled in, up to his waist now, but James kept the sword pinioned through Carlo's chest, holding him to the beach. Yet this time, it did not withdraw enough to allow the Beast to draw breath. Their gazes locked through bloody foam, and Carlo smiled.

"James!"

His head shot up at the sound of her voice, terror filling his chest because she hadn't made it. Which meant it wasn't just him the soldiers would catch, it was Ahnna as well.

Yet it wasn't Ahnna swimming in the waves that his eyes lit upon, but rather Ahnna standing in a tiny sailboat.

"Swim!" she screamed. "Hurry!"

Like iron to a lodestone, his focus went back to Carlo. The Beast was staring up at him through the water, still alive.

"James! Swim!"

He jerked the sword out of Carlo's chest. Reaching into the water, he caught hold of his shirt and jerked up above the surf. "If it is possible, I'll plead mercy for your Nina's life."

Horror filled Carlo's eyes. "No," he choked. "Don't ruin it. Don't—"

James dragged the sword blade across the Beast's jugular and dropped him into the next wave. Shoving the weapon into his belt, he waded out deeper and then began to swim.

He dove beneath the waves and fought the relentless current, fighting his way toward her. Arrows sliced into the water all around him, one carving a line of fire down his side, but he kept going. Because there wasn't anything in this world that he wouldn't go to war against to be at Ahnna's side.

A rope landed in front of him and James caught hold of it, gripping tight as Ahnna went back to the rudder, dragging him out of range of the arrows. He held on for all he was worth, coughing and choking when she lowered her sail so that he could climb in.

"Go," he gasped. "Hurry!"

She only smiled, the wind sending her hair floating about behind her. "We're on the sea now, James. They'll never catch me."

# 52

# KERIS

THE NEWS OF Prince James's death had spread through Harendell like wildfire, and it rendered all of Keris's labors to undermine Lestara for naught. Traitor and murderer she might be, but that was old news compared with Ahnna having slain the beloved James. Alexandra and her ladies all returned to the black gowns of mourning, but in a war of propaganda, the dowager queen now had an extreme advantage. Whether it was because Alexandra knew she'd neutered his threat, Harendellian propriety, or the simple fact that she didn't care if he remained, no one pushed Keris to leave Verwyrd.

And though he knew there was next to nothing that he could achieve by remaining, Keris didn't pack his bags.

He knew better than to allow Lestara inside his head, but the trouble with the truth was that it wasn't just his weapon to wield. As the nobility descended on Verwyrd for yet another royal funeral, Keris had conversations with many nobles with trading interests in the south. Which, in combination with what Saam and the others learned from guards and grooms and servants, painted a picture in which his return to Pyrinat would be far from celebrated.

"The storms have been *foul* this year," Saam muttered as he circled the room with Fiona, the tiny dog sniffing away in her endless hunt for poison, though she'd yet to yield results. "Lots of ships lost, and those who choose to run the gauntlet between the continents are sailing wide because the winds are rarely as bad out in the open sea. But it adds weeks onto the journey, and not all cargo can be so long in transport." He reached down to pat the dog on the head. "I suppose I never realized how much we depended on the bridge."

Keris knew. From Teraford north to Cardiff, merchants counted on the safety and reliability of the bridge. The blockade didn't just frustrate rulers, it destroyed livelihoods, and without coin, people lost everything. Including their lives. "Why don't they understand that Harendell is behind the blockades?"

"They do!" Fiona jumped at Saam's retort, and he murmured soothing words to the dog before adding, "They do, Keris. The trouble is that everyone thinks Harendell is *just*. They blame Ahnna. They blame Aren and Lara. They blame *you*, because everyone knows your bias toward Ithicana. It's perceived that you are putting your own interests first, never mind what it costs everyone else. It's . . . it's not improving your reputation in Pyrinat."

It was all going from bad to worse, but Keris couldn't help but ask, "Have you heard anything about Zarrah?"

Saam shook his head, then unfastened Fiona's leash. The little dog leapt onto the large cushion that Saam had purchased for her and curled up, either content that there was no poison in the room or content to watch Keris die.

"Not directly," Saam finally said. "The rumors are that she's grown reclusive. Arjun and her ministers of office are running the nation. The whispers go both ways. That she's looking to get rid of you or that she's unwilling to accept your steepening descent from grace and no longer cares to rule."

"It's all bullshit. No matter how she feels about any of this, Zarrah would never hide in a corner." Which made him sick with fear that something might have happened to her. Except that Arjun was loyal to his daughter. He wouldn't be able to hide his grief if she—

Keris shoved away the thought, unwilling to even consider it. "She has to be planning something. Maybe something secret to aid Ithicana. Zarrah wouldn't . . . she wouldn't walk away from Aren and Lara, even if she wanted to walk away from me."

"Which she doesn't," Saam said softly. "Keris, you're an arrogant asshole with more confidence than ten men combined. Don't let Harendellian propaganda undermine your certainty in Zarrah."

Easier said than done, given that he'd left with angry words between them. Easier said than done when he knew he was a burden to her rule.

The door opened and a servant carrying a tray entered. "A message from His Majesty."

Saam took the folded paper and waved it beneath Fiona's nose before handing it to Keris.

*I'd have your company. I grow sick of courtiers.*

*W*

Other than platitudes at James's funeral, this would be the first time that Keris had spoken to William since the king had almost stabbed him through the heart. Pulling on his black coat and smoothing back his hair, Keris went in search of the king, Saam following at his heels.

Dozens of voices filtered out of various rooms from the guests who remained after the funeral. But the noise of women laughing drew his attention. As he approached a set of doors to a sitting room, which were flanked by guards, a servant exited, the slowly closing door revealing Lestara surrounded by more than a dozen ladies vying for the queen's attention.

A memory of something she'd said to him filled Keris's thoughts. *Through me, you have the harem. The daughters and sisters and nieces of the most powerful men in the kingdom and beyond. Our influence will sway them to support you, to keep your brothers in check, and to ensure the crown remains firmly on your head.*

For better or worse, Coralyn had trained Lestara, and she was taking advantage of the distraction of James's death to secure new alliances with Harendellian noblewomen. Fighting her own war, and entrenching herself so deeply that nothing he or anyone else did could root her out.

The prince's death had been conveniently well timed. Which was not to say that Keris didn't believe James was dead, because he knew it was likely. Just as it was probable that Ahnna had killed him, albeit in self-defense. It just struck Keris that Alexandra had known James was dead long ago and had kept back the information for a moment when she needed to bolster her cause, much the way a general kept forces in reserve. As to whether the dowager queen had been involved in James's death . . . that was hard to say.

Reaching the king's study, he waited for the guards to announce him, and then muttered to Saam, "Wait here."

William was alone in the room, his black-clad form rendering him little more than a silhouette before the window, but he turned as the doors closed with a click. "Good to see you, Veliant. No hard feelings about that nick I gave you, right? I was deep in my cups and a man has to defend his woman. You understand that, right?"

"Already forgotten." Keris inclined his head. "Again, I am sorry for the loss of your brother."

"Not you too." William scrubbed a hand through his hair. "Everyone has been filling my ears with James this and James that and oh, we must avenge James. Even in death, he's the favorite." His green eyes locked on Keris. "You know what that's like, don't you? With your brother?"

It took every bit of self-control Keris had to keep the disgust off his face as he said, "Brothers. My father had a habit of telling me every time one died that he wished it had been me."

William huffed out a loud breath, then moved to fill two glasses. "If my father was alive, that's surely what he'd say. He told me all the time that he wished James was his heir."

*Because James* was *his heir*, Keris thought, but he only took the glass.

"It's not that I'm glad he's dead. Jamie . . ." William pressed a hand to his face, fighting tears, but then his breathing steadied. "I loved my brother. I wish he was here, but part of me wonders if it's better that he's not. Everyone will take me more seriously without James to compare me with."

People would take him seriously to his face, because he was king. His word was law, and all of Harendell would have to behave. But behind his back, no one would ever respect this man-child who spent his days gambling and reveling while his nation readied for war. Alexandra would make all the decisions, and everyone would know it. Keris could already hear the insults. *Suckling Sovereign. The Coddle King. The Swaddlelord.* No doubt the common folk would come up with even more creative terms in time.

"We received word from Riomar that the Beast of Amarid is dead," William said. "I do wish James was alive to have heard that. Those two *hated* each other. I always thought James would be the one to kill him, but I'm glad he wasn't. Would never have heard the end of it."

"Do you know who killed him?"

"Apparently a nobody who escaped the prison and got lucky with his blade. Though I daresay, the only individual in Amarid who'll mourn Carlo is the Crimson Widow." He snickered. "Now all she has left is little girls as heirs."

For a man wholly under the control of his own mother, William held little respect for the prowess of women, but Keris refrained from commenting.

Silence stretched between them.

"You understand that I can't let this go, right, Veliant?" William finally blurted out, then downed his drink. "I wish it was just Ahnna who had wronged us, but Aren's made such a mess of things. Can't you convince him to give up so that we don't have to do this the hard way?"

"Probably not, no." Keris stared at his drink, trying to think of what he could do that might prevent war the moment the calm season arrived, but he felt as though he'd played all his cards.

"That's a shame."

A knock sounded at the door, then it opened and a Harendellian guard stepped in. "Excuse the interruption, Your Grace," he said, bowing low. "But a Valcottan messenger has arrived who wishes to speak to His Highness."

William gave a loud snort. "Let me guess. It's your man Adrius back from Ithicana to inform us Aren still thinks he can cling to his throne."

"Not Adrius, Your Grace," the soldier said. "She said her name is Daria, and she brings word directly from the empress."

Keris tensed, and William cackled. "Worried that your wife is about to haul you back home by your heels, Veliant? Was fun while it lasted, am I right?" He slapped his thigh, a wild grin on his face, which Keris knew was a challenge for him to defy what orders Zarrah might have sent. "Bring this Daria in!"

The guard stepped out into the hall. A moment later, Keris heard the sharp thud of heeled boots against the floor, and a woman in a Valcottan uniform strode into the room. A woman who was most definitely not Daria.

Keris's heart skipped then sped as Zarrah's beautiful dark eyes locked on his, his tongue so twisted with shock at her appearance that he could not speak.

"Your Majesty." She bowed low to William, then gave a smaller bow to Keris. "Your Imperial Highness."

"Daria," he managed to croak out, his brain racing to comprehend what possible reason Zarrah had to risk the Tempest Seas and violate every protocol by sneaking into Harendell in disguise.

William suffered no such speech impediment, his eyes slowly drifting up and down Zarrah's body, his tone smooth as he said, "Welcome to Verwyrd, Daria. We are most delighted to have you join us."

"It is an honor to be in your presence, Your Grace."

William's eyes lingered on Zarrah's ass, the fabric of her uniform trousers tight across its curve. "It is a pleasure to be in yours, Daria."

Every instinct demanded he beat William bloody for daring to look at Zarrah like that. Instead Keris forced his face into a mask of mild annoyance as William's eyes flicked to him.

"God, Veliant, but I might have to reconsider having women in the military, because I envy you in the women you surround yourself with. Do all Valcottan women look like this?"

Keris gave a shrug. "Daria is quite average in looks, if I'm being honest. Very typical of what you'll see on the streets of Pyrinat."

William scoffed. "You can't be serious. More beautiful than this?" He gestured up and down Zarrah's body. Her expression was unmoved but for a dangerous gleam in her eye.

"No contest." Keris twisted his cuff link in circles. "The empress is, of course, the most beautiful woman in Valcotta, but she is also the most likely to cut your heart out if you look at her the wrong way."

William burst into laughter. "Noted, noted! I wouldn't dare step on your toes, anyway. There is a certain code among friends, but I'm not sure that code extends to bodyguards. You wouldn't mind if Daria joined me for a drink after we're done here, would you, Veliant? I could use some cheering up with all that is going on."

"Not at all." Keris gave his cuff link another twist, because the alternative was to reach for a weapon. "Daria can regale you with stories about her incarceration at Devil's Island. She was the leader of the rebels, and I daresay she took the duty of keeping her followers fed very much to heart. Didn't you, Daria?"

Zarrah inclined her head. "One does what one must, Your Imperial Highness."

William blanched, and Keris gave a small yawn before adding, "If you're willing to risk your cock near that mouth, you're a braver man than I am."

Zarrah smiled at William, and it was all straight white teeth.

"I spoke in jest, of course." William looked ready to be ill. "I am a married man."

Keris rose to his feet. "By your leave, Your Grace, I'll excuse myself to hear what orders the empress has for me."

He started toward the door, but drew up short when Zarrah gave a soft cough. "The empress's message is for His Grace."

"Let's have it, then," William said. "I've other matters to attend to."

"It is a verbal message, for Her Imperial Majesty did not wish to risk her message falling into the wrong hands, given it pertains to the queen."

William shifted on the sofa, frowning. "What could Zarrah possibly have to say about my mother?"

Keris struggled not to cast his eyes skyward at the slip. It seemed even William realized that Alexandra ruled.

Zarrah gave another small cough. "Not the dowager queen, Your Grace. *Your* queen, the lady Lestara. It pertains to the relationship between her and Empress Petra, which resulted in the sacking of Vencia."

"Ah." William crossed his arms. "I find myself disinterested in what I suspect will be unjust slander of my wife. Lestara has made it very clear to me that she was used and manipulated by Petra, who took advantage of Lestara's desire for a better future for Maridrina." He shot an apologetic look at Keris. "You're good fun, Veliant, but you weren't much of a king. No offense, of course."

It was hard not to laugh at William's hypocrisy. "None taken."

"Lestara's only goal was to aid in the rise of a ruler who would have the best interest of the Maridrinian people at heart," William continued. "It was foolish of her, of course, and not a mistake my mother would have made, but Lestara was young and inexperienced. Being raised in Cardiff, as she was, there was no opportunity for her to be educated in the ways of policy, and Petra took advantage of her sweet nature. As did your brother. What was his name?"

"Royce." Keris remembered all too well how easily Lestara had manipulated his half brother.

"That's right! Royce! At any rate, all the casualties in Vencia unfortunately must be set at your feet, Veliant. You turned your back and lowered your guard, leaving the defense of your capital to women. I read the copies of the letters Petra wrote that you sent on to my father. Petra was a sly bitch who took advantage, that much was very clear to me. You were responsible for protecting Lestara, but you didn't. I will not make the same mistake, and beneath my mother's tutelage, Lestara will become a fine queen."

Zarrah reached into the pocket of her uniform and withdrew several pieces of paper. "Her Imperial Majesty respects Your Grace's intelligence and capacity to make informed decisions in all things regarding the governance of Harendell, but she feels compelled to ensure you are in possession of all possible information. To that end, she has charged me with delivering correspondence written by the lady Lestara, which was discovered among Empress Petra's personal effects. These are the original copies, which means they are in Lady Lestara's own hand."

Keris bit his tongue and crossed his arms, noting that William eyed the letters like he'd been presented with a handful of earthworms.

"One passage, in particular, caught Her Imperial Majesty's attention." Zarrah unfolded a page and cleared her throat. *"There is no price I won't pay, no cost too high, to ensure my destiny as queen of Maridrina. Too long has the nation floundered beneath the rule of men, and yet Maridrinians still do not see the merits of female rule. That the Veliants continue to reign is the fault of the people, and it seems to me that they will not see the error of their ways unless they are forced to pay the ultimate price. Perhaps when all they hold dear lies in smoke and ruin and shallow graves, they will reach for the alternative that our alliance provides."*

Nausea twisted in Keris's stomach at the coldness of Lestara's words. There could be no denying that she knew exactly what she was agreeing to by allying with Petra, and had felt no remorse at the death and destruction it would bring down upon Vencia. She could atone for the rest of her life and never make up for half of what she'd done.

William's expression was entirely blank as Zarrah handed the letters to the guard who'd accompanied her in. He circled the table and set them before his king. Keris half expected William to light them up using the lamp flame on the table, but instead he read in silence. A slight tic formed in his jaw as he took in Lestara's words, then he tucked the pages into the inner pocket of his coat. "We thank the empress for her concern."

"By your leave, Your Grace," Keris said, "I'll hear my own reports in private."

William flicked his fingers in dismissal, then reached for his glass.

Keris jerked his chin at Zarrah, who followed him from the room. Saam and the rest of his guard fell into step with them as he walked through the Sky Palace, Saam searching his rooms before giving him a slight nod. "I'll leave Daria to convey the empress's report," he said, nothing in his expression giving away that Zarrah was anything other than a Valcottan soldier. "You will not be disturbed."

Keris wasn't entirely certain that was a good thing, because though Zarrah's expression was bland, he could feel anger seething from her.

Saam closed the door behind him, and Zarrah reached out and put the latch in place.

Silence stretched, and he finally said, "I'm sorry."

She crossed her arms. "For what? Not returning to Valcotta, as you promised me? Or for doing the exact opposite of staying out of danger by diving headfirst into it? Or is there something else you have to be sorry for?"

"I was actually referring to me implying you were a cannibal to the king of Harendell, but it was for your own good. William's a womanizer, and if he'd put his hands on you, I'd have had to kill him. So I take it back, I'm not actually sorry."

Zarrah's eyes narrowed.

He'd thought about what he'd say to her when they were reunited, rehearsed a thousand apologies for having gone back on his word, for not consulting with her before leaving for Harendell, and most of all, for their argument just before he'd left Pyrinat and all that had led up to it. Yet every carefully composed word now tasted sour as lies, because the truth was, he had no regrets.

"When I learned you'd been put on Devil's Island, it felt like I stood alone," he finally said. "It felt like I was the only one who was willing to fight for your freedom, but then Aren and Lara agreed to help. They risked their lives, and the lives of their people, in order to aid me, and then answered my call to war to defeat Petra. Now the desperation is theirs, and I couldn't leave them to stand alone." He swallowed hard, wishing he could read her expression. "Just as you wouldn't leave them to stand alone, and for me to waste precious time asking a question I already knew the answer to would be admitting I don't know your heart as well as I know my own."

He heard her soft intake of breath, saw the slight softening in the tension of her jaw, but his wife didn't speak.

"I know it has been harder than either of us dreamed," he

continued. "But I would rather die from poison in my cup than stop being a man worthy of your love, Valcotta."

Zarrah bit her bottom lip, blinking rapidly, then she said, "I don't want you to be anyone other than who you are." In three quick strides, she closed the distance between them. "But we fight these battles together. Live and die together. You swore that to me when you made me your wife, and that's why I'm here."

# 53
# ZARRAH

I T FELT LIKE she'd been apart from Keris for an eternity rather than a matter of months, and Zarrah's breath had caught in her throat when she'd first stepped into William's office. Like seeing him for the first time but also being reconnected with the other half of her soul. It had made her forget herself. Made her forget all the plans she'd forged in the arduous journey north, which had taken far longer than she had hoped. Every second of it plagued with fear for her own life, Keris's life, and the lives of all those she held dear.

But now she was reunited with her husband, and in his presence Zarrah's fears melted away as she inhaled his familiar scent and drowned in the azure ocean of his eyes.

Keris caught hold of her and pulled her close, and Zarrah didn't resist. Allowed herself to be tucked against him, his heartbeat rapid but steady in her ear, and she drew in a shuddering breath, throat tight with too much emotion.

"I've hated every second away from you." His fingers tangled in her loose curls, which had grown past her shoulders, and a soft whimper escaped her lips as he tugged, tilting her face upward.

"Even when you were gambling, drinking, carousing, and womanizing with William?" She gave him a slow smile. "I heard all sorts of rumors when I reached Sableton."

"Cover for my scheming." His lips brushed hers. "Keeping up with that idiot man-child was more torturous than Devil's Island. I'd rather spend an evening with our old friend Flay than with the king of Harendell. At least Flay was consistent and focused, and he didn't need his mother to achieve all his goals for him."

Zarrah let out a choked laugh, and the last of her tension faded away. Reaching up, she pulled loose the tie holding his hair back, the lengths falling to his shoulders. She rose onto her toes and kissed him, fingers of one hand tangling in his silken strands even as she unfastened the buttons of his coat.

As their kiss deepened, their hips met, and the hard length of his arousal met the juncture of her belly and thigh, sending a jolt through her core. Zarrah couldn't stifle the low moan that escaped her lips before she pinched them shut, aware that not everyone who might be listening was on their side.

"Saam checks the rooms daily for listening holes," Keris murmured as he kissed a line of fire down the side of her throat. "Walls and doors are thick."

"They'll just think you're sleeping with your bodyguard. No one will suspect it's me."

He pulled back, brow furrowing. "I don't want them thinking that. I don't want anyone thinking I'd betray you."

Her chest warmed at the vehemence in his voice, and she bit his bottom lip. "I know you wouldn't, and that is all that matters. Now kiss me."

"Yes, Imperial Majesty." He tucked a curl behind her ear, then claimed her mouth, tongue stroking over hers. Zarrah bowed into him, their bodies pressing even closer together as he trailed a hand down her spine and squeezed the curve of her ass. Lust surged through her, the desire to forgo foreplay making her body tremble, though vanquished by a primal need to have him inside her. To be reunited again in all possible ways.

She fumbled with the buttons of his shirt, wanting to tear them off but knowing servants would find that sort of evidence. It made the moment feel illicit and dangerous the way it had been when she was a prisoner in Vencia, and her breath came in small gasps as she struggled to maintain control.

Keris allowed her to pull off his shirt, and she hissed in anger at the wound on his bare chest, part of her wanting to storm through the palace and put a knife through William's heart for harming what was hers. But the thought fell away as he unbuttoned her coat, casting it aside, and then lifted her shirt over her head, a soft moan escaping him as her breasts were bared.

"I had forgotten what true beauty looked like," he whispered, holding her gaze as he dropped to one knee, then the other before pressing his lips to her stomach. Her heart beat staccato as he unfastened her belt, easing her trousers over her hips as he kissed his way down her body.

Zarrah swayed, barely managing the balance it took to step on the heels of her boots and kick them off. His knuckles grazed her skin as he removed her trousers, weapons thudding against the floor, her body entirely naked. "I need . . ." she whispered, words failing her as he kissed her knees, the insides of her thighs, her nipples tightening in the cool air.

"I know what you need, love."

He caught hold of her thighs and pushed them wide, then bent his head to claim her. His normal tortuously slow teasing was absent, betraying that his control teetered on the same brink as hers. His fingers slipped inside her as he sucked her clit, her body jerking with pleasure even as she caught hold of him for balance. Her climax was rising, and Zarrah clenched her teeth tight, feeling a scream of pleasure rising with it.

"Not yet," he murmured, then stood, lifting her with him.

Zarrah wrapped her legs around him as he carried her to the bed, laying her across the velvet coverlet. She could feel his arousal pressing hard against the apex of her thighs, and she reached for his belt, but Keris only shook his head.

He bent over her, drawing one nipple into his mouth while his fingers worked between her legs, and Zarrah pressed her forearm to her mouth to silence her moans.

"Come for me," he murmured. "You break for no one but me, Valcotta."

She bit down on her forearm as his tongue took the place of his fingers, the sound of his belt unfastening nearly her undoing.

His trousers hit the floor, and then he slipped two fingers inside her. Stroking in time with his tongue, stringing her as tight as a bow until she snapped with a cry, pleasure rushing through her in waves.

Keris didn't give her time to come back into herself before his mouth found hers. He gripped her wrists, pinning her, and then plunged into her, filling her completely and making her cry out as his hips met her ass in one hard thrust. She wrapped her legs around him, pulling him deep as he filled her over and over again.

She tasted blood as she bit down on her wrist to keep from sobbing, her body tensing and building in a way that made the tension she'd felt before feel like a drop of water in a sea of desire, and Zarrah thrust her hips against him, hunting a release that she half feared might drown her.

He moved her wrists so that he could grip them with one hand, and with the other, Keris caressed the swells of her breasts and teased at their peaks, and that sent her over the edge a second time, her body tightening around his length as her toes curled and her back arched, her heart threatening to tear from her chest as she felt him fall over the edge with her.

"God, Zarrah," he groaned into her throat, collapsing against her. "I love you."

Tears burned in her eyes, all the walls she'd built to keep herself together crumbling down. "Never leave me again."

"Never. I swear it."

Every part of her wanted to cling to this moment. To let silence reign, the only conversation touch and soft breath. For there to be only the two of them, all the world outside the room falling away.

But they were at war, and the fight waited for no one, so Zarrah said, "We need to tear the crown from that bitch's head."

# 54

# KERIS

KERIS PULLED HIS wife against him, eyeing the dying light of the sun through the expansive windows, longing for darkness to fall and, with it, any reason to leave this room. But it was not lost on him that the stakes were too high to lose himself in his wife for long. "Which bitch?"

"As much as I'd love to say Alexandra, I mean Lestara. I know you have been working to undermine her and the Cardiffian alliance. What progress have you made turning William against her?"

"None. The letters you brought were timely, but in truth, I don't think they'll be enough to sway William. Lestara has his measure and has dug her claws in deep. Plus, she's pregnant."

Zarrah released an aggrieved sigh. "Of course she is. God have mercy on that child to be born to such a family."

"I'd thought Alexandra would move swiftly to be rid of her, but now I'm not so sure. I think she'll keep Lestara in play until she's ready to move on Cardiff, which is likely to be years from now."

"Maybe." His wife's expression was thoughtful. "Lestara makes emotional choices, which Alexandra won't like. If I were a betting woman—"

"Which you are."

She smiled. "My bet is that Lestara won't survive the birth of the child. It's risky business at the best of times, and it would be nothing for Alexandra to arrange to give her something that causes her to bleed out. Ronan can hardly blame Harendell for that, and he still has the advantage of a grandchild sitting pretty as heir. As long as Harendell agrees to move on Amarid, he may be content. It's not as though she's a favored daughter."

Keris frowned, a memory crawling up from the depths of his mind. "Sara said something to me when I first discovered what Lestara had done. She said that she'd overheard the harem discussing Lestara and that Coralyn had been grooming her for . . . err—" He winced. "—me."

Zarrah lifted one dark eyebrow. "Coralyn did love to meddle."

He rolled onto his back, staring at the bed's canopy. "Why would Coralyn choose Lestara as her successor to rule the harem?"

"Maybe because Lestara was young and beautiful?" She bent over his chest and examined the healing wound on it, frowning. "I feel compelled to also point out that Lestara was the only one who hadn't given birth to one of your half siblings."

"Minor factors." When she grimaced, he added, "In Coralyn's mind, at any rate. She would have backed the woman she believed would lead me to the greatest success. I can't begin to fathom why she believed Lestara was that woman."

"Coralyn died before Lestara showed her darker attributes. She seemed to get on well enough with the other women while I was imprisoned with them."

It was not a topic that he relished discussing with his wife, but Keris couldn't let go of the sense that he was missing something. "Coralyn would have had her measure. Would have sensed her ambition and selfishness. What about Lestara was worth saddling me with such a risk?"

"Get Sarhina to ask the other women in the harem?" Zarrah shifted so that she was looking down into his eyes. "Though beyond how poorly Lestara took your subsequent rejection and the fact that she'll surely kill you if she gets the chance, I don't really see why Coralyn's intentions matter."

Keris didn't either, and yet . . . "She told me that Ronan would kill her for failing if I sent her back to Cardiff."

"Her position secured a trade deal with Maridrina."

"A minor one. We aren't in high need of furs in Vencia." He rubbed at his temples. "*Fuck.* I wish I'd paid more attention to the things she said to me, but every thought in my skull was getting you off Devil's Island. Ronan had to have known there was no chance of her becoming queen of Maridrina, prophecy or no. What was his goal for her? What was she supposed to achieve?"

Zarrah curled up next to him, her fingernails tracing lines up and down his chest. "The Cardiffians put a lot of weight into prophecy, Keris, and I've heard that Ronan's queen, Calythra, is a seer of renown. I'm not sure you can rely on logic to understand the things they do."

"Except if we are to break the alliance between Cardiff and Harendell, we need to understand it." He sighed, distracted by his wife's touch and wishing he could lose himself in her for days on end. But there was no time for that.

"Lestara knows your face and knows it well," he continued, rolling onto his side. "The Harendellians won't take it well to learn that the empress of Valcotta is roaming the Sky Palace in disguise. You can't stay, Zarrah. Especially given what is happening back home with the herds."

"It was Harendellian cattle that brought the disease. Cattle that somehow escaped from their isolation to join other animals." Her face hardened. "Seems rather *timely*, don't you think?"

His anger rose, much of it directed at himself. "Alexandra neglected to mention that Harendell was the source."

"The animals were premium bulls sent via ship *before* Edward died."

Zarrah's tone was steady, but he could feel her fury. "Do you think he's responsible?"

"Hold that thought." His wife slipped out of bed and crossed the room to her discarded clothing, only to let out a yelp. "What is that?"

Fiona had appeared from the sitting room and sat watching them expectantly. "Oh. That's Fiona. She's a poison-sniffing dog. Saam bought her."

"Did he now?" Zarrah stooped to stroke Fiona, then shooed the dog into the other room before picking up her jacket.

She extracted a letter that showed signs of having been read many times and handed it to him. Keris frowned at the sight of Eddie's familiar handwriting, skimming the letter and then turning it over to reveal where Zarrah had helpfully decoded the hidden message.

*I will have wed William to Lestara by the time you receive this. Forgive the seeming betrayal of our friendship. As one who has risked all for love, you will one day understand everything, but know I regret the hurt my actions will cause you and your family.*

"It arrived after you left."

"I know," Keris muttered, because this was the actual letter that Cormac had intended his forgery to replace. He swiftly relayed all that had happened since he'd left Pyrinat, leaving out no details. Darkness had fallen by the time he'd finished.

"Harendell is living up to its reputation." Zarrah curled against him, staring up at the canopy. "It's not a matter of one plot. Every cursed person in this court is scheming, and it all tangles together until the plots can't be separated. It's clear that Edward aimed to take the bridge and put James on Ithicana's throne as well as name him heir. Just as clear that Alexandra now aims to give William as much and more. Maridrina was never in a position to aid, but infecting Valcotta's herds was a surefire way to keep us out of the fray. The question is whether it was Edward's plan or Alexandra's? Has she picked up the reins of his plots, or was she scheming the entire time and has only now stepped to the fore? Given James's legitimacy, my gut tells me the latter, and I can't help but question whether she's behind Edward's death."

"It makes sense, but Ahnna has profound motive and the martial skill to have done it. She threatened Edward before a ballroom full of people and then was caught red-handed attacking Alexandra by James and his men, who followed bloody boot prints from Edward's rooms. Did I mention that Edward was stabbed forty-seven times and he didn't die quickly? Alexandra doesn't have the skill or strength for such a feat."

"Perhaps she used Ahnna, then it got out of hand when Ahnna realized she'd been tricked?"

"Maybe. But the only one who could tell us is Ahnna, and I doubt she's still alive. There is no proof against Alexandra, and William is entirely under her control." He watched the clouds that were gathering, slowly cloaking the view beyond. "I'd suggest assassinating them both, but blame for that will only fall back on Aren. The Harendellians see possessing the bridge as a possibility, so whoever claims the throne will only leverage the deaths of the Ashfords to go for the same goal. Cardiff is too goddamned obsessed with revenge against Katarina to see the threat they face, and as it is, William seems unwilling to see Lestara for who she is. As much as I hate it, Amarid feels like the only lighthouse in this storm."

"Katarina knows she's in danger—that's the only reason she's clamoring for an alliance." Zarrah shook her head. "My father and Daria are working to prove the cattle were deliberately sabotaged and to find proof of who is behind it. If we can tie it to the Ashfords, Valcotta has grounds to retaliate. My father is playing up that I've gone into seclusion because of conflict with you, and I'm hoping that Alexandra, if she's guilty, will take the opportunity to try to foster a coup against me by backing one of my cousins, because she has to want to get rid of me. If she does it, she'll play right into my hands."

"She's clever. She might not bite." Cleverer than he'd realized, and Keris wasn't unaware of the certainty growing inside him that he was outmatched by Alexandra. She was smarter than he was, and he didn't like it.

"Very clever, but if all our suspicions are true, she's woven so many threads, north and south, that she risks tangling herself. My father played the propaganda game with Petra for years, so he's got the skill to entice her into making a move." She sighed. "The question is whether we have time for this strategy. The calm season is coming, and then it will cease to be a war of blockades and words. An alliance with Amarid will be the only chance in that situation."

"The enemy of my enemy is my friend." But God, he wished it was anyone other than the Crimson Widow.

A knock sounded at the door, and Saam's voice called through. "It's important."

Keris tensed, but Zarrah was already reaching for her clothes. "Get dressed," she said. "Put yourself together."

"Saam knows what we've been doing," he said, reaching for his own clothes.

"This palace has eyes everywhere."

Fixing his hair into its usual knot at the back of his head, Keris went to the door and unlatched it. Saam pushed his way inside, shutting the door behind him. "There's something you need to see."

Going to the window, he pressed his hands against it. "Look."

Keris looked down the incredible drop of the spiral to the city below, which was awash with the glow of lanterns. "What am I looking at?"

"The procession on the river. Do you see it?"

Keris could indeed see a tiny carriage surrounded by mounted horsemen with torches. They crossed the bridge, then headed north. "What are we looking at, Saam?"

"Two things. The first is a messenger who has been sent to retrieve Princess Virginia and her entourage."

His heart sped, but it was Zarrah who asked, "And the second?"

"Lestara is in that carriage," Saam said with a grin. "Whatever you two did worked. She left the palace in tears."

Keris nearly choked on the thickness of his relief, bracing a hand against the window. "We've done what we can. We need to leave, Zarrah."

The glass was cold beneath his hand as he waited for his wife to respond, but Zarrah only watched the procession of torches slowly disappear into the trees. Finally, she said, "Not yet."

Turning her back on the view of Harendell, she drew in a deep breath. "There's one more thing we need to do."

# 55

# AHNNA

STIFF WINDS SENT them hurtling down the coast, Ahnna pushing the tiny vessel to the limit of its capacity in her hunt for more speed. First to evade capture, and then because she was on the hunt.

Yet as fast as they flew over the whitecaps, in her heart, she feared it wouldn't be enough.

The Amaridian merchant ships carrying the grain were built for speed and rough seas, and the captains had the nerve required to open all the sails to the wind. Especially given their need to evade the Harendellians. They also had a full day's head start.

"Let me fix the splint on your arm."

These were the first words they'd exchanged that hadn't been her shouting orders at him like he was a member of her crew, and for reasons Ahnna couldn't explain, her chest tightened.

Sucking in a mouthful of air, she dug her nails into the wood of the rudder, fighting for composure.

"Ahnna?"

"I didn't think you'd be alive." Her voice came out as a croak. "I left you, and I thought I was too late. That he'd . . . that he'd . . ."

James frowned at her. "You thought that *Carlo* would best me in single-handed combat? Carlo, who has only *one eye* and *one testicle*, would outfight me? I'm insulted, Princess."

A laugh that sounded like a sob exploded from her lips. "You're right. How foolish of me."

The corner of his mouth turned up, and though James was battered, bloodied, and weeks away from a razor, he was so painfully handsome that her breath caught in her chest. His hand tangled in her hair and he tilted her face up. "Carlo's dead."

"Are you sure?" She'd seen the soldiers running to the Beast. Pulling him out of the waves. "Drowning isn't . . . it doesn't always take, you know?" And it felt like Carlo had a shocking ability to survive that which would kill any other.

"I stabbed him in the chest and slit his jugular, so I'm fairly confident it *took*." James pulled her against him, and Ahnna rested her cheek on his chest, hearing the steady beat of his heart. "Our list of problems is long, but the Beast is no longer one of them."

"Katarina will be after our blood for killing her son."

"Let her come." James's hand slid down her right arm, fingers dancing over the splint, which was hanging on by a thread. "Let me fix this."

"I don't need the splint anymore, so just take it off. One of the positive things about sitting in the Furnace is that it gave my arm time to heal."

"Not enough time." His other hand ran down her back, and an ache formed between her thighs. "It will snap if you put too much strain on it without proper splinting, so let's fix that."

What she wanted was to stay in his embrace, but Ahnna reluctantly took a half step back. James knelt before her while she kept her left hand on the rudder, her eyes on the horizon. But her focus was entirely on him.

James took apart the wooden slats that made up the splint, his fingers running over the twin breaks in the bones of her forearm. The site was still sore, but his touch made her feel things other than pain. Made her remember the sensation of his fingers inside her body as he brought her to climax in the Furnace. Reminding her that there were no longer any walls between them, and only open seas surrounding them.

"By some miracle, this is actually healing well," James murmured as he began resplinting her arm. "How you managed not to rebreak it while escaping from the Furnace, fighting through guards, and swimming through the open sea to commandeer a boat is a mystery to me."

"Just lucky, I suppose."

He didn't answer, and Ahnna tore her gaze from the horizon to look down. James was still on his knees, but he was looking up at her with an expression that made her stomach flip. "What?"

"You are the most stubborn, fierce, and extraordinarily loyal woman I have ever met," he replied. "There is no woman alive who is your equal, Ahnna Kertell."

Warmth rose in her cheeks. "I . . . That's . . . If you think that, you haven't met many women. Lara—"

"I've met Lara. My comment stands, and given that Lara once told me that Harendell's gain was Ithicana's loss, I suspect she agrees with me."

Her eyes pricked with tears and Ahnna blinked rapidly, remembering how Lara had been the only one to stand on the pier at Northwatch and bid her farewell. Remembering the dress she'd sent. The necklace. A tear rolled down her cheek, because Katarina had taken it, and she had no idea how she'd get it back.

But what she hadn't taken was the memories Ahnna associated with it, and the sudden desire to make things right with Lara filled her.

"We'll get there in time," James said, seeming to hear her thoughts. "You'll see them soon."

She wiped her wet cheeks. "I'm afraid, James. Afraid to hope, because me wanting something feels like ensuring the exact opposite result. I don't get what I want, not ever, and part of me wonders if I should stop wanting anything at all." The words came out in a flood, sounding like gibberish, but at the heart of them was her fear of hope. "I'm sorry. None of that is important."

"What you want is important to me." His voice was low, and

Ahnna's toes curled against the deck. "Tell me what you want. Something that's small. Something that is just for you."

She looked behind them at the ship's wake, hunting for signs of pursuit because it felt selfish to think about small things. But then she whispered, "Lavender soap and warm water."

"What else?"

"My horse." Her voice cracked, because though Dippy had been sent back to Harendell, she feared for his fate.

James made a noise of sympathy, and she knew he had the same thoughts about Maven.

Ahnna bit the insides of her cheeks, listening to the sound of the waves slapping against the hull, adjusting the rudder as the wind shifted. Words sat on the tip of her tongue, wanting to be unleashed into the silent tension between them, but this want still felt forbidden. "You. I want you."

James gripped the rudder with one hand, then pulled her left hand free of it.

"James, what are you doing? You're going to lose the wind and . . ." She trailed off as he lifted her left hand to his lips, gently kissing her scraped and scarred skin.

"Our future looks bleak." He brushed his thumb over her knuckles. "The chances of us surviving this war are not good, and even if we do, I'm not sure what our futures will hold. But no matter where life takes us, I want to be at your side every minute of it until my heart ceases to beat. I love you, Your Highness. I love you in a way that will never be eclipsed by another emotion, and I want you to be my wife."

The world seemed to stand still. As though it too were taking a breath. The ship and the sea and the wind all fell away so there was nothing but her hand in James's, a question she'd never dreamed he would ask on his lips. Never dreamed of, because those who served the crown as she and James did were not given the opportunity to choose. Especially not to choose the enemy.

But God help her, Ahnna wanted to say yes. Wanted to be his, because she loved him in a way that made her heart burn like the sun.

Even if her own hand was not something she could give.

"It's not my choice," she finally managed to say. "My brother. You'd have to ask his permission, and I don't think—"

"I don't care what your brother has to say on the matter," James interrupted. "The only answer that matters is yours. And if you say yes, there is no crown or power in this world or the next that will keep me from wedding you, Ahnna."

Her whole body was shaking, because her soul wanted this. Yet to say yes would be the purest form of selfishness, because as Ithicana's princess, her hand held value. Even with her name tarnished by Alexandra's false accusations, Aren could use her to secure other alliances now that everything had fallen apart with Harendell. For her to take that opportunity away from him, after the hell she'd put Ithicana through, was not right. Even if doing so would cut out her heart and leave her a shadow of the woman that she was, for Ithicana, she'd do it.

A tear trickled down her cheek. "Every part of my heart says yes."

James tilted his head, his amber eyes narrowing slightly. "For anyone but you, I'd say that is all that matters, but you're unwilling to give your heart anything that might have consequences for Ithicana."

"I know it doesn't feel like it, but we are on opposite sides of this, James." *Opposite sides, yet the idea of pulling my hand from yours is the worst thing I can imagine.* "Ithicana and Harendell are enemies now."

"No." He gave a slow shake of his head. "The enemy is Alexandra and those who support her schemes. The people of Harendell are as much a victim of her manipulation as we are. They've been tricked into supporting a war they never asked for and never wanted, and if they can be made to understand the truth, they will turn on her and this war will be over."

Keeping a firm grip on the rudder and their course straight as an arrow shot, James stood. His fingers trailed up the inside of her arm, the sensation sending sparks of lightning through her body. "We are on the same side in this, Ahnna. Alexandra arranged for the murder of both my parents, and then tried to trick me into murdering you. She's torn apart my family and embroiled my people in a war they didn't want, and I think it won't be long until she turns on my family in Cardiff. You and I are allies in every possible way, and I will have your back in this fight, in every fight, until we take our place in the stars."

He so rarely invoked Cardiff's mythology around her, and it made her heart race because it was proof of how deeply he trusted her. That around her, the walls all came down and he gave her, and only her, his true self.

Maybe protocol demanded her fate be controlled by Ithicana's crown, but it wasn't just her heart that screamed he was the one for her. Her mind also screamed that there was no man in this world who would be a better ally to Ithicana than James Ashford. "My answer is yes."

The world was still trembling from the chaos they'd left behind, but in James's arms, Ahnna found something solid—something she could choose. Her breath hitched as he cupped her face, not with urgency, but reverence, like she was something sacred, and when his lips met hers, the ache in her chest finally broke. The kiss was trembling and fierce, threaded with the weight of everything they'd survived and everything they still might lose. "I will be your wife."

No sooner did the words exit her lips than the wind gusted, tearing at her salt-crusted hair, and gooseflesh rose on Ahnna's arms. Turning in James's embrace so that her back was pressed against his chest, she looked up into the clear skies.

"What is it?" James asked. "What do you see?"

Fear pooled in her stomach, and Ahnna swallowed hard. "Tie everything down. It looks like the tempests will go to war against Ithicana's enemies tonight, and we are going to get caught in the salvo."

# 56

# JAMES

How Ahnna had known what was coming, James couldn't have said, because the skies seemed clear and the seas obliging. The perfect sailing conditions.

Right up until the moment they weren't.

As dusk fell, the skies blackened with something far more ominous than the loss of the sun. The brisk breeze shifted into violent gusts, and the swells deepened as lightning danced across the swirling clouds.

"The Amaridians will have to fight this storm too," he shouted over the noise. "With luck, the storm will sink them."

"They are big ships, and the Amaridians are excellent sailors," Ahnna shouted back, her hair whipping across her face. "Whereas this is a fucking pleasure craft and my only sailor is *you*."

She wasn't the only one who regretted that fact—James knew nothing about sailing a ship like this. "Can we go wide?"

She shook her head. "This storm will blow us straight out into the open seas if we let it, and we don't have any supplies. If we cut east, we'll run afoul of the Harendellian navy. The Amaridians are going straight through it, so we will as well."

"How . . ." He trailed off, catching sight of flickers of specks of lantern light in the distance. It should have been impossible to catch up to the three-masted ships, but somehow, Ahnna had done it. And from the fierce determination on her face, James knew she intended to attack them the moment they got close enough to do so.

"If we can catch them in the night, we can get aboard and kill the sailors," she shouted, validating his thought. "Sink at least one of them."

*Or the storm will smash our tiny craft to pieces, and we'll both drown.*

James's lips parted to tell her to ease off and get out of the path of the tempest, but he bit down on his words. She'd fought too hard to give up now, and James knew that was how she'd see it. Because if that vessel beat them to Ithicana by even half a day, people would die. Ithicana was too starved for grain to hold back on opening a sack or two, and so instead he tightened his grip on the rail.

The tempest worsened, waves washing over the deck and the single mast groaning from the strain of the vicious wind in the sails. He lost his footing over and over, only the ropes securing them to the helm keeping them both from going overboard, but Ahnna remained on the wake of the Amaridian ship.

Thunder crashed overhead, punctuated by waves swamping the deck, and James struggled to get a breath in the deluge of rain.

Ahnna had her shoulder wedged beneath a wheel spoke, face twisted with strain as she fought against the pull of the water.

How he heard it over the noise, James didn't know, but the sound of ripping fabric filled his ears.

"The sail," he screamed in her ear. "It's tearing! We need to lower it now!"

Because if they lost the sail, they'd be lost at sea. Either to die from starvation or dehydration, or to be picked off by one of their endless enemies.

Ahnna didn't react for what felt like a lifetime, and then she gave a wordless scream and turned the wheel. The ship turned, the sails flapping as they lost the full weight of the wind, and then she was forcing his hands onto the helm. "Keep it here."

James did as she ordered as she scrambled forward, clinging to what she could when a wave rolled over the deck. For a nightmarish heartbeat, he was certain the seas had taken her. But the sails ceased their flapping as they were lowered, and in a brilliant flash of lightning he saw Ahnna's silhouette as she tied them down.

She stumbled back and clung to him, shoulders shaking as she sobbed. James held her through it as the storm and the sea took them where they willed, the lights on the Amaridian ships fading into blackness.

# 57

# AHNNA

As soon as the storm eased, Ahnna set to repairing the rip in the sail with a small kit of supplies. The ship was tiny, but whoever had stocked the pleasure craft had done so mindfully, which would save their lives.

Except there was nothing in the supplies that would turn back time, and as she corrected their course, Ahnna prayed that she wouldn't be too late. Prayed that the tempests had sunk the Amaridian ships. Prayed that Ithicana's sharks had consumed those who sought the deaths of all her people.

Yet as they moved into Ithicana's waters, familiar islands filling the horizon, Ahnna's eyes caught sight of sails in the distance.

It was one of the Amaridian ships, heading north, sitting high on the water.

"Do you know where they will have unloaded the cargo?" James asked, the first words they'd exchanged in hours.

Ahnna gave a stiff nod, fear choking her. There were only a few locations this far north suitable for unloading ships of that size that would be safely out of sight of patrols and with good access to the bridge.

None of which they could reach quickly, because the winds were against them.

Conversation felt impossible, her throat tight as her mind ran through scenarios. She suspected that Aren would have moved everyone he could farther south out of easy reach of Harendell, which meant it would be mostly active soldiers who were at risk. It would have taken time to unload the ship, time to move the product into the bridge, but if what Katarina said was true, her people had been months without bread. They'd have surely cracked open a sack to make pan bread, which meant at least some of those charged with unloading the cargo were not long for this world.

But worse was knowing that the poison didn't act immediately. How many of those sacks were already on the move, heading to various outposts and islands to supply those defending against Harendell? How could she ever warn all those at risk before they ate any of the poison?

Ahnna knew the answer: She couldn't. Worse still, there were two more grain ships laden with poison heading to other locations farther south.

The bridge came into view, mist curling around the gray snaking length, but it felt like no homecoming to her. Ahnna sailed the ship through a narrow gap between islands, then approached a small, heavily forested island that had a small beach suitable for taking up cargo. There was no one there, but deep marks in the sand suggested heavy traffic. Yet it was to a single empty burlap sack sitting on the beach that her eyes went, her stomach dropping. "They were here."

"But no longer." James turned, a hand lifted to his eyes as he scanned the horizon. "Where would they have taken it?"

Her bottom lip trembled, because this was her worst nightmare coming to pass, and a thought reared in her head. *What if Aren was here?*

"This island isn't secure," she forced herself to say. "It's easy to attack, which is why there's nothing of importance on it. They'd have split the freight up, taking it by boat to various outposts nearby.

The rest would have been brought into the bridge to take north for distribution."

James gave a slight nod, and she knew he was waiting for her to make a decision. This was her home, her people, and . . . and . . .

"You can't save them all, Ahnna," he said softly. "Focus on how to save as many as you can."

A tear rolled down her cheek. "The bridge. We can catch the shipment heading north and warn any patrols of the poison. They can track down where the rest went."

"How do we get in?"

She scrubbed the tear away and buried fear and grief down deep. There'd be time for that later: Right now, she needed to remember what it was to be one of Ithicana's commanders. "I'll show you."

The access door here was much like the one at Midwatch, set into one of the karst piers but only visible at low tide, which had passed. But they weren't carrying supplies, which meant they didn't need an easy way in.

Ahnna sailed to another one of the karsts supporting the bridge, and at her order, James lowered the sails so that they were drifting. "Drop the anchor," she said. "Any closer and we'll run afoul of a hazard." Because beneath the surf were thick spikes intended to sink the vessels of anyone who tried to access the bridge. Her eyes picked up flashes deep beneath the waves.

"We need to get onto that karst and climb up," she said, pointing. "Behind that foliage, there will be a rope we can use to access the bridge top. Watch for snakes—they like the nooks and crannies, and most of them are venomous."

James scrubbed a hand through his hair, which had grown long since that fateful night in the Sky Palace. "All right. How do we get over there?"

"Swim."

He looked over the edge. "I don't suppose those are dolphins."

Ahnna had already noticed the sleek gray shapes. "No, those would be tiger sharks. You can see their stripes. They've been following us."

"Why?"

She tightened the cord holding her salt-crusted hair back from her face. "Because in Ithicana, a ship like this suggests potential dinner."

There had to be fear coursing through James's veins, but he didn't show it as he said, "All right. So dive in, swim faster than the man-eating sharks, try not to be dashed against very sharp rocks, and if I manage to get that far, climb up a rock formation full of venomous snakes."

"Yeah, but also, there are spikes set into the karst about three feet down. Stay shallow, or you'll be skewered like bait on a hook. Do you want me to go first?"

He huffed out a breath. "I'd always heard that this place was impenetrable. That the loss of life required to take it by force would be enormous, yet I didn't believe it until now. Now I think Alexandra is mad to believe she can take this place at all."

Once, Ahnna had believed that too. Believed that all the defenses, in combination with the natural violence of the land and sea, would keep her home safe. Silas Veliant had taught her otherwise, and she'd never make that mistake again.

Sucking in a deep breath, Ahnna dove in.

There was no time to think, only to swim as hard as she could, keeping shallow enough to avoid being stabbed by the spears. She felt the sharks racing toward her, but there was no point thinking about it. She'd make it or she wouldn't.

A wave caught her, and Ahnna braced as she was flung up onto the rocks. Her nails scratched against stone as she clung to the side of the karst, and when she looked down, it was to see a large tail lashing as the shark swam away.

"What the fuck was that?" James shouted, his eyes wild. "You could have warned me!"

"Next time," she called back. "I'm going to distract them. When I shout, you swim, all right?"

For all the confidence in her voice, Ahnna felt sick with terror as she circled the base of the karst. It was one thing to risk herself, to swim like mad with death at her heels, and quite another to watch the man she loved do the same thing. Retrieving a branch that had been torn from a tree during a storm, she edged down to the waterline and used the branch to slap the water, the splashes mimicking a floundering swimmer. As fins darted in, she shouted, "Now!"

A loud splash filled the air, and the sharks darted away, understanding that a better prize than a branch was in the water. Heart in her throat, she scrambled around the side of the karst.

James was swimming hard, but just behind him were fins. A scream tore from Ahnna's throat as a wave surged, flinging him high on the rocks.

Ahnna lunged, catching hold of his arm. "Feet out of the water! Out of the water!"

James jerked his legs up right before jaws snapped.

"Bloody fuck!" he shouted. "This place is not rational. This place is not reasonable. Why does anyone want to live here?"

"Because in Ithicana, you will always feel alive," she replied, helping him climb higher. Her blood rushed loud in her ears, vomit threatening to rise, but she swallowed hard. "Climb."

The climb itself was easy by comparison, even with her arm being as weak as it was. She encountered only one snake, which she tossed into the water to feed the sharks, for she always favored the latter over the former.

"I'll climb first and then pull you up," James said when they found the rope, which was fastened to one of the brackets set into the bridge itself. "You're going to rebreak that arm if you aren't careful."

Given how much it hurt, Ahnna didn't argue, and after swiftly reaching the top, James pulled her up with ease.

The view from atop the bridge was incredible, their little ship seeming tiny below, but there was no time to take a breath, much less relish the moment. "This way."

They left a trail of water droplets as they ran down the bridge top, and despite her fear for her people, she still noted his awe at the magnitude of the bridge. To her, it was an old friend, a constant presence in her life, but it was not lost on her that there had been no civilization in recorded history capable of building this sort of structure.

Or the spiral on which the Sky Palace sat, for that matter.

Reaching the hatch, she dropped to her knees. "This opens into the bridge. Be ready for anything."

Then she pressed her palms against the stone.

The mechanism activated and lifted the panel of rock, revealing cavernous darkness. Reaching into the empty space carved into rock surrounding the opening, Ahnna withdrew two small jars and one larger one. She poured the contents of the two smaller ones into the larger one, and immediately, the mixture began to glow. "It won't last long. Fifteen minutes at most."

"Is there another source of light?" James asked.

"No," she replied, holding the jar in her broken arm and then drawing her knife. "There is only darkness."

Then she dropped down into the bridge.

Ahnna's boots hit the stone floor with a soft thud, and as she moved aside to allow James to drop down, the bridge's familiar moan filled her ears. James immediately froze, his eyes going to her. "The spiral makes that sound when the wind hits it just right."

"I know." She set her jar and knife down. "Lift me so I can close the hatch."

His hands closed around her hips and he lifted, her fingers finding the mechanism to close the hatch easily.

"How does it work?" James asked, staring up.

Ahnna only shrugged. "No one really knows, although we think some elements came later than the bridge itself. Millennia ago, or maybe longer, who can say. Some say it was a civilization with tools lost to time. Others say the hands of God. Others believe it was magic. I personally prefer the mystery of not knowing."

Picking up the jar and her knife, Ahnna headed north.

There was no light ahead, no sound other than the bridge's moan, and a chill sank into her skin.

"Hello?" she called out. "Is anyone near?"

No one answered, and a shiver ran over her. James pressed closer, wrapping an arm around her shoulder, his sword in his other hand. "Something doesn't feel right," he whispered softly, looking over his shoulder. "Something smells wrong."

"It's just the bridge stone. It smells like—" Ahnna broke off, because her nose picked up the scent of something decidedly fouler than the bridge's mysterious material.

Vomit. And excrement.

She'd known they were too late, but the proof almost brought her to her knees.

James lowered his arm from around her shoulders and moved to give himself space to swing a sword, glancing back more than once at the way they came.

The shadows came into view. The sides of the tunnel were lined with sacks of grain and flour, but written in red across the walls over and over was one word.

*Poison.*

Her breath was far too rapid, and a wave of dizziness washed over her. Ahnna fought for composure lest she cause herself to pass out, but her fear cared nothing for her efforts.

Especially as the bodies came into view.

They lay against one another, vomit splattering the ground around them, their shirts crusted with crimson blood so fresh it had not yet dried. She'd been so close, and yet not close at all, because Ahnna knew that they'd eaten the poison more than a day ago. It was slow acting by design.

A guttural noise tore from her lips, and she fell to her knees next to the bodies of her people, all of whom she knew by name. Many of whom she'd fought alongside. Men and women who'd survived Silas Veliant with skill and bravery, only to fall to the coward's weapon of poison. She sobbed, horror trying to drown her as a dozen dead eyes stared at her. Blamed her for their fates.

Then a noise caught her attention. Like the sound of a boot scraping against stone.

James tensed and lifted his sword, but Ahnna only held up her light.

A figure shifted on the ground, just at the edge of the glow.

Ignoring James's protest for caution, she scrambled upright and raced down the bridge, her chest clenching painfully as she dropped to her knees next to a familiar form. "Aster?"

The old Ithicanian reached for his sword hilt, ever the soldier, then his eyes fixed on her. "Ahnna?" he wheezed, a rivulet of blood dribbling down his chin. "Is that you?"

"It's me." Tears ran down her cheeks. "I'm back."

"Grain. It's poisoned."

"I know," she whispered, trying to think of a way to help him but knowing there was none. He was too far gone. "Katarina and Alexandra are working together to take the bridge. They aim to poison everyone so they can take it without a fight."

"Cunts."

"Yeah." She took hold of his hand, gripping it tight, but before she could say more, Aster spoke.

"Sent runners and boats after all the shipments we sent out." He gagged, more blood running down his chin as he coughed. "Don't know if they'll make it. Everyone ate, Ahnna. Everyone fucking *gorged*."

"I'm sorry." A sob tore from her. "I tried to get back in time. I tried—"

He lifted a bloody finger to her lips. "You're here now, which means we have a chance. You've pissed me off more than once, girl, but you've never failed Ithicana."

Except she had. Over and over.

As if he'd heard her, Aster shook his head. "You'll make it right, Ahnna."

He gagged, a flood of blood pouring down his chin to splatter his gore-soaked chest. She tried to help support him until the spasm stopped, but he coughed with such violence that she knew the end was close.

"Two more ships of grain sailed past this morning," he managed to gasp out. "One will anchor at Vexis. The other heads for Eranahl."

*No no no!*

"Aren is on Vexis Island," he whispered. "Lara and Delia are on Midwatch."

The tiny island was in spitting distance of the king's stronghold, and Ahnna's stomach dropped.

"Sent runners," Aster choked out. "But they'll die before they make it. Go."

"Aster, I'm not leaving you." He was an asshole who was a prick to his wife and worse to his children, ever a thorn in Aren's backside. But he was *loyal*.

"You won't fail Ithicana." His grip began to slacken. "Save them."

He vomited up one last gout of blood, and then went still, the light fading from his eyes. Ahnna let go of his hand, slowly closing his eyelids.

"I'm sorry, Ahnna."

She turned to find James at her back, sword in hand. Like a shadow protecting her when she was at her weakest. But she did not miss the gleam of tears in his eyes, her grief his grief.

"I can't save them all, can I?" She climbed to her feet. "I have to choose."

He gave a slow nod but said nothing, leaving the choice to her.

"There will be more people at Eranahl," she said. "But my family . . ."

"Which is closer?" he asked, and she lifted both hands, because the distance was too close to matter. Too close to be what made this decision.

She squeezed her eyes shut, and made her choice. "We need to hurry."

Shoving the jar into his hand, she opened the hidden door in the wall that led down into the pier, the door at the base still underwater. But that didn't matter, because the supplies she needed were there. Hooking the large crossbow and quiver of bolts over her shoulder, she handed James a long line of rope and two hooks. "Have you ever ziplined before?" When he shook his head, she added, "You haven't experienced Ithicana until you've flown."

# 58

# AREN

"It is fine weather you're having, your grace," the Amaridian captain said, bowing low as he stepped out of the longboat and onto the shore of Vexis Island. "Our fleet encountered fierce storms in the north. Terrifying winds and waves the size of mountains, which is all to say that you might wait before you open any of the sparkling vintages lest you be covered in foam." The man laughed loudly, his nervousness palpable as he glanced behind him. "We also saw several Harendellian naval vessels on the horizon. You have scouts watching for them?"

Aren's scouts had reported the same, and the man's urgency was understandable. A merchant vessel like this would not stand a chance against a Harendellian ship of the line. "My scouts are watching."

"We still need to be swift. Our sister ship with the grain was close behind, but she will take longer to unload. We anticipated outpacing her, so we brought a few sacks of flour to show you the quality."

Aren took a sack from one of the sailors and opened it. The flour was finely milled with no signs of weevils, and against his will, his mouth watered. Handing it to one of his men, he said, "Get baking. Might as well taste it before we pay them."

The captain gave an approving nod. "Shall we begin unloading while the weather holds and the Harendellians are unaware?"

The deal had been grain before wine, but Aren understood better than anyone the practicality. "Get under way. My soldiers will aid you as needed."

"Yes, Your Grace." The captain bowed low, revealing the bald circle in what was otherwise a dense head of red curls. "It is an honor to speak with you, Your Grace. May the alliance between Ithicana and Amarid be long and prosperous."

"I hope for this as well," Aren replied mechanically, watching the man retreat to begin barking orders at his crew to move swiftly but not damage the product. Then the smell of a campfire caught his attention, and he turned to watch two of his soldiers readying to make pan bread with the flour. His stomach growled.

"I'm not sure I've ever looked forward to eating something so much in my life," Lia said, coming to stand at his elbow. "That sack isn't going to last long."

"Plenty more on the way." He returned to watching the ship anchored in the cove, not wanting to admit his own hunger.

Vexis was a small, crescent-moon-shaped island possessed of very deep water. The entrance to it was hard to see because of the placement of other islands, and Aren had often used it to hide various vessels from other nations that he'd taken in war or in the occasional act of piracy. While the cove had a sandy beach, the long side of the crescent was high cliffs, which made it ideal for this particular exchange, as there was no attacking from the rear. "Get the wine under the trees until we can move it into the bridge," he ordered his soldiers. "The heat of the sun will not improve its quality."

And he desperately needed the revenue it would bring at Southwatch.

Crate after crate was unloaded from longboats, and the smell of cooking bread filled the air. Aren didn't fail to notice how his soldiers kept glancing toward the fire where those doing the cooking were building a pile of flat disks of bread. "Finish first," he ordered, because it would be good motivation to get this ship on its way.

"You want to try it?" Lia asked. "We should test to see if it tastes right. I wouldn't put it past Katarina to give us sawdust."

Aren shook his head. "First unload the wine."

The hours it took to unload stretched on without incident, and then the captain approached, bowing low again. "We will take our leave, Your Grace. Our sister ship is waiting to take our place in the cove."

"Agreed. Safe travels."

Shifting from foot to foot, the captain waited expectantly, then finally gave a nervous cough. "With all due respect, Your Grace, it is my understanding that payment is due for the wines. Those were the instructions my queen gave me, and she is not a woman who is forgiving of a man's mistakes. Especially when it comes to her gold."

Lia's hand moved to rest on the hilt of her blade, and the captain gave another nervous chuckle. Aren smiled. "The gold will be loaded onto the ship that delivers the grain. Grain, then gold. That was the deal."

"Of course! Of course!" The man backed away, bobbing three consecutive bows as he did.

Aren gestured to the sky, faint swirls of cloud beginning to form in the distance. "A word of warning: There is weather coming in from the west, and it will sweep north. I strongly suggest you get ahead of it."

"Wise advice, Your Grace." The Amaridian all but leapt into his longboat, which rowed swiftly back to the ship. Within a matter of minutes, the anchor was rising and the oars were moving the vessel out of the cove.

"Might as well eat," Aren muttered to Lia. "They aren't moving quickly."

"You want to take the first bite? You made this deal happen."

His stomach gave another furious growl, but Aren ignored it. His people were hungry *because* of him, so the last thing he intended to do was eat first. "I'm fine."

Lia shrugged, and moments later, the stacks of pan bread were spread among everyone. Groans of delight filled the air as his soldiers ate, but Aren focused on the towering merchant ship that was easing its way into the cove, sitting far lower in the water than the previous vessel. Full to the brim with enough grain to hold his people through for weeks, if not longer. It held more soldiers than the one with the wine had, which Aren found odd given the other vessel had intended to take payment for the wine, and he frowned. "Lia, send for reinforcements."

"You think they are planning an attack?" she asked around a mouthful of bread, lifting a hand to shade her eyes.

That hold could be full of soldiers, which would account for it sitting so low, and old habits died hard. But his concern was one of the Harendellian ships spotting the Amaridians and investigating. "Best to be prepared." Vexis had no real strategic importance when it came to the bridge, but if the Harendellians took it, the island would be easy for them to hold.

A voice said, "I was lured in by the smell. I wonder how much bread Aster and his crew ate before shipping the rest out."

Aren turned to find that Taryn had come up behind him, alone for once. She and Bronwyn had been nearly inseparable. "Hopefully they are rationing. I had to borrow from lenders to pay for the wine transaction, which Katarina gouged me on. None of this is coming for free."

Borrowed from Valcottan lending houses, and Aren did not care to think about the interest that he'd have to pay the bankers if he was late on repayment. Nor did he care to think about how Zarrah had been entirely silent since this had all begun, and he couldn't help but wonder if it was out of anger over Keris putting himself in danger on Ithicana's behalf.

"It will pay off," Taryn said, shaking her head when Lia offered her bread. "Their wines are the best in the known world, and the South has been sorely lacking in supply. It's a good investment."

"At best, we break even." To soften his words, he bumped his elbow against his cousin's. "I'm glad you're back, Taryn. I realize that the conservatory was your dream, but know that you are wanted here."

She bit her bottom lip, then met his gaze. "It was incredible while it lasted, Aren. Exactly as I always dreamed, and it was so peaceful. Until James *fucking* Ashford kicked in our door." She made a face. "It all makes so much sense now with what Alexandra told Keris. James was after Ahnna from the first day, always at her side, always with the dinners and the riding lessons. Bronwyn and I thought he was just allowing his cock to do his thinking for him by chasing after William's betrothed, but the joke was on us." She spit into the sand. "As though Ithicana would *ever* have bent the knee to him. I'd say that I hope he's dead, but I'd truly love the chance to kill him."

"Get in line," Aren murmured, his temper fouling at mention of the prince, but thoughts of Harendell fell away as the merchant ship's anchor rattled into the depths. The Amaridians, who were always efficient, had a longboat loaded with sailors and several burlap sacks rowing toward the beach in short order, and he went down to the water to meet them.

"Well met, Your Grace!" The captain of the grain ship trotted up the slope toward him, handing over a sack of flour with a dramatic flourish. "Apologies for the delay. We had to evade the Harendellians, but we made it."

Aren handed it to Lia. "Have it sent to Midwatch. Bring a few bottles of wine as well." He was tired of Lara living like a pauper rather than the queen she was. "We'll celebrate tonight. You can also get ready to start loading the gold."

At mention of payment, the captain grinned. "A celebration all around, so I brought a bottle from my cabin to toast." He took a bottle of wine from one of his sailors and pulled out the cork. Filling two glasses, he handed one to Aren. "To Ithicana and Amarid. May this be the most profitable of friendships, and together, let's knock those cow-humping Harendellians on their asses. Cheers!"

Aren clicked this glass against the captain's, the red wine looking like blood in the glow of the sun. "I will toast to that."

# 59
# AHNNA

As though the winds themselves knew the urgency of her mission, they filled the tiny ship's sails while they headed south to Vexis. She and James said little, her focus on navigating Ithicana's dangerous waters and his on scampering around the small ship to adjust the rigging. Despite being in each other's presence every day since their escape from the Furnace, it felt as though they'd barely had a moment to focus on each other since he'd asked her to marry him. Every second had been choked with anxiety, the focus survival, and she wondered if it would ever be any other way. Or whether the stars that foretold Cardiffian fates had decided to dangle that which they most desired before them like a carrot before a donkey's nose, ever leading them on but never to be consumed.

*Focus*, she silently chided herself. *Lives are on the line.*

But her heart still skipped as James turned his head to look at her, amber eyes bright in the sunlight. Unbidden, she felt the sensation of his fingers tracing lines on her wrist echoing across her skin, the memory of his touch through that small hole between their cells in the

Furnace somehow the most poignant of all. He'd been what had kept her sane, what had given her hope, and what should have been the worst experience of her life felt instead like a foundation for a future.

"How much farther?"

Instead of answering, she lifted a hand and pointed to a series of shadowed islands in the distance. A merchant vessel lurked near them. She eased east behind a series of towering karsts to keep from being spotted, but dread pooled in her stomach. The ship sat high in the water, its hold empty of cargo.

A second Amaridian ship was easing slowly into the warren of rocks. *How many fucking ships of poison did she send?*

"Do we wait until they're gone?"

She couldn't wait. Her people wouldn't be sitting on their laurels but swiftly loading the grain into small vessels to transport to other locations. If Ahnna didn't warn them soon, what happened in the north would happen here. "We can't wait, James. All it takes is one sack being opened to make bread for lunch, and every Ithicanian on that island is dead."

His jaw tightened and he nodded. "How do we warn them?"

Vexis could only be accessed through a gap between towering cliffs. Like Midwatch, it had a chain that could be lifted to block access to the cove, and Ithicana frequently used it to hide vessels that had been commandeered. They couldn't reach it without passing the waiting ship—but fortunately, that was not Ahnna's plan.

"We need to be clever about this," she said as James moved next to her, reaching for the shirt he'd discarded on the deck earlier in deference to the heat. The sun was no friend to his pale skin, but he was starting to take on a golden hue that emphasized the sharp lines of his thick muscles, and the faint dusting of freckles on his face was more apparent. He looked handsome and rugged, but she shoved away the vestiges of her selfish thoughts and cleared her throat. "If we go in there shouting alarms and warnings, this will turn into a fight."

And enough of her people had already died.

"There are scouts on the cliffs." He lifted a muscled arm and pointed. "I just saw a glint of metal. Can we signal them?"

She considered the many lookout positions, all equipped with signal horns, but discarded the idea. "Not without also getting the attention of the Amaridians."

"I sense you have another idea," James said. "An idea that I'm not going to like."

"We'll circle wide and come in from the south." Her focus moved from the island to James as he pulled his shirt over his head and retrieved his sword, slipping it through his belt. "There is a route we can take using a series of rock formations that will keep anyone from spotting us. I think we can get onto Vexis without the Amaridians seeing us, and we can sneak around to warn Aren discreetly. We let them drop off the grain and leave, and Katarina will be none the wiser."

Because the last thing she wanted was Amarid's queen determining that her plan had failed and turning to violence to achieve her ends.

"How long will it take to get a ship to Eranahl to warn them?" James asked, his eyes tracking west.

*Too long.* She bit the insides of her cheeks, knowing that she was banking on the heavy surf slowing the process of transporting the grain into the island stronghold, for the merchant ship would be far too large to access the harbor. Except all it would take was a few sacks of flour distributed to make bread, and the whole city would be dead within days. If not for the horror of it, Ahnna might almost admire the perfect efficiency of Katarina's plan.

"The choice is made." James slid an arm around her waist, pulling her against him. "Focus on the battle before you."

Instead of allowing herself to take comfort from his presence and his words, she gave a tight nod and let her mind descend into the place it always went during a battle. She eased the ship wide to avoid the eyes of the ship lookouts before circling around to the scattering of karsts that hid the harbor entrance from easy view from the open sea. Spotting the one she was looking for, she said, "Lower the sail and tie everything off."

James did what she asked, and Ahnna eased the small vessel into a narrow slot between two karsts. "Lower anchor."

It rattled down, and taking hold of a mooring line, Ahnna waited until the vessel swung close to a small ledge of rock and jumped. She landed with ease on the slick surface, then tied the rope to a hook ring embedded in the stone for just such a purpose. "Let's go. Watch for snakes."

"That seems to go without saying," James said as he leapt over to join her, and together they scampered up the sharp rocks. She led him on a path between the rocky pillars jutting from the sea, leaping gaps and keeping low until finally, they had a vantage point that overlooked the cove.

The large ship was anchored in the midnight-blue water, the cove full of smaller boats ferrying sacks of grain to the beach.

And returning to the ship loaded with something else. The something else revealed itself when two of the sailors fumbled a chest, spilling coins across the sand.

"That bitch is taking our gold," Ahnna hissed, her cheeks burning hot with anger as she noted the stacks of wine crates and barrels in the shadows of the trees. "It wasn't enough to poison us, she had to rob us as well!"

And it wasn't gold Aren could afford to lose, given he'd likely had to borrow it.

James shaded his eyes, surveying the scene. "Both ships are packed with soldiers, Ahnna. If it comes to a fight, the casualties are going to be high. It might be better to wait for the transaction to happen and for the Amaridians to set sail."

"No." She ground her teeth. "I'm not letting her have any form of victory here. They are not taking that gold."

He caught hold of her shoulders and turned her to face him. But rather than arguing with her, he said, "You have a plan to stop them?"

Ahnna did have a plan. But it was one she knew he wouldn't like. "I'm going to blow up the ship containing the gold."

James's eyes tracked to the cove, following the multitude of sharks lazily circling the ship in the hope of receiving an easy meal.

"The cove is deep but not unreasonably so," she said. "It will take a bit of time, but we can retrieve the gold."

James didn't look convinced, but all he asked was, "And just how, pray tell, do you plan to blow up that ship without anyone seeing you, Ahnna? They have eyes all around, so they're going to goddamned notice if you row up to the side and start setting explosives on their hull."

"I'll swim. I'll go deep and come up on the opposite side from where they are unloading—they won't see me."

James blanched. "Absolutely not!" He jabbed a finger toward the cove. "It's full of sharks. Sharks with a taste for human flesh, and I've seen firsthand how swift they are. You can't outswim them."

Ahnna shrugged to hide the fear in her stomach, because he wasn't wrong. "I'm aware. That's why you're going to bait them out of the cove. I'll only need a few minutes, and then they can come back and feast on Katarina's soldiers when their ship sinks. Then we'll move on to the other vessel—Aren will have reinforcements nearby."

*Hopefully.*

"No."

Ahnna blew out a long breath between her teeth. "James, if that ship full of gold sets sail, we will never get that coin back. Ithicana can't afford that sort of loss."

"Your arm is—"

"It's healed. Tighten up my splints and I'll be fine." And because she knew what he'd say next, Ahnna added, "I'm faster in the water than you'll ever be, and if a shark decides to take a look, I'll know how to deal with it."

James scrubbed his hands through his hair. "There has to be a better way. A smarter way. A way in which I don't have to watch while you—"

He broke off and Ahnna felt a pang in her chest, because she'd been in this position when she'd left him to fight Carlo on the beach in Riomar. She considered pointing out that she'd done what he'd asked then, despite the risks, but instead she said, "I wouldn't do this if I didn't think it would work. Please trust me."

The muscles of his jaw stood out even with the thickness of his beard, his teeth surely on the verge of cracking beneath the strain of his frustration, but then James said, "Fine. How do I bait them?"

"Blood." She winced. "Ideally, yours."

# 60

# JAMES

"THIS ISN'T GOING to work," he growled, flinging droplets of blood into the water. "This is madness. It's bullshit. It's the worst plan ever conceived."

But there was nothing he could do to stop it.

Ahnna would already be in the water, and if he ceased his baiting, the sharks would return to the ship while she was still within reach of their teeth. Pressing his knife against the cut on his arm, he flung more droplets into the waves. It seemed the purest form of stupidity to think that the sharks would notice, much less be lured, by literal drops in the ocean.

On the heels of the thought, a large gray fin cut through the waves toward the little ship. James instinctively tensed, especially when others appeared and began to circle him, because every instinct in his body screamed danger. But better him than her, so James reopened the cut and flung more droplets of blood into the water.

Something thudded heavily into the bottom of the boat.

"Fuck," he hissed, because at least two of the creatures were twice as long as he was tall. And they were watching. There was no mistaking how they turned sideways, black eyes taking in their potential meal even as their fishy brains considered how far they'd go to get it. He threw more droplets and his heart thundered in his chest as they swam faster, their motions gaining a frenzied rhythm.

But then one of the big ones veered away.

Ahnna had said that it wasn't just the blood that would lure them in. It was certain sounds. Most especially splashing.

Throwing caution to the wind, he leaned over the edge and slapped the water. Again and again, only jerking back as one shark rose right beneath his hand.

But the big one had returned.

"That's right," he snarled at it. "You keep your focus on me."

He flung more blood into the water, counting dozens and dozens of gray shapes circling beneath him.

There was no way to know what step Ahnna was at in her strategy. No way to know whether things were even going according to plan other than the relative silence coming from the direction of the ships.

Sheathing his knife, James grabbed the covered bucket next to him, which was full of snakes that Ahnna had caught. They had been thumping around inside, and not wishing to risk a bite, he hurled the bucket itself into the water.

As if sensing the danger, the snakes immediately began swimming toward the rocks. The sharks were faster. They tore the snakes apart, and then went after the pieces floating between the shards of the bucket.

*Hurry.* He watched them until the frenzy began to ease, then flung more droplets of his own blood into the mix and hit the water with a stick. The sharks slammed into his ship, setting it to rocking, but he kept up the noise. Doing everything and anything to keep them close, but it felt like only a few minutes passed before the sharks began losing interest. As though they understood he was only baiting them, they circled away, none of his splashing or splatters of blood regaining their interest.

*Fuck!* He leapt off the ship onto the karst, and then scampered up the slope with no care for snakes that might be hidden in the foliage as he followed the path Ahnna showed him. He threw up prayers to God, fate, and the stars that Ahnna was out of the water, because there was no doubt in his mind that at least some of the sharks would return to the ships in search of a meal.

James crouched on the tower of rock that faced the entrance to the cove. The Amaridians were still working to unload sacks of grain, the Ithicanians ferrying them back and forth between the ship and the bridge.

But there was no sign of Ahnna.

The sharks were circling the ships, and terror threatened to strangle James as he hunted for any sign of her.

Then motion on the edge of the beach that was more rock than sand caught his attention. Behind a set of boulders, Ahnna climbed out of the water, wearing only her undergarments. James stared, those long legs blasting all reason from his skull, but then she looked up. As their eyes locked, she lifted her hands to signal that all was set. Then she lifted three fingers.

Three minutes until the explosion.

Counting down, James dragged his gaze back to the ship. Ahnna had taken several jars from the supplies hidden in the bridge, but there was no time to explain how they worked beyond that it would blow a large hole in the hull. He searched for signs of the bottles, but she must have placed them below the waterline. The ship would go down fast, and Ahnna said that while the explosion would first scare the sharks off, they'd swiftly come back, drawn from miles around by the sound.

Like a cursed dinner bell.

The door to the captain's quarters opened, and a short Amaridian man stepped out, gesturing to his first mate as he did.

The captain wasn't alone. Walking at his side was none other than Taryn Kertell, Ahnna's cousin, smiling and gesturing happily toward the ship full of grain. They walked slowly toward the ship's rail and Taryn rested her hands on the ladder, about to climb over into a longboat.

James's eyes shot to Ahnna, who remained hidden behind the rocks. She lifted her hand.

One minute.

And Taryn wasn't moving.

The explosion itself wouldn't kill her, but the Amaridians would see it as an attack, and Taryn was the closest Ithicanian to hand. They'd cut her down without thought.

And knowing Ahnna as he did, she'd blame herself.

He had to do something.

Desperately, James flung himself at the supplies that they'd brought up with them, including the large crossbow and bolts that they'd used to get off the bridge onto their ship. Whirling, he judged the distance between the karst and the ship.

He had enough rope, but barely.

He readied the weapon, aimed it at the mainmast, and let the bolt loose.

It soared through the air, trailing the thin cord, and sank into the mast. Several of the sailors jerked at the noise, looking up at the rope in confusion, but James was already moving. Pulling the cord taut, he secured it to a tree, snatched up one of the hooks, and jumped.

An Amaridian soldier spotted him and pointed, several more calling out in alarm. But there was no stopping now.

James flew through the air above the open water. Falling, falling, and then his feet hit the deck and he rolled. His knees screamed but he leapt to his feet. Shouldering aside soldiers and ducking under blades, he ran straight at Taryn.

Her mouth opened, eyes filling with horror and recognition as she reached for her weapon. Her machete was only half drawn as James scooped her up and jumped. His foot struck the railing and he leapt, flying over the longboat below to land with a heavy splash in the water.

*Boom!*

The water surged, flipping James over and over, and he lost his grip on Taryn. He lost sense of up and down, but following the rush of bubbles, he reached the surface and sucked in a breath.

The Amaridian vessel was aflame and sinking fast. Sailors leapt into the water and started to swim to shore, and James caught sight of Taryn swimming as though her life depended on it.

Which it did.

The Amaridians ceased leaping from their burning ship. Instead, they stared down at the water, expressions filled with fear.

Ahnna hadn't lied when she said that explosions were like dinner bells for Ithicana's sharks.

All of her instructions replayed in James's head at once, turning to a drone of noise as his eyes fixed on the fins cutting through the waters.

*Don't be prey.*

He slowed his motions, staying as still as possible. The fins shot past him, chasing after the dozens of Amaridians trying to reach the shore. The men disappeared, one after another, jerked beneath the surf so swiftly most of them didn't have the chance to scream.

*Don't be prey.*

The ship was sinking lower in the water, aided by the weight of gold and silver, and the upper decks were rapidly turning into an inferno. The sailors and soldiers were climbing atop one another, screams mixing with the crackle of flames. Trapped between death from fire and death from teeth. The Ithicanians in the boats were shouting at the Amaridians to jump, to abandon ship, but the soldiers only stared at them in fear.

Everything was chaos, the Amaridians certain Ithicana was attacking them, and the Ithicanians searching the horizon for signs of attack from another source.

*Don't be prey.*

If James went any more still, he'd sink beneath the waves and drown, but his skin was crawling with the certainty that he was being hunted. That was when his eyes lighted on the cut on his arm. Shallow. Inconsequential.

But bleeding.

*Don't be prey.*

James sank beneath the water, and his eyes immediately latched on to a massive shark circling him. Its gray body flexed from side to side as it swam, its white belly marked with countless old scars. Even as fear wrapped around his chest like a vise, James recognized that this creature was old. Far older than he was himself, and it was watching him.

He turned with the shark, vaguely seeing the ship sinking deeper. Bubbles exploded out from the vessel, and smaller splashes turned the surface to foam as the Amaridians abandoned ship. Yet the shark kept circling, ignoring the thrashing swimmers.

Then it abruptly swam toward him. James desperately needed to breathe, but he held still as the shark slowed, a mouthful of razor teeth slightly open as it passed, eyes examining him. As though it was curious rather than hungry. For reasons James could only blame on lack of air or temporary madness, he reached out and let his fingertips trail down the shark's rough side.

It allowed the touch, looked at him one more time, and then exploded into motion. James watched in fascination as it bit an Amaridian man in two, swallowing the upper half, but the show came to an abrupt conclusion as hands caught hold of James's arms and yanked him to the surface.

"Got one!"

James was dumped in the bottom of a boat, where he coughed and sputtered while the Ithicanians worked to pull in Amaridians who hadn't yet been eaten. A half-drowned soldier was dropped on top of him, followed by another who was missing a leg and another an arm.

"It's goddamned carnage," a familiar male voice snarled. "Grab that one! He's the last one I see alive!"

Half buried beneath sobbing Amaridians, James twisted to look up, knowing who the voice belonged to even before he fixed his eyes on the big Ithicanian.

Aren Kertell.

James opened his mouth, but someone stomped on his back. James shifted and tried to get in enough air to speak, but the screams from the injured Amaridians drowned him out.

*Find her*, he tried to say. *Make sure she's safe!*

"Get to shore," Aren ordered, and the Ithicanians immediately moved to obey as he added, "I need to speak to the other ship captain and explain that this wasn't us. Katarina is going to think we double-crossed her and retaliate. We can't afford that."

Someone again stepped square on James's back, driving the wind out of him, but then the boat bumped against the rocks of the shore.

The Ithicanians began removing the injured from the boat as Aren shouted, "Someone get me a white flag!"

A female voice shouted back, "Aren, you are not going out to that ship yourself!"

More bodies were lifted off James, and he sucked in a breath to warn Aren. To tell him that the Amaridians were no ally to Ithicana. Aren reached down and caught hold of the front of James's shirt, lifting him with the obvious intent to hurl him onto the bank, but James gasped out, "Don't go out to that ship! They'll kill you!"

Aren's gaze, which had been on the rocky bank, slowly slid to James's face. Recognition flared, along with white-hot rage, and before James could say another word, Aren balled up his fist and punched him square in the cheek.

James's head snapped back, but he almost instantly doubled over as Aren's fist took him in the stomach. "Where is my sister?"

A good fucking question, but James couldn't get the words out as Ithicana's king slammed him down on the rocks. "It's James Ashford," he snarled. "The Harendellians are here. Warn the Amaridians! There might be more explosives!"

Ithicanians went running in all directions, some shouting orders to check watch towers for Harendellian ships while others ran to warn the other Amaridian vessel.

"No!" James lifted his arm, but the Ithicanians took it as aggression and two of them grabbed hold of his arms and pinned him to the rock even as Aren's boot took him hard in the side. "Ahnna—"

The tip of Aren's curved machete was abruptly pressed against James's throat. "You keep my sister's name out of your filthy Harendellian mouth, you fucking prick!"

James ignored the stinging pain and tried to rip his arms free from those holding him down. "You need to—"

"Shut up!" Aren screamed at him, and James went still as the blade dug deep enough that he was at significant risk of breathing through a hole in his throat.

"Aren, stop!" Lara shouted, and in his periphery, James saw the queen hurrying in their direction. "You can't kill him!"

"Oh, I think I can. I'll show your goddamned corpse to the

Amaridians and then let the sharks get rid of the evidence." Aren knelt on James's chest, angling the blade so that it sliced a shallow line of fire just below his jugular. "By all rights I should do this slowly, but I need to undo the damage that you've done or risk my people starving."

The king of Ithicana's blade dug deeper, and knowing it might be the last thing he ever said, James shouted, "Don't eat the—"

# 61

# AHNNA

AHNNA CAUGHT HOLD of Aren's sword hand as she slammed into her brother and yanked the blade away from James's throat.

She and Aren rolled, nearly falling into the water, but Ahnna ended up on top. "No!"

Her brother blinked in shock. "Ahnna?"

"Did you eat?" she screamed the question. "Did you eat the bread?"

"What? I . . . No, no bread."

There was no time for relief. Ahnna's attention snapped to the soldiers pinning the struggling James. He was alive, but she couldn't see his neck. Couldn't see how deep the blade had cut.

"Let him go!" she barked at them, and whether it was shock at her return or old habit, they instantly obeyed.

James pushed himself upright, glaring at the soldiers as he wiped away the blood from his throat.

*He's still alive. Thank God and the stars, he's still alive.*

Aren's whisper caught her attention. "You're alive. How are you alive?"

She ignored her brother and looked to Lara. Her sister-in-law's blue eyes were the only pair in the whole mix of this chaos that seemed sharp. "Katarina is in league with Alexandra. The grain is laced with poison."

Lara didn't question her. Didn't make Ahnna offer proof. She only shouted, "Everyone who ate, puke it up. The rest of you, get on the water and call in reinforcements. We need to sink that ship!"

Shocked or not, their people were trained, and no one hesitated. Warriors flung themselves into boats and horns sounded, calling everyone within earshot to battle, while those who'd eaten stuck fingers down their throats. She prayed it would work. Prayed that it would be enough to keep them alive.

She scrambled up the slope to James. His throat was covered with blood. "How badly are you hurt?"

"He can hit," James croaked, lifting his hand to his jaw. Ahnna fell to her knees, half in his lap as she looked at the nasty cut that had dug deep just shy of his jugular. Twisting around, she screamed at Aren, "You idiot! You almost killed him!"

"I'd like an explanation for why you don't want him dead!" Aren retorted. "You owe me a *few* explanations, Ahnna!"

"Go fuck yourself!" Her heart was thundering so fast that she felt like she was going to be sick. Only for a far larger threat than her brother to appear on the scene.

Bronwyn was striding toward them, sword in hand and murder in her gaze.

Staggering to her feet, Ahnna reached to her side for a weapon but came up empty. Moving in front of James, she squared her feet. "Bronwyn, I don't want to fight you. Just—"

Bronwyn's sword slashed through the air, only to collide against Lara's blade with enough force that sparks flew.

"Stand down." Lara's voice was low, but it held total authority. "You don't get to pick this fight."

"This is my fight as much as anyone's," Bronwyn shouted, her blade scraping down Lara's as she tried to deflect it, but Lara reached out with shocking speed, her left hand closing on her sister's wrist.

"Then you'll have to fight me first."

The two sisters stared down each other, and in her periphery, Ahnna saw Aren draw his weapon. But then Taryn was pushing through the crowd. Seawater dripping from her sodden clothes, she caught hold of Bronwyn's shoulders, murmuring urgently into her ear. Slowly, Bronwyn lowered her weapon, but the anger remained. "I thought you were better than this, Ahnna," she snapped. "I thought you knew what loyalty meant, but for all your claims, you only ever put yourself first."

Ahnna took a step toward her friend, reaching out a hand. "Bronwyn, if you'd only listen—"

"I don't care to hear how you're justifying all that you've done." Bronwyn caught hold of Taryn's arm, bodily pulling her down to one of the canoes pulled up on the beach.

Grief and guilt pooled in Ahnna's core, and all around her, she felt the weight of condemnation, because they believed her to be the cause of all of this. "I didn't kill Edward."

"Ahnna," Aren said, wiping a hand over his face. "I know what Edward threatened—"

"She's innocent." James's voice cut the air. "And she has suffered far beyond the point where most would have lain down and died to try to stop those who'd see everyone in this kingdom dead. The only reason any of you will live to see another day is because of Ahnna, so you will show her the respect she is due."

Her chest tightened, and despite knowing that no one here would understand, Ahnna turned and fell to her knees before James. Flinging her arms around him, she clung to him, still afraid that she was going to blink and find him dead on the ground.

Except this time, she hadn't been too late.

"How are you still alive?" she whispered, ignoring the mutters behind her. "The cove is red with blood. The sharks killed everyone."

James's arms closed around her back, holding her close. "I stayed still."

"That doesn't work in a frenzy." All logic screamed that he should be dead, because the cove's water was entirely crimson, only *pieces* washing against the shore.

James shrugged, then touched his right cheekbone with a wince, seeming more concerned with his rapidly swelling eye than the fact he was nearly eaten. "A big shark with scars and a missing eye came right up to me and had a good look, but it went after an Amaridian instead."

Ahnna went still, and the muttering behind her went silent.

Heart in her throat, Ahnna turned her face to look at her brother. Aren's face was drained of color. "I saw her earlier. I recognized the scars on her sides."

Ahnna nodded, her chest so tight it made it hard to speak. "If you won't trust me, I hope you'll trust a guardian."

The murmurs burst out among those watching, but Aren only looked away.

"What are you talking about?" James's breath was warm against her ear. "What is so important about the shark?"

Her lips parted, but the words caught in her throat and all she managed was, "That shark is a guardian. One of the oldest in Ithicana."

"What does that mean?"

Ahnna couldn't get the words out, so it was Lara who answered. "There is a myth that if the guardians show a person mercy, it means the person is loyal to Ithicana."

"I see," James said, but Ahnna barely heard him, her memory filled with another moment in which Ithicana's guardians had offered salvation. Of how she'd raged then against putting stock in myths but now desperately clung to the spark of hope it planted in her heart.

Lara knelt next to them, her skilled gaze taking in James's throat. "That needs stitches." Then her focus moved to Ahnna. "I know there is a lot to tell, but what do we need to know right now to salvage this situation?"

Coughing to clear the lump in her throat, Ahnna said, "Alexandra is behind Edward's murder. She inflicted those injuries on herself as part of her scheme to frame me. Her reasons are myriad, but what matters is that her goal is the bridge and she and Katarina are working together. All the grain is full of poison, and the ship that delivered up north already struck its blow." She blinked away the memory of the bridge full of bodies of her people. "Aster is dead. He told me before he died that he sent soldiers by foot and ship to try to stop everyone from eating the poison, but I . . . I don't know if they made it in time."

Aren swore, but Lara's eyes only darkened as she climbed to her feet. She snatched hold of the shirt of one of the Amaridians and dragged him up. "Did you know the bread you were feeding us was poisoned?"

He struggled, trying to get away, but she only produced a knife, which she pressed to his throat. "Half my people on this beach are going to die because they ate your poison. Did you know?"

"They won't!" he squealed. "The sample grain they gave you was good, I swear it! No one here will die from it! Please let me live!"

Lara only gave a snort of disgust and dragged her blade across his throat. She shoved him into the water, then gave one of the wounded Amaridians a sharp kick that sent him rolling off the rocks into the sea with a splash. His screams cut off a heartbeat later, only to be replaced by more screams as Lara systematically shoved the Amaridian survivors into the water.

Lara then took a horn from Lia and blew a series of notes. Commands to attack. Commands to show no mercy.

A ragged breath pulled from her, and Ahnna sagged against James, only now realizing how much she'd feared that they wouldn't believe her. How much she'd feared her family would condemn her for all the tragedy that had befallen them.

Vaguely she was aware of sounds of battle in the distance. Explosions, screams, and the clashes of weapons, her people boarding and taking control of the other ship before it could flee back to Katarina.

She should get up. Should fight.

James ran a hand down her spine. "Let your people have this fight." He rested his cheek against hers, lips brushing her ear. "You did it, love. You saved them."

Saving her people had been Ahnna's goal. It had driven her through fear and pain and suffering, because no part of her had been willing to give in while her people's lives were on the line.

She'd not saved them all, and the weight of those losses would haunt her forever, but Ahnna set aside her grief, because the war had only just begun.

Shoving emotion behind walls and embracing the soldier within her, Ahnna climbed to her feet and started up a path through the trees until she reached the cliffs overlooking the seas. The other ship was listing in the water, a large hole in its hull and its decks swarming with Ithicanians. The Amaridians were on their knees in surrender.

Aren stopped next to Ahnna's elbow. "That grain would have become bread that fed every person in Ithicana," he said softly. "Not just soldiers, but innocents. Children."

"That sort of evil deserves no mercy," she replied, her heart hardening. "Kill them all."

"Lia, ring the dinner bell," Aren ordered. "Let Amarid feed the fish."

Lia strode to the edge of the cliff. She dumped the contents of one small jar into another, then threw it out over the water. It exploded with a loud bang, and Ahnna took a deep breath as her people began pushing the Amaridians off the deck of the ship.

Terrified screams merged with the roar of the surf hitting the cliff base below, and the guardians heard the call of Ithicana.

And came in numbers Ahnna had never before seen. Dozens and dozens of fins, sleek gray shapes shooting through the water with jaws open wide.

It was over quickly, the water soon dark with blood as the ship sank into the sea.

"It's done," Aren said, his eyes on bloody surf, but then a hand closed over Ahnna's.

She turned her head to find James at her side, his expression unreadable. Yet she knew what he was feeling, because she felt the same way. Not righteous justice over the deaths of those who'd aim to inflict such harm, but hollow.

Would it ever end? Would there ever come a day when this sort of carnage was nothing but a distant memory? Or would the villains who ruled forever paint the world red in their desire for more?

"We should head back to Midwatch," Aren said, not looking at her as he headed into the trees. "We need to talk, Ahnna. Lia will get His Highness a place in the barracks until we figure out our next steps."

Frustration filled the hollowness in her, because Aren had to have seen that James was more than just a travel companion and comrade. He *knew*, he just didn't like it.

She'd been raised to obey Aren. He wasn't simply her brother—he was her king and her commander. Ahnna had always been the rock at his back, never choosing anyone over him.

But not this time.

When she didn't move, Aren frowned at her. "Ahnna, *now*."

She stood her ground, ready to fight this fight because no one else would.

"Ahnna will remain with me, Your Grace. Her place is at my side, not yours."

James's voice filled her ears, his tone the cool, cultured accent of the Harendellian court, and Aren slid to an abrupt halt and turned. "What?"

"Did you not hear me, Your Grace? Or did you not understand?"

Aren's hand went to his weapon. "You have a lot of fucking nerve, Ashford. Just because a shark decided you weren't fit to eat doesn't mean you have any power here."

James slid an arm around Ahnna's waist and pulled her back against him. She could feel the rapid beat of his heart and the tension singing through him, no part of him unaware of the risk he was taking. Yet he was taking it.

For her.

"Ahnna is going to be my wife. So unless she desires otherwise, where she goes, I follow."

Machetes slithered out of scabbards and arrows were fitting to bowstrings, but Aren lifted a hand telling them all to hold. Lara stepped away from Aren, her arms crossed and expression unreadable. Not willing to intervene no matter what she thought, for which Ahnna didn't blame her.

"Let me get this straight," Aren said quietly. "You, the son of the king my sister was framed for murdering. You, the asshole who incarcerated my cousin and trussed up my wife's sister like a hog. You, who pursued Ahnna across Harendell with *dogs*, are asking me if you can marry her?"

"No." James's voice was steady in her ear, his grip around her body tight. "I already asked Ahnna to be my wife, and she said yes. I'm only informing you out of courtesy."

Aren drew his weapon. "You arrogant Harendellian prick."

Every part of Ahnna wanted to intervene, but Lara gave the slightest shake of her head.

"If you wish to fight over her, I will oblige," James replied. "But perhaps this time you'll do the fighting yourself and not have your soldiers hold me down while you swing your punches."

Aren's cheeks flushed, the muscles in his jaw bulging as he ground his teeth. Slowly he turned in a circle, as though hunting for composure, but then he met Ahnna's gaze. "This is what you want, then? Of all the men in the world, your choice is this asshole?"

"Yes." She swallowed hard. "Aren, I love him."

Her brother scrubbed a hand through his dark hair, then let out a long sigh and sheathed his weapon. "I know I've done an awful job of showing it, Ahnna, but I want you to be happy. If marrying a pretentious Harendellian prince is the way that happens, I won't stand in your way."

"Thank you." She had to fight back tears. "It means more to me than I can say to hear that from you."

"Thank you, Your Grace," James said. "I wasn't looking forward to fighting you."

Aren gave a soft snort. "Don't thank me yet, Ashford. I know my twin better than you, and she will never give you a day of rest."

"I wouldn't have it any other way." James's fingers tightened on her waist, and Ahnna looked down to cover her smile as her brother stomped down the path to the cove, bodyguard following, but Lara remained where she was.

The queen of Ithicana slowly approached them, strands of her long blond hair blowing in the rising wind. "He never once gave up on you, Ahnna," she said quietly. "He refused to turn on you, no matter the cost."

Ahnna's composure cracked, but as twin tears ran down her cheeks, she saw that Lara's eyes were also glistening.

"I'm sorry we left you alone in that nightmare." Lara's voice was choked. "I should have known . . . Should have suspected the full truth."

"You have nothing to be sorry about." Stepping out of James's arms, Ahnna closed the distance between her and Lara. "You and Keris both warned me of how dangerous Alexandra was, but she still fooled me. Fooled everyone. Besides, I'm the one who owes you an apology."

Ahnna met Lara's blue eyes, and though she'd planned what she intended to say to the other woman if ever given the chance, all those words abandoned her. They stood in silence for a long moment, but finally she said, "There was a moment when I was right to be angry with you, but also a moment when I should have let it go. Instead, I clung to my anger and was awful to you. Awful to both of you, and it wasn't even you I was so furious with."

"It was yourself." Lara tilted her head. "I know. And I won't lie and say it didn't frustrate me at times, but I've understood for a long time that you blame yourself as much as you ever blamed me. Although I still don't know why you feel that way."

Shame built in her stomach, turning her mouth sour, but Ahnna forced herself to say, "Because the reason Southwatch fell so easily is me." In clipped words, she explained what happened that night because of decisions fueled by wine, jealousy, and grief. "I know I couldn't have stopped the invasion, but Southwatch was my command. My responsibility. Aren trusted me to protect it, and I failed him."

Lara's eyes were filled with sympathy. "We all let down our guard that night, if for different reasons. Everyone on Midwatch was in their cups as well."

Ahnna watched her queen bite her bottom lip, then sigh. "I understand you, Ahnna, because I also struggle to forgive myself, and there are days when I think that it is the purest form of selfishness to do so. My guilt is not for writing those instructions to Serin and my father, but for hiding the act from Aren."

The wind was rising higher, and Ahnna smelled the scent of a storm coming on. A charge in the air, as if the tempests of Ithicana had arrived to listen to their conversation even as the guardians feasted on their enemies.

"If I had just told Aren the whole truth, he'd have realized what was in the letter he'd sent and we could have defended Ithicana. But those stupid pages felt like the culmination of everything horrible that

I'd done. They felt symbolic of my betrayal, and I didn't want him to know. Didn't want to face that shame, and didn't want to risk *that* being his breaking point that cost me his love. I believed that I could destroy them and that my transgressions would disappear. He'd never know, and there would be no consequences to me keeping this one secret."

Lara turned her face up, and the first drops of rain fell to splatter against her face. "Looking back, it seems so cowardly, so foolish, so fucking selfish."

"So human," Ahnna said quietly.

Lara made a humming noise, then shook her head. "Maybe. But people died because of me being . . . *human*. Children died. And there are nights when I feel like I might drown in the hate I feel for myself. Keris says that to feel this way changes nothing. That punishing myself does no one any good. But I can't fully forgive myself."

Sudden certainty filled Ahnna, and she caught hold of Lara's hands with hers. "I forgive you."

Lara's eyes widened with surprise, then welled with tears. "Thank you, sister."

They stood hand in hand in silence, the rain gaining intensity, and Ahnna finally said, "Can I ask you for one thing?"

"Anything."

Ahnna smiled. "I'd like to meet my niece."

# 62

# LARA

On the journey to midwatch, Ahnna and James relayed much of what had happened, including the depths of Alexandra's alliance with Katarina.

"She was in league with Silas and Katarina," Ahnna explained. "She paid for and supplied the weapons that were used in the attacks, and I'm sure that's not the end of her involvement. But it goes back further than that—they worked together to murder James's mother all those long years ago."

It was a great deal to take in, the scope of the plots extraordinary, and yet Lara did not struggle to believe any of it. Both queens were known to be conniving and clever, and with everything laid out before her, Lara felt only frustration at herself for not having seen through to the heart of it. For not seeing how the two queens had used Keris, Bronwyn, and Taryn to manipulate her and Aren into trusting Amarid.

If Ahnna hadn't arrived when she had, the grain would have been swiftly and efficiently distributed, and by the time they realized that it was poisoned, countless Ithicanians would have succumbed. They'd have been easy pickings when the armies of the north swept in, the bridge taken almost without a fight, and she and Aren would have been unable to stop it, because they'd have succumbed to the poison.

The rain poured down on them as they sailed to Midwatch and into its familiar cove, thunder rumbling in the distance.

"I have orders to give. I'll find you later," Aren muttered, jumping into the water and wading to the beach without a backward glance. He was tense beyond measure, but Lara wasn't certain how much of that was because of plots against them and how much was because of Ahnna's betrothal to James.

Lara watched him go, knowing exactly where her husband was going and why.

James stepped into the water and held out a hand to Ahnna to help her out of the boat. Ahnna took it with practiced grace, and Lara hid a smile at the small sign of the impact Harendell had made on her. His grip on Ahnna lingered, his reluctance to let go of her palpable as he finally offered Lara a hand. "Your Grace."

Lara took the offer, his grip strong and palm callused against hers. Whatever he and Ahnna had endured had taken a toll on Harendell's prince, but it struck Lara that this was a man who was at his best when the world was at its worst. He let go of her hand the moment her boots hit the beach, crossing his arms behind his back and silently following her and Ahnna.

"How bad a storm will it be?" Lara linked arms with her sister-in-law, watching Ahnna as she turned her face to the sky to regard the swirling clouds overhead.

"Still can't read the weather?" Ahnna asked, but the bite that her words once would have held was absent, and Lara felt another rush of gratitude that Ithicana's princess was home. Other than Aren, there was no one she'd rather have fighting at her back. Ahnna would look death straight in the eye and tell it to go fuck itself.

"Aren says I can't read the weather to save my life."

Ahnna smiled. "Just a thunderstorm, but I think there is a big one on its heels. The Amaridians pissed the tempests off."

"Lia has sent word south of Katarina's plot. They'll keep up a ruse that all is well and accept the shipments, and those vessels will make it back to Amarid to inform Katarina her plan worked. They'll assume the two missing ships were lost to the storm."

"It won't be long until she sends ships looking for proof of her successes. We have only as long as the tempests will give us."

They fell silent as they walked toward the nearly empty barracks, every soldier who could be spared set to cleaning up the mess of the battle. Ahnna tugged on her arm to take her into the barracks, but Lara pulled back and jerked her chin up the well-worn path. "We'll stay at the house."

"What do you mean by *house*?" Ahnna lifted an eyebrow. "Because if you mean a tent pitched on the ashes of his tantrum, we'll stay in the barracks."

"A bit better than a tent."

Lara examined Ahnna as they walked. Like James, she looked like she'd been to war, battered within an inch of her life. Always lean, Ahnna was now painfully thin, her cheeks hollow and her eyes shadowed. Whatever they'd been through had taken a toll, and it would take some time to hear the full story, if Ahnna was even willing to reveal it. Sometimes it was easier to pretend certain horrors had never happened.

A soldier approached, and Lara let go of Ahnna's arm as the man bent his head to her ear. "Taryn and Bronwyn have left, Your Grace. They went into the bridge with the aim of traveling to Maridrina."

Lara clenched her teeth, irrationally angry at her sister for leaving without hearing the full explanation. Although maybe it was for the best. Maybe it was better for them to go somewhere far away from the war to come, where both of them might know peace. "Let them go."

"Yes, Your Grace." The soldier headed back down to the water, leaving her alone with James and Ahnna.

"They are right to be angry," James said, wiping rain from his face. "I treated both of them like criminals. If one of them stabs me in the back, don't hold it against them. It's justified."

His words struck a chord in Lara, because she understood all too well what it felt like to regret a choice that had felt right in the moment it was made. How one almost longed for the punishment because it might offer some respite from the guilt that ate away at one's insides.

"I wouldn't hold it against either of them," she finally replied. "But I would hold them to account for violating my order."

They carried onward up the path, this time in silence, and Lara took the opportunity to watch the two of them. They walked close, James's hand resting low on the small of Ahnna's back, and she leaned into his touch. He said something that Lara couldn't quite catch, but Ahnna looked up at him and gave a soft laugh in a tone Lara had never heard her use before. Yet it was James's expression that made Lara's breath catch—the softening of his typically rigid expression, amber eyes utterly entranced by Ahnna's face. As though there were no one else in the world.

Aren had not missed the mark in his assessment of James's sentiment when he'd crossed paths with the pair in Verwyrd, but it struck Lara that what had been between the two then had grown tenfold in the time since. Love, sure and true, and it hurt Lara's own heart to know that both would suffer for it.

Ahnna abruptly stopped in her tracks. "You weren't lying—this is much better than a tent."

Lara rested her hands on her hips as she admired her house. "On the way to Devil's Island, Aren and I had a conversation in which he promised to rebuild the Midwatch house. Given how lean our resources were, it wasn't a priority, but somehow the Midwatch garrison got word of it. They rebuilt the house with their own hands, using wood from Ithicana's trees and a lot of favors, and surprised us both with it."

"Well, there you go," Ahnna said. "Proof that at least a few of your people don't hate you. Either that, or they're kissing your ass to stay on your good side."

A laugh tore from Lara's lips, the first in far too long, and she gave Ahnna a shove. "I take it back. I'm not glad you're home."

They carried on to the main doors, the guards flanking them grinning at the sight of their princess and voicing their pleasure at her return, although both gave James suspicious glares.

"Aren will be with Delia, likely in the library," Lara told Ahnna, and then she leveled a finger at James. "You, with me. That needs to be stitched before you bleed all over my house."

James's eyes went to Ahnna, but she nodded. "You'll be safe enough. Just don't turn your back on her." She gave Lara a wink.

Lara scoffed. "Better me than Nana."

"Is she in Midwatch?" Ahnna had tensed at the mention of her grandmother, her eyes searching the halls as though she expected Amelie to explode into view and immediately begin berating her. A foolish fear, because the old harridan always waited until you least expected her.

"She goes everywhere Delia goes. How else can she criticize every choice I make?" Lara rolled her eyes. "But she was off island today, so maybe you'll get lucky and have some respite."

"I won't count on it." Without another word, Ahnna headed down the hallway to the library.

"We can do this in the dining room," Lara said to James. "It won't take long."

She left him in the large room staring at Vitex while she retrieved medical supplies and asked the servants to secure fresh clothes for both James and Ahnna, as well as any other items they might need. When she returned to the dining room, Vitex was weaving between James's legs, purring at top volume.

"Interesting choice of pet."

"He makes short work of any snakes that find their way inside the house," she answered. "Be sure to check the bedsheets before you get in. Shoo!"

Vitex hissed at her and Lara hissed back, watching as the cat scuttled off to find Aren, whom he favored. "On the table, please."

"With respect, Your Grace, I'm filthy and not fit for your dining room." James crossed his arms behind his back, and Lara was struck with how, despite being filthy, unshaven, and bedraggled, James Ashford looked undeniably like the prince and soldier that he was. Possessed of a quiet gravitas that she suspected served him well on the battlefield.

*Not just a prince*, she reminded herself. *He's the rightful king of Harendell.*

"It's not the first time my dining room has served such a purpose." She gestured at the large table. "This isn't Harendell. Ithicana is endlessly pragmatic, and given that your soon-to-be wife is Ithicana incarnate, you ought to get used to it. Also, I'm queen and you should really do as I say. It's good manners."

She expected *that* to light a fire beneath him, because the Harendellians were sticklers for protocol, but James only lifted one broad shoulder. "Not my queen, Your Grace."

"That's true." Lara circled the table and retrieved two lamps. "*Your* queen is the murderous bitch responsible for Petra's sacking of Vencia and the deaths of countless innocent Maridrinians. Your prior queen and stepmother is a manipulative monster who murdered both your parents in her quest for power and, apparently, Ithicana's bridge. So perhaps you should behave with a mind not for who holds authority over you but rather for proper etiquette."

"A fair request, Your Grace."

"Lara."

"I'm afraid that's not proper etiquette, Your Grace." A flicker of amusement gleamed in his amber eyes. "It will not do to pick and choose among manners."

"God spare me, you and Ahnna must fight like alley cats when you aren't fighting for your lives." Lara set the lamps down, then slapped the table with both her palms. "You're dripping blood on my floor, so either oblige me or go outside."

James sighed and climbed on the table. Lying back, he exposed his throat and the nasty wound Aren's blade had left. Another layer of skin deeper, and he'd have bled to death.

Uncorking a bottle of eye-wateringly strong spirits, Lara sloshed the clear liquid over the wound and then over her own hands, noting that James did not so much as flinch at the pain. "Your eyes are an unusual color. I've only seen the same hue in one other."

"Lestara, I assume. She's my cousin, and amber eyes are as common to Cardiff's royal line as azure eyes are to the Veliants."

Lara briefly considered how much she wished to reveal about what Keris had learned from Cormac, but then settled on what was now widely known. "We learned the truth about your mother's identity from merchant captains prior to the blockade. Siobhan was King Ronan of Cardiff's younger sister."

"Yes."

An answer, yet no answer, because the depths of that story were something Lara deeply wanted to know. Instead she said, "Keris's creative punishment for Lestara did not work out as intended. Harendell was supposed to make her life a living hell, not make her queen."

"He wasn't mistaken. Virginia and her ladies tormented her for months. The things they did to her were not fit behavior and are certainly not fit to be repeated before a lady of your quality's ears."

Lara threaded the hooked needle, feeling oddly flattered by his chivalry despite very much wanting to know exactly what the Harendellian women had done to Lestara. A question to be posed to Ahnna later. "And yet your father broke William's betrothal to Ahnna in order to wed him to Lestara, and now she is queen of the most powerful kingdom in the north, cementing the alliance with Cardiff, for Lestara is Ronan's daughter."

"My father never intended Lestara to be queen."

Lara pulled a lamp closer and then pulled the jagged wound together before pushing the needle through his flesh. James did not so much as twitch. "Oh?"

"Don't disappoint me by playing dumb, Your Grace," James answered. "I've heard great things about your intelligence, as well as the training you received from your father's Magpie. Although I suppose stories do grow in the telling, so perhaps my hopes were too high."

Lara stabbed her needle through his skin and was finally rewarded by a twitch of pain. "Keris is in Harendell, and he had a meeting with your uncle, Prince Cormac, who provided him with a wealth of information. Edward was married to your mother in secret. Are you aware your uncle was assassinated?"

"Yes." James was silent, his gaze fixed on the ceiling above them, but then he added, "He'll only be the first of many who will die if Alexandra isn't stopped. She holds no love for Cardiff, and I can only assume she intends to extend her reach north, at the cost of my family."

"I'm inclined to agree, although I know Alexandra did not kill Edward out of a desire for conquest. At least, not entirely. She killed him because Edward planned to reveal his marriage to Siobhan, to raise you up as Harendell's rightful heir, to cast Alexandra aside, and to name your half siblings as bastards. She acted to protect her children."

"That's correct."

"But you don't want to take the throne, do you? You have no desire to take the crown from your brother or to harm your sister's reputation by naming her a bastard. You hope that if you give William the truth he'll turn on Alexandra, and you are betting that his affection for Lestara will push him to stay true to the peace you worked for with Cardiff. I say *hope* because you are not certain about your brother's state of mind toward you."

"I see the rumors that you are more than just a pretty face are justified, Your Grace. You'd have done well in Harendell's court."

Lara stabbed him again with her needle. "Mind your tongue, Your Highness, or my husband will cut it out."

James only gave a soft laugh, and it struck Lara that it would take a man of this sort of fearlessness to keep up with Ahnna. But his tone hardened as he said, "William is king."

"Not the rightful one." She knotted the thread. "If you claim the throne, this war would end and true justice could be served. Surely that is worth your siblings' fall from grace. You have the power to bring peace to the north."

"We're finished." James pushed her hand away from his throat and then slung his legs off the side of the table and stood. "William is king of Harendell and I will not be the one to dethrone him. Nor will I be the one to destroy my sister's chances by naming her bastard. Once Will knows the truth about what Alexandra has done, about her conspiracies with Katarina, he'll end this war. He has his faults, but he's good at his core and I have sway with him."

"Are you so sure about that?" Lara jerked up her knife to cut the thread right next to his skin, feeling abruptly infuriated that he'd be so willfully naïve. "Alexandra has dangled the bridge before him like a carrot before a mule. Power has allure that few can deny."

"You're wrong about him." James's amber eyes darkened with anger. "And even if you are not, you are deluded if you think that I can march into Harendell and sit my ass down on the Twisted Throne. Any proof that my parents were wed and that I am legitimate died with my father. Just how well do you think the people will take it if I, the half-Cardiffian bastard, claim that Alexandra—a Harendellian blueblood—was never queen? How well do you think they'll take it if Cardiff claims that William—also Harendellian through and through—is a bastard, and our sister is illegitimate as well? How well do you think they'll take me, the half Cardiffian with an Ithicanian princess for a wife, being raised up to the throne? If you believe that Harendell will stand behind me, *Lara*, you are a fool."

He might be right, but Lara couldn't help but wonder if James's anger had more to do with the threat to hurt his siblings than the weakness of his claim to the throne. "What if telling William the truth changes nothing? You are a military man. You know Ithicana cannot hope to stand against Harendell, much less Harendell with Cardiff and Amarid at its back. We might hold out through this storm season, but the moment the calm comes upon us, we will be crushed. And if you think Ahnna will allow herself to survive Ithicana's fall, it is *you* who are deluded. Are you willing to sacrifice the love of your life for the sake of your siblings' reputation?"

James took a step back, and Lara felt a flash of triumph that she'd struck a nerve.

"If you truly love Ahnna as you say, you'll do what it takes to save not just her, but everything she has fought so hard to protect. Begging your brother to *do the right thing* isn't going to cut it."

"What is it that you want me to do?"

"I want you to use your influence with Ronan to break the alliance with Cardiff. I want Cardiff's armies to back you as the rightful heir to the throne. Lestara might be queen and William king, but you *know* it is Alexandra who rules, and she has no tolerance for pagans. Once Ithicana is broken, Alexandra and Katarina will look north. I know it. And you know it. Do this, and you don't just spare Ithicana, you spare Cardiff as well. Quit hiding behind sentiment for Virginia and William and take the Twisted Throne."

All the color drained from James's face. With total disregard for manners, he picked up a decanter of Aren's favorite whiskey from the sideboard, filled a glass, and drained it in one gulp. "I don't want to be king."

"Maybe not, but do you want Ahnna to be queen?"

James went very still, staring into the empty glass.

"She was born to rule," Lara said softly. "Aren would be the first to say that she ruled Ithicana in his absence far better than he ever did, and if she sat on the Twisted Throne, she would make our world so much better."

Silence stretched between them, the air feeling thick and unbreathable.

"I can't bring Ahnna north," he finally answered. "There's a ransom on her head because everyone believes she killed my father, and Ronan tried to assassinate her once already. Do not conflate Ronan's affection for me with a desire to have an Ithicanian as Harendell's queen. He is not on your side."

"Agreed. Which is why Ahnna must stay here while you go north alone."

James set his glass down with such force that the crystal cracked. "You misunderstand. I will not leave her side."

Sympathy and guilt burned in Lara's chest, because she'd stood in this position before and knew the hurt of it all too well. "Admirable sentiment, but if you don't do this, we are all damned." Closing the distance between them, Lara looked up into James's eyes. "Do you think Ahnna will still love you knowing you could have stopped this but chose not to? Worse, how do you think she'll feel about herself knowing that her love was the damnation of all that she held dear?"

She could feel the rage seething off him as he loomed over her. But Lara had faced down big men over less, and she would not back down now. "You will not prove your worth to Ahnna Kertell by shadowing her every step."

James's lips parted and Lara braced for his anger, but he clamped down on whatever he wanted to say and inclined his head. "Thank you for your medical expertise and for your hospitality, Your Grace, but you'll have to excuse me, I need to find my future wife."

Not waiting for her to respond, he stepped around her and left the room.

Pouring herself a glass of Aren's whiskey, Lara sat at her table but didn't take a drink. Only stared at the liquid while a tear slowly dripped down her cheek. *I forgive you*, Ahnna's voice whispered inside her head.

But as Lara finally took a mouthful, she knew that today would not be the day she forgave herself.

# 63

# AREN

"Look at this," Aren said, pointing at the illustration in the book he was holding. "It's a horse. They are horrible creatures but not nearly as bad as camels. Camels kick and bite and spit. The worst of them is a camel in Maridrina named Jack."

Delia reached for the page and caught it with her tiny fist, forcing him to gently extract it. "You can't rip your books. Your uncle Keris thinks you can do no wrong and he'll blame me. He's already referred to me as *an enemy of the written word* for burning my library down."

In typical infant fashion, his daughter cared nothing about the abuses her father suffered at her uncle's hand and Delia shrieked in protest at being denied the book. Aren gave her a silver rattle, which she promptly hurled to the floor.

"I appreciate a girl who knows what she wants."

Starting at Ahnna's voice, Aren looked up to find his sister leaning against the doorframe, and a band of emotion tightened around his chest so fiercely that he could barely breathe. Ahnna was covered in bruises and scrapes, her right arm in a splint, and her body so thin she looked like a wraith, but she was here.

His sister was alive.

"Fatherhood looks good on you, brother," she remarked. "You appear ready to settle down into middle age and get soft while the younger generation runs about having adventures."

"I literally *just* came from the battlefield. And I'd like to remind you that you and I are the exact same age."

"I know." Ahnna grinned. "But I'm not the one sitting on a sofa with a drink explaining to a baby the risks of associating with a camel named Jack."

"If you'd met Jack, you'd understand."

His twin laughed, then came into the room and walked the length of the shelves. "Where did you get the new library?"

"Where do you think?"

She huffed. "Keris. He does understand that you can't eat a book, yes?"

"I won't pretend to understand what that man thinks."

Ahnna trailed her finger down the spines, but then pulled out a volume and flipped through the pages. "*On the merits of using bronze rather than copper for small coinage*. Sounds fascinating."

"Keris has eclectic tastes."

"Katarina told us Keris is in Verwyrd. Other than being manipulated by Alexandra, what's his reason for risking Lestara's wrath?"

"Officially, to be an intermediary between Harendell and Ithicana. Unofficially, he's my spy, although you're correct that he's not going to be pleased to learn that Alexandra outwitted him."

"Alexandra makes the Magpie look like a bumbling idiot, and compared with Petra, she's alarmingly sane." Ahnna was quiet for a long moment as she stared blindly at the pages of the book. "Yet I think her greatest attribute is that she's profoundly patient. Thirty years, Aren. James's whole life, she's known the truth about Siobhan and the threat it posed to her and her children, but she bided her time until now."

"I underestimated her," he admitted. "Edward was the one person I was confident she would not cross, but here we are."

"Here we are," Ahnna repeated, then crossed the room to sit on the sofa next to him. "May I hold her?"

Delia scrunched up her face in protest as he lifted her off his chest and settled her in the crook of Ahnna's arm, eyeing the splint. "Is that broken?"

"It's more or less healed. Carlo broke it when he caught us to prove a point, and James insists I keep it splinted." She handed Delia the book on coinage, his daughter instantly ripping out pages, cooing in delight at the noise. Ahnna lowered her lips to Delia's ear and whispered, "I'll burn the evidence later so that Keris never knows."

"He'll do inventory," Aren muttered. "Keris is like a goddamned librarian. And he drinks all my best wine." He sighed. "But he's in the thick of it for our sake."

"What about Zarrah?"

A flood of frustrated anger surged through him. "Entirely silent. She hasn't responded to any of my letters, and the Valcottan merchants trading at Southwatch say that she's been out of public view. Lots of chatter about conflict between her and Keris, but Valcotta is also said to have wasting disease in their herds. They've had to do significant culling, which has had the impact you might imagine."

"None of this sounds like Zarrah." Ahnna frowned. "What about Sarhina?"

"She's rendered herself borderline powerless. I got into it with a few of Maridrina's elected representatives, and they've made it clear their interest is the resumption of trade on the bridge, not Ithicana's autonomy. They'll throw us to the wolves for the sake of Harendellian beef. Sarhina has sway with them, but she won't risk her people for personal interests."

"Having endured Alexandra and Katarina, there is something to be said for a queen who puts her people first, even if it is not in our interests. Maridrina needed a ruler like Sarhina." Ahnna adjusted Delia on her lap, watching her niece continue to shred pieces of paper. "We've got weather coming in. The next storm will be a big one."

Thunder from the squall currently over Midwatch boomed, and Delia jerked in surprise and then began to cry. Aren reached for her, but Ahnna tucked the baby closer, cooing and calming Delia's tears.

"I always forget how good you are with children."

"Lots of practice. I lost count of how many I helped Nana deliver before you liberated me and put me in command of Southwatch."

"You're welcome."

Ahnna smiled, stroking Delia's dark hair. "She's perfect. I've thought about her a lot since she was born. Wondered what she might be like. Feared for her when I learned how bad things were. Katarina . . . she . . ." His sister gave a sharp shake of her head. "Never mind."

It was easy for him to imagine the sort of threats that Amarid's queen might have voiced. What sort of threats Edward *had* voiced. "What happened to you, Ahnna? It feels like a lifetime since you fled Verwyrd, but all you and James told us was about Alexandra and Katarina's schemes."

His sister was quiet, but he didn't miss how the pulse in her throat beat faster as though she was reliving a nightmare. "I don't want to talk about most of it." Then she gave him a half smile, meeting his gaze. "Katarina put us in the Furnace, which was where we were for much of it."

Aren's stomach hollowed, because he'd spent time in Riomar and knew all about the horrors of the infamous prison. The idea that it hadn't been the worst thing his twin had endured to get back to Ithicana made him feel sick. "How did you manage to escape?"

"The cells are crusted with decades worth of piss. Using that, a bit of trickery, and a lot of luck, I made a bomb."

"A piss bomb . . ." A laugh tore from his lips, because of course Ahnna had figured that out. She'd always been the cleverer one, especially with making bombs. But then a thought occurred to him. "Katarina has to assume that you and James came here."

"She'll certainly assume we tried." Ahnna looked up as more thunder boomed overhead. "But the Tempest Seas sink many ships, and the vessel we were in was not fit for storms."

"Any Ithicanian worth her salt can ride a raft with a handkerchief for a sail through the worst of storms, and you're Ithicanian to your core."

Ahnna's slight smile fell away, and her bottom lip trembled until she bit down on it. It struck Aren that his twin was hanging on to composure by a thread.

*What happened to her?* Fury filled him that she'd had to endure all of this. Fury at Alexandra, Katarina, and everyone else who'd harmed Ahnna, but also at himself. He'd been harsh with her when they'd spoken in Verwyrd, putting her in a terrible position and showing not an ounce of empathy for what she'd felt.

Ahnna slowly looked up at him, her hazel eyes liquid with tears. "Thank you for letting me come home."

Aren's eyes burned, and he scrubbed a hand across them to push away tears that she'd feared he might turn on her. "Always." He slung an arm around her shoulders, and his sister leaned against his shoulder.

There were so many things Aren wanted to say, but he couldn't articulate them even to himself. The clearest feeling was the profound sense of relief he felt having his twin at his back again, because with Ahnna here, it felt like Ithicana might have a fighting chance of survival. Yet all he said was, "It's good to have you here."

"It's good to be home." She picked up a handful of torn paper and tossed it in the air, Delia smiling as it floated to the floor. "You and James can stand on the bridge top and see who can piss the farthest if you must, but it's important to me that you try to get along with him."

"He hasn't tried very hard to get along with me in *any* of the instances I've been in his presence." Aren picked up his drink and swallowed a large mouthful. "I've never met a man so willing to pick a fight."

"James would do anything for me." She twirled a lock of Delia's dark hair around her finger, her niece drifting in the direction of sleep. "Even stand up to you."

Something in his sister's tone suggested that her words meant more than they seemed to on the surface, and Aren immediately felt defensive. "What's that supposed to mean? People stand up to me all the time."

"Not for me, they don't."

"Lara—"

"She's different, so don't even try using her as an example."

Ahnna's body had gone rigid. "This has nothing to do with her, so don't go down that path."

Aren had no idea what Ahnna was talking about, and seeming to sense that, she huffed out a breath of frustration and said, "No one has ever taken my side over yours."

Despite knowing that it was the wrong thing to do, Aren scoffed. "This is childish. Can we have one moment when you aren't picking a fight about some imagined grievance? Don't we have bigger issues?"

"Don't trivialize me!" she snarled, but then winced and soothed Delia before drawing in a deep breath. "I have been your shadow my entire life, Aren. I have had your back, done what needed doing, and held Ithicana together when you could not. I never begrudged my role. Never wanted more, because you were my brother. The heir to Ithicana and then my king, and I felt pride in my loyalty to you. But from a young age, I knew that you mattered more to *everyone*. I came first for *no one*."

Aren's lips parted to say that she'd come first for him, but then stopped, remembering the moment when that had dramatically changed. When Ahnna had confronted him about bringing Lara to Maridrina and then accidentally knocked Lara off the bridge. How instead of being reasonable, he'd lashed out and told Ahnna he didn't want to see her face again. How he'd refused to have anything to do with her until military matters demanded that he must, and then immediately done his best to continue avoiding her. All because his sister had questioned his actions with Lara.

Even if Lara had been wholly innocent, Ahnna, as the commander of Southwatch, had been in the right to call him out, and yet no one other than Lara herself had said a word in Ahnna's defense. No one. Not. Once.

Not even Jor.

Not even Nana.

"People treated me like I wasn't a person but an extension of you," she whispered, stroking the now-sleeping Delia's hair. "Which meant anything anyone ever did or said to me was done with a mind for how you might respond. No one wanted to upset you. No one wanted to make you angry. Everyone wanted to make you happy. So everyone kept a buffer of distance with me, and if that buffer was crossed in a way you might take issue with, it didn't matter how I felt. All they'd ever do is beg me not to tell you."

"Ahnna—"

"Don't." She rubbed at her eyes, voice choked. "Don't apologize, because it's not your fault. It's a function of who we are in this world, and I don't blame you for it. I only want you to understand why James risking your anger—risking your cutting his throat—for my sake matters so much."

Aren blew out a breath from between his teeth, not entirely certain how to feel about everything she'd said. "Does he have attributes other than a willingness to fistfight me, or was that all it took to win your heart?"

Ahnna gave a choked laugh. "Have you *seen* him?"

"His good looks hold no weight with me. I have heard he's a good fighter, though. Many medals for valor, which is more important than pretty eyes."

Ahnna gave an amused snort, but then her eyes grew distant. "When I am with him, I feel like I am finally whole."

Aren's chest tightened with a swell of unexpected emotion, because he'd never heard his sister speak like that about anyone. Never seen that expression on her face. If it was James who made Ahnna feel like this, then Aren would do his best to like the man. Even if he was an arrogant Harendellian prick.

"Where is she?" Nana's familiar voice filtered through the house, and Aren felt an overwhelming urge to find somewhere to hide.

Knowing that their grandmother would be in a mood after everything that had happened, Aren scrambled to his feet. "Speaking of James, I think I'll find the man in question and see about getting to know him better. Don't move. You should never wake a sleeping baby."

Ahnna glared at him. "Coward."

He grinned at her, then swiftly strode out the door of the library. Nana was half running down the hallway, and he lifted a hand in greeting and then turned to escape, nearly slamming directly into James.

"If you value your life," he said before the prince could speak, "come with me."

James eyed the approaching force of nature, and while he might have been willing to fistfight a king to be with Ahnna, apparently that bravery did not extend to getting in the path of Nana. "All right."

# 64

# AHNNA

"Ahnna?" Nana's voice filtered through the house.

Ahnna held up a finger to her lips as her grandmother exploded into the library, glad to have Delia as a line of defense against the storm that was the woman who'd raised her. But Nana only stepped back into the hallway and shouted, "Lara!"

Delia did not so much as stir at the noise, and a few moments later, Ahnna heard the soft pat of boots against the floor, and Lara appeared. Her eyes were slightly puffy, and she said nothing as she took Delia from Ahnna's arms. "He's fine. Just a few stitches."

"Who is fine?" Nana demanded. "Never mind. It's the tall lad Aren escaped around the corner with, isn't it? Let me guess: The Harendellian bastard prince has abandoned family, king, and country to fall between your skinny legs."

Ahnna sighed. "His name is James."

"As though his name matters. It's his face and his cock that have you making foolish choices, you idiot girl. Stupid, reckless child."

Normally each of her grandmother's harsh words would be a

punch to the stomach, but all Ahnna saw were the tears streaming down Nana's wrinkled face. Not once in her life had she witnessed her grandmother cry like this. Not when Ahnna's father had died. Not when Aren had been kidnapped. Not in any of the catastrophes that Amelie had nursed Ithicana's people through. Yet here she stood, sobbing so violently that Ahnna feared she might drop to the floor from heart failure. "Nana, are you well?"

"I'm fine," her grandmother snapped through sobs. "Why wouldn't I be?"

Getting to her feet, Ahnna gripped her grandmother's arms. "Because you're crying."

"Don't be daft." Nana wiped at her face. "I just came out of the rain, and I'm sweating because I was forced to run up that murderous hill."

Every word came out between sobs, and Ahnna nearly fainted in shock as her grandmother flung her arms around Ahnna's waist, clinging to her. "But you're alive, my beautiful girl. Alive against every odd, which means there is hope left. If you are here, there is hope."

It was suddenly hard to breathe, and Ahnna rested a hand on her grandmother's shoulder even as she met Lara's gaze over the old woman's head. Lara gave her a sad smile, then said, "I'll make sure your room is ready and find you some fresh clothes."

Lara's expression more than Nana's tears filled Ahnna with unease, and her skin prickled as the library door clicked shut.

Nana had regained some of her composure, and she pushed away, wiping her face with her sleeve. "Well? Let me have a look at you, then."

She reached up to push back Ahnna's top lip, then ran her hands down Ahnna's sides before making a noise of disgust. "Good God, girl. It looks like the only thing that's whole is your teeth. When was the last time you ate a good meal? You're skin and bones. A walking skeleton." With practiced hands, she pulled off the remains of Ahnna's splint and checked the break. "It's healed, but no swordplay at least another week so the bone has time to get strong. And I mean *both* sorts of swordplay."

Ahnna's face burned hot at the implication. "I—"

She broke off with a strangled yelp as her grandmother squeezed one of her breasts and then declared, "Not pregnant, at least."

"I could have told you that!"

"You know that if you ate more, you'd have bigger tits. This lad must be one for the legs if he's followed you into this storm, because it wasn't for those mosquito bites. Now let me see the rest of you."

Her grandmother had subjected her to this sort of treatment all of her life and Ahnna had always taken it quietly, but she found she'd lost her patience for it. "Enough, Nana. I'm well enough to fight, and that's what matters, isn't it?"

Nana blew a long breath out from between her teeth, then gave a tight nod. "Lia gave me the sum of things on my way up the hill, but I bring dark news with me. I was somewhat north of here, so I received word about the poisoned grain. Hundreds are dead, and though Aster's soldiers were able to spread the warning swiftly, more will die. The commanders are coming to Midwatch, but it's not war they're going to ask Aren for, my girl. It's surrender."

Ahnna very nearly doubled over, the word like a blow to her gut. "*What?*"

"Never in my life did I think that the Ithicanian spirit would break, and if you had told me that it would be poisoned bread that would do it, I'd have called you mad." Nana drew in a steadying breath. "But it has happened. Spirits in the north are broken, and I think the sentiment will sweep south down the bridge and into Eranahl until all demand that your brother abdicate. They no longer believe the bridge and the life that comes with it is worth the toil. Better to give up power to William and allow the might of Harendell to provide, or to flee south into Maridrina or Valcotta to build new lives where death does not knock every hour."

Ahnna's ass rushed down to meet the sofa, her knees having betrayed her. "No!"

Nana moved to sit next to her, taking Ahnna's hand and squeezing it tight. "Knowing that you are here may rally their spirits, Ahnna. Knowing that you are alive and fighting on their behalf might bolster their support for your brother's reign."

What was one sword? One sword swung by an arm not fully mended. "*Might?*"

Her grandmother's shoulders slumped, and it struck Ahnna that Amelie had grown old in her absence. Old in a way that spoke to an end. "I do not think we can win this fight, my darling girl. Not even with you at your brother's side. Maridrina was a bothersome fly in comparison with the hammer that is Harendell, and they have Cardiff and *Amarid* at their backs. We stand alone, Maridrina too weak and unwilling, and Valcotta silent as they face their own obstacles. If there is hope, it is as thin as a spider's web."

Logically, Ahnna had known how dire the situation was. Known that even if she made it back to Ithicana in time to foil Katarina's scheme with the poison, it wouldn't end the war. The two northern queens would merely switch tactics, and when the storms eased, it would be a War Tides unlike any before. Ithicana didn't have enough soldiers, didn't have enough weapons, didn't have enough of anything it needed to fight back against a united North. It just wasn't possible.

Yet the thought that her people would give up or that Aren would abdicate hadn't even crossed her mind, because Ithicana's will to endure had never wavered.

"Ahnna, do you see a way through this? Do you see something that I do not, because . . ." Nana broke off with a choked sob. "Can you save us?"

Ahnna found herself staring at her grandmother's hand. It had always seemed so strong and capable, yet it was now fragile in her own scarred grip.

"I can't save us," Ahnna whispered softly, ignoring the way her heart wept at what she was about to say. "There is only one person who has the power to save Ithicana."

Except she wasn't certain that James was willing to pay the price.

# 65

# JAMES

"Nana hasn't been the same since Ahnna left Ithicana," Aren said, slinging an arm around James's shoulder and steering him down the corridor. "They'll have a lot to catch up on, so it's best to give them space."

James considered what Ahnna had told him about her grandmother, which wasn't entirely positive. "Is Ahnna all right?"

"Well enough to demand I be nice to you." Ithicana's king looked him up and down. "I'm hoping you have hidden depths, James, because my impression so far is that you're something of an asshole."

"Digging deeper isn't going to change your opinion. I really need to speak to Ahnna."

Aren snorted. "I'll give you credit for being self-aware. You can speak to her later. You look like you've been dragged through hell, and you smell worse. Let's remedy that."

Opening a door, he pushed James through a suite of simple but well-appointed rooms, then into an antechamber full of towels, scrubs, and soaps. He proceeded to fill James's arms with said items, along with a razor, before flinging open another door.

Wind and rain hammered James even as a flash of lightning half blinded him. Thunder boomed, the storm above as violent as James had ever seen, but as he tried to step back, Aren shoved him out into the rain.

Together, they walked down a path through a courtyard at the center of which was a series of steaming pools linked by streams, the lot of it fed by a small waterfall that flowed beneath the bottom level of the house. "I'll leave you to it," Aren said.

Except as James peeled off his filthy and ruined clothing, weapons clattering against the paving stones, Ithicana's king didn't leave. Only stood in the rain, staring at the bolts of lightning illuminating the sky overhead.

What James desperately wanted was to be alone so that he could have time to think about his conversation with Lara, but he sensed that Aren wanted words with him. So he bit his tongue and waded into the scalding water, and then set to scrubbing away salt, blood, and filth. He was halfway through ridding himself of his beard, which had been mercilessly itchy in the Ithicanian heat, when Aren asked, "Do you love her?"

James paused the razor mid-stroke across his cheek, but then continued in scraping away his beard as he considered his response. "I tried not to for a long time, but Ahnna is like the tide. Pulling me back and dragging me under, and I'd rather drown in her depths than ever feel solid ground beneath my feet. There is only her, nothing else."

"A *yes* would have sufficed, but point taken." Aren sat at the edge of the steaming pool, then lay back on the stone, not seeming to mind the rain hammering against his face. "You know that if you hurt her, I'll kill you."

"I've already hurt her." James continued with his shaving. "I hunted her across Harendell and into the Blackreaches, fought her, and shot her with two arrows before I came to terms with the truth of her innocence."

Aren's broad chest rose and fell as though he were taking a

steadying breath, then he turned his head to look at James. "You are not making this easy."

"Would you prefer I lied?"

"No." Aren looked skyward again. "But I would like to understand what she sees in you."

Finishing with the razor, James set it on the edge of the pool and then rested his elbows on the ledge, watching the bubbles of soap move from pool to pool, then out through a grate in the wall where they'd carry on down to the sea. "One of my first memories of Ahnna was after she knocked me off my ship before it blew up. There were sharks circling, attacking everything that moved. She was suspended in the water with her hair floating all around, one hand outstretched to an enormous shark. It gave way to her as though it recognized her authority, and every time I blink, that's how I see Ahnna. Beautiful and fierce and defiant."

James rested his chin on his forearm, allowing his mind's eye to be consumed by the vision of Ahnna as he continued, "She doesn't need to be protected. Doesn't need anyone to fight her battles. Doesn't need anyone for much of anything, if I am being truthful. But she knows that there is nothing she could ask for that I would not give, nothing that I would not do, no one that I wouldn't fight. She will come first until I breathe my last."

Aren was silent for a long time, and then he said, "What's between you two all of a sudden makes a great deal of sense."

Neither of them spoke, content to allow the storm to fill the silence between them, only for the violent peace to be broken by a familiar male voice. "Aren, there's news from the north by way of the bridge."

Jor approached, the grizzled Ithicanian looking far stronger than when James had seen him last. He gave James a nod, then said, "Aster's actions saved a lot of lives, but we've still lost hundreds of soldiers. Either dead already or dying, and Mara is leading the surviving watch commanders to Midwatch to meet with you."

Aren sat upright with his elbows on his knees, head rested on one hand, and James could feel his grief at the news. His guilt, because for better or worse, it had been his agreement with Katarina that had allowed this to happen. "We'll think of a plan of defense for when the storms ease. I'll . . . I'll write to Zarrah again. Or see if Keris can get word to her. I'll—"

"They don't want a plan," Jor interrupted, his face drawn, and James instinctively knew what he was about to say next. "They want you to surrender to William."

Aren stiffened.

"They're done fighting, lad." Jor wiped rainwater off his face, then looked to the sky. "They're beat. Amelie's telling Ahnna this now, and Lara knows already. Everyone north of Serrith has given up on this fight. They think there's a better future to be had under William's rule."

"Except William doesn't rule," James snapped, abruptly furious that Ithicana was so quick to give up. "Alexandra does, and this was every bit as much her plot as Katarina's. Explain that she was willing to poison every man, woman, and child among them and perhaps they will reconsider surrendering to her!"

"Except what is the alternative?" Aren's eyes were fixed on the paving stones. "We can't win this fight. We can't prevail against Harendell and its allies once the storms ease, and if I try, it will only mean thousands more Ithicanians dying, and the result will be the same. Maybe it's time to cut our losses."

"You won't be saving anyone," James retorted. "You think Alexandra will take them into the fold and protect them? Because you're a fool if you do. She'll use them as cheap labor and turn a blind eye to their suffering. We need to get the truth into William's ears, because he will surely turn on her for her conspiracies with Katarina. What Alexandra has done is treason. You just need to hold strong until William knows everything."

"Do you really believe that William will turn on Alexandra?" Aren asked. "Because I've met your brother, and it struck me that the apron strings tying him to Alexandra are as strong as steel."

His brother's face filled his vision, and James forced himself to imagine how Will would react to learning that Alexandra was behind their father's murder. That she'd been scheming with Katarina all these long years. That she was a traitor.

Would it be enough to turn him against her?

Doubt that had long been lurking in the back of his mind pushed its way to the forefront, because James also knew his brother. Knew how Will *coveted* that which he did not have.

And what bigger prize was there than the bridge? What better boost to pride than to take it from a man like Aren Kertell, who was everything William was not? Alexandra would try to convince him that everything she'd done was for him, and though he desperately wished otherwise, in his heart, James knew that his brother would choose to believe her.

There was only one other path forward, but every part of him recoiled from that step. He had never reached higher than his station, never wanted to, and to step on the backs of his siblings to do so? It made James feel sick.

"I'm not willing to see my people go to the grave for the sake of keeping power." Aren squared his shoulders, his tone pulling James back to the conversation. "I refuse to be that sort of ruler. I'll negotiate surrender to William, and also make arrangements with Sarhina and Zarrah to create places for my people to move to, if they wish."

Movement caught James's attention, and he turned his head to discover Ahnna standing well within earshot, her expression one of horror. "No," she whispered. "Aren, you can't do this!"

Ithicana's king exhaled a ragged breath. "Ahnna, I have to protect our people. I have to give them a chance at life, even if it means that Ithicana's name fades into history."

This was a path James had been desperate to avoid at almost any cost. *Almost* any, because as he looked into Ahnna's hazel eyes, James knew she was the one thing he refused to sacrifice.

Aren started to rise, but James reached out and caught hold of the king's wrist. "I know how we might save Ithicana. But I'm marrying your sister first."

# 66

# ZARRAH

THERE WAS SOMETHING freeing about walking through a city and no one knowing or caring who she was. By privilege of birth, Zarrah's face had always been well known in Valcotta. First as the empress's niece and then as a ranking general in the army. Now that she wore the crown of Valcotta, it was next to impossible to achieve anonymity, because her goddamned portrait hung in inns and common rooms across her empire.

In the port trading city of Sableton, there'd been a risk she'd be recognized because there were individuals who traveled to Valcotta, but in Verwyrd, all the people saw was a Valcottan soldier who was part of Prince Keris's bodyguard. At most, she received curious looks, but for the most part she met only polite indifference.

Which served Zarrah's purposes well.

With each passing hour, her certainty grew that the infected cattle had been sent to Valcotta on purpose. Not just sent, but willfully set loose to spread their disease with no regard to the harm that it caused her people. All so that when Aren came begging her for aid, Zarrah wouldn't be able to give it, leaving Ithicana easy pickings. Alexandra intended to gift her son the bridge with no care for the fact it had been paid for with the blood of innocents.

Zarrah had no intention of allowing her to get away with it.

Her father and Daria were back in Valcotta working to trace the merchants and investors behind the imported cattle, but if it was Alexandra, she would have carefully covered her tracks full well knowing that the source would be investigated. Full well knowing that, if she were caught, her actions would be seen as an act of war against Valcotta. Every care would have been taken to leave no trace of the conspiracy for Zarrah to find in Pyrinat, but what Alexandra wouldn't anticipate was Zarrah going to the source for proof.

Proof that, if found, would be what Zarrah needed to declare war on Harendell with the full support and backing of her people. Proof that would allow her to be the ally that Aren and Lara so desperately needed.

An austere stone building loomed in front of her. Zarrah stared at the name carved in sharp letters above the door, then squared her shoulders and went inside the bank.

Where she was immediately met by a smartly attired older gentleman wearing spectacles.

"Good day to you, miss," he said, nodding his head. "I trust you are here on behalf of His Royal Highness, Prince Consort Keris? Was he pleased with the dog? A Fitzgibbons is a most excellent investment if he chooses to get into the business of dog breeding."

Not long ago, Zarrah would have said that the chances of her husband getting into dog breeding were next to zero, but she had not failed to notice how Keris had taken to carrying Fiona around tucked under one arm, despite the animal having yet to prove her worth. "He is most pleased about the dog, but I'm here on behalf of the empress."

"Oh!" The banker visibly perked, the smell of money catching hold of him like a terrier scenting a rat. "Let's take this conversation to my office. Astrid, would you make us up some tea?"

He took her into a large room lined on one side with labeled cabinets. He gestured to a leather chair. "Please, sit."

Zarrah sank into the chair, then smiled at Astrid as the woman set a tea service on the desk while the banker shuffled papers before sitting himself.

"How can I be of service to the empress?"

"You may have heard of the struggles with wasting disease in Valcotta."

"Nasty business, that." He poured the tea, then took one of the tiny cakes for himself. "Harendell knows that disease and fears it like none other. You are young, Miss . . . ?"

"Daria."

"Beautiful name! As I was saying, you are young, Miss Daria, so you won't recall the great culls near the beginning of the late king's reign. The sky turned black with soot from the cattle that had to be burned, and no one would stand beneath the Sky Palace lest they be struck by a despairing nobleman who'd lost everything. Another branch of the Fitzgibbons family raises hounds that can scent the disease on cattle. I'd be happy to direct you on how to invest in their stock. I have close connections with the family, and they'd be delighted to have animals in the empress's service."

"I'm sure she'd be interested in such a creature," Zarrah replied. "But of more pressing interest is replacing lost animals, particularly breeding stock."

"Easier said than done in these troubled times." The banker steepled his fingers, sighing deeply. "We could run them in large numbers through the bridge, but shipping them through the Tempest Seas is risky business. They panic in storms, and even if the ship makes it through, half the animals are dead or dying from injury. Better to wait for matters to be resolved with the bridge, is my recommendation. In fact, I'd suggest purchasing stock now and grazing them in the Ranges until such time they can be transported, because the situation in Valcotta will surely drive prices sky-high, especially given that several herds in east Harendell recently had to be culled after animals presented with the very same disease. There is good profit to be made in investing now and selling high."

The man droned on and on, and Zarrah ate a piece of cake and sipped tea, nodding from time to time as he set out a suggested plan of action.

"This all sounds like a solution," she said when he was finished. "With the authority granted to me by the empress"—she produced her personal seal—"I would like to begin making these purchases."

"Wonderful," the banker declared. "We will draft the purchase agreement on the empress's behalf."

He strode to his cabinets, stopping before the one labeled with a *V*, but Zarrah swiftly said, "The empress desires this business to be conducted under her personal accounts, not with the coffers of Valcotta."

"Ahh, of course. Anaphora, then!" He stepped sideways before the cabinet on the far left, opening it with a small key. Zarrah watched as he thumbed through folders, then murmured, "It seems we've not done business with her directly before. We'll have to start a new file. Excuse me for a moment, Miss Daria."

He left the room, leaving the *A* cabinet unlocked. In two quick strides, Zarrah reached the cabinet, swiftly thumbing through until she found the Ashfords. She pulled out sheaves of paper and shoved them under her uniform coat before sitting back down on her chair.

The pages felt like they were burning against Zarrah's skin as she went through the lengthy process of buying cows for herself under her Daria alias, finally escaping the bank as dusk was beginning to settle. The guards at the spiral offered her no quarrel when she returned to begin the climb.

Her breath came in ragged gasps as she jogged around and around, the majesty of the structure lost on her because her mind was all for the thick stack of papers shoved under her coat. It was a huge risk stealing the banking records of the royal family, but it was her best bet for finding proof of Alexandra's move against Valcotta. It took forever to reach the top. Darkness had already fallen across the city by the time she did, but again, no one stopped her as she entered, weaving her way to Keris's rooms.

Saam stood outside, and he gave Zarrah a dark glare for having gone off on her own, which she ignored. Latching the door behind her, Zarrah all but ran across the room to where Keris was sitting. "I have banking records. We need to go through them swiftly, then find a way to smuggle them back before the bankers notice."

Keris blanched. "This is where you went?"

"We need proof, Keris." She slammed the stack of papers on the table between them, the quantity of information feeling suddenly daunting. "To do the kinds of things Alexandra has done requires coin, and a lot of it. There has to be a paper trail."

He shoved a loose piece of hair behind one ear, then picked up the first document, which had *Edward Ashford* printed neatly across the top. "You think they document treason and assassination with their banks?"

"It won't be that blatant, but yes." She flipped through to Alexandra's records, then traced a finger down them, searching. "They don't just keep gold lying around, Keris. It's all invested in this business and that, which means to pay for *anything* they need their banks. It's why they are so cursedly rich, but also why there is a paper trail of all that they do."

A knock sounded on the door, and Zarrah jumped as Saam called through, "Your Highness, there are soldiers here who wish to speak with you."

"Fuck," Keris hissed. "You know what isn't a Harendellian weakness? Organization! They know what you took and have reported you!" Then he called more loudly. "Give me a minute!"

Zarrah's heart hammered in her chest as she riffled through the pages and pages of charitable donations and transfers of funds to William, searching for any reference to companies the banker had filled her ears with in an attempt to secure investment. For any reference to *goddamned* cows.

"In the king's name, open the door!"

"Put them in the fire," Keris whispered. "Burn them, so there is no proof you took them!"

Except burning the documents meant burning the only evidence she might find. "Keris, we need proof Alexandra sent us infected cattle. I need proof she harmed Valcotta if I have any hope of securing support for declaring war!"

He gripped her hands. "Any proof you find is going to be taken from you, Zarrah. At best you'll get a slap on the wrist for this. At worst, they'll imprison you. This is no minor offense!"

Zarrah had known that going in. Had known that she was risking her life, and Keris's life, on a chance. But Lara and Aren had done the same for her. They'd gone to Devil's Island to rescue her, and then sailed south to war against Petra, risking their lives and those of their people. They were her friends. Her family. Her *allies*. How could she not do the same for them?

Her eyes latched onto a familiar name. Silverhorn & Co. It was one mentioned to Zarrah by the banker, and next to it was a note in his spidery handwriting. *Charitable donation to the Silverhorn Foundation for families impacted by wasting disease*. The shipping records for the vessel that had brought the infected cattle showed that it had been chartered by Silver Exports, Ltd.

"You bitch," she hissed. "You're not going to get away with this!"

Fists pounded on the door. "Open up, or we will force our way in!"

Keris skimmed the page, then shook his head. "They won't let you walk away with this page, Zarrah. Our word will have to be good enough when we get back to Valcotta, because we can't be caught with this."

Every part of her wished that her word was good enough, but in her mind's eye, she could see the faces of her nobility eyeing her with suspicion, every one of them believing her actions motivated entirely by sentiment for Lara and Aren. Every one of them blaming Keris and whispering that she was starting another war because of him. As much as she wished otherwise, Zarrah needed the cold hard proof of these documents.

Which meant she needed to get them out of this room to somewhere safe.

Her eyes went to the window, and all the color drained from Keris's face. "No. Absolutely not."

Zarrah's heart hammered, memory of her aunt *falling falling falling* filling her mind's eye. But there was no other way. "You risked your life coming here because it was the right thing to do," she said to him. "You cannot refuse me the right to do the same."

He grabbed her wrists. "Put them in a bag and throw them out the window. I'll send Saam down to find it."

"They'll think of that."

There was too much risk of it being blown somewhere they'd never find it. Or of it landing smack in the middle of a courtyard full of soldiers. "Signal Saam to get one of the windows below open. He can pull me in."

"Zarrah, no!"

There was no amount of arguing that would convince him. She knew that. Knew that he'd seen too many people fall, and that the thought of it happening to her was more than he could bear. But she was going to do it anyway.

Fists pounded on the door.

"We're coming in!"

Zarrah shoved the pile of pages back under her shirt, making sure they were held in place in the waist of her trousers. Pulling a heavy chair next to the window, she looped Fiona's leash around one of the feet, then fastened the metal clip to the buckle of her belt. She swiftly twisted the length of her belt around her wrist and climbed onto the windowsill.

Keris caught hold of her shoulders. "I can't lose you."

"Then for the love of God, get Saam to open the window in the room below us!"

Taking a deep breath, she edged out the window and lowered herself. Wet mist swirled around her, blocking the lights of the city below, which was a mercy because to have stared down that long fall might have been her undoing.

The air was still without even a whisper of wind, and Zarrah braced her feet against the stone of the Sky Palace as she edged downward to the windows of the room below. The diamonds of Fiona's leash gleamed, and she prayed to every higher power that the leather was as good a quality as the stones, because if it gave, there would be no stopping her plunge. There were no handholds, the windows near flush with the stone wall.

Wood splintered as the door was forced in, slamming heavily against the opposite wall.

"What is the meaning of this?" she heard Keris shout, but the response of the soldiers who'd broken in was too muffled to make out.

*Hurry,* she silently pleaded, her arms trembling from the effort of bearing her weight. All it would take was one soldier noticing Fiona's leash hanging over the window frame and they'd catch her. At best, they'd pull her up.

At worst . . .

Crashing and Keris's angry words of protest echoed down, then a soldier's voice near the window. "Send word down the spiral to search the grounds. He may have thrown them out the window."

"Thrown what?" Keris demanded. "What the fuck is the meaning of all this?"

"Your pretty bodyguard is believed to have stolen the royal family's financial records," the soldier replied. "Where is she?"

"I have no idea. And why would she do that?"

The man didn't respond, only barked, "Search the room. Top to bottom!"

"The king will hear of this violation of my privacy," Keris shouted, but Zarrah could hear the fear in his voice. Knew that he was envisioning her shattered at the bottom of the spiral, his composure holding together by a thread.

"Find his bodyguard! What's her name? Daria?"

*Hurry, Saam.*

Her sweating palms were beginning to slide, her grip on the leather of her belt failing.

She was going to fall. Was going to smash against the stones of the courtyard below, dead before her screams finished echoing across Verwyrd. And though it was madness, Zarrah half swore she could hear her aunt laughing as she whispered, *You deserve this fate.*

"Zarrah!"

Her eyes shot downward to find Saam leaning out the window below.

"Climb down!" he whispered. "Hurry!"

Hand over hand, Zarrah edged down the length of her belt, every breath now a panicked gasp. Yet as she reached the end of her belt, it felt as though her heart seized entirely. Because she was still out of Saam's reach. "I'm at the end!"

Her friend cursed, then whispered, "You'll have to let go. I'll catch you."

How long would it take to fall? How long would she have to regret every choice? How long would she have to beg Keris not to give up without her?

"Zarrah," Saam said softly. "I won't let you fall. Trust me."

Whether she trusted him or not, her grip was failing. *You can do this*, she ordered herself, trying to drive away the vision of her aunt's head cracked open like a melon on the rocks. *You can do this.*

Zarrah edged her feet down until her weight was supported entirely by her arms. Her hands were sliding on the slick leather, and a scream started to rise in her throat. But if she screamed, they'd hear. If she screamed, all of this was for nothing.

Clenching her teeth, Zarrah opened her hands.

And dropped.

Her stomach slammed into her throat, and then Saam's arms were around her. He tightened his grip under her armpits and heaved her into the dark room, where they both landed in a heap.

All she could do was suck in breath after breath, the rush in her veins making her feel so sick that it was a struggle not to vomit.

"They're searching for you," Saam whispered. "They think you stole papers from the bank."

"Because I did."

Saam sucked in a sharp breath. "You two will be the death of me, I swear. I hope whatever it was is worth it."

The paper pressing against her stomach had the power to change everything. "Where are we?"

"I don't know. A suite, but I don't know whose."

Zarrah squinted in the faint light coming in the window, then smiled as she caught sight of a Cardiffian headdress sitting on a table. "Lestara's rooms."

Pulling out the few pages she needed as proof of Alexandra's involvement with the infected cattle, Zarrah hid the rest under the mattress of the bed. "One more nail in her coffin when they find this. Let's go."

Feet thundered past the door, and when they were gone, Zarrah cracked it open and looked both ways. "Let's go."

They left the room, but she immediately walked to the portrait hanging on the wall opposite and tucked the pages she needed behind it. "Saam, when the dust settles, you need to get these south to my father. He'll know what to do with them." Behind the next portrait she came to, Zarrah hid the letter that Edward had sent Keris, grateful she'd had the foresight to keep it on her. "All right, let's get this over with."

# 67

# AHNNA

"I CAN'T BELIEVE Aren considered abdicating." Ahnna paced the room in front of Lara, leaving a trail of rainwater on the polished wood floor. "I can't believe he was willing to concede."

"Yes, you can believe it." Lara looked up from a box of cosmetics she was digging through. "You know full well that Aren would rather fall on his own sword than hurt his people. Giving up power? Giving up a crown? It's nothing to him if he thinks it is the right path. Fortunately, he's now been offered an alternative by your soon-to-be husband."

*A path that comes with its own costs*, Ahnna thought, James's resigned expression filling her mind's eye. He had no desire to rule and even less desire to harm his siblings, but claiming the crown of Harendell was the only sure way to stop Alexandra in her tracks. And *sure* was an enormous stretch, because achieving his birthright would be no easy task.

Lara abandoned the box of cosmetics and approached, gripping Ahnna by the shoulders. "We know what we need to do, Ahnna. For one night, let go of everything that is happening outside this island, because you are about to be married to the man you love." Her azure eyes narrowed. "You do want to marry him, yes?"

*More than life.* "Yes." Ahnna blew a breath out from between her teeth. "But I don't need a ceremony and a feast or guests, I just need him. Our time is better spent on planning our strategy and bolstering—"

"One night." Lara's grip tightened, her expression fierce. "For one night, Ahnna Kertell, you are going to let down your guard and live every second for yourself."

"I can't—"

"You can." Lara's tone was more command than request. "I will stand watch until morning. I will be your proxy. Not just me, but Aren and everyone else. Let us give you this moment, sister."

Ahnna's eyes burned, because it felt selfish to accept.

"All we can be certain of is the moment at hand," Lara said softly. "The future is unknown, and you do not want to look back with regret for not *living* while you had the chance."

It was a poetic way of saying that tonight might be her only night with James, because after meeting with the commanders tomorrow, he'd be leaving to travel north to Cardiff. With luck, King Ronan would turn on Alexandra and support James in a bid for the crown, but there was just as much chance he'd fall along the way and that they'd never have another night together.

Her eyes pricked with tears. "I should go with him. My place is with him."

Lara pulled her into a hug, and Ahnna rested her cheek against Lara's blond hair. "You can't. You know you can't, especially since we need you here. If Mara and the others are as close to breaking as is said, then Aren needs you to back him in this plan, Ahnna. You led Ithicana through the last war—they trust you more than anyone alive."

Between her desire to be at James's back as he took this enormous risk and her need to protect her family and people, it felt like her heart was being torn in two. A tear slipped down her cheek. "Fuck."

"I know." Lara's arms tightened, always so much stronger than her frame suggested. "I know better than anyone, which is why I want you to have this moment. Trust me to watch your back through it."

"I trust you." She felt Lara relax ever so slightly, and it took the edge off Ahnna's sense of selfishness because she knew her trust meant something to the other woman. "Do you have anything I can wear?"

"I thought you'd never ask. Go have a bath and leave the clothing to me."

Curious, Ahnna left her queen digging through her closet and went out to the hot spring, the storm easing overhead as evening fell. She badly wished that James were still here, but Aren had hauled him away with very vocal threats about what he'd do if *illicit acts* took place before the wedding. In the past, such behavior from Aren would have annoyed her, but this felt different. Not like he was trying to control her but like he was trying to give her tonight, much as Lara was, and it caused emotion to swell in her chest as she stepped into the hot water.

A bath alone was a gift, because other than dangerous swims in the ocean, she'd not had a proper wash since she'd been scrubbed and dressed for Katarina's entertainment, and she grimaced as traces of the awful white cosmetics came away with the scented soap. She washed her long hair three times to get rid of filth and tangles, mats floating downstream, and it was hard not to wince at how awful she must have looked.

One of the doors to the courtyard opened, and Ahnna heard James growl, "I just want to speak to her for one minute!"

"Later! Let's get a drink!" Aren replied, and there was a scuffle and the door slammed shut again.

Ahnna smirked, then rested her elbows on the edge of the pool and rested her head on them, feeling the soft rain falling on her upper back. The wind eased, then died, and when she glanced up, the sky was clearing to reveal all the colors of the sunset.

Deeming herself suitably clean, Ahnna wrapped a towel around her waist and carried her belongings inside. Lara lifted her head as she entered, her hands busy with blue silk, steel link, and pieces of armor.

"Hair first." Motioning for Ahnna to sit, Lara attacked with combs and pins, twisting and braiding the dark length into a crown around Ahnna's head and then encouraging the remaining pieces to dry into their usual loose curls. With a deft hand, she then set to apply the faintest trace of cosmetics, highlighting Ahnna's cheekbones and collar with silver dust before fastening earrings to her lobes. Then she turned to the pile of blue silk on the table. "It's been through war and back, but I know you liked it," she said, lifting the garment. "So I modified it."

It was then that Ahnna realized she recognized the hue, the dress the same one Lara had worn when she'd married Aren, but much altered. Instead of cutting down into a low *V* to reveal cleavage Ahnna didn't have, it now wrapped in a tight halter that left her stomach bare, a delicate steel pauldron covering her shoulders. The skirt was sliced into fluttering strips that were fastened to a wide belt formed of what appeared to be chain mail, her legs revealing themselves with each step. Lara fastened a thigh sheath with a sharp dagger beneath the skirt, and slipped Ahnna's feet into silver sandals that wrapped up her calves.

"I found these in Nana's rooms in Eranahl," Lara said, admiring the shoes. "I think they must have been from when she was a spy, because I've never seen them. My feet are too small for them, so they've been in my closet."

Ahnna burst into laughter. "I can't imagine her wearing anything like this."

"Apparently she was quite the seductress in her day." Rising, she led Ahnna to the large mirror. "You look like a warrior princess. A queen of tempests."

Ahnna stared at her reflection, her chest tightening because Lara had made her look terrifyingly beautiful. "Thank you."

"You are most welcome." Lara fastened steel bracers to her wrists, the metal etched with a beautiful design. "You are Ithicana, Ahnna. Truly."

Lara swiftly pulled on a simple green dress, ran a brush through her hair, and then donned a small arsenal of weapons. Linking arms with Ahnna, she said, "He's waiting for you."

# 68

# JAMES

THE STORM HAD mercifully ceased, although Aren had frowned at the sky and said the calm was only a precursor for worse when James had asked. Given Ahnna's ability to judge the weather, James suspected the king was right, but he relished the still air anyway, breathing in the thick humidity as they stood in a clearing near the island's summit. Torches surrounded them, flickering and dancing, a pathway of them leading down to the house where Ahnna was getting ready. "How much longer?"

"How would I know?" Aren responded, handing his infant daughter over to his grandmother, who had been staring at James like he was shit she'd found on the bottom of her shoe. "Lara can be ready in a blink of an eye or take three hours lacquering her nails just so. Want another drink?"

Alcohol was already buzzing through James's veins, so he shook his head and fussed with the cuff of the shirt he'd borrowed from Aren. All his clothes were borrowed from the king, who was fortunately about the same size as him, but he felt underdressed and abruptly certain that Ahnna would take one look at him and inform everyone that she'd changed her mind.

"Nervous?" Jor asked, clapping him hard on the back. "Because you should be. This is no Harendellian lady that you can ship off to the country home to spend her days with needlework and dinner parties."

"No," James murmured, searching the shadows between the trees for signs of motion coming up the path. "Ahnna is untamable."

"He has a way with words when he bothers to speak," Aren muttered, but James didn't hear whatever else he said, because he caught sight of Lara coming up the path. Ithicana's queen nodded once at the drummers next to the torches, then walked to her husband's side.

"Your Grace," James muttered, but his focus was on the path, his heart hammering with anticipation. Only for it to skip a beat entirely as Ahnna appeared, the drummers taking up a fierce beat that somehow echoed Ithicana's storms.

She carried a torch, and in the firelight, the love of his life was as wild as he'd ever seen her. Her hair was pulled back from her face, revealing the sharp lines of her cheeks and jaw, her eyes shadowed dark with kohl and making her appear almost feline. An impression that only grew with each step she took, silent and steady as a predator, the long lengths of blue silk forming her skirt swirling to reveal the endless legs that haunted his dreams. Her waist was bare from just below her breasts to just below her hip bones, the flat plane of her stomach entirely exposed, and God help him, James wanted to close the distance between them. To take her somewhere alone and finally make Ahnna Kertell his, and his alone, but Jor closed a hand on his arm. "Steady now, lad."

Standing still was one of the hardest things James had ever had to do, but he stood his ground as Ahnna made her way up the path and handed the torch to Aren. She held out her hand to James, her skin soft against his as he bowed low. "Your Highness."

"Your Grace." Her knees began to bend in a curtsy, but he met her gaze and shook his head. "You bend the knee to no one, Princess. Least of all me."

It felt as though everyone else disappeared, leaving them alone in a circle of torchlight, and he fought the urge to fall to his knees before this woman who had a spine of steel and yet the kindest heart he'd ever known. But then Jor stepped forward, the drums falling silent.

"Do you, James Ashford, heir to the Twisted Throne and rightful king of Harendell, swear to fight by this woman's side, to defend her to your dying breath, to cherish her body and none other, and to be loyal to her as long as you both live?"

It felt like a lie to hear himself called that. A false promise for a future he wasn't sure he could give her. It was only because fighting for the crown was the same as fighting for Ahnna that he said, "I do."

"Do you, Ahnna Kertell, princess of Ithicana, swear to fight by this man's side, to defend him to your dying breath, to cherish his body and none other, and to be loyal to him as long as you both live?"

Her fingers tightened on his, her eyes gleaming in the torchlight. "I do. I swear it."

Jor extracted a knife, then took hold of James's hand, slicing a shallow line across his palm before doing the same to Ahnna's. He pressed their bloody hands together, then shouted, "Behold the rightful rulers of Harendell! May those who stand against them bleed and those who stand at their backs scream in triumph on the day they reclaim the Twisted Throne. All hail!"

All around them, Ithicanians bowed low, Aren and Lara inclining their heads, and it felt impossible to breathe. The weight of kingdoms, the weight of countless lives, all rested upon his shoulders. The torchlight spun.

"James." Ahnna's voice cut through the rushing roar of blood in his ears, and his gaze focused on her beautiful face. A face to go to war over, if he'd ever seen one, but it was the fire that burned within her that would see them win this.

Slipping his arm around her waist and cupping his bloody palm against her cheek, he bent and kissed his wife.

His queen.

All around them, Ithicanians shouted and lifted their weapons into the air, but they'd celebrate a chance at a future alone tonight. Moving his hand to Ahnna's back, he lifted her into his arms and started down the path.

"Where are we going?" she said with a laugh. "The feast is up there."

"Enough with Ithicana's customs," he replied. "It's time to show you one of Cardiff's."

# 69

# AHNNA

"You can put me down if I'm getting heavy," Ahnna said, despite very much enjoying the feel of James's hand on her bare thigh as he carried her down the path to the Midwatch house.

"You aren't heavy." He turned his head to look at her. "Even if you were, it's bad luck not to carry your bride to your wedding bed. I need to prove my worth to you."

"It's a *very* long walk." She tightened her arm around his neck to take some of the burden off his arms.

James frowned at her. "If you're going to question my capacity to carry my own woman, at least soften the blow by putting those legs around me, Princess."

*Not a princess, if this plan works. A queen.*

The thought made her heart clench with a sudden twist of trepidation, but it disappeared from her head as James turned her in his arms so that her legs were around his waist. He ran his hands up her thighs, then gripped her ass, a soft groan escaping his lips. "Stars, woman, you're not wearing anything beneath this, are you?"

She tightened her grip on his neck with one hand and then hooked her heels together behind his back. With her free hand, she slowly unbuttoned his white shirt, then pulled it loose from his trousers so that the apex of her thighs pressed against the bare skin of his stomach.

James's boot slid in the mud and as he cursed, she gave him a dark smile, rubbing herself against him. "Are you sure you're going to make it to the house?"

"I have to." His grip on her ass tightened. "The stars would judge me weak if I broke and fucked you in the mud, although you're making me question whether I care what they think."

"Do you care?" She was curious, but she also felt the hardness of his cock pressing against her as her heels pushed his trousers lower on his hips and it made it so hard to focus on words.

"The only thing I care about is you, Ahnna." He said the words between panted breaths, his eyes dark as he bent his head to nip at her throat. "You're my wife, and that means you must be treated with respect."

"What if I don't want to be treated with respect right now? What if I want you to lose control and put me on my knees so you can make me yours?"

The response she got was a growl that made her heart skip, and then her back was against a tree trunk. He caught hold of her wrists with one hand and pinned them above her head as she tightened her thighs above his hips.

"I never have any control around you." His mouth claimed hers, tongue delving deep, the demand in it making her body respond in kind. "Just looking at you from across the room undoes the man in me and leaves behind a feral beast driven by impulse and instinct. When you say things like that, what do you think it does to me?"

His free hand caught hold of the bodice of her dress and tore. Beads scattered all around them, scraps of silk dangling from her shoulders as he kissed a line of fire down her throat. Her nipples peaked as wind blew across them, and Ahnna whimpered as he caught hold of her right breast, thumb and forefinger working her sensitive flesh to the point that pleasure bordered on pain.

But she needed that. Needed an intensity that matched the life she lived, needed sensation that pushed her to the limit and beyond.

"I need you in me." It was hard to get the words out, hard to remember what words were as his teeth scraped over her collarbone. "I need you. I need everything."

With her heel, she shoved his trousers down over his ass and released his cock from the confines of the fabric. She forced her hips down, and the feel of the thick tip of him pressing into her made her whole body shudder. "Please."

His body trembled, and she ground her hips against him, trying to overwhelm his willpower so that he'd give her what she so desperately needed. Instead, his hand moved from her breast to her ass, lifting her off him. Amber eyes met hers, and it was like looking into the eyes of a wolf. "Not yet."

The tone demanded she obey, but that was not her nature. So Ahnna dug in her heels, the muscles of her legs flexing as she fought against him, trying to force her body down upon him.

James only stepped back from the tree and lifted her, flipping her over his shoulder. Her skirt was tangled around her waist, and his hand came down firmly on her backside. The sting turned her body liquid with need, and she parted her thighs to feel the kiss of the wind against her sex as he continued down the path.

His left hand dug into her thigh, holding her in place against his shoulder, but his other hand traced up on the back of her leg. The feel of it drove her wild, and she dragged her nails up his back, tearing at his shirt.

"No one touches you but me," he said, fingers climbing higher on her thigh and giving her ass a squeeze where he'd spanked her. "Promise me that."

"I promise." How could she not when he was all she wanted?

He turned his face to kiss her hip, then slid his hand higher, his thumb finding her clit even as his index finger slipped inside her. Ahnna sobbed, nearly climaxing—but if she did, he might stop. If she did, he might not give her what she wanted, so she ground her teeth to keep from falling over the cliff of pleasure.

James worked her body as he walked down the path through the jungle, and it began to rain, cold droplets splashing against her bare skin in sharp contrast with the heat of his hand as he rubbed and stroked her, robbing her of control.

"Open the door."

"What?" She opened her eyes, the world shifting in and out of focus as she fought the climax that was threatening to overwhelm her. Bracing her hand on James's hip, she lifted her face to see the door to the house.

"My hands are occupied." He slipped another finger inside her, angling it in such a way that her body shook. Then his fingers paused. "Open the door."

Ahnna squirmed, trying to renew the friction, but his other hand held her still. "You're cruel."

"So I've been told. Open the door."

She caught hold of the handle and lifted it, then heaved open the heavy door, rewarded as his thumb returned its attention to her clit. She moaned, gripping his sides as he walked inside. The house was lit with lamps, but the light seemed to pulse in time with his fingers as he strode through the corridors to her room.

*Their room.*

"Another door."

Ahnna reached for the handle, desperate to get inside so that he would finally give her what she wanted, but James shifted so that her fingertips could just brush the handle. She stretched her body, trying to get her hand on the door, gasps tearing from her lips as he mercilessly pleasured her.

"Open the door, Princess."

Ahnna stretched her body as far as she could, desperate with need as she clung to the edge of oblivion. Her hand closed on the latch right as he added a third finger, stroking her soaked core and shattering her will.

Ahnna felt her back bow as she wordlessly cried out, her whole body consumed by the pulsing rhythm of her climax. It would not let her go, rolling over her with endless waves until she collapsed against his back, entirely spent.

"Good girl, Princess."

The latch opened, and James carried her into the room, shutting the door behind them.

Though it should have been impossible, desire surged through her again with the promise of what was to come. James set her on her feet and Ahnna met his gaze, lifting her chin in challenge.

The corner of his mouth turned up as he said, "Don't look at me like you're not perfectly capable of getting me to do exactly what you want."

His face softened, and he reached up and began unraveling her hair. "No more games, Ahnna. Not tonight."

The curling tendrils of her hair brushed against the small of her back as she nodded, a sudden swell of emotion challenging desire for supremacy. She reached up a hand, tracing her fingers gently across his bruised cheek, his eye still swollen from where Aren had hit him. The cut on his throat with its stitches was a stark reminder of how close she'd come to losing him. "No games."

She pushed his shirt off his shoulders, the fabric falling to the ground. His muscular torso was marked with yet more bruises and scrapes, the scar from where she'd struck him with her knife in the cabin red against his pale skin. All markers of what he'd endured to get to this moment, and Ahnna knew her body bore the same. She pressed her lips to his shoulder, then looked up at him. "I love you, James."

His fingers tangled in her hair, the expression on his face making her breath catch. "For a time, I felt consumed with regret for the choices I have made. But standing here, I realize I cannot lament a single choice—for each one was a step along the path that brought me to you."

Her eyes prickled with tears, and Ahnna blinked rapidly to dispel them before lifting on her toes to kiss him. She lost herself in the taste of him as James pushed the remains of her bodice to the floor, then unfastened her belt, his fingers trailing over her ass as he let her skirt spill to the floor around her ankles. She untied the laces of the silver sandals, then kicked them away so she stood before him in only her bare skin.

"You are so beautiful," he murmured, running a hand up her side and cupping her breast, his thumb pressing against the scar where Carlo had cut her. "Every time I look at you, it's hard to breathe."

For someone who could be so taciturn, when he chose to speak, James seemed to know exactly what to say, whereas Ahnna was at a loss using language to express how she felt for him. It spooled into frustration in her heart, because she needed him to know how she burned for him. How not a second passed when she didn't think of him. How the sight of him before her was very nearly her undoing.

So she resolved to show him instead.

Taking hold of his hands, Ahnna placed them at her waist, then again rose on her toes to claim his lips. She parted them with her tongue, closing her eyes as she stroked it across his, then bit at his bottom lip. She kissed along his jaw, his stubble rough against her skin, and the feel of it causing tension to coil in her stomach.

Catching hold of his hair with one hand, she bit at his earlobe, her mouth turning up in a smile as his fingers tightened on her hips, his cock twitching where it pressed hard against her stomach.

She pulled harder on his hair, forcing his head back as she licked down his throat, using her other hand to trail her nails over the thick muscle of his shoulder. Tall as she was, he was nearly twice as broad, and she relished the feeling of being enveloped by his strength as she pressed her breasts against his chest, feeling his heart thud against hers.

For a moment, Ahnna remained where she was, struck with a sudden fear of what it would be like if she couldn't feel his heart. As though to prepare herself for that eventual pain, her heart stuttered, and it felt like it was tearing itself apart in her chest. Tomorrow, he would leave. Tomorrow, he would go north.

Then James's arms closed around her, pulling her tight, and as he said, "There is no tomorrow. There is only right now," Ahnna realized she'd spoken her thoughts aloud.

"I'm afraid," she whispered. "I want to break my heart now so that I don't have to worry about protecting it."

"I'll protect it." He kissed her. "In this life, and in every life."

He was the only person in the world she trusted with her heart, so Ahnna gave it over to him. Kissed her way down the hard planes of his stomach until she reached the trousers clinging to his hips, and pushed them out of her way. He kicked away boots and clothes, weapons thudding against the floor.

Ahnna took a heartbeat to drink in his naked body, an ache building again between her legs because never in her life had she seen such masculine beauty. Like a statue carved by an artist with talent beyond measure, except life pulsed through his veins and burned in the amber eyes that looked down at her as she took his cock in her mouth, drawing him in deep.

He groaned, and she felt it in her core as he said, "Stars, woman, I'm not going to last if you do that."

James caught hold of her arms, trying to pull her up, but Ahnna only dug her nails into the hard muscle of his ass and drew him in deep enough that her throat spasmed. He stopped fighting her, his fingers tangling in her hair as she showed him what her words could not tell him, the taste of him driving her wild.

He moaned her name, repeating it like it was sacred, then his fingers tightened on her hair. "Not like this. I need to be in you."

It was his turn to plead. There was a desperate edge to his voice, and it was not one she intended to deny.

She didn't resist as he pushed her back onto the bed, the sheets silken against her oversensitive skin. James pressed down on her, the weight of him alluring, and she parted her legs wide. Lifted one over his shoulder, watching his gaze darken as he traced a finger down her thigh, then pressed the tip of his cock against her.

Ahnna cried out his name, her back bowing as he drove into her, inch by merciless inch until they were entirely joined. James leaned into her, burying his face in her throat, his fingers locking with hers. His breathing was ragged against her skin as he said, "I want you to come for me, Ahnna Ashford. I need it."

He was the only man alive she would accept claiming her like this. Claiming her in every possible way. "Then don't stop."

His fingers tightened, and his hips moved. He thrust deeper and harder, the bed slamming against the wall. Ahnna clung to him, one leg still around his shoulders and the heel of the other digging into the muscle of his ass, because she wanted all of him. Needed him to lose himself in her as she'd lost herself to him.

Every muscle in her body was tense, her breath so rapid that her head spun, her climax rising as she sensed him losing control. "Don't stop."

He caught hold of her other hand, lifting her arms above her head, cheek pressed to hers. Her heart was a riot in her chest, and closing her eyes, Ahnna let all her walls down and gave him everything.

The force of the pleasure stole her breath, her sight, her voice, but she heard him howl her name. Felt the force of her husband's control finally coming undone and spilling into her. He collapsed against her, and with her now-free hands, Ahnna wrapped her arms around his neck, breathing in the scent of him, their hearts slowing and allowing words to form.

But Ahnna didn't speak, only allowed James to curl around her body, her head tucked under his chin and his arm around her waist. In the faint light, she looked at the cut on his palm from their vows, the words they'd spoken repeating in her head as James's breathing deepened with sleep.

Dawn was a long ways off, but she felt the slow march of time, and the fear of what would come with tomorrow came with it. In the silence, she swore her own vow. "No matter how far this war takes you from me, I'll find you. Whether it's in this life or the next."

# 70

# AHNNA

A KNOCK SOUNDED at the door, and Ahnna jerked awake, lifting her head off James's chest. He'd woken as well, and she did not fail to notice when he extracted a knife from beneath one of the pillows, every bit as tense as she was.

"Who is it?" she called out, reaching off the side of the bed to retrieve James's shirt.

"Lara."

Her sister-in-law's familiar voice did nothing to relax Ahnna as she buttoned the shirt and padded to the door. Flipping up the latch, she opened it to find Lara standing in the hallway with a stack of folded clothes and a pair of worn boots in her arms. There were shadows beneath Lara's eyes that suggested she had been true to her word and hadn't slept, but there was no time to express gratitude, for she immediately said, "Mara has arrived, and the rest are just exiting the bridge." She handed Ahnna the clothes. "They are Lia's, so they should fit you well enough. We'll gather in the dining room. You should both come as soon as you're ready."

"We'll be there."

Shutting the door, Ahnna went to the window, swinging the glass pane inward before opening the heavy shutters that protected it from storm debris. It was raining, and though the first rays of dawn illuminated the clouds, heavy mist made it impossible to see more than a dozen feet away. She inhaled the wet scent of the jungle even as she built up walls in her heart to shove every emotion behind, transforming herself into the commander she'd once been.

And needed to be again.

James came up behind her, wrapping his arms around her torso and pulling her back against him. She turned her head slightly, feeling the scrape of stubble against her temple. "We need to get ready. The watch commanders are here to demand Aren's surrender, and I don't want him to have to face them alone."

He gave the slightest of nods but didn't let go of her. As though he too wished to cling to the last shadows of night before daylight tore them away from each other once again. Seeming to hear her thoughts, James said, "I won't leave if you don't want me to."

Ahnna turned in his embrace, then wrapped her arms around his neck. "I don't want you to go, but there is no other way to stop this, is there? I wish we could trust that William would hear the truth and do the right thing, but what if he doesn't? What if he excuses away all that Alexandra has done because the allure of the bridge is too great or because his mother's claws are in too deep? We'll have lost our only chance to stop this before the storm season ends, and there will never be another chance. Taking control from Alexandra means taking the crown from William, and you are the only person who can do that. You'll stop this war. Save lives, and not just Ithicanian lives, but Harendellian, Cardiffian, and Amaridian, because war brings casualties on all sides."

"I know the stakes, love." He bent his neck, teeth scraping the side of her throat and sending a jolt of pleasure through her core. "But if you ask me to stay at your side, I'll stay. Nothing, and no one, comes before you."

It wasn't the same as saying that nothing else mattered to him. James feared what was to come as much as she did if they didn't stop

Alexandra, which made the weight of his words so much heavier. "The only thing I ask is that you swear you'll come back to me. That you swear this isn't it, that last night wasn't the beginning and the end."

Instead of answering, James caught hold of her hips and lifted her. She wrapped her legs around his waist, desire and fear at war in her chest. Desire won, and a whimper tore from Ahnna's lips as he buried himself inside her, all her walls collapsing in the face of what she felt for him.

"I can't swear that." James's breath was hot against her ear, the frame of the window against her back hard and unyielding as he thrust into her. "I can't make a promise to you that I have no certainty of keeping."

Tension rose in her core, an aching building need that threatened to drown her as his fingers gripped her ass, angling her so that his cock could go deeper.

"If you swear it, then it is certainty," she gasped, a half sob tearing from her throat at the feel of him stroking against the most sensitive part of her core. "Because I know you will not fail me. Swear you'll come back. Swear that we'll be together again. Swear it to me and then make it happen."

His breathing was ragged, and beneath her hands, she could feel the thunder of his heart as he claimed her with enough force that it should have hurt. Except she could no longer separate pleasure from pain. "I swear it."

Her climax crested, and Ahnna cried out his name, grinding her body against him and pulling him over the edge.

They stayed in each other's arms, connected in every possible way until the dawn's light reached into the room.

And then they prepared for war.

---

Washed and dressed in Lia's clothes, Ahnna held tight to James's hand as she led him through the house toward the dining room, angry shouts filling the corridor. She rebuilt the walls around her emotions, and as she glanced up at James's face, cheeks rough with stubble he hadn't bothered to shave, it was to find his expression hard and unreadable. As ready for a fight as the sword belted at his waist.

A soldier opened the door at their approach, and Ahnna let go of James's hand. In this moment, she wasn't his wife but Ithicana's princess. The former commander of Southwatch. The former regent. But the forever defender of her people.

The argument taking place died at sight of her, and Mara rose to her feet. "You're here." The aging commander of Northwatch gave a slow shake of her head. "They said that it was you who brought the warning, but I didn't really believe it until you walked into the room."

"Believe it." Ahnna kept her tone cool but circled the room to grip Mara's arms in greeting. "It's a relief to see you alive, Mara. We'll have a better chance of winning this war with you on the front lines."

The commander's lips opened, but then she hesitated. "Ahnna, we—"

"I did not suffer the Blackreaches, the Beast, and the *fucking* Furnace to get back to Ithicana and listen to talk about giving up," Ahnna snapped. "So keep any defeatist words in your mouth."

Mara's mouth shut with a click of her teeth.

Ahnna took her seat at Aren's right and James leaned against the wall next to Jor, all the commanders giving him curious stares as they seated themselves. The space held none of the gravitas of the command room in Eranahl, but the direness of circumstances more than compensated for the setting.

Aren rested his elbows on the table. "You've all been made aware of the information that has come to light about the secret alliance between Katarina of Amarid and Alexandra of Harendell, as well as their conspiracy to decimate our people with poisoned grain and take control of the bridge. You are also aware that Alexandra is responsible for Edward's murder, as well as for framing Ahnna by inflicting injuries upon herself. My sister is wholly innocent of all the charges the Harendellians have leveled against us, and is also the reason all of us are still among the living. Are there any questions about the facts, or may we proceed?"

The commanders all shook their heads to indicate they needed no clarification, and Aren leaned back in his chair. "Commander Ahnna, you have the floor."

Her heart skipped, because she'd wondered what her official

place was in this room, and her brother had taken away all uncertainty by making her his equal. The equal of everyone present.

Drawing in a deep breath, Ahnna lifted her voice. "I understand why you are all here, and I want you to know that I share in your grief. I reached the bridge not long after the first shipment of grain was delivered, and saw firsthand the devastation Katarina's poison left in its wake. Aster was alive when I found him, and it was his quick action that prevented the casualties from mounting higher. Aster was a prick who ground on the nerves of everyone, but he was loyal. More than that, he was defiant to the very end, and I know that he's spinning in his grave to hear talk of surrender now."

The commanders and their seconds all looked down, unable to meet her gaze, and Ahnna felt their shame. Yet she could also smell their defeat. Not just defeat but *fear*, and she knew that inspiring words and speeches would do nothing to change their course. Only hope could do that. She needed to give them a strategy that would light that spark in their hearts, so she cleared her throat and continued.

"You are correct that we cannot prevail against a united force of Harendell, Amarid, and Cardiff. Where your error lies is in your belief that the alliances among those nations are strong. Ronan of Cardiff hates Katarina and desires vengeance against her for the murders of Siobhan and Cormac—murders he is yet unaware Alexandra played a role in. Katarina and Alexandra are working together, but neither holds trust for the other. Their relationship enduring so long has been partially due to common goals, but more to do with checks and balances they impose on each other. Despite the threat James and I posed, Katarina kept us alive as, I quote, 'insurance.' Ronan has reason to hate them both. That is something we can exploit."

Mara coughed, took a sip from her cup, then asked, "Easy to understand how to turn Ronan on them, but he's the weakest of the three. How do we break the alliance of the queens?"

"By turning them against each other."

"How?" Mara asked. "These are not women who are moved by emotion. Nor are they easily deceived."

"Agreed. But there is another attribute they share beyond distrust." Ahnna paused to look around the table. "Ambition."

"You've a flair for the dramatic, Ahnna," Mara said, "but their ambition is what got us here, so I fail to see how it will deliver us. Spare us the theatrics and spit out your plan."

"They are allies of convenience," Ahnna explained. "Except neither of them really wants to share the bridge—they're only working together because they feel as though it's the surest way to success. Once they take the bridge, it's only a matter of time until they turn on each other. They won't be able to help themselves. My plan is to speed along that process."

Everyone shifted uneasily and Ahnna fought the urge to look to Aren and Lara for support. Fought the urge to look over her shoulder at James, because she could not afford to show any weakness.

Lifting her chin, Ahnna stared Mara down. "We allow their plan to work."

Mara blinked.

"We make it look as though the poison swept through Ithicana," Ahnna continued. "Stage a few dramatic scenes for their spies to witness and leave the bodies of those who fell in the north where they are, all while evacuating everyone to the outer islands. Then we see what Katarina does when she thinks the bridge is hers."

"She'll do exactly what she and Alexandra planned to do!" Mara threw up her hands. "You think a sly old wench like Katarina is going to risk the wrath of Harendell because she's flush with the euphoria of being the first through our door? She'll stick to the plan and bide her time. It could be years before she makes her move, if she ever does."

"Which is why we're going to tempt her with an opportunity that she can't resist." Ahnna looked to Aren. "The Maridrinian parliament has been vocal in their desire for trade to resume on the bridge at any cost. If they perceive Katarina as being the new Mistress of the Bridge, they will try to strike a deal with her."

Aren nodded in agreement, and Lara said, "Sarhina has given up much of her power in Maridrina, but her parliament trusts her. I think they'll go this direction on their own, but she can encourage the process. Maridrina is suffering a famine and Valcotta's grappling with wasting disease in their herds, which means they can't aid. While

Amarid does not have Harendell's export capacity, it can still do much to aid against the famine."

"I don't doubt that the Maridrinians will move quickly to make a deal," Mara replied. "But I think that Katarina will cut Alexandra in on it. She is no fool, Ahnna. She will not risk war with the titan of the north by making foolish, greedy choices—Katarina is not Silas. Especially with Cardiff at Harendell's back. Ronan might break the alliance, or he might not. His daughter is queen of Harendell, and that is no small thing. If he breaks the alliance, he loses all that he fought to gain in Edward's reign."

Mara's eyes moved past Ahnna. "You going to let your *wife* do all the talking, Ashford? We are well aware of your part in creating the alliance between your father and uncle, and your willingness to sacrifice Ithicana for the sake of Cardiff. That alliance was hard won, and Ronan now has his daughter on Harendell's throne. Will he sacrifice all that for the sake of a sister twenty-five years in the grave? Will he go back to a closed border and burnings and persecution?"

Ahnna kept her eyes straight forward, her heart pounding in her chest, because James needed to take this step, not her. It had to come from his lips. Her pulse raced faster and faster as the silence stretched, then she heard the scrape of boots against floorboards, and his familiar hands gripped the sides of her chair as James stepped up behind her.

"No, he won't." James's voice was steady. "Because all of those things will be a crime when I take Harendell's crown."

Ahnna forced herself to breathe, but the greater struggle was not reaching up to take James's hands in hers.

"My uncle will back me in a bid to take the Twisted Throne from William," James continued. "Not just in word, but in force. William's unlikely to give up his title without a fight, so he'll redeploy Harendell's forces north right when Maridrina entices Amarid with a deal."

"And with Harendell distracted, Katarina will take advantage." Mara sipped thoughtfully at her drink, eyes distant. "With Harendell embroiled in civil war over the crown, Amarid will become Mistress of the Bridge in truth, little knowing that all of Ithicana lurks in the shadows, waiting to strike."

"Yes." The chair creaked beneath James's grip. His calm voice was an act. "Alexandra will by then have learned that Katarina went behind her back, and so when Ithicana strikes against the Amaridian forces, Harendell will not aid them."

"All while you wage a war between Cardiff and Harendell." Mara's eyes narrowed. "Cardiff can't win that fight."

"Which is why, after Ithicana has driven out Amarid and storm season begins anew, I'll agree to withdraw my claims to the throne if William executes Alexandra for her crimes."

Ahnna's stomach lurched, shock hitting her like a battering ram, because that hadn't been the plan. It must have shown on her face, because Mara eyed her for a moment, then asked, "Do you think he will?"

"I don't know." James sighed, and though Ahnna couldn't see his face, she could see his expression in her mind's eye. Distant, his thoughts all for whether William would be willing to sacrifice to do the right thing. "But I have to give him the chance. As far as we know, he's unaware of Alexandra's schemes. No one has given him the chance to correct his course. I recognize that we can't tip our hand by giving him that chance now, but I won't fight a bloody war to win the throne if William is willing to give us both justice and peace. Alexandra is the problem, the threat, the murderess, *not* my brother. And certainly not my sister, who will be collateral damage in all of this. As it is, once the truth of Alexandra's crimes comes out, the nobility and the people may not give William a choice."

Ahnna bit her tongue, wishing James had told her this part of his plan before, rather than dropping it on her in front of everyone. But she wouldn't undercut him now, especially given that so much would have to go right for them to even get to the point of putting William to the test.

"Cardiff will bear the brunt of this," Mara finally said. "Rightful heir or not, Ronan has a daughter on the throne, which is just as good as a nephew, especially given said nephew has wed the princess of Cardiff's stiffest competition for trade. So this all still circles back to how much your uncle is willing to sacrifice for vengeance."

"The mistake every single one of you is making in your assessment of my uncle is your belief that he sees Lestara as an asset." James gave a soft laugh. "The truth is, everyone in Cardiff believes that my cousin is cursed, most especially my aunt Calythra, who is Lestara's mother. They didn't send Lestara to Silas for better trade terms on furs—they sent her to get rid of her."

Calythra. The witch queen of Cardiff. Ahnna didn't know much about her, for Calythra was reclusive and had nothing to do with politics and trade.

"Oh, but this is a tangled web," Mara murmured, pushing her cup over to Lara to refill. The old commander had lorded over Northwatch for nearly as long as Ahnna had been alive, and she knew the northerners and their ways better than anyone. "So Ronan might actually agree to this."

"There is no certainty in war," James replied. "But there is total certainty in what will happen if Aren abdicates to William. The northern alliance will sweep over Ithicana like a tide, taking what they want and giving very little in return. Some Ithicanians may find work but the pay will be a pittance, and all others will be forced to either live off what they can eke from the Tempest Seas or flee south, dependent on the mercy of Maridrina and Valcotta. Though perhaps the promise of being alive is enough."

"If you can call that living," Ahnna said softly, reaching up to rest a hand on top of James's. "I, for one, would rather die fighting."

Everyone was staring down at the table, many resting their heads in their hands as they weighed the choices they faced. There was no easy path, every direction leading to a grueling uphill climb, and it was hard not to fear that they'd fall into hopelessness.

"The choice is yours," James said, echoing her thoughts. "I'm willing to sacrifice a great deal for the liberty of Ithicana, but I'm not going to pick a fight with my allies already having conceded defeat at my back."

Aren rose to his feet. "I know the northern islands have suffered, Mara. I know that the losses to Katarina's poison weigh upon you, because they weigh upon me as well. If you and the other commanders truly believe you'd rather concede to those who sought our annihilation than fight on, I'll call in the watch commanders from the south and we'll all vote. If you and yours decide you'd rather bend the knee to William than to me, I will not protest. There isn't a point, because if Ithicana has lost the will to fight, then Ithicana has already ceased to exist. We are the fight, or we are nothing."

The decision hung on Mara, Ahnna knew that. She was the eldest and most respected, and the eyes of the other commanders were on her, not Aren. They would follow her lead.

Northwatch's commander gave a slow nod. "It's a mad plan, with a hundred places it could go wrong, but it's the only chance we have against that pair of bitches. We can't best them with force—the only way to win this is to play their game and to play it better."

Aren cleared his throat. "You all understand how this will work, and we don't have the time to debate the minutiae. The Tempest Seas sink ships, but the loss of two will still make Katarina suspicious. She will send reconnaissance ships and soldiers to see whether her scheme has been successful. Time is not our friend, so we must either move swiftly to enact our deception or make ready to face the greatest war of our lifetimes. Those for Ahnna's plan, lift your hands."

Lara and Mara lifted their hands, then slowly, the other watch commanders raised their hands high. Triumph filled Ahnna but only for a heartbeat, then it faded, leaving her hollow with the knowledge of what came next.

Slowly, she turned in her chair to look at her husband, knowing the time they'd be together was coming to an end.

Only to discover James was gone.

# 71

# JAMES

J AMES HAD KNOWN what the Ithicanians would decide the moment they saw Ahnna walk through the door. For more than half of his life, he had served in Harendell's military, and James had seen more than once how a single individual could inspire soldiers to fight against the worst of odds. Ahnna had led Ithicana through its darkest days, never faltering, and she'd returned in the moment when it seemed all hope was lost. James put little stock in higher powers, but it was hard not to believe that something mystical walked in Ahnna's shadow for her to have survived so much and arrived just when she was needed most.

The Ithicanians would follow Ahnna into fire, which is why she needed to remain here while he went north to secure the alliance with Cardiff that would make or break this wild strategy his wife had come up with.

James had walked without thought to where he was going, and he paused to look up into the storm-shredded canopy of the jungle to try to get his bearings. It pressed in around him, thick with mist, inspiring claustrophobia. "There's no space," he said, having sensed Ahnna come up behind him, though she made no sound. "No room to run."

"Do you want to run?" Ahnna asked, and he heard the slight shake in her voice. The uncertainty.

"No. But being here . . ." He rounded on his wife. "My father was mad to think that I could rule this place. It needs someone with tempests in their veins and wildness in their heart. The idea that anyone else could take it and keep it is a delusion. William has to see that this is folly."

Her hazel eyes regarded him, one hand lifting to tuck a loose lock of hair behind her ear. "Do you really believe William can be convinced to turn on Alexandra?"

"I don't know." He closed the distance between them. "But within reason, I have to give my brother a chance, Ahnna. I have to give him the opportunity to be a good king, a good man, before I tear away his birthright."

"It's *your* birthright, not his." Her hands balled into fists. "You were Edward's heir in every possible way, which means the crown is yours."

"Everyone keeps saying that, but it feels like theft!" He instantly regretted the anger in his tone, and added, "All our lives, Will felt . . . inadequate. Was made to feel that way by our father because Will was no soldier, no fighter, although now I understand that much of the way my father treated him was because he perceived William as having usurped my role, never mind that it was by his own design. I was supposed to be my brother's protector, and instead I was the unwitting cause of every bit of his misery. Now I aim to take the one thing that has made him feel worth something." James clenched his teeth. "I might as well just kill him. Virginia will endure, but Will . . ."

"I'm sorry." Ahnna wrapped her arms around his neck, and James buried his face in her hair as she said, "I wish it didn't have to be like this. I wish the world wasn't like this."

He didn't answer, only inhaled the scent of this woman who had stolen his heart the first moment he'd set eyes on her. He wished that he could take her and run. Wished they could escape the horror to come and find a place untouched by greed and violence.

The wind gusted, and Ahnna tilted her head back, her eyes closed as her hair billowed behind her. "I did not truly know what it meant to *run* until I came to Harendell." She gave a soft sigh, and James drank in her face. "I dream of it more nights than not. Of galloping in the wide-open spaces, fast as the wind, and my heart longs for it." Her eyes opened, but though she was staring at him, it was as though she did not see him. "We will fight our separate battles, James, but when we win this, promise me that we'll gallop across the Ranges every day for the rest of our lives."

"I swear it."

Ahnna blinked, eyes focusing, and James's skin prickled, the air suddenly charged. In the distance, thunder rumbled.

"I love you," she said. "This is not goodbye."

Footsteps thudded up the path, and they turned to find Aren approaching. "I've got a Cardiffian vessel in my fleet," he said. "I've sent a crew ahead to get her ready to sail north, but we need to move quickly. There's a storm coming up from the southwest, and my grandmother says that it will linger. You need to get out ahead of it."

The wind whipped through the trees, and more thunder rolled, its tone ominous.

"Be safe." James cupped his hands around his wife's head, kissing the scar that ran down her face. "I love you, and I will come back to you. I swear it."

"Then it is certain." A tear ran down her face, sparkling as lightning flashed overhead. "Whether it be in this life or the next."

If he stayed another heartbeat, James knew he'd stay forever, so without a backward glance, he strode toward the storm.

# 72

# LARA

Lara smoothed Delia's dark hair back from her face, committing every inch of her daughter to memory. The baby watched her with solemn hazel eyes, seeming to recognize the weight of the moment despite circumstances being so far beyond her capacity to understand. She caught Lara's index finger in her chubby fist and pulled it to her mouth, as she did all things, her first few teeth sharp against Lara's skin.

They'd left Midwatch and headed south not long after James departed north for Cardiff. Lara had carried her child through the bridge, allowing no one but Aren to take Delia from her, and even then, only for short intervals. To give up even a heartbeat of time with her baby felt like having a piece of her excised with a knife, because heartbeats felt limited and fleeting as Ithicana prepared for war. Except now they were at Southwatch, the skies overhead gray and swirling, but not half so violent as they were in the north.

"Sarhina's coming." Aren ran a hand down her back, and though she knew he intended to calm her, Lara could feel his tension. His grief.

It made her breath catch, and the selfishness in her core screamed, *Run. Take them and run.*

Instead she said, "Everything is in order?"

"Yes. Sarhina has quarantined Southwatch and has spread rumors that a fatal illness has run through all of Ithicana. The rumors will change to poison when the time is right, but fear of infection should keep everyone well away while we set the stage for Katarina. The storms won't last forever."

Lara knew that, but God, she wished they would. Wished the typhoons would scream their wrath over the Tempest Seas and drive away anyone who dared to attack Ithicana, sinking anyone who thought themselves capable of claiming the bridge.

But War Tides was coming, whether she liked it or not.

Footfalls caught her attention, and Lara looked up to find Sarhina approaching, Athena and Cresta at her heels. Normally seeing her sisters would be a pleasure, but Lara's stomach filled with trepidation.

As though sensing her feelings, Sarhina stopped a few paces back, nodding once at Aren before she said quietly, "I wish I were meeting my niece under better circumstances. Just as I wish I could do more for you in this fight, sister. If not for the need for discretion, I'd fight at your side, but someone must see this act through to fruition."

Lara's tongue felt thick and her throat tight, but she managed to say, "You are certain that your parliament will seek out trade terms with Katarina?"

Sarhina nodded. "As soon as they understand that Amarid has taken the bridge, they'll send messages. Yield was poor in the fields north of Nerastis, and Valcotta has struggled with illness in their herds. It's hard times for all, and to regain trade with the north would be a boon." Her blue eyes flicked to Aren. "I know they angered you in your meeting with them, but please don't judge them too harshly. It is their sworn duty to act in the benefit of those they represent, and they are not politicians trained in tact."

Aren gave a small shrug. "It will make it all the more believable when they approach Katarina with a deal, because she'll have heard about the conflict from her spies."

They continued to discuss the specifics of the plan, but Lara let their words fall away in favor of focusing her attention on Delia. She was starting to frown and fuss, hungry as always, and an answering ache formed in her breasts even as tears stung in her eyes, for this would be the last time she'd feed her child. Even if all went as planned, she'd be long weeks away from Delia, who would by then be firmly on the breast of her nurse.

Lara blinked rapidly, trying to keep her tears in check, only to hear Aren say, "At least you answered our call, Sarhina. Zarrah has not answered a single letter. Not one."

There was anger in his voice, reflective of the betrayal she knew he felt over Zarrah having seemingly turned her back on Ithicana in its time of need. "We came for her," he'd said time and again. "We risked everything for her."

"Zarrah hasn't answered your letters because she hasn't received them," Sarhina said.

Lara looked up sharply. "What? Why?"

"Because she's in Harendell."

Lara's lips parted in shock. "You can't be serious? We've heard nothing, and Keris has said not a word."

"I'm not surprised." Sarhina rocked on her boot heels. "She's posing as Daria, and I doubt Keris would risk her true identity being discovered by sending a message."

"Why would she go to Verwyrd?" Lara demanded. "She needs to rule in Valcotta, and there is far more good she can do from Pyrinat than pretending to be my brother's bodyguard in Harendell."

"She might think otherwise." Aren ran a hand through his hair, then gave a shake of his head. "Keris is at risk, and Zarrah loves him like life. Protecting him might have been her only concern."

Lara narrowed her eyes, every instinct in her body telling her that Zarrah wouldn't have thrown aside Valcotta's rule just to race to Keris's side. He could take care of himself, and Zarrah knew that.

"Lestara." Sarhina spat in the dirt as though saying the queen of Harendell's name had brought a foul taste to her mouth. "Or at least, that was the original reason. Zarrah did not take her rise to the throne well at all."

James's voice filled Lara's head. *Everyone in Cardiff believes that my cousin is cursed, most especially my aunt Calythra, who is Lestara's mother. They didn't send Lestara to Silas for better trade terms on furs—they sent her to get rid of her.*

"Lestara *hates* Keris," Aren said. "Zarrah knows that better than anyone, but if Alexandra's goal is to control the bridge, then she won't risk losing trade with Valcotta by killing off the empress's consort. I think she'll keep Lestara in check."

"Don't be so sure. The second reason Zarrah went north, which I learned from Arjun, is that it appears the Harendellian cattle infected with wasting disease were deliberately shipped to Valcotta. She left believing that Edward was behind it, but she has surely come to suspect that it was Alexandra. If she can find proof, she has grounds to declare it an act of war on Valcotta."

"Which will give her grounds to sail to Ithicana's defense." Aren scrubbed a hand through his hair. "I should never have doubted her. I feel like an ass."

Lara frowned, something picking at her mind that she couldn't quite put her finger on, but she left it for later consideration as Aren said, "I support the need for proof, but Zarrah should have sent someone else to search for it. We need her in the south, in power, able to make decisions. If she's not willing to leave Keris alone in Verwyrd, then both of them need to leave together. Can you get word to them?"

"Eventually, although the storms have sunk more ships than I can count this season," Sarhina replied. "But do keep in mind, Aren, that Zarrah is the empress of Valcotta. Neither you nor I are in any position to tell her what to do."

Thunder rumbled in the distance, silencing the conversation but also bringing them to the moment that Lara had been dreading.

Sarhina eyed the sky. "I need to set sail. You need to say your goodbyes, Lara."

A knife to her stomach would have hurt less.

Aren gave a sharp shake of his head. "I can't ask you to do this, Lara. Go with her. Let me and Ahnna fight this fight."

Her control fractured, tears rolling down her face, and she brushed away those that landed on Delia's cheek, holding her child close. Inhaling her scent and whispering, "I love you. I love you so much, my sweet little girl."

Aren's arms wrapped around them both, and she allowed herself one last moment of the three of them together, then stepped forward to hand her daughter to Sarhina.

Her sister took her niece with practiced hands, soothing Delia as she began to cry. "She'll go into the Kresteck Mountains with Ensel's family," Sarhina said. "Deep in the wilds where everyone knows everyone, and no one trusts outsiders. They'll keep her safe, as they keep my own girl safe, and Athena and Cresta will be with them."

"We'll protect her with our lives, Lara," Athena said, wiping tears from her cheeks. "I swear it."

"Tell her that I love her," Lara whispered. "Tell her that she was loved so very much and that I didn't want to let her go."

"You'll tell her yourself when we bring her back to you." Sarhina bent her head to kiss Delia's forehead, rocking her, but Delia only cried harder, and the sound tore at Lara's heart.

"God, Lara, just go with her," Aren pleaded, and his cheeks were wet. "You have done enough. You do not need to do this. She is safest with you."

Lara wiped her eyes. "If the worst happens, Sar, tell her that she was our greatest love. That we wanted her and never wanted to let her go, and that we fought our hardest to get back to her."

Her baby's wails tore apart her soul, but she kept her eyes on her sister's face until Sarhina nodded. "I swear it."

"Thank you," Lara said, then she turned and strode into the bridge. Picked up the rubble of walls she'd worked so hard to dismantle, and rebuilt them, piece by piece, until her eyes were dry, and she was the little cockroach once more.

# 73
# AHNNA

EVERY WAR TIDES, Ithicanians migrated, so it was nothing to Ahnna's people to begin the process of packing up what they needed to disappear under the cover of night and storm. Only this time, instead of going to Eranahl, they moved to the outer islands. Places far from the bridge that held little strategic use and were unlikely to be investigated by the Amaridians. It was, after all, the middle of storm season, which meant that winds and waves capable of putting ships at the bottom of the sea manifested without warning. And for ships the size that the Amaridians used, there were very few locations in Ithicana capable of offering anything resembling safe harbor.

Aren ordered the evacuations to begin the same day James set sail for Cardiff. He also ordered those who remained to begin digging. Creating countless fresh graves, big and small, to set the scene in locations where the Amaridians were likely to come ashore. The corpses of those lost in the north were mercilessly redeployed and staged, though it would be the ripening smell of rot that Katarina's scouts encountered first.

The storms in the north remained vicious throughout, seeming to be buying them time to set the scene, though it came at a cost. There were multiple fatalities, people lost to storm surge, floods, mudslides, and falling trees, and everyone suffered minor cuts and scrapes from debris in the winds. It was a miserable reminder why the bridge was needed, its indestructible stone untouched by wind or sea. Everyone on Ahnna's team was exhausted by the time they were finished, but their silence had nothing to do with the labor or injury.

It was because very soon the enemy would be coming onto Ithicanian soil. Walking through villages and homes with the same callousness the Maridrinians had employed, and then taking over the bridge. At best, it felt invasive.

At worst, it felt like a surrender.

"A ship has been spotted," Lara said, coming up next to Ahnna. "They're moving in close enough to take a look but staying out of range of the shipbreakers."

Her tone was tight and clipped, and Ahnna looked sideways at her queen. Lara and Aren had taken Delia to Southwatch to place her in the protection of Sarhina, all of it done under a cloak of the greatest secrecy. Neither of them had spoken about their feelings on the separation, but Ahnna sensed the complex twist of emotion the sacrifice had elicited. Delia was safer in Maridrina, but every day they spent away from her was a loss.

*Please let them get back to her*, Ahnna silently prayed. *Please don't let them be another family torn apart.*

Though this was a strategy of playing possum, it would be suspicious if there was no one left alive to fight back, so skirmishes were planned. As Ahnna took in Lara, painted with greens and browns of camouflage and armed to the teeth, it was hard not to feel pity for any Amaridians whom Ithicana's queen came up against.

Aren appeared, seeming to have come out of nowhere. He scrubbed a gloved hand through his hair and then gave a sharp shake of his head. "I hate this. Every instinct in me screams *fight*. I don't want to have to burn another house down."

"We are fighting," Lara answered. "Just not in a way we're used to. And if you burn my house down again, love, it will be me you have to fear, not the Amaridians."

Ahnna laughed softly as her brother frowned, but then all three of them fell silent.

Ahnna dropped lower behind the foliage as the ship moved closer, shifting cautiously inside the range of the shipbreakers as it sailed along the cliff sides. Then closer still, and Ahnna lifted her hand to signal Lia, who was waiting below. A heartbeat later, Lia stumbled out into the open. The front of her tunic was splattered with fake vomit, and Ahnna silently applauded her commitment as she spewed a mouthful of crimson onto the ground and then fell to her knees.

"Help!" she screamed, holding out an imploring hand to the soldiers and crew watching from the ship. "Help us!"

Ahnna's stomach tightened because it felt too real. Felt like she had stepped into an alternative reality when she and James had not returned in time and her nightmare had come to pass. Next to her, Lara took hold of her hand and squeezed as she lifted a spyglass to her face, carefully shading the glass so that the faint light coming through the heavy clouds wouldn't reflect off it.

"They see her," Lara muttered. "They're watching."

The Amaridians dropped the rest of their sails, drifting, and Ahnna's nerves twisted with sudden doubt that this would work. What if Katarina knew that she and James had made it in time? What if she suspected this was a ruse?

"Let me see," Aren muttered, reaching for the spyglass.

Lara leaned away from him. "No. You don't want to see this. Neither of you two do."

Lia crawled slowly to the edge of the cliff. Her chin was covered with crimson, her cheeks slick with tears as she reached out her hand to the ship's crew. Then she shuddered and collapsed to the ground, twitching with feigned death throes with such horrifying accuracy that some primal instinct in Ahnna made her want to go to the woman. Instead, she shifted her gaze to the tiny figures on the ship, the distance making it impossible to see their expressions.

But the way they pumped their fists into the air and spun one another in circles around the decks was painfully clear.

"They are celebrating." Lara's voice was cold as death as she lowered the spyglass, her grip on Ahnna's hand so tight it hurt. "These men are no innocent pawns in Katarina's plan. They knew exactly what was intended."

"Good," Ahnna replied. "That means we will feel no guilt and shed no tears when their *allies* come for their blood."

The first step in their plan had worked, but the next step was entirely out of their hands. James's ship should be nearing Cardiff's waters soon, and everything depended on whether he could convince Ronan to agree to their strategy.

*Please be safe*, she silently whispered, hoping that the wind would carry it north to his ears. *Please come back to me.*

There was nothing else she could do to aid him, so together they pressed back into the wilds of Ithicana to watch Amarid take the bridge.

# 74

# JAMES

THE SHIP SAILED west first and then north, and while they were spotted by naval vessels, the Harendellian crews showed no interest. Why should they, given the ship was Cardiffian in style, flew Cardiff's banners, and had a crew dressed in garments from the north?

James had discovered that the Ithicanians had quite a selection of ships and disguises in their collection. Most vessels had been captured during attacks on Ithicana's shores, but he learned that this particular vessel was a ghost ship.

"We found her floating in our waters with all the passengers dead in their beds and the crew missing," one of the crew told him. "The reasonable theory was that the crew had poisoned the passengers and abandoned ship, but all their wealth and goods remained aboard. So there was some thought that the vessel had been hexed by a witch."

The time he'd spent in Cardiff with his uncles had ensured that James had learned everything about the customs and beliefs of his mother's people. Whenever he was in Harendell, it was easy to dismiss many of the powers and gifts Cardiffian women claimed to possess, but while in Cardiff, it all felt very real. One could not stand in the room with Calythra and deny that she had power, and there had been times in Lestara's presence when he felt the same way. It was that feeling of unease that had fallen over him the moment he'd set eyes on the vessel that would take him north, and learning of its dark history only made the sensation worse. He could barely sleep the entire journey, and what sleep he had was plagued by violent dreams that left him in an irritable fog when he was awake.

It was hard not to feel relieved when they entered the northern bay and Cardiff itself came into view. Heavily treed and mountainous, it was a wild place, and as he had since his youth, James felt the call of this land.

"Drop anchor and row me in under the cover of night," he instructed the crew. "Alexandra and Katarina will both have spies here, so no need to draw attention to my arrival."

The skies were clear when they reached shore, the stars a million pinpricks of light overhead as James stepped into the shallows, frigid water filling his boots. He tightened the fur cloak that he'd taken from the Ithicanian collection, all of it moldy and moth-eaten, but the chill of the north felt welcome after the oppressive heat of Ithicana, where the air had been so humid it had felt like breathing in water.

"Bloody freezing," one of the Ithicanians muttered. "Haven't felt this sort of cold since Devil's Island."

"At least the Cardiffians won't eat you," another one of the men replied.

"They'll just have one of their women capture your soul."

James ignored their speculation over Cardiffian witches and focused his gaze on the dark forests. His uncle's castle was called Bryngaleth, and unlike rulers of other nations, he kept it as his only home. When he left to hunt or to battle, Ronan Crehan slept in the open air, his favored ceiling the stars in the sky. So of all the places in Cardiff to find him, this was the surest bet.

"Thank you for your companionship," James said to the Ithicanians. "Safe travels south and may God, fate, and the stars all keep watch over Ithicana."

"In the tempests we trust," one said to him, and then they both inclined their heads. "Good luck, Your Grace."

His jaw tightened at the title, no part of him having grown used to it during their travels.

James left the Ithicanians to row back to the ship and started walking down the banks of the bay, his boots crunching on the frost-laden pebbles. The moon had risen, and the crescent illuminated Bryngaleth in the distance. The castle loomed like a crag of black stone at the edge of the bay, its towers stark against the sky. Bryngaleth seemed to drink in the moonlight, its walls gleaming faintly, almost alive in their stillness. Yet it was the sounds of the bay, not the castle, that held James's attention as he walked.

The lap of waves against the rocks was soft and rhythmic compared with the violent seas around Ithicana. Both seas were beasts, but this one slept, each wave a soft breath of slumber. From somewhere out in the darkness came the low, mournful cry of a loon, its voice haunting as it drifted over the icy water. Closer, a fox barked sharply, its yip a sudden, wild punctuation to the silence, before it fell still once more.

James glanced toward the edge of the path, where a dark tangle of undergrowth met the slope of the shore. A rustle there, brief and faint, set his nerves on edge. Perhaps it was just the wind worrying at the brambles, or some small creature—a stoat or a hare—scurrying through the frozen brush. Yet the sound lingered in his mind as he walked, a reminder of how alone he was. Of how empty these lands often seemed, despite this being the heart of Cardiff.

Bryngaleth seemed to grow taller, its form sharpening with each step. The castle's gates were dark and closed, a void in the wall of frost-covered stone. Somewhere high above, a single owl screeched, its cry slicing through the stillness like a blade. James paused, his breath misting in the frigid air, and listened.

Not an owl. A signal.

James stiffened right before a voice said, "State your business, traveler. It's late to be out and about on a night such as this."

He turned to find two men dressed in heavy furs standing behind him, one with a sword in his gloved hand and the other with an arrow loosely nocked in a longbow. Slowly, so as not to cause alarm, James pulled back his hood so that moonlight illuminated his face.

Their eyes widened in recognition. Not because his face was well known in Cardiff, for his uncles had kept his presence hidden, but because these men were part of the king's war band. Close as brothers to both Ronan and Cormac, and James knew them well.

"Look who the cat dragged in," Theryn said. "You're supposed to be dead, boy. Dead at the Ithicanian princess's hand. They held a funeral for you at Verwyrd. Ronan took it hard, but Caly told him not to weep over an empty grave."

James's skin prickled, but he ignored the sensation.

"The rumors of my death are grossly overstated," he replied with a shrug. "I need to speak with my uncle, but I also need discretion. For reasons I'll relay to him, there's a target on my back, and I do not care to make it bigger."

Theryn's bushy blond eyebrows rose. "This is bound to be a good story, but good stories are worth the wait. Hood up, lad, and we'll get you to him."

James pulled up his hood and followed them into the town nestled at the base of the castle. Light glowed from around closed window shutters and doors, the air heavy with the smoke of hearths that burned all night to ward off the chill. Nearly every wooden surface was carved with constellations, and wind chimes formed from the skulls of small creatures hung from the eaves of every home.

Yet despite everything that was said about astronomancy in Harendell, none of it felt ominous. How could it when he could hear singing and laughing from inside the homes, the sound of children quarreling about having to go to bed, and from the taverns, reed pipes and drums playing joyful tunes accompanied by the unmistakable thuds of people dancing.

"All seems well in Bryngaleth," he murmured. "Spirits seem high."

"Why wouldn't they be?" Theryn replied. "With the blockade on the bridge, the Harendellians have no choice but to trade north. Edward's treaty of peace lives on with William and Lestara, and while they buy our furs, we fill our bellies with their beef and win the hearts of our wives with their shiny trinkets. We have you to thank for it, Jamie. That will never be forgotten."

James gave a tight nod. He could not feel good about what he'd accomplished for a multitude of reasons, not the least being that he was about to ask them to give it all up. Yet he'd also heard a thread of tension in Theryn's voice, which was confirmed as the man added, "I do not wish to be the bearer of dark tidings, but your uncle Cormac is dead, lad. Poisoned by the Amaridians. Yet when pressed for action against Amarid, your brother gives only platitudes. Katarina has the blood of two Crehans on her hands, and that cannot go unavenged. The stars care not for profit—they care for blood."

"If I have my way, they'll get their blood and more," James replied. "But I don't rule in Cardiff. Ronan does."

Both men grunted their agreement and approval, and they carried on in silence.

They reached the base of the hill and began the climb to the castle itself. The road to Bryngaleth twisted and turned in a relentless series of cobbled switchbacks that clung to the hillside like the scales of a vast serpent. The stones were old and uneven, polished smooth in some places by centuries of wear but fractured in others where frost and time had pried them apart. It was a hard climb, the incline growing steeper with every turn, the switchbacks carving a deliberate, unhurried path upward as if daring anyone who did not belong to turn back.

Halfway up, James was breathing heavily, each inhalation laced with the faint tang of the sea far below. The walls of the castle rose high and unyielding, their stone blackened with age, and the towers jutted upward like broken spears.

The wind picked up, biting and sharp. It tugged at his cloak and howled between the battlements, and James felt the sudden certainty that it was warning him to go back. Which made no goddamned sense given he was safer in these walls than anywhere else on the continent. The gates of Bryngaleth emerged from the darkness and fog, flanked by torches that crackled and sparked. Thick timbers reinforced with iron stood closed, their surface etched with deep scars that hinted at battles long past. Above, the raised portcullis cast jagged shadows against the stone, its iron teeth a silent threat.

Instead of approaching them, Theryn led him along a narrow path beneath the walls and banged his fist on a small banded oak door in the base of the wall. "It's Theryn and Waynne. Open up."

A tiny slot opened and eyes peered out, taking in the three of them. The creak of wood filled James's ears as a beam was lifted off the door and it swung open, allowing them into the castle.

"Who is he?" the guardsman demanded.

"King's business. Get the castle shut up good and tight; there's a bad feeling in the mist and winds tonight."

So it wasn't just him who felt it.

James fought the urge to reach for his sword, instead keeping his hands at his sides as he walked behind Theryn through the castle. In deference to the height of the Cardiffian people, the ceilings were vaulted, but the corridors were narrow and there were no windows to speak of. Everything was solid and heavy, designed and built in the times when the clans warred against one another, before Cardiff had unified beneath one king. So very different from the airy and open palaces of Harendell, most of which couldn't be defended from a mob of grandmothers angered by the rising price of tea.

He'd only been in this particular castle a handful of times and James was swiftly lost in the warren of corridors, the sense that he was walking into the center of the earth making his heart beat quicker than their steps warranted. "Ronan will be in here," Theryn said as they reached a shut door. "Let me speak to him first."

The big warrior went in the door, then shut it behind him, leaving James alone with Waynne.

"Was sorry to hear about your father, lad," the old man said. "Edward was a right Harendellian prick, but better than most, and Siobhan loved him true. He must have loved her true as well for what he did, and he deserved a better end than to be stabbed in his sleep by that southern snake charmer."

James's hands tried to curl into fists at the words against Ahnna, but he forced them flat against his thighs. They only knew what they'd been told, and he'd have the truth in their ears soon enough.

The door opened, and Theryn motioned for James and Waynne to come in. No sooner was he through the door than his uncle's familiar form appeared before him. King Ronan Crehan was a bear of a man.

Nearly seven feet tall and broad as an ox, he was one of the few men who made James feel small. He wore woolen garments and thick furs, which only added to his size, and James's spine cracked as he was lifted off his feet in an embrace.

"My nephew!" Ronan roared. "My boy is alive!"

He set James down with a thump but then pounded his back. "Word out of Amarid is that you'd been found dead in the Blackreaches, and William had your funeral. Caly said there were no new stars in the sky, but I was beginning to give up hope. Where have you been, lad?"

"I'm very much alive." James sucked air back into his compressed lungs. "Though it's been close more times than I can count." He hesitated, then added, "I heard about Cormac. He deserved a better end."

Ronan leaned back, gripping James by the shoulders as he looked him up and down. His eyes were amber as well, though more yellow in hue than James's own, and it was like looking into the face of a wolf. "Was the Crimson Widow who did the deed, but your brother won't move toward vengeance. Little fucker didn't get an ounce of your father's blood."

His fingers tightened on James's shoulders. "I'm sorry for Edward. He was a force to be reckoned with, and he deserved better than what he got. We know you chased the Ithicanian woman into the Blackreaches, and it's not like you not to catch your prey. I hope you gave the bitch an inglorious death."

James grimaced but only said, "I've a lot to tell you."

"I'm sure." His uncle slung an arm around James's shoulder, leading him deeper into the room to where high-backed chairs faced a roaring fire. "Harendell will be wanting the same story, but as luck will have it, you can tell us both at the same time."

James's hackles abruptly rose. The scent of a familiar perfume filled his nose, and above the chair, he saw the gleam of white-blond hair. Hands turning to ice, James slowly rounded the heavy piece of furniture to find a pregnant woman with amber eyes smiling back at him.

"James," Lestara said, hand curving around her swollen belly, "thank the stars you are still alive."

# 75

# ZARRAH

Zarrah paced back and forth across her tiny room in the Sky Palace, anxiety souring her stomach and giving her a throbbing headache. Despite extensive searches of Keris's rooms, the rooms of all his guards, and, in a particularly violating turn of events, all of their persons, the Harendellians remained convinced that *Daria* was behind the theft of the Ashford banking documents.

"She didn't take anything!" Keris had argued with rising vehemence. "She was investing in fucking cows on Zarrah's behalf. It's not her goddamned fault if you can't keep track of your paperwork! Anyone could have taken those documents!"

Yet it appeared Zarrah had deeply underestimated Harendellian organization, because the banker insisted that Daria was the only possible culprit for their theft. As a result, William had ordered that Keris and his retinue be confined to the Sky Palace until the documents were recovered. Which meant that her hard-earned proof of Alexandra's attack on Valcotta was not on the way to Arjun, but still stuck behind a cursed portrait in a corridor.

"Think," she muttered to herself. "Think!"

Except no matter how hard she bent her mind to the task, Zarrah had not been able to come up with a way to get the pages south. For all its beauty, the Sky Palace served remarkably well as a prison, as there was only one way out other than the long drop from the top.

"Maybe the best bet is to arrange for those you left in Lestara's rooms to be found," Saam said softly from where he sat on her cot. "They'll think it was her and let us out of this cursed palace."

"Except they'll notice the pages that are missing." Zarrah kept up her pacing. "Alexandra knows what she did, Saam, and she's desperate to keep that information from reaching Valcotta."

"So we put them with the others."

"Then all of this was for nothing!" She flung up her hands. "My reign isn't half as secure as I might like, Saam. Too many of our people will suspect that I'm fabricating the offense to give myself grounds to aid my *family in Ithicana*. Or they'll think Keris put me up to it. No one wants another war, especially not one with Harendell. I need something no one will contest, and those pages have Alexandra's signature on them."

And she was running out of time. The end of storm season was coming, and William was already making plans for an all-out invasion of Ithicana.

"I don't see what other choice we have," Saam said, then stiffened as a sharp knock sounded at the door.

Zarrah opened it to find a Harendellian man whom she knew to be Lord George Cavendish standing outside.

"Daria of Valcotta, your presence has been ordered by Her Royal Majesty, the Dowager Queen Alexandra. Come with me."

Zarrah's pulse thrummed, but she cast a backward glance at Saam that she hoped would dissuade him from doing anything foolish as she followed Cavendish into the corridor. He led her through the Sky Palace, their boots nearly silent on the thick carpet and the halls unusually empty. Reaching a set of doors guarded by yet more soldiers, she waited in silence while Cavendish went inside. He swiftly reappeared. "Search her for weapons, and then send her in."

They roughly searched her but found no weapons. Everything

had been confiscated except for the tiny blade she had concealed in the twist of her hair. Zarrah went inside, Cavendish on her heels, and he shut the door with a heavy thud before standing against the wall with his arms crossed.

Alexandra sat on a sofa, and backlit as she was by lamps, it was impossible to see her face. Zarrah bowed low. "You wished to see me, Your Grace."

"Yes, Daria. I thought that you and I, being two reasonable women, might get to the bottom of this little conflict. Please sit."

This woman had sent death to Valcotta. The desire to pull her hidden blade and slit Alexandra's throat was nearly overwhelming, but instead, Zarrah did as Alexandra bid her. As her eyes adjusted to the room's lighting, she got the first look at the dowager queen's face. There was a thick scar on her cheek that had healed poorly, and it pulled up the corner of the woman's mouth in a permanent sneer. Her eyes were green, but there was something lifeless and cold about them, especially given how they had sunk into her skull, shadows marring the skin beneath them. She was painfully thin, collarbone jutting through her pale skin above her black dress. A mourning gown for the stepson she surely didn't mourn.

"I'll not mince words," Alexandra said, pouring a cup of tea for Zarrah and then filling her own. One of the cups was chipped, but Zarrah recognized the pattern as the design of a particularly famous artist who had died over a century prior. A priceless antique.

"We know you visited one of our banks under the guise of pursuing investment opportunities on behalf of the empress. We know that you used the opportunity to steal Ashford banking records, and we know that you have either hidden them or passed them on to another party. Our banker swears with total certainty that our records were present when he opened the cabinet, and also that he left you briefly alone in the room, giving you opportunity to hide the documents on your person."

"As has been said many times, Your Grace, your banker is mistaken."

Alexandra pursed her lips. "I see." She took a sip of her tea. "Daria, I do not blame you for your actions. I know that the orders were given by Prince Keris, and that you are loyal to him due to his part in rescuing you from unjust incarceration. You acted out of loyalty, and that is something I would applaud if not for my certainty that he does not share your loyalty."

Zarrah said nothing, only sat quietly, waiting.

"He's using you to do his dirty work, my sweet girl. I know he's as lovely as a painting, but he's a Veliant. He does not respect or care for women—they are only things to be used, then discarded."

If circumstances weren't so dire, Zarrah might have laughed at the clumsy attempt to manipulate her. "That has not been my impression of His Highness, Your Grace."

Alexandra gave a soft sigh. "Do not be blinded by infatuation, Daria. Men like him are dangerous to women, because they wield their looks and charm like weapons. But ask yourself this: When Lord Cavendish arrests you tomorrow for espionage, which, during times of war, is punishable by execution, will Keris step forward to aid you? Will he, knowing that we are unlikely to hang him, take the blame for the orders he gave you?"

The room felt suddenly cold. "I have committed no crime, Your Grace, and the empress will not take the unjust execution of one of her people lightly. You have no proof—nothing but the baseless accusations of a single man. We were searched from head to toe, our rooms and belongings picked apart, and no evidence was found. There is also no valid reason why His Highness would order the theft of personal banking records. What interest has he in how you spend your gold?"

The dowager queen's eyes abruptly burned like green fire. "Keris is no neutral party. He is family to our enemy, and while we put up with his presence, we are aware that he works against us on King Aren's behalf. How he intends to use them, I could not say, but he surely intends harm."

Alexandra's face and tone revealed nothing, but Zarrah could feel her desperation. She knew that if Valcotta discovered what she'd done, the bridge would be rendered worthless to her. She'd overplayed her hand trying to ensure that Zarrah wouldn't be able to aid Ithicana, and now it was coming back to bite her in the ass. "We do not have your banking records, Your Grace. Investigate your own for this crime."

"Tell me the truth, Daria, and you will be both protected and generously compensated," Alexandra replied. "You will live life in safety and luxury, and never again be used by the likes of Keris Veliant. For use you, he surely has."

"We do not have your documents."

"Daria, please think this through!" Alexandra snapped the words. "If you are arrested for espionage, Keris will let you go to the gallows for *his* crime. Do not put your trust in a man who has proven again and again that he does not deserve it. You know that Valcotta suffers, that Maridrina suffers, and yet Keris digs in his heels and aids those who are causing the suffering. That is not the sort of man who deserves your devotion."

It was tempting to reveal herself. To make a fool out of this awful woman who was so desperate to prop up the reign of her idiot son that she'd resort to war. Except that would make Zarrah the fool. The Harendellians would scream *espionage* north and south. Would scream that her actions were an act of war on Valcotta's part, which would give them grounds to kill her. Her people might retaliate. Or they might shrug and accept one of her cousins rising to power.

"Make the smart choice," Alexandra said softly. "Don't let him ruin your life, Daria."

There was no way out of this. If she denied the theft, Alexandra would arrest her and execute her. If she told them where the documents were, she'd still be killed, because Alexandra would need to bury the truth and bury it deep.

She'd come here to aid the friends who'd risked everything to save her life, and Zarrah would not abandon them now. Squaring her shoulders, she stared Alexandra down. "The pages documenting your financing of a scheme to send infected animals into Valcotta are already on a ship sailing south to be relayed to the empress, Your Grace. That proof, in conjunction with evidence that the animals were deliberately released to infect Valcottan herds, will be seen as an act of war. Empress Zarrah *will* retaliate, and she is already preparing to set sail to join forces with Ithicana. Leave off on your aggression toward Ithicana, Your Grace, or face the consequences."

The tiny tells of desperation on Alexandra's face melted away, the green fire fading into cold calculation as the queen slowly clapped her hands together. "You are every bit the woman I knew you would be, Imperial Majesty. All the rumors that honor flows through your veins, not blood, have been proven true."

Zarrah's stomach plunged.

"With luck, my agents will intercept my documents and make them disappear," Alexandra said after taking a long mouthful of her tea. "But even if they don't, the cousin I'm bankrolling to replace you will make short work of the evidence." She smiled. "You were always going to be a problem, Zarrah, given your unfaltering devotion to Lara and Aren, so I've been working to undermine your reign from the moment you took the crown from Petra's corpse. I'd hoped that the assassination attempts would drive you to run away with your lovely husband, but I always have secondary strategies in play. Valcotta isn't going to come to Ithicana's aid, and once my propagandists do their work, your people will be thanking Harendell for ridding them of their greatest woe."

It felt like a vise had wrapped around Zarrah's chest, because she'd played right into Alexandra's hand.

"Georgie, do bring Her Imperial Majesty back to her husband's suite," Alexandra said. "Detain their guards, and put our own outside their doors. Kill anyone who resists."

"Ithicana will not go down without a fight," Zarrah hissed as Cavendish took hold of her wrists. "You might win the day, you unrepentant bitch, but they will make you bleed every step of the way."

"Cling to that hope, if you must." Alexandra reached across the table and patted Zarrah's cheek. "But I think it is better to rue your choice not to take your pretty husband and run away while you could."

# 76

# JAMES

J AMES HAD SPENT all of his adult life soldiering, so no one knew better than him that even the best-laid plans rarely went as intended.

But he had not expected everything to fall apart this soon.

Lestara rose to her feet and then rose up on her tiptoes to kiss his cheek. "Your face is a welcome sight, cousin. The Amaridians discovered corpses in the Blackreaches, and you were declared dead by Ahnna's hand. More schemes on Katarina's part, it seems. But why are you here and not at Verwyrd?"

The truth was a nonstarter, but with both his cousin and his uncle watching him expectantly, he had to give them something. James swiftly weighed what Lestara may or may not know, then said, "Carlo captured me in the Blackreaches, and Katarina imprisoned me in the Furnace."

Lestara gasped and caught hold of her chair for balance before slowly lowering herself onto the cushion. "Stars, Jamie! How did you escape?"

"I know how he escaped!" his uncle roared, clapping James so hard on the back he staggered. "My spies recently reported that Riomar was in an uproar because of an explosion in the Furnace that resulted in a convict escaping. The Beast himself pursued, only to be killed on the beaches of Riomar. It was James who dressed the Crimson Widow in black. The stars demanded blood vengeance for your mother and uncle, and you delivered. Stars, but you delivered! Tell me everything!"

"Carlo tried to apprehend me, so I killed him."

"Jamie, Jamie, Jamie! Never a man to brag!" His uncle pushed him down on one of the chairs and poured him a cup of ale from the pitcher on the table. "While I usually appreciate actions speaking louder than words, in this case, I wish to hear every detail. How did you come to be captured? How did you blow up the Furnace? And for the love of the stars themselves, give me every detail of your battle against the Beast of Amarid!"

James took a long mouthful of his ale to buy himself time. While Lestara was likely another pawn in Alexandra's schemes, she and the dowager queen were still inherently allied by the fact both of them wanted to keep William on the throne. Ahnna's plans would harm Lestara almost as much as Alexandra, and this unexpected conviviality between her and Ronan made him deeply uneasy. He was best served relaying the truth that spies would have reported. "Ahnna Kertell fled into the Blackreaches, and I pursued. A rockslide separated me from my men, but I pressed on alone."

"Did you catch her?" Lestara demanded. "Did you kill her?"

"No, Carlo and his men had come across the border. They captured me and brought me to Riomar."

Lestara's expression turned to disgust. "The Amaridians must have aided her. All of Harendell's spies report that Katarina and Aren are allies. See, Father? I told you, yet you refused to believe me. But I've no doubt you'll believe James." The last came out with an air of petulance.

"James has said nothing of alliances, girl. He has said very little at all, while you jabber on like a jaybird."

Lestara's face soured. "Father, I am queen of Harendell. Accord me the respect I deserve."

His uncle laughed. "This is not Harendell, *daughter*. Do not speak to me as though I were one of your subjects, especially given William has banished you from court."

"He didn't banish me." She twisted her skirts with her hands. "He sent me here to protect me from Keris Veliant."

"The only injury Veliant delivered upon you was the truth of your actions. You made your own bed, girl."

*Perhaps not entirely convivial.*

If Katarina had lied about his death, then she had likely kept Ahnna's fate secret as well. "I don't know what befell Ahnna Kertell." He could give his uncle the truth later when they were alone. "I escaped the Furnace with several other prisoners, but ran afoul of Carlo on the beach, where I killed him and escaped on a stolen pleasure ship." To appease his uncle, he added, "The Beast and I dueled. I stabbed him in the chest and then slit his throat."

"Good, good." His uncle gave an approving nod. "You have struck a blow against the Crimson Widow. The stars will look upon you with favor, nephew."

Lestara's jaw worked back and forth, his cousin clearly struggling to contain her questions.

"Not that we are not glad for your company, Jamie," his uncle said. "But why are you in Cardiff and not Harendell?"

Yet more lies, because banished or not, James didn't trust Lestara with the truth. "I came by way of the North Sea and had to earn my passage with hard labor."

"So here not because you favor your old uncle but because you are hungry and broke."

"Can it not be both?"

Ronan laughed and then drained his cup. "No matter the reason, it is good to see your face, Jamie. Caly swore you lived, but I have less nerve for trusting in things I cannot see than I once did."

Lestara's eyes darkened at mention of Queen Calythra. There was no love lost between her and her mother, and James knew that his cousin blamed Caly for turning Ronan against her. James had always been of the opinion that Lestara had done a fine job of doing that on her own.

"How fortunate that I am here, then," Lestara said. "William will not begrudge my return if I have you with me. His heart was broken when the spies brought word of your death, and seeing you will bring him out of his despair." The wind howled down the chimney, sending sparks flying, and Lestara shivered before adding, "It will bring all of Verwyrd out of its grief if I return with you."

She was ever and always consistent in her self-interest.

"I'm surprised to find you here in such advanced condition, Your Grace," James said, the title still tasting sour on his tongue. "I can understand why William wanted you away from Veliant, but we have many estates that would offer both protection and proximity to Verwyrd."

Lestara preened, smoothing a hand over her round belly. "It is because William trusts me implicitly that he asked me to take on the important role of maintaining the alliance between Cardiff and Harendell. In times of war, we must keep our allies close." She smiled at both of them. "And our families closer."

"The alliance is strong, then?" James hated how part of him hoped relations were faltering, because it would make what he needed to do easier. "Trade flows?"

His uncle grunted. "Trade flows both ways, but that is only half the bargain. Edward promised war against Amarid, but William cares for nothing but claiming the bridge. He is like a toddler in pursuit of a toy."

"Not forgotten, Father," Lestara soothed. "It is only that the matter of the bridge is so pressing. Ithicana has caused terrible harm to Harendell, but worse still, Aren's foolishness is doing harm not just to the nations of the north, but also to Maridrina and Valcotta. Ithicana needs to be ruled by a nation with a strong and steady hand. Once that has been achieved, William will look to punish Amarid for its crimes."

It seemed that Lestara had taken in Alexandra's lies as much as William.

"Is Amarid Ithicana's ally or not, girl?" Ronan snapped. "You speak out of both sides of your mouth, in one breath claiming that Katarina and Aren conspire in all things and in the next that vengeance must be delivered separately."

He slammed his cup down on the table, infamous temper rearing its head. "You speak of the importance of family, but you, the *trusted* queen of King William, seem to care little for avenging the murder of your own blood." He leveled a finger. "Siobhan and Cormac were your aunt and uncle, yet you care more for a Harendellian whose only ties to you are words spoken before the representatives of a god you don't believe in. You say you value this alliance, daughter, yet as always, it seems you only care for achieving your own ends!"

"I am bound by blood to the Ashfords through the babe in my belly!" Lestara shouted back. "The heir to Harendell is your grandson, which means he is your blood, too!"

"Of that, there is no doubt," Ronan answered. "As to whether he is William's . . ." He lifted one shoulder. "I would not be surprised if the child was born with eyes of Veliant blue. All know the ways of the *queen of Harendell*, her only gift that which is between her legs. Perhaps that is why William sent you here, girl."

James grimaced, disliking this line of abuse. If his uncle were to call Lestara out for anything, it should be for treason and murder. She'd had no choice about wedding Silas, certainly no choice about bedding him, and James suspected Royce Veliant was a conquest made out of desperation. Besides, Lestara had been too long away from Maridrina for the babe in her belly to be a Veliant.

Even so, she paled at her father's insults, and James took pity on his cousin. "You sold your own daughter to a man who used women like broodmares, Uncle. Don't forget that."

Ronan gave him an irritated glare, but then a female voice spoke. "Your son will be king of Harendell, Lestara, and the bones sing that the Ashford line will rule the Twisted Throne for generations to come. The stars have always favored you, and they favor you still, but remember that they are souls. And souls can be fickle if they feel betrayed."

James turned to find Calythra walking toward them. The queen of Cardiff embodied everything that Harendell feared about astromancy. She was dressed in furs and her face was painted with the constellation of her ancestors, the skulls dangling from her headdress brushing against the wrinkled skin of her cheeks. Her hair was as gray as steel and her eyes as gold as the metal itself. While Ronan's first wives were political matches that yielded many children, he had eventually married Caly out of love, the pair having been close since they were young. She was equal parts beloved and feared in Cardiff, and while Caly cared little for politics, his uncle heeded her every word when she deigned to opine on matters of state.

James had known Caly all his life, and he respected her deeply. Yet she also made his skin crawl as though a thousand fire ants danced upon it, magic seeming all too real in her presence. It was not lost on him that he'd not heard a door open or shut; the queen seemed to have appeared from nowhere.

"I was sitting in the corner, Jamie," his aunt said, patting his cheek as she passed. "You just weren't paying attention."

Rather than easing the prickling crawl of his skin, her ability to read his thoughts only made the sensation worse. Especially given that, from her expression, Lestara hadn't known her mother was in the room either.

Caly knelt on the thick rugs before Lestara's chair and took one of her daughter's hands. She turned it over and examined the lines, muttering in Cardiffian, which hardly anyone spoke anymore and which he didn't understand. Lestara understood it, though, and James did not miss how the pulse in Lestara's throat fluttered faster and faster, her fear of her mother palpable.

"I was the one who told you that you would be queen," Caly finally said. "And now you sit at the right hand of the king on the Twisted Throne. Tell me, girl, have the other certainties I whispered in your ear come true?"

"Yes." Lestara was trembling, looking on the verge of tears. "Many have come true."

"So you believe the things I see, yes?"

"Yes." A tear trickled down his cousin's cheek, and James grimaced. There was no love lost between him and Lestara, but he hated seeing her terrified.

"Good." Caly pressed one hand to Lestara's pregnant belly, then withdrew a handful of polished bones from a pouch at her waist with the other. Human finger bones and knuckle joints, for though any bones could be used to cast, James knew the lore that the bones of one's enemies told the clearest truths. Caly bounced them in her hand, then cast them carelessly onto the table. Her voice was soft yet somehow as loud as thunder as she said, "Look."

It was like having someone grab him by the back of the head, forcing his gaze to the bones, but James resisted even when he heard Lestara sob, "I can't cast for the child inside me any more than I can cast for myself. Our fates are yet entwined."

"*I* cast the bones. You can read what they say."

Lestara shook her head, her whole body trembling and the hair at her temples dampening with sweat.

Caly snorted in disgust. "James, prove you still remember what you were taught and read the cast."

Against his will, James looked at the table. Except it was not the finger bones his eyes fixed upon, but the tiny skull in the center of them that he swore had not been there a moment before. Above the skull, set in a pattern in the shape of a *W,* lay finger bones, and for all the world it looked to him as though the skull wore a crown. "Power," he whispered, forcing himself to look at the other patterns. "Influence. Leadership. Justice . . . no, *revenge.*"

"What else?"

He saw many things, but James gestured to the skull with the crown. "I've never seen this pattern before, but the meaning seems obvious enough." He pointed to bones that sat in a *V* shape. "A fork in the road, a critical choice. Though there is no way to know whether it speaks of Lestara or her child."

Lestara overcame her fear and looked down, and a gasp tore from her lips as she saw the crowned skull. Caly said nothing, only pulled a bag of blue sand from her belt and let it trickle through her fingers, creating an outline around the fallen bones. When she finished, James's stomach dropped, because it perfectly replicated the shape of Harendell on a map.

"God have mercy," James muttered, rubbing at his temples. His head had begun to throb.

"There is no God here, boy," Caly answered. "You know that."

The queen of Cardiff then rounded on her husband. "Do you still question the legitimacy of the child?"

Ronan stared at the skull, his normally rosy cheeks pale. "No." He then gave a sharp shake of his head. "Peering into the future takes a toll, Lestara. You should seek your bed and the rest that comes with it."

It wasn't a suggestion but an order, and James felt a touch of surprise when Lestara rose to her feet. She nodded to her father, but lowered her head in respect and submission to Caly before walking swiftly from the room. James scanned the corners to ensure there were no additional hidden listeners, and then settled more deeply in his chair.

Caly was staring at him, her head slightly cocked and her golden eyes unblinking. Yet she said nothing, and it was his uncle who broke the silence. "You didn't come from the northern passage, lad. You came off a Cardiffian ship sailed by sailors who know the wind and the waves but whose skin best knows the southern sun. Lestara is gone now, so spit out the truth."

*Your son will be king of Harendell, Lestara.* Caly's words repeated in James's head even as his plans crumbled to dust.

Except what choice did he have but to try? For Ahnna, he would take any risk. "Ahnna didn't murder my father. Alexandra did, and she inflicted her own injuries so no one would suspect her."

His uncle's eyes narrowed but Caly only sipped at her ale, not moving from where she sat on the rugs as Ronan said, "Cormac said you were infatuated with the Ithicanian woman, but I did not think it was so deep a sentiment that you'd be this easily manipulated."

"The only thing Ahnna is guilty of is being the scapegoat in Alexandra's schemes." James drew in a deep breath. "Alexandra knows everything. So do not sit there and say that she didn't have a motive to kill my father, *especially* given the way he treated her their entire marriage. Especially given the way he treated William."

"There is nothing fiercer than a woman protecting a child," Caly whispered, staring at the contents of her cup. "The she-wolf will sink low and then rise high."

Tension crackled, but she said nothing more.

James took a sip from his cup, steadying himself. "Alexandra is allied with Katarina. She was a silent player in Silas's gambit to take the bridge, but their ambition to possess it didn't die with him. Yet their alliance goes back much farther than that. All the way back to when Alexandra believed that the only way to my father's heart would be to kill the woman he loved, and Katarina saw the opportunity to gain leverage over Harendell's young queen. This is not speculation on my part, but a fact confirmed by Katarina herself just before she imprisoned me in the Furnace. They conspired together to kill my mother, and I've no doubt they conspired together to kill Uncle Cormac. I may have struck a blow by killing Carlo, but his death will not have sated the stars' desire for vengeance."

"Because it will not be you who sates them," Caly whispered. "It will not be you who strikes the killing blow."

No one spoke. No one even seemed to breathe, and James swore the fire itself fell silent in the tension.

The metal of his uncle's cup abruptly collapsed beneath his grip, ale sloshing over his hand and clothes, but Ronan didn't seem to notice. Only stared at James, unblinking, like a bear just before the charge.

"Edward was certain," his uncle whispered. "Amaridian poison. Members of Katarina's dark guild spotted racing away from Verwyrd. Nothing could be tied to Alexandra—he looked and he looked hard, which is why rumors flew that Alexandra was behind Siobhan's death."

"Katarina made certain to look guilty," James replied. "Leverage over a dead queen is no leverage at all, and my father would have hanged Alexandra for killing my mother. But Lestara is wrong to believe that Harendell will ever take revenge on Amarid, Uncle. My mother will only fade from memory until she is never again mentioned at all, because that is how Alexandra has planned it."

Ronan abruptly hurled his ruined cup at the hearth, the metal clanging as it hit the stone. Then he doubled over and wept. "Oh, Siobhan. My sweet little sister, I am so sorry. I am so very sorry."

James had seen his uncle rage with such violence that everyone went running. Had seen him laugh with such force that the walls shook. But never had he seen King Ronan Crehan weep, and he didn't know what to do. Didn't know what to say, because while he'd wanted his uncle to rage against Alexandra for her crimes, he had not wanted *this*.

Guilt settled in James's chest, so it took a moment before he realized that Caly was staring at him with her uncanny eyes.

Without him noticing, she'd regathered her bones, and quick as a snake, she reached out to grab James's hand, her long nails tearing open the cut healing on his palm as she cast the bones. "When you were a babe, I read your future, but Siobhan forbade me from ever doing it again, and I honored her request. But I think it is time to see what your mother will tell us from the grave."

James ripped free, blood dripping from his hand, but his anger didn't stop him from looking at the bones scattered across the table.

"Your heart is bound to the south." Caly rose to her feet and circled the table. "To Ithicana's princess, as Cormac believed, but he was wrong to call it an infatuation. You love her, nephew."

"She's my wife." Only a fool would lie to Caly's face, and in truth, James wanted them to know that Ahnna was his, now and until he drew his last breath.

"Death has always surrounded you," she murmured, fingers ghosting over the bones. "Tragedy and heartache too, but this is new, Jamie." Her hand paused over four bones that had fallen interwoven. "Do you know what this means?"

*Sacrifice.*

"Yes," she whispered, though James had not spoken aloud. "But what you will give up, I do not know."

His jaw worked from side to side, and though he did not want to ask, the question needed to be voiced. "What else do you see?"

His aunt walked around the table three more times, and then her golden eyes locked on his. "I see many things, nephew, but there is only one that will matter to you: Ahnna Kertell will never be queen of Harendell."

# 77

# JAMES

James didn't argue with Calythra. He told himself it was because he didn't believe in magic. Told himself that it was all speculation carefully worded so that any number of circumstances would make it seem as though the foretelling had come true.

Except the truth in his heart was that if the bones revealed a different path than Ahnna ruling Harendell, James would fucking change it. She was meant to lead—meant to change the world—and he would not allow the stars to deny her.

"I am weary," Caly said, rubbing at her temples. "Ronan, I will leave you to do what you will with all Siobhan has told you. Heed your sister, not sentiment."

His uncle took his wife's hand and kissed her knuckles. "Rest. But ensure Lestara is in her rooms and under watch. It was your daughter's arrival that shifted the winds, my love."

*Your daughter too*, James wanted to say, but he bit his tongue. It was said that when Lestara was born, she took all the darkness in Calythra's soul into her own spirit. Whether that was true, none could say, but there was no denying that even before the sacking of Vencia, his cousin had left death in her wake. No one dead by her hand, but it seemed that if Lestara touched a person's life, the chances of them surviving diminished. Accidents. Suicides. Sickness. Many claimed she was cursed. More still claimed that she was the one doing the cursing. The only thing that united everyone was a desire to be as far from Lestara as possible, which was why she'd been traded to Silas Veliant in a meaningless agreement for furs.

And it could not be denied that *nothing* good had come to Maridrina while Lestara had stood within its borders.

"I will rest in her room and watch her myself," Caly answered. "She is my darkness."

The queen of Cardiff left the room on silent feet, and James said, "Have you ever considered that Lestara is the way she is because you raised her to believe she was cursed? That maybe if you loved her as you do your other children, she'd have turned out differently?"

"I do love my daughter," Ronan answered. "But some creatures are born wrong, and Lestara is one of them. Your father was a fool to allow her into his house. A greater fool still to allow her to claim the heart of your brother. But we have greater villains than your cousin to discuss."

His uncle rose to his feet. "Let us go out into the air. I need to taste the sea and seek the guidance of the stars while we discuss our path forward."

James pulled up his hood and followed his uncle out into the corridor. Theryn and Waynne stood guard, but both followed as they wove through the warren that was this castle, rising narrow staircases that led up and up, and finally out a narrow door onto the battlements.

"Cormac spoke highly of the Ithicanian princess," his uncle said as they moved to rest their elbows on the old stone, staring out over the village below and the expanse of the bay beyond. "Said she was beautiful and fierce as a lioness."

"Cormac also tried to kill her."

His uncle shrugged. "She lives and your uncle does not."

Typical Cardiffian pragmatism. "Ithicana is not Cardiff's enemy. For a long time, I saw them as the greatest obstacle to peace between

Harendell and Cardiff, and in doing so, I made them into villains. My father did not feel that way. His methods were flawed, but in his heart, he knew that trade and peace could flow both ways, north and south. He believed in a greater alliance than any of us, and I think he had the right of it. Alexandra and Katarina have exploited the cracks I formed between Harendell and Ithicana, and they aim to take the bridge for themselves. If they succeed, you know they will look north not for peace but for conquest."

His uncle gave a soft grunt of agreement. "Tell me everything, lad. From the beginning."

The wind rose higher, coming in fierce off the sea and smelling of snow, and beneath its roar, James told Ronan *almost* everything. He finished with, "We believe that if Cardiff can draw Alexandra's eye—and Harendell's army—north, Katarina's ambition will get the better of her when Maridrina offers her a trade deal. If Alexandra and Katarina turn on each other, neither will have the ability to keep control of the bridge, and Ithicana can retain its autonomy."

His uncle was silent for a long time, and then he said, "Your mother's dream was peace between Cardiff and Harendell, Jamie, and she gave her life for it. For decades, I worked with Edward to achieve that goal, and we made it a reality. Now you ask me to throw that away for the sake of Ithicana?"

"It's not a reality while Alexandra holds power," James argued. "Once Ithicana is crushed and the bridge secure, you know she and Katarina will turn on Cardiff."

"Oh, aye, I don't disagree. But why make an enemy out of every Harendellian when there is only one I have a grievance with? There's no sense in that, Jamie. But you've lost sight of reason—love does that to a man."

"Uncle—"

"I know you're Edward's heir, boy. I know that crown should be yours by every right, which was why I worked with Edward to give it to you. But Caly has said Ahnna will not be queen, which means you will not be king. I'll not pursue an impossibility that comes with such a high cost."

Frustration built in James's chest, but also fear. By now, the

Amaridians would be spreading across Ithicana like maggots on a corpse. Ahnna needed him to do this. Needed him to win this. "It's nothing more than a handful of bones and a mouthful of twisted words, Uncle! Lives are at stake, and yet you wish to make decisions based on yet another of Caly's visions."

The blow came fast and hard, sending James staggering.

"You mind your tongue when speaking about my woman, lad," Ronan said, his eyes dark. "You will show respect, or I'll show you your grave."

James wiped blood from his split lip, grimacing.

"I understand the plight of Ithicana." His uncle returned to resting his elbows on the stone, the breeze ruffling the fur of his cloak. "But the answer is not to take that threat and deliver it to Cardiff's doorstep, which is what you're asking for. If I back you for king and we inevitably fail, what then? War. Burnings. Hunger. Poverty. It will all come raging back, and everything we suffered to achieve will be ash on the wind. Better to set our aim on the woman who is our true enemy."

"That's your plan?" James demanded. "To send assassins in the night for Alexandra? Because I assure you, if you murder his mother, William will never let it go."

"No. No assassins." His uncle spread his palms wide on the stone fortifications of his castle, seeming not to feel the cold at all as he added, "We will give William the truth. We will tell him of his mother's plots, her alliances, her crimes, and demand justice. We will demand he execute Alexandra."

"And if he won't?"

"I have his wife and his heir in my possession," Ronan replied. "I will not give them up until he gives me Alexandra's head."

Fear was choking James now, for his uncle's plan made all too much sense if one cared not for the fate of Ithicana. "And what about Katarina? She's just as guilty."

"Once Alexandra is dead, together, William and I will move against Amarid."

"And return Ithicana's sovereignty?"

The wind blew over them, stealing the warmth from his flesh as he waited for his uncle to respond. Finally, Ronan said, "You'll still be in your brother's good graces given you won't have tried to take his crown, so with luck, he'll give you Ithicana. Which means your woman will be queen."

How had it circled back around to this?

"I don't want to rule Ithicana," James snarled. "I don't belong there! You and my father wanted me to be king. That was your plan. I'm finally willing, and now you refuse to back me?"

His uncle gripped his shoulders. "Jamie, if I had my way, you'd sit on the Twisted Throne. It was a goal Edward and I shared, for you are a better man than your brother by far. But if Caly says it will not be, then it will not be, and I will not take my people to war for a dream that was not destined to become reality. Go back to Ithicana to fight and die at your woman's side if that is what you must do. Better yet, take her and go somewhere no one knows your name. Ithicana will fade into history, but you'll be alive."

Giving James's shoulders a squeeze, King Ronan of Cardiff gestured for his guards to follow and then disappeared inside the castle, leaving James with only the frosty wind for company.

A sudden wave of exhaustion fell over him, and James sat with his back to the stone wall, elbows resting on his knees.

He'd failed her. He'd fucking failed her.

It wouldn't be long until the Maridrinians reached out and made a deal with the Amaridians, and with Alexandra's attention fully fixed on the south, Katarina wouldn't risk trying to hide from her that Ithicana had fallen. And William ... James wanted to believe that, if given the chance, his brother would hear the truth about Alexandra and turn on her, but if her schemes had won him the bridge? James did not think that William would put a noose around Alexandra's neck for the sake of Lestara or his unborn child, because what need had he of trade with the north if he had Ithicana's bridge under his control? He was more likely to take his bride back by force, or to just divorce her and marry someone new.

Why couldn't Ronan see that this was no solution? Why didn't he understand that doing nothing while Ithicana fell only meant that he'd stand alone with the two queens turned on him? Why didn't he realize that he was only delaying the inevitable? Why was he allowing visions and prophecy and *fucking nonsense* to make his decisions for him?

It didn't matter. Ronan was not the answer, which meant James had to find another path.

The solution came to him like a punch to the stomach. It was time he remembered that he was Edward Ashford's son, which meant scheming was in his blood.

Going back into the castle, James returned to his uncle's study. "I'm leaving. I'm going to Verwyrd to try to talk sense into William."

"Alexandra will have you killed the moment she discovers you have returned. She knows you are a threat to William's reign," his uncle replied. "Better to return to Ithicana and your woman, no?"

"If I fail Ahnna, there is no point in me going back to her," James replied. "I need two good horses. Time is of the essence."

"If that is your decision, I won't stop you." His uncle rose to his feet and went to the door. "Have two swift horses saddled and supplied. My nephew rides for Verwyrd tonight."

"Yes, Your Grace," Waynne said, bowing low before departing.

"I would say my farewells to Lestara before I go," James said. "Given it will be some time before I see her again."

His uncle shrugged. "After you tell your brother the truths about his mother, you might also give him my terms: If he wishes to have his wife and child returned to him, he must send me Alexandra's head."

"I'll give him the message." Bowing to his uncle, James left the room. A servant woman guided him to Lestara's chambers and carried on down the hallway.

James lifted his fist to knock, only for the door to open, Caly standing in the entrance. The queen of Cardiff gave him a long stare, then barked, "You've a visitor, girl. Wake yourself."

Without saying anything to James, Caly left the room. James shut the heavy door behind him.

Lestara sat in her bed, the lamp on the bedside table casting a soft glow. "James?"

A life in the Sky Palace had made him wary of listeners, so he crossed the room to the bed and kept his voice low. "If you had to, could you ride and ride swiftly?"

His cousin's eyes narrowed. "I'm pregnant, not an invalid. But why would I have to?"

She wasn't stupid. Was nowhere close to it, which meant manipulating her would require cleverness and as much adherence to the truth as possible. "Alexandra murdered my father. Ahnna was just a scapegoat."

Lestara's eyes widened, her mouth dropping open. "You can't be serious. Why would she do such a thing?"

The next part was the lie.

"Katarina blackmailed her." He sat on the edge of the bed. "It was Alexandra who killed my mother, and Katarina has proof. She's been blackmailing Alexandra all these long years, and she forced her to murder my father as a last effort to forestall the alliance with Cardiff. Katarina is a braggart, and after Carlo captured me and put me in the Furnace, she took a great deal of joy in taunting me with her plans. She's using Alexandra to manipulate William."

"To what end?"

"The bridge." He pursed his lips. "Katarina used Alexandra to threaten the bridge, and then pretended to offer an alliance to the Ithicanians. But it was a trick. By now, they are all dead or dying, and Amarid has control of the bridge. William has no idea, and Alexandra has been instructed to keep it that way or Katarina will tell everyone the truth about my father's murder."

Lestara's face hardened. "The bridge is meant to be *William's*. He is to be Master of the Bridge, and my son after him. Katarina is a fool if she believes this can stand."

"I told everything to Ronan under the belief that he'd march with William to attack Amarid, but he couldn't see past his goddamned rage over my mother's death. He insists that William give up Alexandra for execution, and he's going to hold you hostage until William agrees."

Silence stretched, and James watched the wheels in his cousin's mind turn. His cousin, who'd been used and betrayed by every man in her life, would expect no different from William. "He won't execute his mother to get me back. William is . . . *bound* to her." A tear ran down her cheek. "I hate her, James. She is so cruel to me."

"Which is why we have to put a stop to her. But we have to do it carefully." He leaned closer. "Katarina's dark guild is hunting for me because I'm a liability, but worse, Alexandra will put an end to anyone she thinks knows about her crimes. We need William to learn that Katarina holds the bridge, but I don't think I can get to him."

"I can," Lestara whispered. "Alexandra won't suspect me. She dismisses me entirely."

"Then let's take advantage. Convince him to attack Amarid. Katarina will be forced to withdraw from Ithicana because she'll need the manpower. She'll retaliate by revealing everything about Alexandra in an attempt to undermine William, and it will be the people who force him to execute Alexandra for her crimes, not you and not Cardiff." James gripped his cousin's hands, staring into her amber eyes. "You won't just be protecting yourself and your child, you'll be giving our family the vengeance that the stars demand."

Her brow furrowed, and he could see that she was tempted by the idea of proving her parents wrong in their opinion of her. Of finally earning their respect. "I know I have done dark deeds, James, and I regret my actions more than you know. For as long as I can remember, I have been told that I am a curse. A scourge. And maybe I am, but I don't want that same curse to touch my child." More tears rolled down her face. "I don't want people to look at him the way they look at me."

"Then help me stop Alexandra. Help me rip the bridge out of Katarina's grasp." He tightened his hands. "Give your son the legacy he deserves."

"You stand to gain in this as well, cousin," Lestara said softly. "You will have vengeance for your parents' murder, but I think you also desire to strike a blow against the woman who has treated you so poorly all your life. I know you hate Alexandra as much as I do."

It was all true enough, so James only nodded. "Our biggest obstacle is Ronan. He sees the easy path to vengeance as ransoming you and the child for Alexandra's head, which means we need to sneak you out of the palace. I have horses waiting. We'll have hours of head start before dawn, and I know the land well. All we have to do is get you across the border, and your father won't dare pursue. Can you get out without your mother realizing?"

Lestara gave a dark smile. "I grew up in this palace, so I know every secret tunnel like the back of my hand. As to my mother . . . I picked up a trick or two in Verwyrd. Whatever Caly sees tonight will be relegated to her dreams."

"How long do you need?"

"I'll meet you by the graveyard in an hour."

James left the room, shutting the door behind him. Caly was leaning against the wall in the corridor, and she eyed him with her uncanny eyes. "Ronan says you're going to Verwyrd to try to reason with William."

"Yes." It was the most answer he could manage given that it was because of her that Ronan refused to help. He started down the hallway, hoping to escape, but his aunt followed him.

"Quite a pivot, Jamie. You came here asking for aid in taking your brother's crown, and now you leave with the intention of courting his mercy."

A sudden wave of exhaustion passed over James, and he rubbed a hand over his face, finding it abruptly impossible to untangle the truths he had told from the lies. "What choice do I have, Caly? My wife and her people are hiding in the jungles of storm-battered islands while Amarid pours over Ithicana like a swarm of roaches. The Ithicanians don't have the strength to fight back, and our plan is in shambles because of *Ronan's* pivot." The last came out as a near shout, because his uncle had been the one person he'd been certain about and now he had to rely upon the one person he was least certain about. "William is my only hope. Ahnna's only hope. Ithicana's only hope, so I will risk everything to get to him and pray to God, fate, and the *fucking* stars he is the man I need him to be."

Caly tilted her head, the tiny skulls of her headdress swaying, golden eyes unblinking. "It will not be the acts of men that sway the stars," she whispered, and without another word she turned and walked away.

# 78
# KERIS

"I REGRET TO inform you that I must be the bringer of bad news."

Keris crossed his arms where he stood in William's study, Zarrah at his side. "Bad news beyond the fact you are keeping us locked up against our wills?"

"Espionage is a crime, my good man," the king of Harendell said after looking to Alexandra as though for encouragement. "If the pair of you were anyone other than who you are, I'd have your heads for it. Instead, all you have to suffer is being treated as honored guests until this nasty business is over. Which, in truth, is why I'm here."

Unease gathered in Keris's stomach, and reluctantly, he looked to Zarrah. Her expression was fixed, but he knew she felt the same. "Spit it out, then."

"We won't be going to war with Ithicana," William said, then he grimaced. "Because there is no one to go to war *with*."

It felt as though the temperature in the room abruptly plummeted, and Keris struggled to ask, "What do you mean?"

"It seems there was a reason for Ithicana's silence of late. Plague has swept the nation, and reports say that the casualties are high." William sighed. "May God have mercy on their souls."

Zarrah sucked in a sharp breath and pressed a hand to her stomach, but all Keris felt was rage. "You're lying."

Alexandra pushed a folded piece of paper across the table, and Keris's eyes latched onto Sarhina's seal. With shaking hands, he picked it up, reading and rereading the lines, but his eyes kept catching on certain words. *Plague. Quarantine. Fatal.*

The page fell from his hand back to the table, and next to him, Zarrah whispered, "This is your fault. You blockaded them and starved them. What did you think would happen?"

William's lip curled. "Blame Aren, if you must blame someone. Though he's probably dead."

The world turned red, and Keris balled up a fist to strike, only to be dragged backward by Cavendish. "You keep giving us more reasons to execute you, Veliant."

It was just noise in Keris's ears, because if his family was dead, he'd never forgive himself.

"Weather willing, we'll send in ships to investigate," William said. "But if it's plague, we'll need to keep our distance until it runs its course."

"Or you could help them," Zarrah shouted, leveling a finger at Alexandra. "You claim to be a follower of the faith, but you will be judged for this. The deaths of an entire nation stain your hands red, because this is all the result of your greed. There will be a reckoning."

Alexandra had to have done this. Had to have somehow sent sickness into Ithicana the same way she sent infected cows into Valcotta. They couldn't be dead. Lara. Aren. Delia . . . Keris clenched his teeth, feeling sick on grief and anger and guilt.

William coughed, then took a sip of his drink. "Emotions are high, which is understandable, but practically speaking, something will need to be done about the bridge. Trade must flow, and the fact remains that we cannot allow the bridge to be managed as it has been in the past."

"You greedy Harendellian prick." Keris struggled in Cavendish's grip, but more guards moved to restrain him. "You did this. You *fucking* killed them."

"No, he did not." Lestara's voice filled the room, and Keris turned in his grip to watch her enter the room, dressed in a gown marred by travel. "But I know who did."

# 79

# JAMES

IT HAD BEEN one of the most grueling ordeals of his existence getting Lestara to Verwyrd, and James had never felt more anxiety in his life than he did watching her ride alone across the bridge. Everything he cared about rested in the hands of a woman he had no reason to trust beyond the fact that they shared an enemy.

The type of hate that Lestara felt for Alexandra was not the sort that could be feigned, but more than anything, she feared the dowager queen. Lestara was Cardiffian. Her reputation was dark beyond measure. But worst of all, Lestara was of Edward's choosing, and that was something Alexandra would never tolerate.

"I'm only safe as long as I'm pregnant," Lestara had told him time and again on the journey, pressing her hand protectively to her stomach. "She won't harm William's son. But once he's born . . ."

Hate, James could trust. Fear, he could trust. Yet as days passed and the Sky Palace remained silent, it became clear to him that he'd put his trust in the wrong place. Either Lestara had betrayed him or

Alexandra had stymied her, but regardless, Ahnna and Ithicana still stood on a knife's edge.

Which meant he needed to find a way to speak to William himself.

———

GEORGIE TROTTED HIS horse out of the gates, heading into Verwyrd, passing James where he stood hidden in the shadows. James took in his old friend's expression, which was as grim as he'd ever seen it. Shadows of exhaustion darkened the skin beneath Georgie's eyes, and his cheeks were hollow, as though he'd gone weeks or longer eating not quite enough food. Alexandra's schemes had taken a toll on everyone, even if no one knew she was the one to blame.

With his hood up, James followed Georgie through the streets of Verwyrd to the large home belonging to the Cavendish family. His father, the Earl of Elgin, rarely left their estates in the north due to poor health, so the only other people likely to be here were the servants.

James climbed the stone fence, dropping to the soft turf right as Georgie dismounted his horse and led the gelding into the stables. Glancing around the shadowed yard to ensure no one was watching, James followed his friend inside.

"Boy!" George shouted. "Boy, where are you?"

James rested a hand on Georgie's back. "Give the stable boy the night off, will you?"

His friend jumped as though he'd been stung by a bee, his horse sidling sideways. Georgie reached for his sword, only to freeze at the sight of James's face. "Jamie? Good God, everyone thinks you're dead!"

"Let's keep it that way."

Boots pattered against stone, and Georgie shoved James into a stall before the stable boy appeared. "There you are, lad. Here's a silver to go buy yourself a drink with the other boys."

"You don't want me to stable your horse first, my lord?" the boy asked.

"No, you go on. I need some good honest labor to clear my head tonight."

The boy was silent for a long moment, which was fair given that Georgie was not one for menial tasks, but then he said, "My thanks, my lord. God bless you and King William!"

"God bless," Georgie muttered, watching the boy disappear and then stepping into the stall where James was hidden. "Where have you bloody been, Jamie? Everyone thinks that you were killed in the Blackreaches after you went running off alone like a madman."

It seemed that, for better or worse, Lestara had kept the truth that he was alive close.

"I was captured by the Beast," James replied. "Imprisoned in the Furnace."

"My God!" Georgie gave a slow shake of his head, and then his eyes brightened. "It was you who killed that one-balled menace, wasn't it?"

"Yes, during my escape."

"But where have you been since? You've been gone for a long time."

James's throat tightened on the truth. Admitting *anything* felt like a risk, but Georgie had been his best friend his entire life. They'd fought at each other's backs in countless battles, spent endless hours in the worst conditions in the Lowlands together, and Georgie had *always* had his back. He trusted Georgie with his life, but more than that, James needed allies who had sway in Harendell, and the Cavendishes were the most powerful family after the Ashfords. No one would ignore Georgie—they couldn't afford to.

"Alexandra killed my father," he forced himself to say. "My mother as well. Ahnna is innocent."

His friend's expression tightened. "They say the women of Cardiff are witches, but Ahnna Kertell makes me question whether Ithicana has a better claim to the title. You saw her with the bloody knife in her hand, and yet now you believe her innocent?"

"It wasn't her." James gripped his friend's shoulders. "Alexandra orchestrated my father's murder and framed Ahnna, and that's only the beginning of what she's done."

"Says who? Ahnna? God, Jamie, she must be a sorceress in bed to make you believe this bullshit."

"Katarina confirmed it and more before she locked me in her prison."

George shook his head in disgust. "Right. You want me to take the word of the Crimson Widow, and that Ithicanian whore—"

"Don't call her that."

James's grip tightened to the point Georgie winced and said, "Fine. But I need an explanation. A full explanation, mind you, because a lot has happened in your absence."

"There's no time. I need your help," James said. "I need to speak with William without Alexandra knowing, and I need you there to witness."

"You want me to help you accuse Alexandra of murder?"

"Yes." James ran a gloved hand over his head, relieved to have his friend on his side. "If you're there, he'll have to listen."

Georgie huffed out a breath. "Or he'll just cut *my* head off." When James's lips parted to say that was highly unlikely, his friend interrupted him with a wave of the hand. "Yes, yes. I know he won't do that, but I also don't think that he'll turn on Alexandra so easily. He's a mummy's boy, Jamie. Always has been and always will be. We need hard proof if you want anyone to believe that Alexandra stabbed herself *three* goddamned times in order to frame Ahnna for the king's murder. Who stabs themselves? That's madness!"

James grimaced, because that was precisely why Alexandra's actions had worked so well on him. "She didn't kill my father herself, Georgie. For one, I don't think she's strong enough to have managed it, and two, she'd have been covered in blood, but Ahnna said she wasn't. I think Alexandra watched the deed be done, but someone else had to be the knifeman. If we can find him, or her, and get them to confess, that will be our proof. You have the lists of people in the Sky Palace that night."

George gave a soft snort and then began unsaddling his horse. "Long, *long* lists, Jamie. And short of torture, no one is going to confess to killing the king. I believe you, truly I do. But I'm afraid that if we push this, Alexandra will only find a way to put us both in the ground."

James stepped out of the stall, making room for Georgie, and then followed his friend down the hallway to the tack room.

"Honestly," Georgie said, putting the saddle on a rack and then hanging up the bridle, "part of me questions whether you're better off walking away from this. Go somewhere no one knows your name and live a good life."

Anger filled James's chest. He'd come prepared for his friend not to believe him, but he was not prepared for apathy. "How can you suggest that? How can you stand there and say that I'm better off disappearing rather than seeing my father's murderer brought to justice? Not just my father, but Virginia's father."

"You think I don't know that?" Georgie's cheeks flushed red. "I'd do anything for Ginny. *Anything.* But I fail to see how this benefits her. William has agreed to let me wed her, and she's already begun planning the wedding. He's not going to let the man who condemned his mother marry his sister! If I do this, I stand to lose a great deal."

James clenched his teeth. "So you'll make a life with Ginny while withholding this truth from her? You'll sit down for endless dinners with Alexandra knowing what she has done but not caring, because you got what *you* wanted? Ginny would want to know the truth, and she would not hold it against you if you were the one to reveal it."

"I need to think about it," Georgie snapped. "Goddamn it, Jamie. You've dropped a mountain of shit on me and you won't give me but a heartbeat to think before demanding action? Give me a day to decide what I want to do."

Unease grew in James's stomach. "What will change in the space of a day?"

"Well, with luck I'll have come up with the nerve it takes to rip apart all chances of happiness with the love of my life!" Georgie threw up his hands. "If not a day, at least give me an hour and a bottle of whiskey. Be a friend."

James fought the urge to reach for his sword. "Are we friends, George?"

"Yes." George gripped his shoulders and squeezed. "I have your back until the end. I just need a drink to come to terms with what it will cost me. A drink, I might add, that I'd like to have with you. Let's head into the house and open my father's best. You can stay here and get washed up—you both look and smell like you've been living rough."

There was no one else in Verwyrd who could help him. No one else whom James trusted enough with the truth. If it took a few drinks to get Georgie to commit, it would not kill him.

James allowed Georgie to turn him around and start him down the stable corridor.

Only for a familiar equine head to stick his head over a stall door and whicker at him. "Dippy?"

The gelding tossed his head, and then from the stall next to him, Maven lifted her head and looked through the bars.

Ahnna had asked the fate of her horse when they'd been delivered to the Furnace. Had asked where Dippy had been sent. *On his way back to Harendell with James's mount.* Carlo's voice filled his head. *Those who sought your deaths will understand the message.*

The horses had been sent to Harendell as a message that James and Ahnna had been captured and killed, but they'd not been sent to Alexandra.

They'd been sent to George.

Memory rushed into James's mind, revealing the moment when he'd seen George after his father's murder. George's hair had blood crusted in it, and his throat was covered with a crimson spray that had been smeared, as though he'd tried to clean up hastily. James had believed it Alexandra's blood, but he now realized his error.

The blood had been his father's.

James's hand went to his sword hilt, and he started to draw as he turned.

Only to see a shovel flying toward his head.

James jerked sideways, but the shovel glanced off his temple, pain lancing through his skull as he fell backward. Sparks of light spun in his vision as Georgie lifted the shovel and said as he swung, "I have to say, old friend, Edward put up more of a fight."

# 80
# AHNNA

AHNNA KEPT ENTIRELY still as the snake crawled across her legs, the third to do so in the last hour, although a glance downward told her that at least this one wasn't venomous. It wrapped around her ankle, likely enticed by her warmth, and she whispered, "If you bite me, I will cut off your head and eat you for lunch."

The snake only rested its head on her kneecap, unmoved by the threat.

Perhaps it knew that if Ahnna moved, it would be her who lost her head. Because she was surrounded by Amaridian soldiers, and their ignorance of her presence was only possible with her continued silence.

For endless days, she had watched the Amaridians slowly take over Ithicana. Watched as the Amaridians took the clothes off Ithicanian corpses to make a show for the Harendellian ships enforcing the blockade.

Ahnna had correctly predicted that Katarina had not leapt to inform Alexandra of the success of her plan, but so far, there was no sign that the Harendellians were shifting their focus north to Cardiff to face James's claim to the throne. No sign that the most critical part of their plan was taking effect. The ship that had brought him north had recently returned, so she knew that he'd made it to Cardiff, but there had been no word since. With each passing day, Ahnna's fear for her husband grew in her chest.

But some things, once put in motion, could not be stopped.

And this plan was one of them. Maridrina's parliament was traveling to Midwatch, ready to offer a trade deal with the new Mistress of the Bridge.

*There is still time*, Ahnna told herself even as her heart told her that Katarina would never betray Alexandra with Harendell's focus firmly on Ithicana. *Don't give up hope.*

Voices from above mercifully stole her attention back to the moment.

"Has there been any progress in the hunt for my granddaughter?" Katarina asked.

"I'm afraid not, Your Majesty," a male voice responded. "It's my understanding that Ithicanians often feed their dead to the sea, which is why we haven't found as many dead as we might have anticipated."

Katarina sighed. "It is a mercy that Carlo isn't alive to hear that news. Nina always was his favorite, and he did so hate the ocean."

Ahnna scowled at the false sadness in the queen's voice. She'd sent Nina into Ithicana to make Aren trust her, full well knowing that her granddaughter would fall victim to her poison scheme. A sacrifice that Katarina had been more than willing to make to secure the bridge, and Ahnna wondered if she knew that it was Carlo's anger at her for giving Nina up that had made him an easy mark for Ahnna and James.

"I hate to think of what those Ithicanian monsters did to my granddaughter," Katarina continued. "She would have been a queen for the ages."

And still could be, for the Amaridian princess was very much alive. Nina was on Ornak, a large and heavily fortified island on the very outskirts of Ithicana's territories that had become their interim center of command because it was too far from the bridge to be of particular interest to Amarid. The waters around it were treacherous, and short of a dedicated attack that would cost the attacking force soldiers beyond count, it was impenetrable.

"Is there *any* sign of the Maridrinians?" Katarina's heels thudded as she paced the room. "I want to be gone from this shithole."

"The last report I received was that they were waiting for the tide to be low enough to exit the bridge pier, Your Majesty."

The shithole in question was the Midwatch house. It had an elevated construction to protect it from flooding, which meant that there was space between the ground and the floor. Most of it was constructed from stone, but in deference to recent events, the Ithicanian builders had included escape routes from most of the rooms into the open space Ahnna currently occupied. She had sneaked in through the waterfall and had spent the day lying in the mud with the snakes and the insects, silently listening to Katarina make ready for the Maridrinians' arrival.

As she had done every day since the Crimson Widow had arrived in Ithicana.

A knock sounded on a door, and a moment later, a new male voice said, "The Maridrinian official is here, Your Majesty. He has only a small company of soldiers as escort, and there is no sign they intend violence."

"He may not," Katrina answered. "But Sarhina is another matter. She may not be fooled by the deception that Ithicana was overrun by plague, and might suspect our involvement. We must not forget that she was trained by Silas's Magpie, which means she's more intelligent than most."

"We have scouts watching from lookout points north and south, and heavy forces within the bridge itself," the soldier answered. "Queen Sarhina might suspect, but I do not think that it can be denied that by undercutting her own authority in Maridrina, she lost the ability to take meaningful action."

Katarina gave a soft snort. "Idealistic woman. She's no better than her brother, and God knows that Keris nearly destroyed Maridrina. The time of the Veliants is over."

"As you say, Your Majesty."

"Bring him in straightaway," Katarina ordered. "I have spent enough time in this snake-infested jungle to last me a lifetime."

As if hearing the queen, the snake resting on Ahnna's legs lifted its head, tongue flickering in and out.

Moments later, the space echoed with the heavy thud of boots, and the snake slithered away, threatened by the noise.

"Hector Adrias, member of Maridrina's esteemed parliament," someone intoned.

"Your Majesty," a male with a Maridrinian accent said. "It is an honor. I had assumed I'd be speaking with one of your representatives."

"We have found, of late, that we must do things ourselves if we wish for them to be done correctly," Katarina replied. "We desired to speak with you ourselves so as to judge your intent, for Maridrina has not always acted with honor in recent alliances."

"You refer to the actions of the Veliant kings." The man's voice was stiff, though Ahnna was not certain whether it was from offense or fear. "Maridrina is now governed by a parliament elected by the people, and it acts for the benefit of the people, not to achieve the personal goals of those who hold power by virtue of the blood in their veins."

"We would be one such individual." Katarina's voice dripped with amusement. "But do carry on."

"I speak not of you, Your Majesty," Hector swiftly amended. "Amarid's queen is known to be a fair and just ruler who acts in the interest of her people."

"Is that what we are known for?" Katarina laughed. "I confess, such rumors have never reached our ears, but we appreciate the flattery. Yet what we would appreciate more is if you would speak to what you aim to achieve in this meeting."

"Of course, Your Majesty." The Maridrinian cleared his throat. "As you know, for months now, no trade has passed through the bridge, and with the storm season as violent as it has been, few ships have dared venture across the Tempest Seas. We are aware that this is Harendell's doing in retaliation for the murder of their king, but the nation behind King Edward's murder is no more."

The man coughed and then cleared his throat again, his discomfort palpable even though Ahnna could not see him. "The plague that has decimated the Ithicanians is tragic, Your Majesty, but we also cannot deny the need for trade to flow. While relations with Valcotta are much improved, their herds are suffering from wasting disease and they may face famine of their own. Maridrina has long-established relationships with merchants in Amarid that have been severely disrupted, and this cannot continue. A deal must be struck and the markets reopened, and as Mistress of the Bridge, only you have the power to see this occur. We are at your mercy."

"You are at King William's mercy," Katarina responded. "His blockade on Northwatch remains in place."

Ahnna bit the insides of her cheeks, her heart racing.

"We understand the Harendellians are yet unaware you hold the bridge, Your Majesty," the Maridrinian said. "Although that deception cannot continue for much longer." He coughed. "It strikes us that, given the ongoing conflict between Harendell and Amarid, King William will maintain the blockade and go as far as to attempt to wrest the bridge from Amarid by force. In the meantime, we suggest making hay while the sun shines. We will give you information learned while Maridrina held Ithicana, which will allow you to fill the bridge using access points other than Northwatch. Trade will flow immediately, and while it does, steps can be taken to come to terms with the Harendellians."

Katarina was silent, and Ahnna held her breath, waiting to see if the queen of Amarid would take the bait. *You know you want this*, she silently willed the queen. *You know you don't want to share with Alexandra.*

The silence stretched on and on, and then Katarina spoke. "No. No, we don't think that is how this will go."

Ahnna's stomach dropped.

"You don't want trade to flow?" Hector demanded. "If that is the case, Your Majesty, I fail to see what the point was in claiming the bridge." There was a hint of anger in Hector's voice that indicated he was not quite fooled by lies about plague.

"Calm yourself, sir." Katarina gave a soft laugh. "We will trade, and hunger will be a thing of the past in Maridrina. But we will do it in partnership with Harendell."

*No.* Horror pooled in Ahnna's chest, and she felt as paralyzed as she would be beneath a bed of venomous snakes. It hadn't worked. Katarina hadn't taken the bait, and she and Alexandra were as allied as ever.

Silence stretched, then Hector said, "That would be ideal, Your Majesty, but your two nations are not known for working together."

"Times change," Katarina replied. "Those who fostered the animosity between our nations are in the grave, and those who live on finally have the chance to move toward a new era of collaboration. Harendell and Amarid will share ownership of the bridge, the responsibility of administering trade, and the duty of protecting it."

"I see." Through the ringing of panic in Ahnna's ears, she heard Hector's dismay as he realized his powers to negotiate were not half what he'd believed. "We were not aware."

"It is a new, freshly inked alliance," Katarina said, her tone gloating. "Harendell's representative is late to arrive, but I think it safe to begin negotiations while—"

She broke off as a distant scream filled the air.

No one spoke, and that meant Ahnna heard the clash of swords from down the slope toward the cove. More screams and shouts of alarm.

"What's going on?" Hector demanded. "Is this some trick—"

"No trick," Katarina interrupted. "Guards, investigate!"

Rolling onto her belly, Ahnna crawled to the edge of the foundation. Aren must have seen the arriving Harendellians, realized their plan had failed, and rallied his forces to fight. He was throwing everything he had at trying to expel a unified front of Amarid and Harendell. A battle they were destined to lose.

But Ahnna would fight alongside her brother until she could not lift her sword.

She reached the edge of the foundation, ready to throw herself into the thick of it, only to freeze. It wasn't Aren and his soldiers fighting the Amaridians, it was Harendellians. Dozens upon dozens of uniformed men racing up the slope to the house and cutting down anyone who got in their way.

*What is happening?*

*Has Alexandra turned on Katarina?*

Rolling back under the cover of the house, Ahnna listened to the shouts of alarm coming from within. "We're under attack! The Harendellians are attacking!"

More screams and the clash of blades, and then the Harendellians were in the house, boots pounding over the floor. Ahnna forced herself to breathe as she listened to the Amaridians try to surrender, only for the Harendellians to slaughter them without mercy.

A door creaked open, and a Harendellian voice said, "Well, well, well. If it's not the Crimson Widow herself!"

Ahnna recognized the voice as belonging to one of William's courtiers. A minor nobleman named Archie Bennett who was terrible at cards but good in a bar fight. He wasn't in the military, so Ahnna had no idea what he was doing here—and in command, no less.

"What is the meaning of this?" Katarina snarled. "This was not what we agreed to."

"No, I don't suspect it was," the Harendellian replied. "You thought that you could *murder* an entire nation and take the bridge beneath our noses and that no one would be the wiser?"

"That isn't what—"

"Shut your mouth, old woman," Archie barked, then demanded, "Who are you?"

"Hector Adrias," the Maridrinian replied. "I am a member of Maridrina's lawfully elected parliament and have been sent to represent my fellows' interests. I hope you have not shown violence to our escort, else Harendell and Maridrina will soon find themselves at odds."

Archie gave a soft snort. "Your men are well enough for now, but you chose poorly when you chose to deal with Amarid and not Harendell. This will not be forgotten."

"Trade must flow," Hector answered. "Maridrina will negotiate with whoever holds control over the bridge, though that seems to change by the minute."

"Maridrinian rats," Archie said with disgust. "Amarid poisoned an entire nation. Murdered innocent people. Innocent *children*. Shame on you for your willingness to do business with such monsters. If there is justice, King William will punish your lack of morality, sir. Get out of here and flee back to your sand dunes."

There was a scuffle of noise as the Maridrinians were dragged from the room, then Archie said, "You are a war criminal, Katarina. What you have done is a crime against humanity that will not be tolerated. In the name of King William of Harendell, I am charging you with murder. You will be returned to Verwyrd, where you will be executed for your crimes. May God have mercy on your soul."

Katarina screamed in protest, her small feet drumming the floor above Ahnna's head as she was restrained and removed from the house.

"The captain said there is a storm coming and there is nowhere to anchor for safe harbor," Archie said to whoever else remained with him. "We'll leave as many men as possible to purge the Amaridians north and south. Get your hands on whatever deal the Maridrinians were ready to offer, and we'll bring it to the king."

"Yes, sir," a soldier replied. "Should we look for any Ithicanian survivors?"

"Look, but don't expect to find any. The Amaridians poisoned the lot of them, and any Ithicanians found alive were probably put to the sword. This is an empty kingdom, which means it's waiting for the strongest to claim it, and that, my friends, is us."

"Katarina was mad to think she'd get away with it."

"You saw her." Archie gave a dismissive snort. "She's ancient and probably half senile. Either way, we caught her quick as a wink, and now the old hag will hang."

"Don't see why we don't string her up now and be done with it."

"Queen's orders," Archie said. "She's to be brought to Verwyrd unharmed."

"I hope they make a spectacle of it—watching the Crimson Widow dangle and kick will be a fine story to pass down over the years."

Everyone laughed.

"Before we set sail, plant a flag on the highest point of this island to claim these lands for Harendell," Archie said. "King William is now Master of the Bridge."

The alliance between Katarina and Alexandra was broken, but this was no victory. Ithicana had only exchanged one invader for another.

Ahnna waited until the Harendellians had abandoned the house, then rolled out from under the foundation and sprinted into the trees. Her clothes blended into the jungle as she wove her way to where Aren, Lara, and the rest would be hidden.

"What is happening?" Aren demanded the moment he saw her. "The Amaridians allowed the Harendellian ship to unload without argument, but the moment they reached the beach, it was slaughter."

"I don't know what's going on." Ahnna's fear was rising, choking her. "Katarina told Hector about her alliance with Harendell. Said it was freshly inked, and that he would be negotiating with both nations as a united force. She said that representatives were expected, but then . . . well, you saw what happened. They've arrested Katarina and are bringing her back to Verwyrd to be put on trial for the mass poisoning of Ithicana. They think we're all dead, and they've claimed the bridge for William."

Her brother went deathly still.

"A ruse?" Lara demanded. "A scheme concocted between Alexandra and Katarina to lure us out?"

"I don't know. It was under the queen's orders that she be brought back to Verwyrd unharmed, but they were rough with her. I don't think that Katarina would risk her own neck that way."

"Any mention of Cardiff?" Aren's voice was toneless. "Or James?"

"No."

"Did he betray us?" Anger rose in her brother's voice. "Was this all a trick? Was he in on Alexandra's scheme, and all of this, everything with you, was just a ruse to get us to let them in without a fight?"

"No!"

"Aren, James didn't betray us." Lara stepped between them. "Something has gone wrong in Cardiff. Something has happened. He's loyal to Ahnna, you know that!"

"All I know is that I sat in the jungle and *watched* while we were invaded, and now the most powerful nation in the known world is inside my defenses!"

"I'm sorry." Ahnna's tongue was thick and it tripped over her words. "I . . . I . . ." She trailed off, because she had no defense here. This had been her plan, and it had made everything worse.

Aren wouldn't even look at her. "No need to abdicate now, is there?"

Bile burned up Ahnna's throat, and she swallowed hard to keep from vomiting. "Aren, no. Maybe . . . maybe there is something going on here that we don't know. Maybe James convinced William to take our side and this is just a ruse. Maybe—"

She broke off, because Aren had turned his back on her and was walking away. Before she could go after him, Lara's hand closed over her wrist. "Leave him be."

This was her fault.

All her fault.

Ahnna doubled over, hand pressed against her mouth while the jungle around her spun around and around. There was no answer, no solution, because it was one thing to try to fight Harendell off when they were on the far side of Ithicana's defenses, quite another to expel them from the inside.

She'd done exactly what Lara had done, but unlike Lara, Ahnna could not claim to have done it unwittingly.

Lia sat on a rock and started crying. Others stared blindly into space, while more still just walked away. All of them broken. All of them defeated.

Because of her.

A dark voice inside her whispered, *Do them all a favor and fall on your own sword.*

Except to do so would accomplish *nothing*. It was only the coward's way out of an awful solution, and if she was going to die, it might as well be for *something*.

"Don't let him give up just yet," she said to Lara, and then broke into a run, heading down to Midwatch's cove where most of the violence had taken place. Keeping low, she searched until she found a Harendellian soldier who'd been killed in the fray. She swiftly donned his clothes and then hid his corpse beneath some brush, and with her hair tucked up beneath his hat and a bit of blood smeared across her face, she joined the ranks of soldiers being ferried in longboats back to the ship.

"You hurt, lad?" one of the other soldiers asked, gesturing to the bloodstains on her uniform.

"Nothing serious." She lowered her pitch, mimicking their accent. "It's mostly Amaridian blood."

Several of the men clapped her on the shoulder, and then the longboat was pulling alongside the ship. Ahnna climbed up the ladder, saluting the officer waiting at the top, and then headed belowdecks. She knew ships and knew them well, and ensuring she walked with purpose, Ahnna made it to the hold. There, she hid behind empty water barrels, and settled in for an uncomfortable journey north.

*Where are you?* Her heart screamed the question, desperate to know if James was safe. Desperate to know that there was a chance that they would be reunited.

Ahnna shoved away the thought. Her people were alive, and where there was life, there was hope. This time, she wouldn't disappoint them.

# 81

# JAMES

WHEN JAMES CAME to, it was to find himself gagged and bound in a horse's stall. He fought and struggled, trying to free himself, but to no avail. His head throbbed and blood dripped down his cheek, but the question of why Georgie hadn't just killed him was answered as two sets of footsteps approached.

Georgie pulled open the stall door and checked James's bindings, then stepped out of the way to reveal a shadowed figure. Alexandra removed her hood, looking James up and down like a rat who'd crawled over her shoe.

"You've proven to be a tough man to kill."

He couldn't speak around the gag, so James sufficed with giving her a murderous glare.

Alexandra gave a world-weary sigh. "This would all be going so much smoother if Katarina had put you down as she was supposed to, but fear caused her to make mistakes. She should have trusted me to do right by her, because then our plans would still be going smoothly. Instead, you are alive, Ronan knows too much, William has involved himself, and I have been forced to pivot to a new strategy. Katarina's lack of nerve is going to cost her her life, because if the winds were good, Archie will already have slit her throat."

Through the throbbing pain in his skull, James understood that the silence of the Sky Palace after Lestara's return had been to keep Katarina's spies in the dark as Alexandra moved against the queen of Amarid.

"Just because Katarina is dead doesn't mean we are clear of this, Alex. We don't have long until Ronan comes demanding vengeance." Georgie shifted restlessly, looking over his shoulder to ensure the stable remained empty. "Ronan knows too much."

Alexandra didn't respond, only gave James a knowing smile. "It was a good attempt with Lestara, Jamie. She had every reason to ally with you, but she is fortunately not stupid enough to bite the hand that feeds."

Georgie's hand rested on his sword, and he twitched at every noise in the stable. "We need to get rid of him, Alex. I'll slit his throat and dump him in the river."

"Tempting, but James's death won't solve the problem of Ronan. Nothing will fully solve the problem of Ronan, because thanks to Katarina, he knows all our crimes. It isn't knowledge that can be erased, and if we start with assassinations, it will only serve as proof of our guilt." Alexandra pursed her lips, and her scar pulled up one side of her mouth into a sneer. "If you'd played your cards right, you might have come out on top, Jamie. Dubious heritage aside, the people have always liked you. So honorable and stalwart. The perfect handsome prince. But you rushed into things, putting your faith in risky sources and not thinking things through. It's not like you to be impatient and impulsive, so that means something made you desperate. Desperate enough to risk *everything*."

Alexandra saw everything. Always had. But James suspected that her genius and calculating logic came at the cost of what made a person human. It was a monster that stood before him.

"Ahnna Kertell is no more dead than you are, is she? Love has flourished in the garden of shared trauma and adversity, and you act on her behalf, despite it meaning betraying your family." Her focus shifted to George. "We'll need to be on the lookout for Ahnna. She's dangerous."

"No one is getting into the Sky Palace."

Alexandra was quiet for a long moment, head tilted as the wheels in her eyes turned. "The plot thickens, Georgie. If Ahnna is alive and safe, there is no reason for James to have taken such risks." Her chuckle was cold and cruel. "I think there are survivors of Katarina's schemes in Ithicana, and enough of them that it's worthwhile to attempt wild measures in the hope of regaining sovereignty. Bodies were found, so some of the poison found root, but I think the Crimson Widow was tricked. Ithicana yet lives."

She gave a soft laugh, swaying from side to side in dance, her pleasure palpable. "You aimed to get me to turn on Katarina. Aimed to push her into revealing all my truths. Such a shame the dead cannot speak."

God help him, but James hated her. Yet his anger was drowned by fear for Ahnna, because now the monster knew that she was alive. Knew that Ithicana was alive.

"What are we going to do, Alex?" Georgie did not share Alexandra's pleasure over the scheme, and beads of sweat ran down his face. "Ronan is going to reveal everything. We have to do something."

"Of course. We'll use Ronan's own schemes against him. We have that forgery Cormac gave Keris, which we can use as proof the lot of them were attempting to incite a coup to take the throne for James. No one will believe any of their accusations after that is revealed, least of all William. Everything else we can pin on Katarina, given Archie should be in the process of executing her in William's name. We will be applauded for bringing a mass murderer to justice, and once the dust settles, no one will argue when we formally annex Ithicana."

James closed his eyes, his head throbbing as he pleaded to the stars to keep Ahnna safe.

Wasted pleas, because if it had all gone to shit, Ahnna would be in the thick of it. Fighting for her people right up until her last breath, knowing he'd failed her on every level.

"We can do all that with James dead." George gave a sharp shake of his head. "He's a threat to Virginia, and I can't tolerate that."

"We are united in our desire to protect my daughter." Alexandra's tone was soothing, but her eyes were cold. "Yet I must remind you that William wept when he believed James dead, and grief might incline him to believe Ronan's accusations. Whereas faced with the bastard who made his life miserable, the bastard who is trying to ruin Virginia's reputation, the bastard who is actively scheming to steal his throne, William is unlikely to believe a damned thing Ronan says. Emotion is a formidable weapon, Georgie. You need to learn that."

There wasn't an ounce of decency in her chest, and James's skin crawled as he stared into the monster's eyes.

"We'll keep him alive, then." George picked up the shovel. "But do you also require him to be well?"

"Not at all," Alexandra said with a smile. "Just ensure that he still appears a worthy threat. William has such a soft heart for those weaker than him."

Georgie swung.

And darkness fell once more.

# 82

# KERIS

KERIS STOOD AT the window, staring out at the clouds surrounding the Sky Palace, his fourth drink of the day in hand.

They were dead.

Lestara had arrived bearing the truth of what had happened in Ithicana. Poisoned grain and corpses littered through the bridge, Amarid gleefully taking advantage of Harendell's ignorance. All of Verwyrd was screaming outrage, and William had apparently sent ships to trap Katarina as she tried to make a deal with the Maridrinians. She was to be killed on sight for crimes against humanity.

But her death would not bring his family back.

The family dead at the hands of the queen Keris had pushed them to ally with, and there was a big part of him that wanted to open the window and take the long fall so as to escape the burden of guilt weighing upon his soul.

*Thud.*

Keris flinched, then realized the noise was not a body hitting stone but the door shutting behind him. Familiar footfalls filled his ears, then Zarrah wrapped her arms around his waist and rested her cheek against his back.

"We don't know for sure that they're dead," she said softly. "It's possible that they're in hiding, regrouping, and we need to put our heads toward how to aid them."

"Of Lara, I might believe that. She's strategic and is willing to bide her time." Keris swallowed a mouthful, the liquor burning down his throat. "But Aren would not hide while his people died. He wouldn't hide while Amarid spread across Ithicana. And to fool Amarid, there would need to be corpses. You can't fake corpses. How do we know that one of those tiny graves isn't—" Keris broke off, unable to say it.

"Delia is too young to eat bread, so banish that thought." Zarrah's breath caught, and he felt the dampness of tears soaking through his shirt. "Do not discount them just yet."

"It's my fault." Not allowing his wife to respond, he added, "I came here to be the eyes and ears on the enemy, but I was so obsessed with Alexandra's endgame that I lost sight of how opportunistic Katarina can be."

"No one dreamed that Katarina would poison an entire nation. Even Alexandra was stunned. You saw her expression when Lestara revealed what Ronan had learned, and no one knows Amarid better than Harendell." Zarrah drew in a ragged breath. "I was no better in my obsession with undermining Lestara. Everyone discounted Katarina, and she took advantage. Except—" She broke off with an aggrieved noise, then took the glass from his hand and drained it.

"Except what?" He went to the decanter on the table and poured another, refilling hers.

"Except it doesn't make sense." Zarrah paced the room, riding boots thudding against the carpet, her brown curls bouncing against her shoulders. "Katarina had to know that Harendell would eventually find out what she'd done and retaliate. She had to know that she'd have no chance against them, especially with the Cardiffian alliance. Why would she risk outright war with Harendell for a few weeks of control over the bridge?"

Keris lifted one shoulder. "She risked Harendell's wrath when she allied with my father to invade Ithicana. Harendell could easily have retaliated, which, ultimately, it did. Edward himself led the siege on Northwatch. That I'd already arranged for it to be empty does not negate his intent."

"Even so, it was bold of her." Zarrah pursed her lips. "Katarina is like a spider hunting in the shadows. She likes sure bets and has little tolerance for risk, yet twice now she has tempted Harendell's wrath. Why? Why isn't she afraid?"

Keris abruptly stiffened, the wheels in his mind turning, only for his hands to turn to ice as memory washed over him. A vision of the cart trundling through the bridge toward the entourage his father had assigned him. The men had all stood as it approached, more sober than they had any right to be. All of them looking anywhere but at the wagon.

His skin prickled as it had in that moment, and in his memory, he asked, "What's in that wagon?"

Raina's voice, clear as a bell. "Goods from Harendell. Steel, likely."

She'd been right. The wagon was full of weapons honed to a razor edge, one of which had killed her. Keris had always assumed that the weapons were put into position using bribes, but he'd not stopped to consider *who* had been bribed.

Or by *whom*.

"Alexandra supplied the weapons for my father's invasion. An alliance among Maridrina, Amarid, and Harendell, though Edward was unaware." The rightness of it radiated through him. "And the alliance didn't die with my father. Katarina and Alexandra are working together. Or at least, they were until Lestara returned and threw their plans into disarray." Keris slammed his glass down on the table and started for the door. "I'm going to kill that murderous bitch."

Zarrah caught hold of him, dragging him back. "Not like this. We need to be clever. Need to somehow get the word out of this cursed palace of what she's done, otherwise the only thing we'll achieve is our own deaths."

The door to the suite swung open, and Cavendish stepped inside.

"Veliant, you've been summoned. Her Imperial Majesty can remain here."

He didn't want to be separated from Zarrah, but she gave him a tight nod. "Go."

Well aware that he might be walking toward his own murder, Keris scooped Fiona up and tucked her under one arm. "Prove your worth," he muttered to the dog, then followed Cavendish out of the room.

Cavendish took Keris to the throne room, and to his surprise, it was full of nobles. Until now, Alexandra had kept him and Zarrah entirely separate, treating his suite of rooms like a prison cell. To the best of his knowledge, no one outside Alexandra, William, and their inner circle were aware that Zarrah was in Harendell.

William sat on his throne, Lestara on a throne slightly below him, hand pressed against her stomach. But Keris's focus was all for Alexandra, who sat on a chair next to the dais surrounded by her ladies.

Fiona gave a small yip, and Keris smoothed her fur as he said under his breath, "You're right. She's the worst poison of all."

Alexandra's eyes locked with his.

*Don't react*, he ordered himself even as his fingers itched to wrap around her throat.

The dowager queen gave a tight smile as he approached, the scar across her face twisting. "It is good to see you up and about, Your Highness. Grief drives many into the solitude of a wineglass."

"Wine isn't quite strong enough," he answered. "I prefer the taste of revenge."

Before she could answer, William stood and gave a small cough. "You've all been gathered here today because we wish to announce that the Crimson Widow has been caught red-handed in Ithicana attempting to negotiate a deal with the Maridrinians to restart the flow of trade."

Murmurs spread across the throne room, but William held up a hand. "I will not deny that our conflict with Ithicana allowed Amarid the opportunity to take advantage. Through duplicity, Katarina manipulated King Aren's desperation, and using the coward's method of poison, she slaughtered thousands of Ithicanian men, women, and children. She attempted to conceal her act beneath the guise of plague, but the truth always outs."

Just then, the door to the throne room swung open, and a large Cardiffian man strode into the room.

"His Royal Majesty, King Ronan of Cardiff!" the herald shouted out, the man looking horrified at the breach of protocol.

Ronan resembled his murdered brother, Cormac, but larger. His dark hair was heavily laced with gray, his skin weathered, and though Harendell was warm, he wore heavy furs. Around his neck he wore a necklace of steel that depicted what was surely his family's constellation, and on his head, he wore a crown formed of bone.

"Father!" Lestara stood, then winced, pressing one hand to her stomach. "What are you doing here?"

Ronan ignored her and strode toward the dais. He stopped only because soldiers moved to intercept, though he paid them little mind as he raised a finger and pointed at Alexandra. "Murderer."

Gasps broke out through the room, and Keris fought a smile as Alexandra's eyes widened with shock.

William rose to his feet. "You will mind your tongue when you speak to the dowager queen of Harendell, or you will find yourself without it."

Ronan scoffed, then spat on the floor in front of Alexandra, who remained seated. "You would defend this woman? She is a murderer. A liar. A traitor."

Swords drew all around, Harendellian soldiers baring their blades, but Ronan only looked on with scorn. "Shall I list your crimes, Alexandra? Shall I list the horrors that your secret alliance with Katarina has inflicted? The murder of my sister. Supplying Silas Veliant's invasion with weapons. Poisoning Ithicana to take its bridge." His eyes panned the crowd of shocked nobles. "All things you pissants would forgive, but there is one transgression that might steel your spine against this villainess: the murder of King Edward of Harendell."

Shock stole the breath from Keris's chest, and the whispers and mutters in the room went silent all at once.

"Are you mad?" William finally asked, seemingly as stunned at the accusation as everyone else. "Ahnna Kertell murdered my father, and then attacked my mother. There were witnesses. James—"

"It was James who told me the truth."

William's jaw dropped, but Alexandra gave a slow shake of her head as though this development was not unexpected.

"James is alive?" William demanded. "Where is he?"

"You might ask Lestara that question given that he stole her from under my very nose and brought her back to Verwyrd. It strikes me that she has only given you pieces of the truth."

All eyes moved to Lestara, who sat on her seat next to the Twisted Throne. She bit her bottom lip, then said, "James asked me to keep his presence a secret, because he feared Katarina's dark guild. I've not seen him since."

James Ashford was alive.

Keris didn't know what to make of the revelation. Didn't know who was telling the truth. Who was lying. It was impossible to tell who was pulling the strings, because while it might have once been Alexandra, it now seemed that her house of cards had collapsed beneath her.

The throne room was awash with loud whispers, but rather than appearing remotely concerned that she'd been accused of treason and regicide, Alexandra seemed cool as a cup of water. Rising to her feet, she withdrew a folded letter from the pocket of her skirts. "Before you are so quick to believe these baseless accusations, I ask that you hear me out. What feels like a lifetime ago, when we were still thick in our grief over our dear Edward's death, I became aware of a conspiracy to steal the crown from William's head and put it on James's. A conspiracy masterminded by Prince Keris Veliant."

All eyes snapped to Keris.

*Fuck.*

"This letter, supposedly written by Edward and sent to Valcotta, was found on Prince Keris's person." She held up the letter. "Innocuous on the surface, but the code within it . . ."

"You never said anything about a code, Mother," William protested. "And James would never . . ."

"Because I was afraid what the code said was true."

"What did it say?"

"That James was legitimate and the heir to the throne." A sob tore from Alexandra's lips, and Cavendish reached out to steady her as she swayed. "I believed the letter was real, and that my marriage was a lie. That you and Virginia were . . . *bastards.*"

The outburst of noise in the throne room was deafening, but then Alexandra held up a shaky hand. "So I kept it a secret. When word came of James's death in the Blackreaches, I thought it would be over. That it was done. That it didn't matter. But then Lestara came to me upon her return and told me in secret that James was alive, and that he was telling Ronan lies to secure support for a campaign for the throne. Lestara played along with his schemes only to get her unborn child to safety. It gave me cause to look at this letter again, and I saw the truth. It is a forgery."

Gasps tore through the room, but William only took the letter, reading the coded message transcribed on the back.

"It struck me that Prince Keris concocted this letter because of his hatred for poor Lestara. How better to get rid of her than to depose William?"

"James would never agree to this." William was as white as a sheet.

"Wouldn't he?" Alexandra scoffed. "Read it, my love. Read the scheme they set out and tell me that James didn't have every reason to go along with it. He suffered his whole life being named a bastard, and this gave him the chance to make you taste what he endured."

William looked ready to be sick, and his eyes fixed on Keris, expression murderous. "Veliant rat! You came into my kingdom and tried to start a coup against me?"

"I did no such thing!" Keris's protest sounded weak in his own ears, the words of a man who has been caught out, but if he cast blame, it would undermine Ronan's accusations.

"He's done it before," Alexandra said softly. "Against Silas."

"Bring me his head! Now!"

Guards caught hold of Keris's arms. He dropped Fiona and she barked wildly, biting at the guards' legs as one of them drew a sword. The blade pressed against the back of his neck, and knowing he had no other choice, Keris snarled, "Cormac brought the letter and the scheme to me! He wanted me to pass it off as real, but I declined! Then he died of poison while I was holding the damned thing when

Cavendish tried to arrest me for his murder. He said the facts were true. He said that Edward had aimed to make James king!"

It was a chaos of shouts punctuated by Fiona's barking and soldiers shouting orders.

"He's lying," Alexandra snarled. "He conspired with James, and when Cormac refused to turn on sweet Lestara, he killed him! All this time, they have been plotting together, and Ronan is the victim of their lies. All because Keris can't stand to see Lestara elevated. Surely you see that, William, given all that he has done?"

None of this would hold together under closer scrutiny, but that didn't matter. What mattered was that William believed, and he was the goddamned king. The only person with the power to stop this was Ronan, but if he admitted it was his scheme, William would never believe his other accusations.

"Kill him!" William shrieked, and the guard raised his sword up high. "Bring me his head!"

*I'm sorry*, he silently screamed, praying that Zarrah wouldn't be touched by this. Praying that she would survive this nightmare. *I love you.*

The guard squared his feet, the others holding Keris flat on the ground while one caught hold of his hair.

"Hold." Ronan's voice cut air. "Veliant speaks the truth. Cormac presented him with the forgery. As to what he told my brother, only Veliant and the dead know for sure."

The throne room fell silent, then William whispered, "You call yourself an ally, Ronan? Because this does not feel like an alliance."

As the hands holding him down loosened, Keris pushed up on one elbow. Fiona frantically licked his face, but he barely noticed. Never had there been a mastermind like Alexandra Ashford, and he felt sick with fear over what might come next.

William's focus was not on Ronan but Lestara. "Did you know about this?"

There were tears pouring down Lestara's cheeks, but instead of answering William, she asked her father, "Why do you hate me so much?"

Ronan grimaced, silent as he considered a path through it, because saving Keris's life had cost him all of his legitimacy. Keris's as well, because no one would ever believe that he hadn't leapt at Cormac's offer. All of Alexandra's schemes had been dragged out into the open, but all that anyone would remember was that he and Cardiff had conspired to overthrow the crown.

"Give me one good reason not to close our border," William hissed. "Give me one good reason not to condemn astromancy and allow witch burnings to begin anew."

"You need me, boy. You need this alliance to hold on to your new toy, so I suggest you give me the justice I am owed if you wish to keep it."

"Need you for *what*? Katarina killed everyone in Ithicana. There is no one left to fight."

Ronan gave a slow laugh. "You certain about that?"

Hope surged in Keris's chest, but he remained silent as William's gaze narrowed. "You wish me to condemn my mother with no evidence she has done anything wrong beyond the word of those who conspired to tear the crown from my head? You say this information all came from James? But where is my brother? Why doesn't he come to me himself with these allegations? Why does he hide in the shadows?"

"I'd ask your mother."

William scoffed. "Give me proof, Ronan. Give me proof of any of your claims my mother has committed any of these crimes. Something. Anything."

Ronan crossed his arms, and William gave a disgusted snort. "Because there is no proof. All of this, all these attacks on my mother and my wife, are just schemes to try to undermine my reign. Your word is worth nothing, and if you know what's good for you, you'll get back to Cardiff and abide by the terms you agreed to."

Silence hung over the throne room, but it was broken by a cough. "Your Grace," the herald said, looking as though he regretted every decision that had brought him to this role. "The prisoner has arrived."

"What prisoner?" William snarled.

The herald seemed to shrink beneath his king's glare. "Queen Katarina, Your Grace."

# 83

# AHNNA

Ahnna stared up at the towering spiral, the sky palace itself lost in a haze of clouds. It felt like a lifetime had passed since she'd escaped from its lofty heights and into the night, but also like just yesterday, and her heart thundered with remembered fear.

*Where are you?*

A question that had eaten at her thoughts throughout her journey as a stowaway on the Harendellian ship, growing louder and more desperate as she'd cautiously followed the caravan containing Katarina north to Verwyrd, because instead of James's name being on everyone's lips, she'd not heard him mentioned once. Which meant his plan to gain his uncle's support to claim the Twisted Throne had not materialized. As to why . . . that was as much a mystery as where her husband was now.

It made her feel desperately alone. A feeling compounded by her sense of helplessness to remedy Harendell's hold on Ithicana. She was powerless, and days and nights grasping for solutions only to discard them as unviable sapped at her strength.

Destroying the alliance between Alexandra and Katarina had been her goal for so long. The solution to all woes. Yet it had proven to be no solution at all, because once again, Alexandra had been one step ahead of her. Ithicana was in Harendell's hold and Alexandra's only rival was now her prisoner, soon to be executed for war crimes. Yet another perfect scapegoat for Alexandra, who still appeared innocent in all things.

The only solution that Ahnna kept coming back around to was assassinating Alexandra. While she wasn't fool enough to think that William would withdraw from Ithicana just because his mother was dead, she did think his capacity for conquest would be hindered by the loss of Alexandra's skill for scheming. William didn't have his mother's mind, and that could be exploited. Once the calm season was over and the storms returned, Aren might be able to expel Harendell as he once had Maridrina. Given that William believed everyone dead, he wouldn't be prepared for the fight.

Kill Alexandra. That was the plan. As for how, Ahnna had collected ingredients for poison on her way from Sableton to Verwyrd. She would use her stolen uniform to infiltrate the Sky Palace. She'd put the poison in the wine in Alexandra's study. Then she'd pray that the Harendellians blamed Amarid.

That it was a terrible plan wasn't lost on her, and she desperately wished Bronwyn were here to aid her. But Ahnna was on her own with this assassination.

"You've killed plenty of people before," she muttered. "What's one more? Especially given she deserves it."

Words that did little to calm her thrumming pulse.

Moving into the trees lining the slope of the river valley, Ahnna waited for the column of soldiers escorting Katarina to round the bend, then trudged out to join them. She pretended to fasten her belt as though she'd been in the trees taking a piss. Everyone was tired from walking and listening to the barked orders of their mounted superiors, so no one paid her any mind as they moved through the town and onto the bridge crossing the river.

Security in Verwyrd was higher than Ahnna had ever seen it. Soldiers patrolled the streets and the waterfront was under heavy guard, and as they approached the wall encircling the base of the spiral, sweat began to roll down her spine. The heavy prisoner carriage rolled to a stop, soldiers exchanging heated words, then the gates finally opened.

Ahnna ducked her head lower, keeping her face hidden by the shadow of her brimmed military hat. Her height went a long way toward convincing people she was a young man, but if anyone took a good look at her face, most especially Archie, this gambit might be up. The carriage rolled forward, but when the escort of soldiers began to march with it, Archie reined in his horse to block their path.

"Palace guard will take her from here," he shouted. "Get yourself some libations in the barracks and lift a toast to the end of the Crimson Widow of Amarid. Huzzah!"

"Huzzah!" all the soldiers around her shouted, and Ahnna managed to choke out a *huzzah* as the gates slowly closed behind Katarina's carriage.

She stared at the spiral, her eyes climbing higher and higher to the palace barely visible in the clouds. The palace where her enemy lurked, so close and yet so painfully distant.

But not out of reach from someone born in Ithicana.

# 84

# KERIS

"QUEEN KATARINA OF Amarid, Your Grace," the herald repeated, as though the silence in the room was due to confusion over the Crimson Widow's identity. "She is in the custody of Lord Archibold Bennett."

"What?" William gave a sharp shake of his head. "He was supposed to execute her after she was captured."

Keris heard the words, but it was not William's response that interested him. Alexandra's expression was blank, but all the color had drained from her face, her lips an alarming shade of gray.

Whereas Lestara's skin was flushed pink with triumph.

"Well, well, well," Ronan said. "It would seem proof has arrived. I wonder, Alex, do you think Kat will keep your confidence now that you have stabbed her in the back?"

The way he spoke reminded Keris abruptly of how his father had spoken about Petra, and Petra about him. Rulers in the old guard who knew their enemies so well that they were almost like friends.

"I think she will say whatever she needs to stay to save her own neck," Alexandra replied. "Her word is worth even less than yours."

Getting to his feet, Keris said, "I, for one, would like to hear what the Crimson Widow has to say. If what you say is true, Your Grace, she murdered my family, and I would have justice."

Ronan gave a sharp nod. "I would have the same."

William hesitated, then waved one hand. "Bring her in." Then he leveled his finger at Ronan. "You will be silent. If you lead her with accusations, you will render her testimony useless and all here will know you to be a faithless liar. The stakes are high, Ronan—Cardiff needs this alliance more than Harendell."

It was like watching a pot on the verge of boiling over, but rather than exploding, Ronan inclined his head. "As you like. We will hear the Crimson Widow speak."

Uniformed soldiers brought Katarina into the throne room, and though she was tiny and old and frail, it struck Keris that no one in the entire room, not even Ronan or Alexandra, held the gravitas of the queen of Amarid.

In deference to her rank, servants had dressed her as befit a queen. Katarina wore a crimson brocade gown with a train that fanned out behind her. Her wig was an identical hue, and it had been styled into a tower above her head and woven with chains of gold, giving her at least an extra foot of height. Her cosmetics were heavy, skin painted white and lips red, eyes rimmed with dark kohl. To cover what were rumored to be rotten teeth, she wore a false set made of gold and jewels, the feral smile on her face causing it to glint in the sunlight.

The epitome of defiance, and though nothing she could say would save her life, Keris was struck with the sense that the Crimson Widow yet had a card to play. Though Fiona didn't move from Keris's ankles, she leaned toward the queen, nose sniffing the air, but remained silent.

The soldiers pushed Katarina to her knees before the Twisted Throne, but instead of lowering her head, the queen of Amarid stared William down and said, "You look like a child sitting upon his father's throne playing at king, Your Grace. The crown does not fit your head half so well as Edward's."

William's jaw tightened, but he showed uncharacteristic restraint as he said, "Be silent, woman. There are laws in the conduct of war in the north, Katarina, and in poisoning innocent civilians, innocent *children,* you have violated them all."

William's voice caught on the last, as though emotion had gotten the better of him in the face of such awful acts, and it made Keris wonder what sort of man he might have been if he'd been born to a different life.

A young noble stepped forward, presumably Archibold Bennett. "We caught her in the midst of making a deal with the Maridrinians, Your Grace. Plenty of graves on Midwatch, and if there is an Ithicanian alive, we did not see them. We put a few of her soldiers to the question, and they all admitted to knowledge of the poison plot. She herself has been silent."

*She* had been meant to be permanently silenced, judging from Alexandra's pallor, but William only nodded. Lestara's face was blank, but Keris didn't miss how Bennett's eyes flicked to her and then away again.

"There is no judge or jury, nor king, nor empress who would pardon you for what you have done, Katarina of Amarid. There are too many witnesses, too many corpses, and far too much proof of your guilt. It is fair and right that you be condemned to death."

"Did you murder my sister?" Ronan stepped forward. "And my brother as well?"

"Ahh, we get to the true accusations," Katarina murmured. "No one cares about the Ithicanians, they're just an excuse."

"Answer the question!"

"Well, I didn't personally kill them, but yes, I gave the orders." Katarina tilted her head. "But no one in this room cares about Cardiffians either."

Ronan closed his eyes briefly, naked grief filling his face. When they opened, all that was left was hate. "Did you have an accomplice?"

"Oh dear." Her gaze drifted to Alexandra. "Has that old rumor bubbled up?" Jewels flashed in the sunlight as she grinned.

Alexandra sat back down on her chair, gripping the arms. "Hateful old bitch. Those rumors were of your creation. Your mirth speaks to madness, because you will be executed for all that you have done."

The queen of Amarid shrugged. "It seems the pupil has surpassed the master, and I find that I take some pleasure in that."

"Enough vagaries," Ronan demanded. "Answer the question."

Katarina remained silent.

"Answer!" Ronan roared. "Did Alexandra conspire with you?"

Silence.

William grimaced, sweat dampening his brow beneath his crown. "Speak the truth and tell them you acted alone. Confess to all your crimes, and rather than losing your life, you will only lose your crown and your freedom."

All across the room, brows furrowed, because William had effectively destroyed the legitimacy of Katarina's testimony. Yet Keris didn't think it was an act of strategy, but rather one of desperation. The skin above William's jugular fluttered rapidly, and the underarms of his coat were beginning to soak through with sweat.

"This was not what we agreed to!" The room seemed to shake from the volume of Ronan's voice. "Alexandra is guilty, but you are a grown man still on the teat and you do not know how to live without her. You make yourself look weak. You make Harendell look weak."

"I will not condemn my mother based solely on the word of a known liar," William replied.

A soft rasping noise filled the throne room, and it took Keris a heartbeat to realize that Katarina was laughing. It grew louder, the sound making his skin crawl, and as he stared at the queen, Keris was reminded of the Magpie just before he took his last flight.

"What an unexpected treat to discover I am not the only one who stands accused," she cackled. "I see you, William. See that you are torn between loyalty to your *mummy* and your desperate desire to disprove your father's belief you would make a poor king."

Katarina panned her gaze across onlookers, and when her eyes locked on Keris's, he swore evil itself looked straight into his soul.

Ronan stepped closer, his hand resting on the hilt of his sword. "This is your last chance to speak, Katarina. I will not lead you, as

William has done, because you know the truths we wish to hear. Speak and be done with it. Go to death with your conscience clear."

The queen of Amarid showed no fear, only amusement as she said, "You promise me mercy if I absolve your mother, William, but Ronan promises me absolution if I condemn her. How to choose? More important, will all those watching believe what I have to say?"

"Get on with it, Katarina." The words ripped from Keris's throat. "No matter what you say, you are a dead woman walking for what you did to Ithicana."

"Killing me won't help you sleep at night," she replied. "When you lie awake, remember how you guided Aren toward my outstretched hand. Think of me, Keris. When you finally jump, think of me all the way down."

Keris's blood ran cold, his skin crawling.

"Enough stalling!" The king of Cardiff's hand was balled into a fist as though he might strike her. "Speak your truth!"

"As you like." Katarina smiled, and it was all gold and jewels. "I will tell all that I know, but only to the king of Harendell. Come, William, let me whisper my words in your ear."

"William, no!" Alexandra spoke for the first time. "You are the king! This is beneath you!"

William ignored her. "To what end? Why do you play this game, Katarina?"

Her eyes were cold as frost as she said, "Because the truth is what you make of it."

The king of Harendell rested his hand on his sword hilt, but he didn't move.

"Are you afraid to come close to an old woman?" Katarina asked, baiting him. "Or is it the truth that you fear?"

"I fear nothing," William snapped, then belied his own words by adding, "But I've no interest in playing whispering games like a child."

"That is my deal." Katarina's golden teeth gleamed as she grinned. "Threaten me, torture me, do your worst. But I will only speak the truth into your ear."

Keris's skin crawled, and at his feet, his dog whined and pressed closer to his leg, her small body trembling.

William descended the steps of the dais and closed the distance. "Get up, woman. I bend the knee to no one."

Katarina rose. "My whisper is only for you, William."

"Move back." He waved a hand at the soldiers, the action flippant, but Keris sensed the other man's unease even before he drew his sword, holding it loosely in his hand. "She's only an old woman. I've no fear of her."

*I do*, Keris thought, seeing the gleam in Katarina's midnight eyes as she slowly got to her feet.

William bent his head, and with one hand pressed against his cheek to hold him close, Katarina began to whisper.

Everyone in the room leaned closer, like starving people reaching toward a meal of gossip. Everything that happened today would spread through Verwyrd like wildfire, the theatrics of this moment growing as they were whispered in taverns and tearooms, hovels and estates, until all of Harendell knew what had happened here today. Just as Katarina likely intended it. She knew her enemy.

And she knew them well.

Keris was as close as anyone but he could not make out her words or read her lips, despite the entire throne room having fallen entirely silent. William's lips turned bloodless and his eyes dilated, chest rising and falling rapidly as her truth poured fear into his heart.

Katarina finally fell silent and William straightened. No one spoke as they waited to see what he would do. Alexandra stood frozen before her chair, expression so blank she might have been carved of marble, but the pulse in her throat fluttered like a wounded bird.

"Well?" Ronan finally demanded. "What did she say?"

William didn't answer, his green eyes fixed on the floor.

"William!" Ronan snarled. "What did she say? Did she confirm Alexandra's guilt?"

The king of Harendell twitched, and Katarina said, "Well, William? What did I say? Tell your people my truth. Tell your allies what I whispered in your ear."

Yet Keris heard the real meaning behind her words: *Choose between your mother's life and proving your father wrong.*

William seethed hatred, but above all else, he seethed fear.

"Speak the truth!" Ronan shouted. "Tell us what she said!"

The king of Harendell moved. Faster and with more force than Keris had thought him capable of, William gripped his sword hilt with both hands and swung.

The edge of the blade carved deep into Katarina's neck, striking against a vertebra with a gruesome thunk. William jerked the sword out with a curse, and Keris grimaced as blood splattered him in the face.

Screams filled the throne room, soldiers rushing forward even as the nobility fled backward. Keris only reached down to pick up his dog before she could be trampled, watching the scene play out.

The queen of Amarid had dropped to her knees, blood spurting from between the fingers she pressed against her catastrophic wound. Yet it was not fear of imminent death that Keris saw in Katarina's eyes but triumph as she used her last breath to whisper to Alexandra, "The master should always fear the protégée."

Whether it was because she believed no one would notice in the chaos or whether her hubris had grown to make her feel untouchable, Alexandra gave a small smile.

And William's blade struck a second time.

It sliced through Katarina's hand and her neck, and her head toppled to the floor with a heavy thud. Her body stayed upright for a long moment, blood pumping from the stump of her neck until the heart in her chest finally realized the end had come.

Then the queen of Amarid slumped to the floor.

Keris didn't move as the pool of blood spread out, a slight angle in the floor causing it to flow toward him and around his boot.

William's boots slid in the blood as he stooped to catch hold of the queen's hair, but as he lifted her head, it came away from the wig and rolled to a stop before Ronan's right boot. Katarina's eyes stared sightlessly, her gold and jeweled teeth bright in the sunlight. The king of Harendell gave a wild laugh and cast the wig aside. "She told me my mother was innocent, my good man. That's what the hag whispered in my ear. She called you a liar."

That wasn't what Katarina had said. Keris knew it. Ronan knew it. Every goddamned noble in the room knew it. But the king of Cardiff said nothing. Likely the wise course, but silence had never been Keris's forte. "You said you'd spare her life if she told the truth."

"She whispered the truth in my ear knowing you pricks would never believe me when I repeated it," William spat. "You should be toasting my name, Veliant. It's not just Ronan's family who is avenged, it's yours."

Keris glanced down at the head, his skin still crawling with the certainty that, somehow, Katarina had had the last word.

"You lie!" Ronan drew his sword, and a dozen Harendellian soldiers moved between him and William. "Alexandra is *guilty*. That is what the Crimson Widow told you! Admit it!"

"Stop!" Lestara ran into the fray, pressing one hand to William's chest and another to Ronan's. "Please!"

"Give me Alexandra's head, or the alliance between Cardiff and Harendell is over!"

"No! And I suggest you run, because the first thing I intend to do when I walk out of this room is reinstate every law against your kind!"

"William, please!" Lestara pleaded. "Don't do this. If we negotiate, I'm sure we can find middle ground."

He slapped her arm away. "There is no negotiation, Lestara. My mother is innocent, but more than that, she is a good Harendellian woman and I'll not sacrifice her to witches and stargazers."

Shock filled Lestara's face, but it was swiftly filled with hurt, and Keris couldn't help but pity her as she came to realize that she'd always be second to her husband's mother. A very distant second. He wondered how long until hurt turned to fear, because if Lestara was behind Katarina being brought to Verwyrd versus executed in the field, as seemed likely, Alexandra would make her pay.

"Take the Crimson Widow's head, Ronan," William said. "Take the whole goddamned corpse, and do whatever you bone casters like to do with them. Ask your stars what you should do, but know this:

Harendell is the mightiest nation of the north, and I am now Master of the Bridge. We do not *need* Cardiff when trade with all the wealth of the south is now ours. I hope your stars will tell you that we are better off friends than enemies."

"I do not need the stars to tell me what is clear to my own eyes," Ronan replied, then lifted his fingers as though to test a wind. "A storm is coming, and not everyone will survive it."

# 85

# AHNNA

Ahnna surveyed the Sky Palace, a crossbow resting against one shoulder.

The gates to the wall around the base of the spiral had not opened once since Katarina had passed through them, and while rumors ran wild over what might be going on in the Sky Palace, all of it was pure speculation. The only way to find out what was going on would be to get up there herself.

It was the darkest hour of the night, but patrols in Verwyrd were heavy and the Harendellian soldiers watchful. For the first time in decades, the nation was at war, and it had changed their demeanor in a meaningful way. This would have been much easier in prior days when they'd been so confident in their supremacy that they believed no one would dare attack the capital.

But that was of no matter. Ahnna had spent her life doing difficult things, and she would not balk at one now.

Ahnna had acquired everything she needed to go about this like an Ithicanian, and as she watched the unnatural mist roll toward the

Sky Palace on the gentle breeze, she remembered how this had once been what Lara and Aren had used to escape a king's tower. Tonight she would use it to infiltrate one, and then assassinate a queen.

Holding her place in the shadows, Ahnna waited until the wall of mist was nearly at the spiral, and then aimed the crossbow and let the heavy bolt fly. Wincing at the loud retort, she watched the metal hook soar through the air, trailing behind it a thin length of black rope. Metal clinked against stone several rings up right as the mist enveloped the spiral.

Keeping one ear alert for any sign of alarm, Ahnna held her breath as she pulled the rope, only exhaling when the grappling hook caught on the metal railing of the spiral. Knowing the mist wouldn't last long, she secured the end of the rope. Shouldering her small pack and securing the crossbow, Ahnna took hold of the thin rope and started to climb.

The bone in her right arm was long healed, but Ahnna felt the loss of strength in the muscle as she worked her way toward the spiral. Her heart pounded, half from exertion and half from fear of discovery by the soldiers below, but there was no time to rest. Already, the mist was beginning to clear, and when it did, not even her dark uniform would be enough to hide her against the bright moonlight.

*Faster*, she ordered herself. *Fucking climb!*

Her muscles shuddered as her gloved hands dragged her higher, and though instinct demanded she look down, look to see how much farther she had to go, Ahnna only stared upward at the brightening orb of the moon.

*Hurry!*

Her hand struck metal with a dull thud. Tilting her head backward, Ahnna swiftly examined the railing and then hooked her legs more firmly around the rope before reaching with one hand to grasp the ornate iron barrier. Within a heartbeat, Ahnna was on the other side of it. Watching for a break between soldiers patrolling the base of the tower, she tugged on the second line that was fixed to her belt, which released the primary from where it was mounted below. She swiftly pulled both ropes up, leaving behind no trace for patrols to find.

With the ropes hooked around her shoulder, Ahnna began the

long climb up to the Sky Palace. She moved as swiftly as she could while still maintaining silence, for while the wind moaned through the spiral, Ahnna well knew how the sound of running feet echoed in this place.

Higher and higher, but as she reached the bend that would reveal the gate to the courtyard into the palace itself, she dropped into a prowl. Keeping tight to the shadows, she edged around until she could see the gate.

As expected, it was locked tight, several armed men staring through the thick bars, hands on their weapons. Ahnna backtracked a full rotation, then grasped the railing and leaned out.

Looking up.

The palace reared above her, walls as smooth and unclimbable as she remembered, but the tops of them more heavily patrolled. She marked the distance between glowing lanterns. "Shit." Too close together by far for her to shoot a grappling hook over the top without one of them noticing.

Which meant it had to be a window.

She slowly circled the spiral, searching for a dark window in a location unlikely to have anyone in it at this time of night. Spotting a likely square of glass, Ahnna readied her bolt and its rope, then climbed over the railing. Like the spiral itself, the palace narrowed, the whole of it slightly conical, but the angle was still awful for what she needed to accomplish.

Grimacing, Ahnna fastened her second rope to the rail and then around her waist. Taking a deep breath in a fruitless attempt to calm her racing heart, she leaned back.

Terror threatened to take hold, because if her knots failed, it would be a long drop to the stone below, so Ahnna forced herself to look upward. To angle her crossbow just right to shoot the hook through the small square of glass, which was big enough for her to fit but not so large that the shattering of it would catch the attention of guards above and below.

*Breathe,* she whispered. *Just breathe.*

And then she released the trigger.

The bolt exploded upward at a slight angle, her aim as true as ever as it punched through the glass, the wind carrying away the sound. A few shards fell, and Ahnna winced as the sharp glass cut the side of her head. Birds hit the windows often, and with luck, that was what would be blamed come morning.

Pulling the hook tight and jerking the rope several times to ensure its hold was good, Ahnna began to climb.

Wind buffeted her from side to side as she rose up the thin rope, using the knots she'd tied in it to secure her grip as she pressed higher. Her arms shook with the strain, every muscle in her body agony, but Ahnna clenched her teeth and climbed. She reached the base of the palace itself. It was made of different stone than the spiral, but was every bit as slick.

She climbed carefully past a large glass window through which light faintly glowed, the occupants concealed by heavy curtains.

Higher and higher, eyes fixed on the dark opening above.

All she needed to do was get into that window, and then evade capture while finding a way to poison Alexandra. It had to be poison. Had to be something that could be pinned on Amarid avenging Katarina.

She kept between the large panes of glass that belonged to bedroom suites, almost all of them revealing nothing but thick curtains. Yet as she passed one, Ahnna noticed that the curtains had been pulled too far in one direction, leaving a gap next to the frame through which she could see. Motion caught her eye, and she leaned forward.

To see William speaking with Lestara.

They were arguing, the queen pressing one hand against her very pregnant belly as she pleaded with him about something Ahnna could not hear. Lestara abruptly tensed, and Ahnna frowned as she watched the other woman grip the foot of her bed, all while she continued to argue with William.

*She's in labor.*

Ahnna had delivered enough babies to recognize the signs, but William seemed oblivious as he continued to berate the crying Lestara.

*Climb, you idiot*, she told herself. *It's not like you can hear them, anyway.*

Yet she remained in place, her boots resting against the rock and her arms trembling from the strain of climbing. Lestara reached up one gloved hand to cup William's cheek. Only for him to shove her away. She fell, weeping, and William stormed from the room.

Pity filled her, for Ahnna doubted that Lestara had found any more happiness in this life than she'd had in the harem in Vencia. Lestara peeled off her gloves and flung them aside, then set to work on unfastening her gown. The contractions were close together, but Lestara made no move to call for aid.

*Climb.*

If she delayed any longer, her strength would fail her, so Ahnna progressed higher. Up past the next level, the broken glass of the window that was her target beckoning her with salvation.

Then a tremendous gust of wind blew Ahnna flying sideways. Her body bounced against the palace, sending her twisting in circles. The ground far below spun around her, and Ahnna reached a foot out for the wall, trying to stop the spin—knowing that if she didn't, the motion would rip the hook loose and she would fall. A fall so long and horrifying that she'd have more than enough time to think about how stupid this plan had been.

Her foot bumped the top of a window as she spun, around and around, only for the rope in her hand to go slack.

Ahnna dropped.

A scream tore from her lips, only for it to be cut short as hands closed around her wrists, arresting her fall.

The person who'd caught her dragged her through an open window and Ahnna landed on her back on thick carpets, breath coming in ragged gasps as she looked up into a Valcottan woman's face. She was beautiful beyond measure with warm brown skin, large eyes framed with thick lashes, and loose dark curls that reached her shoulders.

"Fuck me," a familiar voice growled. "It's Ahnna Kertell."

Keris stood beyond the woman, arms crossed but a knife gripped in one hand.

"It's Ahnna Ashford now," she managed to croak out.

"I'll make sure they know that when they carve your name on the tombstone," Keris replied.

"Is James here?" There had been little hope in her heart that James was in the Sky Palace, but she'd hoped all the same. Hoped for some clue as to what had gone wrong with Cardiff, but even more than that, for certainty that he was alive.

"He's apparently near Verwyrd, but if he's smart, he'll stay hidden. He's a wanted man." Keris drew in a steadying breath, and Ahnna noted the signs of exhaustion that were written across his face, his expression as grim as it had been when Zarrah had been a prisoner on Devil's Island. "We know about the poisoned grain. Is—" He broke off, pressing fingers to his temples as though asking the question brought him physical pain.

"They're fine," Ahnna swiftly assured him. "Everyone is in hiding, either in the wilds or the outer islands, but my plan . . . it didn't go as we'd hoped."

"That's abundantly fucking clear." Keris caught hold of the Valcottan woman's arm. "Zar, if she climbed up, we can climb down. We have no choice but to risk it."

*Zar.*

*Zarrah.* Realization struck Ahnna, and she managed to say, "It's an honor to meet you, Imperial Majesty."

Empress Zarrah of Valcotta looked down at her and smiled. "Likewise, Your Highness. I've heard a great deal about you." She crossed her arms. "We'll talk about climbing down shortly, but first, Ahnna, I want to hear why you've risked climbing up."

# 86

# KERIS

"**I**S THE EXPLANATION Lunacy?" Keris snapped the words, well past his breaking point. "Do you know what happens to a person when they fall from such a height?"

*Thud.*

His memory filled with the sound of such a fall, and Keris turned away to hide his flinch. Given that Aren was apparently *not* dead, he'd be the one Keris would have had to tell if Ahnna had been reduced to a splatter on the stone below.

"She's fine," Zarrah murmured. "We caught her."

Fine for now, but the only way out of this palace was the way Ahnna had come up, and he was not looking forward to it.

He went to the table full of decanters and filled a glass. As he did, he noticed the spot of blood on his cuff. Katarina's blood. "What are you doing here, Ahnna? If William catches you, he will kill you to protect Alexandra. He cut off Katarina's head in front of his whole court so that she couldn't implicate her mother."

"Katarina's dead, then?"

"Quite."

"I'm going to poison Alexandra. It might be a long shot, but if William is rid of her influence, we might have a chance."

He laughed, noticing how Fiona was watching Ahnna with sharp interest, nose moving, and then she let out three sharp yips. Apparently the coin Saam had spent wasn't wasted after all. Except Alexandra's dogs had the same training. "You're never going to get close to her. Especially not after tonight."

"What happened? No one in the city knows anything."

Keris took a sip of his drink. He'd already told Zarrah everything, and the thought of doing so again was exhausting. Seeming to sense that, his wife stepped in, swiftly explaining all that had occurred.

"William won't turn on Alexandra," Keris said as she finished. "I'm not sure if he's in denial about her guilt, or if he just doesn't care. He's burned the Cardiffian alliance to protect her, and I don't think there is any length he won't go to if it will keep her head attached to her shoulders."

"He can't keep this all contained," Ahnna argued. "The people are going to find out, and they'll demand justice for Edward. If he refuses, he'll have a civil war on his hands."

"If we had time, I'd say that we could work with that," Keris said. "But when Ronan gave William his ultimatum, he all but told him that there were survivors of the poison plot. Harendell already has soldiers holding the bridge, but the calm season is only weeks away, which means they can move to purge resistance in the outer islands. If he has uncontested control of the bridge, he might be able to buy his mother's forgiveness from the people. Or at the very least, the nobility."

"If we can get out of the palace and out of Harendell, we can take the proof we need for me to declare war and sail to Ithicana's defense," Zarrah said. "But even that will take more time than we have. If we could even find a way to get the proof south, my father has the authority to set sail."

It felt hopeless, but instead of panicked, Ahnna's expression was thoughtful. "I think I know someone who might help. Is Virginia in the palace?"

"Yes, but she's been in seclusion since she returned," Keris replied.

"I've not even seen her, and there is no reason to believe she'll speak with me."

"I guarantee that she will."

"Why is that?"

Ahnna shrugged. "She once referred to you as *the most beautiful man in the world*."

Keris blinked. "Flattering, but I feel compelled to point out the obvious: Virginia Ashford is blind. I could be as ugly as a pig's ass and she'd never know it."

"She is now but wasn't always," Ahnna replied. "Which means descriptions mean something to her, and you've been waltzing about the Sky Palace in full view of all her ladies-in-waiting, which means the descriptions have been confirmed."

He cast a sideways glance at Zarrah, who appeared amused by his discomfort. "I find this all very reductive."

"I doubt that," his wife answered. "And Virginia is not wrong."

Heat rose to his cheeks, and Keris covered the reaction by saying, "Where are you going with this, Ahnna?"

"Virginia was quite intrigued by you, and she said, I quote, 'It's a shame he's wed.'"

"I disagree." Keris saw the direction this was going, and no part of him liked it.

Ahnna's eyes flicked between him and Zarrah. "I think she would leap at the chance to speak to you alone, and I think there is a good chance she'll help you."

Reaching out, Ahnna took Keris's drink and finished it, then flopped on a sofa, her mannerisms reminding Keris deeply of her brother. "No one knows Alexandra's nature better than her own daughter, so she will not struggle with believing her mother capable of all of this. Virginia loved her father dearly. She loves her brothers and is loyal to them, and she will not take well to any of this."

"Are you sure?" Keris replied, going to a chair and sitting on the back of it, not caring that his boots were on the plush upholstery. "Keep in mind that Alexandra's actions benefited Virginia. If Edward had lived, it wouldn't have been just William who was discovered to be illegitimate, but Virginia as well. Her value, and her pending nuptials to that asshole George, would have been ruined. I do not think we'll find an ally in Harendell's princess."

"Dip your toe in the water and see what she says."

"I might dip my toe in these waters and find myself pulled under when she goes to William with everything that was said and he decides to go through with cutting off my head this time." Keris rocked the chair back, balancing it on two legs as he considered whether what might be gained with this scheme was worth the risk. Zarrah met his gaze and gave the slightest of nods. "But we need to find a way to get you out of here, Ahnna."

"My rope is dangling from the spiral railing, so I can't go back the way I came." Ahnna picked up a pen that was sitting on the table, dipped it in the ink, and began writing on a piece of Keris's stationery. "Nor do I intend to."

He tried to read what she had written, but other than the flourish of her name, he caught none of it before she folded the page. "Ahnna, you aren't going to be able to get to Alexandra. At the best of times, she's more protected than William himself, and with what happened today, no one will get near her."

"Alexandra is no longer my goal." Ahnna extracted a vial, which she tossed into the fire. Then she tucked her hair up into a uniform hat and started toward the door. "If you find James, please tell him I love him and that I'm sorry I broke my promise."

"What are you doing?" Keris reached for her, trying to stop her, but she was too quick. His fingers brushed the sleeve of her uniform as she took hold of the doorknob, and the last thing he saw of Ahnna was a flash of hazel eyes as she said, "You claimed that William will do anything to protect Alexandra. I think it's time we put that to the test."

# 87
# AHNNA

Stepping through the door, Ahnna kept her head down and adopted an annoyed scowl. "Can't take his complaining any longer," she said in a low Harendellian accent. "One of you go in. Cavendish wants eyes on them at all times."

Not giving them time to get a good look at her or to question why they hadn't known a guard had been assigned within Keris's suite, Ahnna strode down the corridor. From behind her, she heard one of the guards say, "I don't want to go in. The empress is friendly enough, but he's a prick."

"Draw straws?"

"Fine."

It had worked, but Ahnna suspected her luck couldn't last.

William could be in any number of locations in the Sky Palace, but her gut told her that he'd gravitate to the place that had long been Edward's center of power.

The halls were nearly empty due to the late hour, and with her head down, her stolen uniform served its purpose as she strode through the corridors. Guards glanced in her direction but saw no further than her Harendellian uniform, complacent in their certainty that no one was in the Sky Palace who wasn't supposed to be. Her instincts proved accurate as she caught sight of two guards standing outside the doors to what had once been Edward's study.

"Message for the king," she said in a low voice, holding out her message. "I was told to wait for a response."

One of the men took it, then knocked on the door and entered. "A message for you, Your Grace."

William's voice was faint, but she heard him say, "Give it here, then. Who is it from?"

"I don't know, Your Grace."

Silence stretched, then William said. "Send in the messenger, and then close the door. No interruptions."

"Yes, Your Grace."

The guard stepped out, then gestured at Ahnna. "He wants to speak with you."

She nodded, drew a deep breath, and stepped into the study. The door closed with a heavy thud, and Ahnna's eyes skipped around the familiar room. Past the roaring fireplace and expensive artwork. Past the large cart full of bottles of all shapes and colors. Past the velvet curtains that covered the window from view. Finally landing on William, who sat on a sofa with a blue drink in one hand and his sword in the other. A half-consumed glass of wine sat on the table across from him; everyone in the Sky Palace seemed to be in their cups tonight.

"Drop your weapons on the floor or I call back the guards." William's voice was wary, his fingers flexing on the hilt of his sword. He wasn't the swordsman his brother was, but Ahnna knew he was more than capable of using the weapon. He'd proven that today with Katarina.

Unsheathing her various knives, Ahnna left them in a pile next to the door and slowly approached.

"Who did you murder to get that uniform?" he asked, looking her up and down. "I'll add them to your tally."

"I took it off a corpse on Midwatch." She took him in, wondering if he was aware that his wife was giving birth to his child as they spoke.

William appeared exhausted and unwell, his normally clean-shaven face rough with stubble and his green eyes bloodshot. The facial hair made his delicate beauty more masculine, and she saw echoes of James in his features. It made her heart ache, but she couldn't succumb to her fears for her husband right now. "An Amaridian killed him in the fight to take Katarina. We watched it all."

"Ronan indicated that Katarina's poison wasn't as effective as she'd thought." His fingers flexed on the hilt of his sword. "Is Aren alive?"

"Hundreds of people died choking on their own blood. Perhaps more." Her mind's eye filled with memory of the bridge. The bodies with their unseeing eyes. The sharp stink of vomit mixed with the copper tang of blood. "They were hungry, and everyone who had the chance to eat, ate. Not one of them deserved to die—they were just an obstacle that stood in the way of Katarina's greed. Alexandra's greed. *Your* greed."

"I didn't know." He let go of his sword to scrub his fingers through his hair. "I wouldn't have agreed to that. Poison is a woman's weapon."

"Oh, fuck you, William!" Her disgust got the better of her. "This was the weapon of someone with no regard for human life. An expedient choice that ensured nearly certain success with no cost in gold or soldiers' lives. You sit there trying to wash your hands of culpability, but the truth is that you were content to allow Alexandra to rule and scheme and murder in your name while you drank, whored, and threw away money at the horse races. You are king of Harendell, which means you are responsible for all that your kingdom does."

"It's not my fault everyone lies to me!" He downed his drink, then slammed the cup on the table. "I don't even know what the truth is anymore, Ahnna, because everyone twists it to their own ends. Giving pieces and holding back others, and how am I supposed to know what the reality of circumstances truly is?"

"Because it's your *duty*. It is your birthright."

"But it isn't, is it?" He gripped both sides of his head. "It's James's birthright, wherever he is. If he's even alive."

*He's alive*, her heart screamed. *He has to be.* To William, she said, "A birthright he had no interest in claiming."

"Well, others seemed damned intent on claiming it for him!"

"Have you asked yourself why that is?" Ahnna couldn't keep the frustration from her voice, every part of her wanting to grab hold of his shoulders to shake sense into him. "Have you stopped to consider that it has nothing to do with legitimacy or birthright and everything to do with you being a puppet controlled by Alexandra?"

His face flushed dark. "She doesn't control me—she supports me! And she's the only one who ever has!"

"Really? Tell me, William, what part of this strategy was yours? By your own admission, you were kept in the dark and lied to, so what part of it do you claim? The deception? The murders? The attempted genocide? Or do you just claim the results, which is a fancy bridge to put in your toy box and wealth to fund revels for all your friends?"

"She did the dark things so I didn't have to! She was only protecting me!" He was shaking, looking nearly ready to burst into tears. "If I'd known—"

"You know now. What are you going to do about it?"

William stared at his empty glass but didn't answer. For all he acted foolish, he was not a stupid man. His weakness was not intellect but spirit, and that made this not a war of logic but of emotion. Under the guise of protecting him, Alexandra had made it so that William *needed* her. Had made it so that he could not begin to comprehend life without her, and that was what everyone was asking him to do.

Watching him tremble and shake, then reach for more liquor to steady himself, Ahnna knew that William would rather cut off his own arm than cut the apron strings linking him to Alexandra. That he would do everything and anything to keep her at his side, which meant that was what Ahnna needed to offer him.

"You're in a tight spot, William," she said, taking a seat across from him. "Half the nobility was in that throne room today, and while you can keep them all locked up in the Sky Palace tonight, you can't keep them all locked up forever. Word of what happened will spread, and people are going to believe the accusations because the way you silenced Katarina makes you look so very guilty. They don't care about Siobhan or Cormac or all of my dead people, but they do care about Good. King. Eddie."

William lifted his head.

"Your people might have accepted regicide if you'd done it with that sword, like a man, but your mummy had him murdered in his sleep. It's not very kingly, William. They might not risk their lives to pull the crown from your head, but they will never respect you."

As the words left her lips, Ahnna noticed that the rim of the half-full wineglass was marred with pink lip stain. Her hackles rose with the sudden sense she was being watched. "You can come out, Alexandra. I know you are listening."

"She's not—"

William cut off as a bookcase against one wall swung open on silent hinges, revealing a narrow hiding space. Alexandra stepped out.

It was the first time Ahnna had seen her since her flight from the Sky Palace, and she was struck by the toll that injury and strain had taken on Alexandra. The cut in her cheek had healed poorly, the skin puckering as the muscles in her face moved, all the more pronounced given how gaunt she'd become. Like a skeleton with skin stretched over it, though her green eyes were as sharp as ever.

"Ahnna."

"Alexandra."

The older woman sat on a chair perpendicular to Ahnna, then reached over and retrieved her discarded glass. She sipped deeply as she eyed Ahnna. "Give me one good reason why I shouldn't scream. Give me one good reason why we don't just have you arrested."

"It's the same reason it's always been." Ahnna rested her boot heel on her opposite knee, trying to project confidence she didn't feel. "You need me to get away with your crimes. You need a scapegoat."

"Your note said you wished to offer us a deal."

"I wish to offer *William* a deal, not you." It was a struggle to keep her voice level, because she was afraid of what was to come. But there was no going back now, so Ahnna turned to face the king of Harendell. "I'll take the blame for your father's murder. I'll stand before a judge and jury and tell them that I killed Edward in a moment of rage, and then you can execute me for his death. I will be the scapegoat your mother always intended me to be, and all of Harendell will exonerate her of your father's murder. In exchange, you will withdraw from

Ithicana and work with Aren to create a treaty with not just Ithicana, but also Amarid, Cardiff, Maridrina, and Valcotta, to secure peace."

"You want us to give up the bridge when two days' worth of work during the calm season will see it ours?" Alexandra's tone was flat. "The bridge that I have sacrificed a great deal to take control over."

Ahnna ignored her and said to William, "A sacrifice for a sacrifice. Rather than being the king who is remembered for a *poison plot* and the slaughter of a nation, you will be remembered as the one who secured peace from Valcotta all the way to Cardiff. That is a legacy to be proud of."

His lips parted, but Alexandra scoffed loudly. "Why shouldn't we just call the guards and have you arrested? All of Harendell believed you guilty once, so they will do so again. I will have my cake and eat it too."

"If you believed that arresting me would work, you'd have already screamed," Ahnna said softly. "But you know that you need my confession to silence the rumor mills. I've named my price. Either pay it, or roll the dice to see how the world treats your son after knowing the truth. Perhaps all the cake will be yours, Alexandra. Or perhaps William will lose any chance of ever being respected."

"Don't listen to her, William," Alexandra snapped. "Rumors can be managed with propaganda, and no one will care when they are all making gold hand over fist with unencumbered access to the bridge and trade in the south. The history books will write of the Golden Era of Harendell, and you will be the king responsible."

William gripped the upholstery of the sofa, digging his nails in as though he were attempting to ground himself, and Ahnna could smell the sweat pouring off him. He didn't have Alexandra's ambition, but with that came an inability to say no to her.

So Ahnna played her last card. "Lestara is in labor. When I was climbing the Sky Palace, I saw you arguing with her through the window. She hid the contractions from you, but it was apparent afterward. Your child will soon be in this world."

"Lessy is in labor?" William stood up abruptly. "I—"

"Sit," Alexandra snapped. "You are of no use in the birthing room. I'll send for a midwife when we are through here."

"But—"

"Remember that it was Lestara who arranged for Katarina to be brought to Verwyrd alive. We would not be in this position if not for that idiot girl. Now sit!"

William sat.

"I've no fondness for Lestara, but I think she was trying to do right by you in trying to get rid of your mother. Or at the very least right by your child."

"Don't be a fool." Alexandra drained her wineglass, then stared at it angrily. "Lestara is an ambitious whore. She wants to be the one to control William, but I won't allow it."

William's jaw tightened, and Ahnna said softly, "Everyone is controlling you, William. If you don't break the shackles, they will do the same to your child. Break this cycle, and be the father this child needs. Take my offer, send Alexandra to live on some remote estate, and carve your own path."

Alexandra's lips pulled back to reveal her teeth. "William, you would do well to remember that it was *your* error with Katarina that brought us to this moment, not mine. We could have had *everything*, yet now we cling to power by the skin of our teeth. Cling to our very lives."

William flinched, and it struck Ahnna that for all he had been used to Edward's harsh words, he'd never heard criticism from his mother. He deflated beneath it, and Ahnna swallowed a wave of pity for him.

"This *savage* pleads to your kind heart, but remember that she stole James's loyalty from you. He was ever your guardian until she sank her claws into him, and since, he has turned on you. Conspired against you. Tried to steal what is rightfully yours."

"Where is James?" William rose and went to the window. "His name is on everyone's lips, but where is he?"

"I don't know," Ahnna replied, and though she wasn't sure if it was the right course or not, she added, "He married me before he left Ithicana to go to Cardiff. Our families are united now, for what that is worth."

Alexandra made a noise of disgust and went to refill her wine.

"Enough of this, William. Let's call the guards and be done with it. Then you can go to Lestara."

William pressed a hand to the glass, looking out. "Do you love him?"

"With all my heart." And she was never going to see him again. Never hear his voice, never taste his lips or feel his hands on her body. Never again would she wake in his arms to watch the dawn or race him on horseback through open fields.

"We need to find him. I need to speak with him." William dropped his hand from the glass. "I have loved and hated him in equal measure my whole life, but never have I doubted James's word."

"Then you're a fool." Alexandra flung her glass across the room, spraying the wall with wine. "He *ruined* your life! He planned to take everything from you for the sake of this bitch."

"I want to speak to him, Mother. I know you know where he is, because you know *everything*. If he has been against me, then he will admit it."

Silence stretched, and in it, Ahnna felt her heart begin to shatter because she *knew*.

"That's impossible." Alexandra's chin jerked, and then she smoothed her skirts once, twice, three times. "James is dead."

Noise filled Ahnna's ears. A high-pitched ringing, and her whole chest spasmed, pain tearing through her body. *No. No no no.*

"Did you kill him?"

"He was trying to destroy you, my darling."

William let out a sob, then rounded on Alexandra, but the words they exchanged were faint in Ahnna's ears. Like she was falling away from this world, all sight and sound slowly diminishing, leaving nothing but pain.

James was dead.

"You promised you'd come back to me," she whispered. "You promised, and you never break your promise."

Then hands took hold of hers, and she looked into William's eyes. "I agree to your terms. On my honor, on the life of my child, I swear that I will withdraw from Ithicana and call for a treaty to be signed."

It was hard to breathe, but she managed to say, "How can you not kill your mother for what she has done? How can you still be loyal?"

His hands trembled. "I cannot harm her. I know what she is. I see her clearly. But I cannot blame her when all that she has done was for me." His grip tightened. "I'll send her away where she can do no more harm."

The only place that Alexandra could do no more harm was in the grave. Ahnna shoved him away, lunging for his sword where it still sat on the sofa, but it fell beneath the table.

"Guards!" Alexandra shouted. "Help!"

The men were in the room in an instant, pinning Ahnna to the ground. William stepped close. "I'll hold to my word. Just make sure you hold to yours."

"I curse your whole fucking family," she sobbed, each word a choking gasp. "You are monsters. Every last one of you."

William stepped back and squared his shoulders. "Announce to the city that we will have an execution. We will have justice for my father's murder."

# 88

# KERIS

"SEND A NOTE to Virginia now," Zarrah said, striding to the writing desk and pulling out a card. "We need to take advantage of the distraction that Ahnna is giving us."

"Do you know what she's planning?" Visions of Ahnna going on a killing spree through the Sky Palace filled Keris's mind.

As if seeing inside his skull, his wife shook her head. "She's going to confess to Edward's murder in exchange for Ithicana's liberation."

Keris felt the blood drain from his face. "They'll execute her." He started to the door, but Zarrah caught his arm. "Zar, this plan is mad! They'll take her up on her offer, and when her body isn't even cold, they'll purge Ithicana. There's no way to hold them to their word."

"There is. The one she gave us. We need to get Virginia on our side."

It felt like a shot in the dark, the stakes high and the chances of success next to none. "She has nothing to gain from aiding us and everything to lose."

"Do you have another suggestion?" His wife slammed her fists down on the table. "We are trapped, Keris. Trapped in this palace in the sky, and the moment the storms ease, the Harendellians will slaughter our friends and family. Everyone in this place is too loyal or too afraid to help us. So write Virginia a note poetic enough that she steps out of isolation to meet with you."

She shoved a pen into his hand, and Keris stared down at the card, his mind as blank as the paper.

"Just write whatever you'd have written to me to entice me to invite you into my room."

"No," he muttered. "Some words are for you alone. Besides, Virginia can't see to read. This . . . this is not how to get to her."

Tossing the pen on the table, he caught hold of his wife's beautiful face, his fingers tangling in her loose curls. He kissed her, tasting her, then said, "If this all goes to shit, you need to get out."

"I'm not leaving you."

Her eyes narrowed with stubborn defiance, and he kissed her again before adding, "Obviously not. You'll escape, and then plan my rescue. I look forward to being the damsel in the tower this time."

Zarrah scoffed, then cast her eyes to the ceiling. "I'm glad you reserved these words for me. Don't say anything so foolish to Virginia."

The humor was an act, but Keris smirked anyway. "Our future does not end beneath Harendell's stars, love. If for no reason other than it's impossible to see them in this cursed foggy country. We will make it home, and then we will make everything right."

He reached for the door just as it opened, a guard staring at him in surprise. "I need to take my dog for a walk."

The man blinked. "At this hour?"

"She ate one of my shoes. I think her stomach is distressed, and being stuck in this shithole is bad enough without it being covered in actual shit."

"Fine." The guard jerked his chin at his fellow. "Watch her."

Clipping the leash to Fiona's collar, Keris went into the hallway and then made his way outside into the courtyard where the dog did her business. The guard dutifully followed him as he went back in through another set of doors, strolling through the lower corridor until he found the painting he was looking for.

Loosening the slack on the leash, he pretended not to notice as Fiona circled the guard's legs, tangling him up.

"I thought these dogs were supposed to be well trained," the guard muttered as he tried to unravel himself. Keris took the opportunity presented by the distraction to slip his hand behind the portrait where Zarrah had told him she'd hidden the documents referencing cattle and wasting disease.

There was nothing there.

Was it the wrong portrait? Or had they been found?

He kept walking, then slipped his fingers beneath another portrait, finding the worn page of Edward's letter, which he shoved in his pocket.

The guard managed to untangle himself from Fiona, turning a glower on Keris. "Control your animal, Your Highness." He shoved the end of the leash into Keris's hands.

The banking documents were no longer his asset, which meant his strategy needed to pivot. "Fiona is quite uncontrollable, I'm afraid."

They carried on, walking past the rooms he knew belonged to Virginia, a single guard standing outside. Light filtered out from beneath the door, but he kept walking to the next set of doors.

"Hold on to her." Keris dropped Fiona's leash, and she kept trotting down the hall. "I'm going to find something to read, and she's prone to chewing books." Fiona reached a potted plant and made to do some business behind it.

Cursing, the guard raced after her, leaving Keris to his own devices. The library doors were richly carved to resemble bookshelves, the metal handles molded to resemble book spines. He went inside and shut the doors behind him. A single lamp burned on one of the tables, and he turned it up bright.

He'd already pursued the contents of the Ashford library many times, so Keris swiftly found the book he was looking for. Sitting on a chair beneath a portrait of a queen of old, he flipped through the pages and began to read aloud. It was an old epic, filled with romance and heartbreak, and through the hole behind the portrait, he suspected that Virginia Ashford could hear him clearly.

It was just a matter of whether she was willing to talk.

She delivered something better than a conversation through a hole in the wall, for it was not many pages later that a set of bookshelves swung inward and a young woman stepped through the opening. Virginia wore a velvet dressing gown of black with matching slippers, her light brown hair pulled back from her face in a loose braid. She used a cane, but it struck Keris that she barely needed it in this room, for she moved with total confidence to sit on a chair across from him.

"Don't stop on my account, Your Highness," she said. "You read very well."

Though time felt short, Keris carried on until he reached the end of the poem, then shut the book. "It's a pleasure to make your acquaintance, Your Highness."

Her mouth curved. "In the middle of the night, luring me in with romantic poetry and your reputation."

"Is that what I did?" Keris hated this. Hated using tricks to manipulate this princess who had barely stepped into adulthood. A young woman who wore grief as thick as the black velvet of her garments.

"Yes, and I confess that I'm disappointed." She smoothed her dressing gown. "I'd heard your love for the empress was a story for the ages. That you lived and breathed for her. That you had eyes for no one but her. It gave me faith that such love was possible, and to find you seducing me when she's in another room in this very palace is . . . heartbreaking."

Keris considered her words, never forgetting that Virginia was an Ashford. Born and bred for manipulation, and by the rumors, she was the cleverest of the three siblings. She had the capacity to manipulate him, but there was a hollowness to her that could not be easily feigned. "Put the pieces of your heart back together, Your Highness. I did lure you here but not for the purposes of seduction. My wife is the only star in my sky."

Virginia gave a dreamy smile. "She is fortunate."

"On the contrary, the night she tried to light my palace on fire was the most fortunate night of my life."

The princess's smile turned into a grin and she kicked her feet, settling back farther onto her chair. "My faith is restored. Now shall we turn to the reason for this secret sojourn, this conspiracy of the darkest hour."

"You know of all that has occurred today?"

"Yes. Including your role with the forgery." Her unseeing eyes tracked to him, and though Keris knew she used the sound of his voice to place his position, it still felt like she could see him.

Keris cleared his throat. "The letter was a forgery, but the information within it was true. Edward wed Siobhan Crehan and was wed to her still when he went before the altar with your own mother. James is Edward's only legitimate child, and Edward aimed to name him heir to the Twisted Throne."

Virginia was silent for a long time. "Is my brother alive?"

"I don't know." Keris hesitated, then added, "He married Ahnna."

She made a soft humming sound, a small smile forming on her face. "I knew James fancied her, but I thought she had villainous intent, so I was not always kind to her."

Withdrawing the real letter Edward had sent him, he set it on Virginia's lap. "Your father sent me this before his death. The code says: *I will have wed William to Lestara by the time you receive this. Forgive the seeming betrayal of our friendship. As one who has risked all for love, you will one day understand everything, but know I regret the hurt my actions will cause you and your family.* I'm sure you have the resources to confirm its authenticity, should you so desire."

To explain the relevance would have been an insult to her intelligence, so Keris only sat silently while Virginia considered the tangled web of truth and lies. Finally, she said, "My father loved Siobhan with all his heart; this I know for certain. It makes sense that he married her, but if I believe that, then I must believe everything else. Like a row of dominoes, one truth knocking into the next and the next. I must accept that my mother murdered my father."

"I'm sorry." Keris knew her pain, because his father had murdered his mother right in front of him.

"I've always wondered if my mother was born cruel. Whether there is something in the blood that disposed her toward schemes and manipulation." Virginia toyed with the tie on her dressing gown. "My heart tells me no. My heart tells me that once upon a time, Alexandra was just a girl who dreamed of love, family, and being a good queen, but then my father tore those dreams apart by loving another. What pain to know that her life was a lie, and that everything that mattered to her was at risk unless she did horrible things to protect it. All with no escape, because her tormentor was her king. My father made my mother the way she is, and he died for it. I loved him, but perhaps he deserved his death."

Keris grimaced, Alexandra's absolution not his goal in all of this. "It is the least of her crimes."

"Another domino."

Silence stretched, and time grew short, because once Ahnna was arrested, they'd come for him and Zarrah.

"To have suffered does not excuse causing suffering in others," Virginia finally continued. "My mother will say that she acted out of love, but what she has done to William is not love. What she has done to me is not love. Love should not leave horror and death in its wake."

*It shouldn't, but it often does.*

"I don't have the ability to condemn her, if that's the reason you are here," Virginia said. "William will only send me away. He already did once, because whenever she sees me, Lestara is reminded of how I leashed her like the bitch she is. Yet another thing I won't forgive my father for."

"That's not why I'm here. I need your help."

"I can't get you out, either, but I suspect you know that."

"Ahnna is in the Sky Palace." Keris moved straight to his point, because he might only have minutes left. "To save her family and what remains of her people, she is meeting with William. She intends to take the blame for Edward's murder on the condition William withdraws from Ithicana. She's going to die because William refuses to hold your mother accountable for murder and treason."

"Die for nothing," Virginia murmured. "My mother's word means nothing, and William always does as she says. As soon as the storms end, Ithicana will fall for good. It never ends."

"You know that Valcotta has been recently plagued with wasting disease?"

"Yes."

"Alexandra arranged to have infected cattle sent south, then for them to escape into the herds to spread the disease. The proof was in her banking records, which she seems to have recovered after their unfortunate theft. But if you were to send that information south, the powers in Maridrina and Valcotta would believe it coming from your lips."

"You wish me to send information that will cause Valcotta to declare war on Harendell?" She huffed out a breath. "You are bold."

"Desperate. The lives of those I love most are at risk. I don't think I can save Ahnna, but I can try to save those in Ithicana."

"There has to be another way besides war."

"If there is, I no longer see it."

Virginia was quiet for a long moment, then she said, "They said that James was somewhere near Verwyrd watching events unfold." Her brow furrowed. "He loves Ahnna, so he won't let her do this. If he does not intervene before she's executed, it means he is dead."

*If he is dead, it was Alexandra's doing*, Keris thought.

Silence stretched, then Virginia abruptly sat up straight, putting her feet back inside her slippers and tucking the letter into a pocket. "I thank you for the poem, Your Highness. You truly have the loveliest reading voice I have ever heard."

Shouts of alarm filled the corridors, then alarm bells began to ring. *May God, fate, and the stars have mercy on you, Ahnna*, Keris thought. He stood, needing to leave before anyone discovered that he was with Virginia. She had the power to turn the tide, and only time would tell what she did with it.

Taking her hand, Keris kissed her knuckles. "God rewards the pure. Fortune favors the brave. But the stars smile upon those who are true to their hearts. I hope that yours finds the love you seek." He lowered her hand to her lap. "Good night, my lady."

# 89

# JAMES

J AMES DREW IN a shallow breath, then coughed, bits of flour from the sack George had put over his head choking him with each inhalation. His wrists and ankles were bound tightly, and while he couldn't be precisely certain, James suspected his *best friend* was keeping him in the wardrobe in one of the house's many bedrooms.

He had no way to be sure how long he'd been locked up. George came at irregular intervals to give him water and some food, and his attempts to shout for help yielded no results beyond fists to the stomach and a gag shoved back in his mouth. Either the servants had been dismissed or George had paid them off, and the grounds were large enough that his shouts wouldn't reach beyond the walls.

George wanted him dead, that much he knew. James was a liability, and years as a soldier had made George practical about prisoners. Yet he abided by Alexandra's orders, and it was terrifying to see how deeply she had George under her control. Not by threatening to reveal that he was a knifeman, but by manipulating his sentiment for Virginia. George believed he was protecting Ginny, believed his actions were righteous, and nothing James could say dissuaded him of that belief.

He drifted into a sleep fraught with nightmares, only to be torn into consciousness by the ringing of cathedral bells. They rang joyously as they had when Delia Kertell had been born, though James felt none of the sentiment. Lestara must have given birth to an heir, and James felt a pang of grief for the child who had been born into this nightmare.

*Lestara.*

As her name echoed through his thoughts, so, too, did Alexandra's voice. *She had every reason to ally with you, but she is fortunately not stupid enough to bite the hand that feeds.*

Clear enough that Lestara had betrayed some or all of what James had told her to Alexandra, and yet something about Alexandra's phrasing suggested that she did not trust his cousin. Now that Lestara had given birth, Alexandra would be looking for ways to get rid of her, and he hoped Lestara did not go down easily. Hoped that Alexandra had underestimated his cousin and would pay the price.

Small, petty hopes, because it was unlikely that he'd live long enough to see the two women collide.

A door slammed shut, and James listened to the steady thump of boots coming up the stairs, drawing closer. Doors creaked, and a draft of air brushed against the bare skin of his neck just before the sack was pulled off him.

James blinked in the light, his eyes focusing on George. He crouched before James with a knife in one hand.

"Sorry for leaving you alone for so long, Jamie," he said. "But it was an eventful night. You've a nephew, healthy as an ox and screaming like a banshee. Good news to distract the masses from thinking too much about Katarina's death."

The Crimson Widow was dead.

He'd fought for that, but given George's demeanor, it was obvious that it wasn't the blow that he'd hoped.

"You made a right mess of well-laid plans, as did Lestara, and if you'd asked me yesterday evening, I'd have told you that things were fucked. That everything we'd done, every plunge of that knife into

Edward's chest, was for nothing. But then God delivered upon us salvation in the form of your wife."

*Ahnna.* He couldn't breathe.

"You should have stayed gone, Jamie. Should have run away with your girl and never looked back, but if it's any comfort, you'll soon be together in the next life. Or in the stars, since apparently you're more Cardiffian than I knew."

*No no no!*

Panic clawed at his insides, and it must have shown on his face because George gave a slow nod of affirmation. "That wild creature you called a wife scaled the spiral and climbed into the palace using a grappling hook. Wouldn't have thought it possible if I hadn't seen the broken window and ropes, but she did it. Word we're spreading is that she was conspiring with Keris and Zarrah, but I'll give you the truth. She managed to get to William and Alex alone, and she cut a deal with them. She'll confess to Eddie's murder and take the blame for everything in exchange for our withdrawal from Ithicana. Say what you want about Ahnna, but she's got bigger balls than most men. Shame she needs to die."

James snapped.

He threw his weight at George, but trussed up as he was, it amounted to little more than rolling out of the wardrobe onto the floor. He didn't care. He screamed around the gag, trying to break the ropes without care for how they cut into his skin, his muscles straining to the point of agony. He had to get loose. Had to stop this. Had to save her, because he'd promised he'd get back to her.

George only stood up, watching him twist and struggle with grim eyes. "It will be quick, Jamie. I promise you that. She'll confess from the gallows, and I've already ensured they are set up for a long drop and a snapped neck. She won't suffer, and you'll be waiting for her."

He looked at the knife in his hand, then sheathed it. "William's gone sentimental, and Alex no longer sees your life as having any value. You're a liability in every possible way, so make your peace, my friend."

James screamed in wordless fury as George retrieved a pillow from the bed. He shoved James down, then knelt on his chest with the pillow in hand.

"I'm sorry for this. Truly, I wish none of this had come to pass, but I had to protect Ginny. One way or another, you were going to destroy her, which I know you never wanted. Hold on to the knowledge that I'm saving your little sister. That I love her and will marry her and keep her safe until the end of her days, just as she deserves. Take comfort in that."

James thrashed and screamed, fighting for all he was worth to break free. But it was all for nothing as the pillow descended.

# 90
# AHNNA

THEY KEPT HER gagged and bound in a cell for the balance of the night, but in the wee hours of the morning, the sound of footsteps tore her from her misery.

Hazel approached with two guards, one of whom carried a washbasin and pitcher, the other a lamp. Hazel herself had white garments over one arm and a pair of white slippers in her other hand.

The guards opened the cell, and the one with the lamp pulled the gag from Ahnna's mouth.

"Your Highness." Hazel bobbed a curtsy. "Her Grace, the dowager queen, requested that you be dressed as befits your station so that you might have dignity for your execution."

Ahnna gave a soft chuckle that held no humor. "You know that most people piss themselves when they are hanged, right, Hazel? It's hard to maintain dignity with urine dripping off your corpse's ankles."

"Then perhaps you should refrain from drinking."

To be contrary, when the guard unfastened her shackles, Ahnna picked up the cup of water on the floor of her cell and drank deeply.

Hazel had been one of Alexandra's agents, which meant the girl was no friend of hers.

But Ahnna held her tongue, not wanting to do anything that might disrupt the tenuous deal she'd made with William and Alexandra.

*Do this, and you will save Ithicana,* she silently repeated to herself, knowing that if William's resolve slipped, her death would be for nothing. "I thought we were friends, Hazel. Why did you betray me?"

Hazel's fingers paused in untangling Ahnna's braid. "You remember you and I once talked about how having skill with arms allows you to fight to defend those you love?"

A conversation that felt like a lifetime ago, but Ahnna remembered it. "Yes."

"Well, there is more than one way to fight." Hazel continued working on her hair. "My father works for Cartwright Foundries. I think you're familiar with the name."

*C.F.*

"Was my father who took the bribe and smuggled sharpened weapons onto the bridge, though he had no knowledge of how they would be used. He's not a thinker, my pa." The maid gave a frustrated shake of her head. "After the invasion came to pass, Edward ordered an inquest into the source of the weapons. It was discovered my pa was behind it, and he was arrested. Was to be tried for treason, despite his only fault being that he was a greedy idiot."

"Alexandra was behind that bribe."

"I know that now, but I didn't then. Then, she was my salvation. She came to me and said that she'd use her right to grant pardons to save my pa if I came to work for her in Verwyrd. It seemed like a dream being offered the chance to work in the palace washing the sheets of fancy ladies, because we'd been living in Sableton's tenderloin, which is a miserable place. Moved my whole family with me to Verwyrd, and I never stopped to question why Alexandra had come to my rescue, because she was known to be so charitable."

Hazel passed the comb down the length of Ahnna's hair and then set to braiding. "The first favor she asked of me was nothing. Just a bit of spying on one of her ladies and reporting back. But her requests kept coming. Planting objects and delivering messages, and one day, replacing a lord's glassware in one of the suites with a set she gave me. 'He deserves the finest,' I remember her saying. Just as I remember her saying, 'We hold you in our hearts in your time of grief,' to his widow when he dropped dead of a heart attack the next day." Her fingers tightened almost painfully on Ahnna's hair. "That's how she does it. Twists you up in her schemes until you are as guilty as she is. So if she goes down, you go down with her."

"I'm sorry."

"I'm the one who is sorry, my lady." Hazel tied off the braid. "It's the charities, that's how she does it. That's how she bribes and incentivizes, all under the guise of good works. Her banking records are her insurance, because if you follow the flow of gold and silver, it is to the accounts of all the individuals she's twisted up in her schemes. If she were to go down, she could take half of Harendell's nobility with her. Her banking records went missing recently, and I daresay that she's not slept a wink since. Nor should she." Hazel's voice turned cutting. "It's hard to hide dirty laundry from those who do the cleaning, and we have ways of getting information where it needs to go."

Ahnna didn't press, but she silently put a fervent wish out into the world that Hazel, or others, would bring Alexandra down in due course. "I hope someone makes her pay."

"As do I, my lady."

"She murdered James. They'll blame someone else, but it was Alexandra."

Hazel's breath caught, her grief thickening the air. "There is no end to her cruelty."

Ahnna didn't fight the tears that rolled down her cheeks as Hazel formed a crown around her head with the braid. Didn't fight the grief that pooled around the pieces of her broken heart, because they'd had so little time. So little time, and most of it had been spent fighting for their lives. Ahnna allowed Hazel, the guards, and the cold cell to fade away, losing herself in the memory of that one blissful night they'd had together. The taste of his lips, the feel of his hands, and the exquisite pleasure of being filled by him. She let the memory replay in her mind, hoping that if there was a Great Thereafter, it would be living in that moment for all eternity.

*I love you*, she silently whispered. *For as long as I draw breath, I will love you, and when my breath ceases, I will find you. I swear it.*

Hazel pulled the simple white dress over her head and fastened the buttons up the back. It had a low neckline, leaving her throat readily exposed for the noose to tighten around. Next came the soft white shoes, which Hazel carefully laced. Last was a white cap that covered the coronet of braids. Dressed like a martyr, and Ahnna hated the choice because no part of her felt that way. It would have been better to be dressed as a warrior, because this felt like dying in a battle so as to win the war.

"She's ready," Hazel murmured, and one of the guards bound Ahnna's wrists behind her back and led her out of the cell.

The soft lambskin of her slippers made little pats against the stone as they brought her up a narrow staircase and out into the Sky Palace's courtyard. More soldiers waited with the small carriage pulled by Buck and Brayer, the mules watching her with bored expressions as she blinked in the dawn light. Yet before she could take a step farther, shouts rang out through the Sky Palace: "A prince has been born! A new baby prince!"

"It is not auspicious to have an execution on the baby prince's birthday," Hazel muttered. "The execution should be postponed." The maid abandoned Ahnna to the guards and went into the palace, but Ahnna knew she'd be wasting her breath. Inauspicious or not, Alexandra wanted her name cleared, and Ahnna's confession was the only way to achieve it.

Archie stepped into the courtyard, his uniform crisp and his boots polished. "Bring her down," he said to the guards. "I'll go ahead to be sure all is as it should be."

With swift strides, he exited the gate and disappeared down into the spiral.

"Let's go." The guard holding Ahnna's wrists shoved her forward, and she stumbled over her own feet, nearly falling. They loaded her into the carriage, one sitting next to her, the other across, both with weapons in hand. There was so much hate in their expressions that Ahnna lowered her eyes to her white skirts as the carriage rocked into motion, the mules making their painfully slow progress down the spiral.

Around, and around, and they were not halfway down when the cathedral bells began to ring, spreading the news about the birth of the heir to the Twisted Throne.

Her nephew.

The corner of her mouth turned up as she considered that fact but then fell as her consideration turned to the legacy he'd know her by. A murderer and a traitor who died by execution. Would he even know that she was his aunt, or would Alexandra erase Ahnna's marriage to James from existence? Would it be as though it never was, remembered only by the handful of survivors who were there the night she and James swore to defend each other to their dying breaths.

James had honored his vow, Ahnna knew that in her soul. He would never have given up, and she wanted to scream and scream because Alexandra would never be punished for what she'd done to him.

Her body shuddered with a rough sob, and Ahnna rested her cheek against the carriage window, watching as they descended below the clouds. Down and down, and it felt all the world to her as though they were descending into an underworld from which she'd never escape.

A large escort of soldiers awaited them at the spiral's base as she was transferred to a larger carriage, and then they began their winding passage through the streets. It was a strange dichotomy to hear the bells still tolling joy for the new prince even as the citizens of Verwyrd jeered and threw rotten food at her carriage, screaming their hate, and Ahnna knew that Hazel had the right of it that her death would be forever entwined with the baby prince's life. She wondered what his name was. Wondered what he looked like. Wondered if he'd break free of the darkness in his family tree and become a good king to all these people.

The carriage rolled into the square. It was normally a teeming marketplace, but all the stalls had been cleared to create space for the crowd that had gathered. Uniformed soldiers were everywhere to hold the crowd back from the gallows that had been erected, along with a viewing gallery that had been assembled to keep the royalty out of the misting rain while Ahnna said her piece. Keris was there, as was Zarrah. She wore her Valcottan uniform but still outshone all of Alexandra's ladies in their fancy gowns. An enormous man she didn't recognize stood behind them, dressed in leather and furs, his expression grim and unyielding. Cardiffian, for certain, and though she'd thought he'd left Verwyrd, her guess was that he was King Ronan. Which meant that he knew that her confession was a lie. She could only pray that he didn't try to interfere.

Alexandra sat on one of the chairs, eyes down, but Virginia was absent, as was William. His absence made Ahnna uneasy. Made her fear that Alexandra had changed his mind, and that he'd hang Ahnna and then set sail to destroy Ithicana.

Her guards pulled her forcefully from the carriage, mud staining her white shoes and splattering her dress as they pulled her up the stairs, her ears filled with jeers and bells. One of them pulled the noose over her head and tightened it, and then they left her standing on the platform alone.

Fear filled her veins, and every instinct in Ahnna's body screamed *fight*. Not once in her life had she backed down. Not once had she surrendered. This was not who she was, and her body shook with the need to take action.

*It's not surrender*, she told herself. *It is a sacrifice that will save lives. It is a victory.*

Except her words sounded hollow as the black-clad executioner walked toward the platform. Alexandra gave the slightest nod, and the big man cleared his throat. The crowd fell silent, and he said, "Princess Ahnna Kertell of Ithicana, you have been charged with the murder of King Edward of Harendell, the assault of the Dowager Queen Alexandra, and the murder of Prince James—"

*What?* Her eyes shot to Alexandra, the cruelty of the woman beyond reason.

"—treason, and sedition," the executioner intoned. "You have confessed, and with your guilt certain in the eyes of the law, King William has condemned you to be hanged by the neck until you are dead. Do you have any final words?"

*One last battle. One last swing of the sword in this life before you go find James in the next.*

Ahnna coughed, trying to clear her throat, but the noose already felt like it was strangling her. "I . . ."

She trailed off as the crowd parted, revealing a familiar figure on horseback, and the whole crowd erupted.

# 91

# JAMES

THE PILLOW PRESSED down on his face, and though James tried to suck in a breath, no air came. He struggled and fought, trying to get out from under George, but the other man only leaned down harder.

He needed air. Desperately needed a breath, and James pulled at his restraints, feeling them move against the slickness of his bloodied wrists. But not enough to get free.

His heart beat frantically, his pulse a loud roar in his ears. He could not die. He could not die, because he'd promised Ahnna he'd fight for her. Promised he'd be at her side until his dying breath, and he refused to break that promise.

James slammed his knees up, catching George in the balls, but though the other man cried out, he didn't let go.

"Why won't you just die?" George hissed. "Why won't you accept that no one wants you to live?"

"George?" A voice called. "Georgie, are you here? I hear banging.

My goodness, why does it smell like spoiled milk? Have your servants abandoned you?"

*Ginny.*

George froze, then slowly lifted the cushion from James's face. "I'm . . . I'm just busy with something, Virginia. What are you doing here? You shouldn't be here."

He drew his knife and pressed the tip to James's jugular, deep enough that it stung. "Stay silent, or you bleed out," he whispered.

"Is there a woman in there with you? I heard you speaking to someone."

"No!"

The door handle turned, and George shouted, "Ginny, you cannot come in here."

"Why not?" James's sister demanded. "Who is in there? What are you doing? If you have some hussy in there, I swear to God I will end our betrothal and have William banish you to the swamps."

"There's no woman!"

"Prove it!"

"There's no woman in here! I swear it."

James didn't want Ginny caught up in this, but she was his only chance to save Ahnna, so he willed his sister to be true to her stubborn self.

"I'm coming in."

The door flung open and Virginia appeared. She was dressed in black with a veil over her hair, her cane in one hand.

"There's no one in here," George repeated, his knife tip digging deeper into James's skin. "If you go downstairs and wait, I'll finish what I'm doing and take you to join Alexandra for the execution."

James watched his sister's face, seeing the focus in her features as she leaned into senses that had grown acute to compensate for her lack of sight. "George, do you know where my brother is?"

"With Lestara. Or at the execution. I don't know."

James felt blood dripping down his neck. Heard the faint splats as it hit the wooden floor beneath him.

"Not William. *James*. Do you know where James is?"

"What?" George said the word a touch too quickly. "Ginny, you know that Ahnna has confessed to his murder. But we're still looking for his body."

If it weren't his wife and his life that were being discussed, James might have admired the genius with which Alexandra tied up loose ends.

"I find it hard to believe that Ahnna killed him."

"Why? She's a murderer, Ginny. You know what she did to your father."

Ginny tilted her head, lips pursed the way they always did when she played cards with James and William, listening for tells. Her nostrils flared, scenting sweat and blood. "You are lying."

"I'm not. I don't know—"

"James?" Ginny interrupted. "Are you here?"

He didn't dare move. Scarcely dared breathe, given that George's hand was trembling.

A tear trickled down Ginny's cheek. "Let James go, Georgie. If you love me at all, you will not harm my brother."

"I can't." George's voice was strangled. "It's because I love you that I can't let him go. There are things you are better off not knowing, Ginny, but I promise you that everything that I've done was to protect you from the worst of truths."

"Which truth would that be?" she asked, taking a step closer. "That I'm a bastard? Let me guess, my mother enlisted you to aid her schemes because she feared for my future and reputation, is that right? What has she manipulated you into doing, Georgie? What else have you done?"

George didn't answer, but his knife hand was shaking now.

"What else have you done?" She shouted the words, and George flinched, his blade digging deeper.

"It wasn't that I didn't believe my mother was guilty." Ginny took two steps closer. "It was that I didn't understand how she could have done it. She's not strong. Not brave. And my father was a big man who knew how to defend himself. It had to be someone else, and that someone else was you, wasn't it?" She drew in a shuddering breath.

"You stabbed my father forty-seven times. You took him away from me, and now you aim to take my brother as well."

"To protect you," George whispered. "Edward was going to ruin you. Ruin us. Ruin everything. James intended the same!"

"How would it have ruined us?" She snuffled, wiping her nose with a gloved hand. "I would still have been me. Or am I to understand that your affection's limit is my legitimacy? That I am not worthy of being your wife unless I am a princess?"

"Virginia, I love you!"

She sliced her hand through the air, cutting off further protest. "Prove it. Let James go. I can smell the blood and hear his breath, so don't insult me with more lies. Prove you love me and face all the consequences that your actions have netted, or kill us both, because I will not allow this to stand. Which will it be, George?"

James didn't know what George would do, because it felt like the man he'd been friends with since they were children didn't even exist. George had stabbed his father to death and betrayed James in every possible way. What was it to him to add Virginia to his victims, since she'd made it clear she'd never forgive him?

"Choose!"

"That is no choice." George's voice was choked. "Because I will always choose to make you happy."

He lowered the knife, and James immediately rolled away. A heartbeat later, Virginia was next to him, hands on his face and pulling loose the gag. With his next breath, he gasped out, "Ginny!"

"Oh, James." Her tears struck his face as she bent to kiss his forehead. "It is good to hear your voice, but you must go. They are bringing Ahnna to the gallows where she intends to confess for all my mother's crimes. They're going to hang her."

She was alive. Ahnna was still alive. There was still hope.

Virginia used George's discarded knife to saw through the ropes binding his wrists. James took the knife from her and freed his ankles, and then rose to his feet. Virginia's hand closed around his wrist. "You can't kill Georgie. He's the one witness everyone in Harendell will believe, because in condemning my mother, he condemns himself. And you will confess, won't you, Georgie? You will do this for me?"

George didn't answer, but he did withdraw his sword and hand it to James. "I'm sorry, Jamie. I . . ."

"Convince him to do the right thing, Ginny," James said, and then he bolted through the door.

*Please don't let me be too late.*

# 92
# AHNNA

THE CROWD PARTED as William rode into the square, a wrapped bundle in his arms. A hush fell over the onlookers—nobles pressed forward in the viewing gallery, murmurs breaking out among their jeweled ranks, while the civilians craned for a better view, voices rising in confusion and anticipation. Soldiers tightened the perimeter, the clink of armor and weapons audible as they moved to contain the growing tension.

Dropping the reins, William pulled back the fabric to reveal a newborn baby. Gasps rippled through the crowd.

He held the child aloft and shouted, "Behold, my son!"

A wail burst from the infant's lips, thin and sharp, cutting through the stunned silence. The baby's cry echoed off the stone buildings, and a wave of murmured reaction followed—some awed, others bewildered.

In the gallery above, Alexandra surged to her feet, one hand clutching the rail as if ready to leap over it, her lips parted in horror. Her knuckles blanched as white as the handkerchief clutched in her hand.

"Today, we celebrate the continuation of the Ashford line," William declared, mercifully lowering the child back to the crook of one arm. The king's face was flushed, one cheek unusually red. "My family has shepherded Harendell for generations. Beneath our rule, the kingdom has been strong and prosperous and, until recently, a place of peace. That peace has been sorely tested by the actions of one woman, who attacked not only my family but our entire nation."

A chorus of disapproving mutters rolled through the square, but it wasn't unanimous. A few voices cried out—"Warmonger!" and "Look to the dowager queen"—before being swiftly silenced by soldiers with barked warnings and drawn weapons. Children clutched their mothers. Old men whispered behind gnarled hands. The nobles, faces like masks, observed with sharp, calculating eyes.

Though this had been her plan, Ahnna's stomach still twisted. This was how the people would remember her. One moment. One lie. A lifetime undone.

William rubbed at his red cheek with one hand as he continued, "Ahnna Kertell's violence set us on a spiraling course toward war that allowed other villains to take actions most nefarious. But today, with the birth of my son, I will put a stop to that spiral. We will have justice, and in that justice, we will have peace restored to the north."

More cheering. More clapping. Some sounded genuine; others felt mocking. Soldiers flanking the square cast hard glares that discouraged any shouts.

William turned his head and met Ahnna's gaze. In his green eyes, she saw the truth: He meant what he said. For the child in his arms, he would cease his quest to claim the bridge and work toward peace.

Her death would not be in vain.

Ahnna's fear faded. She cleared her throat, ready to confess to a crime she hadn't committed. But before she could speak, a shrill voice shattered the illusion of order.

"William!"

Lestara—hair tangled, nightgown stained—stumbled from the press of onlookers, Hazel and a handful of soldiers trailing in her wake. Civilians gasped and shrank back, some crying out at the sight of her. Nobles leaned forward, some scandalized, others enraptured by the drama unfolding.

She doubled over beside William's horse, her body trembling from the lingering pains of long labor. "Give him to me!" she demanded. "You should not have taken him!"

William gave a chuckle. "You see your queen's protective spirit? She will instill this into our son, and he will be a king like no other."

Applause followed, though scattered and uneven. Lestara's expression twisted as she reached up, arms shaking, to take her baby.

William passed the infant down, but his body swayed in the saddle. He caught the horse's mane, steadying himself with a frown and a shake of his head. Then he gestured toward Ahnna.

"Do you have any final words?"

This was the moment when she needed to confess to uphold her part of the bargain, but the words vanished from her tongue as she focused on his cheek—no longer just red. Blisters, angry and swollen, now mottled the flesh.

Poison.

William coughed, the sound wet and hacking, and he pressed a hand to his chest in pain. "Confess to those you have wronged, and go to death with a clear—"

The rest drowned in a gruesome tide of blood. He gagged and vomited, spraying crimson across the horse's white neck. The beast reared, screaming, and panic cascaded through the crowd.

Ahnna heard screams from the gallery. Soldiers surged forward, struggling to keep order. Civilians shouted in confusion, mothers scooping children into their arms, but rather than fleeing, they pressed closer for a better view.

Lestara screamed, cradling the baby to her chest as she stumbled back from the terrified horse. "William!"

Another wave of blood spilled from his lips, and then William collapsed, hitting the cobblestones with a sickening thud.

Ahnna's knees gave, only the noose around her neck keeping her upright. She needed William. Needed him to make good on his promise. Without him, there would be no leash on Alexandra's fury.

And Alexandra was screaming. Skirts gathered in her fists, she raced from the gallery, barreling past stunned nobles and shoving through soldiers. "Get the physician! Get the physician! Hurry!"

But it wouldn't matter. The blisters were bursting now, William's limbs jerking in grotesque spasms. Blood gushed from his nose, ears, mouth. The crowd recoiled as one, horrified. Several people vomited. A noblewoman fainted in the gallery. A soldier crossed himself.

There was no medicine for this. No cure.

William gave one final gurgle, then went still. The silence that followed was total, as though the kingdom itself held its breath.

Alexandra let out a howl not meant for human throats and fell to her knees beside his body, rocking him like a child. Blood stained her hands, smeared across his lifeless face, his eyes open and glassy.

The baby began to cry again, a desperate wail that echoed across the square.

And Ahnna knew, with bone-deep certainty, that whatever future had been promised, it had died with William.

Lestara screamed and screamed, the baby's wails cutting through the rising cacophony like a blade. The square stank of sweat and horses, blood and fear—a nauseating blend pressing down like a wet shroud.

Clutching the baby, Lestara pointed a shaking finger at Ahnna. "You did this! This was all a scheme, a trick to get close enough to William. You murdered him!"

Gasps rippled through the crowd. Some noblewomen covered their mouths, eyes wide in horror. Others leaned forward, hungry for blood.

Lestara's face was a twisted ruin of grief, cheeks streaked with tears and sweat, but her amber eyes—those were clear. Cold. Calculating. "In the name of my son, William's heir, I order you to kill her!"

The executioner, pale and slick with sweat, hesitated only a moment before moving. The crowd held its breath as he reached for the lever, and Ahnna's body tensed. Her heart was a drumbeat in her ears, loud enough to drown out the crowd, the baby, the cries of confusion.

This was it. This was it.

"Stop!"

The voice rang out like a thunderclap, silencing the square. Heads turned. Ahnna's gaze snapped from Lestara to the far side of the crowd.

James.

He sat bareback astride Dippy, the gelding's flanks heaving from the run. Dust coated his shoulders. His clothing was torn and his face marred with dark bruises. But he was alive.

He was alive.

Gasps swelled into shouts, the crowd shifting like a tide. Nobles leaned over the gallery rail, craning for a better look. Civilians surged against the soldiers holding the perimeter. One called James's name. Then another. And another.

Lestara turned on him, fury making her skeletal, monstrous. "Seize him!" she screamed. "He is a traitor! A slave to the snake charmer's wiles!"

She lunged toward the executioner, her nightgown torn and filthy, her legs streaked with blood. "Kill her!"

Still, neither soldiers nor the executioner moved.

James was their prince. The man they'd fought beside, bled beside. Lestara . . . she was their queen by marriage marred by a dark reputation, her authority weak.

"They murdered your king!" Lestara shrieked. Spittle flew from her lips as she spun toward the nearest guards. "James and Ahnna conspired together because they want the crown! Kill them!"

The crowd had gone volatile now—hot with uncertainty, pressed shoulder to shoulder. Someone shouted that it was Ithicana's doing. More still that it was the work of Amarid. Chaos swirled like a rising tempest.

James spurred Dippy forward, the crowd parting in gasps and cries. Hands reached out, trying to touch him. He ignored them all, gaze locked on Ahnna.

"Alexandra, do something!" Lestara hissed. "Stop them!"

There was a long, sickening pause.

Then the dowager queen slowly lifted her head.

Ahnna's breath caught.

Alexandra had clawed her own face in grief—blood striped her cheeks in jagged crescents, mixing with smeared cosmetics and tears.

Her mouth trembled, but her eyes ... her eyes were pure, undiluted fury as she rose to her feet.

"Execute the prisoner." Her voice was hoarse, inhuman. "And arrest that traitor!"

Gasps. Screams. Shouts of protest from the crowd.

But the executioner obeyed.

He nodded once and pulled the lever.

The world vanished beneath Ahnna's feet.

She screamed as the platform dropped, her stomach rising into her throat as she waited for the rope to snap taut.

She kept falling.

Falling—

Pain jolted up her legs as her slippered feet slammed into the cobblestones. Her knees buckled. The noose was still around her neck, but it dangled loose, cleanly severed.

Above her, an arrow quivered in the wooden backdrop of the gallows.

An Ithicanian arrow.

The roar came next, shattering the stunned silence.

"For Ithicana!"

On a rooftop, silhouetted by the sun, stood her brother. Her king.

Bow still raised, eyes blazing.

Pandemonium erupted.

Figures shed Harendellian cloaks to reveal Ithicanian tunics of green and gray. Hidden warriors burst from alleyways, from shadows, from within the crowd. Civilians screamed and scattered. Soldiers turned, but too late.

And James—

He vaulted from Dippy's back, arms catching Ahnna around the shoulders just as she crumpled.

"You're alive," she gasped, clinging to him as best she could with bound wrists, her fingers clutching his torn shirt. The scent of sweat, leather, and blood clung to him, the marks of physical violence, old and new, written in the injuries to his face.

"I made you a promise, Princess," James said, lifting her onto Dippy's back, the saddleless horse lathered from the gallop here.

"And there is no power in this world that would prevent me from keeping it."

He vaulted up behind her, his chest pressing into her back as he seized the reins. Then Dippy surged into a gallop, his hooves pounding like war drums against the cobblestones as they fled the square.

They flew past Lestara, who shrieked curses after them, her voice fraying with hysteria. Behind them, the clash of metal rang sharp as Ithicanians fought to carve a path through the chaos. Aren's voice cut through the din. "Get downstream!"

James nodded, already veering down a narrow street. Ahnna twisted in his grip, heart lurching. "We can't leave them! I need to—"

"Aren has a plan," James snapped. "Let's not fuck with it!"

They tore through the winding streets of Verwyrd. Dippy's hooves struck sparks from the uneven cobbles, and the scent of smoke blew over them from fires that had been set in the city, probably by Aren. It was the same path Ahnna had taken the night she'd escaped—and now, like then, the walls felt too tight, the corners too sharp, the chance of a fall as deadly as being caught.

Shouts rang out behind them. The harsh clatter of hooves. The blare of horns.

Worse were the shouted orders.

Not to capture them.

To kill.

An arrow sliced through the air and clattered off a building wall to her right. Another hissed past her ear, and then another. Dippy squealed, his stride faltering.

Ahnna's heart seized.

"Just grazed his haunches," James said grimly. "He's fine."

The river's tang hit her nose a second before it came into view—wide and rushing, gleaming in the sunlight. The bridge loomed upstream, gates clanging shut as soldiers took up positions. Archers swarmed the fortifications, bristling like thorns.

*Faster*, she silently begged her horse. *One last time, save me.*

The wharf came into view, stacked with crates and lined with soldiers bearing shields and pikes. There was no way through.

James didn't slow.

Instead, he wrenched the reins, and Dippy veered toward the wide gangplank used to load taller riverboats.

"No," Ahnna breathed. "He won't do it. He'll balk."

But Dippy did not hesitate. With the stride of a champion, he thundered up the ramp and leapt.

The wind tore the breath from her lungs. For a suspended heartbeat, they flew. The river rushed beneath them, wide and deep and waiting.

Then they fell.

Ahnna had just enough time to suck in a breath before they hit.

Water swallowed her, pulling her off Dippy's back. Cold. Crushing. Blinding. Panic shot through her chest because her sodden dress was dragging her down. She kicked. Twisted.

And broke the surface with a gasp, the taste of the river bitter in her mouth.

"Hold on to his mane!" James shouted, pushing her onto Dippy's back. One hand on the reins, he guided the swimming horse, cutting through the current with powerful strokes.

Ahnna clung to her horse's rough mane, coughing and gasping. Around them, figures leapt from the banks—more Ithicanians, plunging into the current and swimming with practiced ease.

Upstream, soldiers scrambled into boats, oars slapping water.

But the real threats were the mounted soldiers thundering across the bridge, racing along the river road. They would outrun the current in minutes.

Hope surged as the river pulled them around a bend, and sails appeared. Shallow hulled Ithicanian ships were tied off along the far bank, only their masts visible above the reeds. Men and women leaned out of them, hauling swimmers aboard.

Relief hit Ahnna like a punch as she saw Aren climb aboard one of them.

James guided Dippy toward the vessels. As they passed, Aren caught Ahnna's arm and hauled her unceremoniously aboard. She hit the planks hard, dress sodden, lungs burning, but before she could say anything to her brother, he leapt to the next boat.

James was removing Dippy's bridle, teeth clenched as he struggled to control her horse. The current threatened to pull him away, but just before he was swept past the final vessel, Aren reached down and caught his hand, dragging him aboard.

"Lia, give me a count!" Aren barked, already searching the banks for threats.

"We lost two," Lia called, clutching a bleeding arm. "Everyone else is here."

"Let's go!"

The ships cast off, the current gripping them fast and flinging them downstream. They weren't meant for river sailing, but her people were endlessly adaptable.

In their wake, Dippy swam ashore, clambering up the far bank before stopping to shake like a drenched hound. He turned, watching them go.

*Be safe*, Ahnna thought. *Live with the cows in the Ranges.*

"What were you thinking?" Lia dropped to her knees in front of her, knife already sawing at the ropes on Ahnna's wrists. Beyond, Aren was leaping between boats again, making his way toward them.

"I made a deal with William," Ahnna said as the ropes fell away. She grabbed the knife and hacked off her sodden skirt until it bared her knees. "He was going to go through with it, so don't look at me like I'm insane."

Aren landed beside her—but barely had time to straighten before James barreled into the space, nearly knocking him over. Shoving Lia aside, he dropped to his knees and pulled Ahnna into his arms.

"Why?" he demanded, his voice low and ragged, his hands trembling against her back. She buried her face in the hollow of his neck, his skin smelling of river water. "Why would you let them do that to you?"

"She likes being a martyr," Aren muttered. "Always has."

"I do not." She pulled back with a scowl. "It was—"

"You do." Aren crossed his arms, glaring. "You always want everyone to blame you. Which is irritating enough, but to the gallows, Ahnna? Really?"

"Would you have preferred that Harendell kept the bridge?" she snapped. "Because that was the alternative. It was all going to plan until . . ."

She trailed off, her gaze locking with James's. "I'm so sorry about William."

He gave a tight nod, hands sliding down her arms until they closed over her fingers.

"They'll blame us for William's poisoning," Aren said, scanning the tree-lined banks, tense as a bowstring. "But any idea who it was? Amaridians, maybe? Revenge for Katarina? Or was it Alexandra? She's got an heir now—a baby's easier to control than a grown man, and she would not have liked the deal you made with William."

Ahnna's vision blurred, not with tears, but with memory.

Alexandra's face, shredded by her own nails. William's body in her arms, his face blistered in the shape of a handprint. The vision faded away, replaced by William and Lestara arguing in the Sky Palace. Lestara had cupped William's cheek with a gloved hand, only for him to shove her away. After he'd left, she'd cast her gloves across the room before giving in to labor.

Ahnna's breath caught.

"Not Amarid," she whispered. "Nor Alexandra. I think . . . I think the manipulators of this great scheme have become the manipulated."

"By whom?" Aren asked sharply.

James's voice came first, tight with fury, his grip firm on her hands.

"Lestara."

# 93

# ZARRAH

Zarrah's nails dug into Keris's hand. She'd held him back as chaos erupted before them, every warrior's instinct in her screaming to join the fray. Her heart had pounded against her ribs, not just with fear for her friends, but fear for what their deaths would mean for Ithicana. It was only the empress in her that defied emotion in favor of logic. It would be her crown, not her blade, that would serve her allies now.

And so she'd held Keris back, knowing that if Aren fell, her husband might never forgive her restraint.

The square, moments ago brimming with noise and movement, had become an eerie place of echoes and shadows. Civilians had scattered like frightened birds, slamming doors and shuttering windows. The coppery scent of blood still lingered in the air, mingling with smoke from a fire burning in the city, the damp scent of the river carried on the wind that swirled Zarrah's hair. Soldiers had vanished in pursuit of the fleeing Ithicanians, Aren and his fighters melting into the city's alleys like smoke, leaving behind only the dead, the grieving—and the vultures waiting to feast on power.

In the gallery, Alexandra's ladies had collapsed in swoons, fans fluttering like dying moths in the hands of frantic maids, but Zarrah didn't fail to notice that the swoons were feigned. The nobles who had fled at the first sign of violence now crept back like rats to a battlefield, eyes gleaming with the prospect of gossip more lethal than the steel Harendell was famed for.

Ronan stood unmoving, one elbow on the railing, his expression carved from stone. When he met Zarrah's gaze, his voice was resigned. "There is no honor in this nation, and never has been. They are spiders, every one of them—building webs and waiting for poison to do their work so they can devour the remains."

Zarrah couldn't keep the hollowness from her voice as she said, "And now your daughter rules. Queen of spiders."

The king of Cardiff gave a slow nod. "Her mother cast the bones when Lestara was seven. Calythra saw she would not just be queen—she would rule. But also that death would follow her. Her name would become a curse. We should have killed her then, but Caly also saw that Lestara would give birth to a prince who would deliver our people into a brighter era."

A gasp from a noblewoman nearby reminded Zarrah they weren't alone, and that more spiders were listening.

"I thought," Ronan continued, "that sending her to Silas would dull the prophecy. A nation without queens, a king who refused to grant any woman power. But Caly warned me—you cannot manipulate futures written in the stars. I hoped we could claim the good without the horror." His mouth twisted bitterly. "But my wife, as always, was right. Lestara has borne the son who may bring a bright future, but all I see right now is death."

Below them, Lestara rocked, her scream-raw voice cracking as she clutched the crying babe. Her face was soaked with tears, but her arms held the child too tightly, like a crown rather than a son. *Does she mourn William,* Zarrah wondered, *or the loss of his shield?* Alexandra still ruled, and Zarrah doubted the dowager queen would suffer Lestara for long.

Alexandra sat on the cold cobbles beside William's body, his hand clasped in hers, her expression empty. It was not maternal grief Zarrah saw, but calculation derailed—rage unspooling inside a woman whose every plan had shattered.

Movement at the edge of the square drew all eyes.

Virginia Ashford, supported by George Cavendish, limped forward, her cane striking stone with an uneven rhythm. She shoved his hand away and pressed on. Her dress was soiled at the hem with mud, her face streaked with tears.

"William?" she called out, voice trembling. "Will, where are you?"

"Ginny . . ." Cavendish reached for her arm, attempting to hold her back.

"Will, answer me!" Her voice rose in ferocity like surf in a storm. "You know I hate this game. Please, please, just answer."

"He's dead, you idiot girl!" Lestara snapped, her hatred for the other woman palpable. "Ahnna used her confession to poison him. He's dead before your feet!"

A guttural scream tore from Virginia's throat, and she dropped to her hands and knees, crawling the last distance to William's body. She pressed her forehead to his chest, her sobs keening through the square.

The onlookers, noble and commoner alike, stood stunned—frozen between pity and dread.

*Spiders*, Zarrah thought again, her heart aching. *But spiders that loved one another dearly.*

A soldier approached the huddle of royals and bowed low. "The Ithicanians have escaped downriver, Your Grace. They had vessels waiting. With wind in their sails, they are already outpacing us."

"You let them escape?" Lestara lurched to her feet, still clutching the child. It struck Zarrah that she hadn't looked at her baby's face. Not once.

Ronan's exhale beside Zarrah was nearly imperceptible, but she knew he had noticed his daughter's behavior as well.

"We will relay horses and follow by river," the soldier said, glancing at the gathering nobles. "They will not get far."

"If they make it to the Tempest Seas, they *will* escape," she shrieked.

"Like snakes slithering into holes, where they'll bide their time before biting again! Alexandra, do something! Make them fix this!"

Alexandra stirred as though waking from a trance. "Send pigeons to every port," she rasped. "The birds will outpace the ships."

"You will do no such thing!" Virginia screamed the words, everyone around her recoiling from the feral rage on the princess's face. *This spider had had enough.*

The noblewomen who'd feigned swoons were climbing to their feet now, moving to the railing for a better view.

Harendell's princess climbed upright, batting aside Cavendish's attempts to help her, and with unerring precision, she pointed a finger at her mother. "I know the truth, Mother. William is dead because of *you*!"

Alexandra's face hardened under her bloody mask. "Everything I do is for you and your brother, Virginia. I would die for either of you. Would gladly exchange places with William, if such a thing were possible." Her voice cracked on the last, but then she squared her shoulders. "This is Ahnna Kertell's doing. Ithicana's doing. How is that not clear to you?"

"It's Ahnna *Ashford*," Virginia spat, "because James married her! And he would never harm William." Turning to face the rising murmurs of the onlookers, the princess raised her voice. "I spoke with James not an hour past, and he confirmed all that King Ronan claimed about my mother's crimes. She allied with Katarina and together, they murdered Princess Siobhan. Together, they conspired with Silas Veliant. Together, they plotted my father's murder. And together, they attempted to slaughter an entire nation so as to control a *bridge*!"

"Lies," Alexandra snarled. "You're overcome with grief. Be silent."

"No." Lestara had ceased weeping, her voice now filled with authority. "Let Virginia speak."

Alexandra climbed to her feet, her desire to protect herself overwhelming her grief for her fallen son, and she gave Lestara a sharp look before rounding on her daughter. "I know you love James, but he has been taken in by that Ithicanian snake. Corrupted by her sensual wiles, for he has the weakness of all men."

"Sensual wiles?" Virginia laughed, high and brittle. "You think James betrayed everything for *sex*? No. You're just angry because Father never loved you. And William is dead because *you* killed him. You conspired with Katarina, and she poisoned him before she died!"

Beside Zarrah, Keris stiffened. "Not Katarina," he whispered. "Fiona was with me. She'd have smelled it. She didn't bark."

*Then who?* Zarrah's thoughts spun.

"Virginia is lost to grief and is being manipulated by stronger minds." Alexandra crossed her arms. "We stand in a dangerous moment, and Harendell needs leadership, otherwise villains will capitalize. Ithicana will capitalize—laughing, because they have been exonerated by the emotional bleating of a woman barely out of girlhood. You are all grown men"—she surveyed the noblemen—"and you must be more discerning in the information you choose to believe."

Virginia sneered. "Then let someone else speak. A man. A discerning man." She turned to Cavendish. "Georgie. Tell them."

Cavendish looked like a man on the edge of collapse.

"If you ever loved me, you will speak the truth." Virginia wiped tears from her face. "Speak, or I will know that every word of affection that you've ever spoken to me was a lie."

"Speak, George," Lestara urged. "If you have knowledge, you must share it."

He swallowed hard but then spoke. "The accusations are true. Alexandra brought me into her schemes. I murdered King Edward on her orders. Her injuries were self-inflicted to frame Ahnna."

Silence swept the square like the shadow of a passing storm.

In hindsight, it made so much sense. Virginia had always been collateral damage in Edward's plots, and Cavendish's love for the princess would have made him an easy target for Alexandra's manipulation.

"This is damning." Lestara's words filled the square. "This is treason and regicide, and the court cannot continue to deny the truth."

"Oh, be *silent*, you stupid slut!" Alexandra shrieked. "You're a Cardiffian whore—good for birthing and nothing else!"

Lestara smoothed back her hair, voice cool as water. "Oliver is king apparent. And under Harendell's law, *I* am his regent. That makes *me* queen."

Zarrah's blood turned to ice. Beside her, Keris whispered, "It was Lestara. She poisoned him."

Alexandra's face lost all color. "You will not listen to this woman!" she shouted to the crowd. "She is a traitor. A Cardiffian witch!"

Keris broke from Zarrah's grip, descending the gallery stairs like a storm. "Neither of these women should rule!" he shouted. "The child has an uncle! Name *James* as regent. Or Virginia. Anyone but this monster!"

"Not James!" Alexandra shrieked. "He and Ahnna murdered William!"

"It is you who are responsible for William's death, not James," Virginia shouted over the noise. "Quit blaming him!"

"I did not kill my son!" Alexandra clawed at her blood-streaked face. "All of this—*everything*—was for *him*! I killed Siobhan for him. I killed Edward for him. And if not for *you*"—she pointed at Lestara—"William would have been the greatest king Harendell had ever known!"

Lestara only gave her a smile of condescension. "No, Alexandra. You just got tangled in your own web."

For all his size, Ronan of Cardiff moved as silently as smoke. He flowed down the stairs, drawing his blade as he walked. With one swing, he cut Alexandra's head from her shoulders.

The noblewomen swooned in truth this time as the head rolled, coming to rest just below the gallery platform. As Zarrah looked down at it, Alexandra's green eyes gleamed with the last thought she'd ever had, and Zarrah would swear until her deathbed that it was fury at discovering that she'd been outmanipulated.

"Cardiff has what it came for," he said, then bent to wipe his blade on Alexandra's dress. "I will leave Harendell to untangle this mess."

As he walked away, Lestara called out, "You should be proud, Father. Of all your children, I have achieved the most, and I hope our alliance will remain strong."

"You are everything the stars said you would be, daughter." Ronan did not stop walking, only joined a group of waiting Cardiffians and disappeared from sight.

Lestara smiled, and it struck Zarrah that the woman had taken her father's words as a compliment. Then she cleared her throat. "We've seen enough death today. George Cavendish, it is clear that you were a victim of Alexandra's lies and manipulation, and to that end, I pardon your role on the condition that you remove yourself from Verwyrd and return to your family's estates in the north. You will take Lady Virginia with you so that she might recover from this ordeal. I hope that time together will repair your fractured affections."

"I'm not going anywhere!" Virginia snarled. "I led you around on a leash, you little bitch. Do not think that you can tell me where to go, and do not think that I will stand by and let you take power!"

"Virginia, I assure you that I will *never* forget how you treated me like a dog," Lestara purred, and the princess took an abrupt step back, seeming to finally realize the dangerous position she stood in.

"She will come with me, Your Grace," Cavendish said, taking hold of Virginia's arms and tugging her back. "We will leave straightaway."

"You cannot do this." Tears flooded down Virginia's face. "I will not let you do this."

Cavendish's lips were close to her ear, his expression urgent as he whispered words Zarrah could not make out but knew were pleas for her to recognize the danger she was in. To flee and fight another day. And the princess did not resist as he pulled her away.

As they departed, Zarrah noticed that William's friend, Archibold Bennett, was circulating through his noble peers, murmuring something into their ears. Each time, the individual in question stiffened and paled. He had a stack of paper under one arm, and as he moved past Zarrah, she recognized the letterhead. It was the banking records she'd hidden in Lestara's rooms, and her gut told her that there was more damning information in them than she'd realized.

And she'd all but delivered them to Lestara's hands.

"Are you all going to stand here and do nothing?" Keris shouted at the gallery. "You represent the most powerful houses in Harendell, and you just stand there while this monster"—he pointed at Lestara—"takes control?"

The men all exchanged looks, then one lifted a shoulder and said, "She breaks no laws, Your Highness. The baby prince cannot rule, and Lestara is the queen mother, which makes her a strong choice for regent. Stronger still, given that James has shown his loyalties are not with us and Virginia is . . ." He trailed off, waving a hand before his face. "You know my meaning."

Keris huffed out a disgusted breath. "You would rather let a monster rule than a blind woman? Lestara leaves thousands of dead in her wake, whereas Virginia has caused the death of no one."

"That is not a virtue when one has enemies all around," the man responded. "Besides, all rulers leave death in their wake. Dead soldiers. Dead civilians. Dead children. You are a perfect example of this, Veliant." His eyes flicked to Zarrah. "As is your empress. As is every ruler who has lived, making decisions that others pay for with their lives. Most claim a righteous path. A greater good. Perhaps that is so, but it does not make the victims of their chosen course any less dead."

Zarrah tensed, wanting to intervene, but this was Keris's fight. Even if it was one she knew he'd lose. What would come next was on her, and Zarrah was ready.

Lestara gave him a sideways glance, eyes gleaming with vicious triumph, and then she began to circle William's body and Alexandra's headless corpse. She cut a striking image, dressed in bloody birthing clothes, baby prince in her arms, her bare feet leaving crimson prints as she trod through the blood of the fallen. "Alexandra was guilty of many crimes, but the one we cannot rest on her shoulders is the death of King William. Ahnna conspired to get close to him to deliver a poisoned blow, and King Aren was clearly complicit given it was he who rescued her today, at the cost of many of our good and true soldiers. Their purpose was clear: to send Harendell into a tailspin of turmoil over who will lead so as to take advantage and reclaim their precious bridge. But they have sorely underestimated us."

Rage rose in Zarrah's chest, hot and fierce, as the men nodded their agreement.

"You're a liar, Lestara." Keris stepped up to her, only to be pushed back by soldiers. "This was your poison. Not Katarina's. Not Ahnna's. Put a poison dog in your rooms, and I'm sure we'll find the evidence to prove it."

"The only evidence you'll find is of my labors to bring William's heir into the world." She gave Keris a disgusted shake of her head.

"I was in labor all through the night with midwives watching on. I did not even see my husband until he took Oliver from his cradle and went running from the Sky Palace, and my heart breaks that we did not get one final chance to share words. To share in the accomplishment that is our son."

She turned away from him again to address the gallery. "The bridge is the greatest wonder of our world. Created before living memory by a power we can't begin to understand, but its purpose is clear: to connect nations and allow trade to flow. That is why it exists, but its purpose is continually stymied by the fact that the nation that controls it is weak. That weakness makes it an endless target for those who desire control, but all that is ever achieved is a disruption of its very purpose."

Again the men all murmured their agreement, nodding vigorously, and Zarrah swallowed her anger. Lestara had claimed control of Alexandra's arsenal of blackmail materials, and their agreement was only a desire to protect themselves.

Lestara raised her voice higher. "The bridge needs to be controlled by a nation powerful enough to protect its interests. A nation whose might is such that no one will contest the ownership, and in the peace that will come from that certainty, trade will flow without disruption. All nations will benefit, as will the people, low and high, because all will be able to carry out business without fear. Harendell, my friends, is the only nation capable of achieving this. The only nation capable of promising the certainty of undisrupted traffic through the bridge, and for this reason, we cannot give it up. For this reason, we must set sail with all force and claim the Bridge Kingdom once and for all."

The crowd of men erupted into cheers, but they fell silent as Zarrah walked down the steps from the gallery to stand at Keris's side.

"Empress." There was a hint of mockery in Lestara's tone, and more still in the curtsy she gave, holding her stained nightdress out as though it were a gown.

"Spare me the performance, Lestara," Zarrah said, keeping her tone measured despite the fury in her heart. "And speak clearly. Is it your intent, then, to annex Ithicana by force of arms so as to control the bridge?"

"It need not be by force," Lestara replied, ignoring her baby's hungry cries. "We would embrace the Ithicanians if they laid down their arms and accepted Oliver's rule. We would nurture and protect them as our own people, and they would thrive under the stability we offer. But Aren has been given the opportunity to abdicate before, and he has always chosen deception and violence instead. It would do well if the Ithicanians rebelled against his selfish choices, but if they remain loyal to his weak rule, we will move with force. It is for the greater good."

"No, it is not." Zarrah stared Lestara down, and it was the other woman who looked away first. "You do this because you desire power. These men do it because they fear the consequences of their own greed. *Goodness* has nothing to do with it, and on my honor, if you do not withdraw from Ithicana, as was William's intent, it will be *me* you come against. Harendell might be the queen of the north, but Valcotta is empress of the south, and we know war *far* better than you. Do not test me."

Lestara's jaw tightened, and she glared down at her crying child before remembering herself and forcing a smile back to her face.

"Bold words, Zarrah," she finally said. "Bold words for a woman whose rule is hardly secure. You cannot even keep your consort safe from your own people, because the Endless War has not been fully extinguished. How well will they react to discovering that you intend to stop trade with the north? How strong will support be when you destroy their livelihoods for the sake of another nation? And poor, hungry Maridrina . . . what of them? How will they react to learning that you are the reason their children starve? How long until the flames of the Endless War burn anew, and both you and your *consort* find yourselves the first victims?"

Lestara's mouth curled up in a smirk as she bounced the baby prince. "I think your threats are empty, Zarrah. I think that you, and your consort"—her eyes slid to Keris—"are impotent in this conflict."

She'd grown clever under the tutelage of the Harendellians, but Zarrah had never been one to back down. "Are you willing to make that bet?"

Lestara pantomimed shaking dice in a cup, casting them out into the air, to the amusement of the men watching on.

"So be it." Zarrah eyed the Harendellian nobles, who were looking everywhere but at her. "This investment is going to cost you dearly."

"I find myself growing weary of your threats," Lestara snapped. "You were never invited here, and your presence is unwelcome. Leave, and on your way south, do let Aren know my terms."

Zarrah looked at the face of the prince who was supposed to achieve such great things, her heart aching for the life he'd been born into through no fault of his own. "Long live the king," she said.

Then she took Keris's arm, and together they walked toward war.

# 94
# AHNNA

THE RIVER STRETCHED out before them like a green ribbon winding toward the sea—but to Ahnna, it felt like a noose wrapping around all their necks.

They were all going to die, and it was because they came to rescue her.

She crouched low in the narrow canoe, fingers white-knuckled against the wood, every muscle braced as arrows flew overhead. Her sodden dress clung to her skin, blood seeping from a shallow cut across her forearm, but none of it registered over the pounding of her heart.

*They should have left me.*

Another arrow thudded into the wood beside her knee, then the mounted archers gave up their pursuit, their mounts spent. A moment of respite, but like all the others, it would be short-lived.

James was crouched next to her. His face was set in grim lines, his shirt torn and wet with river water, one of his eyes swollen almost shut. He hadn't left her side during their flight down the river toward the sea.

Yet part of her still struggled to believe he was alive.

"You're too quiet," he said, not turning around. "Talk to me."

She shook her head, and though her throat felt too tight for words, she managed, "She said you were dead. Said that she'd killed you. I . . ." She didn't know how to put into words that her heart had been shattered, and even with him living and breathing right next to her, she was still struggling to put the pieces back together.

"Is that why you went to William with your plan to take the blame?"

Ahnna shook her head. "No. But it made it easier to go through with it."

He shifted to look at the opposite bank, but she didn't fail to notice how his jaw flexed and unflexed beneath the scruff of beard. "I'm angry at you."

It was awkward having this conversation with her people pressed in all around them, the threat of another force of archers coming upon them putting everyone on edge. Yet with death lurking around each bend in the river, no conversation could wait. "I didn't see another solution."

"It was never a solution." He rounded on her, amber eyes flashing. "William would have kept to his word for a time, but Alexandra would *never* have let the bridge go. She'd have worked away at convincing him that he deserved the bridge, or that Ithicana needed his guidance, or whatever strategy she came up with, and Harendell's navy would have set sail. Your death would have been a bandage, would have hidden the wound, but that wound would have continued to fester beneath."

"Well, actually, given Lestara had already poisoned William when I went to meet him . . ." She trailed off as James's glower deepened. "I'm sorry."

"No, you're not."

Ahnna bit the insides of her cheeks. "What would you have had me do? What would you have done, if you'd been me?"

Instead of answering, James lifted an arm to point. "Aren, archers!" Everyone lifted shields and weapons, but he met her gaze again. "We tried to be clever. We tried to defeat our enemies with manipulations and schemes to avoid a war, but here we are. All that is left is to fight. All that is left is to pit Ithicana's defenses against the might of Harendell and hope that we can hold out until the storms come again. What I would have you do is pick up your sword and fight at my side until the end."

In answer, Ahnna lifted a shield above their heads, her arm shuddering as an arrow struck the wood. "You'll fight, even though it's against your own people?"

"I chose you, Ahnna. I married you. Your fight is my fight until my heart beats its last." He caught hold of her waist, and pulled her against him, kissing her hard even as shouts sounded from shore.

A volley rained from above. Arrows tore through the air, some splashing into the river, some striking the other vessels, others punching into shields. Ahead, one of their ships faltered, caught sideways in the current. Archers targeted it mercilessly.

"Give them a volley!" Aren shouted, and Ahnna retrieved a bow, launching an arrow at a soldier. It hit his arm, not a killing blow but enough to render him helpless in the fight, and she moved on to another, catching him in the shoulder.

Her countrymen were less discerning, and soldiers fell off the backs of their horses, dead before they hit the ground. Ahnna's stomach soured, but she kept shooting until the attack ceased.

"They've sent pigeons to garrisons along the Eldermoor," James shouted. "Which means that they'll have sent the message to Elmsworth. It's a military port, so there are hundreds of soldiers in that garrison. Worse still, we have to pass beneath the city's six bridges, the first and the last of which have the capacity to lower chains to prevent passage. How the fuck did you get past them coming upriver?"

"Portage," Aren called back. "We carried the boats from the beach up past Elmsworth under the cover of night, then sailed upriver. We didn't know what we were getting into until this morning when we heard about the execution, but we came to get Ahnna back, so we adapted."

James stood, shadowing his eyes as he stared downriver. "Portage won't work. They know we're coming, which means they'll be sending patrols up the river. We can't outrun or hide from them carrying boats, and if we abandon the boats, we have no way to get back to Ithicana."

Ahnna stood next to him. "It will be night when we reach Elmsworth."

"They'll have torches. They know we are coming. We can't sneak through an entire city without them noticing, if that's what you're suggesting."

"That's exactly what I'm suggesting." She rounded on Aren. "Submerged tow?"

"We could. They use the river as a sewer, so the water is filthy and full of debris." He jerked his chin toward the banks. "There are reeds aplenty."

James frowned. "They'll have the chains down. The boats will get caught up, and while we can swim under, we can't swim to Ithicana."

"Did you bring our usual supplies?" Ahnna asked, then watched a smile grow on her brother's face as he said, "You do love your explosives, Ahnna."

She bowed with a flourish. "One last scheme."

---

AS DARKNESS SETTLED, everyone was still under the water and holding on to a network of towropes fixed to the rear of the two vessels they needed to keep. Each of them breathed through a reed, and they'd filled the water with floating debris to hide them. The two other vessels floated well ahead, explosives set up inside of them.

Her heart thrummed, because all too easily, Ahnna remembered how she'd tried a version of this scheme to evade Carlo, only to be caught in his net. *Not this time*, she silently whispered. *This time, it's going to work.*

Through the murky water, the lights of the city grew brighter. Elmsworth was large—larger than Sableton or Verwyrd—and as they passed into it, there was no mistaking the filth that poured from the sewers into the water. She could taste it on the air she breathed through the reed and feel it bumping against her, foul as anything she'd ever experienced. But the filth provided cover, not even the light of soldiers' torches enough to pierce its depths.

A light flashed.

*Boom!*

The river water shuddered with the force of the explosion. The first vessel had hit the chains and tipped, the powders they'd set igniting with enough force that the whole bridge would have collapsed.

The lights of the torches began moving and bouncing, the men holding them running. Shouts faintly emanated from above, and alarm bells rang. They'd have spotted the identical setups in the next vessel, as well as the false setups in the ships she and the others floated behind.

"They'll think that we abandoned ship upstream and send forces to hunt us down," James had said when they were planning the strategy. "They'll lift the chains on the next bridge rather than lose it to an explosion, and they won't board the vessels for risk of them going off. Safer to let the boats drift into the sea and deal with them there."

"Except instead, we'll climb back in and sail away."

"They will pursue," he'd warned. "That harbor is full of ships, and they're ready for war. *Fast* ships."

Aren had only shrugged. "I've never had anyone catch me yet."

Still, it was hard to cling to that bravado as the river swept them downstream. Ahnna's legs bumped into rubble from the collapsed bridge, flames bright on either side of the river from where nearby structures had been set ablaze. Yet more distractions for their escape, but she hoped they didn't spread.

*Boom!*

Ahnna's stomach lurched, because there was no way the second vessel had reached the last bridge. Either someone had tried to board it or it had run aground and triggered the explosion. Either way, if the other bridge chain was still lowered, they'd lost their only way to get past.

*Stick to the plan.* She could all but hear James's voice in her head. *They won't risk losing the bridge—they'll get the chains up.*

Ahnna clenched her teeth around her reed, sucking in breaths of the rank air above the river, then her control snapped. She let go of the rope and swam underwater until she reached the banks. Carefully lifting her head, she watched the two ships drift downriver, swarms of soldiers with torches keeping pace on the roads that ran alongside the banks.

Keeping low, she clambered up the rocks and raced into the city. Everyone was awake and out in the streets, shouts of alarm and cries of terror filling her ears. Fire had broken out from the explosions, and bucket brigades were racing to put them out. The chaos made it easy to run without drawing notice, and Ahnna sprinted down alleys and streets, keeping parallel to the river. Her side cramped, her breath coming in rapid gasps, but she couldn't slow down if she meant to get to that bridge before the two remaining vessels.

The roar of surf grew loud enough to match the shouts, the ocean growing nearer with every passing stride. Ahnna cut toward the river, wary of the masses of soldiers gathered along the bank to watch the ships. None of them were venturing closer, the false explosive set up inside each of the vessels working as a deterrent.

Ahead, just before the harbor, a large bridge stretched across the wide river. It was built of thick stone with endless adornments, two large piers supporting it in the middle, between which dangled chains half submerged in the water. Winches were rattling as men struggled to lift the heavy links high enough that they wouldn't catch the masts, shouts of "They're coming! They're coming!" flying above the noise.

Relief filled Ahnna's veins, only to drain away in a heartbeat as she caught sight of heavy ropes being dragged across the water. Men worked in teams to lift them parallel to the river to catch the masts as they passed, detonating the explosives where they could do no damage.

"Goddamn it!" Everyone floating beneath the surface would be forced to let go and drift down to the sea, and unless they could swiftly steal a ship, they would have no escape. Ahnna had no doubt the Harendellians were swarming the ship docks, waiting for any such attempt.

She had to cut those ropes.

In her periphery, the ships drifted closer, but Ahnna focused on the group of men holding the rope on this side. They were tying it off to an oak tree on the riverbank, those on the far side doing the same to a mooring pillar.

"Get back!" the captain in command shouted. "Get out of range of the explosion!"

The men rushed back between the building lining the boulevard, their eyes on the mast drifting around a bend, the second vessel not far behind. Half a minute, no more.

Drawing her sword, Ahnna sprinted toward the oak tree. The soldiers shouted, and she dodged a swift one who got into her path, but she'd always been quick on her feet.

Lifting her blade, Ahnna put all her strength into chopping down on the taut rope, only for it to fall limp at her feet before her blade could strike.

*What?*

Her gaze snapped across the water to find a dripping wet James standing on the opposite bank, a sword in hand. "Run!" he roared.

Ahnna didn't hesitate. Parrying a sword from a howling soldier, she dodged an arrow shot and broke into a run. Not toward the water, but away. Drawing the attention of the soldiers away from her people hidden beneath the surface of the river.

She flung herself into an alley, leaping over broken crates and debris, her bare feet slipping in refuse. The rush of fear in her veins gave her wings, but exhaustion was rising, her sides aching.

*Faster.*

She leapt onto a barrel and jumped, catching hold of a balcony railing and climbing atop it. Balancing on the narrow beam, she reached for the roof and hauled herself up, immediately on her feet and running. Most of the buildings were row houses, and once she leapt onto the top of one, it was a long stretch of open roof.

*Slick* open roof, with mold and moss from the humidity turning it treacherous. Her feet slipped, then one went through a weak spot and she sprawled, losing her weapon.

Cursing, she got upright and kept running, the sound of pursuit loud from below.

Arrows flew past her, catching at her clothing, but there was nothing to do but run on. She leapt to the next row house, stumbling as the roof sagged beneath her weight. Ahnna threw herself into a roll, nearly sliding down the steep pitch, but her nails caught on the wooden shingles.

But it was the sight of chaos on the far side of the river that stalled her progress. Soldiers were running, torches bright in a long line as they chased a shadowed figure through the alleys.

*James.*

Ahnna risked a glance at the ships. They had only the last bridge to pass through, but it was the one with the chains. As she watched, the soldiers began lowering them, willing to destroy the bridge in an explosion rather than allow her and James to escape.

"I don't think so!" she snarled, leaping into a tree and letting it slow her fall, heedless of the branches scratching deep into her skin. Her feet hit the cobbles, and she ran straight toward the winch station.

Soldiers turned to meet her. Ahnna ducked beneath a swinging blade and came up with her fist balled. It took the man in the face, and he stumbled, allowing her to rip his sword from his grip. She dueled with another soldier, sending him sprawling, and then lunged, her sword sliding between the links. The mechanism kept going and then caught with a groan, the force bending the sword into a sharp *V.*

But it held.

"Ahnna!"

She ran toward James's voice, breath coming in ragged gasps as she hurled up the slope of the bridge. They half collided in the middle, the ships passing beneath them, the tide causing them to pick up speed as they were sucked into the harbor. Arrows flew, clattering against the stone of the bridge, and armed soldiers ran toward them.

"Jump!"

He lifted her onto the railing and leapt up next to her, and then hand in hand they jumped.

An arrow scraped across her leg as they fell, then filthy water closed over her head. It wouldn't stop an arrow from hitting them, but it would ruin their aim, so Ahnna dragged James deeper. She kicked hard, following the current toward the salvation of the sea.

When her head broke the surface, Ahnna sucked in a breath and searched the waves. "There!"

Aren and the rest were climbing into the small ships, but her brother immediately began to panic. "Ahnna! Ahnna!"

"Here!"

She and James swam hard, fighting over the surf to reach the bobbing ships. Hands caught hold of them, pulling them inside, but they hadn't reached safety. Not even close.

"Sails!" Aren shouted. "Go! Go!"

No one hesitated, and the sails unfurled, catching the wind. But on the docks, other ships were making ready, and signals were being sent to those anchored on the water.

It wouldn't be long until the large vessels were on the hunt, and on the open sea, they'd be much faster.

Strong hands caught hold of her shoulders, and James pulled her against him. "They won't find us in the dark." Then he caught hold of her hand and lifted it to the sky, using her index finger to point at the gathering of stars. "South," he murmured, his heat chasing away the cold of the river. "Follow them, and we'll make it home."

# 95
# AREN

There was no respite on the seas.

James identified the ships pursuing them as clippers, and the fastest the Harendellians had at their disposal. Aren couldn't argue that as the three ships flew over the waves, endless white canvas sheets stretched open to catch every bit of wind. His two ships were outmatched in every possible way.

Except for the crew sailing them.

"These are the nimblest ships in Harendell's fleet," James said, his hand held over his eyes to shade them. "But it's like watching three lumbering bears trying to catch two rabbits."

It was true that the larger vessels were unable to match them now that they were among the obstacles of the endless islands and outcroppings of Ithicana, the small ships backtracking and weaving, sailing over shoals and sandbars to evade pursuit. But it was not lost on Aren that if they hadn't escaped during the night, they'd never have survived this long.

It was not sustainable.

Everyone was exhausted, as were their supplies, and to beach on any of the islands would allow the ships to capture them with ease.

They needed rest. They needed food, but above all else, they needed *water*.

Aren tilted his face to the cloudless sky, squinting in the brilliant light, his tongue dry as sand. What he wouldn't give for rain.

"It would be timely for one of Ithicana's tempests to rear its head," James muttered, also looking at the sky.

"Every other nation calls this season *the calm*," Ahnna said as she scampered along the length of the vessel to retie a line, sensing what Aren needed without him giving an order. "But we have another name for it."

"What do you call it?" James had shifted and was now staring back over his shoulder at the ship gaining ground. Aren didn't need to look over his shoulder to know that archers lined the decks, ready to loose arrows the moment they came into range, and there was nowhere to hide.

"War Tides," Aren muttered, then shouted, "Lean!"

Ahnna and James joined those catching hold of lines, throwing their weight, the vessel heeling over at a dangerous angle. But as the wind caught the sail from a different angle, it flung them sharply between two islands, the passage between them narrow enough that the clippers couldn't follow. Their other vessel tracked the opposite direction, forcing the clippers once again to choose which ship to hunt.

"We can lose them when the sun sets," Ahnna called to him, one hand locked on a rope and the other trailing in the waves. She still wore the remains of the dress she'd nearly been executed in, her legs bare from the knees down, her naked toes gripping the wood of the ship. Painfully thin, she was marked with bruises and injuries, and—though she put on a fighting face—exhausted beyond measure. "Get onto one of the smaller islands and stock up. They'll never find us."

"We can't." Aren shifted his weight, adjusting the rudder. "Ornak is the obvious place for us to be headed, and if they manage to encircle the island, we'll never get through. Lara's there."

His queen was there ruling in his absence, and readying for the war that was about to come down upon their heads.

"Can it be defended?" James asked.

Ornak was an island on the outskirts of the archipelago. It was the largest on the eastern half of Ithicana, so it was where many of the Ithicanian warriors were gathered because of its proximity to the threat of the north. Unfortunately, it was also a location known to the Harendellians because of its size and visible defenses, which meant they'd suspect that was where her people were hiding. Eranahl as well, but that was much farther south.

James's words garnered worried looks from the others aboard, but he wasn't wrong, and they all knew it.

"Harendell is ready for war," James continued. "On the assumption Alexandra is still in control, she'll be out for revenge. She and her supporters will surely have the people convinced that Ahnna poisoned William. Though in truth, she may hardly need the justification given that Ithicana is going to seem like easy pickings. They'll smell the profit. We have a day's lead at most. Maybe less, given we've hardly taken the straight shot south."

He looked in no better shape than Ahnna. One of James's eyes was swollen, his left cheek was a mass of bruises, and his lip was split. "A shovel," was the only response he'd given when Aren had asked. From the way he moved, his injuries were worse from the neck down. Still, he could fight.

If he chose to.

James had proven in Elmsworth that he was willing to fight his own people for Ahnna's sake, but whether he'd choose to fight Harendell on Ithicana's behalf was yet uncertain.

And not something he could worry about now. Aren scowled as he caught sight of one of the clippers moving to cut them off, shouted orders, and then guided his vessel between two islands that looked like blades of rock sticking out of the sea. "We get as close as we can to Ornak, then make a run for it. If we can get inside of the range of the shipbreakers, we'll be safe."

Though not for long.

How long could they hold out against the full might of Harendell's navy? Maybe they could hold them off with shipbreakers and the island's other defenses until storm season came, but when it did, the bridge and all the islands would be firmly under Harendell's control, trade merrily flowing unless Zarrah and Keris were able to do something about it. Ithicana had fought back Maridrina and regained sovereignty, but circumstances were a thousand times worse now, and Aren did not see a way back to where they'd been before this all began.

He guided his ship out from between the islands, heading toward another scattering of rocky outcroppings while one of the clippers pursued, gaining on them.

"They're almost in range," James shouted, his eyes on the clipper as it closed the distance. Closer and closer. "Everyone who can, get down."

Aren held his ground, their lives depending on his sailing skill.

Two arrows splashed into their wake. James caught hold of Ahnna and pulled her low, ignoring her growled protests as he protected her body with his own. More arrows soared toward them, striking the wood of the vessel with heavy thunks. One grazed Aren's shoulder, leaving a line of fire across his flesh. He swore but didn't duck down. To give an inch would see them overtaken.

And then they were between two cliffs, pursuit left in their wake.

They wove and twisted through the islands of Ithicana. Backtracking and hiding in small coves, using every trick Aren had garnered over his lifetime, but they could not shake their pursuers long enough to escape. Almost like the Harendellians had a strong idea of where they were going.

And it was no longer just three ships.

Other naval ships that had been in the area joined chase. No longer a trio of bears hunting two rabbits but a fleet. Aren managed to evade them time and again, but their other vessel was not so lucky.

As he watched in horror, arrows punched through one of their sails and the ship lost speed. In what felt like a heartbeat, the clipper ran straight over the small vessel. His people dove into the water as their vessel smashed, but the archers picked them off from above.

"Don't say it," Aren snapped at Ahnna as the Harendellians aboard the clipper cheered and punched their fists into the air. "Don't even think it. Even if we threw you and James overboard, they'd keep coming. You're both an afterthought in the scheme to take the bridge."

She stood, but James caught hold of her, his hair soaked with seawater and plastered to the side of his face. "He's right! Listen to your brother!"

"I am listening! When we get through this group of islands, it's a straight shot across the open sea to Ornak, but we're not going to make it," Ahnna shouted. "We're not fast enough!"

"We'll make it," James argued. "The wind is picking up, which will make it hard for the archers to have any degree of accuracy. With sails intact, we'll make it."

"We won't!" Ahnna pulled out of James's grip and stepped over the others in the boat until she was face-to-face with him. "Aren, let me sail. I'm faster than you, and you're heavier for a counterweight."

No part of him wanted to relinquish control in this moment. Lara was on Ornak, and if he didn't make it back to her, she'd have to stand alone. Fight alone. All it would take was one mistake on Ahnna's part, and that nightmare would become a reality.

Yet as he stared into his twin's eyes, he saw the half of a whole who had never faltered. Never failed. Who'd go to the brink and scream defiance into the void, then dive straight in. Because his sister never *ever* gave up on Ithicana.

"Don't flip us," he growled, then handed her control of the rudder. "If we end up in the water, we are all dead."

"I won't." She switched positions with him, dress fluttering around her legs as they flew down a narrow channel between island cliffs, gray rock and brilliant green jungle blurring past them. "When we get past these islands, we are going to be hit hard by the crosswind. But with everyone on the port side, it will be enough weight to keep us upright."

*We'll flip*. Aren could see the wind bending the trees on the clifftops, and fear screamed that it was too intense for her plan. That the vessel would overturn, and the clipper would crush the wreckage into splinters while picking them all off. *I have to get back to Lara. I have to get back to her.*

He clenched his teeth. "Do what she says."

Everyone made ready, taking handholds where they could. They were reaching the end of the channel, and beyond, across open sea, was a hazy blob.

Ornak.

It was armed to the teeth and Lara was in command, which meant they needed to make it inside shipbreaker range, and they'd be safe.

"Ready!"

As they flew out from between the islands, the wind exploded against them, and the vessel tipped, the port side hull lifting out of the water.

"Lean!" Ahnna screamed, and Aren and the others threw their weight outward, trying to counterbalance the intensity of the wind.

The ship flew, faster and faster, seeming to barely touch the waves. Rope cut into Aren's hand as the port side rose higher, lifting him and the others into the air.

*We're going to flip.*

Aren's lips parted to scream a warning at Ahnna, but from deep within him, something stronger and more primal than fear bellowed, *Trust her.*

Sea spray stung his eyes, but Aren fixed his gaze on the island that was their salvation.

*Faster.*

Ornak grew in the distance, and Aren made out a few flashes of steel. Motion in the dense jungle across the cliffs. Most important, the tiny opening into the cove, and the gleam of chains being lifted.

*Almost there.*

Against his will, Aren looked backward, and *almost there* felt nowhere near close enough. Two clippers were right on their wake. Their decks were swarming with soldiers, archers with arrows nocked, and a heartbeat later they let a volley fly.

Aren watched the arrows soar through the air, knowing that there was no way to evade them. No place to hide, because to move from his position would see the ship keel over and they'd be overrun. "Steady!" he screamed.

Ahnna's expression was tight. Focused. Not once did she look over her shoulder, and he knew there was nothing but the wind, the ship, and the safety of the cove ahead. They'd either beat them, or they wouldn't. They'd either all fall to arrows, or they wouldn't. Ahnna sailed on a razor's edge, her nerves not faltering.

Surf hammered against the hulls of the Harendellian ships as they gained ground, and Aren could see the individual faces of the archers. The anger on them, because they believed that this pursuit was just. Believed that Ithicana was the enemy.

*Crack!*

The noise was faint, but Aren spotted a boulder soaring through the air to land with a splash in the water.

Not much farther.

An arrow thudded into the deck. Another grazed his forearm, but Aren barely felt the sting.

Another boulder hit the water.

So close. They were so close.

Lia screamed, an arrow jutting from her side. Aren reached for his friend, but their fingers only brushed as she fell, disappearing into the waves.

"Lia!" Ahnna screamed, her weight shifting, and Aren shouted at her, "Stay the course!"

But more arrows were falling.

Two pierced the sails, and two more screams cut the air, figures falling in Aren's periphery.

The vessel tilted precariously, Ahnna forced to turn away from the wind lest they go over entirely.

They had been so close. So damned close. The clipper was nearly on them, but Aren stared at the island where the love of his life was watching. "Lara!" he screamed, not wanting her to see this moment.

*Crack!*

A boulder flew over his head, sending a wave of water over them as it struck the sea.

*Crack!*

Another boulder flew, but this time, his ears filled with a crunch instead of a splash. It had struck true, taking out one of the clipper's masts. It fell sideways, taking another mast with it.

*Crack!*

A boulder landed square on the deck, punching all the way down to the sea, turning the clipper's deck to chaos.

The other clipper veered away, sailing out of range of the shipbreakers, not quite ready to court this battle.

"Get us to that cove," Aren shouted, knowing that tears mixed with seawater on his sister's face as she sailed onward, beneath the raised chain and into the cove.

Familiar shouts called their names, and the beach was filled with the faces of comrades as they dropped the sails and drifted up onto the sand. But Aren's eyes were all for Lara as she sprinted down the beach. He leapt into the water and met her as she flung herself at him, her arms going around his neck.

"Are you all right?" she demanded, and he couldn't tell if the rapid thud of a heart he felt was his or hers.

"Yeah. But Lia . . ."

"We saw." Her body tensed in his arms as though she fought a sob, and then she let go of his neck and settled into the knee-deep water. "We saw it all."

Aren straightened, taking in everyone watching. "A lot has happened, but suffice it to say, William is dead. Harendell is coming for blood. We have a day, maybe two, until the Harendellian fleet arrives and begins its attack."

Lara gave a tight nod. "I've sent word to Maridrina and to Valcotta begging for aid."

"Zarrah was in Harendell with Keris. I imagine they'll be trying to get back south, but they are in no position to help. And I think Maridrina's parliament cares more for trade than they do for who holds the bridge."

"This is it, then?" Her blue eyes met his. "The battle is upon us?"

Aren pulled his gaze from hers, surveying the Ithicanian warriors watching from the sand. Every single one of them stood square-shouldered and defiant, ready to make this last stand. And they needed to be ready.

Because in this fight, Ithicana stood alone.

# 96

# JAMES

"**H**OW MANY WARRIORS do you have on the island?" James asked, fighting the weariness threatening to overtake him. When was the last time he'd slept? He couldn't remember.

"Five hundred, give or take a few," Lara replied, adjusting the sword belted to her waist. "The issue is supplies. We've stockpiled as best we could, but five hundred mouths is a lot to feed if we can't access the sea. Now that the storms are over, the trees will produce fruit, but we have a few weeks yet until that happens. Likewise, water may become an issue if it doesn't rain. Our freshwater basin is full right now, but without rain, we'll drink it dry soon enough."

It was like being trapped in a fortress under siege, and the only thing capable of breaking the line of ships that would soon form around the island was a storm, as had happened in the siege of Eranahl. Perhaps the tempests would come to the aid of Ithicana twice, but James wouldn't bet on it. Or at least, not soon enough.

He glanced down at Ahnna, who had been silently listening to

Lara's update on the situation. She still wore that awful execution dress, though it was shredded and stained with dirt and blood. Her dark brown hair hung in salt-tangled clumps, her arms and legs were marked with cuts and bruises, and she was barefoot. She limped slightly from the cuts on the bottoms of her feet, and he fought the urge to pick her up. But he knew better than to undermine her like that.

The group approached a midsized building. It was formed of blocks of stone that had gone green from moisture and mold, the wooden roof layered thick with moss. Trees had been cut back so no branches stretched overhead, likely in deference to the violence of the storms, but even so, it would be easy to miss, it blended into the jungle so well. There were several smaller buildings set nearby he suspected were more quarters for soldiers.

They went inside, and James blinked as his eyes adjusted to the dim light from the lamps set around the windowless room. They stood in what seemed to serve as a common room, stacks of supplies sitting to one side, and a series of tables with benches taking up most of the space. Doors lined the back wall, probably leading to more sleeping quarters.

"It's tight, but we'll make space for you," Lara said. "Have something to eat and then get some rest. By the morning, we should have a better idea of what we're up against."

A woman approached with a pile of clothes and a pair of worn boots, which she passed to Ahnna. But his wife only put on the boots and set the clothes aside. "I want to have a look now."

Without another word, she left the building. Aren scrubbed a hand through his hair. "She's busy blaming herself. She thinks this is her fault, but it's not."

"That's not what she's thinking. She's trying to think of a way to win this." James grabbed a few pieces of jerky from a plate on the table, then filled a waterskin from a barrel. "I suggest you do the same."

He strode out into the fading sunlight, breaking into a jog to catch up with Ahnna as she wove through the jungle. "Eat," he said, pushing a piece of jerky into her hands, then he skidded to a stop, realizing they'd reached the clifftops. Below, the sea smashed into rock, spray bursting high with each wave. Not a fall one was likely to survive. At least, not for long.

Ahnna ate the jerky and scowled at the ships in the distance, which were only shadows on a sea painted orange and gold by the setting sun. Leaving her to think, James walked over to where a massive ship-breaker was bolted to the rock. Two Ithicanians stood next to it, and behind them was a large pile of rocks. They didn't protest as he examined the mechanism, noting how it rotated on its mount so that it could be aimed in various directions. Before it was a screen of woven vines that hid the machine from ships on the sea. There was another one about thirty paces farther along, but it was of different construction.

"It can throw farther," one of the Ithicanians said. "This one can throw heavier."

"But not that far?" James pointed to the distant cutters.

The Ithicanians shook their heads. "They'll keep out of range."

"Can't stay out of range if they want to take the island." James muttered, going back to where Ahnna stood as he considered how he'd attack if he were in command. Sea battles weren't his expertise, given most of his time had been spent in the Lowlands, but he knew enough to say with certainty that taking this island quickly would cost a lot of lives.

Ahnna was sitting at the edge of the cliff, bare legs hanging off while she chewed on the jerky. James sat next to her, ignoring the lurch of vertigo inspired by the long drop below.

"The one we hit with shipbreakers sank."

He handed her the waterskin.

Ahnna drank, then wiped her mouth on the back of her arm. "When darkness comes, we'll sneak out small vessels with good crews to use explosives to sink the ships."

"Those on the ships will be watching for them." He drank some water. "We know too many of your tricks."

"*We?*"

James didn't answer, his eyes on the banners flapping in the riggings of the ships, distance and fading light making it impossible to see them clearly, but every time he blinked, he could see it in his mind's eye. Harendell's colors, which he had fought beneath all his life.

They sat in silence, the sun turning the sea red as blood. Shadows stretched long, and the humid air clung to him like a second skin, the churning water below seeming alluringly cool.

Ahnna's hand found his. She didn't look at him, just laced their fingers together and stared hard at the horizon. "Will you be able to do it?" she asked quietly. "Fight them?"

His countrymen. His comrades in arms.

James considered lying. Saying yes without hesitation. But that wasn't what she needed from him. And she'd see through it anyway.

"I'll fight." The words stuck in his throat, and he coughed to clear it. "But it will be one of the hardest things I've ever had to do. The men on those ships are fighting for false justice. Fighting because they were ordered to, and to throw down their arms is treason. Fighting because it's how they earn the wage that pays for their families to live back home. I wish there was a way to spare them as much as I wish there was a way to spare us."

Her hand tightened in his, and this time, Ahnna looked at him. "They brought the fight to us."

"You know that's not how they see it." He watched the sun slip below the horizon. "People died on Ithicanian blades in Verwyrd, all down the river, and again in Elmsworth. It will make the task of manipulating them to support the cause easier." James couldn't keep the bitterness from his voice. "It doesn't help that they'll see this as an easy victory."

"It won't be." As the last rays of the sun faded, leaving the sea black as ink, all the lights on the distant ships began to wink out. Ahnna swore softly, shaking her head in frustration, and then said, "You're right about them knowing too many of our methods. We can't find them on the open sea with no light, and if we can't find them, we can't sink them."

James wrapped an arm around her, disliking how, in the absence of the sun, it seemed their legs hung into a void.

"Don't suggest trying to escape." She rested her cheek against his shoulder. "Anywhere we go, they'll follow. Not just you and me, but Aren and Lara. We can flee south from island to island, but unless we abandon Ithicana entirely, at some point we have to make a stand. Everyone on this island knows it, and those who don't wish to fight to the end will be gone by morning."

"I think they'll be here when the sun rises and the horns call to battle," James replied. "As will I."

His wife let out a shuddering breath.

"I've made my choice, and that choice is you. Blade, body, and soul, I am yours, Ahnna." He swallowed hard. "To not fight tomorrow would be the same as bending the knee to my enemies, and I refuse to do that."

"Can we win?"

James shook his head. "No, but we can spill their blood across the history books."

A north wind blew against them, carrying with it a chill, and Ahnna shivered.

"Let's go inside. They won't do anything until the rest of the fleet arrives, and we'll fight harder with rest."

James helped her to her feet, his arm slipping around her waist to support her weight. She didn't protest this time. The limp had worsened, and even her stubbornness had limits.

Back at the barracks, most of the soldiers had disappeared into rooms or bedrolls, the low murmur of voices dimming to an exhausted quiet. Lara sat at the table, and she silently gestured to one of the doors. Inside was a single cot, a rough blanket folded at the end. Bare stone walls. No window. Just the steady drip of water somewhere in the distance and the muffled thrum of insects in the dark.

James sat on the cot and began removing his boots. Ahnna stripped off the remains of the execution dress and pulled on the shirt and trousers she'd been given earlier, though the latter fit too loosely around her waist, barely clinging to her hips. She rinsed her hair using a small amount of water, fighting with the tangles until he took it from her. Carefully, he unraveled the knots and tangles until it hung in a curtain of loose curls down her back, gleaming in the lamplight.

Reaching, he turned down the lamp until it winked out. "Sleep."

"I don't want to. I don't want to waste what might be our last moments."

He pulled her down on the cot, wrapping an arm around her and holding her close. "It's not a waste. This is the dream, love. This is the peace we fought for, and even if it won't last, cling to this one moment of it."

She curled into him immediately, tucking herself into his side with a sigh that sounded like surrender. Not to the enemy, but to this request.

Her fingers traced idle lines along his chest. "I'm glad we get one more night."

"One night with you is worth a lifetime without."

Silence stretched between them. Her breathing slowed. And for the first time in what felt like a lifetime, James felt his muscles unwind, the relentless press of vigilance finally giving way to stillness. He pressed a kiss to the top of her head.

They lay there in the dark, the cot too small for two, their limbs tangled, hearts steadying against each other. And despite everything—the pain, the fear, the dread of what was coming—sleep came. As did the dreams of a life that would never be . . .

Until a horn bellowed, ripping James back into wakefulness.

It was a low, dull sound, and it reverberated in his chest as he wiped away the confusion of heavy sleep, unsure what time of the night it was.

Ahnna was upright in his arms. "That's the alarm."

James was already grabbing his boots, tossing Ahnna hers.

They were out of the room in seconds, the common room alive with noise. Warriors ran past, some still buckling weapons and armor, all while the horn kept up its bellow. Ahnna caught hold of his hand and dragged him outside, both of them following the warriors racing down to the beach.

Lara and Aren stood on the beach, the king shouting orders to get the chain up.

"What's going on?" James demanded.

"That's a long list," Lara responded. "I didn't want to wake you, but news came in during the night. It sounds like it all turned to chaos after you fled Verwyrd. Virginia called out Alexandra, George Cavendish confessed to being Alexandra's knifeman, and then Alexandra herself confessed to the murders. Ronan took off her head, and now Lestara rules as the baby king's regent. She wasted no time picking up the reins of Alexandra's plans, and they now sail to war."

It was almost too much to take in, so James only asked, "What else?"

"A Maridrinian merchant vessel has arrived. Just one." Aren's tone was clipped. "They're lit up like a light show with banners hanging everywhere, so the Harendellian ships know who they are. We've let them inside shipbreaker range, and there are longboats on the approach."

One merchant ship wasn't going to make a difference unless it was the front-runner bringing news of the impending arrival of the Maridrinian fleet, but James kept his mouth shut as the longboats drifted under the chains and into the cove. The first rays of sun began to glow from the east, the night having passed while he'd slept with Ahnna in his arms, and now the fight would begin.

Against all hope, James prayed to the fading glow of the stars overhead that they would not fight alone.

Then a woman got out of the first longboat to hit the beach, pulling back her hood. She was pretty, her hair long and dark, expression regal. Though it was too dark to see color, every one of James's instincts screamed that this woman's eyes were Veliant blue. As would be the eyes of every woman who stepped out of the boats, their bodies dripping with weapons, and their expressions promising death to any who stood against them.

"Sarhina." Lara's voice was choked with emotion. "Is Delia . . . ?"

"She's safe."

Queen Sarhina of Maridrina bowed low, a feral grin on her face. "In the darkest hour of Ithicana's night, the Veliants have come to fight at your side. May God, fate, and every fucking star in the sky have mercy against those who come against us."

# 97
# AHNNA

THERE WERE NO words to describe the swelling in her heart that Ahnna felt as Taryn and Bronwyn pulled back their hooded cloaks. They stood behind the other sisters, both of them staring at the water lapping the beach, and even from where she stood, Ahnna sensed their worry that they weren't welcome.

"Taryn! Bronwyn!" she called, taking two steps into the water, equally worried that she was the last person they wished to see. But they lifted their faces, and all doubt about sentiment vanished from her chest.

Wading through the shallows, Ahnna flung her arms around her cousin, then caught hold of Bronwyn and pulled her in close. "You came."

"Yeah." Taryn stepped back, smoothing her dark ponytail, expression rueful. "I have to say, we didn't hesitate when Sarhina came knocking."

Bronwyn huffed out a breath of agreement. "Turns out living your best peaceful life away from all woe isn't all that wonderful when you know that your family and friends are suffering and dying."

"Alas, our garden was sowed with cowardice and shame, so none of its yields tasted sweet." Taryn slung an arm around Ahnna's shoulder and another around Bronwyn's, directing them toward the sand. "So we are here to fight, and probably die, but at least we will go into the Great Beyond with songs of glorious death ringing in our ears rather than songs about squash and potatoes."

Ahnna laughed, and the sensation of it almost brought her to tears because she couldn't remember the last time she'd had something to laugh about. "Can't say I see you two wielding hoes."

"You and Ensel's mother both." Bronwyn spit on the sand. "That mouthy cow is cut from the same cloth as your grandmother, Ahnna, because she never saw or heard a damned thing that she didn't feel a need to voice an opinion about."

"Well, rumor has it that Nana is on Ornak, so consider yourself warned," Ahnna said, then her eyes tracked to where her brother and Lara stood in deep conversation with Sarhina. Lara looked like she was barely holding her emotions in check, Aren's arm wrapped around her and Sarhina holding one of her hands. "Is Delia okay?"

"Right as rain and busy crawling around in the dirt with her cousin as they plague the chickens," Bronwyn answered. "Ensel and his people in the mountains have made Delia their own, and they'll protect her unto death. He's as good a man as you could ask for, kind and patient with children, but fierce as an angry bear when he needs to be. Loves Sarhina like life, but he knew what he was getting into with her. Knew that he'd be holding together hearth and home while she changed the world, so he's prepared for the worst."

The worst being that Sarhina never came home to her daughter and husband. That Delia was never reunited with her parents. War tore apart families, and Ahnna couldn't help but wonder if there would ever come a time when their world was free of it. Or if it was a miserable inevitability that greedy and power-hungry people would always rise to the top, leaving death and suffering in their wake as they reached for *more*.

"Where is Keris?" Bronwyn asked. "And Zarrah, for that matter? Sarhina said she'd gone north."

"We don't know." Ahnna swiftly explained what had happened,

finishing with, "They were alive when we left them, but I don't know if they managed to get out of Harendell."

"Lestara is treading on dangerous ground if she thinks that Valcotta won't sail to Zarrah's defense."

They reached James where he was standing far up the beach, and Bronwyn took one look at him and said, "You look like shit, Ashford. What happened to your face?"

"Shovel."

"Someone try to bury you?"

"Yes."

"They the ones who ended up buried?"

"More or less."

Bronwyn cast her eyes skyward and shook her head. "For Ahnna's sake, I hope you are a better lover than a conversationalist, because your skills in the art of small talk are sorely lacking."

James only shrugged. "You'll have to ask her."

"Oh, we will," Taryn chimed in. "We intend to learn all the details."

Ahnna hid a smile as her husband's composure slipped, but then shouts rang out from the lookouts on the cliffs surrounding the sea. "More Harendellian ships have arrived! They are shooting warning shots at the Maridrinians! They're driving them off!"

"Signal my ship to go," Sarhina shouted back. "We have what we need."

Yet Ahnna barely heard the woman's orders, because all she saw was the way the color drained from James's face. Without saying a word, he broke into a run, heading for the narrow path leading from the cove to the clifftops. Letting go of her friends, Ahnna raced after him. "James!"

He didn't stop, and fast as Ahnna was, she couldn't match his long strides. He already had a spyglass in hand by the time she reached the top, and was watching the two ships facing down the Maridrinian vessel. Its deck was full of panicked crew rushing to get sails up, and within minutes, they were heading south.

James handed her the spyglass. "Look at the front of the ships."

The sun was still rising, the light poor, but Ahnna focused on the Harendellian vessels. Her blood instantly ran cold, because mounted on the foredecks were catapults of some kind. As she watched on in horror, one of the monstrous vessels turned and the soldiers on deck worked as a team to load a rock into the catapult.

*Crack!*

Her stomach lurched as she watched the boulder sail through the air to land with an explosion of water perhaps a hundred paces from the base of the cliffs. Ahnna sucked in a breath, then shouted, "Return!"

*Crack!*

A shipbreaker was released, the rock soaring through the air toward the ship but falling just short with a splash that soaked the crew aboard. "We have the advantage of the clifftops," she said. "Greater range."

"If they come close to use those, we'll sink them," one of the soldiers manning the shipbreaker muttered, then gestured to the pile of boulders behind him. "We've got rocks for days."

They'd have to risk an entire ship that had to have well over five hundred men aboard, but Ahnna couldn't shirk the sense of dread pooling in her stomach. Especially when she noticed that James had left her, running along the edge of the cliffs that circled the island. Exchanging a worried glance with Aren, she chased after him, the light growing with each step she took.

Her breathing grew rapid, heart thundering as she circled around and around until she reached James at the northernmost point. He stood frozen, watching the shadows of the island stretch, the sun revealing more of the sea with each passing second.

Shadows emerged. Great ships with bright white sails, decks full of soldiers, and all of them bearing siege equipment mounted to the foredecks. Five, six, seven, she counted, and then the numbers leapt into the dozens and she gave off counting. With them was the familiar shape of the *Victoria,* royal purple flying in her rigging.

Harendell had been prepared for this moment, and the full force of the jewel of the north had arrived.

Ahnna caught hold of James's hand, her palm slick with sweat as she whispered. "God have mercy on our souls."

# 98

# AREN

"EVERYONE TO THEIR positions!" Aren shouted, his mind filling with flashbacks of the siege of Eranahl. Countless ships pressing in, steel and flame flying through the air, and defenses falling one by one as Silas tried to pull out the island's gate.

This was a thousand times worse.

"Don't show them your true range," James said, falling in alongside him. "Let at least a few of them find out the hard way. The debris and sinking vessels will get in their way, and they'll have to deploy ships for rescues."

Nothing he didn't already know, but Aren gave the orders to keep the shipbreakers at the ready, no deployments. Then James grabbed his arm, his amber eyes intent as he shoved a spyglass into Aren's hand. "It's not just weapons those decks are mounted with. They've adapted siege towers and other mechanisms that we'd use to gain entrance to fortresses. They aim to use them to get soldiers onto the island."

Aren lifted the spyglass, focusing on each individual ship.

"It's warfare we haven't used in a generation." James's expression was grim. "Someone did their research, and this doesn't feel like something Alexandra would have included in her plans. These retrofits couldn't have been accomplished so soon after my father's death. They were in the works well before, I think."

"Edward's own designs."

James gave a tight nod. "I think so. Sea warfare isn't my expertise, but it was my father's."

"And we gave him all the information he needed to take Southwatch from Silas."

"He'd invested in the shipyards," Ahnna said from where she was strapping on weapons that Sarhina had brought with her in the longboats. "It was marked as repairs in his banking records. I suppose now we know the truth."

"I assume you didn't know, James, so it's not your fault." Aren tried to pull out of James's grip, but the other man's fingers tightened.

"I'm not apologizing for my father's ambition—I'm telling you he would have aimed to command this sort of battle himself. Would have been preparing and doing his own calculations and strategies in secret, because he didn't want anyone to know his endgame. He's dead. Which means whoever is in command is unlikely to have the skill or knowledge needed for this. He'll make mistakes. That is where our advantage lies, because none of them"—he waved a hand—"have done this before. You have."

"They're dropping sails and running out oars," Lara called. "Forming a line. They're not waiting. This is happening now."

Aren's eyes filled again with Eranahl, his ears ringing with the screams of the injured. The shriek of steel dragging against rock.

Lara, dead in his arms.

His breath caught, chest tightening so fast it hurt. He wasn't on the cliffs of Ornak—he was back in the harbor of Eranahl, crushed beneath the weight of loss, grief strangling his will to go on.

Aren blinked, forced air into his lungs, and shook his head roughly. *Lara is alive. And you won that battle.*

*Lara won that battle.*

And from the way she stood surveying the threat, the queen of Ithicana intended to do the same thing again.

The sea surf was quiet, belying the chaos that was about to unfold atop it. The Harendellian fleet was moving into formation with their typical efficiency, sleek cutters flanking heavier ships loaded down with siege towers and catapults, none of it anything Aren had seen in his lifetime. Sunlight flashed on the spray made from oars moving in perfect unison. Glistened off the shields and weapons of the uniformed soldiers lining the decks.

The line of ships curved, spreading outward and encircling Ornak like a noose.

He turned and took in the lines of Ithicanians stretched across the cliffs. Warriors—his people—waiting with weapons ready. Brave and determined, but very much targets.

"Everyone get behind cover!" Aren shouted. "Do not let them see you. Do not let them see so much as a glint of steel. I want every third shipbreaker removed from its mount and put behind obstacles that can take a direct hit. The rest need to be kept behind vine screens. They are the targets, so don't make it easy for them!"

Voices called back, affirming the order. Then came the clatter of movement—grunts of exertion as the crews scrambled to obey. The grinding sound of heavy bolts being unscrewed from stone. The massive shipbreakers, painstakingly mounted to defend Ornak, were dragged back under jungle cover.

Ahnna remained on the cliff edge, silhouetted against the water. Her hair was pulled back in a tight braid, and though his sister's face was grim, her eyes were alive with calculation.

"We need to get every vessel we have out of the cove," she said, watching the ships move closer. "They may try to damage the entrance, but at the very least, they'll take shots at anything that comes out."

Aren jerked his chin at two of his soldiers who waited to relay orders. "You heard her. Make sure they are well crewed and armed with all the explosives they need. Fire is going to be our best weapon."

"No," Ahnna murmured. "Fear will be our greatest weapon." Her eyes flicked sideways, meeting his. "You have chum barrels?"

Aren gave a nod. They'd been sitting far from camp, their stench enough to make hardened soldiers gag.

"Then let's ring the dinner bell."

Ahnna retrieved one of the clay pots they'd prepared days ago—pitch sealed and primed to burst when it hit the sea. With the smooth motion of long practice, she hurled it far out over the cliffs.

*Boom!*

The sound rolled back toward them, muffled but ominous. She threw another.

*Boom!*

All of Lara's sisters had joined them and were watching with interest. Ahnna said, "The sharks know that sound means a battle. They know it means bodies falling into the seas. They'll come, and the Harendellian captains will find their crews far less willing to risk a sinking ship when they see gray fins circling the water."

But fear would only serve them if first they rattled the fleet's confidence.

"Lara and I will hold the north," he said to Ahnna. "You and James take the south. Jor, the east. Taryn, the west."

Everyone departed without argument, Sarhina quietly splitting her sisters into pairs and sending them in various directions.

Aren returned to Lara, behind one of the vine screens hiding a shipbreaker. Her face was streaked with sweat, her eyes narrowed behind her spyglass.

"They're moving in slowly," she muttered. "Waiting for us to deploy so they know our range."

"They'll discover our range when they're inside it."

Below, the Ithicanian ships were exiting the cove and moving like a swarm of angry bees readying to attack.

Aren knelt beside his wife, peering through the screen of vines and leaves. One of the ships in the first row of the Harendellian fleet had soldiers scrambling around a catapult. The rope tightened. The load lifted.

He gritted his teeth. "First volley's coming."

The catapult fired.

A large block of stone shot into the sky. Aren's stomach clenched as he tracked its arc. Time slowed.

It fell short—hitting the sea with a thunderous splash, just missing one of the Ithicanian ships.

Next to him, Lara let out a loud breath.

Another shot came. Higher. Closer.

Still short.

"Everyone hold!" Aren shouted. "We know we have better range. Once they have their first strike, we'll know they're inside it. Then we send death down on their heads."

He felt the tension building in the jungle, in the cliffs, in his spine. His hands flexed on his machete hilt, the wait always worse than the fight.

"The next one will hit." Lara's voice was tight. "They know it. That's why the other ships are making ready."

It was why they were using fire.

The third projectile, this one covered in burning pitch, arced through the air. Like a star falling from the sky.

Aren's body went still. He could feel the pressure shift in the air.

Could see the faint spiral of flame as it began to fall.

The sound came a second later.

*Boom!*

It struck the edge of the cliff line, flipping and rolling into the jungle, destroying everything in its path. The air reeked of burning pitch and charred vegetation, but there were no screams.

Instead, a hush fell over the island, and in it, Aren roared, "Deploy!"

Lara had moved to man the shipbreaker, brow furrowed as she rotated the machine slightly left. Then she pulled the lever.

*Crack!*

All along the cliffside, shipbreakers deployed with deafening cracks. Boulders flew through the air, nothing but shadows soaring toward the front lines of the Harendellian fleet.

But Aren didn't watch them strike, because coming toward the island were six balls of flame.

# 99
# AHNNA

As Ahnna raced around the island to the southern edge, thick greasy smoke rolled over her.

She scrambled up the rise with James close behind, her boots sliding in the damp earth. Ash fell in soft spirals, catching in her eyelashes and coating her tongue with its bitter taste. But worse were the screams.

"Commander!" someone called out, but Ahnna's gaze was fixed on the sea. Harendell's ships edged closer, the oars protruding from them reminding her of great centipedes, their decks blossoming bright with fire every time a projectile was lit. Each crack of a catapult being loosed made her twitch, fire soaring through the sky with the promise of death.

A burning ball flew overhead, trailed by a tail of smoke. It exploded into the jungle canopy, tearing through trees and leaving behind a line of char.

Ahnna winced, throwing an arm up against the heat, but her eyes never left the battlefield. If the ships got much closer, they'd be able to hit the structures at the center of the island. Structures that contained all the food, all the supplies, and all the injured whom Nana and her assistants would be struggling to keep alive.

The crews on the shipbreakers were loading and shooting as swiftly as they could, and damaged ships listed in the waves, one of them actively sinking.

"The vessels with the catapults aren't loaded with soldiers." James lowered his spyglass, his face glistening from sweat. Ahnna knew hers was the same because the heat was intense. "It's the ones with the towers, and they're holding back."

"They're not within range."

"They'll come when they think our shipbreakers are destroyed."

As if in answer, a ball of fire flew toward the clifftop. Those manning the shipbreaker dove to either side right as the war machine exploded, sharp pieces of wood and metal flying in every direction, the base catching fire.

The screams were horrible, and Ahnna raced to shove down the soldiers whose clothes had ignited from the spray of fire. The damp earth smothered the flames but did nothing for the burns.

"It hurts! It hurts!" sobbed the woman beneath her. "Make it stop!"

Ahnna lifted her up and shouted, "Get the injured to Nana. The rest of you, keep hitting them." Sickness pooled in her stomach. "Use fire!"

"Should we bring back the other shipbreakers?" someone demanded.

"Not yet." She struggled not to look at James to beg forgiveness for her next order. "We wait until they commit the ships with soldiers."

It had been so much easier when she'd given orders to defend Eranahl, because she'd been fueled by anger and hate. Not so now. There was only one person she wanted dead, and if she was here, Lestara would keep well out of reach.

Runners brought forward clay pots filled with tree sap that were kept in a trench behind lines, and within moments the shipbreakers were launching incendiaries of their own.

Fire exploded across a ship as one projectile clipped a mast—not with enough force to break it, but the burning sap sprayed over the sails and over the sailors below. Too far to hear the screams, but they echoed in Ahnna's head all the same.

The Harendellians returned the attack, ships moving to take the places of those that were damaged beyond use. Dirt and fire and rock exploded all around, the noise deafening. James aided with one of the shipbreakers while she directed fire, forced to scream over the uproar for anyone to hear her.

The sea was full of damaged ships. Full of fire and debris. But they kept coming.

And one by one, they picked off Ornak's shipbreakers. Worse still, with each strike on the island, more of her people fell. Men and women sat in the dirt burned beyond recognition while others lay still, their eyes as glassy as the pools of blood around them.

Then there was only one shipbreaker left under her command.

James heaved a rock into the sling, their stores of sap and pots long ago spent. With the aid of two Ithicanians, they shifted the machine so that it was directed at a ship, then let it loose.

*Crack!*

The large rock soared through the air, but the very same ship let loose a fireball at the exact same time. Ahnna's chest tightened as the projectiles passed each other, and then she took note of the trajectory.

"Move!" Her scream was loud and shrill as she lunged at James. Her shoulder hit him in the side and they both rolled, going off the side of the cliff right as the fireball struck the breaker.

Ahnna clawed for purchase on the tree roots, then her whole body jerked as her fall was abruptly arrested. "I've got you," James shouted, one hand holding tight to her belt and the other latched on the roots. "Climb!"

She scrambled up, her burned hands screaming in pain against the rough roots, then rolled over the top and helped James up.

The shipbreaker was nothing but a smoldering mess of charred wood and metal, a human form half melted against it. The other soldier who'd been working it sat a distance away, hands pressed to her ears and rocking side to side.

Ahnna stumbled to her, falling to her knees. "Are you hurt?"

The woman stared at her, and Ahnna realized she was just a girl. Sixteen, if a day, but old enough to have joined the service. She carefully pulled the girl's hands from her ears. "Are you hurt?"

"Why are they doing this?" the girl asked. "What did we do to deserve this?"

"Nothing." Ahnna pulled the girl against her. "To find meaning in why Harendell is here is the path to madness. Instead, remember why you are here. To defend your home. Your family. Your friends. Know your own heart, and care not for the hearts of those who try to take what is yours."

"Ahnna!" James shouted. "They're coming!"

She twisted in the ash and debris, eyes fixing on the ships with siege towers, their decks teeming with soldiers with shields. The other ships were parting to make space for them to sail through, giving her a first good look at them. They'd been reinforced, especially on the bow, with thick wood and metal plates to protect each ship as it came up against the cliffs. The weight of the vessels had to be extraordinary, and they sat low in the water, primed to sink if she could hit them just right.

"Bring forward the other shipbreakers," she shouted at her remaining soldiers. "Get them mounted and then shoot at will! Archers, get ready!"

Ahnna dragged the girl to her feet. "Help get the injured to Nana. Go!"

All she was doing was delaying the inevitable, but Ahnna didn't want a child on the front lines of the fight to come. Getting to her feet, she ran to help James and the others moving the three shipbreakers they'd kept hidden.

The war machines were murderously heavy, and sweat streamed down her back as she pushed one up the slope on top of log rollers. Fireballs still flew overhead, striking the island with thunderous booms, but the pace decreased as they made way for the other ships.

A teen boy raced up to her. "Commander, Jor sent me. He says that the boarding ships are focusing on the south and west sides of the island because the surf isn't as fierce. We're sending reinforcements."

"Any word from the other quadrants?" Her real question was

whether Aren was well. Lara, Taryn, and Bronwyn. Though in truth, she knew almost everyone on this island, so every loss was a knife to the chest.

The boy only shook his head.

"Go find out." She gave him a push to the path leading into the jungle. "Go across."

She wasn't protecting him any more than she had the girl. There was nowhere to hide once the island was taken. Nowhere to run. Yet she couldn't fight the desire to stand between death and those who'd barely had the chance to live.

"One more push!" James shouted, and they heaved the catapult onto its mount, two soldiers falling to their knees with tools to secure the heavy bolts. The other machines were moving into place, but as Ahnna stood, it was to find that the ships were close enough that she could see the faces of the men. See their panic.

Oars tangled up as they tried to reverse course, but it was too late. "Shoot!" she screamed, the crack of it deploying making her ears ring. The rock shot through the sky and exploded into the siege tower, carrying onward to smash through the deck behind it. The tower swayed, then collapsed on the deck full of soldiers, but Ahnna didn't pause to watch the carnage. "Another! Don't stop!"

Rocks flew, smashing into the ships as they tried to retreat out of range, but the weight of them made it impossible for the oarsmen below to reverse progress. Oars tangled or broke, and Ahnna knew that belowdecks, those manning them would be suffering. Injured and crushed by the heavy wood, splinters driving into flesh. Not even soldiers, just desperate men willing to take on the hard labor for a bit of coin.

Fire flew from the Harendellian ships as they resumed bombardment, and to her right, the cliff collapsed beneath one of the shipbreakers from the force of impact, its crew falling screaming into the waves below.

"Get the chum ready!" Ahnna screamed, wanting to give those who'd fallen time to swim to the cove even though she knew they'd never make it, for dark shapes were already moving in the sea, called by the noise.

James helped lift the barrel of blood and guts, then it was flying into the water, spraying the gore across the white froth of the sea. Instantaneously, the sharks rose, the sea swirling in a chaos of crimson foam, and Ahnna watched the soldiers and sailors take notice. Felt their fear as much as saw it, because that was what waited for them if they landed in the water.

One crew mutinied, throwing the captain to the deck, the vessel turning and sailing back through the lines.

But Ahnna felt no satisfaction. More fire bloomed overhead.

James caught her arm and dragged her sideways, the rest of the crew racing for cover, and the shipbreaker exploded. The last remaining machine managed three more shots, then it succumbed.

And one of the boarding ships struck the cliff.

Ahnna swore the whole island shuddered from the impact, great pieces of the cliff falling into the sea or onto the deck below, judging from the screams and crunches.

"Archers!" Ahnna shouted. "Volley!"

Arrows soared in a dark cloud, coming down on the ship below. Screams filled the air, but so did pings of metal against metal, and Ahnna suspected most had been blocked by shields. "Again!"

In the distance, she saw several explosions, Ithicanian vessels risking archers to veer close enough to throw bombs up onto the decks, and the air above the fleet was black with smoke. Ithicanians burst through the trees to flank her, Jor sliding to a stop at her right. "They're focusing on the south and west quadrants," he said through gasps of breath. "Aren and Lara are moving to the west to reinforce. You got us."

"Volley!" Ahnna screamed, wishing she had a bow. Instead, she drew her sword. "I'll take this ship. You take the one coming in."

Jor motioned for his soldiers to follow up the edge of the cliff while her soldiers readied behind her.

"Ready!" she shouted.

Everyone hefted their weapons, the archers now shooting at the soldiers climbing the towers.

Another ship hit the island with a shudder. James had found a bow and was shooting arrows dipped in burning tree sap into the rigging. Onto the decks. Great clouds of smoke wafted upward, but chains rattled.

"They're coming!" James shouted, slinging his bow over his shoulder and drawing his sword. An arrow flew up from below, but he sidestepped it. Then he pointed to another ship coming up fast. "Ten with me!" and he raced to meet the threat.

"Steady!" Ahnna shouted, and then the drawbridges affixed to the towers dropped. For a heartbeat, the soldiers waiting in the tower just stared at them; then they screamed in fury and exploded across the drawbridge, which bucked and swayed with the motion of the sea.

"For Ithicana," Ahnna screamed. "Make them bleed!"

The two forces collided with a clash of weapons and words, and Ahnna lost herself to the fight. There was nothing but the opponent before her, the blade in her hand, and a burning need to save everyone who depended on her on this island.

The ground beneath her feet turned soupy with mud and gore, bodies tangling up and getting kicked off the cliff, but soldiers kept coming. Kept climbing up through the tower, and both left and right, Ahnna knew it was the same with all the ships that were pressed against the island.

She had to do something.

"With me!" she screamed, then shoved her sword into its sheath and took a running leap at the tower. For a heartbeat, she thought she'd miss and fall to her death, but then her hands caught hold of wooden beams.

She scrambled downward, toward the deck, doing her best to keep out of sight of those still aboard. Above her, more of her people followed, easily climbing after her.

"Get the sails up," she whispered beneath the noise of the Harendellians shouting triumph as they met no resistance getting off the drawbridge. "Kill anyone who gets in your way."

Together, they gathered in the gap between the tower and the rail, the drawbridge overhead and bits of rock raining down, then Ahnna hissed, "I'll distract them, then you go."

Drawing her blade, she exploded out from their cover, running toward the quarterdeck. Shouts of alarm rose from the crew, but she sidestepped and dodged, heading toward the helm with murderous intent.

Soldiers got in her path with blades high, and she met them head-on, parrying and slicing. Then her feet found the stairs and she was flying up them. With ruthless efficiency, she cut down the sailors standing with the captain, then embedded her sword in the helmsman. He staggered sideways, and she caught hold of the wheel and twisted.

Beneath the ship, the rudder turned, the force of the sea slamming into it again and again. The ship shuddered where it was hung up on the rocks, the stern moving toward the cliff with painful slowness. But it was enough to pull free the drawbridge from where it rested across the clifftops, and it came crashing down. The tower moaned, then fell sideways, and above her, a sail unfurled.

The crew on deck were in a panic, but Ahnna's people knew ships and they knew them well. They worked together to get the sails up while fighting off interference, and with a mighty groan, the ship pulled entirely free from the cliff face beneath the sea.

The waves caught hold of the vessel as it turned perpendicular to the cliffs, and the ship groaned as it raked along the rocks. Then the wind caught the sails more fully, pushing them away from the cliff face.

Ahnna clenched her teeth and guided the heavy vessel straight into the ship that James was battling. The armored bow punched through the starboard side, and the siege tower lifted clear off the deck as the ship was shoved sideways. It fell apart with a splash, soldiers spilling into the water.

The wind was gusting harder now, and her vessel kept pushing the other one sideways, slowly but surely.

Hooks flung up to catch hold of her ship's railings, and then more Ithicanians were climbing up from the small vessels that had come alongside. They fell upon the remaining crew and soldiers, slaughtering them until she had total control of the ship.

"Ahnna!"

She lifted her face to see James standing on the clifftop, sword in hand and face splattered with blood. She'd not said goodbye. Not told him that she loved him, and there was no time now. Instead, she willed everything she had in her heart onto the wind, praying that it would deliver it to him, and she spun the wheel.

Her ship tore loose from the vessel it was pushing, and she veered away from the cliffs before shifting back to strike yet another vessel unloading soldiers onto Ornak. The impact slammed her against the wheel, but she righted herself and carried on.

She knocked loose two more ships before the first strike came. An explosion of fire across the deck, burning oil splattering.

"Abandon ship," she shouted at her crew, knowing that Ithicanian vessels were keeping pace and would take them aboard. But everyone held their positions, and someone shouted, "Not until we sink as many as we can!" They raced to throw sand from barrels on the flames.

Ahnna cast one backward look to Ornak, seeing James standing with Aren at the edge of the cliff.

Then she turned toward the enemy.

# 100

# JAMES

"WHAT IS SHE doing?" Taryn shouted. "Has she lost her mind?"

Ahnna hadn't lost her mind, but watching her sail away on a burning ship felt like having James's heart torn from his chest. In one risky move, she'd struck an incredible blow to Harendell's attack, and while there were still skirmishes going on across the island, she'd bought Ornak time to take a breath.

Even if that breath only gave clarity that the worst was yet to come. Already, more ships were moving in to resume bombardment. Dozens upon dozens of them, and with every shipbreaker on the island a ruin of char and splinters, Ithicana had no way to fight back.

Except for Ahnna, twenty Ithicanians, and a burning ship.

A hand closed on his shoulder, and James turned his head to see Aren. The king of Ithicana's face was splattered with gore, and blood soaked his shoulder where an arrow had torn a gash through skin and muscle. "Our people are trailing her," he said. "She might intend to ram as many as possible until it sinks, then she'll abandon ship and escape on one of our vessels."

Even if that was Ahnna's plan, she'd be sailing through ships with catapults that had already struck her once. Ships full of archers, and she stood on the quarterdeck entirely exposed. And beneath all of it swam sharks that had been stirred into a frenzy, which meant no one who went into that ocean was coming back alive.

But ramming ships wasn't Ahnna's plan. "She's going in pursuit of the *Victoria*. It's flying purple, which means there is royalty aboard. It means Lestara is aboard."

Everyone was silent, and though the island was alive with the noise of waves striking cliffs, swords clashing, and screams of the wounded, it all felt distant as he watched Ahnna's ship set its track north to where the *Victoria* watched on. It was possible that killing Lestara would end this. Just as possible that it would enrage his people, because they would perceive Ithicana as having taken yet another of Harendell's rulers.

"Aren." Lara's voice seemed loud, and James twitched as though he'd been struck. "They're readying for another wave."

Ships were moving in, and James suspected they'd be more cautious this time. That they'd turn this island into nothing but rubble and ash before risking more men.

The side of Lara's face was crimson from a cut at her temple, but tear tracks cut pink lines through the blood. "Athena and Cresta are dead. Sarhina is with Nana—she took an arrow to the stomach. But that's just the beginning, isn't it?" She doubled over with a sob, but when Aren reached for her, she pushed his hand away and straightened. "I'm fine. We fight on. It's what we do."

A fireball soared into the air, swiftly joined by two rocks as ships drew nearer, and all three struck the island with force. They rolled through the jungle, tearing down trees, but before they ceased their carnage more came on like a hailstorm of flame.

All while Ahnna sailed to strike the one last blow they had in their arsenal, even if it meant her death.

Aren abruptly stiffened. "Do you hear that?"

All James could hear was the noise of battle and the hammering of his heart. No . . . not his heart.

War drums.

Jor abruptly exploded from the trees. He had an arrow punched through one arm above the elbow, and his face was red with blood, but his eyes were bright with elation as he shouted. "The Valcottans are here! And they aren't alone!"

Spotting a spyglass laying on the ground, James lifted it and looked through the smoke, past the Harendellian fleet, south to where dozens of ships were pounding through the surf, Valcottan and Maridrinian banners flying in the rigging. On one Valcottan ship, purple banners of royalty gleamed in the sun.

It was impossible. Utterly and entirely impossible that Keris and Zarrah could have reached Valcotta and returned with a fleet, short of some form of witchery. Yet there was no denying that they were here.

Aren wavered, then caught Lara's arm and broke into a run toward the south end of the island. Jor remained. "I saw what Ahnna did," the old warrior said, seeming to barely notice the arrow stuck in his arm. "You going to go after her before she gets herself killed?"

"How?" James's throat clenched down on the word as he returned to watching the rear of Ahnna's ship. In another few minutes, she'd hit the first ships in the northern line, and he knew that if he lifted his spyglass, it would be to see the archers making ready to shoot. "I'd swim after her if I thought I'd get more than ten strokes before getting eaten." Even then, he was sorely tempted to leap into the sea.

"I can get you to her," Taryn said. "I can signal one of our ships, but you'll need to jump and swim quickly. Even then, the water is teeming, so . . ." She pressed a hand to her side, closing her eyes tight for a heartbeat, then opened them and nodded. "But it's possible."

From a pouch at her waist, she withdrew a vial of powder, which she poured on the ground. Then she kicked a piece of burning wood atop it. It immediately flared bright, red smoke billowing into the air. One of the Ithicanian vessels caught sight of it and veered away from where they'd been harrying a Harendellian ship, heading straight toward them.

"When they're ready for us, we jump," Taryn said. "Then we swim like hell and pray they pull us in."

"Taryn . . ." Bronwyn looked ready to be sick. "I can't swim."

"You can't come," Taryn responded, then bit at her bottom lip. "It will be okay, though. Make Jor get some help, and then go help Lara." She gestured toward the mass of ships in the south. "Looks like we might see the other side of this, and then we can go back to the potatoes."

"Fuck the potatoes." Bronwyn caught hold of her and pulled her in. "I just want you for the rest of my life."

James stepped away to give the women their space and watched the Ithicanian vessel skip over the waves toward them. Behind, explosions rattled the island as the bombardment continued, though he'd seen several ships turning to face the incoming threat. What was coming was a sea battle for the ages, but he didn't care. All that mattered was that the love of his life was on a ship growing smaller by the second. All that mattered was catching her, and being with her to whatever end they reached.

"Take off your boots." Taryn had moved next to him and had kicked off her own boots. She began securing her weapons. "We jump together. Running start to get as far from the cliff as possible, and then swim like hell. Hopefully both of us make it, but if not, the other goes to fight at her back. Clear?"

"Yes." James let Ahnna's cousin take his hand, drawing him back even as the island shuddered from impact after impact, the air thick with choking smoke.

The Ithicanians dropped their sails, and one of them lifted a hand. "Go!"

With Taryn holding tight to his hand, James broke into a sprint, and together they leapt into the air.

# 101

# KERIS

Long before they could see the ships, they saw the smoke.

Though all eyes were on the great cloud of black that rose like a demon in the sky, no one said a word. But for his part, in the silence, Keris prayed to every higher power that they weren't too late.

That there had been even a hope they might make it in time had felt like a miracle. After swiftly gaining passage on a Valcottan merchant vessel in port in Elmsworth, the city still reeling after failing to prevent Aren and the others from escaping, he and Zarrah had sailed south ahead of Harendell's fleet. The horror of seeing the siege equipment mounted to the naval vessels was a thing that would haunt Keris's dreams. Was a thing that now haunted his reality as they drew closer to the cloud of smoke over Ornak and the enormity of the fleet came into view.

"Drums!" Zarrah shouted, one hand resting on the rail of the quarterdeck. "Let them know we are not here to negotiate. There is only one outcome in this fight, and it is Lestara's capitulation!"

The beat of the drums should have fired his heart, but instead it turned his stomach sour, bringing back old memories. Bad memories that he now feared would soon have company when they tormented his dreams.

He'd been so sure that they'd make it when they had come into sight of the Valcottan fleet, the Maridrinians with them, already past the midpoint of the bridge. He and Zarrah had boarded the flagship to find Arjun in command.

"We received your message," Zarrah's father had said, and when they'd looked at him in confusion, he added, "Alexandra's banking records, which we easily tied to the proof we'd discovered of her conspiracy to infect our herds. We'd already been preparing to set sail with the calm season, but this broke all resistance within the nobility. And also revealed conspiracies within our own ranks. We sent the information to Vencia with all haste, and their parliament took equal issue with Alexandra's crimes."

It was a relief to learn that his people had not lost their nerve. That they still had the capacity to fight for what mattered.

"Alexandra is dead. Lestara rules, and her fleet is set to destroy the last remaining Ithicanian resistance on Ornak Island," Zarrah said. "We must sail with all haste for there to be any hope."

"Lestara." Arjun spat on the deck. "That will light a fire in the Maridrinians, sure and true." Then he lifted his voice and bellowed, "Sails up! North with all haste!"

Zarrah went with him, adding in orders of her own, as well as signals to be sent to the other ships in the fleet. But Keris had held back with Saam and motioned to Daria. "The last time we had those banking records was when Zarrah hid them behind a painting. Then they went missing. How did you get them?"

Daria flung her arms around Saam, but over his shoulder she said, "A maid in the Sky Palace named Hazel. Do you know her?"

The Sky Palace had been full of servants, every one of them seemingly loyal to the Ashfords.

"She was one of Alexandra's maids," Saam said. "But she'd been Ahnna's maid before that."

"Ahnna must have made quite an impression."

The moment had felt like hope. Like salvation delivered from the least expected hands, but as they drew closer to the battle and the carnage became clear, it felt like a fool's hope. Dozens of ships were damaged and sinking, the water covered in debris, but the island was what stole Keris's focus. The cliffs were scarred, the jungle around the perimeter crushed and burned, and lines of black crisscrossed the island, smoke rising from multiple fires. It seemed impossible that anyone was alive, but from the crow's nest, a scout shouted, "There are survivors! Ithicana fights on!"

"Do you wish to offer them the chance to surrender?" Arjun asked Zarrah, but she only shook her head. "Ramming speed. I want them to know that we are here to sink them, and we shall see what they do with that certainty."

The fleet moved into lines, decks full of archers and swordsmen, their eyes hard and ready for the fight. As Keris lifted a spyglass to his eye, he saw chaos on the decks of the Harendellian ships as they pivoted to meet the threat. Closer and closer the fleets drew together, the thunder of drums matching the beat of his heart.

"Brace!" Zarrah shouted.

And Keris drew his sword.

# 102
# AHNNA

"WHAT'S THE PLAN?"

Ahnna twitched at Mara's familiar voice, not having realized that Northwatch's commander had been one of those who'd boarded to assist.

Mara scowled at her. "Well? We can't ram them all. Where do you want to start?"

The Harendellians left aboard had all been forced into the hold, so only Ithicanians were on the decks of the enormous ship, it taking all of them to manage the rigging. Wary of the reinforced bow, the ships of Lestara's fleet had been doing their best to get out of Ahnna's way, but some were moving to get alongside, archers at the ready.

She couldn't outrun them. Not in this vessel.

"The *Victoria*." Her voice was raspy, so Ahnna coughed to clear her throat. "It's flying royal purple, which means Lestara is aboard. We sink it and turn her into shark shit. That's the goal."

"Right." Mara rested her elbows on the rail, her face heavily lined from a lifetime of being outside in the sun. "Except that murderous tit isn't Silas and there isn't a typhoon staring the Harendellians down. Killing Lestara isn't going to send them packing—it's just going to piss them off while they finish the job."

"How many ships do you suppose I can sink with this tug?"

Mara shrugged. "Three. Maybe four. We're already taking on water from the other collisions, and it's not going to be long until this thing goes down like a rock."

"Will sinking four ships win this fight for us? Will it make them surrender?"

"Nah, we're done. It's just a matter of how many of the bastards we can take down with us. Word's been sent south, and everyone will be fleeing to Maridrina and Valcotta. Ithicana dies today, Ahnna."

Not just Ithicana, but everyone she loved. Lestara would surely execute any survivors on Ornak once the island was taken, and Lara and Aren wouldn't flee. They were going down with the ship.

And James . . .

Her eyes burned, her vision filling with his expression as she'd sailed away, and she desperately wished he was with her. Wished that they could fight through this final moment together, rather than dying apart.

*I'll find you*, she silently whispered. *Whatever comes next, I'll find you.*

Then she squared her shoulders. "If Ithicana must fall, let's make this last battle about giving tomorrow to those who survive us." Ahnna shifted the wheel, then ducked as an arrow shot over her head. "Harendell has a baby king, Mara. With Lestara as his mother, he has no more chance than William did with Alexandra. We're going to give him a chance. Give him a chance to be better, because if Ithicana is to be ruled by a Harendellian, I want them to be ruled right."

"Killing Lestara won't guarantee that. He's got a lot of years of growing, and who knows who will rule until he's of age."

How much different would the baby king's life have been if he'd had the chance to know his uncle? What sort of man would he have grown into with James at his side? It broke her heart that she'd never find out.

"Virginia will rule." Ahnna lifted her chin. "She'll do right by him, if given the opportunity."

Mara cracked her knuckles, then retrieved a shield from a dead soldier who still held the grip. "There are worse things to die for. Get yourself a shield and something to hold on to, friends," she shouted to those in the rigging. "We aim to give the *Victoria* to the Tempest Seas, but we'll have to fight our way through to her!"

Ahnna set the *Victoria's* bulk in her sights, but she could feel the ship sinking lower in the water. There was nothing nimble about the vessel she sailed—it was like a battering ram, all strength and momentum.

She clipped another vessel, and it heeled over with a groan, spilling soldiers into the water before it righted itself, but her ship didn't alter its course. Deep in its bowels, she heard it groan as water poured in through the gashes and gouges in its hull, its fate certain.

But not yet.

Arrows rained down on the deck, Mara and another Ithicanian protecting her with shields, but above, she heard a scream. Then another, and a body fell from the rigging to hit the deck with a heavy thump.

Ahnna kept her course.

They struck another vessel, the crunch of wood deafening, and below, those they'd imprisoned in the hold began to scream. The ship shifted lower, moaning its death knell, but Ahnna ignored it, her eyes on the *Victoria*.

The jewel of Harendell's navy seemed to understand it was a target now, but the sailors weren't moving quickly enough. Sails billowed, and the ship rotated, but it was pinned in by the ships intended to protect it. The wind chose that moment to die, every sail falling limp, and Ahnna smiled.

Then her smile faltered. Because standing on the deck, dressed in a golden gown, was Lestara. And in her arms was a child.

*No.*

Across the waves, Ahnna swore that Lestara gave her a smile of triumph, and a scream of fury tore from Ahnna's lips. With a heave, she threw her weight against the wheel, trying to turn the dying ship. Trying to avoid a direct strike that would kill the very child she'd aimed to save.

The ship moaned, momentum driving it onward, turning slightly to port. Then a bit more. And then it shuddered as the rudder broke free.

The sailors on the *Victoria* were making progress, but it wouldn't be fast enough. Ahnna howled, and the ships impacted.

Her great fortified monstrosity scraped down the side of the flagship, splintering oars and sending everyone aboard toppling. Ahnna was knocked off her feet, but in a flash, she was running. Leaping down stairs and heading to the starboard rail. Her boot hit it, and she leapt, tumbling across the deck in a roll.

She was on her feet in a heartbeat, sword in hand, running toward Lestara, who was sprawled on the deck with the crying baby in her arms.

*Kill her. Kill her, and end this!*

Weaving between soldiers who were trying to regain their feet, Ahnna angled her sword so that she'd hit Lestara but not the baby, only for a heavy weight to strike her in the side.

In a heartbeat, soldiers were piled on top of her, driving the air from her lungs.

Her sword was ripped from her hands, and her wrists were tied behind her back.

"Would you like me to slit her throat, Your Grace?" a familiar voice said, and Ahnna turned her face to find Archie Bennett holding a knife to her throat.

With the help of servants and soldiers, Lestara had righted herself, though she ignored the sobs of the child in her arms.

Her goddamned shield.

Righting the crown on her head, Lestara gave a serene smile. "That is not proper conduct, Archie. Keep her restrained. She might be useful in negotiations for surrender."

"Yes, Your Grace."

"Are we damaged?" She gave the baby a slight jiggle, then an annoyed glare when he didn't cease crying.

"Casualties among the oarsmen, but we're seaworthy," the captain called, then from above, a voice shouted, "The Cardiffian fleet has arrived."

"Wonderful of my father to be on time." Lestara sighed. "Keep the princess on deck. Let her watch as we finish this."

# 103
# JAMES

"WHY IS SHE turning?" Taryn shouted. "Why isn't she ramming them?"

James didn't know. But whatever the reason, Ahnna had made the decision too late. While the blow wasn't direct, her ship still scraped alongside the *Victoria,* the sound of crunching timber loud as the vessels slid past each other.

As the ships parted, the *Victoria* seemed seaworthy, but Ahnna's vessel gave a mighty groan and began to sink, bow first.

"Go!" he shouted. "Hurry!"

Arrows flew down around them as they wove between ships, most striking water but two finding flesh. Yet the Ithicanians sailed on, teeth clenched against the pain of their injuries as they raced to save those on the sinking ship.

They came alongside it, and James searched the deck for Ahnna's face, not finding her among the Ithicanians aboard. Screams of those trapped in the ship filtered through the hull, and as he watched, an older woman he recognized as one of Aren's commanders unlatched the hatch before sprinting to join her fellows.

With ease, they leapt down onto the craft, though it sank deep beneath the weight of so many people.

"Mara!" Taryn said to the woman. "What's going on?"

"Where is Ahnna?" James couldn't keep the panic from his voice, because she'd been on the ship moments before. "Where is she?"

"On the *Victoria*," Mara replied, pointing. "We were going to sink it, but Lestara has the baby. She's using her own child as a shield. Ahnna went after her."

*Alone.* She'd gone *alone* onto a ship full of soldiers who wanted her dead.

"We need to go!" one of the Ithicanians shouted. "She's going down!"

Going down, and all those who had been trapped in the hold were trying to escape. Lifting longboats and hurling them into the water, many men falling in, and below, James could see the flash of gray fins.

But on the other side of the sinking ship was the *Victoria*.

And his wife.

James jumped, catching hold of the rail of the ship, then dragging himself up the tilted deck toward the stern. It was rising higher and higher, barrels and ropes and stars knew what else sliding down, some of it striking him, but James didn't stop. He made it to the back of the ship as the bow dipped fully underwater, the ship bobbing like a top and then beginning to sink.

From this vantage, he saw that a fleet flying Cardiff's colors was sailing in from the north, the flagship moving away from the rest. But his uncle's arrival didn't matter—Lestara didn't need her father to win this. What mattered was that James could see Ahnna on her knees, restrained by *fucking Archie*, while Lestara gestured toward Ornak.

Getting his footing on the slick wood, James broke into a sprint and leapt off the side of the stern, landing hard on the *Victoria*'s deck. He rolled, then came to his feet with no less than three arrows leveled at his face.

"James!" Ahnna's voice filled his ears, and it was like music, because he hadn't thought he'd hear it again.

"Hello, cousin." Lestara looked at him as though he were vermin. "I wish I could say this was a pleasant surprise." Raising her voice, she said, "Seize Prince James. He's a traitor and will be dealt with once we've won the day."

"Don't count your victories so soon, Lestara," James snapped as hands shoved him to the deck. "A united fleet of Maridrinian and Valcottan ships has arrived. I suspect we'll see smoke rising in the south soon enough."

Lestara's cheeks blanched. "That's not possible."

"And yet there they are." He jerked out of a soldier's grasp and glared at him before adding, "What do you think the chances are that they've discovered Alexandra was behind the infected cattle and worsening famine?"

His cousin's lips parted ever so slightly in shock, and James scoffed. "What? Alex didn't tell you?"

"I know nothing about this." Lestara roughly jiggled the crying baby in her arms, then looked around at the stunned soldiers. "He's lying."

"You can plead innocence as they chase Harendell's fleet north," James replied. "I can only imagine Empress Zarrah and her consort have joined their fleet, and we all know what they think of you. What is it they call you in Maridrina? Butcher of Babies? Queen of Carrion?"

"Gag him!" she shouted. "I am the queen mother and you will not allow this traitor to speak to me so!"

Calling Lestara a mother was the worst abuse he'd ever heard of the word. She held the baby with as much affection as a block of wood, his nephew nothing more than a tool she'd use to hold power.

"She murdered William," he shouted. "Lestara was the poisoner! You've allowed her to lead you into this nightmare of a battle, and for what?"

"For the bridge!" Lestara shrieked at him. "My son, the king of Harendell, will be Master of the Bridge, and all its wealth will belong to Harendell! That is why we are fighting! Every one of you will be wealthy as a king!"

James gave a bitter laugh. "Is that what you think?" He jerked his chin south. "You think that Maridrina and Valcotta brought warships to negotiate trade? The only thing they came for is retribution. Lestara promises you the wealth of kings, but she will make you bleed like pawns. There is no victory to be had here!"

The men around them shifted uneasily, because this had become a harder fight than they'd bargained for.

"He's a liar and a traitor," Lestara shouted. "He's fallen prey to this Ithicanian snake." She kicked at Ahnna, nearly losing her brocade slipper and stumbling. "He's betrayed his kingdom and family to do her bidding! Do not listen to him!"

James's lips parted to retort, but Archie kicked him in the mouth. "Gag him!"

Dirty fabric was shoved inside James's mouth and his wrists were bound, as were Ahnna's, but if James could have smiled, he would've, because nearly every sailor aboard was staring south where the fleets were colliding.

"Your Grace, the Cardiffian flagship is coming alongside," a lookout shouted. "They're asking permission to board."

Lestara smirked. "Granted. Hopefully he's coming to beg my forgiveness for his tardiness."

James watched Ronan's ship come alongside the *Victoria,* the vessel not nearly as tall, though that proved no problem for his uncle, who climbed into the rigging and jumped aboard. His feet made a loud thump as he landed. "Daughter."

James's skin prickled at the tone of his voice, but Lestara didn't seem to notice.

"You're late, Father."

"Late would imply the battle is over, but I see Ithicana yet holds strong against you."

Lestara scoffed. "Hardly. What you are seeing is the arrival of the Maridrinians and Valcottans. Likely stirred up by some grandiose speech Keris has given, because he's far too good at convincing people to die for him. Which, with your arrival, they surely will. Victory will be ours."

Unless Keris used some form of magic, the prince consort had nothing to do with that fleet's arrival, but James didn't try to speak. He didn't need to, given the amusement on Ronan's face.

"Can't blame Keris Veliant for all your struggles, girl. It seems you and yours have suffered mightily against naught but an island defended by a handful of soldiers, and I think that's to do with your leadership of this battle. You know nothing about war." He gave a cold chuckle. "Though I see you brought yourself a shield."

"Do not call me girl." Lestara's knuckles whitened where she held the baby against her chest. "I will accept your advice, but I am leading this battle, Father."

"Oh, of course!" Ronan rocked on his heels. "Well, let's have at it, then. Carry on with your speech."

Lestara cleared her throat, then smoothed her skirts with one hand. "My brave and loyal soldiers, we would have won this handily on our own, but our ally Cardiff has arrived."

The sailors and soldiers didn't seem to be paying attention to her, their eyes all fixed south, but Lestara only shouted louder, as though volume would make a difference.

"My father, King Ronan, has our backs, and together we will show every nation, north and south, that Harendell will not be made a victim. We will rule, and beneath King Oliver, a golden era will dawn!"

"That last bit is true enough, given your mother saw it in the stars," Ronan said. "Cardiff sailed for King Oliver. A new alliance has been negotiated, but it is not with you."

To James's amazement, the Cardiffians lifted Virginia onto the deck of the *Victoria*. Hazel was with her, one hand steadying his sister's elbow as she walked across the deck, and Theryn and Waynne walked behind them, hands resting on their weapons.

"Lestara, give me my nephew!" Virginia demanded. "A baby has no place on a battlefield."

"I will do no such thing." Lestara stepped away from him, tripping on her skirt. "What is Virginia doing here? What is going on?"

"*What's going on* is that Keris left me his dog as a gift," Ginny snarled. "Good girl that she is, Fiona found gloves hidden under your bed that were covered with poison. The same poison that killed William."

Lestara's eyes bulged. "That is a lie."

"I'd tell you to burn the evidence next time, but there isn't going to be a next time." Virginia's lip curled with derision. "There are no men left for you to work your particular form of power on." Her head tilted. "Archie, I suggest you sit this one out."

The man in question was busy trying to look invisible, and he twitched in alarm when his name was called. James had no doubt that Virginia had endless proof of his treason given that Theryn was watching him with hard eyes.

Expressions on the deck were hardening, because his sister was beloved. But above that, his sister was Harendellian, and for better or worse, that mattered.

Lestara saw the shift, and her voice had a desperate edge as she said, "Virginia is trying to frame me to take power! That's all this is!"

"I saw you, Lestara." Ahnna spoke from where she remained on her knees. "I saw you through the window of your room. Saw you touch William's face and then discard the gloves."

"Your word is worth nothing!" Lestara shrieked. "These are all lies to discredit me! Why is no one doing anything?"

"They all sense the wrongness in you. They all know that it was you who brought them to this moment." Ronan waved a hand toward Ornak. "Now hand over the baby to Virginia."

"No!" Lestara stumbled away, coming up against the railing. "The stars said I would be a powerful woman and queen. They said my deeds would never be forgotten, and what greater deed is there than claiming the bridge?"

"What else did the stars tell us about you, Lestara? What else did Caly see on your seventh birthday?"

"That I'd give birth to a prince who'd deliver our people into a brighter era. And I have done it! Against all odds, in defiance of every monster you gave me to, I have done it!"

"What else?"

Lestara didn't answer.

"What else?" Ronan roared, and when she still did not respond, he continued, "That your name would be a curse, and death would follow you. That you would one day face a choice, and that day has come. Take off the crown and give Virginia the child, and death will cease to follow at your heels."

"I hate you." Lestara spat the words, her eyes glowing like suns. "I have hated you and Mother all my life. All of this is to prove Mother's power, because if she isn't right about me, how else has she led you astray? Fuck you, Father. I will give you nothing! You threw me to the rats, and I climbed higher. They threw me to the spiders, but I crushed them all beneath my heel. Now the last spiders think to throw me to the snakes, but I will burn this nation of serpents to ash."

James wanted to pity her, because the world had been unkind to his cousin. But it was hard to pity her given the harm she had done to those who'd had no part in the hurt done to her.

"Is that your choice, then?" Ronan demanded. "You choose power?"

"I choose the bridge," she spat. "I don't need Cardiff, because I am the queen of Harendell. I sit on the Twisted Throne. I will be the Mistress of the Bridge, and all the world will bow to me!"

No one spoke. No one even seemed to breathe, Lestara's words having reached the ears of everyone on deck, and though it was midday, James swore the world darkened. Like all the stars in the sky had turned their backs, and not even the sun could make up for the loss of their favor.

His cousin looked to the sky, and her throat moved as she swallowed hard.

"Ships spotted to the north," a voice shouted from the crow's nest, whoever it was seemingly oblivious to the conflict below. "Amaridian! It's the Amaridians!"

"That would be Queen Nina and her fleet," Virginia said. "It seems she was quite won over by the Ithicanians during her time here. Enough that she answered the call to sail in their defense."

"They're surrendering on the south side," another voice shouted. "The fleet is surrendering to the Valcottans! To the Maridrinians!"

Ronan crossed the deck, and none of the soldiers protested as he said, "You truly think that James is the traitor? James, who fought at your side all these long years? Let him go, you daft fools."

The ropes unraveled from his wrists, and James ripped the gag from his mouth as Ahnna was also unbound.

"It's done, Lestara," James said, moving cautiously closer to her as she backed to the edge of the deck, resting one hand on the rail. Ahnna moved to the other side, her eyes fixed on the baby. "It's over."

"No!" Lestara gave a rapid shake of her head. "The stars saw it, James. They saw my future. That I would be queen. That I would rule, and my son would bring in a golden era."

"And you did rule. Queen of the most powerful nation in the known world, Lestara. But Caly never said you'd rule for long, did she? What did she say?"

"She said that death would demand payment," Lestara whispered. "But I have paid and paid and paid."

As he kept Lestara's focus, Ahnna moved in from behind.

"Let it end, Lestara," James said. "Quit paying, and turn away from this path. Give us Oliver and surrender."

"No!"

"You can't win."

Lestara tilted her head. "If I can't claim the golden era, James, then neither can you."

He lunged, sensing her intent, but Lestara was too quick. In a flash, she hurled herself over the side of the ship, plunging toward the shark-infested water with the baby clutched in her arms.

Ahnna didn't hesitate.

His wife leapt onto the rail and jumped, falling toward the splash that Lestara had left in the sea.

"Ahnna!" James screamed, trying to go after her, but his uncle caught hold of his arms. "No!"

It was a churning mass of wave and foam, and James screamed at the Ithicanian ship, wordless demands that they help her.

Then Ahnna's head broke the surface, the baby clutched in her hands. She shoved Oliver into Mara's grip, but then she was yanked under.

"Ahnna!"

He fought against his uncle, trying to get free.

"You can't go in! It's full of sharks!"

As though he couldn't see that. As though there was any mistaking the gray shapes surging through the churning sea. But it was his wife in that water. It was the love of his life. It was Ahnna.

Another Ithicanian vessel approached, Aren at the helm.

"She's in the water," James howled at him. "Get her out!"

The king's eyes widened with panic, but before he could move, the froth and foam turned crimson red.

# 104

# AHNNA

Fingernails dug into her legs, Lestara's grip seeming preternaturally strong as Ahnna tried to kick her free.

*Get out get out get out!*

The panicked words blurred into one in her head, because all around were sleek shapes and fins, the sharks lured by the battle. But Lestara wouldn't let go, and Ahnna sank beneath the sodden weight of the other woman's gown no matter how hard she swam.

*Fight.*

Ahnna twisted downward, drawing back a fist to strike at the other woman. Her fist connected with Lestara's face, but not before Ahnna saw the gleam of steel. Pain exploded in her abdomen. The bubbles around her turned red, and Ahnna barely managed to get her arm up to block Lestara as she tried to stab Ahnna again.

The knife flipped out of Lestara's hand, sinking into the sea.

But the damage was done.

Blood pulsed from the puncture, crimson clouds of it staining the water. Ahnna knew all too well the sort of madness it caused in Ithicana's sharks, and the flashes of fins all around her moved faster.

They'd come for her soon.

And Lestara wouldn't let go.

With a viselike grip, she clung to Ahnna's clothes. The golden fabric of her gown billowed out around her, layers upon layers of skirts, and they were like a lead weight as Ahnna tried to drag them both up to the surface. Her lower abdomen was in agony, her lungs burned, and with every passing second, the surface grew darker.

She punched her fist into Lestara's face again, then at her fingers to try to get loose, but Lestara only smiled at her through the darkening water.

Harendell's queen wasn't trying to live, and what was pain to someone who sank toward death's embrace?

Except Ahnna wanted to live.

She slammed her forehead into Lestara's face, then reached down and fumbled a knife out of her boot. Her arm carved an upward arc, the blade slicing a red line across Lestara's face. Blood bloomed red, but the taste of it in the water drew the sharks closer. A tail fin struck her hand, knocking the blade from her grip, and it disappeared into the darkness.

*Down and down and down.*

Her strength was faltering, the loss of blood and the need to breathe turning her legs weak.

Lestara pulled herself close, the churn of fins causing their bodies to circle as they stared into each other's eyes. The queen's eyes were manic and wild, and Ahnna swore she could hear the woman's voice in her head as bubbles trailed from her lips. *I have won.*

Then a gray shape shot toward them, jaws gaping wide.

Lestara was torn away from Ahnna, and the world turned red.

Harendell's queen hung in a cloud of floating skirts and blood, half her torso ripped apart. The eyes locked on Ahnna's were now filled with terror.

Bubbles exploded from Lestara's lips as she screamed, but then the mass of sharks was upon her. Tearing apart pieces of the monster who had tried to slay Ithicana, gulping chunks of flesh down. In what felt like a heartbeat, all that remained was red water and scraps of golden silk floating on the current.

*Swim.*

Ahnna kicked, knowing that they'd come for her next.

Knowing there was no chance she'd reach the surface, because dozens and dozens of sharks circled in a rising frenzy. Light reached for her even as darkness moved in to claim her, the pressure in her lungs beyond measure, all her strength seeping out with her blood into the sea.

Fins bumped into her legs, the torrent of water the circling sharks created pulling at her hair and clothes as they pressed closer.

Ahnna couldn't see as blackness consumed her vision, her lips parting to take the breath that would be her end—

Only to feel strong hands grip her face, lips pressing over hers, and as Ahnna inhaled, it was air that went into her lungs. She blinked to find James holding her, kicking upward.

*To my dying breath . . .* She heard his voice in her head saying the vow he'd sworn when he'd married her.

*I'll find you*, she silently whispered as a tail slammed her shoulder, open mouths full of teeth all around them. *Wherever we go next, I will find you.*

It was the last thought she had before everything went dark.

# 105

# JAMES

His head broke the surface, and James lifted his wife's face above the waves, only to find her limp in his arms, her eyes closed.

"Pull them out!" Aren shouted. "Get her out!"

Ithicana's king lifted his sister out of the water, screaming Ahnna's name even as other Ithicanians caught hold of James, dragging him to the safety of the Ithicanian vessel.

"Ahnna!" He shoved people out of his way to get to her side.

*Sacrifice.*

The word filled his head, whispered by Caly's voice.

*But what you will give up, I do not know.*

"Not her," he screamed. "Anything but her."

Lara leaned over Ahnna's still form. "She's breathing!"

But it was little relief, because there was blood everywhere.

"Where's the bite?" He couldn't control his panic. "Do you see a bite?"

Lara tore at Ahnna's clothes, her face a mess of blood and tears.

"Stabbed. She's been stabbed!"

The world faded in and out as his eyes fixed on the wound above Ahnna's hip bone. It pulsed blood with each heartbeat until Lara pressed her hand down on it.

*Sacrifice.*

"There is no room to move!" Lara shouted. "We need to get her onto the ship! I need space to save her." Then she caught hold of James's hand and pushed it down on the knife wound.

Ahnna's eyes fluttered open. "James?"

"I'm here." All around was chaos as the Ithicanians moved the ship closer to the *Victoria*. "You're all right. You're out of the water."

"Oliver?" She turned her head, eyes searching. "Where is he?"

"He's safe." Alive because of her.

The fear in her eyes faded, and she smiled up at him. "That's all that matters."

It wasn't all that mattered. Not even close.

"Get her in the longboat! Move! Move!"

James scooped her up and half fell into the boat that the *Victoria* had lowered, Lara and Aren following. It lifted into the air, the noise of the winches loud, but none of it mattered. Only her. "You're fine," he said to her. "You've had worse. This is nothing."

"I can't see."

"Press down hard!" Lara shouted at him, then screamed instructions to the crew above as they were lifted higher.

"I love you," Ahnna whispered to him, staring at something beyond James's head, and then her lids slipped shut.

*Sacrifice.*

# 106

# AHNNA

Her panic faded like a retreating wave, because if she'd accomplished nothing else, she'd saved the baby's life.

Ahnna stared at a night sky, taking in a sea of stars. A thousand constellations. Ten thousand, and she swam toward them, hearing their call.

"Ahnna!" She blinked and saw James's face, then it faded into the night sky.

"Bandages!" Lara's voice. "I need to stop the bleeding! I just need to stop the bleeding!"

It all felt so distant as she swam from star to star, listening to the stories they told her.

"Ahnna!"

She reached out a hand to a glittering ball of silver, and a woman's voice whispered, "The she-wolf will sink low and then rise high."

"What does that mean?" Ahnna asked, the voice both familiar and not.

James's shout made the stars shake. "Look at me!"

She opened her eyes, but the pain that came with it was so fierce that she slipped once more back to the sky.

"No, no, no—Ahnna, *stay with me!*" Ahnna could feel his hands cupping her face. "You promised me. You promised to stay at my side."

"Until my last breath," she whispered, remembering that breath. Remembering the feel of his lips against hers as the sharks circled around and around.

"Which is not today, because you are not done fighting." His voice was raw thunder. Desperate. Commanding. "The war is over because of *you*. Ithicana is safe because of you. Oliver lives because of you. But *I*—" His voice broke, cracking wide open. "I cannot endure without you."

She wanted to tell him she'd done all she could. That it was time to let the sea have her. Time to let Ithicana's tempests carry her last breath away.

But James's eyes burned into hers, his gaze full of fury and fire and *love*.

"You don't get to fight for everyone and then give up on yourself." His forehead pressed against hers. "You don't get to give up on me. That's not our ending. You *stay*. Do you hear me, Ahnna? You *stay and live*."

For him, she could do this. For herself, she would do this.

Ahnna coughed, agony racking her frame—but her fingers found his, and she clutched him with what little strength she had.

Her lips moved. A whisper. A vow.

The battle was over.

But their story had just begun.

# 107

# JAMES

For all he'd grown up in the Sky Palace of verwyrd, it still felt strange to be walking around the spiral, and James suspected it always would. It would always carry a hint of threat and danger, the lurking sense of being unwelcome, and that he'd always feel a sense of relief every time he reached the bottom.

But with the love of his life currently recovering in the palace, James climbed the spiral as quickly as he could without breaking into a run.

Aren had wanted them to remain in Ithicana, but Ahnna would have none of it. "We're not abandoning him," she growled from her cot, swathed in bandages and as white as the sheet she lay upon. "And Oliver needs to return to Harendell."

So they'd returned on Ronan's ship with Virginia, Harendell's defeated fleet hobbling behind them while the other nations went home to lick their own respective wounds. Ahnna's grandmother had traveled with them. James had come to respect and loathe Amelie in equal measure. Though Ahnna's recovery was much to do with Amelie's skill, he would not weep to see the back of her when she returned to Ithicana.

Passing through the gate, he nodded at the guards on duty and then entered the palace, coming face-to-face with his uncle in the grand foyer.

"Where have you been?" Ronan asked, crossing his arms. "Your presence is wanted."

"I had an important task to take care of." James fell in alongside his uncle as they walked through the corridor, eventually reaching the offices that had belonged to his father. He entered, and it was like stepping back in time as he took in the endless bottles of spirits on the sideboard. The familiar artwork on the walls. The smell of leather upholstery, paper, and ink. Except instead of Edward Ashford sitting at the large desk near the window, James found his sister sitting there, a white dog at her feet.

"Where have you been, Jamie?" Ginny demanded. "No one knew where you had gone, not even Ahnna."

"Riding."

"Riding *where*?" She made a face. "Never mind. You're here now. Which means you need to settle the statement you intend to give from the throne. Everyone is well enough aware of the rumors that you are legitimate—all that remains is for you to claim the crown and sit on the Twisted Throne."

James rested his hands on the back of a sofa, casting a sideways look at Ronan.

"Don't do that," Virginia growled. "Speak your thoughts instead of making faces at each other that you know I can't see."

"Apologies, Lady Virginia," Ronan muttered. "It has always struck me that you see more than you should. You must have Cardiffian blood in you, generations back."

Ginny snorted. "Hardly. It's that you're both sighing in a very particular way that tells me you don't agree with what I'm saying."

James's fingers tightened on the leather, and he stared at the table before it, remembering the last time he'd sat there. How he'd listened to his father's revelation of his heritage and his grand ambitions for James's future. Not once had his father asked him what he wanted, and yet it was his father's voice James heard now.

*What do you want to do?*

"I understand that you taking the throne will have consequences." Virginia reached down and picked up the dog, settling the ball of white fluff on her lap. "But Harendell has endured a great deal, and it needs a steady hand. The hand of someone it can trust. Someone the people won't suspect of nefarious ambition, and that, brother, is you. They know you. They respect you. And Ahnna . . . well, I think we all know how sentiment toward her has shifted."

An understatement.

"We've also a number of judgments that need to be made. My mother's records are rife with proof against individuals. Murder. Theft. Treason. Fraud. The gallows will be full." Virginia stroked the dog's fur, mouth downturned, and he knew that she was thinking of how George would be one of the individuals who'd hang. It could be no other way, but James suspected that his sister still grieved the life that might have been.

"You know my thoughts, Jamie," Ronan said. "You saw how the bones lay on the table."

"Ahnna will be a good queen," Virginia said. "Father knew it. In hindsight, I think he cared more about her sitting on the throne than you."

James huffed out a breath of agreement, then said, "I appreciate your insights, but if you'll excuse me, I need to go find my wife. You both seem to believe that this is my choice, but I go where Ahnna goes."

―――――

AHNNA HAD REQUESTED they stay in her old rooms in the palace and asked Hazel to return to her service. Before they'd sailed back south, Keris and Zarrah had explained that without the maid's act of defiance against Alexandra, the Valcottan and Maridrinian fleets might never have come. Which would have made for a very different end to the battle. Hazel had never picked up a weapon, but she'd fought all the same.

As he approached the door, Amelie exited. As she spotted him, she quickened her stride. "I've had enough of your miserable cold palace, boy. Ahnna's recovering nicely, though you'd do well to keep your hands to yourself for another few days. I'm leaving. Get me one of those pretty riverboats that are always floating by, not a carriage.

My ass will never be the same after the pummeling it took on the carriage journey here."

"Your will, my word, my lady." He bowed.

Amelie made a rude noise. "Won't miss that nonsense, either. It's no small wonder that you lot get anything done with all the bowing and bootlicking that goes on. Goodbye, James. Take care of our girl."

"Goodbye, Amelie," James said, and went inside the room.

Ahnna sat on a chaise at the far end of the room with Oliver lying on her knees, kicking his little feet in the air. She didn't seem to notice that James had come in, and he leaned against the doorframe to watch his wife play with the baby. Ahnna's hair was pulled back in a tail behind her head, revealing old scars and new, her cheek mottled with purple-and-green bruises and her lip healing where it had been split. The dress she wore was loose, because beneath were the heavy bandages protecting the wound that had nearly taken her from him. Next to her was a sheathed sword, and through the fabric of her dress James noted the slight bulge of a knife strapped to her thigh.

A warrior through and through, and yet beneath the violent exterior was a kindness that took true bravery. The sort of empathy and selflessness that always carried a higher price than most people were willing to pay, and it shone through as Ahnna made silly faces to amuse the heir to a family who tried to destroy everything she held dear, laughing when Oliver cooed and wiggled.

The stars help him, but James loved her. Loved her so hard that it stole the breath from his chest and made his knees weak, and he thanked every higher power for bringing her into his life. And for keeping her in it.

"James, are you going to stand there the rest of the afternoon or are you going to come in?"

James pushed away his thoughts to discover his wife was watching him through her lowered lashes, a slight smile on her face. "I was enjoying the view."

The flush that pinked her cheeks made him of a mind to entirely disregard Amelie's instructions.

"Where have you been?" Ahnna asked. "Ronan and Virginia were looking for you."

He crossed the room and sat next to her on the chaise, kissing her on the forehead between various scrapes and bruises. "I tracked Dippy down. He was on the Ranges grazing, and he was a right ass about being caught. I think he'd decided to become a cow. He certainly shares their intelligence."

"Do not insult my horse or you might find yourself stabled with him."

"Noted." He ran a hand through his hair, wincing as he jostled one of his own bruises. "He's in a stall next to Maven. We'll take them out when you're healed. Or if you decide you want to escape all this pomp and ceremony."

"Tempting." She smiled. "But I think I'm content where I am."

For his part, he was content anywhere that she was.

"He's a good baby." Ahnna tickled Oliver's toes. "A happy baby. His nurses adore him."

James looked out the window, a dull ache always forming in his chest when he was in the presence of his brother's child. He tried to remember the last time he and William had spoken. Tried to remember the last words they had exchanged, but beyond knowing it must have been in Sableton before James left in pursuit of Ahnna, he could not remember. Which was maybe for the best. It was better to remember William from a time before the knives had fallen and the poison had flowed, when they'd been brothers and united in all things.

"William was going to hold true to his word," Ahnna said, seeming to read his thoughts. "He was going to withdraw from Ithicana. The threat to Alexandra might have been what caused him to agree to the plan, but I do think that in the end, he wanted a better legacy for his son."

"At the price of your life." It was the only thing William had done that had been wholly unforgivable. The thing that tarnished every memory of his brother, and for Oliver's sake, James knew he should let it go, as Ahnna had. Except while his wife was blasé about all the hurts she had endured, James was decidedly not.

True to form, she said, "We're alive. Our hearts beat in our chests, whereas all those who tried to hurt those we care about are in the grave or in the stomachs of Ithicanian sharks. From Valcotta all the way north to Cardiff, we are bound by blood shared and by blood spilled on one another's behalf, which is stronger than signatures on paper. We need to relish this moment for as long as it lasts, because eventually, new villains will rise."

Ahnna wasn't wrong, especially in Harendell where greed and the desire for power seemed to run deeper than in other nations. The war had ended with Harendell's surrender in the face of a united force greater than had ever been seen in recorded history, but in truth, the people had been happy to finally abandon the ambitions of too many rulers with a taste for *more*. A taste that was only ever satisfied by stepping on the backs of soldiers and civilians, their lives nothing but numbers on a list of casualties deemed acceptable next to the accounts of profit set beside them. James believed that was why they'd been so swift to accept his return—because he and Ahnna brought both the promise of peace and the willingness to defend those who were so often stepped upon. The story of Ahnna diving into shark-infested waters to save Harendell's infant king had spread through the nation like wildfire, and her name had become synonymous with a different sort of rule than Harendell was used to, but one they were desperate to keep.

Which was what they needed to talk about.

"Virginia wants me to make a statement." He kept his eyes on the view out the window, taking in the river valley. "To declare my parents' marriage and my legitimacy, and then to claim the throne."

Ahnna leaned her shoulder against his, still tickling the baby's feet, the child's content noises so at odds with the heaviness weighing upon him.

"You are a constant in the eyes of the people, James. I know you don't always see it, but they trust you to do right by them in a way they trust few others. They will support you."

"And you."

She made a soft humming sound, then bent to kiss the baby's forehead. "I think they understand that I'll fight to defend them, and that means something. They want a ruler who will protect them."

Ahnna had been the people's princess in Ithicana—beloved because she never put anyone above them, least of all herself. She'd be the people's queen in Harendell, of that James had no doubt.

Destined to rule and to rule well.

"Do you want to hold him?"

James glanced at her, then away again. "I don't know anything about holding babies."

"It's not hard. Just don't drop him."

Before he could answer one way or another, Ahnna scooped up his nephew and deposited him in James's arms.

Every part of him went rigid, and seeming to sense it, the baby began to cry. "Ahnna . . ."

Her hand curved around his face, forcing James to look at her. "I know it hurts," she said. "But we are all he has now. We are all that stands between him and a very hard world. He's ours, and we are his."

James stared into her beautiful hazel eyes. "It's not fair to ask you to raise the son of people who tried to murder you. He's not your blood. He's—"

"What does blood have to do with anything?" Ahnna tilted her head, hazel eyes thoughtful. "I chose you for no reason other than that you were all my heart wanted. I choose Oliver because my heart tells me that is what it wants me to do. To be bound by love is a far more powerful force than anything that flows through our veins—you and I are testament to that."

His throat felt tight, emotions threatening to drown him, not the least of which was fear. Yet James made himself look down at his nephew. The moment he did, Oliver stopped crying. Amber eyes framed with dark lashes stared up at him with the trust that only comes with innocence. "Ahnna, if I claim the throne, he will suffer for it. So will Ginny, though she says she doesn't care."

His wife didn't answer, only stroked her fingers through his hair, and James knew that she was waiting for him to voice the fear in his heart.

He swallowed hard. "If I claim the throne, it comes at the cost of William's legacy, which is . . . already fraught. The truth will paint my brother not just with the criticism he earned but as a false king. A pretender to the crown. A bastard. And as much as it should not, that legacy will cling to Oliver like a stain, and there will be nothing he can do to escape it. I know, because I've lived it."

James drew in a ragged breath. "He deserves better than that. I want him to have better than that." He lifted his face to look at her. "But I also want Harendell to have you."

"I know." She leaned forward and kissed him. "I think it also deserves to have you."

She reached beneath one of the chaise cushions and extracted a large, leather-bound book that James recognized from the law library. Ahnna opened it to a marked page, then took Oliver from him. "Read, James. And then choose."

James picked up the book, taking in the laws surrounding the coronation of a child, who could not rule on his own until the age of majority. Until such time, a regent would rule in his stead with all the authority of the crown. His eyes moved over who should be named to the regency, and then he slowly closed the book.

Caly had cast the bones and seen his future, and in it, she'd seen that Ahnna would never be queen.

Not that she would never rule.

James pulled his wife and child into his arms, the future he wanted as certain in his heart as the stars in the skies. "I choose this life."

Ahnna smiled, her eyes liquid bright. "And we will show no mercy to anyone who tries to take it from us."

# EPILOGUE
# AHNNA

AHNNA LEANED OVER Dippy's neck, urging him for more speed as he raced across the Ranges, hooves like thunder in the tall grass.

*Faster*, she willed him. *I want to win.*

As always, her horse heard her thoughts, and his stride lengthened, the world around them nothing but a blur as they flew past the markers, James and Maven following, albeit several paces behind.

"He's getting slow in his older years," her husband remarked as he drew alongside her. "We nearly caught you."

Ahnna laughed, tilting her head back as the wind flowed through her hair, the air smelling of rain and wind and freedom. "You should be sympathetic to his plight."

James gave a soft snort, then reached over and pulled her out of Dippy's saddle, settling her in front of him. "I take it back. He's in the prime of his life."

"Oliver told me that he caught you pulling a gray hair out of your beard."

"Little traitor." James kissed her, tongue stroking over hers, and the thrill it sent through her was the same now as it had been five years ago. Five exhausting years of love, passion, and dedication toward building a kingdom for the nephew they were raising together.

"Don't pull them out," she teased. "They give you gravitas."

"I didn't realize that was something I lacked." He kissed her again, hand curving around her ass and pulling her against him in a way that promised he'd make good on her teasing later. Or right now.

"Last time, a cowherd came upon us and proceeded to tell everyone he met that he caught Harendell's regents fucking in the cow pasture," she reminded him. "And Hazel had to pick thorns out of my backside when we got back. You'll have to wait for the comforts of our bedroom."

"A saddle is comfortable enough." He moved her so she was facing him, and desire pooled in her stomach as she felt the hard length of him against her. She kissed him, burying her fingers in the beard he'd taken to wearing, and then licking a line down his throat.

He groaned, and she unfastened his belt—

And then she scrambled back into Dippy's saddle. "If you want me," she called. "You'll have to catch me."

Digging in her heels, she left her husband cursing and buckling his belt, and then Maven was in pursuit. Thunder rolled, a storm rising in the east, and Ahnna lifted her face as the first droplets of rain fell.

This was the life she'd dreamed of. The life she'd fought for.

A life worth living.

———

AND A LIFE worth sharing.

Ahnna watched with anticipation as the longboat drew closer to the entrance to Eranahl.

"Is this it, Auntie?" Oliver asked, his eyes wide with excitement. "Was this where the battle was?"

"Yes." She took his little hand and used it to point to the cliffs. "Right up there was where I shot the line that Lara used to rappel onto King Silas's ship, where she dueled and slew him before all of his soldiers. Then she swam through shark-infested waters to get back to Aren, who was on the other side of the gate."

He looked down into the water right as a gray shape passed beneath the vessel, and he shifted closer, gripping Ahnna's hand tight as the great portcullis lifted and they sailed into the cavern.

It glowed blue with the light of dozens of jars full of algae set into niches, every breath seeming to echo as it bounced off water and rock, Eranahl as magical as ever. Aren waited on the narrow dock, and her heart skipped, for they'd been too long apart.

"That is King Aren of Ithicana," James murmured to him. "Remember your courtesies."

"He's so tall!" Oliver replied, the childish fixation on growing taller of critical importance to him of late. "Taller than you. Nearly as tall as Great-Uncle Ronan."

"He is not taller than me," James muttered, and Ahnna hid a smirk as the boat bumped out of the dock.

Aren reached down a hand to help her out, and she hugged her brother tightly. "It's good to see you."

"Likewise. No Virginia?"

"She's keeping an ear on the spiders. She's also not forgiven how your cat tried to eat her dog the last time we were here."

"That ball of fluff isn't a dog."

"You'll get no quarrel from me on that front." She stepped sideways as James lifted Oliver out of the boat, her nephew squaring his shoulders and approaching. Looking up at Aren, he inclined his head slightly, then said, "Your Majesty, it is my greatest honor and privilege to be invited to visit Ithicana. Our kingdoms have a union forged with blood, and I am proud to continue that bond. May our friendship grow ever stronger under our reigns."

Aren's expression was serious as he inclined his head. "You honor Ithicana with your presence, Your Majesty. The bond between our peoples is one I hold sacred, and I am grateful to stand beside a ruler who values it as deeply as I do. May our shared legacy be one of strength, peace, and unwavering loyalty." Then his expression turned sly. "Might I entice you with a game of rock throwing on the cliffs today? Whoever achieves the greatest splash is declared the winner."

Oliver's face brightened. "Oh yes. I'd enjoy that very much. Is it true that you were once catapulted out of one of Ithicana's shipbreakers? Could we try that?"

Aren laughed. "Not unless you want your aunt to shove me off a cliff."

He slung an arm around James's shoulders, pounding him on the back in the way men always did. "It's good to see you."

"It's good to be free of the spiderweb, if only for a little while." James rested a hand on Oliver's back, gently pushing him up the stairs, then he reached back to take Ahnna's hand. They climbed up and out into Eranahl, Oliver forgetting all his training as he shrieked with delight at the city hidden within the volcano, but Ahnna's eyes were all for Lara and Delia, who were staring each other down with equally matched glares. Lara held a hairbrush in one hand, and the princess's wild tangle of dark hair seemed her obvious target.

"They have a difference of opinion on the matter of personal appearance," Aren said, nearly drowned out as Delia shouted, "I don't care!" She then turned and stuck her tongue out at Oliver before bolting off into the city.

"Oliver, if it is peace you wish to have with Ithicana, you had best hope I live forever," Aren said with a sigh.

Another young girl with tidy dark braids skidded to a stop before them. She dropped into a polite curtsy. "Well met, Your Grace," she said, and then grabbed the brush out of Lara's hand. "I'll get her to do it, Auntie." She bolted after Delia, a pair of Ithicanian soldiers trailing after the girls.

"Sarhina's daughter, Oriana," Aren said. "She and Delia are thick as thieves."

"Is she here?" Ahnna asked.

"In the palace arguing with Keris about something," Lara replied. "You three are the last to arrive."

"May I go with them, Auntie?" Oliver asked, looking up at her. As always, she was struck with how his eyes, despite being identical in color to Lestara's, held nothing of the dead queen in them. He was quick as a whip, but as kind a child as one could ask for, and she loved him with all her heart. "If you like."

"He's brave to want to face those two girls." Aren reached up into a tree and pulled a boy with curly brown hair out of the branches. Ahnna hadn't even noticed him there. He looked to be a little more than four years of age, and the eyes glowering at Aren were a very distinct azure blue. "Does your father know you're climbing trees?"

"You going to tell him?" the boy asked sullenly.

Aren bent low. "I'll make you a deal. You keep your cousins from knocking Oliver off a cliff or tricking him into eating worms, and I won't tell your father that you escaped again. Deal?"

The boy, who was clearly Keris's son Lucas, considered the request, then nodded. "Don't tell my mum either." Then he grabbed Oliver's arm and dragged him in the direction the girls had run. Aren gestured, and more Ithicanian soldiers broke ranks to follow the children.

Ahnna approached Lara, pulling her sister-in-law into a tight embrace. "I missed you."

"At least this is a happy reunion."

The last time Ahnna had been in Ithicana had been for her grandmother's funeral. Nana had been a force to be reckoned with right up to the moment she'd dropped from a heart attack while shouting at Jor for getting water on her floor. Lara had taken her death hard, because for all Amelie had driven her to the brink, she'd been a grandmother to her as well. Taking Lara's hand, Ahnna circled the lake with her, leaving Aren to walk with James.

She and Lara exchanged letters regularly, so there was no need to ask for updates about Ithicana. Instead Ahnna asked, "Are you happy?"

Lara looked up at her, blue eyes gleaming in the sunlight. Her face was marked with scars from the battle of Ornak, but she seemed to have grown more beautiful with age. "Yes. It's been a journey, but yes, I'm happy. Although my daughter might be the death of me." She rolled her eyes up at the sky. "Aren said that it's Veliant blood, because all of the cousins are positively feral, except for Yrina. She's a miniature Zarrah, which of course means she's the apple of Keris's eye. But what about you?"

Ahnna looked over her shoulder at James, who was animatedly explaining something to Aren. "Harendell comes with endless challenges, but peace has brought profit, and that makes them happy.

I saw an Amaridian vessel anchored. Is Nina here, or just Bronwyn and Taryn?"

"Nina as well. She and Keris's sister Sara have become fast, if somewhat unexpected, friends. Sara aims to travel back with her to Riomar when she leaves here, and Bronwyn and Taryn will return as well. They like Amarid, and it is good to have them at Nina's back. She's funding a new music school, which Taryn will chair. And you didn't answer my question."

Ahnna lifted a hand to greet the Ithicanians who had come out of their homes to call her name, their faces familiar. "I think part of me is afraid to admit that I'm happy, because to do so might cause it all to come undone." She closed her eyes as the wind caught hold of her hair, and her mind filled with her and James galloping through the Ranges. "I have everything my heart desires, that I know for certain."

"That sounds like happiness." Lara squeezed her hand, and then they stepped through the open doors of the palace.

Ahnna's nose breathed in the familiar scent, the building cool and filled with the tinkling sound of fountains. Familiar faces scurried in all different directions as the staff prepared for dinner, and Ahnna waited to be struck with the sense of coming home.

Except this wasn't home anymore.

Home was Verwyrd. Home was Fernleigh House or Whitewood Hall. Home was Harendell.

"Ahnna!" She turned to see Jor approaching. He'd lost his arm below the elbow from the wound he'd taken on Ornak, but years of peace had done him well. He looked fit and healthy, and the arm that wrapped around her was strong. "You're late."

"James wouldn't let me sail the ship. He says that I scare the crew too badly."

"This I believe." Jor moved on to speak with Aren and James, and Lara led her down the hallway, raised voices growing louder with each step. Ahnna opened the door to the dining room to find both Keris and Sarhina on their feet, each waving a book at the other, neither seeming to be listening to a word the other was saying. Bronwyn and Taryn sat near them, watching with amusement. Zarrah and Ensel sat at the table conversing with their hands, a small girl with curly dark hair and dark eyes sitting between them with an illustrated book in her lap.

Everyone stopped their conversations as Ahnna entered, then in a heartbeat, they all began again as if there had been no interruptions. Family, as family was intended to be, and Ahnna took a seat next to Zarrah, Lara taking the one next to Ensel. James and Aren sat with Bronwyn and Taryn, and it was then Ahnna noticed Nina and Sara seated in the corner, heads together as they whispered. The young queen of Amarid lifted a hand in greeting as her eyes locked on Ahnna's, but though she was Katarina's granddaughter and Carlo's daughter, she had proven intent on changing Amarid for the better.

"Ronan sends his regrets that he wasn't able to come," Ahnna said to Zarrah. "You made quite an impression on him."

Zarrah smiled, then leaned over to hug Ahnna tightly. "I've invited him to Pyrinat, so we'll see if he makes the journey. I'm glad to see your face, though. James's as well. Where is Oliver?"

"With the other children. Lucas has been charged with his defense."

Zarrah grimaced. "That's . . . not a comfort. Yrina, go find your brother and make sure he's not causing trouble. Take Saam with you."

The little heir to the Valcottan Empire gave a world-weary sigh, snapped her book shut, then rose. "Yes, Mother."

Once she was gone, Zarrah looked around, then smiled. "A gathering for the history books, if not for the secrecy. Wouldn't do for certain people to know that half the rulers of the known world, and their heirs, are all in one place."

Lara took a sip from the glass of wine Ahnna poured for her, then said, "It wouldn't be wise to attack this gathering. Many have tried, and they all rest six feet under."

"I still know how to run a shipbreaker." Ahnna flexed her hands and laughed, though she could feel the weight of too many wars, too many battles, too many losses stretched among the three of them. It was a weight none of them would ever shake free from, and one they'd all fight to keep the next generation from experiencing.

The servants began loading the tables with food, and moments later, the children all exploded into the room. Oliver's clothes were muddy and his coat was torn, but his cheeks were flushed with happiness as he conspired with the other children in the corner. The noise grew, everyone laughing as they moved from conversation to conversation, the children eventually tucked into their beds, and it was well after midnight when Ahnna found herself face-to-face with her husband.

She wrapped her arms around James's neck, the hum of chatter all falling away. "I haven't spoken to you all night."

"I was defending Aren from Keris. That man is merciless."

"Didn't look like defense. Looked more like you and Keris were ganging up on him. Is it because my brother is slightly taller than you?"

"Between you and Oliver, my ego will not survive this trip."

"It's good for you." She pulled him closer, desperately wanting to be alone with him. "Would you like to go for a walk with me?"

"Gladly."

Ahnna linked her arm through his and led him out of the room, through the palace, and out into the night. All of Eranahl was celebrating, music and laughter pouring from the homes lining the slope of the volcano, but Ahnna passed them all by, taking James up and up.

Until they stood at Eranahl's summit.

Ahnna set down the lantern she was carrying and turned the flame low so it would not take away from the view. The night was clear as only the calm season could bring, and the sky was an explosion of glittering stars that reflected off the mirror of the sea.

"It's beautiful," James said, turning in a circle. "I've never seen the sky quite like this."

"You should see it during a typhoon."

"I'll pass on that." He caught hold of her hand, and then rested his other on her hip. "Dance with me, Princess."

With only the wind and the waves as music, her husband led her in a waltz across the rough ground of the summit. She'd danced with him a thousand times over the last five years, in palaces and ballrooms and in their bedroom before he'd take her down to the sheets and make her his own, but to dance beneath Eranahl's stars felt like a different sort of magic.

"I love you," she whispered, resting her cheek against his shoulder. "Thank you for giving me this life."

"I wish I'd given it to you, love." His breath was warm against her hair. "But you fought for it yourself. You still fight for it, even though the battle is won."

"Is it won?" As soon as she said the words, Ahnna regretted them. "Don't listen to me. Too much wine has me saying things I don't mean."

"You had one glass. And I heard what you said to Lara."

Ahnna pulled out of his grip and walked a few paces, staring out over the sea. "It was nothing."

"I hold you every night, Ahnna, through all the nightmares that plague you. Watch how you never go anywhere without an arsenal of weapons. I see how you are always on guard, asleep and in your dreams. That's not nothing."

He wasn't wrong, but no part of her felt willing to relax. To do so felt like inviting disaster to fall down upon them, because happiness felt like something so easily torn from her hands.

James came up behind her, wrapping his arms around her and pulling her against him. "Before we left Verwyrd, a package arrived from Caly."

He let go with one arm, then held a small velvet bag out in front of her. Curious, Ahnna took it and sat on the ground next to the lantern, turning up the flame. She opened the bag and poured the contents onto her palm. Then promptly dropped them in the dirt. "Good God. James, these are human finger bones. Knuckles."

"The best bones are those from your enemies, but she didn't say who they belonged to. Though I wouldn't put it past Caly to have robbed Alexandra's grave." James sat across from her, legs crossed. "In Cardiff, you can see a person's future in the patterns the bones form when they fall. It's called casting. If you want, I can read your future in the bones you just threw on the ground in front of you."

She knew about the things Caly had said about Oliver bringing a golden era of peace, and how she'd foretold Lestara's fate. It had all felt like cleverly chosen words, but as Ahnna glanced down at the haphazard mess of white bones, then away, her skin prickled with the sense that powers she could not comprehend existed in this world. Powers that had created the bridge. Powers that spoke down from the stars. "I have known you for six years, James. And not once did you mention that you know how to read the future."

"Caly taught me when I was a boy." Reaching across the bones, he took her hands. "If it will give you peace, I'll tell you what your future holds."

"Have you already looked?" she whispered. "Do you already know?"

James shook his head. "I won't unless you ask me to."

Ahnna slowly lowered her gaze to the bones between them, examining how they rested against one another and trying to decipher the patterns they formed. Would knowing what the future held give her peace? If James told her she'd live a long life with him, would that make her happy? If he told her that she'd do right by Harendell, would she relax? Or would the hints and clues only serve to torment her, the lack of specificity magnifying the tension that plagued her days?

"I don't want to know." Letting go of one of his hands, she knocked the bones, destroying their pattern. "You swore that you'd be at my side until the end came for us, and I swore that I'd find you in whatever comes next. That is the only certainty I need in my life, even if it means I must live every day as though it may be my last."

For a heartbeat, she feared that she'd see frustration in his eyes at her unwillingness to let down her guard, but her husband only said, "I thought you might say that."

James pulled her into his arms before gently lowering Ahnna to the ground—the very earth she had spent her life fighting to protect. "I do not think tonight will be our last night, Ahnna, but let's make it one to remember."

# ACKNOWLEDGMENTS

Writing "The End" on this novel truly represented the end of an era. In 2017, I was at a point where I feared that I'd have to give up my writing career to go back into the workforce. There was no interest from publishers on the novel I had on submission, my first series wasn't making a living income, and I had two very young daughters who required a certain amount of pragmatism from me when it came to life choices. It was dark days and I feared the worst, but everything changed when my agent received a phone call from Audible Originals. Audible produced the audiobooks for my first series, and they wanted to know if I was interested in writing original content for them to be published as an audio exclusive. I had, at the time, the very beginnings of a passion project that I was working on about a princess named Lara. We sent the first seven chapters to Jessica Galland, who fell in love with what I had written and offered me not only a publishing deal but one that would allow me, financially, to continue writing.

It was a really big moment for me, but something else that made it special was that Audible Originals didn't make me revise the story to make it young adult. At that time, publishers weren't really interested in putting out adult fantasy novels with a lot of romance, and there was tremendous pressure to age down the characters and make it appropriate for teen readers. I had a very unique opportunity to write a story that drew from the fast-paced, character-focused style of young adult but was about older characters exploring mature situations and have it released by a large publisher. It feels hard to believe, given how hot all things fantasy and romance are in 2026, but trust me when I say: No publishers wanted this type of book in the adult section in 2017.

It was also my first step into independent publishing. As Audible Originals only published the audiobooks (and exactly zero publishers were interested in the print/ebook rights), it was on me to put out the print and ebook editions. I must credit the incredible Elise Kova for coaching me through the process, because I truly don't think I'd have managed without her. I learned an incredible amount about the publishing industry through putting out these editions, and I have made so many indie author friends (looking at you, NOFFA!).

The biggest moment for *The Bridge Kingdom* came during the pandemic when a few readers on Booktok took a shine to Lara and Aren. The love and support those individuals gave this series truly changed the trajectory of my career, and I hope they all know how grateful I am to them!

The success of *The Bridge Kingdom* and the shift in the publishing industry into the romantic fantasy space were the stepping stones to first Michael Joseph (UK) and then Del Rey (US) acquiring the print and ebook editions of The Bridge Kingdom series. Under Del Rey's stewardship, the series was treated to gorgeous new covers, and it also hit the *New York Times* bestseller list for the first time.

*The Tempest Blade* focuses on James and Ahnna, but it is truly an epic finale for all six Bridge Kingdom series characters. Writing this book was one of the most enjoyable experiences of my career but also bittersweet, because I'm saying goodbye to a set of characters who have been with me for many years and who changed my life.

All the thanks in the world to my family for having my back through all the ups and downs I've experienced with this series. The demands of this career are a challenge for us all, and I am so grateful to be blessed with such an incredible family.

Jessica, thank you so much for taking a chance on Lara and Aren all those years ago. I am grateful for Audible Original's support, as well as to the incredibly talented narrators who voiced all six characters.

A huge thanks to Emily Archbold for your love for this series and all your hard work on each of the novels. I appreciate your enthusiasm and tenacity on ensuring these editions were absolutely perfect for the stories. Endless gratitude to everyone else at Del Rey, Michael Joseph, and PRH Canada, especially Jordan, Madi, Ashleigh, Tori, Scott, Julie, David, Keith, Regina, Sarah P., Meghan, Sabrina, Maya, Erica, Emily R, Megan C., Polly, Rebecca, and Jorgie. We've had a whirlwind few years of releases, and so much of the success is because of the incredible amount of effort and enthusiasm of everyone involved.

To my agent, Tamar, you were there for every step this series took, including learning a lot about self-publishing, which I appreciate more than I can say. Celsie, thank you for your foreign rights efforts and for ensuring I never miss a deadline. Amy, I could write a novella about all the things you do—thank you for everything, but most especially your fondness for Aren's biceps. Melissa, you've stepped in so many times when I needed help, and I am forever grateful for your guidance.

Over the years, I've had the opportunity to work with a tremendous number of artists, and I want to thank Annabelle Moe, Dominique Wesson, Richard Anderson, Eevien Tan, and Pandora Young for the beautiful covers of various editions, as well as thank all the fan artists who have created stunning images of my characters to show their love for the Bridge Kingdom world.

Last, but not least, I have the privilege to have one of the kindest and most supportive readerships. Thank you so much for coming on this journey with me, and I hope you will venture off into new worlds with me in the future.

On a station platform, with nothing to read,
and a four-hour train journey stretching ahead of him...

That's where the story began for Penguin founder Allen Lane.
With only 'shabby reprints of shoddy novels' on offer,
he resolved to make better books for readers everywhere.

By the time his train pulled into London, the idea was formed.
He would bring the best writing, in stylish and affordable
formats, to everyone. His books would be sold in bookstores,
stationers and tobacconists, for no more than the price
of a ten-pack of cigarettes.

And on every book would be a Penguin, a bird with a certain
'dignified flippancy', and a friendly invitation to anyone who
wished to spend their time reading.

In 1935, the first ten Penguin paperbacks were published.
Just a year later, three million Penguins had made their
way onto our shelves.

Reading was changed forever.

—

A lot has changed since 1935, including Penguin, but in the
most important ways we're still the same. We still believe that
books and reading are for everyone. And we still believe that
whether you're seeking an afternoon's escape, a vigorous debate
or a soothing bedtime story, all possibilities open with a book.

Whoever you are, whatever you're looking for,
you can find it with Penguin.